Christopher Koch is of Irish, English and German ancestry. All his forebears arrived in Australia in the 1840s – among them a Prussian architect, an English merchant sea captain, and a young Irishwoman who was transported to Van Diemen's Land as a convict at the time of the Famine.

Koch was born and educated in Tasmania. For a good deal of his life he was a broadcasting producer, working for the Australian Broadcasting Corporation in Sydney. He has lived and worked in London and elsewhere overseas. He has been a full-time writer since 1972, winning international praise and a number of awards for his five previous novels – many of which are translated in a number of European countries. One of his novels, *The Year of Living Dangerously*, was made into a film directed by Peter Weir. He has twice won the Miles Franklin Award for fiction: for *The Doubleman* and *Highways to a War*.

In 1995, Koch was made an Officer of the Order of Australia for his contribution to Australian literature.

By *Christopher Koch*

The Boys in the Island
Across the Sea Wall
The Year of Living Dangerously
The Doubleman
Crossing the Gap: Memories and Reflections
Highways to a War

Out of Ireland

VOLUME TWO *of*
Beware of the Past

Christopher Koch

V
VINTAGE

Published by Vintage 2000

2 4 6 8 10 9 7 5 3

First published in Australia by Doubleday, 1999

First published in Great Britain by
Vintage, 2000

Vintage
Random House, 20 Vauxhall Bridge Road,
London SW1V 2SA

Random House Australia (Pty) Limited
20 Alfred Street, Milsons Point, Sydney,
New South Wales 2061, Australia

Random House New Zealand Limited
18 Poland Road, Glenfield,
Auckland 10, New Zealand

Random House (Pty) Limited
Endulini, 5A Jubilee Road, Parktown 2193, South Africa

The Random House Group Limited Reg. No. 954009
www.randomhouse.co.uk

A CIP catalogue record for this book
is available from the British Library

ISBN 0 09 933171 3

Papers used by Random House are natural,
recyclable products made fromwood grown in sustainable forests;
the manufacturing processes conform to the environmental
regulations of the country of origin

Printed and bound in Great Britain by
Bookmarque Ltd, Croydon, Surrey

For Robin

Out of Ireland have we come.
Great hatred, little room,
Maimed us at the start.
I carry from my mother's womb
A fanatic heart.

W. B. YEATS, 'Remorse for Intemperate Speech'

EDITOR'S INTRODUCTION

The diaries of the Irish political exile Robert Devereux were kept between 1848 and 1851. They lay hidden for one hundred and twenty-five years, on a hop farm in southern Tasmania.

The farm was founded by Devereux and his partners, James and Bess Langford. The journals – together with an oil painting of Devereux by Doctor Neville Howard, the Colonial Surgeon of the time – were bequeathed to me by Devereux's great-grandson, my friend the late Michael Langford.

They consist of two thick volumes bound in calfskin, with entries made on both sides of the page. They were lodged in Devereux's writing-slope, together with a number of personal letters. When Devereux fled the island for America, these things were left behind. He also left behind an infant son, Thomas – who was born out of wedlock, and who was reared as their own by the Langfords. The boy was named Thomas Langford, presumably to cloak his illegitimacy; and Devereux – for reasons I've not been able to discover – never brought his son to the United States.

Michael Langford and his brothers were ignorant of this history, and of the facts about their ancestry. Their father, John Langford – Thomas Langford's son – had read Robert Devereux's diaries, but made sure that his own sons did not, by keeping the journals locked in his storeroom. There they remained throughout his lifetime. The sons were thus unaware of the fact that they were descended from Devereux on the paternal side, and that Devereux, not Langford, should have been their family name. Instead, John Langford led them to believe that Devereux was a maternal great-grandparent, of whose background little was known.

After old John died, in 1969, Devereux's journals and portrait remained in the storeroom for some years. Marcus and Cliff Langford, who now worked the farm, displayed no interest in these relics, and intended eventually to hand them over to Michael, who lived and worked abroad as a war photographer. Michael's early death prevented this, so the papers and the portrait came to me, as he had wished.

That his brothers had not read the Devereux diaries after their father died may seem surprising. It doesn't surprise me, knowing these men as I did. They were simple farmers; unlike Michael, they had no taste for reading anything but the newspapers, and I know what effect on them these two thick notebooks would have had. Devereux's old-fashioned handwriting would not have been easy to read, and anything to do with history or the past they found tedious and vaguely troubling. They would have put the journals aside without a second glance.

Only a native Tasmanian of my generation will understand why old John Langford concealed his grandfather's journals as he did – and why he was so deeply ashamed of so prominent an ancestor.

Robert Devereux had been transported to what was then Van Diemen's Land as a convict. This would have been all that mattered to John Langford – this, and the fact that Thomas Langford was illegitimate. In other words, John had to live with a double shame: his father had not only been a bastard, but the son of a transported felon. I am using the harsh and unforgiving terms of John Langford's day, and of my own youth – terms that would have been used by all John Langford's neighbours, as John very well knew. And John himself was a harsh and unforgiving man. So

Devereux was locked in the storeroom out of shame; and in Tasmania in those days, to discover convict ancestry was the ultimate shame. No doubt Thomas Langford (of whom I can discover nothing), had felt the same shame – and perhaps he resented the fact that his natural father had abandoned him.

Robert Devereux was in the Langford blood; but he wasn't wanted there. So he was hidden, but not destroyed. Many other Tasmanian families did the same with their convict ancestors. It was called 'hiding the Stain'.

According to Marcus Langford, his father had once let drop that Devereux had been Anglo-Irish, of 'good family', and had been transported as a convict because of some kind of political trouble. And that was all. Marcus had learned nothing of Devereux's eminence as an Irish patriot; nor, I believe, did he know that a political prisoner was different from a common convict, or that other noted Irish patriots had been exiled to Van Diemen's Land with Devereux. It was all too long ago and unreal for such a man to deal with, and his knowledge of history was very rudimentary – as I imagine old John's would have been. The Irish exiles of 1848 would have meant nothing to the Langfords, in their silent and changeless valley.

I am an amateur historian, and to come into possession of the Devereux diaries was deeply exciting for me. Editing them has been a labour of love. The Young Ireland rebels – spiritual fathers of Sinn Fein and the IRA – have come to fascinate me. I've carried out a study of their history for my own information that has caused me to neglect my legal practice, and which took me at one stage to Dublin.

There, going through the Young Ireland papers in the National Library of Ireland, I made a wonderful find: a long and detailed letter by Robert Devereux, sent from California following his escape, and addressed to his fellow-exile in Van Diemen's Land, Thomas

O'Neill. It's quoted in full at the end of this book, since without it, Devereux's story would not be complete. It was placed in the library by one of O'Neill's descendants – who was good enough to receive me at his home in Dublin. From him I learned that Thomas O'Neill was eventually pardoned, and returned from Van Diemen's Land to live out his life on the family estate near Ennis.

Now that my task is done, and the Devereux diaries donated to the Archives Office of Tasmania, I find it difficult to believe that I'll no longer live with the man who wrote them. Devereux stood on the brink of the modern world, and he has seemed very close, at times: his voice would sound in my head as I worked, and I'd sense the nearness of his spirit. I'll cease to hear that voice now – but his portrait continues to hang on my study wall, staring at a point somewhere behind my left shoulder, his truculent lower lip projecting, a glint of sardonic humour in his eyes. It's a face in which arrogance, hardness and a refined sensibility mingle: the face of a man of double nature.

There's little to be said about the editing of these journals. I've deleted entries here and there which seemed to me to have no narrative or other interest – and have also removed some of Devereux's more windy diatribes against the British. Otherwise, if long gaps occur, they do so simply because Devereux neglected his journal.

The diaries have been in my possession for twenty-three years. Cliff, the last of the Langford brothers, died last year. Out of respect for him, and knowing that he would not have wanted the family's ancient secret displayed to the public, I have not published until now.

Fellow-Tasmanians will understand.

Raymond Barton,
Launceston, Tasmania, 1999

CONTENTS

PART ONE

PROMETHEUS BOUND

Here is Prometheus, the rebel:
Nail him to the rock; secure him on this towering summit
Fast in the unyielding grip of adamantine chains.

AESCHYLUS, 'Prometheus Bound',
translated by Philip Vellacott

1. FELON

Aboard the hulk '*Medway*'
June 21st, 1848

They are talking about me, through the wall.

Invisible in my kennel, I'm separated from them by two barriers of planking, with a narrow passage between. But when the gangs come in to their quarters for dinner, and their interminable arguments begin, I can clearly make out barked obscenities, as their voices rise and shout. At times, whole sentences reach me.

My name, hateful on their English lips, has sometimes leapt like a trout above the canine growling and snarling. But I've made out nothing more, until tonight. A few minutes ago, as I sat here at my table, one Liverpool voice penetrated with absolute clarity. Raised in a hound-like falsetto, it made me flinch.

– Bugger his eyes! What is he but a convict, like the rest of us? That's right! A buggering, bloody convict!

I can picture the brute, cursing my eyes. His own eyes, red from their work, have no doubt met mine from a distance, on the pier; or perhaps they've looked up in resentment to where I pace the quarter-deck. As well that he can't get his hands on me. And of course he's right, even though my disbelieving heart is chilled by his words. I'm a convict, just as he says. But what sort of convict?

I wear my own clothes. I'm forced into no coarse blouse like his – that linen garment of shame, stamped with the Queen's broad arrow. I do no labour. I carry no chains. Instead, I sit writing in this diary, at my own table, in my own cabin, with shelves for my books, attended by a convict servant who brings my meals, and carries away my chamber pot. Although I call this my dog-house, I come and go as I please. It's clean, with a porthole giving light and air, and commands a view of the dockyard. And in the mornings, after my unknown enemy has trudged off along the breakwater, with the rest of his gang – chains jingling, wearing his palmetto hat against the Bermuda sun – I'm to be found reclining on the breakwater's seaward side, in the southerly breeze, contemplating the bay and its islands, or reading. Or else I'm found strolling on the quarter-deck, conversing with the British officers – who greet me with respect, and touch their caps to me.

British gentility; British hypocrisy! My gaolers touch their caps to me; and why? Because I'm a gentleman! My own cap remains on my head, as they salute me; and the convicts, who must doff their straw hats to the lowliest guard, see all this. As well, every day, some of them on tasks about the hulk glimpse me pacing the quarter-deck, where they may not even set foot. I've seen them scowl on such occasions, and mutter curses across the distance that lies between us. And although my captors maintain a fiction that I'm some sort of privileged tourist, the convicts are right. It's nonsense; I'm a felon like them: 'a buggering, bloody convict'; a prisoner of hateful Albion. My heart won't admit it, but my mind knows it's true.

In commencing this journal – an occupation I hope will prevent me from going mad – I shall begin by writing an account of the past two months. This is the period that has elapsed since my arrest in Dublin, my trial, and the pronouncement of my sentence. Two weeks after that, Catherine and I exchanged our farewell kisses.

Catherine! She has now become a mere, exquisite profile, in the coloured Gluckmann daguerreotype sitting on top of the bookshelves. A shaft of white-hot sun, coming though the barred porthole, catches and illuminates her. But this remorseless sun doesn't make her portrait glow, as the gentle beams of Ireland would do: instead, it seems to be fading the picture as I watch; to be bleaching it to a white shadow; to be consuming it altogether. An illusion; but I have just got up and moved it into the shade.

∾

I have no more tears, for now. I shed them all on the night of May 26th, when I found myself on Spike Island, in Cork Harbour.

I was met there by Mr Walker, the prison Governor – a thin, elderly man with fine-spun white hair and a Roman nose, whose wistful courtesy was enough to make one tearful then and there.

– So you are Mr Devereux, he said.

We were standing in a small courtyard, on one side of which was an open door. No other prisoners were to be seen. A turnkey waited at attention, and the two blue-uniformed naval officers who had brought me by ship from Dublin stood to one side. Mr Walker pointed out my cell – which lay though the door. His faded, blue-grey gaze was mild and regretful, as though I were an admired colleague who had somehow fallen into disfavour, and whom he wished to help but could not. His white choker collar was a little too large for his thin, aged neck, and his hands, the colour of old registers, were marred by ropy blue veins. Another of these veins stood out on one of his narrow temples, making him seem vulnerable and sickly. This, and his low, slightly tremulous voice, made one feel almost protective, and not wish to alarm him. He seemed more like a parson than a prison Governor, and although I wanted to hate him, I could not.

Why is it that British tyranny's agents and gaolers are so often gentle and unremarkable, making one feel a brute if one defies or opposes them? Ah, this is where Britannia is most cunning: so many of her representatives and even her warriors are like this! And we who are under her heel are made to feel like churlish oafs if we protest at what she does!

The naval officers, both men of my own age, with the open faces of boys, now took their leave of me, telling me with ludicrous courtesy that they hoped we'd meet again in happier circumstances. We had got on well on the trip from Dublin, and they seemed truly to pity me. Mr Walker and the guard accompanied them from the courtyard, and I was left here alone.

It was five in the afternoon; above me curved pale blue sky with sailing clouds. Invisible birds twittered, farewelling the day, and the sound had a sad, sharp gaiety I seemed never to have heard before.

The sky was all I could see of what lay outside; the walls hid all sight of the Bay of Cork and its tender green hills. Cold fingers gripped my entrails. For how long would the beauties of the world be hidden from me? I began to consider the idea that my eyes might meet little else but stone and bars for the next fourteen years.

Absolutely quiet: no sign of life. My cell was the only one here; and the Governor had told me that the courtyard was solely for my use. I walked to the open door, my boot heels loud on the cobbles, and went in.

I found myself in a normal room – no gaol cell at all, really, except that the single window looking out onto the courtyard was barred. There was a high, vaulted ceiling, and the room was furnished like a bedchamber in some country inn: a tall bed with an old red coverlet; two armchairs; a table; a basin stand. My portmanteau had been placed in a corner. And a sense of strangeness – of dreamlike bewilderment – came over me. Was I a prisoner or not? What would they do with me next? I had not worn fetters since the night of my arrest in Dublin, when I was hurried from Newgate Prison to the Government steamer that had brought me here. Was this sort of leniency to continue?

I hadn't long to ponder before Mr Walker returned, motioning me to one of the armchairs and taking the other for himself. The turnkey lurked by the open door – keeping an eye, no doubt, on his master's safety.

– Now, Mr Devereux, the Governor said, there are some things I wish to explain to you.

He had placed a papery hand on each arm of the chair, like an aged king. His voice still had its slight quaver, but had become self-consciously grave.

– I have written instructions concerning you from Dublin Castle, he said, and I shall communicate these quite frankly to you. It is recognised that you are a person of education and a gentleman, and my instructions are that you should be treated as such.

He gestured delicately at the room.

– As you see, you have your privacy and your personal effects, and you are not being lodged under the conditions of a common

6

convict. Nor will you be placed in contact with convicts.

– Am I not a convict? I have been convicted, I said. And I am labelled a felon.

He looked at me with his former quiet regret.

– Let me be a little clearer. You are a celebrated man – although not in a way that Her Majesty's Government finds attractive. And you are, of course, a political prisoner: that is, a prisoner of state.

I held my tongue and waited. I had already resolved to hold no converse with the penal authorities concerning the issues that lay behind my conviction. I would be a silent and circumspect prisoner, until opportunity for action presented itself. Mr Walker cleared his throat, and went on.

– It is therefore the Government's intention that you should be treated scrupulously, and that the deprivation of your freedom is the only humiliation you will suffer.

– A mere trifle, that. I'm comforted, I said.

His protuberant eyes became sorrowful, and his voice even softer.

– I'm not unconscious of the dreadfulness of your position, he said. Which, of course, you have brought upon yourself. I'm sorry for you, nevertheless.

– I have no complaint to make to you personally, Mr Walker, I said. You merely carry out the orders of those who are responsible for your system.

His face relaxed, and he pinched his little chin reflectively.

– I'm glad to hear it. You are young – thirty-two, is it not? – and you will still have life ahead of you when your sentence is served.

To this, I said nothing.

– You will no doubt wish to write to your loved ones, said Mr Walker. I'm afraid the regulations require that the letters be submitted to me before they are despatched – but this will be done promptly, I assure you. You may ask that clothing, books, and other personal things be sent to you. I see that you brought very little with you. Is there anything I can supply you with in the meantime? Tobacco, perhaps?

– I'd be grateful, I said. But it's books and writing materials I should welcome most – especially since I take it I'll have no other employment here.

I watched him, wanting to ask what my future would be for the next fourteen years – but knowing I would not allow myself to do so. For how long would I sit in this room, before being transported? To what region of the globe would I be sent? The remorseless Empire has its convict colonies everywhere: at Gibraltar; Bermuda; Van Diemen's Land; the settlements in New South Wales. On Britannia's penal network the sun never sets.

– Of course, said the Governor. Books: I'll be only too pleased. I have a modest library of my own; I'll have some sent down to you. Do you enjoy the novels of Walter Scott?

– He can keep one amused, I said. Most grateful.

I was being polite; Scott's plodding romances bore me to death. Aloud, I asked:

– Do you by chance have the latest novel by Mr Dickens? Or any of the works of Victor Hugo? No? Some essays by Leigh Hunt, perhaps – or the poems of Shelley or Wordsworth?

He was shaking his head to all of these – but he did have the plays of Shakespeare, which he promised to send along to me with Scott's *Quentin Durward*. He stood up.

– If you have any other wants or concerns, you have only to let me know, he said.

He sighed and hesitated, his eyebrows arched in sad surprise. Then he said:

– I do find it hard to understand that a man with your natural gifts, who has benefited from every advantage that society has to offer, should have placed himself in this situation. You practised at the Irish Bar, I understand, before you turned to those activities that have put you outside the law. And yours is an Ascendancy family, is it not? What a tragedy this must be for them!

– You need not puzzle yourself over my situation, I said. I'd hardly expect an Englishman to understand it. As to my aged parents, and others in my family – I can assure you, Mr Walker, they have every sympathy with my struggle. They are appalled, as I am, by the condition of our people – ejected from their homes by your landlords, and allowed to starve on the roads by your Government.

I had allowed my blood to rise a little, and instantly regretted it. There was no use in a display of passion to Mr Walker, whose face had closed like an affronted maiden lady's.

– However, I said, these are things that you and I need not discuss. I look forward to your books, sir. I may not love Britain's empire, but I do love her poets.

Slightly mollified, his careful smile in place again, Mr Walker took his leave of me.

I sat on, in my armchair, a sort of numbness stealing over me. It was sunset, and the empty courtyard outside was now filled with shadow. Only one door-shaped panel of sun was left on the grey cobbles, and I gazed at it with a sort of longing.

The guard was still there, in his dark blue uniform and peaked cap. He marched slowly to and fro with faint jinglings of his keys, boots clicking, humming a little tune to himself. He was a stocky, middle-aged Englishman with ruddy cheeks, grey side-whiskers and round dark eyes like a bird's that glanced at me as he passed. Now he paused in the doorway, clearing his throat and looking at me openly, his expression solemn and faintly wondering. He rocked on his heels, still humming his soft, music-hall tune.

– Tell me, I said, am I a beast in a cage for you to stare at?

He blinked, and I saw that he had a decent, well-meaning face.

– No sir, he said. But I'm set to guard you. I must have you under my eye at all times, and not leave you alone until lock-up hour. Those are my orders, and I can't help it. I've no wish to be here, sir, I can tell you, and lock-up hour can't come soon enough for me. I'll be glad to go for my tea.

And he took out his pocket watch, consulted it solemnly, and paced off with an affronted air. I laughed under my breath then, in rueful self-mockery. Of course: a beast in a cage was just what I was, for all the room's shabby-genteel fittings; a beast that needed to be watched. Mr Walker's respectful treatment had made me forget this.

9

Twenty minutes later, the turnkey came back and locked and bolted my door, carrying out the ceremony as loudly as possible.

Now I was a prisoner indeed; and the room's dim furnishings became suddenly intolerable. Bed, armchairs, basin-stand and table seemed to send out fusty emanations: invisible cords, seeking to bind me here for ever; to enmesh me in this comfortable tomb until the world forgot me. There was a sudden welling-up in my throat, and I lay down on the bed and wept.

I wept out of sheer anger, in a way that I'd not wept since childhood – and this made my weeping difficult to check, since my anger had no bounds. But checked the weeping was, at last, and I went to the basin-stand, poured out water from the china ewer, with its domestic pattern of roses, and washed my face. Then, breathing hard, I straightened myself up and smiled. It was over, and I would not weep like this again.

I am ready for you, I said. *Fate, I defy you!*

The obliging Mr Walker sent the promised books and tobacco by the guard that night, together with my supper. The next morning, having exercised by walking in the courtyard, I carried a chair out of my room and sat in the sun, reading *Macbeth* and smoking my pipe.

I found I savoured every word and every puff of smoke: the deprivation of one's freedom gives a new sort of intensity to things, it seems. I've always loved the fearsome beauty of this play, and have a sort of sympathy with Macbeth, who was drawn along his path of blood like a man mesmerised. What a man, for all his folly! He never turns his eyes from the consequences to which his actions are leading him. Thank God for Shakespeare, I said. I suspected I'd depend on him henceforth – and on many another poet and novelist of genius – at least as much as I depended on the dreary but adequate food my gaolers were providing.

Some days later a trunk arrived, despatched to me by my father. It contained, among other things, a selection from my library. So now I'd have sufficient reading matter to solace me for some time: the sort of literary powder magazine not to be found in sedate collections like Mr Walker's. Rousseau; Montesquieu; the sprightly and deadly Voltaire. But would my gaolers allow me to keep such dangerous French companions?

That afternoon, I had a visitor: the prison surgeon. He was a brown-bearded, comfortable young Irishman with a kindly face and an early inclination to plumpness. He was disposed to be friendly, and was possibly in sympathy with our cause – although I didn't try to draw him out. He made very careful enquiries about my health: so careful, that I began to wonder what his motives were. I assured him that my health was excellent.

– But you must have *some* congenital weakness, Mr Devereux, he said. Think.

His eyes widened and shone, trying to send me a message. When I merely looked puzzled, he pursed his bearded lips.

– You have certainly a good physique, he said. You are nearly six feet tall, I imagine.

– A little less, I said.

– And what complaints have you had in the past?

– Well, I have had asthma quite badly – but at present I'm perfectly free of it.

– Asthma! Good! That will do very well, Mr Devereux.

He smiled in delight, while I stared at him. Then he leaned forward, and lowered his voice confidingly.

– Mr Walker is very sympathetic to you, he said. As you see, he hasn't put you in convict dress – and nor does he wish to set you to prison work. But we may need to send a certificate to satisfy Dublin Castle: to testify that your health isn't equal to it, do you see?

He smiled reassuringly. Everyone was being very reassuring. Packing his medical bag to leave, he looked up at me: a look that was both whimsical and diffident.

– The whole of Ireland is talking about you, he said, so it won't surprise you to hear that there's some excitement in Cork at your being held here. You have many well-wishers – not least the ladies. Your portrait is hawked about the streets, and they declare you very handsome.

He drew from his bag a number of prettily-bound booklets.

11

– I wonder if I might ask you a favour, he said. Some lovely young ladies in Cove have begged me to get you to sign their autograph albums. I hope you won't think it a nuisance.

I signed half a dozen of the silly, scented little books, which looked as out of place here as flowers, or lace handkerchiefs.

– I wish the girls much joy, I said.

And I saw in my mind's eye these young Irish gentlewomen tittering over my signature in the parlours of their comfortable homes. Many were full of generous, romantic feeling, I had no doubt; but what would they or their close-mouthed parents ever do for our suffering country? They sympathised with Young Ireland; they read my newspaper, and murmured in fervent agreement. But when Paul Barry and I called for pikes and guns, and for the blood of our oppressors – then they shrank back, in their parlours. I knew them. Next month, when in all probability I should be confined on some foul British transport in mid-ocean, the young ladies would have a new idol: perhaps a singer with perfumed hair.

I saw how low my spirits were getting. I must guard against this, or risk losing my balance – even my resolve.

Three days later, I had a visitor.

As I was taking a turn about the courtyard, my shadow the turnkey called out to me. He was standing by a door in the high grey wall which led into another enclosure. He'd opened this door with one of his keys, and spoke to me in a manner that seemed furtive and almost nervous.

– There's a gentleman to see you, sir: a friend of yours. Will you come this way?

A friend? My thoughts flew to Paul Barry, and to Thomas O'Neill. Was it possible that one of these comrades had been allowed to visit me? I stepped to the door, heart beating fast, and found myself in another courtyard, larger than my own, and empty except for the figure of a man of medium height, in a black suit. He was pacing slowly about with his hat in his hand, half turned away from me, and my heart sank: it was neither of the cherished friends I'd hoped for, and I didn't seem to know him.

My guard stood in the doorway, hands clasped in front of him, looking into some private distance above his head with his sharp bird's eyes. I walked up to the gentleman in black. His funereal suit was decent but creased, I saw, and a little the worse for wear. He turned; amber eyes sought mine from behind round spectacles, and he held out his hand to me, his expression one of delight.

– My dear Devereux! It's good to see you looking so well, he said. But I should have known you'd look well.

And now I saw that it was Matthew Casey.

He and I had been at Trinity together. We'd taken our degrees in the same year, but I'd seen little of him since – even though he was a member of Young Ireland, as well as of the St Patrick Club. He had moved to Cork some years ago, and seemed to visit Dublin only seldom. I'd heard he'd become a journalist, and was working on a newspaper here. I knew little more about him; but the years had not outwardly changed him very much. His reddish-brown hair – of that straight, spiky sort that resists all grooming – still stood up in a tuft on the crown of his head, to prevent him from ever looking elegant. He had never seemed to have much money – or if he had, he plainly hadn't spent it on himself. He came from the people; his father had been a prosperous butcher, I recalled: an Anglican convert who wanted his son to get on in the world, like so many other ex-Catholics who sent their sons to Trinity. His upper lip, like mine, remained clean-shaven, but he'd grown a pair of side-whiskers, bronze and luxuriant, like a fox's brush, and quite out of keeping with the rest of him – as though Nature, having made him plain, had compensated with these hirsute decorations. He now had a small, dignified paunch that bulged his waistcoat – incongruous in a man who was otherwise somewhat thin and hungry-looking.

Setting all this down, I see that it looks as though I scarcely regarded him as a friend. But he had been one once, in our youth at Trinity – usually as a face among crowds of others, walking with me through the streets of Dublin, or seated in lecture halls or taverns. Yet although he was one of my group of confidants, there was a sense in which he wasn't quite *there* for a good deal of the time. He was one of those people who tended to disappear and then turn up again, at unexpected moments – suddenly surprising you by their presence. He was the born man behind the scenes, scheming on behalf of others; and he and I had never shared those secret ecstasies and longings which can only be comprehended by like minds, like spirits – who thrill to discover that their souls miraculously have counterparts. I didn't read aloud from Shelley, Coleridge, Byron and Goethe with Matthew Casey, as I did in the flickering midnights with men such as O'Neill. Had I done so, Casey would have grinned his obliging grin and made polite noises: but I believe he lacked those particular strings that have to be inside a man for the breeze of poetry to visit him, and to draw forth its music.

He stood looking at me now with what I can only call an ingenuous slyness.

– I came as soon as I could, he said.

There was a quick glint in his eyes which I remembered: a look both cautious and alertly calculating. His voice dropped: it was slightly nasal, and carried easily.

– Our good friend the guard was most helpful, he said. He doesn't approve of you, but he's sorry for your plight – and a little in awe of his celebrated captive.

He winked so swiftly that I almost thought I'd imagined it.

– I could have worse warders, I said. In fact, I'm quite well treated. It's good of you to come here, Casey. I'm heartily glad to see you.

– The least I could do, sir, he said. The very least.

With this jesting use of 'sir' – an old affectation from our college days – he lightened the situation. A somewhat ponderous and mannered jocularity had always been Casey's style.

– You're in all our minds, he said. Has no-one else visited you yet?

– No-one, I said. And I'm amazed that you've been able to do so, Casey. The Castle and the penal authorities are at pains to keep all members of the public away from me. There was talk of a rescue attempt in Dublin, and this has made them frantic to keep me isolated. So how did you manage to get in?

He grinned, revolving his tall black beaver hat by the brim, his fingers moving nervously, though the rest of him was still.

– A journalist can penetrate most barriers, he said. As an editor, you know that, I'm sure. It seems we both took to the pen, Devereux – although I've hardly done so in the distinguished way that *you* have. I'm a mere crime reporter on the newspaper here in Cork; but the police and the authorities know me quite well, and extend the occasional favour for favours done. At the moment I'm reporting on a rather tragic murder case. The man is a respectable bank employee who killed his wife with a poker. She'd betrayed him not once, but many times, and quite openly. Plainly he was driven beyond his normal bounds. He's been tried and sentenced, and awaits execution. I came here to interview him; it proved to be easy enough to gain access to you as well.

– And did the interview with your murderer go well?

– Sad, he said. Sometimes I'm glad I've not married. But I hear that *you're* engaged, Devereux – to a very beautiful young lady. From a Dublin family called Edgeworth, I believe.

– You're very well-informed about me, Casey.

– I read of your betrothal in the press. And mutual friends spoke of it as well. You're much reported on, sir.

His face became solemn; almost reverent.

– I can't express to you how much I've admired you, Devereux. I've never missed an issue of the *New Nation*. Your articles on the Famine brought me to tears – as they did so many others. The rest of us went off to our comfortable livings – but you! You, who could have followed a career at the Bar, and achieved success and affluence! I tell you, Devereux, as you stand here today, you are the man in all Ireland most to be admired; most to be envied!

At this, I couldn't resist glancing ironically at the grey stone walls that rose above us; nor could I help the brief laugh that escaped me.

– Forgive me, Casey, I said. It's somewhat difficult for me to appreciate my situation's enviable nature just now.

He looked chastened.

– Of course: your situation is appalling, my dear fellow. Please don't think I make light of it. I meant –

– I know what you meant, and thank you for it. But being incarcerated really does simplify one's notions. One concentrates on getting through each day. And my thoughts dwell a good deal on my parents, my brother and sister, and above all on my fiancée, whose distress is greater than mine.

– Terrible, he said. Terrible.

And then, delicately, with a glance under his brows:

– Miss Edgeworth will wait for you, I trust?

– For fourteen years? I would hardly expect that, I said. I would release her from the engagement, if that proved the situation. But I believe the British will eventually transport me to one of their colonies, and I hope that they may allow me a measure of freedom there. Then perhaps Miss Edgeworth might join me, and we still might marry. A faint hope – but it's all I have, at present.

– Yes, he said. Yes. Should it come to that, I'm sure she'll be true to you. But look here, Devereux, you won't actually serve out that whole fourteen years – I'm sure of it. You've committed no violence, even though you may have advocated violence. There'll be something done.

– A pardon? I think not. I'm convicted of high treason: I'm fortunate to have been let off execution. And under their wonderful new Treason-Felony Act, I'm actually a common felon: the first Irishman to be convicted of a felony for demanding liberty for his country. They've been very clever.

Casey made no immediate reply, pinching his chin between thumb and forefinger. Then he said:

– I imagine you regard such a conviction as an honour, rather than a disgrace.

– Their so-called treason is indeed an honour, I said. But felony? That's another matter. A common felon is a man disgraced. And so I am disgraced. My parents feel it deeply. They see our name as sullied for ever. I have seen my father weep over it. I love him, and his sorrow is the worst thing I've had to bring away with me.

– I'm familiar with the Act, Casey said. 'Levying war against the Queen; inciting others to do so by speaking, printing or publishing.' Of course, Devereux, it was framed to entrap you personally. It's a measure of the greatness of their concern about you. The Viceroy is thoroughly alarmed by Young Ireland – and by you and Paul Barry in particular.

His voice grew confiding; his expression earnest and intense. It was a journalist's intensity, feeding on the excitement of great events.

– The revolutionary situation in Europe is what's dominating Lord Clarendon's thinking, of course. Extraordinary, these last few months! Hungary; Italy; Prussia: all of them challenging the old order! And I know from reliable sources that the Castle sees Young Ireland as part of the revolutionary epidemic – with you as its most dangerous leader.

– Wonderful months, I said. A wonderful year. The British do well to fret; and the Castle does well to fear us. The day of the old order's done, Casey; suddenly everyone can see it. Even Metternich won't stem the tide.

Casey was half-smiling as I spoke, but at the same time shaking his head.

– All very fine, sir. Inspiring, he said. But this is why your position is so serious. Given that what you say is true, they *had* to arrest you. Lord Clarendon and his masters in London see the violent revolution you have preached in the *New Nation* as the signal for a larger storm, about to burst on them.

– As well they might, I said.

Casey's eyes were fixed on mine almost wonderingly.

– As well they might, sir, he said. The authorities imagine rifles and pikes everywhere – and here you are in your newspaper urging the peasantry to take up arms. It was your railway article that caused most alarm at the Castle.

– You speak as though you have connections there.

– I have my informants, like any good journalist. And I'm told Lord Clarendon sees you as a sort of Communist. You saw those placards, plastered up on walls by his orders? No? They warned respectable people that Red Republicans and Communists would rob them of their property, and murder them in their beds.

– What nonsense it all is! I said. I'm no Communist – and I don't give twopence for Republicanism either, except as the way to Irish freedom. As to my railway article, that's another matter. Who controls the railways, controls the nation's nervous system. If we engage in struggle, the railways will carry the troops who will try to crush us. And so we must strike at the railways, and tear up the lines – just as we must prepare for battle in the streets. You have seen how it is on the Continent, Casey: it's in the cities where ideas ferment – and in the streets of the cities where revolutionary struggle is decided.

Casey's expression had now become grave; no hint of amusement remained.

– You must have known the risks in advancing such ideas, he said. And you must have suspected that the people wouldn't rise. Even your Ascendancy supporters don't want bloodshed, do they? Not even your colleague Fitzgibbon wants it: he advocates peaceful means. You must have known that the Castle would seize you eventually. Why did you go so far, sir?

– As to whether the people will rise, I said, I have my own opinions on that. But it wasn't some foolish attack against the power of British arms that I advocated in the *New Nation*. I simply asked that the people deny their harvest to the British; that they pay no rents; that they defend their farms. That would have been a beginning. I took a gamble, and I lost.

– You thought they wouldn't pack the jury?

Casey had always been shrewd: he seemed, down here in Cork, to know as much as though he had been living all the time in Dublin.

– You follow very closely, I said. You are right. Here we have a Whig Ministry in London, piously proclaiming its liberal principles, and condemning the Tories for packing juries in the past. Very well; I decided to gamble on their principles: I challenged them in print to try me. No unpacked jury in Ireland would convict me; I knew that. And if they did pack, they would infuriate the people.

– Yet they did it.

– They did it. No Catholics at all – and no fellow-Protestants who were not my enemies. The people saw this, and are outraged – and so my hopes have been answered.

– Your *hopes*?

– Of course. What has been done to me has hastened our revolution – don't you realise that? Dublin Castle realises it, I can assure you.

Casey shook his head; then he gave me a quick, nervous smile.

– Well, there's one thing that can't be denied, sir. You've now become a hero and a martyr – whom the mass of the Irish people can look up to.

He took my arm, and began to lead me off across the courtyard.

– Let's walk, he said. You must surely need the exercise.

We paced to and fro, while the turnkey pretended to watch the sky. And now Casey spoke in a whisper, bending his head towards me.

– You say that the Clubs in Dublin wanted to take up arms to rescue you?

– Yes. But their leaders persuaded the clubmen to give it up, I said. I learned of that with disgust. Think: I am falsely convicted, put in fetters, and taken aboard a convict ship in what is actually an act of kidnapping – and not a counter-blow is struck! Where is our Irish manhood, Casey?

In spite of myself, I found I was beginning to indulge in the old, seductive ecstasy of anger. But Casey's sideways gaze, although seemingly sympathetic, had a quality of detachment which cooled my ardour. He said nothing; he paced on, and waited to hear more. He had always been a listener.

– What I have tried to make clear to everyone, I said, is that so far as I am concerned, we are at war. And my trial and conviction are really a sort of victory in this war. I may be transported; I may even die in one of their penal settlements; but what has been done to me will rid the faint-hearted of any notion that change is possible through constitutional means. The young will see it: they will see now just what sort of enemy we are dealing with. And all Europe will see it.

Casey halted, and looked at me in a sort of sober wonder. When he spoke, it was still very low.

– You are a truly dangerous man, sir.

– I hope so, I said.

He went on examining me, as though to assure himself of something. Then he asked:

– You really do want to see blood on the streets?

– If it will free us – *yes*. I have said it in my public speeches; I have printed it in my articles. I have called an end to the charade of negotiation.

– You have certainly done that, sir, he said. But could you not have waited for your revolutionary ideals to take root a little more, before you began to act on them? Could you not disseminate them underground, as it were?

– *No*. We've already waited too long. And what you suggest implies plotting and secrecy. I've no time for plotting in corners, and sly little deceptions. If a thing is true, it will stand the daylight – and be damned to those who don't like it.

He looked at me now with a curious expression: almost disconcerted, as though I'd rubbed on some hidden wound.

– You will never be a cautious or secret man, he said. That's plain. But what I've come here to say to you is this: that I will give you any help I can. I'm already making enquiries through every avenue I know concerning ways of getting you a pardon.

– Thank you. But I have a feeling that I shall be gone from here in a few days. My fiancée wished to travel from Dublin to visit me, and they discouraged her. They said there would not be time.

– Well then, we must work for your release – even if you are transported. And I shall visit your parents and your fiancée, if I may, to express my sympathy and support.

– My parents will be glad to see you, I'm sure. But alas, Miss Edgeworth's parents view with horror what has happened to me. They thought me a good match for their daughter until now. They tolerated my activities as misguided excesses of patriotism, and were impressed at how widely my articles were read. But now they find their daughter engaged to a terrorist and a felon. So they may not be so welcoming when you call. But thank you, Casey. You are a good friend.

20

I meant it, and took his hand. As though this had been a signal, the turnkey approached us deferentially, with soft throat-clearings.

– I'm sorry, Mr Casey, but I must ask that you come away now, and that Mr Devereux return to his cell. I'm to be relieved very soon, and it wouldn't do if –

– Of course, of course, Casey said. He turned to me, taking my hand again.

– I'll be working on your behalf, Devereux, you may be sure. I have a few acquaintances in high places.

– Bless you, Casey, I said. Write to me.

I was being polite: I had little faith in his 'acquaintances in high places'. We murmured final goodbyes, released each other's hands, and Casey was led away towards the door.

I watched his retreating, black-clad back as though he were the last normal human being I should see, the courtyard extending between us like some stony desert place where I must wander for ever. He had told me that I was to be envied; but in a few moments he would walk free through the world outside, seeing trees, crowds of faces, shops and secure houses: the blessed complex of the ordinary, which for me had already become the invisible and extraordinary. So it was I who envied him: even though I suspected there was not much to envy. With his plain, somewhat plebeian face, his hopeless lack of style, his respectable shabbiness and his wistfully eager interest, he was one of those people destined to be an eternal onlooker: a vicarious enjoyer of other people's joys and risks. He saw me as occupying the centre of the stage, just as he'd done in our student days: that I now trod a pathway towards a miserable fate had not altered this view, apparently.

Well, I thought, I'd be happy to change you places.

But then I thought again, and reflected that I wouldn't really choose this, if the price were to become Matthew Casey.

– Are you ready sir?

It was the turnkey at my elbow, mournful and respectable, waiting to see me back to my cell-disguised-as-a-bedroom.

2. A DREAM OF SUMMER ISLANDS

My prediction to Casey was fulfilled the very next day.

In the afternoon, I was visited in my room by a sullen, dark-browed, red-faced man in a chocolate tail coat. I'd been warned of his coming by the guard: his name was Inspector Broadbent. He seated himself heavily in one of the armchairs, and addressed me in a flat, throaty voice with a London accent.

– Good afternoon, Mr Devereux. You are well, I take it?

– Quite well, thank you, I said.

– You have no complaints to make?

– None at all.

– I'm glad to hear it. You could scarcely have grounds to do so.

The Inspector glanced about at the comforts of the room with contemptuous disapproval. Then he looked back at me in silence, hands on fat knees, with the dull and thwarted menace of a choleric man. I returned his stare with an air of quizzical good humour which I hoped he found irritating. Finally, he spoke again.

– I now have the duty to inform you that Her Majesty's Government has decided to transport you out of Ireland.

– I see, I said. May I ask when?

– Tomorrow morning, sir.

– Indeed? And may I ask where?

– Bermuda, sir. You'll be taken by the *Nemesis*, at present lying in the harbour. A war steamer.

– Really? The latest thing. I'll be interested to see over her.

The corners of his mouth grew sulky.

– No doubt you shall, he said. I have to inform you that Mr Walker has already been on board, and has had a meeting with the Commander, who's got sealed orders concerning you which was given to him in Portsmouth. The instructions apparently direct that you're to be treated on the voyage as you've been treated here. As 'a person of education and a gentleman'.

His voice had become heavily sarcastic, uttering this last phrase. He began to cough extensively, growing even redder in the face, and holding a handkerchief over his mouth. When he'd done, he stared into the handkerchief with sombre satisfaction, breathing heavily. Then he looked up at me.

– What else the instructions say concerning you will no doubt be made known to you when you reach Bermuda. But if they was to direct that your position should be as easy there as it is here, I'd be very surprised. Very.

He stood up, and I did the same.

– But I entirely agree with you, Inspector, I said. The situation is absurd. The British Government says I'm a felon – and an educated felon is surely as bad as any other. How does education entitle him to special privileges? The Government should prosecute me with the utmost rigour. I ask no special favours. But perhaps the Government finds severity impolitic. Perhaps it's embarrassed by the scrutiny of the world. Perhaps I'm *not* a felon, after all. In which case, the Government must be the felon. It's one or the other, isn't it?

His mouth squeezed itself up like a fist. His muddy eyes widened, and I saw that he badly wanted to strike me. I smiled insultingly, letting him know by my expression that my wish to strike him back was just as strong. But he gained control of himself, and spoke in a soft, hoarse voice.

– Be thankful, Mr Devereux, that it isn't me that's got to decide your fate.

I continued to smile.

– It makes little difference to me, Inspector. One of you is the same as another.

He moved to the door, and then turned.

– You are proud, he said. They'll break that pride, on Bermuda.

At eight o'clock next morning, I found myself being rowed across Cork Harbour in a boat full of Marines.

I was leaving without having had a letter from Catherine; but there was still a last chance of hearing from her. Mr Walker had offered to bring out to the ship any letters that might arrive today before we sailed. It was grey, cold and windy, with showers of light rain; but after my confinement, the harbour's wide reaches were wonderful to me. Beside me in the stern were my humble port-manteau and the trunk full of clothing and books sent by my father. As the sailors pulled at their oars, they shot glances at me. Many of them had those cheerful, steadfast faces of rural England which I cannot help liking. The first lieutenant of the *Nemesis* stood by me in full uniform: young, blond and serious, with cocked hat and sword. Patently dutiful, he was like the sort of boy who is made a prefect at school; but he could hardly be seen as hateful either.

Port of departure! Port of tears! The rain, in what seemed a ceremony of sadness, was letting down veils of grey gauze. It trailed them across Spike Island, where the grim, nude buildings of the prison receded behind me; it shrouded the ketches of poor fisher-men, and tall British brigs and schooners, distant and close at hand. It came and went, concealing and then revealing the green Cove of Cork, with a church spire and huddled white houses; it veiled final, grey-blue hills, which became like territories of Faery. And I spoke silent words, then.

Farewell, my country, my mother and my queen! Am I truly leaving you for fourteen years?

No, I said: I would escape my gaolers. I would come back – unlike those desperate emigrants who had crowded the quay at Cork since the Famine began, their hopes set on America, and New South Wales. On a previous visit to Cork I had watched them with pity, never dreaming I might join them: the young men in their many-patched jackets and tall, battered hats; the wives in their eternal cloaks and shawls, clutching their bundles and their babies,

24

taking leave of parents they would never see again, who knelt down in front of them on the cobbles: the fathers weeping and praying, the old mothers keening as though for the dead.

Ahead, about a mile off, and rapidly drawing nearer, lay HMS *Nemesis*: a rakish, steam-powered auxiliary frigate with a black hull, two funnels, and three masts for sail, waiting to carry me away. But animal spirits can't be subdued, at my age. As I looked at her, I found I had the fast-beating pulse one always has when setting out on a voyage, and a paradoxical illusion of freedom. Appalling though my situation was, there was also something tremendous in the prospect of being borne three thousand miles across the Atlantic, clad in my grey summer frock coat and old, dark-blue cap, with its glazed peak. So contradictory is the human heart! In particular a heart such as mine, since I am a man of double nature.

Very soon, I was climbing the companion-ladder that hung from the warship's side, preceded by the blond lieutenant. He held out a polite but unnecessary hand to help me onto a long, unbroken deck, and I was met by sudden smells of coal and tar, informing me that I had entered another world: the machine-world of her Britannic Majesty's navy. Following where the lieutenant led, I looked up into the rigging and at the tall, strange funnels, which seemed to me like towers from some realm of troubled fancy: a life yet to come, perhaps, or one just being born, shaped in the iron womb of England. A mortar sat close to the mainmast; a long gun was set above the bow. Tan-faced English sailors hurried by, glancing curiously at me, many of them with eyes of that particular vivid blue which seems (although surely one imagines it), to be peculiar to men who follow the sea. Three of them were carrying my trunk and portmanteau across the deck to some unknown point in the ship, like obliging porters. Somewhere out of sight, a voice shouted an order; and I began to feel incongruously like a guest being taken into some splendid hotel, rather than a prisoner. It was a not unpleasant illusion, and would persist, since these conditions would also persist.

The lieutenant led me up a companionway on to the quarter-deck, where he presented me to the captain of the *Nemesis*, who was pacing to and fro. Captain Wood lifted his cap, and gave me a searching yet courteous glance of appraisal. He was an angular, dark-haired man of middle age, whose skin had a yellowish tinge, perhaps as a result of serving in the tropics. He had a brooding, thoughtful look that seemed more scholarly than seamanlike: but perhaps this is a breed of officer the new steamships are producing.

– I think you'll find your quarters adequate, he said, and asked me to follow him below.

When I did so, I was startled to discover just how adequate my accommodation was. I'd been placed in a small but well-fitted sleeping-cabin in the stern, which adjoined the ship's main cabin. Both were lit by the handsome, inward-sloping stern windows, which curved from one side of the ship to the other. The main cabin was quite spacious, with a mahogany dining-table, two couches, and a set of chairs. The captain and some of his officers took their meals here, but I was told by Captain Wood that I might use it as I pleased during the day.

– I trust that you'll not be averse to dining with us on most evenings, he said.

I told him that I'd be delighted to dine with them, and that I hoped my company would not be a burden on the voyage.

– On the contrary, he said. We grow rather dull at times, and will welcome fresh conversation at dinner. You have, I believe, some original notions on various subjects.

His mouth bent in a smile that revealed a sense of humour, and he turned to go. At the door he paused and spoke again, his polite tone unchanged.

– I'm sure we'll manage well enough, Mr Devereux – but I'm obliged to consider you a prisoner. A Marine will be stationed at the foot of the companionway outside. You may go on deck when-ever you please, but you will have to inform him, and he'll then call for a sergeant to escort you. Breakfast will be sent down to you shortly. The prison Governor, Mr Walker, is expected on board at any time: I believe he has some mail for you. I'll delay sailing until he arrives.

I thanked the captain for his trouble – everyone was going to a good deal of trouble – and sat down in the main cabin to wait for Mr Walker. My spirits had risen higher at the mention of mail. There must surely be a letter from Catherine: the first communication from her since we'd parted in Newgate Prison. Soon I heard feet coming down the companionway outside.

Mr Walker entered the cabin accompanied by a red-coated Marine, his tall hat under his arm. He was carrying a single envelope which he held out to me between two fingers – delicately, like an expensive gift.

– I sent in to the office at Cove to see what they had for you, Mr Devereux. This had just arrived.

I thanked him, and looked at the envelope. The handwriting was not Catherine's.

Mr Walker was still talking, but I no longer heard him; my bowels seemed to fill with a hateful, cold gruel. I forced myself to look up, and to encounter his piously concerned, protuberant old eyes.

– Trust that your news from home will be good, he was saying.

I managed a reply to the effect that I was sure it would be; and he held out a papery hand.

– I must take my leave of you now, Mr Devereux, he said. I do wish you well. I hope that your stay in Bermuda will not be too greatly prolonged. It is my belief that the authorities will allow you to make a new life there in comparative freedom.

– I'm in young Queen Victoria's hands, I said. But I believe I'm a troublesome charge for her. More than she can deal with, perhaps.

His face closed at this veiled and gentle disrespect for his sovereign.

– Goodbye, Mr Devereux. I fear you have a strange destiny – but God be with you.

– Goodbye, Mr Walker. You've been most kind.

When he had gone, I sat down at the table and opened the letter. It contained a brief, scented note from an unknown lady admirer, assuring me that Irish hearts were beating for me in my dread situation. And she enclosed, for my comfort and inspiration,

27

a religious tract. I crumpled it in my hand, and sat absolutely still for some time.

Poor Mr Walker! He'd gone to some pains to bring me this wretched letter in person – while the *Nemesis,* with all her leashed power, had been held on my behalf. Why had no letter come from Catherine? She had promised to write quickly. In my bitter disappointment, I tried not to blame her in my heart. Perhaps she'd delayed writing for a few days more to give me extra news; after all, she could not have known that I'd be transported so suddenly. Well, I would not know the answer now for many weeks. Her letter – when she wrote one – would follow me to Bermuda, and I must wait for it until then.

Somewhere in the bowels of the ship, the sound of engines began: muffled, slow, but terrific.

A steward entered, carrying on a tray a hearty breakfast of eggs and smoked kippers and coffee. They did themselves well, in the British Navy.

It blew hard, in the evening. There were creakings in the walls of my cabin, and I could dimly discern white-topped waves rearing grey in the dusk through the stern windows. We were out of sight of land now, and moving solely under sail – which we'd done since clearing the coast of Cork that morning. I had gone out on deck then, escorted by a sergeant of Marines, and had stood watching the hills disappear in the rain until I could see no more, while the shrouds of the *Nemesis* rattled, and her sails boomed. Now I was a man without moorings: a man without a home or citizenship.

There was a knock, and the steward came in: a small, cheerful Londoner with thin, fair hair and prominent front teeth. He told me that the captain would not be dining in the main cabin tonight, and asked if he might bring me some supper. But my stomach had begun to grow queasy with the pitching of the ship, and I asked him to bring me nothing but a pot of tea and some arrowroot.

– She's rolling a bit, eh? Yes: arrowroot's a good idea, sir, if you're seasick.

– Will there be a storm?

– Bless you, no, sir. This ain't going to be a storm – just half a gale of wind. And there's not much a storm can do with the *Nemesis*.

When he'd gone for my tea, I lay on the bunk and felt easier. And I found myself wishing that a storm would come: the biggest the ocean could brew up. A curse on the halfness of the half gale! I wanted the sea to grip and pound this warship to the limit of her capacity to endure it: not just to test and try her, but to test and try me. But no storm came.

All that night, with the steward's words in my ears, I lay fitfully sleeping and waking, pitched and tossed in a half-world, by 'half a gale of wind'. The bunk would rise under me, borne on the shoulders of old Ocean, and hang static for many long seconds; then, with a giddy, gliding motion, we would be let down into a trough, a place of churning uncertainty, to await the next wave. It became an actual region, this trough: a boiling yet icy netherworld, without life or hope or peace, resembling the deepest circle of Inferno.

The motion of the ship was not entirely novel to me. But its power and force were – since the vessels that had taken me across St George's Channel, or over the English Channel to Calais, could scarcely have been said to have gone to sea. I was truly at sea for the first time; and I contemplated the fact that HMS *Nemesis* was moving out into the Atlantic, carrying me away from Europe altogether: away from all that was civilized, known and loved.

The next morning I woke feeling well, and more cheerful – even though the wind was blowing stronger, and the ship pitched and rolled to a degree that would have been alarming, had it not been for the steward's reassurances. It continued to blow for the next two days – during which I saw nothing of Captain Wood, and ate alone in the main cabin.

Late in the afternoon on the second of these days, I went out on deck and stood at the slanting rail. There was no rain, but the world was darkened and the sun blotted out by bruise-coloured clouds. I watched the little storm petrels – birds of the half-light – skimming and wheeling above the huge, dark green rollers. I had got my sea-legs now, and found that I revelled in the croon of the wind in the shrouds, the sway of the deck, and the flight of the petrels, which danced above the sea's surface like spirits of upheaval. And I had a sudden premonition: I would not be suited by the tropics. O wild North Atlantic! Native zone! Borne away to those other, opposite regions of heat, calm and languor, I saw how utterly I belonged not there, but *here*. I am a North Atlantic creature: a trite and obvious statement, perhaps, but it is one thing to know this as a fact, and quite another to discover it in one's soul, as I now did, in the moment of exile.

A voice spoke at my elbow.

– Mother Carey's chickens. Eh?

It was Thompson, the sergeant of Marines who'd been appointed as my keeper: half formidable, half absurd, in the red coat, white webbing and curious black hat with the curling brim that these Britannic sea-troops are obliged to wear. He was a big, balding fellow with a smiling face like Humpty-Dumpty's, and entirely hard eyes. Always friendly, he seemed to regard it as his duty to keep me entertained. He was pointing now to the petrels.

– That's what we call them, sir – Mother Carey's chickens.

– So I've heard. The souls of lost sailors, don't they say?

– They do say so. Would you like to take a stroll about the ship, sir?

He led the way down the main deck, where we came upon a mixed group of Marines and sailors being drilled. Britannia is thorough: on a man-of-war, her sailors as well as her Marines are drilled as soldiers, and these were all armed with muskets, cutlasses, bayonets and hatchets – which I had no doubt they were adept at handling. Easy to see that the English were once notorious pirates: these fellows could have been taken for well-disciplined buccaneers. The ship was rolling so much that it threatened to pitch them across the deck and so impale Thompson and me on their bayonets; but they balanced themselves so cleverly on toes and heels that the drill went on perfectly, every face wearing that particular look of hard cheerfulness that is peculiarly English: the same expression that Thompson wore.

It's deceptive, this look; I half despise and half admire it. It sometimes causes these men to be considered harmless. It's a mindless
cheerfulness which comes from their servant mentality, and has turned
them into battle-fodder for all of England's wars – just or unjust,
reasonable or atrocious, it makes no difference to them; they obey.
They lack the Irish rebel instinct that makes us question such things;
they lack our wild daring. They go at war like good-humoured labourers getting a job done; like mechanics repairing an engine. But they
win wars, while the reckless so often lose them. They lack true independence, and that divine madness which I call the Celtic leap – that
jump into the fire or into the dark without heed of consequences.
But the treacherous Norman Englishman in my blood had begun to
trouble me, whispering that men such as these, with their ultimately
terrible stubbornness, were those who always prevailed in the end.
They had broken Napoleon; they had subdued India, and all the other
territories around the globe that make up the Empire: they were the
rocks on which the iniquitous Empire was built. The Roman legion-
aries must have had faces like these, I thought. Very likely they'd
worn the same patiently cheerful expressions as they stood in their
cohorts to face the enemies of Rome, javelins and short swords in
their fists. And I found myself remembering my schoolboy study of
Caesar's *Gallic War*, and his caustic remarks on the character of the
Celtic tribes: brave, eager for war, but also unstable, credulous,
scatterbrained and disorganised – given to both anger and panic.
Because of these weaknesses, Rome and Caesar had prevailed.

We haven't changed. When will we learn?

That evening, for the first time, I dined with Captain Wood and
two of his officers in the main cabin. One of them, Millington, was
the blond first lieutenant who had brought me aboard; the other,
Campbell, was also a lieutenant. Stocky, with reddish hair, Campbell
had a friendly yet immobile Scots face that I liked.

We were all very polite with each other throughout the meal,
which consisted of onion soup, a fine cut of beef, and fresh peaches.
We drank a good claret, followed by a sunny Madeira, and it became somewhat difficult to remember that I was a felon.

Over the Madeira and peaches, the captain became inclined for conversation, and addressed me directly.

– Well now, Mr Devereux, I believe Sergeant Thompson has conducted you over the ship. What do you think of her?

– A remarkable vessel, Captain: truly a creature of 1848.

– Yes, I believe she is. We shall live to see the day when these steam vessels will replace sail entirely.

– The prospect of such juggernauts must be exciting, for the Navy, I said. But surely there's nothing so beautiful as a sailing ship.

The captain grew tolerant, as experts do with amateurs.

– I agree with you, he said, but it isn't beauty that wins battles at sea. With these auxiliary steamers, the British Navy is truly unbeatable. A fast ship under sail may outrun us for a while in a fair wind; but in the end, we will outrun her every time, since we can call on our engines. We cannot be stopped.

– I don't doubt you, Captain, I said. Unstoppable as the Empire itself, I imagine.

There was a short silence, during which the wholesome, blond Millington absorbed himself in slicing a peach, and Lieutenant Campbell glanced at me; I thought I caught a glint of amusement in his grey Scottish eye. The captain smiled, but said nothing. Then he picked up a box of cigars from the middle of the table, opened it, and pushed it towards me.

– Do you like cigars, Mr Devereux? I fancy you'll find these good, he said.

We each selected one, and lit up. As we got them to draw, Millington did his duty by directing the conversation back to its original safe channel.

– Steam power isn't easily accepted, he said. It's been the same story with Sam Cunard's passenger liners, on the Liverpool to Boston run. At first people called them tea-kettles. Now everyone wants to travel with Cunard, and get there quicker.

– True, Campbell said. But I have to agree with Mr Devereux: we may never make such a lovely thing as a sailing ship again. No doubt you've read Charles Dickens, Mr Devereux. Aye; well, he went across to America a few years ago on Cunard's *Britannia*, and didn't think much of her. He said that her dining saloon was like a hearse with windows.

We all laughed; and in this moment of ease and good humour, I raised my glass to Captain Wood.

– It can't have resembled this handsome saloon of yours, Captain. Your good health, gentlemen – and my thanks for your hospitality.

– Our pleasure, sir, said Captain Wood. We hope you find the voyage agreeable, and we regret the circumstances that oblige you to make it.

His tone grew neutral; he sat back in his chair, and his dark eyes examined me with a thoughtfulness whose nature I couldn't read. Not for the first time, I wondered about the contents of his sealed orders concerning me.

– We hear all manner of stories about Ireland, he said. I know little of your country, to be truthful with you. What is all this talk about packing juries?

I explained as objectively as I could – avoiding, as was my policy, any direct reference to my own trial, or any complaint. The three men listened to me in silence, their faces composed. But there began to be a doubtful expression in the captain's eye; he looked at me sideways, as though considering for the first time that I might be a fanatic, after all.

– Well now, he said, and ashed his cigar. I'm glad none of it concerns me. I've never cared for politics.

– It's a happy man who doesn't have to, I said. Your ship is your world, Captain, I fancy.

– Aye, true, he said briefly; and after this the talk turned to other topics.

When they had gone, and the steward had cleared away, I withdrew to my cabin next door. After a time, there came a tapping on the door, and Lieutenant Campbell peered in.

– I brought ye this, he said, and held out a book. It may interest you. It's one o' the best accounts I know of serving under sail, and what it means to be a sailor.

The book was *Two Years before the Mast,* by the American

33

Richard Henry Dana: a work I'd heard of but not read. I thanked Campbell, and he held up his hand, dismissing my thanks. He turned to leave the cabin, obviously not wanting to linger.

– We officers have a small library on board, he said. Ye'll be most welcome to make use of it. We've all agreed we're happy for ye to do so.

I thanked him again. I had intended to be cold, formal and withdrawn with these captors of mine; but it was proving difficult.

The *Nemesis* throbbed towards Bermuda at the rate of a hundred and eighty miles a day. When she wasn't driven by fair winds, she would call on her infernal engines, and the smoke from her black, weird funnels would rise to stain the sky.

To serve these engines, half-naked sailors laboured below in a pit like a compartment of Hell, their sickly-white bodies like those of underground grubs. Pouring with sweat, their coal-dusted skins reflecting the flames they served, they worked with shovels, bending and straightening as though they too were machines, feeding the coal into the mouths of roaring furnaces. These were no longer sailors, I thought: except that they worked for pay, their lot was surely as bad as that of ancient galley slaves. But the results of their efforts were impressive. In less than a week, the grey-green northern seas were left behind, and we passed the distant peaks of the Azores, tantalising as the mountains of lost Atlantis – which they may be, for all I know. We had entered the regions of sun, and blue water.

I had never seen such blue. It was the deep, luxurious blue of the edge of the tropics: of a zone of extravagant intensities. Vivid and profound, the colour of depth and infinite distance, it kept me fascinated for many days, as I stood at my post on the main deck. I revelled too in the sun, which at first was delicious and mild, bathing my face with healing kindliness. But with each passing day, it grew stronger and more remorseless, and I began to retreat into the shade, and finally into my cabin, where I lay reading Charles Dickens's *Nicholas Nickleby*, and many old copies of *Punch* – borrowed from the officers' little library. Paddle-wheels churning through a glass-smooth sea, the *Nemesis* was carrying me into latitudes as enigmatic as my future, and I ought to have remained alert; yet a lassitude overtook me which I finally called boredom. I'm not sure that this term will do, though, since the ship's routine was always at bottom unreal to me: a sort of strange day-dream, relieved by small diversions of a magical nature.

Standing on deck with the friendly Lieutenant Campbell, I found that we had entered a region of flying-fish. They appeared from nowhere, as though materialising out of atoms; and they seemed to me as miraculous as morning dreams. Bursting from the water in brilliant little explosions to skim above the swell, they were like the incarnation of those rare moments in life when a surge of remarkable happiness overtakes us, for no apparent reason: moments that open a door on the land behind appearances. They would fly, disappear and reappear a number of times; then they would drop into the blue for the last time: a shower of silver sparks, not to be re-kindled. At this, I would find myself searching the ocean's plains to ask that they change their minds: that they leap into being just once more, and bring back joy. And when the water's surface remained implacable, and would not yield them up until the next time, I found my heart sinking like a disappointed boy's.

Then, with a stab of fear, I realised what was happening to me, and what my future in captivity might be like. My good spirits would depend on things as small as the flying-fish.

Next, the dolphins came. The dolphins, with their bulbous, shining baby heads, were even more miraculous than the flying-fish: they burst through bottle-green windows in the sea across two thousand years, emerging into reality from ancient coins and frescoes, leaping into being while I cried out in amazement, and Campbell smiled. Frisking around the ship like clever dogs, the dolphins actually seemed to smile too, and one sensed a silent laughter. One of them, jumping high as I craned over the rail, appeared to glance sideways at me, with the light of human intelligence in his eye. I imagined this, of course; but every day, I grew more childish in my notions, as this strange tropical reverie extended.

My other diversions were the appearance of Portuguese men-of-war – jelly-fish with lovely rose-and-purple sails – and the brown

Gulf weed that began to surround the ship, and which Campbell told me drifted all the way from the Gulf of Mexico. And one morning the steward hurried into the cabin to inform me that a sail had been sighted: an event of some moment, at sea. I went out on deck and watched her pass, Europe-bound: a French sailing ship, a big West Indiaman, flying her proud tricolour. And I longed, with a poignancy that almost made me cry out, to be plucked across the space between us and set aboard her: to be carried to Le Havre or Nantes, in that country which is the capital of liberty and beauty; home of the free mind and the free spirit.

I watched her sails until they dropped beneath the horizon, and then went below to my cabin and lay for an hour quite still, staring at the cabin ceiling.

The heat increased still further, as the days went by, to a degree I had only imagined, and never before experienced. After breakfast, and a stroll on the deck, I would lie on my bunk with coat and waistcoat off, sweating like the men who laboured below at the furnaces, but with no exertion to justify it.

When I stood on deck with my guard Sergeant Thompson, he would wipe his brow constantly, his egg-like countenance flushed, his heavy uniform plainly a burden to him. The water was hot in the tank; the wine that the steward brought to Captain Wood's table in the evening was warm in its bottle. There was not a breath of wind on the sea; had we been a sailing ship, we would have been becalmed. But we churned on, engines remorselessly throbbing.

We had not sighted land since the Azores, and I began to have the irrational feeling that we'd never do so again. But Thompson now informed me that we'd reach Bermuda in two days.

– Perhaps we may miss it, I said lightly, and sail on, like Columbus.

He shook his head; he was a literal-minded fellow.

– Our navigation's better than that, sir, he said. However much you may wish it wasn't.

And he grinned, glancing at me with his genial killer's eyes, a sudden hint of sardonic amusement showing beneath his veneer of respect. It was the first time he'd alluded to my real status and condition, and I saw that his deference was a mask. They all wore masks, these English. No doubt at Bermuda the masks would be taken off, and I'd discover that this was no tropical holiday after all. They were playing with me. My bowels went cold; but I steeled myself. I'd been letting myself grow soft; instead, I must be ready for the worst they could do.

Two more days.

At ten o'clock in the morning on the second day, a sailor at the masthead gave the call: *Land-ahoy!*

I was standing already at the rail, smoking my pipe, and the sound of that call sent a thrilling shock through me. Officers and ordinary seamen crowded to the rail beside me; others hurried up and down companionways, talking with a special animation. The whole ship was astir, voices rising like those in a gay and busy marketplace: everyone wanted a glimpse of the familiar element we had so long lost sight of, and these seasoned sailors had an eagerness no less sharp than my own.

I peered ahead, to where a sort of amber mist lay on the horizon, thinning as the sun climbed higher; but I could make out no land. Lieutenant Campbell, more spruce than usual, his dark blue uniform and cap looking freshly cleaned, came hurrying along the deck, chewing an apple. He halted beside me, and threw the apple half-eaten into the sea, as though anticipating better pleasures on land. His firm-fleshed, square face was freshly shaven and raw-looking.

– Ye'll no see Bermuda from there, Mr Devereux, he said. Come up on the paddle-box.

Together we climbed the steps up the half-moon of casing that housed one of the paddle-wheels, bringing us a good way above the deck. A number of other officers already stood there, all gazing in one direction. And now, following Campbell's outstretched finger, I made out on the horizon several low hummocks of land, seemingly quite close.

Bermuda! My heart rose and sank like a ball on a string, and when I turned away from my scrutiny, it was to find Campbell regarding me with his narrow grey eyes, his face expressionless yet somehow hinting at good will, in that particular way he had. But his next words had a brutal directness.

– There's your gaol.

– So I see, I said.

The other men had gone down; there was no-one to overhear us. Campbell and I had conversed pleasantly during the voyage – mostly about ships and the sea; sometimes about books. He was a well-read man, and intelligent, but plainly not cursed with imagination: the sort of man I trust and feel comfortable with, but can never be like. To be with him was comforting; he made me think of homely things, and of the sort of boyhood friend who now belonged to a lost, simpler world which I no longer inhabit, and never can again – but which such men, in their plain, decent serenity, still do. And always, although he said nothing, I seemed to glimpse in Campbell's reliable, clean-shaven face some sort of sympathy for my position.

He took off his cap and scratched his head. His faded, coppery hair had some grey in it; he was older than I: perhaps forty.

– May it not be too trying for ye, he said softly.

He squinted again towards the islands out in front of us.

– I'm sorry that ye'll be away from those who are dear to ye. I know what it is to miss my wife and boys for even a few months.

– Well, I've brought it on myself, I said.

He looked at me hard.

– Ye're a bold man, he said. But a rash one. Ye'll not beat them this way, ye know. We learned that in Scotland.

– You fought them bravely, once. You should have fought on.

He smiled without amusement and shook his head, his gaze still steady on me.

– An idealist is a terrible thing to be, he murmured. It's an illness. A young man's illness. I wish ye good luck, Mr Devereux. Ye'll need it.

Without further words, we came down the steps to the main deck. We were joined here by Lieutenant Millington, who lent me a glass with which to spy out the land, and began to point out its features. Unlike Campbell, he seemed to want to maintain until the end the fiction that I was really a sort of tourist whom it was their duty to entertain.

– In all these three hundred islands, he said, there's not a single stream. So they're devilish short of water here. The people have to trap rainwater.

– Aye, a thirsty place, said Campbell. The rocks are porous. They drink up the water that falls on them.

No streams! Something in my soul shrank back. I thought with pure pain of the streams of green Clare, bubbling over smooth grey stones, running deep and dim under overhanging trees; and I thought of the lovely Shannon. All my life I've loved streams and rivers; now I'd been exiled to a place entirely devoid of them. The islands I was spying through Millington's glass had a brownish tinge underlying their greenery – an arid undertone never seen in northern Europe – and the nearer we ran to the shore, the more the thirstiness of this land was confirmed. Low hillocks were sparsely covered by dark cedars: no other kind of tree was to be seen. The brown soil was hungry-looking, and the rocks of which Campbell had spoken were an unnatural white, glaring in the sun in a way that made one squint. White houses without chimneys began to appear under the cedars, next to which were outhouses for cooking, their inhabitants visible in the open doorways. Through the glass, I could clearly make out African faces, and bright, outlandish clothes like those of gypsies. There was no sign of cultivation, except for small kitchen gardens.

But by questioning Millington, who loved to impart information, I discovered that this barren impression was somewhat misleading. Bermuda was fertile, he said, and produced an abundance of fruit, vegetables and fish. There was quite a large population, with two towns – and of course, the dockyards and barracks of the Empire. So it seemed the place flourished; and watching the islands glide by, I tried to raise my spirits by conjuring up their literary associations. These, after all, were the 'remote Bermudas', the islands of eternal Spring, riding in Marvell's magical poem; these were the models for Waller's *Dream of the Summer Islands*, and the place where

Prospero sent Ariel to fetch dew. Might I not achieve a sort of lotus-eating, exile's happiness here, if they allowed me 'relative freedom'? And if Captain Wood's sealed orders permitted it, might I not look forward to bringing Catherine here, to live with me in a white cottage by the sea, enjoying the eternal Spring?

We arrived at our anchorage at sunset: an island at the extreme north-west of the group, whose name, of all things, was Ireland Island. I stood with a group of officers on the main deck. Nearly all of these men, I noticed, began to be vivacious, and to laugh frequently; it was as though they had all taken a tot of brandy. Everything about this place conspired to stir youthful British senses, since here, on this remote Atlantic island, a sample of the might of their Empire had burst into view. As for me, I viewed it as a prisoner of Rome might have done, coming for the first time into one of her more important colonies in Asia, and seeing how Roman arms imposed themselves everywhere.

We were dropping anchor opposite a naval dockyard of a magnitude quite novel to me. Certainly it had no counterpart in Ireland. The stone-built stores and offices, and the wet dock itself, were on a vast scale – their brutal massiveness truly Roman. Ireland Island was basically a huge, complex fortress. Behind the dockyard's crescent, a low, mound-like hill rose in terraces, on which a series of cannon squatted, pointing out to sea. On top of the central hill was a barracks: a set of monumental buildings of the same pale stone as the rest, with arched, bomb-proof roofs; and on a high, arrogant standard like the mast of a ship, tyranny's Union Jack waved in the light breeze. From this centrepiece, the eye was led away around a long, sweeping line of fortifications that connected the barracks hill with another on the north of the island. Distant batteries brooded there in a threatening red glow – for on all these frowning fortifications the sun was now setting fast, tinting them with the theatrical hues of the sub-tropics, as though preparing them for some dread imperial drama.

Meanwhile, a coolness was arriving which made me realise that the Bermudan climate was softer than I'd imagined. A moist, delicious south wind came in across the sea, ruffling the pale green water of the port; and such a variety of shipping rode around us that the mind reeled back. Many of the sailing ships had strange and exotic rigs, and on our starboard side, the *Great Western* lay at anchor. I gazed in fascination at this titanic, trans-Atlantic steamer, which I'd seen until now only in pictures. With her great black funnel, four tall masts, long, lance-like bowsprit and giant red paddle-wheels, she dwarfed the *Nemesis*; and the officers grew quite animated, pointing out her features. She was the first, they said: the pioneer steamship of the Bristol-New York run; and they gazed on her with that sentimental pleasure the English usually reserve for their horses and dogs. They are falling in love with their new machines, I believe.

On our port side was a line-of-battle ship of seventy-four guns, a square red flag fluttering at her masthead – which meant, Lieutenant Millington informed me, that an admiral was aboard. The admiral was old Lord Dundonald, he said: hero of many naval battles, from South America to Greece – where the navy had given support to local patriots fighting for their freedom. I smiled, but said nothing, wondering what Lord Dundonald thought of Irish patriots fighting for their freedom. Meanwhile, speaking in a low, cautious voice, Millington had gone on to tell me that Captain Wood must soon report to the admiral, bearing with him his sealed orders concerning me. The admiral would then communicate with the Governor of Bermuda, and tomorrow these two great men would make my fate known to me.

To this, I made no comment, and Millington took his leave of me. My watch-dog Sergeant Thompson was not about, and I lingered here alone, as the *Nemesis* moved slowly towards her anchorage.

The dock was sheltered by a long breakwater, where more ships lay; and skimming everywhere among the world's proud traffic, like dragon-flies on the light green water, went small Bermudan boats with stained and ragged sails, manned by black African crews. They were market men and washerwomen, and they had piled their craft dangerously high with fruit, vegetables and baskets. One of these, handled by two tall Negroes in palmetto hats, came quite close to the *Nemesis*. A young woman in a blue-spotted turban and bright

orange dress sat in the stern, and she attracted the attention of a row
of young sailors some way along the deck. Spruce for shore-leave
in their straw hats, blue round jackets and white, bell-bottomed
trousers, they leaned far over the rail and began to chaff her, yelping
with laughter. The African men on the boat called back, and then
laughed in high falsetto, slapping their knees. But the woman sat in
straight-backed silence, looking ahead with an expression of queenly
and contemptuous indifference that made the noise of the sailors
seem foolish. She was probably a mulatto, and had a strange and
ancient beauty. Her skin was the colour of milky coffee, and her
face, with its outcurled lips, was like a carving out of old Egypt. So
was her stately figure, its high, frank, prow-like bosom delineated
by the scant orange bodice of the dress. She was the first woman
I'd seen for two months, and I confess that I gazed at her with the
same degree of curiosity as the young sailors did – but not, I hope,
with the same lasciviousness.

A quiet voice spoke behind me.

– There's the hulks.

I swung round; it was Lieutenant Campbell, who had no doubt
been directed to keep watch on me, lest I try to escape in the
confusion of arrival. I stared at him as his words sank into my mind.
He was pointing across the harbour towards the dock, looking at
me as he did so, the peak of his cap pulled low over his eyes. Hulks?
I tried to understand: the word at first made no sense. And yet its
implication had struck home before I recalled its meaning. *Hulks*:
the very word trailed ragged grey streamers of gloom and wretchedness; despair beyond despair. It was a word that had nothing to
do with me, or ought not to have done: a word out of some bad
English dream, lying in wait for the spawn of England's gutters. But
looking to where Campbell pointed, through the fast-falling tropical
dusk, I saw that here indeed the prison hulks lay.

There were three of them, moored inside the breakwater: disgraced remnants of ships whose masts had been felled, to leave them
floating in stoic humiliation, like clumsy, many-tiered Oriental
junks – the long, ominous roofs that had been added to them
recalling those of Britain's factories. My thoughts now had the

42

quick irrationality of panic. Under such roofs, men would be turned into vermin. Was I really to be housed in one of these?

– I believe it's possible ye'll be lodged in one o' them tomorrow, Campbell said.

– Really? I said. Not so handsome as the *Nemesis*, are they?

– No.

Into this one monosyllable, drawn out in the Scottish manner, Campbell managed to inject much meaning.

We both stared in silence over the rail, in the fading evening light: the attitude of men bound on a journey together, which I saw as a cruel irony. Figures could be made out, moving on the decks of the hulks, and I realised what they were. Convicts! Every man wore a white linen blouse and a straw hat: the palmetto hat of Bermuda. On every man's blouse, indecipherable at this distance, were numbers of some kind; and I could clearly make out felonry's broad arrows.

I clenched my teeth, and summoned up a cheerful tone.

– Well, Lieutenant Campbell, no doubt from tomorrow I'll be enlisted in that little army, and will wear my numbered blouse and straw hat, and go out to the Bermuda rock quarries.

– Oh come now, I think not. They'll no do that, I feel sure of it.

Campbell's tone was abrupt and uneasy, undermining his attempt at reassurance – as did his glance.

– I'm glad of your optimism, I said. But do you know that for a fact?

– I don't. No-one knows what the orders are concerning ye until they're delivered to the Governor. But they'll no make a common convict of ye. They wouldn't dare.

– There's only one thing I feel hopeful about, I said. That the fresh sea-creatures of Bermuda will appear tonight on Captain Wood's table.

Campbell smiled reluctantly, and shook his head.

The next morning, which was June 20th, another steamer moored in the channel: a big West India packet, just arrived from Southampton, her decks crowded with passengers. Two of these

43

steamers rendezvous here once a fortnight, carrying mail and news-papers. Lieutenant Campbell, who was officer on guard, went across and boarded her at ten o'clock.

Alone in the main cabin, I sat drinking a cup of the excellent coffee the steward always brewed at this time, trying to savour every mouthful – since this, I told myself, might well be the last good coffee I'd taste for years. But I barely noticed the taste. I was waiting for Lieutenant Campbell, all my nerves on edge. Surely he would carry back to me much news from home – and most important of all, Catherine's lost letter.

I'd just finished the cup when Campbell hurried in. He placed a thick pile of letters in front of me, and sat down on the other side of the table.

– Mail, Mr Devereux, he said. I'm sure it will be welcome.

My heart thudded; feeling his eyes on me, I picked the letters up and began to shuffle through them. There was only one I was looking for, and I found to my embarrassment that my fingers had begun to tremble. It was here: her round and unmistakable hand leaped up at me from the envelope, and without being able to help myself, I smiled in delight. Raising my eyes, I found Campbell smiling back, his amused yet respectful gaze unwavering on my face.

– Yes, I said, and coughed. Thank you, Lieutenant Campbell; I'm much obliged to you for bringing these.

There was no way I could be so unmannerly as to begin to break the seal of Catherine's letter in front of him, and nor did I wish to; I wanted to read it alone. I put the letters down, hoping that he would go. But he didn't; instead he threw a newspaper across the table. It was the London *Morning Post*.

– Ye should read this too, he said. Ye figure in it prominently.

I found that he was surveying me with that childlike curiosity which seems to affect even the most sensible, ordinary man when he finds that someone he knows is written about in a large newspaper. It's as though he imagines that the words printed there proceed not from the brain of some hack, but from an elfin wordsmith whose task it is to choose both the fortunate and the disgraced for a special destiny in print. Well, the very smell of newsprint has a heady specialness – I'm not immune to it myself, especially when the newspaper is my own – and this romantic effect is perhaps natural; yet how quickly the edge of that entrancing scent fades: as quickly as news itself! Here was the *Morning Post* of nearly three weeks ago, limp and dog-eared from much handling; and the high importance and sharpness of the newsprint smell, which would have been fresh on June 1st, was now gone. I held in my hand a limp, sombre artefact: a shard of history.

– Ye're even more famous than I realised, Campbell said, and gestured at the paper, which he'd folded open.

My own picture confronted me: a somewhat theatrical pen-and-ink likeness, showing me standing in the box at my trial. Below it was a leading article devoted to 'the convict Devereux'; and its author proclaimed me to be not only a felon but a scoundrel.

A question had been asked in Parliament, it seemed, as to whether my sentence was being carried out; and the Member who had asked the question was sympathetic to me. He had spoken on my behalf, commenting on the extraordinary nature of my conviction, and asking whether the Government was really going to make me serve the full extent of 'this monstrous and disproportionate sentence'.

The reply of the Minister was very interesting to me, and I forgot Lieutenant Campbell's presence as I read. Her Majesty's Government, the Minister said, 'had sent strict instructions to Ireland to ensure that the convict Devereux would indeed serve the full extent of his sentence'. And he rebuked my defender for daring to protest against 'a fully justified sentence properly pronounced in due course of law'. The hack who had written the article then went into a diatribe approving the Minister's remarks, adding 'dangerous terrorist' to his other labels.

I looked up to encounter Lieutenant Campbell's concerned, steady gaze.

– At least ye have someone speaking out for ye, he said. But they do seem bent on making ye serve your full sentence. I cannot believe they'll stick to it, though.

– But why should they not? The gentleman who tries to defend me is wrong, in fact – a well-meaning simpleton. It simply isn't true that my sentence is monstrous and disproportionate – *if* I've been properly tried. But I haven't been — that's the real point. It's the nature of the trial the Honourable Member should have been questioning, not the sentence.

I was half amused and half angry, just thinking of it; but Campbell seemed not to understand. He shook his head, stood up, and sighed.

– Ye're in waters too deep for me, he said. But now I have my duties. I'll see ye once more, Mr Devereux, before ye leave us.

I watched him march from the cabin. I would miss his bemused concern and his straight, decent gaze; he had almost become a friend. Now that the hulks were waiting, I had a wistful wish that he would not disappear.

This, of course, was the sort of weakness I would need to guard against. I could not afford to become sentimental about any of my captors.

Moments later I was in the solitude of my cabin, the letter from Catherine in my hands, the others flung onto the table. I found that my fingers were trembling again as I broke the seal.

Dear God, what a heartless and immense distance separates us! A few days' delay, a missed ship, and silence descends for weeks! Paper has become something more than paper, reaching me here; and writing is something more than writing. There were runes inside the envelope I held which would either spell out a message of absolute happiness, renewing my resolve to hold on, or else push me down into the deepest pit of wretchedness.

* Dublin,
May 30th, 1848

My dearest Robert,

They will not tell me how long you will be at Cork, but I do hope that this letter will reach you before you are removed from there. I hope too that you still have with you the portrait of me that you liked, so that you will not forget my face, and so that I am somehow there with you – wherever it is those creatures finally imprison you. Please wear your warmest clothes at all times; it would be terrible for you if your asthma should come back.

Robert, Robert, although you warned me so often that this could happen, I simply cannot believe it. I never quite agreed with you that the English were perfect tyrants (how you rebuked me for that!) – however badly some of them may have treated our poor people. But now I see that the authorities in London and Dublin are all you have said they are.

Don't lose heart, dearest. I know you won't; you are always so full of spirit and pride. Everyone says that you will surely not serve the full fourteen years. I have visited your parents, who received me with great kindness, and I have spoken with your father about your situation. He is making enquiries of highly-placed friends, and has been told that in a case like yours, a pardon is always possible. I have begged your father to find out what is planned for you through his connections at the Castle; but they have told him it is too soon to discover anything definite at this stage. The intentions concerning you in London are simply not known.

Your father and mother are being very comforting, despite their own distress. Neither of them, as you know, will ever understand what has driven you to act as you have done. Your father says that you have destroyed your life to no good purpose. Don't be angry; you know how he thinks; and indeed, he loves you dearly. He is quite bewildered, and keeps saying that he cannot believe that a speech, and something printed in a newspaper, can ruin a man's life. I am afraid my own father and mother say much the same.

Yesterday the police seized your newspaper office – no doubt on Lord Clarendon's orders. Terence Butler was there, watching over things on your behalf. He has been a very good friend to you – and is most kind to me. The police had a warrant which they showed him, and they seized everything: types, stores of paper, and all your books and financial records. I know how this will anger you, but you must put it from your mind for now. Please think of nothing else but convincing the authorities to pardon you; I am sure this is possible if you show the smallest regret. I know how proud you are, and know what you will say to this; but Robert, think of us.

I must get this letter off, in the hope that it will reach you at Cove before you are taken abroad. I shall think of you every night. I am weeping; I can write no more just now. My dearest, please believe that I am with you day and night. I love you. I love you.

                                                                          Your

                                                                          Catherine

I stayed in the cabin for the rest of the morning, reading and re-reading Catherine's precious letter, and all the others from home: from my parents, from Paul Barry and Thomas O'Neill, and from many other comrades and well-wishers. They filled me with new hope and strength, these silent, loving voices, like draught after draught of some wonderful elixir, giving me the courage to face whatever was to come.

It came after lunch. The Cockney steward brought a note into the cabin from Captain Wood, informing me that he had been instructed by the admiral, Lord Dundonald, that I was to be taken aboard the hulk *Medway*, and that a boat would come to the *Nemesis* for me at four o'clock.

I began to pack my trunk and portmanteau, moving automatically, shutting off thought. While I was doing so, there came a knock on the door, and I opened it to find Lieutenants Campbell and Millington. They shifted on their feet awkwardly, embarrassed as schoolboys: each bore an armful of books, which they deposited on the table. I saw immediately that the books came from their modest 'officers' library'; *Two Years before the Mast* was among them.

– Put these in your trunk, Mr Devereux, Millington said. An addition to your collection. Knowing what a great reader you are, we thought you might run through your supply pretty soon, out here.

He seemed pinker than usual, and one hand fiddled with his flaxen side-whiskers. Beside him, Campbell nodded, his thin smile fixed.

– Aye, he said, and blinked.

I immediately protested.

– No, gentlemen, I can't let you do this. It's very good of you, but these are most of your library; I can't let you give them to me.

– Take them, man, Campbell said, and his tone had become

almost terse. You'll need them more than we do; we can always buy more. Take them.

– Yes, do, Millington said. Really.

He was stiff with English embarrassment, but smiled encouragingly. In the end, foolishly moved, I insisted that I would take only two: one book from each pile. This being argued out, I selected *Two Years before the Mast*, and a collection of poems by S.T. Coleridge. Then I shook hands with both officers, and thanked them for their kindness.

– We'll not say goodbye, but *au revoir*, Campbell said. The *Nemesis* will be back here pretty regularly, and I understand from Captain Wood that we'll be permitted to visit you on the *Medway*. So we'll meet again – maybe in six weeks or so.

– I'll be very glad to see you, if you care to call, I said.

When the words were out, I heard how foolish they sounded, and laughed. The two officers joined in; but then we all grew constrained, and they took their leave.

I have not seen them again; nor will I.

When they were gone, I sat at the table in thought. I had suddenly seen the ignominy of what had happened. I realised now that I should have refused their books; and I struck my fist on the table in chagrin and self-contempt. What had I done? I'd accepted presents, and therefore charity, from officers of the Queen of England's navy! More; I'd shown pathetic gratitude to my captors.

And yet I knew that there was something artificial in my shame and anger. How, I asked myself, would I have been able to spurn the good-hearted gesture of those two men? They had, I felt sure, no ulterior motive; and to haughtily repel genuine kindness is not in my nature; I simply can't do it.

I'm not, I'm afraid, a very satisfactory revolutionary.

Four o'clock found me standing on the main deck beside Captain Wood, watching two boats approach us from the naval dockyard. They moved quite fast through the harbour's green glitter, amid the traffic of other small craft. Too fast.

They were rowed by those figures that had made my heart sink, in their white, numbered blouses and palmetto hats; and they were coming for me.

– Some of these fellows have never seen an oar when they come here, Captain Wood said. They soon learn.

He spoke of the convicts as though I had no more in common with them than he did; and I suspected that he was saying anything that came into his head, to fill the awkward silence between us. He coughed, formal in his full regalia with cocked hat and sword, and we fell quiet again; I found myself standing erect as he did.

When the boats came alongside, they disgorged three naval dignitaries, also in blue frock coats and cocked hats, their gold epaulettes gleaming in the sun. As they came up the companion-ladder, our sailors stood at fierce attention, and Captain Wood moved forward to greet his visitors. I sauntered behind, like a schoolboy with his master. A little ceremony then took place, with a bare minimum of words.

The leader of the naval trio was a short, powerfully-built man with rope-coloured hair cropped short. He announced himself as Captain Thorpe, superintendent of convicts. His expression was pugnacious: almost challenging. The other two – taller men, of less chilling demeanour – he introduced as Commander Moffatt, in charge of the hulk *Medway,* and Doctor Howard, a naval surgeon who was medical officer here. Doctor Howard looked at me pleasantly from behind round spectacles. When Captain Wood had formally identified me, the superintendent of convicts allowed himself to survey me with a single hard glance, big chin out-thrust, warning me not to smile.

I smiled, and Captain Thorpe continued to look at me hard for a few more moments. Then he turned to Captain Wood and passed him a piece of paper, which I gathered was a receipt for my body. I'd been transferred, like a parcel. I turned towards the gangway, and Captain Wood farewelled me, with a last look which seemed to me to mingle sympathy with his usual faint melancholy.

The two boats pulled fast across the harbour – one of them, it seemed, having come expressly to transport the superintendent of convicts, myself, and my luggage, together with two junior officers who were no doubt here to restrain me should I prove violent.

None of these men spoke during our little voyage, and nor did they look at me; but the convicts at the oars shot many glances from under their straw hats. They were all English – no Irish among them – and they were very different types from the sailors of the *Nemesis*; the brutality of many of their faces was repellent. I gazed away over the water, and behaved as though the proceedings had little interest for me. The marine and vegetable scents in the soft, warm air were much stronger out here on the water, sending an incongruous thrill of elation through me. I longed to set foot on land, and wondered when I would do so.

In a few minutes, I found myself on the quarter-deck of the *Medway*, the innermost of the three hulks, standing at attention in front of my three blue-coated keepers. All of them had their hands behind their backs, and all of them examined me with a sort of restrained wonderment, as though I were an odd new animal in their private zoo. In the background, observing proceedings with a respectful dubiousness, was a lean, white-haired old seaman who proved to be the hulk's first mate.

– Have certain things to inform you, Mr Devereux, the superintendent said.

He tended to bite off and swallow his words, and his gaze seemed contemptuous; but perhaps the look was habitual with him, and merely impersonal. His voice was extraordinarily resonant and deep: a bullfrog's. He had a very broad chest from which this voice boomed forth, and a firm-looking middle-aged paunch which caused the many gold buttons of his frock coat to curve outwards; altogether, he looked like a blue-swathed cask.

– For the present, he said, you will be allowed to wear your own attire, and will not be sent out on the works as a common convict. You will not go ashore at all, in fact. You will remain on this hulk.

The first part of this little speech had caused my hopes to rise; but at the second part, which Captain Thorpe seemed to utter with malicious satisfaction, they sank again. Not to go ashore, but to be imprisoned indefinitely on this rotting ruin of a ship! This didn't bear thinking about. But I kept expressionless, and merely nodded,

51

as was my policy at such times. Then came the question with which I was becoming familiar.

– Have you any complaints?

None, I said, as I'd done on all other occasions. No matter what they did, I would not complain. At this, the superintendent looked slightly baffled; even disappointed.

– Have you any money?

– A few shillings, I said.

– Any credit in the colony?

– None.

He sniffed once, as though in satisfaction. Then the bullfrog voice was raised to full boom.

– Mr Wall!

This was a summons to the old seaman in the background, who now hurried forward.

– Take Mr Devereux's money, the superintendent ordered, and place it to his credit.

The mate hesitated. Plainly I was unlike any convict he had dealt with before, and he was not sure how to proceed. Was he to lay hands on me? I decided to help him, and took out my French tri-coloured purse, which I unfastened and held out.

– Take it, I said.

He opened his large, rough hand, and I poured the few coins into it. He stepped back in evident relief, glancing at his master.

– Now, the superintendent said to me, you will find, Mr Devereux, that nobody here has any intention of harassing you. No-one is going to add to the annoyances you must already suffer. In fact, no severity of any kind will be shown you.

His eyes, which were pale and wide-set, remained entirely cold as he spoke: quite at odds with his words. He was reciting, I felt sure, orders from on high of which he didn't approve, but couldn't question. But Commander Moffatt, nodding his cocked hat, seemed almost benevolent.

– None, he said. You will be treated according to your station.

His solemn voice was almost as deep as the superintendent's, but lacked its threat, and his long face with its oak-coloured side-whiskers was distinguished. But a narrow forehead and heavy-lidded, puzzled grey eyes gave an impression of slow-wittedness: even stupidity. Perhaps this was why he stared at me as though trying to work something out. Meanwhile, Captain Thorpe continued as though the commander had not spoken, still looking fixedly at me.

– Provided, he said, that you observe the rules of this place. Is that clear, Mr Devereux?

I nodded.

Doctor Howard spoke for the first time.

– How is your health, Mr Devereux?

His accent, which was well-bred, had a faintly northern colouring: Yorkshire, perhaps. He had taken off his cocked hat and held it at his side, surveying me with a shrewd yet genial expression through his glasses. He was in his late forties, and had a high, bald forehead, tanned by the sun, and a fringe of curling brown hair sprinkled with grey. The effect was somewhat scholarly, but there was a naval crispness about his speech, and a physical fitness about his erect posture which was neither scholarly nor unworldly.

– I'm very well, sir, I said.

– I'm glad to hear it, he said. We're informed you have asthma, however. You've not been troubled by it on the voyage?

– Not at all – I believe I'm rid of it.

– One never really gets rid of asthma, he said. He's a nasty foe. He has a way of returnin'. I'll come and visit you from time to time, and see how you are.

The superintendent cleared his throat, plainly impatient at the Doctor's solicitude.

– Let me make clear something else, Mr Devereux. You are to have no connection with public affairs here, or politics of any kind, and you are not to interfere with any of the prisoners on board. Do you accept that?

– Of course, I said. I would hardly have expected to be involved in public affairs in this place, even if such a thing were possible. Nor do I have any desire for the pleasures of intercourse with your other prisoners.

53

A faint smile appeared on Doctor Howard's face, and the dully noble features of Commander Moffatt also seemed amused. But the superintendent's eyes became empty windows; he turned away as though from a distasteful object, and raised his bullfrog voice in command again.

– Mr Wall! Show the prisoner to his quarters.

I bowed slightly to my three gaolers, and followed the first mate off the quarter-deck, going down the companion-ladder to the main deck, and so into a dim wooden passage that led into the bowels of the hulk. We encountered no-one else here. The old man hurried ahead, looking back at me once or twice as though he feared I might break away. There was a smell that I couldn't identify: something dank and sombre. Perhaps it was the odour of old fear.

Mr Wall halted at a low, cavern-like doorway. Inside was a compartment not much larger than a dog kennel, and very much resembling one. He led me in; we had to stoop, and I peered about me almost in disbelief, while the mate watched me do so with an expression that managed to be both non-committal and unfriendly.

– Here's your place, sir, he said.

Neither of us could stand fully upright. The smell was much stronger in here, and it was hot, stuffy and dark, the only natural light coming through two dim bull's-eyes set in the boards of the deck above, which formed the ceiling. There was no porthole, this being the heart of the hulk; and I saw that this place was simply the cavity where the main-mast had once been fixed, before the ship was dismembered to make a gaol. The great beams that had held the mast in place ran across the ceiling, causing me to stoop still further when I passed under them. The whole area was about six feet square, and one half of the floor was raised about a foot; in that section it would not be possible to stand up at all. For furniture, there was one wooden stool.

I sat down on this, stretching out my legs so that my feet reached to a corner of the compartment, and looked up at the mate.

– Very well, I said. I presume I can have my portmanteau? And my trunk?

– That I can't say, sir. I'll ask.

– Do.

I did not look after him as he left the cabin, but commenced to fill my pipe. As I lit it, attempting a philosophical calm, a movement in one corner caught my eye. A creature scuttled across the floor which at first I took to be a mouse. But it proved to be a reddish-brown cockroach, of a size so large I could scarcely believe it. Plainly there was a race of cockroaches on Bermuda beside which their European cousins were pygmies. I stood up. I have a loathing of vermin, and this creature – spawn of darkness, ordure, and the fetid tropical heat in which all growth is monstrous and rapid, and in which all things decay just as rapidly – produced in me an irrational alarm. I let out an exclamation of disgust. No insect should be so big, I thought. More like an animal than an insect, it halted at my movement, waving its feelers, and seemed actually to look at me, with a crafty intelligence. I stepped towards it in a rush of hatred, intending to stamp on it; but it ran away, fast and horribly clever, disappearing down a crack.

I sat down on the stool again, and began to re-light my pipe. My fingers were trembling, and my heart was racing with anger.

This wouldn't do. I struggled to calm myself. The hulk must be teeming with these creatures; and after all, they didn't bite. I was going to have to get used to them – and I would probably soon have to face more serious enormities. The fact that I'd been relegated to this hole seemed to signify that the superintendent's reassurances had been ambiguous – perhaps even false. What had he said? *For the present, you will not be sent out on the works as a common convict.* But later?

Well, I said, the worst they could do would be to put me in the dreaded linen blouse of a convict, stamped with my name and number, and send me out to the limestone quarries, pick-axe in hand. Let them. I was as strong as the next man, and in good health; asthma had not attacked me for a year. I would endure, I said; they wouldn't break me.

Now Mr Wall reappeared, followed by two brawny, grinning sailors in blue jackets and white duck trousers, who carried between them my trunk and portmanteau. They set these down and quickly moved out again; the kennel was uncomfortably crowded until they did so. They were followed by a convict servant, in his arrowed blouse: a small, slyly glancing man with a broken nose, carrying a mug of black tea and a lump of bread on a dish. These he set down on the raised platform, and shuffled out again. Mr Wall watched him go, and then turned his disapproving old face to me.

– The Commander has asked me to tell you that you're free to walk about on deck, sir, he said. There are no prisoners housed on this part of the deck, except the servants. You're also allowed to go down on the breakwater, to take the air. If you want to bathe in the sea tomorrow morning, you can do that too, sir.

He took a long breath to continue, and his voice became almost nagging.

– But you must get up at four-thirty, and have your bathing over with before the gangs turn out to work. You're to have no contact with the gangs.

– I've been given to understand that already, I said.

I made my gaze as cold as possible, and his own eyes were the first to drop; he turned and went out, leaving the door ajar.

I was eager to leave this kennel, and to walk on the breakwater; but I drank some tea, gnawed on the hard lump of bread, and sat on my stool for some moments more reviewing my situation. It could be worse, I said. It seemed I was free to emerge when I wished from my suffocating dog-house; even to escape from the hulk itself, and walk on the pier. This was good. And better still, they had left me my trunk, my books, and this journal that I write in; all my small personal possessions. They had not even searched my luggage; nor had they searched me. I was still not a prisoner of the lowest degree.

But the night brought horrors.

After my promenade on the breakwater, a meal of mutton chops and vegetables was brought to me in my kennel. Later, Mr Wall and the convict servant set up a cot on the raised platform, where I eventually lay down to sleep.

Sleep came quickly; but in the middle of the night I woke up with the sensation of being touched by a hundred cold little fingers:

on my face; my feet; my hands. I looked down in disbelief. In the faint, cold light that came through the bull's-eyes above me, I saw that my hands and bare feet were black with cockroaches – as was the single blanket that covered me. A living carpet of the creatures was moving over me.

With a cry of rage and loathing, I jumped up, banging my head against the ceiling. I began to dash the insects from me; they fell in showers, and my greatest horror came from their having been on my face. I must have danced there like a madman, crouched in my kennel, slapping and exclaiming until all the vermin were off me. They scuttled thick about the floor then, like an angry mob in some Lilliputian public square.

I was close to vomiting; I felt faint. When I lay down again, I told myself again that the things had no poisonous sting; and I tried to be calm and rational. But it was their size and foulness that I dreaded. I slept no more that night, but lay watching the hordes move about the floor. Now and then one would ascend the cot near my face, feelers waving, and then retreat when I slapped and shouted. But they always came back.

And now I believed I knew what kinds of punishment were in store for me. Nothing official; nothing open and honest; instead, sly filth and degradation.

3. NAIL HIM
TO THE ROCK

July 2nd

Five-thirty in the morning. Fresh from my regular swim, which is the one moment of unfailing joy in my day.

My body still glows as I write this, like a free man's; my hair is damp with brine. Dawn is coming, pink through the porthole; roosters crow on the island, and I've blown the candle out. The shuffling of convict gangs and the jingle of their chains float up from the breakwater as they move out to their work.

Swimming, I'm liberated – or rather, I have that illusion, freed not only from my gaol but almost from the confines of my body; from clogging reality itself. I dive naked from the breakwater in the dark, there being no-one to see me except a lone Marine, who stands guard under a lamp by the gangway of the hulk. He always greets me cordially enough, and with a somewhat proprietary air – as well he might. I've learned that he's set there especially on my account; and on my account too, another Marine has been placed by the bridge joining the breakwater to the fortifications. Since my arrival here, persons coming to the hulks after sunset must get special passes to show to these guards. What on earth do the authorities fear that I'll do?

There are few sounds out here but the rasp of the Marine's boots, and the lapping of water. The air is still, and curiously warm for such an hour; it seems seldom to be cold at all in these summer islands. The lolling sea is wonderfully fresh, but without the numbing cold of the North Atlantic, so that I float through dark water and dark air in temperate delight, hardly distinguishing one from the other: an experience quite novel until now, except in dreams. Dreamlike too, the lamps around the empty breakwater, and the lights of ships riding far off, like the outer districts of some vast marine city, beyond the horizon. O, to swim out there! Out, out of this suffocating trap, in which I've been penned for a month!

The blue-black of the sky is lightening; a faint streak has appeared on the horizon; the last stars burn high in the west, strange as the other lights around me. Freed from gravity, I let my limbs go limp; I turn and lie on my back; I follow the white shape of an early gull, while mackerel of a colossal size move like rumours in the dim green below me. And I think of Catherine, whose face always glimmers among the day-faded lights. Soon, I say, I'll soar away from the wretched *Medway* altogether: a citizen of another dimension.

But now the Marine is signalling; I must haul myself onto the breakwater, where my towel and clothing lie, and disappear like a goblin before the gangs come out, on their way to the quarries.

Of what region am I really a citizen? Certainly not of Bermuda. Except for my promenades on the breakwater, I never set foot on Bermuda. Nor, after a month on this hulk, have I come to share the fate of the other convicts. My fears of the first evening here have proved groundless: I've not been sent out upon the works; yet I remain a peculiar prisoner of Her Majesty's Navy: a man without citizenship, not quite on water and not quite on land; a lone passenger on a fourteen years' cruise, on a ship that doesn't move. Bermuda for me is a set of pictures, glimpsed beyond the naval dockyard; a half-real middle distance, mild and monotonous, at which I gaze like a sickly child, forbidden by its parents to leave the confines of its house. I'm exiled not just from my country, but from *terra firma*; from the natural world itself. An ingenious way of dealing with me! I've been taken out of reality.

However, my living conditions here have now changed, and are really very tolerable.

Whether the primitive arrangements of the first night on board were contrived to frighten me, or were simply carelessness, I've not discovered; but things began to improve the next day. Mr Wall informed me that I was to have better quarters, and I was brought out of my windowless, cockroach-ridden dog-house and shown to this cabin in the stern, on the half-deck. This section of the ship seems to be where the mates, the steward and the surgeon have their cabins. As I've already recorded, the quarters of the convicts are separated from my cabin only by a corridor, and two wooden walls. But an invisible line seems to have been drawn at this point, and the convicts have no communication with the half-deck. I have dubbed this compartment a kennel as well, since it somewhat resembles one, being long and low: fourteen feet, with a six-foot ceiling, and only five feet wide. But it's perfectly clean, only the occasional cockroach appears, and it really deserves a better title, having two chairs, a good-sized oak table, a basin-stand and shelves for my books, and a cot at one end. Best of all, it has a gallery window admitting fresh air, and a view of the dockyard. True, the window is barred, but its glass lattice opens and shuts, and admits plenty of light.

The food I'm brought, although limited and crudely cooked, is nourishing and good: fresh beef or pork daily, fresh vegetables, pea soup, tea and loaf-bread. I'm not being given special treatment with this diet; this is what my fellow-prisoners eat too, and many of the poor devils have never eaten so well. I'm also supplied with tolerable tobacco for my pipe. And I do as I please, reading or moving freely about on the hulk and the breakwater during the day. But I'm reminded of my status at night, when I'm locked into the cabin to sleep. This ceremony is carried out by Mr Wall, who seems to have been given special charge of me; and at ten o'clock he returns, accompanied by a guard, looking in with his expressionless, thin-lipped old face to make sure that I haven't escaped. At this time, I'm usually awake, reading or writing at my table here, and I nod briefly; but there are two more visits to come during the night.

The first of these, at midnight, nearly always wakes me. Comes the soft rattle of the key in the lock; when the door opens, I pretend to be asleep, lying in my cot with my face to the wall. There's a low muttering; the mate has the guard with him, and prepares to check me more closely, like a tiresome, fussing old grandfather.

– Bring the lantern over, he mutters, and I sense the swing of shadows in the cabin, and the light held above my face. He grunts, satisfied that I am truly lying here; then the light is withdrawn.

I'm seldom woken fully by the last visit, at two o'clock; but the knowledge of its imminence often keeps my sleep uneasy; I dream about the mate, who frowns above me. I have no plans for escape at this stage; but if I ever wish to try it, these attentions are going to make it very difficult.

A knock on my half-open door. Lane, the convict servant, comes in with the breakfast tray.

– A nice bit o' fish for you this morning, sir.

I'm beginning to realise that Lane has special instructions about my diet. My victuals aren't always as scrupulously identical to those of the other convicts as I at first thought; I very much doubt that they ever get fish. And there are times when I'm secretly glad of these little variations; food, in my state of confinement, begins to assume an importance it never had before, and mealtimes become great events in the day.

– It's mackerel, Lane adds.

His nasal London voice has an enticing tone; and as he sets the tray down on the table he stoops very low, in his arrow-stamped blouse, like a waiter in a fashionable restaurant. His sideways smile wishes to please, but the effect is essentially cunning. He's unusually tall and lanky for a Cockney, with a horse-like, sallow face, a horse's liquid brown eyes, and a long head whose prison-cropped stubble resembles a horse's coat. Perhaps his stooping is merely a reflex because of the low ceiling; but sometimes I suspect it's a parody of obsequiousness: a crafty joke at my expense. And who could blame him? He, a convict, is waiting on another convict. I wonder, not for the first time, what he has to say about me to his fellow-felons.

Lane is one of the small number of prisoners kept on the half-deck as servants, instead of being sent out in the gangs. He's been assigned here especially to attend to me, it seems. Great care is being taken to keep me from contact with any of the other convicts. The half-deck area, I find, is set aside for the cabins and pantries of the mates, the surgeon, and the chief steward, and has no communication with the fore part of the hulk: this peculiar, motionless vessel that carries on a dismal pretence of being a proper ship with a proper crew. In addition to Mr Wall, who is second-in-command, we have a second mate and quartermasters, while the military turnkeys are termed 'guards'. The ship's company are the convicts, and they are distributed into 'messes' and 'watches'. The half-dozen like Lane who are set aside for special duties – swabbing decks and manning boats as well as acting as stewards – are known as 'boatswain's mates', and have achieved this situation through good conduct. It's easy to see how Lane would have managed this: his air of obliging deference is very convincing, whatever my suspicions about it might be. And indeed, after a month of his regular appearances in the cabin, I've allowed myself to be lulled into the assumption that for the most part, he truly wishes to play the perfect servant. His motives are another matter. Perhaps he thinks I'm close to the authorities, and imagines I'll report well on him. Certainly he wishes to ingratiate himself; to linger and gossip.

But although I welcome most diversions to lighten the slow, empty hours of my day, I carefully discourage him. Some instinct warns me not to allow Lane to become familiar with me. It isn't so much the gulf in our stations that makes it hard to be at ease with him, but something else. There's a faintly repellent quality under his comforting ministrations: something I can't identify, but which causes me to present him with a fairly stiff surface. Yet he never seems discouraged; he always tries afresh; he always lingers, as he's doing now.

– You've been sent a present, sir, he says.

He nods and smiles at the breakfast tray. Next to the piece of fried mackerel and the plate of bread is an object covered with a white napkin; he draws the napkin away like a conjuror, to reveal a large pineapple. Treasure indeed! Here on the hulk, we're given only lemons and occasional oranges, against scurvy; I've been longing for other fruit, and have already heard that the pineapples on Bermuda are superb – but beyond reach. The scent of this forbidden object fills the cabin, and I smile with involuntary pleasure. Then I ask him where it comes from.

– Aha, says Lane, as though rewarding a child; then he lowers his voice confidentially.

– A gift from the surgeon, sir – Doctor Howard. But he asked me particular that you shouldn't mention this to anyone. Prisoners ain't generally allowed dainties like this. Not even a gentleman prisoner like yourself, sir.

I look at him without speaking, and his sly smile falters. Then I say:

– And what about you, Lane? Will you mention it to anyone?

He looks shocked.

– O' *course* not, sir. Doctor Howard knows he can trust me. He knows I'm a close one, sir.

He winks, but I remain expressionless. This is pompous of me; but I can't help the effect Lane has on me. He attempts invasion through every crack and crevice; he even stands too close, bending over me like some tall, arrow-marked bird, so that I have to fight down an impulse to draw my chair away. Instead, I say:

– Wait just a moment, Lane. I'd like to send a note of thanks to Doctor Howard. Can you deliver it?

– I'll be happy to do so, sir. He don't always sleep on board, and he's ashore at the moment. But he'll be back this morning, to see to the sick prisoners. There's a bit of the Yellow Fever about at the moment, and a lot of dysentery: I had the dysentery myself, not long ago, something fearful. The Doctor has lunch with the Commander, and I'll be serving. I can slip him the note then, sir, and none the wiser.

He makes this sound conspiratorial, but I ignore his glance. I go to the other end of the table where my writing-slope is, scribble a note and hand it to him. Then I resume my place in front of the breakfast tray and begin to eat my fish. But still Lane lingers. Chewing, I look up enquiringly.

– Doctor Howard often asks about you, Lane says. He seems concerned about your state of health.

– Really? I can't imagine why.

– Do go on with your nice fish, sir, it'll get cold. Yes; Doctor Howard has asked me to let him know if you seem at all poorly.

– How they fuss, Lane. No doubt they want us in good health to appreciate our punishments.

Lane sniggers through his nose.

– I believe you, sir.

Encouraged, he draws closer again as I eat.

– But you know, sir, some of the lags that gets hulked, they think they're in heaven. They ain't never had food like this in their lives. Some of them Irish in particular, sir – they ain't scarcely ever *seen* food like this.

He sniggers again, while I sip my tea.

– Yes, Lane, I'm sure that's true. They starve, while your rulers squeeze them off their land.

– Is that the way it is, sir? Well, the gentry can be hard-fisted, when they like.

Smoothly, taking advantage of the length of this conversation, he says:

– But you're one of the gentry yourself, sir, ain't you? You have an Irish way of speaking, but you're still one of the quality – anyone can see that.

– I'm Irish, Lane, and there's an end to it.

I say no more and resume eating, hoping that he'll go. But he doesn't; his dark gaze continues to probe me. I decide it's time to dismiss him, in case he becomes even more familiar. But before I can do so, he is speaking again.

– It's very noble of you, sir, I'm sure, to be concerned about the common Irish. But it's made a lot of unnecessary trouble for you, ain't it? And for *us*.

I look up, at this.

– Us? What can you mean by that, Lane?

– Why, what I say, sir. Surely you know what's going on? How Marines has been placed on the pier, all because of you? How all Irish prisoners and Irish guards has been taken off this hulk? And you've noticed them soldiers, sir, haven't you, that are camped up there by the fort, day and night, looking down on us? It's all on account of *you*, sir, we all know that.

I push aside my plate and begin to laugh.

– That's why the soldiers are up there? No, Lane, I didn't know they were going to all this trouble on my account. Surely they don't imagine I'm capable of leading an uprising?

He glances over his shoulder at the door, and licks his lips. Suddenly, he begins to seem nervous.

– Before you come, sir, us convicts used to be able to walk on the breakwater in our hours off, like you do. And we was even able to read the newspapers from home – those as could read. Now that's all been stopped; any man caught with a newspaper can be flogged, or put in solitary. And a lot of the lags hates you for it. They say they wish you'd been sent to Botany Bay, or hanged. Of course, I understand you're not to blame, sir – but there's some here with pretty thick skulls.

His voice drops; crouching, he glances swiftly around again.

– I know what's going on, sir, you see. It's all on account of your Irish friends in New York, ain't it?

– New York? What on earth are you talking about, Lane?

His eyes widen; his glance at the half-open door is repeated like a spasm; he's plainly half-afraid, but his desire to gossip is stronger than his fear.

– You mean you truly don't *know*, sir? No, I can see you don't. O' course: they keep you so cut off that I suppose no news from your American friends has got through to you. And none of *us* dares to speak to you on deck: I can only do it because we're alone in this cabin.

His voice becomes sickly-intimate, and he bends even lower towards my ear.

– Well, sir, I serves Commander Moffatt at dinner, and I keep my ears open, see? And the story is that when the Irish in New York heard about you being nabbed, they raised a real shindig. They've vowed to equip some ships, and sail down here to rescue you. So the traps have made things ready for them if they try. It's really put the wind up the traps, I can tell you.

He straightens, head on one side, to study my response. And I can't help smiling into space.

– I think my supporters in New York have little hope of success, I say.

Then I look up to meet his eager smile, and remember who it is with whom I'm speaking.

– Thank you, Lane, I say. You may go.

His expression changes; but he isn't disconcerted.

– Yes, sir. I'll be sure to get your note to Doctor Howard, he says.

He slips out of the cabin, tray in hand, his arrow-stamped dress more than ever suggesting the livery of an outlandish footman.

This present from Doctor Howard is surprising – apart from being against regulations.

He and I have exchanged a few words on deck occasionally – usually remarks dealing with the weather – and sometimes he's passed on scraps of information concerning the invisible colony on shore. But then, all the officers I encounter on my daily promenades about the decks are friendly and respectful, and Doctor Howard is no more or less so than the others. He turns out to have moved in Dublin society for a time, and knows some of the people that I know; and I have the impression, despite his blandness of manner, that he's concerned about me in some way. Whether it's a medical interest in my reported asthma, or something else altogether, I can't imagine.

July 19th

My life has now settled into a painless, joyless pattern, here in the narrow galleries of the hulk.

Commander Moffatt has lent me fresh books, and has given me permission to obtain more from home – provided they are 'not of a political nature'. I have fresh sea air, limited exercise, good food, and paper and pens. Very supportable, over a few weeks. But how am I to endure it for fourteen years? Alone – though surrounded by polite captors – for fourteen years! The notion is simply not real.

The hulks have given monotony a new meaning. The sun blazes down each day on my changeless little vista of dockyard pier, Britannic stonework and distant glimpses of the rocks and dark cedars of Bermuda; and in all the four weeks I've been here, not a single shower of rain has fallen. It is an arid, shimmering mirage, this place, its light blindingly bright. Locked on the borders of a mirage! It would be easy to go mad here, and my constant task will be to keep my feet away from that path which runs into the country of lunacy. The heavy dew that Ariel was sent to fetch falls here at night, and even by day. The air is weary and humid, clogging any salt or sugar left uncovered, even in our dry hulk. This humidity is carried in the south wind – which blows, so the officers tell me, for the whole summer. It tempers the sun, however, and makes the mornings and evenings here very pleasant – as well as bringing life to the vegetation, and ripening such delicious fruits as Doctor Howard's pineapple.

In the mornings, after the gangs have gone out, I stroll to my favourite spot on the seaward side of the breakwater, and stretch out at my ease. The sunlight is almost white, coming through the sea-haze. I read the newspapers, or one of my books: Aeschylus, or Victor Hugo, or my friend and mentor Thomas Carlyle, or one of my favourite English poets: lately, Samuel Taylor Coleridge. Or else I simply dream, watching sailors of many nations at work on nearby ships; or I peer at the multitude of fish that move through the glass-green depths straight below me: mullet, bonito, and the great Bermudan mackerel, over three feet long, whose flesh I relish, and which cruise in threes and fours, like undersea warships. Meanwhile, the flat, glittering sea, with its carnival of shipping, stretches away to the north-east, reaching the rim of the world: a line of deep, seductive blue.

And I muse on this rim for hours, in a state which is not contentment, but its sad counterfeit. Straining my vision, I sometimes seem to see the spires of that phantom city whose lights beckon me on during my dawn bathe. But at other times, deliberately indulging fancy, I pretend to discern the cloudlike, minute and utterly far coasts of lost Europe, and of that particular green island where all my thoughts are concentrated; and then my belly hollows with bitter yearning. Am I falling into the mindless trance of exile? For how long will it console me? And for how long will my books and my strolls divert me? Soon, surely, my feet will wander onto that terrible, empty little footpath where a warning signpost stands, lettered with a single word: *Lunacy*.

When the heat grows too intense, I go up to the *Medway*'s quarter-deck, which then becomes more pleasant to walk on than the break-water, being partly sheltered from the sun, yet open to the air on both sides.

From here, where the officers stroll, and where the convicts may not set foot, one has a view of the whole dockyard, the ships at anchor, and the barracks. In the other direction, the wide anchorage opens up, and the myriad islands beyond – all of them low in height, and seemingly identical; all of them composed of the same lime-cement, encrusted with sea-shells, which is Bermuda's basic substance. These are the white rocks which the convicts must quarry; and the glare injures their eyes. I'm informed of this by Lane, who tells me that many of the prisoners grow 'moon-blind': this being the term they use for the reddening of the eyelids and damage to their vision that the glare inflicts – damage which causes them to stumble over the stones as they walk. Moon-blind! Yes: Bermuda, with its bleached and blighted crust, might well be a fragment of the moon.

I grow morbidly curious about the convicts. I'm separated from them by the narrowest of lines – a line which authority may presumably abolish in an instant, should it choose to do so. In the morning, after my swim, I watch from my cabin porthole as they're mustered on the breakwater in the sunrise, coming in their hundreds from all three hulks, to be marched away in gangs to their work in the quarries or on the new government buildings – the stiff, red-coated soldiers of Britannia's army of tyranny shouting commands at them. And I see that many of them do indeed stumble as they walk. Nearly all of them, in their broad-brimmed straw hats, have their heads drooping on their chests as though from the weight of unalterable sorrow. I watch them again at sunset as they come trudging back, some of them with faces drained and grey from effort, others – the tougher ones, no doubt – stoically unchanged: some even grinning and laughing. There are always a number of them carrying irons on their legs, as punishment for some misdemeanour or other, and the clink and jingle of these chains is wellnigh constant, floating up through the porthole, or sounding from hidden quarters of the ship.

This grim jingling stitches itself into my thoughts, mingling with the cabin's odour of scrubbed planks: an incongruous mixture, since the scent of clean, plain wood has always, in my mind, been the essence of simplicity and goodness. The jingling comes constantly from a distance: that distance where the convicts move like figures in a frieze.

On Sundays, though, when a church service is held on the main deck, I have the opportunity of observing them more closely. On the first Sunday I attended it (a thing I am not compelled to do), I was profoundly interested.

I seemed at first to be viewing a tribe of alien creatures. They sat quietly on their benches in the clean morning sun, in their Sunday-clean blouses, with neckerchiefs knotted at their throats – like bad schoolboys subdued into pretending to be good. This illusion was heightened by the physical smallness of the majority of them: children of the rookeries of London, and of those other cities Britannia has made monstrous through her new industries, in the last hundred years. Penning the poor creatures in those foul warrens, she has actually stunted their bodies, as though through some evil magic; she has produced a new race of metropolitan dwarfs, whose impulses are either vicious or futile. And the close-cropped heads of these stunted little men, together with the enforced shaving of their whiskers, made them fundamentally naked and exposed. How sad and vulnerable is the shaven human head! Poor, knobby, white egg! This one furred with brown, that one with ginger, another sandy (and all obediently bowed, waiting for the chaplain to appear), they seemed to belong to creatures too fragile to threaten anyone. Yet many of these men were ruthless robbers and murderers. At first, as I studied them, this was hard to believe. But as I examined the rows more closely, I began to find men who were bigger, and powerfully built, with visages that were truly fearsome: the faces of brutes already inhabiting some criminal Hell – who were most unlikely, I felt sure, to be reached by the chaplain's prayers, or by anything else. Morbidly absorbed, I examined a toothless, gash-like mouth here, and a pair of fierce, blinking grey eyes there – eyes which darted quickly to intercept my stare, and flashed a chilling threat. Other daunting faces secretly returned my scrutiny: a dangerous chin was thrust out; a broken nose turned to point a furtive warning. But there were some whose looks were more pathetic than frightening, their skulls and faces somehow not properly formed: infantile.

Commander Moffatt came up to where I stood by the gangway to the quarter-deck, a pleased smile on his dull face, his sleepy-lidded eyes friendly.

– Good to see you in our congregation, Mr Devereux, he said. The service does us all good, I'm sure. What?

He lingered, erect and attentive, fidgeting with the braid on his uniform, wanting to make conversation. The dull sometimes have a sympathy which is more soothing than that of the intelligent, and this was the case with our hulk's Commander. I asked him about the condition of the convicts, and whether he believed that many of them were ever reformed.

Not many, he told me. He had a deep, burring voice, which seemed to come through a panel, and which now took on a tone of puzzled regret.

– Most of your Irish, for instance, have come here for stealing sheep and poultry and so on, because they're starved at home. They're astonished to find how well off they are here. There's no vice in 'em, as I'm sure you know; they're not rogues; not really turbulent or dishonest. But after being here with our London thieves and murderers, they're soon as finished ruffians as the rest. It's very sad. And then there are the young boys. They come here at twelve or fourteen, and when they get among the men –

He broke off, and sighed.

– One does one's best, he said, but they keep coming back, you know. Some are in their third terms. There are fathers and sons here whose families have been hulked for generations.

He smiled in reluctant amusement at this, and I was forced to smile too: there was something morbidly comical about it. Burglars and murderers from the womb! It seemed that most of them were doomed from the beginning; that there truly are born criminals, as some theorists maintain. Yet as I search the congregation each Sunday, I begin to find faces that puzzle me, and which don't fit the mould: faces that seem intelligent and pleasing. You could meet such faces on any day of the week, going up Dame Street, and feel quite drawn to them. What is one to make of this? Are these men actually innocent, and unjustly convicted – or superbly cunning hypocrites?

I am in low spirits tonight. Tomorrow, I'm told – being the 20th – the July mail steamer should arrive, bringing (please God) a letter from Catherine. I sent a long and cheerful letter home to her in June, telling her of my easy conditions, and of my hopes for the future; but this went on the 21st, by the mail steamer that passes through from the West Indies, and I can't expect an answer to it before the 20th of August.

July 20th

A letter from Catherine arrived on the mail steamer today. But it wasn't quite the letter I've been longing for over the past month.

When I went up to the quarter-deck this morning, full of anticipation, knowing the steamer was in, I found myself the subject of mysterious looks. Two young convict 'boatswain's mates', at work cleaning the deck in the bright early sun, actually drew away from me as I passed, crouching furtively over their holystones. Their expressions were almost frightened. Others that I passed behaved in the same manner. I seemed to be marked as a dangerous shipmate.

Lane tells me that the rumour of the projected rescue bid by my comrades in New York has now thoroughly alarmed everybody. Preparations to meet it are still going on; but I don't for a moment believe it will eventuate. Breathing in the southerly wind, I greeted the officers on deck here. Usually easy and friendly, they now touched their caps without smiling; but I affected to notice nothing. I paced the deck with an expression of innocent equanimity, a copy of Virgil's *Eclogues* in my hand. I spoke to no man, and no man spoke to me. From time to time I stole a glance at the line of tents on top of the fortifications on shore, where numbers of redcoats must now spend their nights on my account. The steamer lay at anchor close by, and the sight of her set up a churning in my vitals. I waited to be informed of letters, my impatience growing more difficult to conceal by the minute. But mask it I did, keeping a phlegmatic exterior; I wasn't going to beg my captors for my mail.

At eleven o'clock, the squat figure of Captain Thorpe, super-intendent of convicts, appeared on the quarter-deck. He was accompanied by Commander Moffatt. After being saluted by the officers and exchanging greetings with them, the superintendent beckoned me over.

I saw that he had in his hand a thick packet of letters. He greeted me in his profound bass voice, not smiling, but affecting a studied courtesy. Commander Moffatt, hands behind his back, smiled faintly but benevolently, as though I were a promising but difficult pupil summoned to the front of the class. Captain Thorpe's glance went briefly and questioningly to my cap – a thing that always happens when we meet. He clearly thinks I ought to remove it – or at least touch it to him. But my old blue cap remained where it belonged. He can't help himself, this supreme ruler over convict desperadoes: despite his orders concerning my status, my failure to recognise his exalted position is putting a severe strain on his self-control. His mouth twisted slightly to one side, as though he were exploring a hollow tooth.

– As you see, Mr Devereux, the mail steamer is in, he said, and jerked his head at the vessel beyond the rail.

I agreed that it was, without letting my eyes go to the letters in his hand.

– Here are your letters, he said, and held them out. You seem to have a good number of correspondents. Trust there'll be good news of your family.

His entirely cold expression was at odds with these words. Unlike my other captors, he possibly nurses a genuine hatred for me; or for what I represent.

– You'll note that all the letters are still sealed, he said. We are entitled to open them, but the Governor, Captain Elliott, has elected not to do so. Think you should also know that His Excellency himself wrote to your father as soon as you arrived, to inform him of your situation and to set his mind at ease.

– That was very courteous of him, I said. Please convey my thanks to His Excellency.

– However, Captain Thorpe said, His Excellency has asked me to communicate to you that he expects you to give up any letter for examination that may contain matters relating to politics or public affairs.

– Certainly, I said.

I carefully controlled my expression at the fatuousness of this request; it was a promise I had no intention of keeping. I then made to depart. I was anxious to regain the privacy of my cabin, there to discover whether letters from Catherine were among those I held in my hand.

– A moment.

The absurdly penetrating voice was raised a little higher, and the gaze had become even colder.

– One other matter, Mr Devereux. Afraid you can no longer be allowed newspapers.

I was amazed and angry enough to frown. This was a considerable affront, and I spoke with difficulty.

– May I ask why?

The official British gaze looked through rather than at me; the large, beefy face still showed no expression.

– Think you know why. The world beyond this hulk is still a little too concerned about you – and you may in turn grow over-interested in the world. We think this measure advisable, for the foreseeable future. Governor's orders.

– I see.

I was determined to maintain my resolve to meet all indignities

73

in silence; but it now took all my strength to do so. My captors knew very well, I saw, how to strike at me most fundamentally, while keeping me in comparative comfort. Henceforth, I would be in total ignorance of events in Europe and in Ireland; I would vegetate here like a savage, not only suspended in space, but in time. History's story would cease for me from today.

Commander Moffatt now interjected, in his dull, soothing burr. He looked faintly apologetic.

– Plenty of other reading matter is available to you, Mr Devereux. Some new books I sent to London for have just arrived on the steamer. I'd be happy to lend you any that are of interest.

– Thank you, Commander. You're always kind. I'm happy to find that I'll still be allowed to look at print.

I was no longer looking at the superintendent, but it was he who answered me. His bass voice was soft, but it carried clearly.

– You may look at print, Mr Devereux – and we'll be looking at *you*. Make no mistake about that.

Despite his phlegmatic mask, his eyes now conveyed the direct and primitive menace by which one man attempts to intimidate another. I did not let my own gaze falter, and I gave him back a look into which I put all the contempt I could muster.

– Thank you, Captain Thorpe. I fear I won't have much scope to justify your curiosity.

I took my leave, and moved towards the companionway going down to the main deck. Commander Moffatt watched me go with mournful puzzlement, and three young officers by the rail also watched my retreat, while pretending not to.

As I went back along the half-deck to my cabin, I shuffled through the letters in my hands, anger making me half-blind. I recognised the handwriting of three friends; and here were letters from my parents, and from my sister and brother. Then I found a letter from Catherine. I quickened my pace to reach my cabin, and began to break the seal of her letter as soon as I was inside. With a glance at the calm eyes in the daguerreotype by the porthole, I began to read.

My dearest Robert,

Soon after my last letter, we were informed by the authorities that you were being exiled to Bermuda. I am told that it may be well into July before this letter reaches you.

That this action was taken without warning was dreadfully cruel. I'm told that the English believed that had their intentions been known, there would have been an attempt by the Clubs of Dublin to storm the ship. And Terence Butler tells me that the Clubs did discuss doing so, and were very vehement about it. But sometimes I think that talk is all the Clubs are capable of.

Oh Robert, for how long will we be separated now? Your father is trying to discover whether you will be allowed to live in Bermuda as a free settler – and whether I might hope to follow you, and marry you there. But the authorities will divulge nothing: they simply say that for the time being, you are to continue as a prisoner. They refer to you as a convict, and so does the London press.

'The convict Devereux'! It fills me with shame and horror, and I'm beginning to grow afraid. Forgive me, dearest, I know I should be brave about this as you are being, but I can't be; I begin to have the most terrible misgivings. You try to cheer me up in your letter from Cork, and you tell me you are respectfully treated and have hopes that we will be re-united – but what real grounds do you have for this? How can you count on being freed on Bermuda – or anywhere else? They've made you into a convict, and they are able to do what they wish with you. I shall pray for you every day, until I hear from you in Bermuda; and every day I shall be wondering whether you are labouring in irons.

I shouldn't be writing in this way, I know, but I can't help it. I've never allowed myself to believe that we would be separated for more than a few months – but I'm now fighting against the dreadful idea that we may be separated for years. Robert, tell me this won't happen! Speak with your captors there, and beg them to re-unite us. Be humble, I beg you, if that will help – even though you hate to be humble. Already I lie awake weeping every night. Already I long for your arms about me again. How is the notion of years of separation to be contemplated?

Were all your politics and your hatred of English rule worth this? I have never spoken so before; I see your face as you read, and am half ashamed — yet I don't take this back. You are a man of high ideals, whose integrity cannot be bought: in other words you are stronger than other people, and you act without fear of consequences. But there's also a violence in you — a need for violence (even though you have personally committed none in your life), that I cannot but fear, and — forgive me — cannot approve. This is why you called on the people to rise, and it is this, surely, which has most provoked the anger and hostility in the authorities that has brought you to the present terrible pass — while others live their lives in peace. It is this that causes them to call you a terrorist; it is in you, Robert, and I am compelled to ask again: was it worth it? Or has not the price been too high?

I can't write more; I'm unable. I'll wait every day for your next letter, and will have no peace until I learn what they have done with you.

All my love.

Your
Catherine

★ EDITOR'S NOTE: Letter found in Devereux's writing-slope.

R.B.

What am I to make of this letter of Catherine's?

At first, despite its distress, the anxious love I found in it was reassuring. But as I re-read it, its questions and gentle reproaches grew in importance. I know, of course, that her pain makes these questions natural; but I'm troubled by an ill-defined premonition, given rise to by something more than her anguished words: by a sense of something else behind the words: a shadow behind a shadow. As I write these lines, in this hateful Bermudan afternoon which decays outside time, I begin to fear that she no longer understands what I am, or that I can do no other than what I do. I even fear that she never did understand — or didn't wish to.

This is wrong, and unjust. It must be.

I've not gone back on deck since my exchange with Captain Thorpe. I sit here at my table, or pace my few feet of cabin, unable to bear going out, yet scarcely able to bear being here. Nowhere,

nowhere to go! With its low timber ceiling mere inches above my head, and its long, narrow shape, this accursed box of mine puts me more and more in mind of a coffin.

For the past month, dazed and stupid with the tedium of captivity, lulled by Bermuda's narcotic warmth, my brain has been asleep. Now it's been thrown into turmoil: invaded by the world. Paul Barry has written, and so has Thomas O'Neill: long, wonderful letters, giving me glimpses of events in Ireland and all across Europe as well, where nation after nation strikes out for its liberty in this great and extraordinary year – which the press is now calling a year of revolutions. British fate is moving ever nearer to these comrades, but their tone remains gay, cheerful and defiant. We are no longer alone, in Ireland. We are part of a larger music, our struggle just one theme in a symphony of revolt: a music reaching its climax in all those lands where Austrian power is being broken, and the Empire of the Habsburgs is dissolving.

Paul Barry tells me he was arrested again a month ago, and carried off to Dublin, his crime this time being 'a seditious speech' – but he's currently out on bail. Martin Fitzgibbon at present remains free too; but a warrant is out against Thomas O'Neill, also for sedition, of course: in his case, for an article published in the *New Nation*. Well, Barry and O'Neill will no more get fair trials than I did. Will they join me here, I wonder?

In his letter, Barry says that all three of our newspapers were stopped by the police, and even confiscated from the newsboys on the streets. All their offices, like mine, were broken into and searched for secret documents.

Good! I like this. Let all Europe see what tyrants are ruling us – just as it now sees Austrian tyranny unmasked in Prague! Because the game is by no means over; the forces of reaction are hitting back, Barry tells me. Newly independent Bohemia is reeling – its infant democracy bombed into submission by the wolfish commander Prince Windischgrätz – who now rules as a dictator, in the Emperor's name. And in Italy, alas, the ancient Marshal Radetzky has given the Emperor some victories over the Piedmontese, Venetian and Papal troops – those triumphant armies which seemed assured, when I left Ireland, of taking Young Italy to freedom. But the reactionaries won't check the tide for ever: not in Bohemia, not in Italy, not in Ireland.

My prisoner's peace is gone as I study and caress these letters. I can't sit still: for the first time, the full agony of confinement has seized me like nausea. These challenging, cool northern voices will not stop sounding in my head – and they now carry the only news of this shattering chain of revolts that I'm ever likely to receive. But where at first they excited me, now they begin to torment me. From the Danube to the Seine, Europe is convulsed – *and all this is going on without me!* This is what I can't bear. Rumours of the struggle come to me here like furious echoes; like a far, exalted music that's only half-heard. Ah, God! My captors have buried me – neither on land nor on sea, neither in the world nor out of it – and the ceiling of this wretched cabin presses down to suffocate me. Yet to go out on deck would be worse, just now. There, I'd be tormented by the sight of the officers and guards scanning the forbidden newspapers, passing them from hand to hand: those tantalising sheets which carry the story's latest chapters in every detail – but which I may not read.

News! News! I lust for it. I'm a creature of the world, and the world is denied me. They have found a perfect way to torture me, and surely my head will burst. Although the porthole is open, the air remains listless; lifeless. I've been walking up and down; I've torn open my collar. I feel I can't bear to live through the next few hours; not even through the next five minutes. Yet I must; and only writing in this good, thick journal is helping me to do so. I've tried to pray, but can't. God is absent, as he so often seems to be now; there's nothing but the void. Several times, strangled cries have come from me, which I can only hope my captors have not had the satisfaction of hearing.

Cot; bookshelves; littered table: I'm ready to smash them all to pieces! The few possessions from which I take comfort – my books, the picture of Catherine, and the little mahogany writing-slope in which I keep my pens, paper, ink and letters – these are of no more comfort. Objects, mutely persisting, become unbearable; the universe itself becomes unbearable, to a prisoner. Perhaps the universe is only ever bearable because we move and divert ourselves, and because we love: and I can do neither, now.

I've just dealt the table a tremendous blow, making a cup and pen jump, badly bruising my fist. I want to go out and dive from the pier; I want to attempt some mad, impossible flight. I want –

But hold hard. Not yet. Patience. Turn away from the little path with the sign on it saying, *Lunacy*. What my gaolers want is to see me take that path. Captain Thorpe wants it, certainly; but he'll not have that satisfaction.

I'm breathing hard, empty, like a man who has exerted himself beyond his limit; and my thoughts swim like trapped fish towards Catherine.

Late at night. Better.

Much has happened since writing the above: things I wish to record before I sleep.

Seconds after I struck the table, the convict servant Lane entered the cabin with a handful of books. I glared at him. He hadn't waited for me to bid him enter after he knocked, and I could see from his expression that he'd heard the crash of my fist, and was curious. But when he scrutinised my face, what he saw there apparently warned him against asking questions.

– These books was sent to you by Commander Moffatt, sir, he said, and set them down carefully on the table, straightening the pile fastidiously.

He always gave himself an expert air, his style varying with each task: this evening he was a librarian.

– I expect you'll be glad of them, he added.

– I expect I will, Lane.

My voice was lifeless; I remained motionless in the chair into which I'd just sunk, trying to bring myself to a normal state of calm, waiting for him to go.

But he didn't go; instead, like a conjuror, he produced a bottle of French brandy from about his person, setting it down with a triumphant gleam in his eyes, and a gloating smile.

– And this was sent to you by Doctor Howard, sir.

I leaned forward to examine the bottle, while Lane smirked at the surprise in my face.

– He said as how it's for your health, sir. A lovely drop, I'm told it is. Put some heart into you, I shouldn't wonder.

He eyed the bottle with ill-concealed avidity; but I frowned at it as though it were a bomb. A pineapple was one thing; this was quite another. For a prisoner to be in possession of alcohol was a flogging offence. I had not seen Doctor Howard since sending him my note of thanks for the pineapple; and I began to wonder what his motives were, and whether this was some sort of trap.

– Is there any other message, Lane?

The servant produced and handed me a sealed note.

– This, sir.

He hovered, eyeing the letter as though he thought I might share its contents with him. Instead, I put it aside and looked at him enquiringly, waiting for him to leave. But he did not.

– There's something else, sir, before I go – something I thought I should tell you.

He licked his lips in a way that was unaccountably lascivious. Clasping his hands, he bent his long body like a hinge, bringing his face uncomfortably close to mine and smiling as though about to impart some unclean secret. I responded with a discouraging grunt, and said nothing. Something about him had warned me this would come; he was the sort of man who seemed to smell of stale bodily secretions, and to be privately dwelling on foul fancies.

– There's to be a flogging, he said.

I stared.

He bent even lower, and I caught his breath, which smelled like drains.

– A dose of the cat, he said. It'll be on the main deck, in an hour's time, when the gangs come in from work. We'll all be mustered to watch. All except you, sir, that is. *You* don't have to watch.

– I see. Why are you telling me this, Lane?

– Because you'll *hear* it, sir. The place where they'll string him to the gratings isn't far from this cabin – so you won't be able to *help* hearing. I thought I ought to warn you.

80

– Indeed. And what is the fellow being flogged for?

– Giving cheek, sir. They'll probably give him twenty-five.

– Really. Isn't that rather severe?

– Nah, sir, that's just a tickling. There's some coves gets a hundred or more, for more serious capers. A good flogger can lay your backbone bare – and our quartermaster's a fierce flogger. He won't do that today – but this chap who's getting the twenty-five is a lily-liver, so I promise you'll hear him howl.

And he grinned, as though this news would give me pleasure. My stony expression of distaste told him otherwise, and the grin faded. I scribbled a note of thanks to Doctor Howard and gave it to him, and he finally slid from the cabin.

Doctor Howard's note to me, which I now opened, was clever.

Dear Mr Devereux,

Please accept this cognac with my compliments. I think you'll find it a reasonable one, and I trust it will be of help in keeping you in good health, and warding off that asthma of yours. At night – especially when winter comes – it can grow a little chilly and draughty on this hulk, and this gives me some concern, knowing of your weakness. I prescribe this to you as your doctor, to be taken in moderate amounts each evening. Perhaps it will also have the pleasant effect of cheering the idle hour, and making your regrettably isolated condition more tolerable.

Thank you for your recent note; I had intended to call on you before now, but Yellow Fever among the prisoners has kept me much occupied. I hope to step in and see how your own health is after eight this evening.

Neville Howard

I sat puzzling. What was the reason for Doctor Howard's attentiveness? Was he genuinely worried about my health – and if so, why such persistent concern? Did they fear that I would die on their hands, and embarrass them? Whatever the reason, I frankly looked forward to his visit; I had so little else to divert me.

Five-thirty found me absorbed in writing letters. Suddenly I became conscious of a low murmur of voices from somewhere outside.

These were then stilled by the arrogant, petulant-sounding bark of an English voice, raised in command. At first I took little notice, and had returned to my writing when a new sound made me start. It was a hissing report, of which at first I made nothing. But when it was repeated, I remembered what Lane had warned me of, and slowly got to my feet. The flogging had begun.

I have never witnessed a flogging, and had never before heard the sound of a cat-of-nine-tails being brought down on human flesh. I have no objection in principle to convicted felons being flogged, if it's absolutely necessary to prevent the breakdown of order and discipline. But principle is one thing; this merciless ceremony of punishment was another. The reports were like gun-shots; no wonder the flesh is cut to ribbons, as I'm told it is. And I found my shocked mind asking whether in fact this should be done to the miracle of human flesh: any human flesh.

I didn't want to consider the question. I didn't want to hear. And yet I listened with horrid attention. Somehow, the fact that I couldn't see made it worse. Between each stroke there was a frown-ing pause, during which, each time, I bit my lip and wondered whether it was nearly over. But then, after each hiatus, the terrific, whistling lash would connect again, machine-like and remorseless, an engine which neither pleading nor defiance would alter. And yet a human being wielded it!

When at last it was over, I found myself physically chilled, despite the mild air, and actually trembling a little. Sub-tropical sunset glowed outside the porthole, colouring the ramparts of tyranny above the dock with a dramatic pink I normally admired. But this evening it seemed like the manifestation of some vast, ethereal injury: a haemorrhaging in the sky. The cabin darkened, and I took my first glass of Doctor Howard's excellent cognac. (They have provided me with a glass and a cup, in the cupboard; my dishes and cutlery are taken away at the end of each meal.) This briefly heartened me; but a ghost of the trembling continued, and I sat staring into space, glass in hand.

This was what it had come to, then, I said. I was not clear what I meant – except that the savagery of the British penal system had now been unmasked for me. This, I said, was what underlay everything: the scrupulous manners, the strict and conscientious order. And what had the poor devil done? 'Given cheek', Lane had said. Well, I had heard the way such felons were addressed by their keepers, the military guards; and no wonder they occasionally 'gave cheek'. Every order was given with contempt, as though to something sub-human; and nearly always it was preceded by a variation on the oath that wished injury on the subject's eyes. There seemed a peculiar cruelty in this, when the eyesight of the prisoners was so often injured by the glare of the alien rocks where they were forced to labour; and I found myself recalling an elderly convict with a narrow, stubbled grey head, bucket in hand, stooped, resigned, and blinking his ruined, red-rimmed eyes at the second mate, a young man with the face of an enraged spaniel, who cried at him:

– Damn your bloody old eyes! Do you call this deck clean?

Thinking of that old convict, I had a sudden fellow-feeling for him, and for all the felons. This evening, the thin span of fabric separating me from their endless toil and bleeding flesh seemed very thin.

And then a wild wailing began.

It came from the dimming esplanade opposite the breakwater, and I jumped to my feet as though summoned to witness some fresh torture. Peering out the porthole, I found that it was a platoon of the 42nd Regiment of Highlanders, all in their bonnets and kilts, marching towards the barracks with their pipers playing 'Scotland the Brave'. They had done this on other evenings, and I had enjoyed it; but tonight the strains of the pipes were grim, in the grim sunset, and seemed to me the music of Hell.

– Sitting in the dark, are we sir?

It was Lane again, with dinner.

– I'll just brighten things up, he said.

He set the tray down, found matches, and lit the two candles on the shelf above the table, shooting a look at me of unusual penetration, as though he'd been eavesdropping on my thoughts. The candle-light struck his long face obliquely, making the hollows

83

in his cheeks cavernous, and giving to his somewhat bulging dark eyes a glossy brilliance, so that they reminded me again of those of a horse.

– You're looking low, sir, he said. No bad news from home, I hope?

And he glanced at the pile of letters at the end of the table.

– No, Lane, I said. Nothing's wrong.

He removed the napkin that covered the plate of boiled beef and vegetables he had brought, shaking the cloth in his imitation of a waiter, and laying it in my lap.

– Well then, he said, that's something to be thankful for. But you don't look yourself at all, sir.

Standing to attention, he glanced at Catherine's picture.

– I expect you're missing your intended, he said. A very beautiful young lady, if you don't mind me saying it, sir.

– I'm glad you think so, Lane.

It was the first time he'd ventured such a comment, and normally I would have discouraged him; but in the mood I was in, even Lane was half-welcome. More and more I found myself adrift; and while I drifted, the reality outside my cabin was breaking in. I found I welcomed the sound of any friendly voice – even if its friendliness was suspect. And in this moment of weakness, I told myself that I might have misjudged Lane, who was perhaps well-meaning and even good-hearted; why should I repel his every attempt at kindness?

As usual, he was hovering; and instead of indicating that he should go, I looked up with a reasonably cordial expression to see what he would say next. Encouraged, he moved a little closer to Catherine's portrait, and stooped with an air of reverence to examine it further.

– Very beautiful, he repeated. A real lady. But then, you're a handsome gentleman, sir, as I'm sure your young lady would agree.

I began to feel uncomfortable again, and said nothing to this compliment. Unabashed, he gestured at my plate.

– *Do* eat, sir – it'll put some heart in you.

I picked up my knife and fork; I had little appetite, but began to eat mechanically, seeking for something to say to him that would show a little more friendliness.

– What brought you to the hulks, Lane?

It was the first time I'd asked him any personal question; a bridge had been crossed, and I saw, too late, and with a sinking heart, how quickly he would grasp this advantage. His face became both pleased and sly; he moved closer and bowed over me, clasping his hands, his voice taking on a low huskiness that acknowledged our intimacy. And his language became suddenly coarse; he lapsed into the half-comprehensible thieves' cant of the London streets.

– What brought me? You might say a woman did, he said. It was Peg, my own bloody natural, who grassed on me to the peelers. She wanted to see me put away so she could go off with another cove she fancied. I had a good little business in Seven Dials: a nice little shop. A curiosity shop, you might call it: antiques and second-hand goods. And that bloody woman squealed to the traps that some candlesticks I had was stolen.

– And were they?

I began to be interested, in a squalid sort of way. He raised his brows, grinned, shrugged, and spread his hands.

– I took anything people brought me, sir – anything I could sell. As it turned out, these same candlesticks was stolen by the bloody villain that sold them to me. But I never knew nothing about it – how could I? Yet up I went at the Bailey for receiving.

He had plainly been a fence; but I made no indication of my scepticism, and went on eating.

– Yes, sir, he said. It's the women that can bring you low – the wrong women, that is. I tell you, I don't miss the morts, most of the time; I trust men more. I mean, a good chum won't let you down, will he? But a mort will, whenever it suits her, without looking back.

– You've just been unlucky, Lane. There are good women and bad, just as there are good men and bad. And after a few years on these hulks, I imagine men nearly go mad, missing their women. Isn't that so?

At first, bent over me with both hands thrust into his trousers

pockets, he didn't answer. The expression he wore now was odd –
a kind of eager leer – and his breathing seemed uneven. Too late,
pushing my plate away, I realised that I should never have pursued
this conversation.

– There's other things besides cracks, he said. Who needs cracks?

He winked, and appeared to be fidgeting with something in his
pocket. Before I could check him, or object to the increasing
brutality of his language, he went on – his voice sinking almost to
a whisper, his fawning stoop bringing him even nearer.

– After a while here, sir, you look at these nice fresh young
boys as gets transported, and they begin to look prettier and prettier.
Do you get my drift, sir? Does it interest you?

For a moment, I was too astounded to speak. Then I said:

– No, Lane, it doesn't – and I don't much care for your
language, or this conversation. It's time you were gone.

But he would not be stopped. The shine in his bulging horse's
eyes was now like a veneer which prevented him from seeing me
clearly: he saw only whatever writhings were taking place in his
own brain, and the left hand in his pocket grew worryingly busy.

– There's quite a few of these boys that takes to me, he said.
They call me Long Lane. Would you like to see why, sir?

Before I could answer, he had drawn from his pocket what at
first looked like a white eel. He must have worked it through a
hole in the lining.

This is why, he said, and grinned at my horrified astonishment.
You've got to admit it's long, sir, ain't it?

The shadows in the cabin seemed to draw closer; the candle-
flames trembled upwards, then dropped again, illuminating the pallid
thing Lane gripped, which seemed no part of himself at all, but
some blind, unwholesome creature he would presently release into
the cabin. I could scarcely believe his insolence; scarcely bring
myself to speak. Was he mad? Did he really believe he could behave
like this without consequence? I rose to my feet.

– Get out of this cabin, I said. You won't enter it again. I'll
report your behaviour to Commander Moffatt, depend on it.

His grin vanished; he went a sickly colour, and cringed – still holding his wretched, corpse-like member, like someone with a gift which had been rejected.

– No, sir, he said. No, you mustn't do that. I only –

– Go! I shouted. Go quickly, before I deal with you myself!

The anger in my own voice surprised me; it was as though all the inward rage of the past weeks was directed at this one corrupted creature – and I suppose what heightened my rage was the idea that Lane believed that he could do this with impunity, and that he surmised that the gap between myself and the other felons was narrowing.

I advanced on him now, raising my fist, and he drew back in alarm; his hands rummaged frantically at his clothes, and the eel disappeared. He grabbed the dirty dishes from the table and fled from the cabin, not looking back.

I sat down in my chair again, my chest heaving, my temples pounding.

– Dear God, I said.

Then I began to laugh. I laughed until I almost wept.

About an hour later, there was another knocking on the cabin door. Thinking it might be Lane again, I threw the door open with what was no doubt a menacing expression – only to find myself staring at Doctor Howard.

He blinked at me, his spectacles reflecting the candle-light: tall, erect and trim in his dark blue naval frock coat, his tanned, balding head tilted far back, so that he peered, as it were, downward. If he found my demeanour unusual, he gave no sign, but smiled with pleasant geniality.

– Ah. Mr Devereux. Am I disturbin' you?

He had a resonant, pleasing voice, and that habit of dropping his gs which is common among some members of his class. It was a voice that was accustomed to authority, but without pomposity.

– Hardly, Doctor, I said. I'm not over-occupied. Come in.

I stepped back, and gestured at the interior of my dog-box.

– Thank you, he said, and moved past me into the cabin. He was holding a bottle of wine in his hands.

– I've been meanin' to call, he said, ever since I got your note. But the fever among the prisoners has kept me pretty busy.

Facing each other, our heads almost touching the ceiling, we made the cabin seem even smaller than usual. I indicated one of the two straight-backed chairs by the table.

– Do sit down, I said. I'm afraid the hospitality I have to offer is somewhat rude, but –

He laughed, placed the bottle on the table, and seated himself carefully, looking up at me.

– This will do very well, he said. I thought we might enjoy a glass of wine together.

It was a fine Bordeaux – an 1838 Chateau Lafite – and the sight of it was extraordinarily festive to me, after so many monotonous weeks without such pleasures – the exception being the Doctor's brandy, hoarded in my trunk, to be taken in small amounts when I needed to hearten myself. I'm not a heavy drinker, and it was not so much the prospective stimulus of alcohol that made the sight of the Lafite such a treat, as what it represented. It was like a reassurance that some small fragments of civilization were still within my reach; and I picked up the bottle and looked at its label like a child examining the wrappings of a Christmas present.

– It looks very fine, I said. But surely such luxuries are somewhat irregular for a felon?

He narrowed his eyes, head tilted back, continuing to smile.

– Medicinal, my dear fellow, he said. I am responsible. And it's no-one else's business but ours – d'you see?

I sat down, and we looked at each other across the table.

– Yes, I see, I said. Well, I'm most appreciative, Doctor – for this and your other gifts.

After the events of the afternoon, I found his appearance here extraordinarily welcome. He had the sort of easy cheerfulness that would have raised my spirits in any circumstances; and it was undeniably pleasant to be in the presence of someone of my own kind: someone with a friendly face. Yet I had to remind myself that the whole situation was ambiguous, since this man, friendly or not, was one of my captors.

He was shaking his head now, and holding up one hand to check my polite thanks.

– Not at all, not at all, he said. Very small comforts, I'm afraid, in your situation.

He produced a corkscrew from his pocket, and began to work it into the cork with long, powerful fingers.

– Have you two glasses, by any chance?

I went to the little cupboard under the porthole and produced my glass and cup: the only drinking vessels supplied to me. I sat down as he poured the wine; he pushed the glass across the table to me.

– The cup will do for me, he said. You'll enjoy the wine more, in a glass. Next time I'll bring an extra one. I do hope there'll be a next time?

I raised my glass to him.

– Certainly, I said, if you don't mind sitting in this little kennel of mine. Your good health, Doctor.

The claret was excellent: rich and mellow. Sipping it, I observed Doctor Howard carefully. His eyes, slightly magnified by his spectacles, were pale green and fish-like. They watched me shrewdly, as he raised his cup in response to my toast, and expressed cordiality; but they gave nothing away. Nor did his bland, big-chinned face, which was that of a much younger man – its tight, tanned skin contrasting with the curling, greying fringe of hair, and the bald head. He drank, then let out a small gust of breath, his open lips tightening over his teeth. He had a firm, well-disciplined mouth; yet the lips had a fullness that hinted at sensuality. Certainly this was a man who enjoyed life; and he was making my kennel into a pleasant parlour.

– Yes. Your good health also, Mr Devereux, he said, and gestured with the cup again. Speakin' of which, how *is* your health?

– Never better, I said. It's kind of you to be so concerned.

– Hm.

After this sound, he remained silent for some moments, the glassy, piscine eyes examining me dispassionately. He leaned further back in his chair, legs extended across the cabin, his left thumb hooked in his waistcoat, the cup held in his right. The confident, backward tilt of his head, cocked slightly to one side, was plainly habitual – perhaps as a result of constant diagnosis. He must spend a good deal of his time attempting to peer through men's skins. Finally, he said:

– I've read your medical report. Your robust appearance is deceptive. I realise you've had no asthma since you've been in custody; but we understand that you have a history of quite bad attacks, and that one or two of them nearly killed you.

– True, I'm afraid. Britannia knows everything.

He smiled.

– She tries to do. But she doesn't always succeed. Be that as it may, I hope you'll ask for me should you feel an attack comin' on. Will you do that?

– Certainly. There's not much to be done about asthma, Doctor, as I'm sure you know. But I'll have every confidence in your advice.

He refilled his cup and my glass.

– Good. You're right, of course – asthma is a wretched and bafflin' thing, for which we've no cure. It's important you keep warm, of course. But one of my observations is that it's affected by the patient's state of mind. If you're in low spirits, that may bring it on.

He smiled, his expression becoming confiding.

– You don't *seem* in low spirits, I must say. It puzzles Commander Moffatt that you're not. He's convinced that you're a deep one – but a lot of things puzzle Moffatt. He's a kind fellow, y'know, and is genuinely concerned about you. 'That man is unhappy inside, depend on it,' he says. I must say, it's a reasonable assumption. You wouldn't be human if you were not depressed under these circumstances.

Once again I was struck by the peculiarity of my situation. The free and easy way in which Doctor Howard spoke to me, a prisoner, about the hulk's commander – even hinting humorously at Moffatt's limitations – was surely most irregular. And it was done with the most easy assurance, as though the surgeon held a position that allowed him to do and say whatever he chose.

– Truly, Doctor, I'm not at all depressed, I said. I've placed myself in these circumstances by challenging your Government's rule in my country, and I accept the consequences.

– Ah. You're a true revolutionary of the new breed, I see.

Again the magnified green eyes studied me, without giving anything away; and his spectacles, reflecting the candle-light, made his expression even harder to read. He drank, and then smiled again, like a man recalling a piece of choice gossip.

– As for Captain Thorpe, he said, he's very uneasy about you indeed, since news came through of this idea of a rescue attempt from New York. An organisation called the New York Irish Directory, I understand.

He waited, as though hoping I'd confirm this. When I said nothing, he went on; and his tone remained humorous, even lightly mocking, as though he discussed notions that were nonsense.

– The superintendent's convinced you're merely biding your time – waiting to lead Irish prisoners in a patriotic uprising on these hulks. You're known to advocate force of arms; you're seen as a dangerous terrorist, so you can understand his thinkin', I'm sure. That's why he's had all Irish prisoners and guards replaced with English. And he even had an English guard removed who was heard to make sympathetic comments about you. Nothin' escapes him, in this little wasps' nest of ours.

He wiped his wine-wet mouth fastidiously with his forefinger.

– Yes, he's really most concerned, is Captain Thorpe. The Government surveyin'-steamer has had her bulwarks pierced for guns, ready for your band of comrades to appear over the horizon from America.

His expression invited me to laugh, and I did so.

– There'll never be any rescue ship, I said. Such a thing simply isn't feasible. Your fortress here is far too formidable. It's just a wild, generous notion which I'm sure my compatriots will by now have thought about twice.

Howard nodded.

– I agree; I see you're also a realist. And that's what I told Captain Thorpe myself. But our superintendent has no sense of humour. The vision of those brave New Yorkers sailin' down here with a squadron occupies him a good deal, I'm afraid.

He chuckled, and drank again.

There was an especially large knot in one of the boards that lined the cabin, over by the door, at which I often stared; I did so now, trying to marshal my thoughts. Out of the corner of my eye I saw the Doctor's long brown index finger rest on the lid of my polished mahogany writing-slope, which stood on the table in front of him: he stroked and tapped on it lightly, in an absent yet enquiring manner, and I wondered what he was actually up to with me. Was he simply a friendly man who enjoyed gossip, and who wished to offer me sympathetic company? Or was he trying to draw me out – perhaps to report on me? What he said next made him seem to read my mind.

– Difficult, on these hulks. Everyone spyin' on everyone else. The guards spy on the prisoners; the prisoners spy on one another. Unhealthy atmosphere; not one I like. The latest matter for spyin' is the possession of newspapers. The penalties for a prisoner havin' a newspaper on board since your arrival are rather extraordinary. Irons; floggin'. Captain Thorpe's orders again. And of course, the stool-pigeons gain favour by informin' to the guards if they know of a man who has a newspaper tucked away. That's how their sort get special treatment; they make themselves into trusties.

He leaned forward, and poured more wine. Looking up over his spectacles as he did so, he said:

– Your servant Lane is a stool-pigeon, y'know.

– I'm not surprised, I said.

I picked up my glass, and leaned back. Then I said:

– I have a favour to ask in regard to that man, Doctor.

– Oh?

His face became blandly neutral.

– Perhaps I should be discussing this with Commander Moffatt; but I'd be grateful instead for your private help, if that's possible. I don't wish to lay a complaint against Lane, or to get him into trouble: I stress that. Nor is he a bad servant. But I'd simply like to request that he cease to bring me my meals. My reason is that he seems somewhat depraved, and makes me uneasy.

Howard raised his eyebrows, rubbing his chin.

– What exactly has he done?

I explained that Lane had subjected me to a dissertation on his lascivious interest in boy prisoners, and had given me an unwanted display of his private parts. When I'd done, we stared at each other in silence, straight-faced.

– Good Lord, Doctor Howard said finally. How very beastly.

Then, as though in spite of himself, he smiled; and I could not help smiling myself. The next moment, we were both guffawing until the tears came. Finally Howard controlled himself, sniffed, and removed his spectacles, wiping the corner of one eye with his cuff.

– I'm sorry, he said. It's no laughin' matter – quite serious, in fact. We get a lot of buggery on these hulks, of course, with men cooped up. We try to check it, but it's difficult.

He replaced the spectacles and took on a mildly official air, head thrown back again.

– I'm glad to see you have a sense of humour, Mr Devereux. But you should never have been subjected to such annoyance, he said. Lane's had strict instructions not to be familiar with you, and to serve you as he would one of our officers. If you care to report this formally to Commander Moffatt, we'll make it a floggin' matter.

– No, no, Doctor, I don't want that. Nor do I wish him to lose his position as a trusty. Just remove him from attending to me, if you will.

– Very well, he said. I admire your charitable attitude: the fellow's more foolish than vicious. We'll simply assign him to other duties, without any fuss. We'll find a more steady man to serve you. And be assured that Commander Moffatt and I wish to make your situation here as tolerable as we can. Is there anythin' else I can do for you?

– There is one small matter, I said. I was very sorry to be deprived of the newspapers. I've not complained about any of my circumstances –

– Yes. That's been noted, he said quickly.

– Nor will I. But the deprivation of all news means that I'm cut off from the affairs of the world as effectively as though I'm imprisoned on the moon. Since I'm essentially a journalist by profession, this is more of a hardship to me than being deprived of the other comforts of normal life. Is there any hope that Captain Thorpe may eventually relax his edict?

The Doctor pursed his lips, swirling the claret in his cup and studying it.

– Not much, I'm afraid. He's pretty set. Has to be, of course, in most things; and he takes his cues from the Governor – who's somewhat suspicious of your intentions. I'll speak to the superintendent on your behalf – but I'm afraid I can't be optimistic.

He looked towards the door, as though concerned that we might be overheard. Then he said:

– But if it will cheer you up, *I* can be a sort of newspaper for you. Let you know from time to time what's goin' on in the world. Would that help?

– It would indeed, I said. But won't it be frowned on by the superintendent? After all, it would undermine the intent of his prohibition, would it not?

Howard smiled; but his green stare still told me nothing.

– Well now, I can act as a censor as well, can't I? I'll pass on to you only those affairs that are not to do with Irish rebellions. There's much else of interest goin' on. That way, Devereux, neither of us can get into trouble.

He'd dropped addressing me as 'Mr', I noticed, but this carried no hint of impoliteness; his assumption of a degree of informality between us already seemed natural. He leaned to pour more wine for me, concentrating on the tilted bottle. As he did so, he said:

– Somethin' that brought on this newspaper prohibition, by the way, was a report on certain events in London that took place in the last few months. Some of them directly concerned *you*.

– Oh?

– Yes. You'll know of the Chartist riots in April, with their call for votes for everyone, and a British Republic, and God knows what else. It seemed that your year of revolutions had come to Britain, didn't it? The Chartists were led by a fellow with a background similar to your own: a lawyer and newspaper editor called Ernest

Jones. Well, the Duke of Wellington's garrisons soon snuffed that out. But the Chartists tried again, a few weeks ago: they planned a real armed uprisin', like the mobs in France, startin' from a place in London called Bishop Bonner's Fields. No go again, I'm afraid. The police were ready – and it rained so hard that the mob gave up their attempt; their guns would have been useless. It simply fizzled out – and Jones and others are in prison. There'll be no British revolution now, I'm afraid.

– I'm sorry to hear it.

– I'm sure you are. But you see, Devereux, England's not the right soil for revolution: it always does fizzle out – or gets rained out. One of the reasons is that we've already *got* most of the freedoms the rest of Europe's askin' for – so it's hard to whip up much anger. It's the Frogs who do that sort of thing best – with all the nasty consequences that follow.

He spoke without heat or rancour, and I found it difficult to resent his words; he seemed entirely uninvolved, as he no doubt would be when he dissected a body, or diagnosed a disease.

– But here's somethin' to cheer you up, he said. Before that, some of the Chartists held a meeting in Clerkenwell Green, at which they declared their sympathy for *you*, and condemned your conviction. Jones was quoted as sayin' that Robert Devereux would one day return to his country in triumph, while Lord John Russell and Lord Clarendon would be transported.

This seemed genuinely to amuse the surgeon; he observed me from under lowered lids and chuckled, and I stared back at him in deep surprise. Here he was passing on the sort of inflammatory news that Captain Thorpe and the Governor expressly wished to hide from me!

– Inspiring times, I said. A year as good as the one that produced this wine.

He smiled and raised his cup.

– From your point of view – of course. But not for those who want to see civilized order intact, and Europe at peace. The forced abdication of Louis Philippe in February caused a good deal of worry in London, and in most other capitals, as you'll know. Not so much because the monarchy gave way to a Republic again, but because of the way it was done: through riot and mob rule in Paris. Revolutionary violence spreads like a contagion – we saw that in 1789. And y'know, Devereux, it may not end by bringin' people more freedom at all. Take Germany, for instance. *Their* revolution's actually in the hands of conservatives, and it's all about a new, united German state – one that'll include a new Austria and a new Prussia. And this Parliament of theirs at Frankfurt has decided that the new Germany will be monarchist, not republican – did you know that? That could lead to a new sort of Habsburg Empire, it seems to me – with many races subject to the Kaiser. Is that what you want? It's all not as simple as you young firebrands think, Devereux. So many things are goin' into Revolution's pot, on the Continent. Nationalism. Liberalism. Socialism. Monarchism. What a mixture! Its real name may be Chaos.

I smiled, looking at Doctor Howard with renewed interest. He was certainly well informed about current political events, and clearly no ordinary surgeon.

– The monarchs and despots like to tell us so, I said. But that's because they fear it, and know it's the final end of feudal power in Europe. France has ended it once and for all, with the overthrow of that vulgar little middle-class king. Paris is once more the moral capital of Europe.

Howard drained his cup, set it down on the table and rose, looking at me with an expression of quizzical amusement: one that seemed almost affectionate.

– Not quite the way *I* see the place, he said. Not after all the horrors it's seen in these last fifty years. If that's what moral fervour brings, then I'd rather do without moral fervour. But I realise that for an idealist like yourself, Devereux, it's wonderful to believe that there's a city or a country somewhere that's the capital of all your hopes. Even if such a country exists only in dreams.

I had stood also, and Howard held out his hand.

– I must say good night to you now, and be off to my bed – even though I could talk all night. It's a pleasure to get good conversation: in short supply on these hulks, I'm afraid. I'll come again in a couple of days, if I may.

– Do, I said. And just ignore my rant, Doctor. Be my news-paper, and I'll be deeply grateful, and hold my tongue.

He smiled, turning to the door.

– No need, he said. No need to hold your tongue with me. I'd be sorry if you did.

July 22nd

A new attendant has entered my life.

I waited uneasily in the cabin this morning to see whether Lane would appear with breakfast, or whether Doctor Howard had already carried out his promise. A light tapping sounded on the door; I called 'come in', and a convict I'd not seen before entered with the breakfast tray.

– Good morning, sir.

It was a confident, throaty voice, with an undertone of good humour: the sort of voice that compelled one to be alert. The accent wasn't Cockney, but from a county I couldn't place; I guessed it to be somewhere in the south of England. Putting the tray down on the table with a neat quickness that was quite unlike Lane's ceremony, this man also differed from Lane in being of medium height, but robust and solid-looking, with a broad chest and powerful shoulders. He had an upright, almost military posture which gave dignity to his coarse linen blouse, and neutralised the shame of its pattern of arrows. In fact, I strongly suspected that he'd once been a soldier: one somehow saw the ghost of a military moustache on his longer upper lip – though of course he was clean-shaven, like all the felons. He was perhaps forty or forty-five – the thick, rust-brown thatch of hair that fell over one eye (of greater length than seemed to be generally permitted the convicts), having touches of grey in it.

– I'm Langford, sir, he said, and straightened up. James Langford: Doctor Howard's servant. He says I'm to attend to you.

– I'm glad to hear it, Langford.

– Yes, sir.

His wide smile, showing a gap of unusual size between two strong front teeth, was appealing, and in spite of a resolve to keep a good distance between myself and this new attendant, I found myself feeling cordial. There was nothing sly or insidious in this smile, and no hint that he knew anything of the reason for his replacing Lane. Nevertheless, it wasn't an easy face to read. It combined a pleasing geniality with a ruthlessness I saw as criminal; and this ruthlessness was mainly in his eyes, which were arresting: of a kind I think of as 'tiger eyes'. Grey-blue and wide-set, transparent yet unfathomable, they had very small pupils, and that strange, feline emptiness which is like a distant sheet of water. Rigid-looking top lids gave his gaze an unnerving fixity; and it made me wonder if his crime might have been murder. I wasn't left to wonder long.

– I expect you'll have heard of me, sir, he said.

I looked up guardedly from my sausages and eggs.

– Heard of you, Langford? No; Doctor Howard has told me nothing about you.

– Not through Doctor Howard, sir. Through the newspapers.

He waited with quiet confidence for this to penetrate, the disturbing eyes steady on my face, hands at his sides in military fashion.

But I shook my head.

– No. Never heard of you, Langford, I'm sorry.

He smiled tolerantly.

– You're just not remembering, sir, I expect. The South Eastern Railway Gold Affair, four years ago. It realised a matter of five thousand pounds. I'm *that* James Langford.

He watched me now with the quiet certainty of a man who did not need to advertise himself. I put down my knife and fork and stared back; but without comprehension.

– That's right, he said quietly. Five thousand pounds, and not one farthing of it recovered by the authorities. Surely you recall the case now, sir?

– I'm afraid not, I said. It's all most fascinating, Langford, but I don't read much about crime in the English papers, and I've truly never heard of this great railway robbery of yours.

And I resumed eating, with an air of indifference that was scarcely genuine. I'd not encountered a bandit at close quarters before.

– Well, sir, he said, you do amaze me. I thought everyone in the world had heard of the Gold Affair, there was so much fuss in the papers at the time.

Then his tone became tolerant.

– Maybe not so much notice was taken of it in Ireland. But believe me, sir, I made a bit of a sensation when I first arrived here on Bermuda. I've been reckoned the first man in the colony – until *you* came, that is.

– I?

– Well of course. A prisoner of state; a patriotic martyr, discussed all the time in the press. You've cut me out, you might say.

His smile was both generous and ironical, and I was compelled to smile back.

– You do me too much honour, Langford, I said. I can't presume to compare with you. Five thousand pounds is more money than I ever saw at once in my life. How can a mere patriot compete with such an achievement?

For a moment, his smile disappeared, and the tiger eyes looked at me with a chilling blankness. There was a silence, in which we each tried to stare the other down. Neither of us succeeded; but as the seconds went by, I sensed the hidden violence in him. Then he chuckled throatily, and his look became mock-indulgent: an expression that was itself a form of aggression.

– You're chaffing me, sir. Well, I can't blame you for that. But no need to get on your high horse.

This last remark was really more insolent than anything Lane had ever offered; yet it didn't seem so, and I couldn't be annoyed. The power of this rogue's personality was so strong, and his manner so fearlessly direct, that I would have felt pompous trying to curb him. Moreover, I felt fairly certain that he would in the end observe some sort of limits with his familiarity – if only because Doctor Howard had sent him to me.

– I ride no high horse, I said. There's not a horse to be had on this hulk. We're all on foot, Langford, aren't we?

He looked at me for some moments before replying.

– You're right there, sir, he said softly. We're all on foot. Not a nag to be had.

I resumed my breakfast, and as I did so he began to chuckle again, as though something beyond my remark was amusing him. His chuckle went on until it ended in a cough; his face reddened, his eyes began to water, and I found myself laughing too, not really knowing why I did so. We watched each other, both of us laughing immoderately. It did me good, this silly mirth.

Finally, I picked up my knife and fork and began to eat again, and Langford sobered. He thumped his chest to settle his cough and wiped his mouth with the back of his hand; then as though continuing an uninterrupted story, he said:

– So I'm doing very comfortably out here, you see, sir. It's a very nice berth, serving Doctor Howard. I haven't had a day's illness; I'm in a very good mess, and I move about these islands a bit with the Doctor. And they have their attractions, sir, I can tell you. Devilish pretty brown girls.

His grin came back, his voice sank, and he winked.

– I have a little friend on that island across the bay, where Doctor Howard keeps his cottage, and his ducks and goats. I go over there and tend them for him, see? And that little brown girl's always looking out for me.

I was considerably surprised by these confidences. Had he been Lane, I would have checked him; but by now Langford so interested me that I let him run on. He added savour to my breakfast. If this was the condition of a convict, no wonder some of the soldiers committed crimes to become felons themselves, considering it an easier life. Clearly, though, Langford was no ordinary felon.

– I'll leave you to finish off that breakfast, sir, he said. Oh, by the way.

He drew from his blouse a small package which he handed to me. It was a very fine Virginia pipe tobacco.

– From Doctor Howard, sir. He said you might be running low.

– Give Doctor Howard my grateful thanks.

– Yes, sir. Doctor Howard has told me to look after you in all ways possible, and rest assured I'll do it, sir. Anything at all.

– Thank you, Langford.

Still he stood.

– I've ways and means of getting most things I want here, he said. Is there anything you'd like?

His look managed to hint at illicit satisfactions: brown girls, perhaps. But I returned it blankly.

– I don't think so, Langford.

He seemed quite unaffected, like a man dealing with a somewhat moody invalid.

– Well, sir, if there ever *is* anything, you've only got to say the word.

Briskly, he picked up my empty plate, leaving me with my tea, and crossed to the door: when he walked, he seemed to limp slightly, favouring his right leg. At the door, he turned.

– I believe they've stopped you getting any newspapers, he said, and his tone was neutral.

– Now there's a different matter, I said. If you can get *those* for me, I'll be very grateful.

– Risky, he said thoughtfully. Very. I'm not anxious to do solitary, sir. But there's more than one way to skin a cat. Let me think about it.

And he winked again, his expressionless face managing to make the wink respectful rather than impertinent. Then he was gone, and I sat digesting both my meal and my thoughts about this extraordinary new servant.

Somehow, I'd ended by tolerating a far more frank familiarity from him than I'd ever done from Lane. Dangerous, this, since he was probably the Doctor's spy, and could be leading me into some sort of trap. But I have the presentiment now that I'll tolerate greater familiarity yet, if Langford goes on serving me. He's outside my experience: I've had very little to do with a man of his kind, yet his personality threatens to dissolve the social barriers between us. And because of the tedium and isolation of my situation, where small things loom larger and larger, I have the novel and probably foolish sensation of welcoming this, rather than rejecting it. Here am I, a prisoner as Langford is, my life in tatters, my very reason threatened by boredom; and here is a man whom my instincts tell me will stop at nothing – and I inwardly welcome him.

Setting this down, I'm not entirely sure what I mean by it. I find I'm entertaining the curious fancy that Langford has been assigned to me not just by Doctor Howard, but by fate, and that somehow he will influence my future.

Boredom, surely, is reducing my mind to childishness.

July 23rd

Tonight Doctor Howard appeared again as he'd promised to do, bearing another bottle of fine Bordeaux. He also held two tall crystal wine-glasses, which he set down on the table.

– There, he said. Now we can drink like civilized men. Put these away in your cupboard afterwards, for our future meetin's.

Humiliating though it is to set this down, I'd waited for his coming like a boy for an expected treat; and this indirect promise that his visits would continue filled me with pleasure. The two glasses, twinkling on the table in the candle-light, transformed the cabin into a civilized room, as Howard's very presence did: he fills this wretched kennel with an atmosphere of vivacity and hope.

When he'd poured the wine, we raised our glasses to each other and drank, and Howard exhaled with satisfaction.

– Well, now, he said. I've been scannin' every journal about the place, fillin' my head with news on your behalf. Before I have too much wine and get fuddled, where shall I begin?

– Begin with France, I said. How goes the new Republic?

– Ah, yes, your capital of noble dreams.

Doctor Howard extended his legs at full length, hooked his thumb in his waistcoat, and thrust out his lower lip: humorous and judicial. I saw more and more how this man relished discourse, as I did: and we both knew his news would lead to discourse.

– You'll have been out of touch since late May, he said. Isn't that so?

– I was allowed to read one London newspaper on my arrival, dated June 1st, I said. I recall its outrage at the establishment of the Republic, and its hopeless call for the return of Louis Philippe. Since then, for a month, I've seen nothing.

He smiled faintly.

– In that case, you'll not know of the events of June in Paris – what they're callin' 'the June days'. You had the details of the April elections, of course?

– Yes. A satisfactory outcome, I thought. The Republic legalised; the people's wishes democratically realised.

– One might look at it that way. But you heard what happened next? The second Paris revolution in mid-May?

– An attempt to overthrow the National Assembly by Red Republicans and Socialists – yes. I gather they were easily thwarted – if a paper like the *Morning Post* is reliable on the matter.

– Oh, it's pretty reliable, I think. And certainly the uprisin' was carried out by a mixed bag of left-wing agitators. Democracy didn't suit them, apparently. The will of the people hadn't provided them with the sort of government they wanted: *their* sort of government, that would steer for total power. Instead, the people had elected conservatives and moderates. Very disappointin' for the radicals. Didn't suit 'em at all.

His smile was now openly derisive.

– But a much more serious uprisin' followed a few weeks ago, he said, durin' June. Large numbers of out-of-work labourers came into Paris demandin' work – and these provided troops for the Socialists. They set up barricades in the streets, and there was outright civil war. But the new Republican Government put them down pretty savagely – swept them from the streets usin' grapeshot.

– Good. I'm glad to hear it.

He raised his eyebrows, while I took out my pipe and tobacco.

– Comin' from a man of your views, that's a surprisin' remark.

– But you don't really know my views, Doctor.

– It seems not. Would you care to expound?

– I believe that France is the world's best hope, in the new era we're entering. She is truly the capital of freedom and the new order – and I believe it's every man's right, however humble, to be free. So I rejoice that every man in France may now legally vote to decide who will govern him. This is truly the will of the people, matched only in the United States – and nowhere else in Europe. But I put it to you that Socialism threatens this ideal – and that in fact, Socialism and feudalism are brothers under the skin.

Howard was watching me closely, his eyebrows still high.

– That's a novel notion – almost a paradox, isn't it? The Socialists would maintain the very opposite.

– I'm sure they would – but they'd be wrong. You've made the point yourself that the Socialists have sought to over-ride the expressed will of the majority: the outcome of a vote based on universal manhood suffrage. Such revolutionaries and Utopians are no better than the feudal aristocracy they seek to replace. Theirs would be the will of a minority imposed from above, all over again: this time, a minority of intellectuals. They would claim that they spoke for the masses; but the people would be their puppets. And they would seek to seize power by force, just as the feudal barons did. But unlike the old aristocracy, they would be free of the hereditary responsibilities that the warrior caste accepted as the price of rule. We saw it in the French Revolution, which the Jacobins debauched so hideously. This caste would not rule by valour and the sword, but by secretly managed insurrection; the dagger in the back; the sinister committee – a consolidation of tyrannical and petty power. The rule of envious plunderers, in other words. So you see, Doctor, I can only applaud the action of the current French Assembly. True democrats, true liberals, should never make common cause with power-seeking Utopians of any colour – red or otherwise. There must be no return of the Jacobins.

I paused to light my pipe, and then took another sip of the excellent claret, which had loosened my tongue more than I intended. Howard was sitting with his near-empty glass suspended in his fingers, studying me as though trying to learn something beyond what my words intended.

– Interestin', he said. I take your main point, and can only agree with it. But it still surprises me, comin' from a leader of Young Ireland. It was the property-ownin' middle class who rejected the radicals in France – and you sound like a member of that class, Devereux, defendin' his interests. You do seem to be a man of contradictions: privileged land-owner; defender of the Parliamentary system; bloodthirsty revolutionary.

– I'm hardly in a position of privilege any more, I said. A few years ago, just before the Famine, my father was forced to sell 'Deer-park', our estate at Sixmilebridge in Clare. It was a very sad day for him, and for all of us – it had been the family home for some two hundred years. My father had inherited debts, and much of our land had been repeatedly remortgaged; but like so many of his friends, he wouldn't take such problems seriously, or change his way of life. He continued to entertain lavishly, and to purchase fine hunters and so on. He's a charming man, but not very practical; in the end, most of our farms had to be sold. Now he and my mother and sister live modestly in a house he bought in Dublin. And I merely rent a house in that city – I own no property at all.

– I see. You're not destitute, I hope?

– No. My father's a generous man, and divided a good deal of what money was left from the estate between my brother and sister and myself. Some of it helped me to launch the *New Nation*; and my brother John, who is a doctor, used his inheritance to set up a practice. But we are scarcely rich, any of us.

– Nevertheless, yours is an old Anglo–Norman family, with a history of land ownership – that's the point I'm makin'.

– It's true that we're descended from that monstrous Earl of Essex who carried out such slaughter in Ulster for Queen Elizabeth. I take no satisfaction in my descent from bloody Walter Devereux, I assure you – nor do I admire the second earl, my namesake, whom Elizabeth beheaded. I'm a good deal more proud of those ancestors of mine who truly became Irish, and who went down at the Boyne against your armies, fighting beside the Gaelic gentry. We were good Norman Catholics then, although it's true we're Protestant now. And we Old English are no longer yours, you know. More-over, it's my conviction that the day of the aristocracy is finally drawing to a close. So if you accuse me of being middle class, Doctor, I'll proudly wear that label.

– You're rejectin' your ancestry – is that what you're sayin'?

– Of course not: I can't do that, nor would I wish to. But I recognise that my family belongs to an age that's dying. It's the merchant class who are now nurturing most things that are civilized.

From the dung heap of commerce, all flowers grow. All else is tyranny, in one form or another. The middle class home is truly a castle, giving its children the protection and leisure for music and poetry, philosophy and dreams. I'd be proud to be labelled middle class, which means: neither a feudal sheep nor a Utopian sheep. So here's to the middle class!

I raised my glass, and Howard did the same, still watching me closely. Then he said softly:

– I really cannot fathom you. You are imprisoned in this hulk for urgin' violent revolution. You have urged your country's peasantry to take up arms against the Crown. You have preached sedition. So despite all that you say to me, Devereux, I still have to ask: how do you reconcile your distaste for the revolutionaries in France with wishin' to use the same methods as theirs?

He remained as bland as ever, and I continued to find him agreeable. But he'd shown me his steel, and I sobered and sat up straight, putting aside my pipe.

– Let me be plain, Doctor. I recognise no such label as 'sedition' where rule is immoral or illegal. The people of my country are a conquered people, living under the dominance of a ruthless foreign power. We have no universal suffrage, as the French have. And you know about the Ejectment Acts, I'm sure. You know what the Famine has done to our people: you know that Irish peasants have been uprooted from their farms and flung upon the roads by your absentee landlords.

– I know, he said. Yes.

He had suddenly become uncharacteristically subdued, and his eyes avoided mine, behind their glasses. But I went on.

– Last winter was the hardest ever known in Ireland – yet the peasants whose potato crops had failed, and who could no longer pay their rents, were turned out of their cabins to freeze and starve to death. How do you justify that? Their houses were torn down in front of them by your soldiers – and even some of the soldiers were ashamed of what they did. If I had been armed, I believe I might have gone out to try and defend them; but I was not armed.

– I understand your feelin's, he said.

– Do you, Doctor? But you have not seen what I have seen – what all of us have seen in Ireland. We may try to turn away, we who are well enough provided for, but we are followed in the streets of the towns by walking skeletons, whose children are crying with hunger. I have seen peasants wandering the freezing roads, men and women, with nothing to cover their nakedness but sacks, carrying the naked corpses of their children. Whole families have walled themselves into their cabins to hide their shame and misery, and to die there. Two years ago I went back to Clare, and visited the lands we had lost. I found a scene of desolation. I went onto a farm we once owned at Sixmilebridge, to look for the tenants there: a family I used to visit as a boy. They were good people: people I was deeply fond of, who used to invite me in for a meal of potatoes and milk. I went there with gifts of food; but too late. Grass grew in front of the door, and when I looked inside, I found five corpses, gnawed by rats.

Doctor Howard wrinkled up his nose and stared at me directly, saying nothing.

– And all this time, I said, our people watch food taken out of Ireland under military escort, bound for England. Ship after ship goes down the Shannon, laden with enough grain and butter and eggs to feed every one them. And this Jack Russell calls free trade – and refuses to allow food to be sold below the market price. I will never forget or forgive these things. I will die myself, if need be, to oppose what has caused them.

My breath was coming a little fast, now, and I broke off. Howard was frowning. He set his glass down and finally spoke, his voice subdued yet measured.

– I don't wish to justify nor defend what you speak of, he said. Except to say that I know the British Government has worked constantly to distribute grain and to provide relief. I don't admire the ruthless landlords you speak of – but not all are bad, and I do know that some, like the Earl of Kingston, have given half their rents to relieve the distress. But none of this has been enough, and I understand and respect your anger. We have much to be concerned about, in Ireland.

– I'm glad to hear you say that, and I'll not distress you further with my anger, I said. But you see, Doctor, this is what has made me a patriot. The Famine decided me. I wish to see my country gain its freedom; and I have had to realise that England will never grant this peacefully. I'm no passionate Republican – but I see that it's the tool that will bring us liberty: the sort of liberty France has.

– You certainly do admire the Froggies, he said. He stretched his legs out further to ease them, and smiled at me quizzically again.

I had been carried away by my rhetoric, and because of his soothing courtesy, I had half imagined that Howard might have been responding to it. But now, with a little jolt, I saw that I was dealing with a thoroughgoing Englishman: self-contained, good-humouredly immovable, and anti-French.

– My admiration is not uncritical, I said. As I've told you, I have no time for the excesses of such men as Robespierre and Saint-Just. What I admire in the French is that despite those old catastrophes, they have once again set about completing the great work of sixty years ago. France is leading the way into the future; she is prepared to end feudalism once and for all, even if it means facing all the swords in Europe to do it: even if it means flames and blood. That is what I admire.

– I begin to see, Howard said. And if it does come to flames and blood, and if we have war throughout Europe again, with England drawn in, Ireland may gain some sort of independence as a consequence. Is that what you're hopin'? Is it hatred of England that's at the heart of your theories?

It was time to draw back. I wondered how much of this conversation would later be recorded, and passed on to some higher authority – even to London. I told Howard now that I had no hatred for the English people; only for their rule in Ireland.

– I'm glad to hear that, he said. I'd be sad to find you hated *me*. You're an interestin' fellow, Devereux, and I enjoy talkin' to you – although I do hope we never see your flames and blood. Much of what you say no generous man could disagree with; there are many young men in England who think as you do – and a few older ones. But what interests me is the contradiction in these things. For instance, there's a paradox at the heart of this new revolution in

France, as I think we both see. It's ended in a victory for conservatives and moderates who are determined to defend order and property – and who have the sanction of the people to do so. It seems the ordinary people have no use for flames and blood, in the end – and the French peasant hates such excesses most of all, since he fears for his land. Once the peasant had the vote, it ensured the defeat of the radicals. They really should have foreseen that.

He stood up, smiling, apparently preparing to go. But then he paused, and drew out a leather tobacco pouch and a handsome briar pipe, which he proceeded to fill. I stood also, watching him light a twist of paper at one of the candles, which he then held over his pipe.

– Are you a Tory by conviction, Doctor?

Puffing, he glanced at me quickly over the flame.

– I sail under neutral colours, Devereux. I merely note the facts. But I'm inclined to think that your flames and blood are never worth their price, and that the best reforms come without 'em, when their time's ripe. That's an English way of thinkin', which you'll view with impatience. And yet it seems you've no time for mob rule either. A problem, isn't it, the mob? All civilized men fear it. Rome was undone by it; and now we face the same problem.

– The same? How so?

He released a single puff of smoke, squinting at me.

– As I see it – and I'm merely a surgeon, not a political leader – there's a philosophical problem at the bottom of all this that ancient Greece and Rome didn't solve, and neither have we. Namely: how far do we take these rights to representation, education and equality for the broad mass of the people? If we take 'em as far as they'll go, we'll presumably end without any sort of ruling class, and men will no longer see public service as a duty, but as an outlet for the lowest ambitions. The most crudely aggressive and vulgar will come to the top: not only in government, but in the arts, education – everythin'. We may well be governed and diverted by self-seekin' rogues and fools. By the mob, in other words. And that can result in less freedom in the things that matter – not more. So freedom doesn't necessarily beget freedom. There's no worse tyranny than the tyranny of the stupid, the half-educated and the crass. The Greeks knew that.

He smiled again, took his pipe from his mouth and turned towards the door.

– But we'll perhaps debate this next time – it's growin' late. I'll see if I can provide a Chambertin for our next session. French wine inspires me, even if French thinkin' doesn't.

When he'd gone, I sat nursing a glow whose source was not only the wine.

The pleasure of good discussion is like no other. It has a sort of bloodless beauty; and at its best, it has no hidden consequences or false motives. It's not a cloak for something else. Consequently, if it's conducted without egotism or the desire to dominate one's opponent, it's the calmest, cleanest and most reassuring of pleasures. Unlike the towering and stormy pleasure of love, it has no subterranean roots; no strange flowers are latent within it, to bloom and disturb us when they are least expected. Strangely, despite my rational suspicion that Doctor Howard's hidden aim was to report on me, my discourse with him had seemed to be of this kind. It had even caused my worry about Catherine to dwindle and seem less crucial: to take on its true position in the scheme of things.

I have written long into the night. Soon the chief mate will come in and find me still up, and click his tongue in disapproval.

I have a strong feeling now that new events are about to take place, and that my situation will change.

July 24th
Late morning.

A few minutes ago, as I sat here vacantly at my table, the sound of a woman singing floated through the open porthole. Many sounds come through this porthole by day: the mewing of gulls, shouts of soldiers on the breakwater, confused, alien cries from the many small craft that scud about among the world's great ships. And I have come to half ignore them, as one half ignores most sounds. But the singing that came to me now, from somewhere quite close, plucked at my attention.

The woman had a clear, contralto voice which I might have

thought beautiful, had it not been so outlandish and wild. The singing was like nothing I'd ever heard, and in no language that I recognised. The melody was attractive, in a mode that was almost familiar; but then the voice would take a note and soar away with it into reaches quite strange to the European ear. The note would be whiningly distorted, and the voice would waver like a bird with a broken wing, setting one's teeth on edge. But just when one thought it had lost itself in grotesque and wailing discord, it would recover and return to the melody: a melody which charmed the senses with its plaintive and raffish beauty.

Curious to see the singer, I stepped to the window and looked out through its iron grating.

Almost immediately below me, in the space of green, lolling water between the hulk and the stone dock, was the rocking, rickety vegetable boat I'd seen on the day of my arrival, with its two long-bodied black men, and its brown mulatto woman in her orange dress. It was she who was singing – seated in the stern as before, her clothes exactly as before also, her long hands clasped about one upraised knee, her head thrown back in its spotted, blue and white turban. She sang, her eyes closed, oblivious to everything about her; and while she did so, the two lanky Negroes in their palmetto hats were holding aloft baskets of oranges and bananas, grinning enticingly to someone invisible to me on the main deck above them. They took no notice of the woman's singing; she apparently sang to please herself.

Moments later, on a final soaring and wavering note, she stopped. Turning her head, no doubt in response to some sixth sense, she looked up and saw me at the window, and I met her dark gaze. She stared, straight-backed, high-bosomed and proud as royalty; and so imperious was her expression that I almost shrank back. But then she smiled, with a mysterious familiarity, showing me her shining white teeth.

I came away from the window, and sat down again at my table, my heart beating somewhat faster. Here was a new trial, I said. Caged in my dog-box a thousand miles from Catherine, I was becoming a prey to empty, bizarre temptations: temptations like dreams, arbitrary and unwanted, which would present me with neither the danger nor the hope of fulfilment. The mulatto woman's smile must be put out of my mind, for my mind's peace.

A light thump made me start.

Someone had thrown a package through the half-open door, and I heard retreating footsteps outside. I peered out, but the corridor was empty. I picked up the package, which was wrapped in brown paper, and tore it open.

Inside were newspapers from London: the forbidden batch from the latest mail steamer. My train-robber had been as good as his word: and he'd amassed this treasure in only two days. No ordinary felon, this.

Linkage with the world! I'm inhaling the newsprint odour like incense. My door is closed, lest anyone passing should see me with my booty; my fingers tremble. That mere newspapers should mean so much!

Here is the June news, and the *Morning Post* devotes much space to Ireland. My comrades have shown great courage; but even as I write, they're no doubt in the process of being charged with felonies. A copy of the *Post* nearly three weeks old publishes a prospectus of the *Irish Felon*: a new weekly newspaper put out by Paul Barry and Thomas O'Neill in response to our other papers being closed. The two of them announce that the paper has been established to preach the doctrine of 'the convict Devereux', and 'to promote the sacred principle of Irish felonry'. Good, by God, good!

Dear Barry: poet and singer of our cause, with your sand-coloured hair and your narrow, joker's face: half youthful, half ageless! To you, even this act of suicidal defiance is no doubt like some huge prank, or is one of your songs become actual. I'm filled with a glee like drunkenness; and you seem to be grinning just behind my chair. What you and O'Neill have done will drive the Castle and London to fury – and must surely compel the waverers in our cause to become felons like me. If they don't, they must whimper to John Bull that they meant no revolution at all, and show themselves as the lickspittles they are.

I've been reading for an hour, my pulses racing. Occasionally I break the silence of my still, close, wood-odorous box with an involuntary exclamation.

No wonder that my captors wanted to keep all this from me. Across the Continent, the months of May and June have seen the great tide of rebellion reach its height. The 'June days' in France of which Doctor Howard told me are dealt with here in detail; and in item after item, the collapse of the old Vienna system is documented. In Germany, the Frankfurt national Parliament, elected by the people, has declared itself sovereign and above princes, and is working admirably; in Hungary, led by the hero Louis Kossuth, the Magyars now have a constitution of their own that seems secure, a free press and freedom of religion; in Vienna, the revolutionary students and free citizens continue to establish popular rule, with the exiled Habsburgs at Innsbruck giving way inch by inch to the calls for liberal reform.

Whispering feverishly to myself, the newspapers pushed aside, the white light of noon glaring through the window, I sit thinking. In a moment I'll hide these papers in my trunk, lest the mate come in and discover them, an inquisition begin, and suspicion turn on Langford. I rather suspect that Langford's accomplice in getting me these precious journals was Doctor Howard: but why would Howard do this? And why does he wish to keep me abreast of these events, when the Governor and Captain Thorpe so urgently wish to keep me in the dark?

Is Howard friend or foe? Ally, or spy – or double spy? What are his purposes? Life grows interesting.

4. A CANDLE IN THE DARK

August 20th

Nearly a month has gone by, and I've neglected this journal.

Why scribble here? Why pretend that I record some sort of voyage – some sort of motion forward – when I'm trapped in a ship that doesn't move? These scribblings will probably never be read; but if they are, they may cause me trouble. At any time, I presume, my journal could be seized by the first mate and delivered to the superintendent of convicts; I have to remind myself of that, since I'm theirs to do with as they wish, and I've resolved to weight the book down and pitch it overboard, should I ever have warning of such a move.

But why write here at all?

For the reason that my journal's thread is the thread on which my sanity hangs. It makes me believe that although so little happens to me, my life still has shape, like a free man's; that I still have a personal identity. If I'm not careful, I suspect, that identity may slip away. So I'm fond of this journal of mine: unreasonably fond. Taking it up, I sniff its calfskin cover and its pages with a melancholy, animal pleasure.

Well, then; what's to report?

Doctor Howard continues to visit me regularly; and I continue to enjoy our talks, which are the highlight of my motionless life. But he still hasn't shown his hand. Whether he's to be regarded as a secret friend, or a spy set to record my every opinion, and perhaps to encourage me to inform on my comrades, I still can't tell. Obviously, if I were a cunning fellow, I'd assume the second possibility to be true, and act accordingly at all times. But I've never been very cunning, I'm afraid. Playing double games isn't my style, and if a man shows me friendliness, I find this very hard to reject or to treat cynically – even though he comes from the heart of the enemy camp. I won't fawn on him, or give any quarter in areas where we disagree; but I'll deal with him openly, since I know no other way to deal. So without telling Doctor Howard anything I don't want his masters to know, I receive him as the friend he wishes to be.

His personality makes this easy to do: he's bland, but he manages at the same time to appear frank, forthright, and free of guile. This, of course, is true worldliness, since I'm sure he's actually full of guile. He's a man of many parts, well read in the classics, and with a considerable knowledge of history. He's also an amateur painter of surprising ability: in his spare hours, in his little cottage on the island, he produces water-colours and pencil sketches of the Bermudan landscape, of the natives, and even of the convicts at their toil. He often brings his sketch-books to show me, and I'm greatly impressed: they are vivid and lively glimpses of the hidden world beyond the docks, and I enjoy poring over them. As well, he does portraits in oils; he's completed one of Commander Moffatt which he brought and showed me. It's excellent: he sees beneath the outer man, as he no doubt does in his medical diagnoses. He captures not only Moffatt's empty handsomeness, but also his placid, kindly dullness – yet in so subtle a way that the subject himself must surely be unaware of it. And in fact, the Commander likes it so well that Howard has made him a present of it.

An intelligent man, then, despite his conservative and even reactionary cast of mind, with an intellectual range quite surprising in a naval surgeon (if that is all he is), and one with whom I delight to debate. He, and he alone, now acts as a substitute for all my lost friends and comrades; for my lost social life. He's a widower, with one grown-up daughter in England, now married. I've yet to learn much detail about his personal background, except that he comes from a little village in Yorkshire called Brotherton, and that his father was Vicar there. His father wasn't rich, he says, and there were three other brothers and a sister to provide for; but Howard was sent to St Peter's, a good school in York, and then to Edinburgh Medical School. He had a medical practice in York for many years; but when his wife died, he wanted change, and entered the Royal Navy as a surgeon. He says nothing about his wife, which makes me suspect that either he loved her greatly, or not at all. He's made voyages to China and Australia, and says he likes the life of travel. The time he spent in Dublin society was brief, and took place some years ago, before the potato famine; but he's met some of the less politically-inclined men and women of substance there who are among my acquaintances. He even remembers meeting Thomas O'Neill on one occasion. So we're able to enjoy light gossip, as well as debate; and gossip is something in which the Doctor plainly delights.

I look forward to his visits – and to occasional encounters with him on deck – more than is good for me. I must not become dependent on his company.

August 22nd
Yesterday the August mail steamer arrived, with more letters from home – including one from Catherine, mercifully more understanding and hopeful than her last.

The energetic James Langford has also brought me the newspapers, delivering them at nightfall in his usual invisible manner. They contain some extraordinary news concerning my comrades.

A rising, I find, has already been attempted, and has failed.

It took place in the last days of July. Paul Barry seems to have roused the people in Waterford superbly – but the main revolt was in Tipperary, and was led by Martin Fitzgibbon, with Barry playing a supporting role. A revolution led by Fitzgibbon, the man of peace, the opponent of all violence! The attempt was doomed at the start; and a poor wretched thing it was, by all accounts. Shots were exchanged with the police on the property of a widow named MacManus, near a village called Ballingarry; but the attempt was quickly put down, without much loss of life. The British press are enjoying themselves hugely with this, terming it 'the Battle in Widow MacManus's Cabbage Patch' – and they make great mock of Fitzgibbon, portraying him as a vainglorious coward, crawling among the cabbages. *The Times* calls him 'the King of Tipperary', and declares him of unsound mind.

I am gnawing my knuckles so that the blood has come. I am cursing these lying journalist jackals with every foul oath I can summon. Fitzgibbon is an upright man, for all his distaste for the warrior virtues: he would never have played the coward, and nothing would have shaken his calm and logical mind. But it should never have been Fitzgibbon who led this attempt: it should not have been tried now, and it should never have been him! Oh Christ, why wasn't I there?

Fitzgibbon and Barry and others went briefly into hiding, I learn, but were captured in the early days of this month. Now they lie in Kilmainham Gaol in Dublin, awaiting trial on charges of high treason. Thomas O'Neill is also imprisoned there, awaiting trial on the same charge: in his case for publishing a seditious article in the *Irish Felon*. No doubt their juries will be packed, and no doubt they will end by being transported as I have been. Shall we be reunited, here or at Botany Bay? Dear Lord, I hope so.

There's another revelation in these papers. They have acquainted me with a scandal of which I'm the unwitting centre; and at the same time have cleared up a sad little mystery.

Five days ago, the *Nemesis* put in again for the first time since carrying me here. I waited with pleasant anticipation for the promised visit of my friends Lieutenant Campbell and Lieutenant Millington. They didn't come; and yesterday the *Nemesis* sailed again without their having appeared. This depressed me; I thought they'd simply not troubled themselves; but now I've come upon a story in the papers which reveals the real reason.

It seems that the unfortunate Captain Wood was severely censured by the admiral on the station for not treating me like a common convict on the voyage from Ireland. There has been, apparently, much discussion in England of my 'privileged' treatment. Worse: according to *The Times*, questions were asked in Parliament. Ministers were badgered about instructions regarding the usage of 'the convict Devereux'; and Members demanded to know where I dined on the *Nemesis*. Was it true that I actually took victuals and wine with Captain Wood and his officers? British 'public opinion' has been outraged; and the Admiralty was in a fury. Much of the wrath fell upon the unlucky Captain Wood; and there was even a danger for a time of his being dismissed from the service. But a lying excuse seems to have been invented to save him, and presented in Parliament.

Here, in *The Times*, is the Member for County Armagh, embarrassing the Ministers by demanding to know how 'convict Devereux' is faring on Bermuda? Is he kept at work in the rock quarries? And is his hair kept properly cropped in the convict fashion? (Involuntarily, as I read, my hand rises to my somewhat over-long locks.) And what is the real truth about his treatment on the *Nemesis*? In answer to all this, the Lords of the Admiralty have lied shamelessly.

What, in God's name, are their reasons for these fictions? And what are their ultimate intentions concerning me? How much longer will I be penned in this hulk?

August 24th

– You'll find there's a bit of a flutter on the hulks today, sir.

James Langford sets down the breakfast tray, his light, unwinking grey gaze commanding my attention.

– Two prisoners escaped last night. Men from the *Medway*.

His glance seems to give this last fact particular importance.

– Really? Enterprising fellows. Are they still loose?

– They are. Have a look at that signal.

And he jerks his head at the porthole, through which, from where I'm sitting, the telegraph station is visible, on the hill above the dockyard. Flags fly from its mast against fresh blue sky, but I'm unable to read their meaning.

– 'Prisoners escaped'; that's the message, Langford says. Poor silly buggers; they'll be run down, soon enough.

His firm, throaty voice gives the fleeing wretches no chance, and contains no particular emotion.

– How can you know that? I ask. Sometimes convicts get clean away, don't they? There are so many islands here – some so close you could swim between them, I believe. They might find a boat on one of them, and be off.

But Langford is implacable.

– They've already tried that, sir. News travels fast in these hulks, and we all know what's happened.

He clears his throat, one hand on his hip, the other resting easily on the edge of my table, and begins his tale, confident that I'll want to hear it.

– These two coveys was both at the evening school that's run for prisoners in the *Coromandel*, see? It seems they asked leave to go out on the breakwater to take a piss.

I glance up at this coarseness; but he seems not to notice. He's always basically respectful; he always 'sirs' me; and yet in many ways he manages to talk to me as if I were one of his fellows. I imagine that Langford deals with every man he meets in much the same way – with very slight adjustments for those in authority. Timidity isn't in him; and somehow he makes himself seem my equal. I have to keep reminding myself that this man is a train-robber.

– It was raining very hard, he says, so no-one bothered to go with 'em – and then they was off. Jumped in the sea, swam across the entrance of the breakwater, and away into the island. Robbed a store and got biscuits and rum; then they got hold of a boat, and tried to set sail for America. *That's* been done, sir – three smart lads got clear away to Charleston last year, and was never caught. But these two wasn't so clever or so handy.

He smiles with cold amusement.

– They run aground on a sandbank, and left the boat there; it was found this morning. So they're still on the islands: and that means they'll be taken – London to a brick.

I'm deeply interested by this story. If it's possible to reach Charleston, mightn't I try it myself? If no change occurs in my situation, I may well have to attempt it. Strange how intoxicating the thought of escape becomes to a prisoner: even escape by others generates a sort of secondary exhilaration, and I find I want these two fellows to succeed.

– They might have found another boat, I say.

– No, sir. My information is that no other boat's missing. And all boats are watched, now. The traps can comb every last flea from Bermuda, when they want. Which they *do* want, sir, very particular, in this case. Captain Elliott reckons that if these two escape while *you're* here, it sets a bad example – or so I'm told. So he's ordered out the troops.

– Dear God, I say, why must it always come back to *me*?

– Well now, I wouldn't distress yourself, sir. They always gets cross about coves scarpering, you know; especially when it's done by a trusty. And one of these coves was a trusty. They'll flay him alive when they bring him in. He won't have much skin left.

His wide mouth parts in a smile, revealing the gap between his strong front teeth. But I begin to feel sick.

– You seem almost to relish his plight, Langford.

– No, sir, I don't relish it. But my heart don't bleed for him either. The mate he took with him was a boy that he fancied – if you get my meaning, sir. There's some of 'em takes boys as sweethearts, and that's what this chap does. Most of 'em can't get women, so I suppose it's not surprising. Me, I'd rather do without – but then, I'm *not* doing without, so I don't generally judge 'em for it.

He gives me his quick wink, his face entirely expressionless.

– But this particular trusty – he's a *dirty* cove, Langford goes on. And here he's gone and convinced this boy to go with him. Not nice; not nice. And Captain Thorpe ain't going to like it much, *that's* pretty certain. The boy'll probably just get a birching – he's only sixteen or so – but I reckon the superintendent will see that the trusty gets enough of the cat for both of 'em.

He opens the door; then turns and looks at me.

– I think you know this particular cove, he says. He was your servant before me. Lane, his name is.

He favours me with a last, feline smile, and moves out.

My feeling of faint nausea is increased. Lane still revolts me; but the thought of his fate is dreadful. I hope he's not caught.

August 25th

They are caught.

I first had the news from a group of young officers on deck this afternoon. It's taken only twenty-four hours to flush out the miserable Lane and his companion. They were in one of the limestone caves that hollow this island like bubbles. Lane was disguised in women's clothing – which has caused some mirth.

It seems that Captain Thorpe and even the mild Commander Moffatt looked on this escape as setting a very dangerous example, just as Langford said; capture was seen as essential, and there was quiet triumph among my group of officers. They were friendly enough, but kept shooting glances at me. As we spoke, Commander Moffatt and Captain Thorpe appeared on the quarter-deck, and the young men in their dark blue uniforms stiffened a little, and their remarks became self-consciously manly.

Captain Thorpe nodded to me with just sufficient courtesy, and I saw a special glint in his eye: a sort of triumphant warning. His bulky body was encased in its blue naval frock coat as usual, but he was bareheaded, his short, rope-coloured hair fluttering in the light breeze. Everything about him is so rigid, it was almost surprising to me that his hair should be so human as to flutter. A young lieutenant now eagerly addressed him: a narrow-faced fellow whose spurious liveliness was all ambition.

– So the foxes are taken, sir?

Captain Thorpe's jutting chin jutted further still, and his pale Britannic eyes grew narrower, looking into the dancing afternoon light. For a moment he didn't answer, and the quarter-deck was silent. I have to admit that despite his shortness, this pompous creature has presence; his paunchy massiveness makes him dominate any space he stands in. When he spoke, his ponderous, booming voice carried to every part of the sunny, elevated deck.

– Yes – they are taken. The wretched boy will merely be birched, and put into solitary for a time. He was led astray by that God-damned trusty. We put our trust in a wrong one, there.

His empty gaze moved from face to face.

– I've made special arrangements for Lane, he said. We'll set an example with him that the other felons won't forget.

His gaze came to rest on me. A small, uncharacteristic smile lifted the corners of his mouth, and everyone, including the sleepy-lidded Commander Moffatt, turned their eyes on me as well. But I turned away and studied the harbour, where small boats went swift as thoughts across bottle-green vacancies, driven by the delicate south wind.

– Usually, I heard Thorpe say, a delinquent prisoner is flogged aboard his own hulk, as you gentlemen know. But what we shall do with Lane is flog him through all three.

I looked back at him; he was still looking directly at me.

– Forty lashes on the *Coromandel*; thirty on the *Dromedary*; and thirty more here on the *Medway*, he said. A hundred in all. We'll carry it out at first light tomorrow. The gangs will be mustered to watch before going out to their work. I want them to remember it. I don't think there'll be any further escape attempts for a while after that.

– Good, said the narrow-faced lieutenant. Good, sir.

He was smiling with eager pleasure; but he was alone in this.

– Has to be done, Commander Moffatt murmured soothingly. An unusually heavy punishment – but we must set an example.

His expression was regretful; even a little uneasy. The other officers wore looks that were intent, sober and perhaps ambiguous; they said nothing, and I believe they were somewhat shocked. But the superintendent of convicts seemed pleased with the silence he'd created; his set mouth expressed satisfaction.

As for me, my first impulse was to walk off and go below. But I would not give Thorpe that gratification; I remained impassive. Despite my hostility to what he represented, I'd seen the super-intendent until now simply as a British naval man: arrogant, yet correct and proper within his narrow limits. Now I saw that he actually enjoyed his legal sanction to torture. I stared at him, and did not lower my eyes.

His own flickered, and he ceased to smile; I believe he'd read my contempt.

August 26th

It's over.

The gangs, having been treated to the superintendent's carnival of blood, have gone out to their day's work. The troops, who were drawn up on the pier while it took place, have marched off to their barracks. And no doubt by now the floggers have washed the blood-gouts from their arms and faces, and have changed their crimson-spattered clothing.

Lane was flogged here on the *Medway* last, having taken the first two stages of his punishment on the *Coromandel* and the *Dromedary*, as Thorpe promised. I've been spared no details of the three stages of the ordeal, since Langford, who seems to know everything, related them to me at breakfast, after it was over. There was no hint of amusement or gloating in Langford's manner: he gave me the facts in a terse, soldierly way which increased my good opinion of him.

It seems that Lane endured the flogging quite well at first, showing surprising grit. During his forty lashes on the *Coromandel*, he uttered not a sound.

– But his back was cut up bad, Langford said. The old cat was laid on hard.

He was then carried to the *Dromedary* with a blanket thrown over his bloody back, instantly stripped again, and strung up for his next thirty.

– And this was bad news for him, Langford said. The flogger there is a cruel bastard. I know him: he's a quartermaster that *likes* flogging, and he's an expert at crossing the cuts. After he'd laid on a dozen, they say Lane's back looked like a skinned bullock. He started singing out, then – and he passed out. So they stopped for ten minutes while Doctor Howard examined him and brought him to. They say the Doctor didn't look none too happy. But when Lane come around, Captain Thorpe ordered the quartermaster to carry on and finish the thirty. They tell me the super seemed to be enjoying it.

They had wrapped Lane in his blanket again then, more dead than alive, and carried him here to the *Medway* for his final thirty.

– It was bad here, sir, Langford said. I had to watch it, o' course.

And this quartermaster's just about as bad as the other. Some coves who stood closer than I did say they heard Doctor Howard tell him not to lay on too strong – he's got a good heart, has the Doctor – but the God-damned flogger didn't take a blind bit o' notice. Encouraged by Captain Thorpe, I shouldn't wonder. The old super stood there watching like the cat that swallowed the cream. He wanted a real example made of Lane, they say. Well, they did that, all right. He was screaming his bleeding eyes out, in the end.

– I know, I said. I heard.

But I had not merely heard, although I didn't tell Langford this. I had seen.

I wish I hadn't. I most earnestly wish I hadn't.

As usual, at that early hour of the day before breakfast, I was sitting here in my cabin, where I'm required to stay until the gangs go out to work. It was the most golden of Bermudan mornings, with a clear sky, a glittering green sea, and a sort of half-visible, crystalline dancing in the blue and amber air. The flogging was to take place on the main deck, at the companionway leading up to the quarter-deck.

All was quiet, and this was uncanny, since hundreds of invisible men were mustered outside. Some troops were drawn up on the pier, visible to me through the cabin window, and stood absolutely silent, stiff as toys in their red coats, watching the hulk. Everyone was waiting for the final butchering of poor, silly Lane. Men some-times die under a hundred lashes; and this possibility, I felt sure, was in all their minds. Then the weird whistling of the boatswain's pipes rose, and the sound of drums beating the Rogue's March: the signal to begin. This made me cold to the roots of my hair. That I'd found Lane distasteful made no difference to the emotions I now experi-enced; and I was suddenly seized by a desire not merely to hear what was happening, but also to *see*. I really can't justify this. I suppose I was impelled by that terrible curiosity which brings the vulgar to the scene of an accident. But I think I imagined that what I'd witness would prove to be less grim than what my mind was picturing. In this, I could not have been more wrong.

I came out of my cabin on to the half-deck and crept along the passageway, making for the forward part of the hulk. I encountered no-one, and soon came to a door that led onto the open area of the main deck. It was slightly ajar, opening outwards. Here I hesitated, unwilling to show myself on the deck; and in that moment, the drums stopped. A gaping silence followed; a voice barked a command; then the cat made its first report.

He shrieked immediately. It was not like the shriek of a man at all; more like the wail of some sad brute, tried beyond endurance. It was a wail which said that he had given up manhood; and yet it contained anger. Biting my lip, listening to each cry with absolute attention, I suddenly heard words wrung from him: high, half-strangled, raging, and obscene: yet human. I set them down here only because they will never be read.

– *Bastards! Fucking bastards! Don't cut below the mark, bugger you!*

I knew what this meant, from my talk with Langford; the lash was going about his loins – which is against regulations. Flinching at each measured stroke, I lingered alone in the corridor, gnawing my tongue. I wanted to go back, or at least, to stop my ears; but I did neither. The laceration was punctuated by those pitiless pauses that were somehow worse than the strokes – and although I'd not been counting, soon I said that he must surely have had his thirty lashes; must surely have endured all the suffering required of him, and need be flogged no more.

But the quartermaster's nine-tailed cat was deaf to such notions. It paused for its customary interval, and then hissed implacably down again. And as Lane shrieked and cursed, I found that the most horrifying thing of all was the response that his cries were summoning from me. Mingled with pity was something else, which was pity's antithesis. A secret, unworthy part of me began to scorn the poor creature for his cries; and a brutish voice inside me whispered: *Let him be flogged until he faints! Get it over with!* This demonic voice is one that many must admit to having heard, if they are honest with themselves: it accounts for much of the cruelty in the world. And it's not really engendered by heartlessness, or by a lust to see pain: it comes when we are forced to witness suffering which we cannot stop, and cannot bear; it's our last squalid resort when we wish to shut suffering out.

I had to see, I decided. I would not show myself on the main deck; instead, very carefully, I pushed the door out a little further, opening a space of some two inches between the edge of the door and the jamb. I peeped through this; and the scene that flashed upon my vision caused a leap of the heart that made me dizzy.

I didn't look for long, but retreated to my cabin. Once inside my refuge, I bent over the basin-stand, half expecting my stomach to give up its contents. This didn't happen; but I rinsed my mouth out anyway with water from the jug, and stood breathing deeply.

Framed in the crack of the door had been an abattoir for human beings, presided over by civilized men: Captain Thorpe, Commander Moffatt, and my friend Doctor Howard. They were standing not three feet from me, to the right of the door, next to the gangway that led up to the quarter-deck: spruce, erect and grave in their blue uniforms and cocked hats. Rank upon rank of little convicts stood on the main deck, in their sad grey blouses; and the object of their scrutiny was the dark, balding, keg-shaped quartermaster, feet apart, drawing the nine-thonged scourge through his fingers. He did this to free it of blood, which fell in great drops to the deck, and there were spatters of red as well on the shirt that stretched across his paunch. His expression at first had appeared to be a smiling one; but then I'd seen that it was rather a fixed grimace, expressing a satisfaction too profound for levity. His round, opaque, mud-brown eyes were of the sort that never seem to contain any expression; and this, combined with the grimace, made him very repugnant to me. He was wholly concentrated on the corpse-pallid carcass of my former servant.

Lane hung in profile, roped by the wrists and knees to a grating upended beside the gangway, his hair glued to his forehead with sweat. And his face consumed my vision: his face, not the red, streaming meat of his ruined back, at which I only looked once, and could look no more. Laid against one of his naked, up-drawn arms and turned in my direction, this face was no longer that of my cheeky and lascivious Cockney attendant. It frowned; and the frown was that of all men who ever suffered atrocity: half amazed, half protesting, ignominious yet noble, despite the gaping hole of the mouth and the saliva that hung from it in a long, shining thread.

Noble? What nonsense am I writing? How could Lane's frown be *noble*? I only know that it appeared so, and that it was a frown I couldn't bear. Uninvited, the thought flashed upon my mind that Christ must have frowned so on the cross. God forgive me, what blasphemy is this? Christ and Long Lane! But hadn't my attendant entered the same region of pain and ignominy into which our Saviour descended? A region of which men like me know nothing? Yes; his frown told me so. Thus, at any rate, the two thieves must have frowned, on Christ's left and right.

And this, I see now, is the second face of Albion: the face of this tortured criminal. It frowns on the ease of my own position; and I must no longer forget for a moment that I'm in the hands of bloody tyrants: creatures who inflict cruelty with relish, and to monstrous excess, as Thorpe has done – or else who blandly connive in it, as Doctor Howard has done. For even that civilized and refined gentleman must inspect the mangled bodies of Albion's victims, in order to pronounce them fit for more torture – whereupon he goes off to heal the sick, or to debate with me over a good claret.

I accept that criminals must be punished and controlled; I don't quarrel with this. But somehow I also know that Heaven cries out against what I've seen today: a thing which is not punishment at all, but something else, wearing punishment's mask. And knowing it, I find that every nerve in my body shrills at me now to get out: to escape from this coffin-cabin; from this foul catacomb that was once a ship; from this cursed scatter of bleached, mid-ocean islands with their blinding, waterless white rocks.

But any attempt at escape by sea plainly has small chance of succeeding – and I have very little knowledge of handling a boat. I must make my move at a time and in such a way that ensures success. And I can only do this if the tyrants transport me to one of those penal colonies where I have freedom of movement.

But when? When?

November 18th
Asthma! The enemy has returned. I had thought him gone for ever – as I always do, when he stays away for any time. But I see

127

now that I'll never be safe from him: not even should I follow the morning around the whole curve of the globe.

He's been with me for over a month now. I'm weak and listless, and lose interest even in my scribblings in this journal: hence my long silence. Doctor Howard can no more rid me of my demon than any other doctor, despite the doses of Stramonium and the balsam inhalations he prescribes: they soothe, but don't cure. I've grown much thinner, and suffer from sleepless, gasping nights. Howard seems more and more concerned, and ponders over me in a preoccupied manner which betrays his helplessness.

I had thought the change of climate would go far to ridding me of this disease; that in these 'summer isles' I might even be cured. But I find that Bermuda actually has a winter: the nights now are quite cold and dank. Remnants of icebergs float into these waters at this time of year; and the dankness at night is proving more trying than the good, sharp frost of home, even though the temperatures here are higher, and the days remain bright. Bermudan cold is not an honest cold: just a humid, miserable chilliness that eats into the bones and the lungs, and which fills me with a congestion I can't get rid of. There's a damp and bitter north wind, which works its way into the cabin with such force that it often blows the candle out. I keep the gallery window closed, but this will not stop the wind. The ship is old, and her portholes much rounded away at the edges, so that the glass no longer fits properly. And they give me no fire in this kennel, so that when I sit up in my chair in asthma's grip, as I was forced to do all through last night, I'm shivering like a dog.

The end of November: near to the end of this mighty year in which I've played my part, only to be forced from the stage. Its drama is still carried to me here, but is less and less convincing. Its gunfire, its frenzies and its high alarums grow fainter and fainter on my inner ear: sounds carried on a breeze, from somewhere immensely far off. The world's no longer real: it's a place I'm told stories of, as tales are told to an invalid, or a child.

It's nearly six months now since I sailed out of the bay of Cork. For the first time, I begin truly to fear that they mean to leave me on this hulk for the whole of my sentence. Six months out of fourteen years leaves one hundred and sixty-two months yet to serve. What mortal man could keep despair at bay for so long?

I ache for home.

In the dank, sleepless nights of this wretched box, I go back again and again to the place I love most on earth: to a certain empty hilltop on the north-west coast of Clare.

It belongs to childhood: to the the time of our annual holiday at Liscannor Bay. My father would rent a lodge in Lehinch; we rode horses on the strand, and John and Margaret and I bathed every day in the sea. Friends from Dublin would accompany my parents as guests: the ladies found this wild part of Clare very romantic. They would sketch the rocky crags, and expeditions would be made to view the cliffs of Moher, which drop six hundred feet into the sea. The Atlantic waves broke on those rocks with a particular fury: a fury that thrilled me, and which entered into my soul. I never tired of looking over that edge, where the men of the region lowered themselves on ropes to catch puffins, which they sold for their down – swinging without care above the sickening drop, while my mother and her friends gave cries of horror.

One day, when I was eight years old, I tired of the company of my brother and sister, and went walking by myself into the hills behind Liscannor Bay. It was a bright, sunny afternoon. My solitude was an adventure, as it is at that age, and made everything I saw take on a silent meaning: a meaning I believed I'd decipher, if only I roamed far enough. I moved inland, walking east; and soon I found myself on the top of a low hill. There were no human beings to be seen; the only signs of life were wandering cattle, and curlews wheeling overhead. The strange limestone plateau of north-west Clare extended all around me: that treeless country of grasslands and white rock of which Cromwell's soldiers had complained that there was not enough water to drown a man, and no tree to hang him on. But I found a tiny pool, glinting among yellow-green tussocks.

Here I stopped, and sat on a smooth grey stone, and looked about me. *This is the place,* I said, and smiled in a sort of wonder.

I had discovered my *place*: the place which I had always sought, and had seen in another life. Treeless and empty it might be; but I loved its very emptiness, and its tufted, dark green grass and rocks, and its pure, unvisited air. Above all, I loved the scene it commanded. Behind me in the west was the glittering blue bar of the Atlantic; but it was what lay inland in the east that held my gaze.

I was looking into a shallow valley, extending to violet hills. It was a perfectly ordinary valley: one of a type I had often viewed before. And yet it was not ordinary; it was a place of enchantment. I stared at it for perhaps an hour, trying to discover its riddle – which I knew was the riddle of the world. Green, cultivated fields stretched away there, divided by dry-stone walls; I could see men ploughing with horses. Tender blue spires of peat-smoke rose; and scattered here and there were the small stone cabins of the people, with their thatched roofs. I could imagine the smells of seaweed scattered to fertilise the fields, and the smells of smoke and farmyard dung; and I gazed and gazed at the far, slumbering cabins of the peasantry.

Sitting on bread-pale slopes among the gorse, they were infinitely strange to me. It's a strangeness whose savour can scarcely be recaptured, belonging as it does to boyhood. Why did they interest me so much, those crouching little cabins? Why did they have such mystery? All I remember now is that in my fancy, extraordinary lives were lived beneath their roofs: the lives of a wild people of the West. I conjured up reckless, handsome men, and girls of an otherworldly loveliness – the same and yet not the same as the people I saw in Lehinch: the men in their grey frieze coats and sheepskin trousers; the barefoot women in their red petticoats and short jackets. The people I imagined, beneath those thatched roofs in the valley, had a special, elusive strangeness about them: the strangeness of a fairy race. Of the poverty and hardship of the real people down there I knew little, in those days.

Every summer, I went alone to my hill above the bay, and sat on my smooth stone, and looked out to sea, or pondered on the mystery of the fields and the cabins. Like all true mysteries, it remained unsolved; and the hilltop remained my secret. It was the refuge of my childhood, and the solace of my manhood: I would always return there, when I went to Liscannor Bay.

Now, in my waking dreams, I seek it out night after night. I climb that hillslope, as I gasp and cough, and longing for it makes me groan.

I long above all for Catherine, and to hold her in my arms.

Courage. Courage. Something will happen soon.

November 22nd

Worse again. This has been the twelfth night I've sat in this chair without sleep; without even being able to lay my head on the pillow. Twelve nights! When shall I breathe again like a normal man?

The enemy's attacks often come when I'm most cast down – and this is certainly the case now. Yesterday the mail steamer put in, bringing letters that have thrown me into turmoil.

The most distressing is from Catherine. She comes close to reproaching me for the length of time I've been marooned here – and she seems to reproach me as well for not knowing when my incarceration will end. Meanwhile, my father writes that he comes up against a blank wall when he tries to discover from Dublin Castle what plans the authorities have for me. He is merely told that at present there are no plans to let me off this hulk. So I can't begin a normal life in the colony, and hopes for a future with Catherine are frozen and suspended.

Catherine's letters over the past months have grown steadily more despairing, and I can scarcely blame her for this. Her protests until now have been directed against the authorities who've kidnapped me – even though she's so often asked me whether what I've done has been worth it; even though she's suggested that my beliefs and principles have resulted in nothing but disaster. But yesterday's letter actually begins to blame me directly for my situation. No doubt it was written in despair; but I'm forced to face the fact that although she may be loyal to me, she will not necessarily be loyal to what I am.

And worse; much worse. The mail has also brought me information that raises a doubt about her constancy.

Having written this down, I feel almost certain that entertaining such a doubt is unjustified and unworthy: the product of my isolation. But it won't be dismissed; and I have little else to do but think about it, and no means of confronting it.

November 23rd
Let me analyse this matter calmly and rationally.

The information I referred to in yesterday's entry comes in a letter from Matthew Casey: the second letter I've had from him since coming here.

His first, which arrived a couple of months ago, was one I welcomed, and replied to. He too, as he'd promised, had been trying to discover from acquaintances at the Castle what plans existed for my ultimate fate; and he too was fobbed off with vague answers. But I was grateful for his efforts; and his profession of journalist is one that seems likely to help him in gaining this vital information. He told me about the persecution of O'Neill, Barry and Fitzgibbon, and cheered me with predictions that I would not long be held in this hulk, but freed to lead a life on Bermuda. He gave me news as well of Catherine and my parents, having kindly called at their houses a number of times. And he mentioned the fact that Terence Butler was calling on Catherine quite often – apparently to discuss my situation with her, and to offer his sympathy and support.

At the time I thought little of it, since Butler is a member of Young Ireland, and has long been a friend to both Catherine and me. But Casey's latest letter has thrown a different light on Butler's attentiveness.

Last night, in the cold, wretched hours before dawn, wheezing and choking in this chair, I found myself wrestling a suspicion that was a far worse enemy than the asthma. The suspicion grew, and focused itself on Catherine's reproaches, borne to me on the same ship as Casey's letter – until finally, as I sweated and fought for breath, I was convinced that my worst fears were true.

But now, with the placid and elementary light of day coming through the window, rationality has returned, and I must ask myself: how seriously should this infection of suspicion be taken?

I'm inclined to say: not very seriously at all. I've re-examined

Casey's letter: and what does he actually tell me? As before, that Terence Butler continues to call frequently at the house of Catherine's parents, and that he offers her comfort and reassurance. Innocent enough; and I wrote to Butler not long ago expressing my gratitude. But what is disturbing is the last paragraph of Casey's letter, which ran endlessly through my head last night, and which I now transcribe before destroying it.

Please don't misunderstand me, Robert, when I say that despite his undoubted loyalty to you, and his unselfish desire to help, Butler is perhaps a little excessive in his devotion to Catherine. This devotion, I hasten to say, is surely blameless; but he is, I believe, a somewhat lonely bachelor, despite his successful law practice, and Catherine's situation is an unusual and difficult one. Tongues wag easily in Dublin society, as you know, and I think it of the utmost importance that this unhappy separation be ended soon, that Catherine join you at Bermuda, and that you two are united in matrimony . . .

Is Matthew mischief-making? I have to ask myself this question. But thinking of his earnest, amber eyes behind their spectacles, and his frank and good-humoured face, I can't believe this. He may be something of an alarmist; he may exaggerate out of concern for my welfare; but he doesn't lie, of that I feel pretty sure. And there's nothing in what he says to tell me that Catherine is anything but faithful to me.

No, Catherine is not faithless – but Butler is possibly treacherous towards me. This is the conclusion I've come to and must live with, in this dog-box. And Casey is therefore right: Catherine and I must be reunited, and soon.

I clench and unclench my fists. I stare helplessly out at the break-water: at the free, gliding gulls, and the stiff, pacing Marine who is set there to prevent my escape.

November 24th
Bad again, last night.

At midnight, just after old Mr Wall had made his second visit to see me locked in, I sat with my head in my hands, with Casey's accursed letter once again repeating itself in my brain. I was wheezing, but not so badly, and I decided I might actually find sleep in the cot tonight, and blessed oblivion.

I undressed, crawled in, and closed my eyes.

A little earlier, I'd been re-reading *The Rime of the Ancient Mariner*, in the volume of Samuel Taylor Coleridge's poems given me by Lieutenant Campbell; now I summoned up whole stanzas in my head, to bring me calm. I'm more and more impressed with this strange and wonderful poem, which has a particular power to bring me pleasure and solace at present – possibly because of my quasi-marine existence – and I have committed much of it to memory. Mr Coleridge's life seems to have been marred by a certain instability in his nature, and a tendency to indolence. There are those who despise him, and say that there is really very little in his poetry – poetry which they see merely as fragments of dreams, with no more meaning than dreams have. As to that, I have always found much meaning in dreams: significances far deeper than those easy meanings to which we have access by day. But they are not significances which can easily be summarised in rational propositions. So it is with *The Ancient Mariner* – which now gave me comfort as I lay coughing, dragging dank air into my chest, and imploring sleep like a lover.

> *O sleep! it is a gentle thing,*
> *Beloved from pole to pole!*
> *To Mary Queen the praise be given!*
> *She sent the gentle sleep from Heaven,*
> *That slid into my soul.*

I slept.

But perhaps an hour later, my demon woke me: and never before had he attacked so fiercely. Only once before in my life, half-strangled in his grip, had I feared the terrible end which hangs above all asthmatics: death by suffocation; death for lack of air. This time, in my absolute isolation, locked in my pine coffin, my fear was far greater than on the previous occasion, when I'd been in my own bed in Dublin. Here, in the pitch dark, coughing deep in my chest with the squalid profundity of the worst attacks, I had the absolute conviction that my end had come. I tried to call out for the mate, who I hoped might still be awake, lurking about on watch; but I had not sufficient breath.

What had woken me had been the sensation of drowning. I was sinking into a place where to draw breath at all was impossible, and death towered above me like a cliff; I had the sensation of falling upwards. I sat up blindly in the cot, my breath whistling and rattling in my chest with a peculiar loudness that did not seem to come from my own body. Then, for many terrifying moments, I could not breathe at all.

I fought, clutching my chest, gaining such small amounts of air that hope seemed lost, and even my terror became confused. A line of Coleridge's poem was all that rang clear in my head: *To Mary Queen the praise be given . . . To Mary Queen the praise be given . . .* It was a sort of prayer. Then Catherine's name rang in my head too, and her face appeared above me: her calm hazel eyes; her clear white brow. As my senses began to swim, and nothingness, like a grey jelly, began to set around me, Catherine's face became the face of the Holy Mother as I had seen her in the pictures and statuary in Catholic churches. Then the two faces became one, and I believe I prayed to Catherine to save me. She was all love, all sweetness, all safety. But then I remembered her letter, and the grey jelly thickened.

I continued to fight grimly for breath: without hope now; without there being a shore to strike out for. But still I fought.

The difficulty with asthma is not to get air in, so much as to get it out – to empty the lungs so that one can take another breath. Little by little, I found that I was managing to do this again. I was forcing out pitifully small amounts, as I coughed, but it was being done. In a few more moments, I'd summoned enough strength to crawl out of the cot.

It's of vital importance to be upright; and this I now achieved. I sat in my chair, wheezing like a broken engine, chest heaving and aching, so weak I could barely raise a hand. But I did raise it, and searched for matches on the table. The bitter north wind was roaring outside again, and whistling through the edges of the casement. It was cold, and almost totally dark, there being no moon; a dim and distant light came from one of the lamps on the pier. I lit the candle, which flickered wildly in the gusts through the casement; but it stayed alight, and now I could see familiar things: the volume of Coleridge I had left on the table; my writing-slope with a pen beside it; that knot in one of the boards by the door which somehow helps me to meditate. Should I call for help? There seemed little point, now. Doctor Howard doesn't sleep on board, but sensibly repairs to his little cottage on the island, usually accompanied by the fortunate James Langford; and no-one else here could help me. I continued to cough, trying to bring up the mucus that filled my lungs. If I succeeded, the attack would end. Pulling my old greatcoat on, I prepared to face the rest of the night in the chair, my fingers rigid with cold, my feet numb as stone.

A small looking-glass stands on the table, and between bouts of coughing, I caught sight of my face in it. The wretchedness of this sweating visage, lit like a mask by the candle, was such that I could scarcely believe it mine. My loss of weight has made me hollow-cheeked; and my eyes, in deep sockets, stared out like those of a hunted hare. And indeed, I am hunted, since my enemy hounds me every night, riding in the hours of darkness, defeated only by the morning.

Thus Mr Wall found me when the red and gold of dawn was seeping through the window. The distant voices of healthy, free human beings rose from the breakwater, and from the small craft on the harbour. The cabin had grown a little warmer, and I had brought up enough mucus now to breathe more or less normally; but the effort had exhausted me. I must have looked unusually ill, because the old mate frowned in stern alarm.

– You've had another attack, sir?

I said I had, but was now better; all I needed was hot water for an inhalation. That said, I found myself too weak to speak further, but simply sat staring at him.

Mr Wall's concern generally has a sour and sceptical quality in it, and I think until now he has suspected me of manufacturing asthma for my own purposes. This time he apparently changed his mind; he hurried out with an anxious air, and reappeared shortly with a jug of hot water – a task usually carried out by Langford. The mate hovered over me, still frowning, as I poured Doctor Howard's balsam into it; then he passed me a towel to put over my head. Veiled, inhaling the fumes, I heard him mutter:

– I'll send Doctor Howard as soon as he's aboard. Langford'll bring you some broth.

Then his heavy boots retreated.

When Langford arrived, he was lively as always; and the sight of his robust figure cheered me. It also made me wryly aware of the contrast of my own state with his. He stood at attention with the tray, grinning down at me as though my condition were something of a joke, like the penalty of a night's carousing.

– Well, sir, *you're* a sorry sight, he said. But that's the trouble with gentlemen like you; the constitution gets over-delicate. I've seen the same thing with high-bred dogs.

I was too weak to rebuke him for this, even had I wanted to; instead, I smiled feebly back. I begin to feel a curious sympathy with this bandit: which is absurd, of course. But there's a sort of paradoxical decency about him, and a vigour I can't help admiring.

He dragged the other chair in the cabin next to mine and sat down, still holding the tray. Then, to my startlement and confusion, he dipped the spoon into the broth and held it matter-of-factly to my mouth.

– Here, he said. This'll put the roses back in your cheeks, sir. You look bloody awful, if you don't mind me saying so.

I struggled to a more upright position and held up my hand in protest.

– No, I said. Thank you, Langford, but there's really no need. I can feed myself.

But even raising my hand had cost me an effort. Meanwhile, the blank tiger eyes with their rigid-looking top lids remained steady on my face; the spoon remained steadily poised, and Langford's expression became faintly threatening. It was not a serious threat – with Langford, there's always a hint of humour – but it nevertheless produced in me an irrational reluctance to defy him: no doubt a product of my debility.

– Come, sir, he said. Just drink it. You're as weak as a cat, anyone can see that. No point in spilling it down your front, is there?

He elevated the spoon, and I allowed him, with a certain sense of humiliation, to push it into my mouth. He did it deftly and neatly, as he did everything; and when he repeated the action, the situation began to seem matter-of-fact. It was an excellent chicken broth, and by the third mouthful, I felt a hint of returning strength.

– Had a pal in the Marines who lost both arms, Langford said. I had to feed him like this. Poor bastard, he only lasted a few days. Gangrene. Just as well, I expect.

– You were in the Royal Marines, Langford?

– That's right, sir.

His face became expressionless, and he dipped carefully into the broth.

– Enlisted as a drummer boy at fourteen, he said. Silly young bugger that I was.

– You might have had an honourable career, I said. What turned you to crime?

Again his eyes seemed to hint at warning; the spoon remained poised in mid-air, and for a moment he didn't answer. Too late I recalled that such a question had caused me trouble with Lane; but in the present odd circumstances, being spoon-fed as though I were a child, it had somehow seemed natural. Finally, Langford said:

– I did have an honourable career, sir, as a matter of fact. I was wounded in the knee at the Battle of Navarino, when we blew the Turks out of the water. I was a sergeant then, at twenty-two; and I was honourably discharged because of this gammy leg of mine.

He slapped the right knee; his slight limp was now explained.

– But you try living on honour, he said, at twenty-two.

He fed me the spoonful. Was his expression bitter? I couldn't tell; but his tone closed the subject.

– Come, you're looking better, he said. Got to keep your strength up, haven't you, if you want to get out of here?

I looked at him quickly. Was he talking about escape? But he didn't pursue the topic. Instead, his eyes went past my shoulder to rest on the portrait of Catherine, on top of the bookshelves. Like Lane, he'd once asked me about her, and had expressed his respectful admiration. I wondered if he was now going to offer further comment, and prepared wearily to discourage it; I could not bear to discuss Catherine today. But he didn't do so; instead he said softly:

– It's no life for you, sir, stuck in this hulk alone, and not even getting ashore. You're being treated worse than us lags, in a way. At least we do get ashore, and see a bit of life. Aren't they even going to let you set up house on these islands?

– It doesn't seem so, Langford. Who knows, I may end up like the Man in the Iron Mask: confined alone for the whole of my sentence.

I began to cough again, and he watched me, spoon poised. When I recovered, he fed me a final mouthful, and set the bowl aside. Then he said quietly:

– *That's* not to be put up with, sir, surely. You'd have to do a flit.

– Yes, Langford, I believe I would. But it doesn't seem easy to do here – as our friend Lane has demonstrated.

– Anything's possible, sir, if you put your mind to it. And there's not much that can't be got, if you know how to go about it. Even here.

He waited, like a big, attentive cat, as though expecting me to put in some request; but I remained silent, lying back in my chair. Finally, dropping his voice to a throaty murmur, he said:

– For a young man like yourself, sir, it must be devilish hard without a woman. Do you mind if I speak plain?

– I dare say you will anyway, Langford.

I half-guessed the nature of what was coming, and my impulse was to stop it; but I didn't want to lose his good will – if only because of his faithful delivery of the newspapers. And God help me, if I tell the truth, I'm beginning to actually value his company and his ministrations, even though I know it would be foolish to trust him. He sat forward with an air of enthusiasm: no longer the servant, but the confidant.

– You'll have seen from the breakwater, sir, what fine young women there are among the natives here. And they're friendly – very friendly. A few small gifts and they'll do anything for you.

He chuckled, watching me.

– That's maybe what you need, sir, to cheer you up. A fine brown girl. Would you like me to arrange a visit from one?

All this in the same cheerful manner as he wore when serving breakfast. Staring back, I found myself thinking involuntarily of the woman on the vegetable boat; and it seemed to me that he must know it. This, and shame at my blind impulse to an act of infidelity – if only in the imagination – made me more brusque than I might have been.

– Certainly not, Langford.

His face went dead. To mollify him, I adopted a jocular tone.

– Anyway, man, you surely can't be serious. You speak of the penalties of smuggling in newspapers – so what would be the penalty of smuggling a woman on board?

He raised his eyebrows.

– Drastic, sir – drastic. But I've got arrangements so that I *don't* get caught. I've got friends, and I've got ways. You'd be safe as houses.

The outrageousness of this caused me to laugh, and he grinned back happily.

– Well then, sir, will you change your mind? Shall I arrange it?

This time I softened my tone.

– Of course not, Langford. I appreciate your kindness, but it's misplaced. I'm engaged, as you know.

– And I've got a wife I'm very fond of, he said, who's been my right hand. But she's in old England, and I've been out here over four years, with ten more to go – and she understands that I'm a man of flesh and blood.

– That's as may be, I said. But I'll not betray my fiancée, however long they pen me up here.

– Ah. I see.

He stood, picking up the bowl and spoon, and coughed regretfully, glancing at Catherine's picture.

– I understand, of course, sir. And I do respect it. No offence
meant, you understand.

– None taken, Langford.

On his way to the door, he paused and glanced once more at
the picture, and then back at me, his expression unreadable.

– But it's still going to be a mortal long time without her, he
said. Think about it, sir.

He nodded once, and was gone.

An hour or so later Doctor Howard arrived, entering the cabin
quickly after knocking, carrying his medical bag.

He drew up the chair that Langford had vacated, so that he was
placed directly in front of me. For a few moments, his hands spread
on his knees, elbows out-thrust like wings, he surveyed me in
frowning silence, head back-tilted at its usual angle. He didn't return
my greeting; instead, he reached out and took hold of my left wrist,
checking the pulse. Having done so, he compressed his lips. This
somewhat abrupt behaviour was not like him, and I waited to see
what he would do next.

– You've got into quite a bad way this time, he said. Have you
taken your Stramonium regularly?

I said I had, conscious that I still wheezed badly as I breathed.
He took out his stethoscope, I unbuttoned and drew up my shirt,
and he applied the instrument to my chest and back as he'd done
many times before – but this time at much greater length, tapping
me frequently with his fingers.

– I should guess that this was one of the worst attacks you've
had, he said finally. Was it not?

I agreed that it was, but told him I was now much better. He
put away his stethoscope and snapped his bag shut. He was looking
at me severely; but I read it as the severity of concern.

– Better until tonight, he said. And then you may well grow
worse again. You've never had such constant attacks before – didn't

141

you tell me that? It's been goin' on for more than a month, and they're growin' more severe.

He paused; then his voice grew softer.

– Look here, Devereux, Bermuda is a very bad climate for asthmatics, in my opinion – and your bein' confined under these conditions makes it worse. It's far too humid and dank in the winter.

He looked at me insistently, as though expecting me to ask a question. When I failed to do so, he spoke somewhat brusquely again.

– I have to tell you plainly that if you stay here, you'll almost certainly die.

We stared at each other in silence for a moment.

– Why then, I said, I must die, Doctor. The Government has condemned me, and there's no help for it.

I found I cared very little about this, today.

– Nonsense, Howard said. You *must* get out – and in your case, I believe something may be done. You're a man of qualities, and a decent fellow, despite your wrong-headed call for blood in the streets. I've no intention of watchin' you waste away.

He smiled, for the first time this morning.

– Now, here's the way we must proceed. You must write to the Governor personally, informin' him of your state of health. You must tell Captain Elliott that I have made the diagnosis I have, and say that in my opinion your continued confinement here will soon lead to your death. And you must ask to be removed to a penal colony with a more healthy climate, where you'll no longer be confined. I would suggest Van Diemen's Land. The island's climate is said to be superb. Bracin', and similar to that of southern France – which should appeal to a Francophile like you.

He cleared his throat.

– I've been meanin' to tell you this, Devereux: I'm goin' there myself, very soon: just after Christmas, in fact. A man-of-war's callin' here then that's goin' direct, and I'll join her. I've been appointed Colonial Surgeon, attached to the Hobart Town Hospital.

– Congratulations, Doctor. I'll miss you.

I meant it; and an extraordinary desolation assailed me at the thought of being penned up here without my talks with Howard. He leaned forward.

– We can resume our acquaintance at Van Diemen's Land, in a very short time, he said. Do what I ask, Devereux: take your pen and write. A simple, brief letter is all that's needed.

– I'm afraid I can't do that, I said.

He frowned.

– Can't? Why on earth not?

– Since they made a felon of me, I said, I've not asked for any indulgence from the British Government. Nor will I do so. That's my resolve, and I won't break it.

Doctor Howard now lost some of his usual calm; he frowned, and raised his voice a little.

– But you *must*, man, or you condemn yourself to death. Can I be plainer?

I sat up a little.

– I'm not such a fool as to want to die, I said. But by doing what you suggest, I'd acknowledge myself to be the felon they pretend I am. I won't do that. I'd thereby betray the whole stand I've taken.

He blew out an impatient breath.

– My dear Devereux, you're not bein' asked to betray yourself. Simply write to His Excellency and inform him of your condition – that is all I ask. Captain Elliott is a humane man, and I'm sure will be receptive. I shall do the rest. And I'll be in a position on Van Diemen's Land to see that your situation there is made very tolerable. I think you'll enjoy most of the privileges of a free man. You'll certainly not be incarcerated, as you are here.

– Then, with respect, Doctor, can you not put the position to the Governor on my behalf?

His agitation grew. In this normally cool man, it manifested itself in very small signs: a tightening of the mouth; the long fingers lightly drumming on the table.

– That is not possible, he said. It must be you who does so in the first instance. I'm not permitted to intervene officially, do you see. I can only involve myself *after* you yourself have notified the Governor of your condition. The proper form has to be complied with. Then, I assure you, I can do my best on your behalf.

– In other words, I'm to put in a petition – observing the proper forms. I'm trapped inside English rigidity, and English rigidity will kill me. Doctor Howard, believe me, I'm very grateful for your kindness, and for the feeling that makes you urge this on me. I believe we have become something like friends.

– We have. Most certainly we have, he said.

– But I shall never petition the British Government, or throw myself whining on their mercy. No; I will not do it.

What he now saw in my face apparently made Howard realise that further argument was useless. He stood, picking up his medical bag and looking down on me with an air of frustration.

– Very well, he said, I see your mind won't be changed. This sort of mad stubbornness is what has brought you to this pass. You are your own worst enemy, Devereux.

He stepped to the door; then turned.

– I should tell you, he said, that some weeks ago I applied to the Governor myself to have you removed to a hospital ship, in order to get you out of this wretched cabin here, and under proper care.

– Really, Doctor? You didn't consult me.

– I wasn't obliged to, damn it. Why are you so stiff-necked? If any other prisoner had been in your condition, I would have sent him to the hospital weeks ago, and wouldn't have had to apply to Captain Elliott to do it. But the authorities are obsessed with certain notions about you – among them the idea that these Irish rescue attempts will be mounted – and my request was refused. It's madness. They are killin' you, keepin' you here. Your only hope is to do as I've asked. You're a talented man, and your life is bein' wasted. You could find yourself in a very pleasant situation in Van Diemen's Land, with any amount of outlets for your abilities. Your fiancée could very well join you. I won't believe you'll let yourself be trapped here to die – and although it's probably useless, I ask you to take time to reconsider. Good evenin' to you.

I saw to my surprise that he seemed somewhat moved. He thrust the door open and went out, gripping the small leather bag which contained no nostrum that could save me.

December 17th

Lurking in my zone of shadow, I stand at the edge of a field. There's a weak, unsavoury light here, more like that of the moon than the sun.

A most curious field. Instead of trees, tall iron pillars stand about, which resemble the funnels of steamships. There are also old chairs here, and office tables with stacks of documents on them. On the horizon are dark, ragged cedars, and the roofs of massive buildings which ascend in tiers, like Chinese pagodas. Yet they are not Chinese: their stonework is imperial British: oppressive.

A small crowd of people appears in the distance. They dance along as though to some gay music, yet there's no music: only a windless silence. These people are mostly natives of Bermuda: black African men in straw hats, ragged cotton shirts, and trousers of jean fustian; but among them are British convicts, in their arrowed blouses. They all jig and caper together, and gesture at the sky; but as they come closer these gestures are like a parody of gaiety, being fierce and despairing, like the spasmodic leaps and twitchings of victims of St Vitus' Dance. And now that their faces are close enough to be discerned, I find that they all frown, and their frowns express anguish.

At first, the crowd appeared to be entirely male; but now I see that there's a female among them, gyrating and capering and frowning as they do. I recognise the mulatto woman from the vegetable boat, in her spotted, dark blue turban: her brown bosom rocks as she dances, scarcely confined by the orange dress. A British convict with a stubbled flaxen head holds one of her arms, and a lanky, loose-limbed African in a palmetto hat holds the other. It's as though they keep her prisoner between them; and I realise that she suffers as they do. As the group dances by, the woman's sombre eyes turn on me, and my heart jumps in sick excitement. I want her to stay, and not to dance on; I smile, but she gives me no smile back: instead she stares accusingly, her head turned, as though I'm

145

the perpetrator of some terrible wrong. They all caper off into the distance, and the field is empty.

But soon two more figures appear: Catherine, accompanied by Terence Butler.

They are walking directly towards me, passing a smoking funnel, and she trustingly holds his arm. Her head is slightly bent; he is half-turned towards her, a lock of his thick black hair falling over his forehead. They're in sober conversation, like a married couple. He's dressed in a dark, broadcloth suit of good quality, and is carrying a tall round hat; she has on a coal-scuttle bonnet trimmed with flowers, and a skirt of brown satin with a matching, V-shaped bodice. She's sedate as always; but she holds Terence Butler's arm and walks with him like a wife. When they draw near to me, they stop beside one of the office tables. They don't see me; I'm invisible to them, and I know that should I call out, they wouldn't hear me.

Butler begins to turn over papers on the table, while Catherine sits down in a nearby chair, hands folded in her lap, watching him with a trusting expression. He looks solemnly at a document, and I see that he's become pompous and self-important: it's an affliction that takes hold of almost every man who practises the Law, and makes me glad that I gave it up. At Trinity, Terence had an eager boyishness – even a sort of naivety – that was pleasant and amusing; but little is now left of this boyishness. I recall now that when I became engaged to Catherine, he told me how much he admired her, and how fortunate I was. I used to feel pleasure in this; but now I tell myself that I should have read the signs that accompanied his declarations about Catherine's virtues: the deepening of the voice; the intense gaze. Catherine, for her part, often said that she was fond of Terence; but this seemed an innocent fondness, as for a relative, and never troubled me. Butler professed admiration for my political stand, and cautiously supported Young Ireland; but he was never to become involved directly. I had little respect for his caution; but Catherine regarded it as sensible.

She gazes at him now with a smile of serene admiration – and somehow I become aware that his perusal of this document is going to decide her future, and therefore mine as well. As I realise this, the landscape insidiously darkens, and the chimneys and cedars behind the couple fade to silhouettes. Butler goes on studying the document; but Catherine stands up from her chair, and begins to undress.

First, she removes her bonnet and puts it on the chair; then she unpins her hair, and its long, fair coils tumble down her back. She reaches behind to unfasten the stiff brown bodice. At this, I want to cry out, and to beg her to stop; but I'm voiceless. She struggles unsuccessfully with the hooks behind her back; then she turns to Butler and asks him to help her, though her voice makes no sound. He smiles with the indulgence of a husband, and moves behind her to oblige, his head bent close to hers. And now her eyes look directly into mine, with a mute, mild appeal for understanding. I try once again to cry out, but my voice is choked in my throat; I make only guttural noises, and I seem to grow colder and colder, in my zone of shadow.

Butler has finished his task; the dark brown casing of the bodice collapses, revealing the delicate, embroidered chemisette beneath. He places the bodice on the chair. Smiling her thanks, Catherine steps out of her skirt, and Butler regards her with open appreciation. She stands, in the darkening field: erect and slim in her chemisette and petticoat, hands folded under her bosom.

I choke. I can't breathe; I can't get air, and the field has gone much darker: dark around the whiteness of Catherine's naked arms and shoulders, and of her chemisette and petticoat. Soon I can make out nothing but the upright candle of her body in the gloom; and that too is being obscured. I fight to breathe; my chest rattles, and I'm deadly cold.

There's light in the cabin. The white candle on the shelf is alight, and flickers crazily in the draft through the porthole. Old Mr Wall is here, holding his lantern high near the ceiling, and peering fiercely from under his peaked cap.

I sit up in the cot, coughing profoundly, dragging in air, searching for a handkerchief as I bring up mucus. I lie back on the pillow, wheezing. Then I see that another man is here, sitting at my table and watching me.

It's the superintendent of convicts, Captain Thorpe.

– Good evening, Mr Devereux, he says.

I stare, too amazed to answer, and with no breath to do so anyway.

– As you see, I've decided to visit you, he says.

He speaks more softly than usual, but his bass voice fills the cabin. He is sombre and official, in his eternal dark uniform. He leans forward with his hands clasped on the table, his eyebrows politely raised.

– What remedy do you take for these attacks? he asks.

At first, when I try to reply, I merely bring on another bout of coughing. I sit up, fighting for control, while the superintendent waits, eyebrows still raised. Mr Wall, standing behind him, looks from me to his master with a dubious expression, as though I'm deranged. The sound of my own obscene whooping humiliates me in front of Thorpe; with a great effort I overcome it and begin to breathe, my handkerchief in front of my mouth. Remorselessly, Thorpe waits for his answer, and finally I manage one word:

– Stramonium.

– Do you need it now?

– No, thank you.

I find I can now inhale reasonably well; the attack is not so bad as last time. But even if it were, I would accept no help from the superintendent. What is he doing here, invading me like this? To gain time and collect myself, I pretend that I still can't breathe easily; I lie back and look at him.

– I thought I should see how you are, having heard of your current condition, he says. Plainly, you are not well at all.

– May I ask you the time?

My voice is thin; I resolve to strengthen it. He draws a pocket watch from his vest. In the candle-light, his ocean-cold eyes have deep shadows around them; it makes him look more threatening than usual.

– It's five past midnight, he says. Why?

– I'm honoured, I say, that you visit me in person. But I wonder why you choose to enquire after my health by waking me in the middle of the night?

His eyes narrow, and his lower lip creeps out; he waits before replying.

– This is the time that the mate always checks your cabin, is it not? And he tells me you are usually awake at this time.

– That's right, sir, the mate puts in. Usually at his books.

The superintendent looks at him.

– You may leave us, Mr Wall.

He waits until the mate has gone; then he says:

– So: I must apologise for disturbing your rest, it seems.

I have evidently angered him, as I intended.

– However, he says, you are a prisoner, Mr Devereux, even if a somewhat privileged one; and we have the duty of watching you at all times. At some cost to the British taxpayer, I may add.

I resolve not to be spoken to like this while reclining in the cot; it gives him an advantage. I struggle up, cross the floor in my night-shirt to the peg where my greatcoat hangs, and draw it on. He watches this with a sardonically pitying expression; no doubt I cut a wretched figure. But a man feels less vulnerable in a greatcoat, and I sit down at the table opposite him with a renewed sense of dignity, and fix him with my gaze.

– The British taxpayer might well have been spared all this expense, I say, had things been conducted in Dublin according to law. But there's little point in my commenting on that now.

– You're right. There's none whatsoever, he says. You would do well to make no observations at all on your situation, which is a very lenient one. More lenient than you have any business to expect.

He speaks very low, and his lips are tight. I begin to sense that he may be on the verge of breaking his policy of courtesy towards me, and my heartbeat increases.

– That may be so, I say, if you call permanent isolation in this freezing hutch leniency. But the conditions under which I exist are really not the point, Captain Thorpe, so far as I'm concerned. Your Government has already done its worst, through the original atrocity of transporting me here.

– *Atrocity?*

149

At last he's lost control: his beefy face goes a deep pink, and his jaw works.

– God damn you, sir, for your bloody insolence! How dare you speak to me like this?

In spite of myself, I go colder. At last the pretence has been abandoned; the line has been crossed. I'm no longer a gentleman whose movements merely happen to be restricted, and who may not be bullied or insulted; alone here, without witnesses, I'm the felon, he the keeper, and he can say and do what he likes. I suspect that this is why he's come here; but I find I'm not concerned or cast down. Instead, my loathing for Captain Thorpe is accompanied by a sort of wild exhilaration which is banishing my debility. At last I have a true enemy to attack; at last battle is joined! He is the British Empire personified; I intend to defy and taunt him as much as I am able, and all tonight's grief and anger will be in it: I care nothing for the consequences. Let him send me to the rock-quarries, if he likes! But I say nothing to his rhetorical question; I return his hostile glare, and hold my fire. After many seconds, he speaks again, his voice dangerously soft.

– Let me tell you something, Mr Devereux. You should thank your stars that your sedition is being dealt with by the Government of Great Britain. In any other realm, you would find yourself in a dungeon – or worse.

I laugh outright, and he blinks.

– Do you think I don't know, sir, I say, that the only reason I'm not slaving in chains like the other wretches here is your Government's hypocrisy? Do you think I'm unaware that what is done to me is noted in Europe? And that you therefore don't wish to be seen as tyrants? That in my case, your vaunted freedoms and your British justice have been made a mockery of, and you dare not go further for fear of the civilized world's opinion? I think you shouldn't boast to me of your Government's leniency, Mr Thorpe. I know its real motives.

There is silence in the cabin; his jaw slants sideways, and his eyes, fixed on my face, blaze up as though he's been struck. I can hear him breathing; and at the same time I'm fighting with all my might to keep my own breathing regular. There's a natural hatred between us, and we both know it.

Finally, he speaks: hoarsely, and almost in a whisper.

– You will apologise for that speech, Mr Devereux – or you'll regret it.

– I'll apologise for nothing, I say. What will you do, Captain Thorpe? Have me flogged for your pleasure, like that miserable Lane? Do so. Do whatever you see fit.

Saying this, giving release to all the anger of months, I'm filled with savage joy; but at the same time, I find my body is betraying me. My breathing has gone shallow again, and I'm sweating; the accursed blockage in my lungs returns, and my enemy renews his attack, while Thorpe stares. Within seconds, I'm barking and wheezing in front of him again, my hand clutching my chest. I fight vainly for air; and as I do so, he leans forward, hands on the table, studying me as though I'm a sick animal. Then he smiles, with a restored air of superiority.

– I'm sorry to disappoint you, he says, but you're clearly too feeble to have flogged at present. Much as you'd like us to, wouldn't you? That's what you want, Devereux – to be a martyr. Well, we shan't oblige you.

My eyes water, as I cough helplessly; his dropping of my title makes me angrier, but his face is becoming dim. He now rises, takes hold of my upper arm with iron fingers, draws me from my chair, and leads me across the cabin. His rope-yellow head only comes a little above my shoulder; but by using his bulk, and taking advantage of my weakness, he's able to push me down on the cot. I want to resist, and to tell him that I need to sit up; but I'm too weak. I lie back gasping against the pillow, and the superintendent stands over me, his shape growing vague in the half-dark. I find I'm getting faint; cold sweat runs down my forehead, and as I struggle to keep hold of my senses, Thorpe's pink face is lowered close to mine.

What on earth is he about? Playing the doctor, or trying to intimidate me? His huge, gargoyle-like visage (lit from one side by the candle, deeply shadowed on the other) is now only inches away, as though he intends to kiss me. I wheeze desperately; I'm truly choking, and perhaps this is what he intends.

The gargoyle speaks, and I smell brandy on its breath.

– You call for those Irish peasants of yours to take up the gun. Have you ever had a gun in your hands, Devereux – other than to hunt birds?

I make no answer; I haven't enough breath.

He sits on a chair beside the cot, but leans forward so that his face is still close.

– Before I took this thankless post, he says, I commanded a ship of the line. I'd like to see you given a taste of some fighting at sea, Devereux. I wonder how much stomach you'd have for it, when the gun-trucks were rolled out? I wonder if you'd keep your taste for blood then?

He smiles: it's a mere, malicious grimace; and I'm certain now that he's drunk.

– Look at you, he says. Do you imagine your precious followers would give twopence for you now? Do you think your female admirers would find you such a dashing fellow if they could see you these days? You're dying, do you realise that? You may have some notion later of complaining of your treatment, or making public the way I am speaking to you now. It will do you no good; there's no-one to witness this discussion. And I tell you that you are certainly going to die here, unless you heed Doctor Howard's advice. The Governor has already shown you great kindness. You'll do well to ask that he show you some more. A present for Christmas, perhaps.

I'm gaining a little air; but I continue to lie quiet, and to stare at him with a contempt I hope he reads correctly. And now he does an extraordinary thing: he gets up, moves across the cabin, and picks up Catherine's portrait. He studies it; then looks across at me, and replaces it without comment.

– I'll give you some advice of my own, he says. Renounce some of your more violent views, and seek a conditional pardon. Lord Grey is offering them to certain prisoners who are prepared to start a new life in the colonies. That is the best you can hope for,

Devereux. You might then be re-united with your future wife.

He smiles: and the smile is both sardonic and faintly lewd. Another fit of coughing seizes me as I try to answer, and I close my eyes. When I open them, the cabin is empty.

I sit up, shivering. It's as though Captain Thorpe was never here – or was simply another bad dream.

December 18th

For the past twenty-four hours I've waited for some sort of summons from the superintendent. No prisoner, I'm sure, has ever spoken to him as I did; and despite my peculiar position, I believe he'll impose some sort of penalty on me. His pride will insist on it.

My asthma bad again last night.

December 24th

Christmas eve. My thoughts circle around my parents and friends in Dublin, and Catherine. Is Terence Butler at her parents' house today, sharing their Christmas?

I can't afford to dwell on this. I must numb my mind, through this season of joy and of family happiness.

A week has gone by, and still Captain Thorpe has done nothing about my defiance. Anti-climax! When he saw me yesterday on deck, he nodded once, and then stared through me. So I assume now that those above him frustrate him from taking revenge, and that London's policy in regard to me actually renders me immune from convict punishment – within certain bounds. What those bounds are, who knows? I may have to test this question further, very soon.

Asthma continues to come every night, and I'm now almost too weak to drag myself on deck. Doctor Howard says that death could come to me at any time, if I continue to deteriorate; and I do not wish to die.

No; I shall not die at young Queen Victoria's pleasure, in this dog-box. I have come to a decision. I shall apply to the Governor for removal to Van Diemen's Land, after all.

I've thought about this carefully, and have discussed it with

Doctor Howard, who seems genuinely delighted at my change of mind. I've concluded that I'll not be betraying myself or my cause by taking action in the way I intend to do. I shall not petition for a 'pardon', as Thorpe has suggested. Nor will I plead with the Governor for mitigation of my sentence – or any other favour. Were I actually condemned to death, the situation would be different. Then, I would not be able to plead for mercy and still keep my honour. But that is not the situation: I don't believe they actually *wish* to kill me; they are simply making my demise likely through neglect – or stupidity. Therefore, it's reasonable to draw the Governor's attention to my physical condition, and to ask, as Doctor Howard has suggested, that I be removed to a penal settlement whose conditions will allow me to survive, and so serve out my sentence.

Is this ignominious? I think not; although it fills me with distaste to ask anything of them. But I have no intention of dying at Britannia's hands if I can help it. I wish to live; and to fight. The only other answer to my present plight would be suicide: an option I actually considered in one of my lowest moments. But although my religious belief is wavering at best, and rendered increasingly uncertain through my explorations of current thought, I still have a blind belief that my life is not my own to take. And when I shake off my weakness, my faith in regaining the world against all odds returns, and I know that I still have a destiny beyond this hulk.

Already, having made my decision, I feel hope flowing back into me – and a vast excitement simply at the prospect of removal from this box.

December 25th
I've written to Captain Elliott.

Doctor Howard came in this morning for a Christmas drink with me: a kindness I was touched by. We toasted each other in my 'medicinal' brandy, and he took the letter away quickly – before I could change my mind, he said.

He has said that he'll give the Governor medical advice to the effect that I'm a dying man unless I'm removed from Bermuda; but

I must wait nearly two months for the result, since the Governor must apply to London. So I must hope to survive for that time. The dubious looks Doctor Howard gives me aren't reassuring, but I believe I'll get through; my hope already makes me a little stronger, and this lone Yuletide a little less cheerless.

Commander Moffatt also looked in a little while ago to wish me the compliments of the season. He suggested I attend the Christmas church service on the main deck in an hour, and I believe I'll try, although I'm very unsteady on my feet, and have to stop every few paces to breathe. The human need for community on such a festival is very insistent: better to celebrate it with my gaolers and with London thieves than with no-one!

I've written to Catherine, telling her that I may now be removed to Van Diemen's Land, where I expect to live more or less free, and where I hope she may come to marry me – if my position is one where I can offer her security and comfort.

Christmas day; and here I sit alone, wrapped in my greatcoat, reading Aeschylus. My Greek, which was rusty, is improving: I have a dictionary. How superb, pitiful and haunting is *Prometheus Bound!* Prometheus, whose defiance could not be broken! Has not his fate become my own? Am I not also nailed to a desolate rock? Am I not also tormented by tyrants, who seek to break my will?

To pass the time, I've begun to make a translation:

> *O Goddess of the sky, and fleet-winged winds;*
> *O running, racing rivers!*
> *O laughing ocean waves beyond all number!*
> *O Gaea, mother of all life!*
> *To you, and to the sun's all-seeing disc, I cry:*
> *Look what is done by gods to me, a god!*

February 14th, 1849
Voyage!

Word has come: Doctor Howard informed me last night that my request has been granted. The Governor, it seems, has had directions from London to remove me to Van Diemen's Land, where

I'll probably be given 'comparative liberty'. Escape from Bermuda! Escape from confinement! My spirits begin to soar. I begin to take in what even 'comparative liberty' will mean, after eight months in this box.

I'm also told by Doctor Howard that a transport is leaving London at the end of next month: the ship *Sir Stamford Raffles*, of 700 tons, with a cargo of male convicts to be deposited here at Bermuda; after which she'll set sail for Van Diemen's Land with another cargo of male convicts, of whom I'll be one – and James Langford another. Even the wretched Lane – who actually made some sort of recovery from his flogging, after a spell in the hospital ship – is going. He and many others aboard will be 'recommended' prisoners: men who've served most of their sentences, and will now be freed as settlers: what are termed 'Ticket-of-Leave men'. But Langford, of course, has some ten years of his fourteen-year sentence still to serve, and will no doubt be hired out as a convict servant.

May the north wind which torments me at night blow the *Stamford Raffles* to these islands at full speed! My health has been improving for the past month, and this news has sent a wave of strength coursing through me. I'll now serve out my time as a living man, and not one trapped in a wooden coffin – and to hope that Catherine may join me is surely not to hope for too much. Doctor Howard, at least, encourages me to think so.

He spent some time with me yesterday evening, after delivering the news. He brought with him the usual bottle of wine, and announced that this must be our farewell: his man-of-war brig would arrive within twenty-four hours, to bear him away to Van Diemen's Land before me.

– I shall miss our debates, he said, even though you're such a turbulent fellow, Devereux. But we'll meet again soon, if your ship has a good passage. She'll be sailin' from here in April, I understand.

– Well then, I said, may we meet again in Van Diemen's Land, if fate wills it.

My words were sincere. This doctor and I have now reached a considerable degree of ease with each other – almost of genuine friendship. The prisoner begins to love his gaoler, and I've been lulled into accepting Howard as he wishes to be accepted. Yet at times I suspect that he's no mere naval surgeon: or at least, that he's privy to secrets of policy beyond this rank. It's almost as though he has charge of my destiny in some particular and secret way.

But it's easy to imagine such things. Soon my mind, like my body, will be free; and ghostly suspicions will cease, or become mere memories.

April 22nd

Nine a.m. My last day on Bermuda: a bright Spring morning. The dancing green harbour has seldom looked prettier; but I doubt I'll give it a backward glance, when we sail at two o'clock. Farewell, bleached summer isles!

Going out on deck after breakfast, with James Langford beside me, I find that the mail steamer is in the bay – which means that I'll have letters from home before sailing. Langford and I pause, side by side at the rail of the half-deck, and gaze across to the dock where the *Raffles* now lies: moored astern of the flagship, sails furled, tiny figures of sailors swarming about her decks. In spite of myself, I'm impressed by her steep, fortress-like sides, her great yardarms, and her look of hulking power.

Langford's hair, I notice, is combed with special care this morning, and he's very well shaven: he has an air of returning to military service, and I find this somehow touching. How vulnerable to hope and how frail in their hopefulness are even the hardest men! He and I are drawn together at this moment, on the bright, deserted half-deck: we're poised on the brink of a common destiny. As he looks across at the *Raffles*, Langford's eyes gleam with a quiet excitement; and no wonder, since this vessel may well be carrying him out of imprisonment. Captain Thorpe has told him that when he reaches Van Diemen's Land, he will probably only have to serve a short time as a convict, before being given his Ticket-of-Leave. He's fortunate indeed: I'm surprised that the penalty for a crime such as his should be reduced. But I imagine he's unlikely ever to see England again.

He knows everything, it seems. Talking softly, he gives me much information about the *Raffles*: and the interest I show is a mask for my own exultation at escape from Bermuda. It's deliverance that he and I are actually discussing, not the ship – and we have the careful solemnity of men who are secretly drunk.

The *Raffles*, Langford says, began life in Asia, plying as a merchantman between the Indian ports and China. But for many years now, she's appeared in the sea lanes in her grim incarnation as a convict transport. She's named, of course, after that enterprising gentleman who founded the island colony of Singapore – thus securing Britannia's covetous grip on the Eastern Seas. She's one of the imperial Indian ships: a very durable breed, according to Langford. He narrows his eyes professionally in the sunlight, leaning on the rail with both outstretched hands, his forelock fluttering in the breeze.

– Made of the best East India teak, he says. At least as old as me – and good for years yet. You can't wear 'em out, those Calcutta-built ships.

He seems as proud of her as though he owns her; and not for the first time I wonder at the patriotism that surfaces in English rogues: enemies rather than admirers, one would have thought, of their own society. And once again, I have to remind myself that a rogue is what he is, this stocky ex-Marine with his throaty voice. How little I really know him! Bit by bit, through casual questioning, I've extracted the basic facts of his background; and yet, for some reason, they don't seem to add up to a totality that explains him. He's always apparently frank, friendly, and forthcoming; and yet I feel sure that large areas are shrewdly withheld: he manages to remain mysterious.

He comes from Kent, where he grew up on a small hop farm, the youngest of eight children. His father, he says, didn't do very well at farming, and the property wouldn't support them all. James got a sort of education at a village school – he's certainly quite literate and well-informed, being an ardent newspaper-reader – but he was sent away from home at twelve to be apprenticed to a cooper, somewhere in London. The cooper beat him a lot, and he ran away. There followed a year or so of wandering in the stews of

London – about which he's deliberately vague. He was fourteen when he joined the Marines, which seems to have suited him well: he rose rapidly in the ranks. Then, after he was wounded, he became a merchant seaman for many years. He married somewhat late.

That he was a good fighting man and sailor, I feel sure. He conveys the warrior's certainty of his own strength; the deceptive calm of the genuinely formidable. Yet there's nothing vicious or surly about him, and his friendly good humour is unfailing – although I have to remind myself that it may be assumed for my benefit. About his life as a criminal he's far less forthcoming. He's happy to boast, in a general way, about his railway robbery; but when I ask for detail, I find that his replies actually tell me very little.

No; I really don't know him. The gap is too great.

– I wonder if they'll let you continue as my servant on the *Raffles*, I say now.

– That I don't know, sir. They haven't said. But it would suit me very well if they did.

– It would suit me too, Langford.

Suddenly, the moment and the brink on which we stand impel me to tell him something I hadn't planned to do.

– It's as well we're being shipped out. If it hadn't happened, I was planning something difficult, and I might have asked for your help.

– Really, sir? What was it you was planning?

– I wanted to try an escape by boat, I say. As soon as I got rid of the asthma.

For a moment he says nothing, but shoots a quick glance at me. Then a slow smile begins.

– That *would* have been difficult, sir, he says. You're pretty bloody rash, I must say. I believe you'd have tried it, too.

He begins a throaty chuckle; it ends, as his chuckles often do, in a brief, wheezing cough – a symptom, I suspect, of over-indulgence in his secret supply of cigars.

– Yes, he says, wiping his mouth and blinking, I believe you really would have tried. And I'd have done what I could, sir, of course, short of coming with you – my Ticket being likely, you understand. But a gentleman like yourself, steering an open boat for the coast of America? No, your chances wouldn't have been good. I can see why they call you rash.

I look at him soberly, refusing to respond to his amusement.

– It would have been better than rotting here, Langford.

– You're right, sir; your position was bad. When things are that bad, better to jump and damn the consequences, I agree. But it's all changed now, ain't it?

He looks over his shoulder, checking to see that we're still alone.

– It'll be a new story now, he says, when we get to Australia. Plenty of room to move, if you see what I mean. A lot of possibilities. Then you and I might talk again, and make different plans.

I have no idea what he might mean by this surprising statement, and think it better not to pursue it. I say something about having to pack, and we part. He hurries away briskly down the deck, limping almost imperceptibly, light on his feet as always. Watching him go, I reflect that I was probably somewhat foolish to confide in him as I did; especially when it was no longer necessary. I'm not quite sure what made me do so; but it can hardly matter now. In a few more hours I'll be aboard the *Raffles* – flying for my life through seventy degrees of latitude. And this time, please God, I'll outstrip my demon.

A boat is to come for me in a few hours, to deliver me to the ship. Will I be searched on embarkation? If so, they may discover and read this journal. Should I destroy it? No; I think not. They've shown no interest in searching me so far; they're apparently indifferent to what I put on paper.

My trunk and portmanteau are packed. Even now, I must make an effort to realise that I, Robert Devereux, convict number 2017, with just thirteen shillings in my tricolour purse, will actually voyage to the utmost south of the globe, under strange constellations – leaving my thwarted enemy behind, among the moping cedars of Bermuda.

5. FLIGHT

Aboard the *Sir Stamford Raffles*
July 12th

The zone of calms, lying across the equator.

The sun doesn't shine here as I thought he would do; instead, the sky is tin-coloured, and we float in a strange twilight. The air's a warm gruel, causing one's face to be constantly slippery with perspiration. The sea is a brooding, dark green oil. The *Raffles* hardly moves; we seem actually to have drifted into some still and eerie region of the dead.

Today another convict was pitched into the sea, after a perfunctory burial service: the seventh death so far. And every one of them Irish.

No wind: we're becalmed.

It's well over two months since we sailed from Bermuda: but the extraordinary fact is, this far into July, that we're still thousands of miles from the Cape of Good Hope. We've crossed the line no less than three times in our attempts to find a wind, and I'm told that the captain has now given up hope of reaching the Cape without touching at a port in Brazil for provisions and water. So we're bound for Pernambuco: by inches.

Nearly three months at sea, never once in sight of land! And it could well take another three months to reach Van Diemen's Land; or even longer. Sickness grows among both prisoners and soldiers: mostly scurvy, whose effects on its victims are dismal to see. Since I'm granted the diet of an officer, getting some vegetables with the salt beef on which we all live, I'm thus far unaffected. But there's fever aboard now: all seven deaths were caused by it. We're pent up in the unhealthiest region of the globe, within three degrees of the equator, and the wonder is that no more have died so far.

Langford still serves me, but only infrequently. Sometimes he fails to appear for weeks, and is replaced by other, less attractive felons. My bandit remains resourceful: he shows no sign of scurvy, and has managed to arrange for himself an extra supply of limes – some of which he brings to me. There's something indestructible about Langford: my admiration for him grows.

A small, stuffy and dirty cabin has been assigned to me here, its window looking out over the quarter-deck. And I'm isolated on the *Raffles* far more than I ever was on the hulk.

On our first day out from Bermuda, my situation was explained to me by Doctor Richards, the surgeon-superintendent in charge of convicts – who supervises most matters on board, it seems, except navigation. He appeared in my cabin in the late afternoon, and his purpose – concerning which he clearly felt awkward – was quickly revealed. He'd come to tell me that I must live as a solitary through-out the voyage.

He's a quiet, courteous man, impossible to take exception to. Very thin, with sober grey hair and a long, sober face, he has a sincere, serious manner that's more medical than naval. It's a curious British practice, this placing of naval surgeons in charge of convict ships; perhaps London feels it gives their merciless business of trans-portation a stamp of humanity. Not wanting to look at me, Doctor Richards took refuge for a moment in examining his hands, turning them over to look at the backs.

– I'm afraid that you can have nothing to do with the officers on this ship, he said. I'm sorry about that, Mr Devereux. I realise the isolation for many months will be hard for you, and unnatural. I wouldn't have the least objection myself, but –

He broke off.

– But if you allowed it, questions would be asked in Parliament, I said. As they were asked concerning Captain Wood of the *Nemesis*. And then you and your officers would risk court-martial. Is that it?

– Exactly, he said, and looked up from his hands. That is exactly the case. After that matter, we're all afraid of unpleasantness.

– Make your mind easy then, I said. Since I've become a prisoner, I'm happy with my own company, and don't wish for the society of my gaolers.

He looked relieved and disconcerted all at once, and soon took his leave.

If only Doctor Howard were in charge on the *Raffles*! I miss our talks. Loneliness has taken on a new dimension.

July 15th

I peer out of my window at the quarter-deck.

I know every detail of this little stage by heart now: its gratings and slow-turning wheel; its swinging fire-buckets. Its sounds have taken on an eternal quality, like sounds known for ever: bellowing voices of command; low rumble and laughter of men gossiping; sweetly monotonous *ting-ting-ting* of the bells marking the watches. Beyond the quarter-deck's gangway are the main deck and the forecastle: forbidden territory, the territory of the convicts, who mill about or silently idle down there, in their arrowed blouses. As on the hulk, they may not come aft: the quarter-deck and the poop deck are out of bounds for them. And also as before, these are the areas in which I'm permitted to exercise – this time under the eyes of two red-coated officers of the military guard.

The quarter-deck is the hub of the ship, where a succession of seamen, in their striped shirts and flapping, bell-bottomed trousers, patiently handle the great, mahogany wheel: brown hands on the spokes, hour upon hour. It's also a hub of official and social life for the transport's officers and guardians; a sort of elevated promenade, its stainless white boards patterned with the complex shadows of the rigging, where our black-bearded, morose captain and his various blue-coated lieutenants and midshipmen appear and disappear in due order, and red-coated, off-duty soldiers smoke their pipes and chat. To listen to their talk, either on deck or as they pass by my window, is one of my few entertainments.

Soon I'll go out and look down on the distant thoroughfare of the main deck, where the convicts who aren't sick lounge and gossip and trail fishing lines, or play cards. At night there's singing among them there, and even step-dancing, which is tolerated by the watching soldiers.

Last night, standing at the gangway in the dark, smoking my pipe, I heard singing in Irish float up from the forecastle. There are some two hundred Irish aboard, all of them young men and boys; but they're too far removed for me ever to see them properly. I glimpsed them only when we boarded: some of them were very handsome fellows, and nearly all of them had the fine, open, faces of the countryside – utterly different from the sharp grey visages of the London burglars milling around them. It filled me with pain to see them. Victims of the Famine, they had stolen not to starve; and I cursed the tyranny that had made them criminals for it, and had torn them from their homes and hillsides, and exiled them for ever.

The song they sang, in the becalmed stillness, was infinitely strange and melancholy. I'd heard it before, although its name now escaped me. It was Paul Barry who had once drawn my attention to it, as we passed a little cabin in the countryside not far from 'Deerpark', in the days before the estate was lost. I have little Irish, but Barry is fluent in it, and draws the inspiration for many of his songs from those of the people. A middle-aged woman was singing, sitting by an open door, and Barry told me that this was an *aisling,* or vision-song. He gave me the burden of it. Wandering through a valley at dusk, a poet had met a lovely woman, and had thought at first to make her his love. But this was a fairy: a *spéir bhean,* or sky woman, whom the poet saw as fallen Ireland. In this guise, Erin in her bonds could be sung of without fear of English prohibition.

Now, as the young male voices floated up to me, I was suddenly ashamed that I had no proper knowledge of the tongue of my people. Except in my boyhood, when I was close to the servants in my father's house, the people have always been at a distance from me. I've occasionally entered their cabins, and accepted their hospitality, but the truth is they're almost like a race of trolls or elves to me: I scarcely know them. And tears stood in my eyes for these young Irish prisoners whose voices went out above the dark sea – and for the fathers and mothers who'd reared them. They had cherished their sons, and sung them to sleep in their cradles, only to lose them to this: a foul British prison ship, and the ends of the earth.

July 17th
Still becalmed.

We're all on half rations of the endless salt beef, and on a half allowance of water. The water has turned hot, black and foul, and is filled with some wriggling form of life. We take it mixed with lime juice against the scurvy, but I don't drink more than I can help. Instead, I wait on deck for the blessed downpours that occasionally relieve us, and trap rainwater in a cup. Tormented by thirst, yet ever hopeful, my tongue like paper, I sit thus for hours on the deck, watching swollen rain clouds on the horizon. I will them to release their bounty; and occasionally they do so two or three miles off, showering their precious liquid into empty ocean, while we on the ship helplessly gnaw our lips.

I never knew before how exquisite simple water could be, both as drink and as a balm to the body. Last night, I went out naked onto the gangway of the quarter-deck in one of the sudden downpours, head flung back, glorying in this natural shower-bath. And strangely, I have never felt so free as in that solitary moment: I, a prisoner. Despite our trials, I'm sanguine and hopeful. I'm well again: asthma has so far not followed me into this zone of gloomy warmth, and I thank God for it every day. Everything is interesting: even this unearthly region of Dis, where our ship moves by inches, the water slopping dully at her sides. The sound is like that of some huge, naked creature being slapped; and the voices of convicts, soldiers and crew come to me dully, as though through wrappings. My only real disquiet is at being so long out of touch with Catherine; but even this anxiety is muffled. I must wait for her letters to reach me at the Cape.

By day, I lie in the heavy heat on deck; by night I drink brandy with which Langford keeps me supplied from some secret store he has access to, and smoke my pipe, and am reasonably content. I work when I can on my translation of Aeschylus; but I do so in a very desultory manner, since this strange and ominous heat saps the brain, and makes one reluctant for mental activity. The tropics are no Paradise; to live here for ever, it seems to me, would be a sort of Hell, turning one slowly into a creature of dull impulse, the intelligence and the higher instincts rotting.

Last night at about ten there was a brief squall. For a quarter of an hour the *Raffles* actually moved as a ship should – timbers and blocks creaking, rudder grinding, flying through the underworld gloom. I went out on deck, suddenly inspired by the old vessel, now that she'd come alive. Seamen hung like ragged white birds on the tilting yards in the dark, at a sickening height. Orders were shouted, and a throng of officers stood with the midshipman of the watch on the lamplit quarter-deck, heads back-tilted. The ship was coming on to a starboard tack, lurching and shuddering; then she ceased this, and found her way.

Avoiding the crowded quarter-deck, yet sharing its excitement, I climbed to the poop, which I found to be deserted. From here, I found myself watching unearthly blue fires that flared in the pitchy water astern. And I whispered a snatch of the *Mariner* to myself, as I do more and more often lately:

> – *About, about, in reel and rout*
> *The death fires danced at night* . . .

Breathing in the thick, warm air, I peered in exaltation at these icy, dancing fires of Dis. Voyage! How vast the world, and I alone in it!

August 11th
At sea again.

An hour ago, we sailed from Pernambuco – that white-walled town with its tolling Portuguese church bells that Langford and the sailors called 'Pennybooker', since pronunciation of its true name was beyond them.

We lingered for over three weeks, lying two miles out from land, and taking on supplies; but I was never permitted to set foot there, and so have had nothing to record. Pernambuco, like the whole bottle-green coast of Brazil, was locked off from me, as Bermuda had been. But I tasted its sweet water, and devoured the

166

delicious oranges, yams and limes which cured the ship of scurvy. And the ever-resourceful Langford, going ashore as a servant to Doctor Richards, found English newspapers there, and smuggled a small batch to my cabin.

They were papers dating to the second week in June – and a copy of the *Daily News* for that month carried an article that caused me to sit chuckling with joy.

It reported that an appeal to the English House of Lords against death sentences for high treason by Paul Barry, Martin Fitzgibbon and Thomas O'Neill, had failed. It further reported, however, that mercy was to be shown to the prisoners, and that their sentences would be commuted to transportation for fourteen years. All would be sent to Van Diemen's Land – the sentence to be carried out early in July. So all three, like me, are no doubt now on the high seas, and are bound where I am bound. We may well arrive in the Antipodes at much the same time.

My feelings at first, when I read this article, were mixed: anger at Albion's latest atrocity, but admiration for the heroism of my comrades – whose characters are such that their transportation is Britain's shame, not theirs. But what predominated was selfish joy: joy that I'll not be alone in that wild island prison; that whatever we face there, my comrades and I will face it together.

In a May copy of the same paper, I found an article devoted to myself – or rather to what my captors believe to be my imminent death. The British Home Secretary was quoted as follows:

During his imprisonment at Bermuda, Mr Devereux's health declined to such a degree that a further prolonged stay there was out of the question. It has therefore been decided to transport him to Van Diemen's Land, where he will probably be allowed a Ticket-of-Leave, in order to serve out his sentence. However, judging from recent accounts of his health, it seems doubtful that he will survive the voyage to the colony.

This too made me laugh. I will disappoint the Secretary, and all my other captors.

September 12th

A month from Pernambuco, and a thousand miles from the Cape. Little to record.

We now have a steady wind, which often increases to gale force, and the old ship flies along, day after day. She's been released into the dimension she was made for, and is several degrees south of the Cape: well down into the southern hemisphere. September is the southern Spring, and we're into a region here where all heaviness and torpor are gone: a region of brisk days, and keen air. But I begin to feel a touch of ice in these gales. And with this breath from Antarctica, the shadow of the enemy sometimes falls on me.

Yet his attacks have been light ones. Last night I sat wheezing for an hour or so; but then I cleared my chest, and slept. I won't believe that the demon has any strength, in these southern latitudes; I treat him with contempt.

Outside my cabin is the vast blue circle of the globe, at which I stare half the day. From it, a profound yet inaudible reverberation comes, like that which goes on emanating from a struck gong. It softly fills all things, as the *Raffles* slides down the glassy walls of the waves; it tantalises the inward ear like the music of the spheres; it comes and goes in the pure, face-whipping breeze which continues day after day, here to the south of the Tropic of Capricorn.

At night, as I stand on the poop deck, the mighty arch of the Milky Way is close above me. Gazing up, I count myself privileged by accident, since even if I should die tomorrow, I'll have heard the silent singing of the world. This titanic tune is not heard by every man; thousands, after all, living out their lives in Europe's warrens, die without having heard it. The poorest tar on this ship, carried to these unsullied regions, is richer by far than such people; and I'm made richer for life.

September 16th

Afternoon. The gale blows hard again. The *Raffles* heels, masts leaning, and dips its prow in the spume, racing towards the Cape at a speed of eight knots.

We have only a few hundred miles to go: we shall see Table

Mountain the day after tomorrow. Charming little white-breasted birds like petrels, which the sailors call Cape pigeons, follow us day after day. Sometimes the seamen try and lasso them for sport; but these little creatures of the fresh-breathed south are too fast for their traps.

Behind them, on the starboard side, comes a great white albatross, coasting on its giant crescent wings. It too has followed the ship for some days, appearing and disappearing like a portent, riding the air-channels like an angel in brute form. One of the sailors is trying to trap it, watched and cheered on by a group of other sailors and some convicts. He's a tall, lanky, grotesquely ugly fellow of middle age, whose head is totally bald, and burned the colour of walnut. I've noticed him before. He appears to be entirely toothless, his sunken mouth an inverted U; and he never smiles. It's a skull face, cruel and hard, devoid of any signs of humour or human sympathy; and his eyes have a dangerous, almost mad glint. I pray that he'll fail in his efforts. This majestic and harmless bird surely can't be snatched from the freedom of the air!

Yet this is what he's trying to do. He's baited a hook with a fish on the end of a heavy sounding-line, and he flings this into the air – his long legs flailing about the deck with a horrid, jerky vigour, in their flapping white bell-bottomed trousers, his bare feet slapping, the ends of the black kerchief at his throat snapping jauntily in the breeze. The albatross swoops at the bait, and the watchers cheer. The bird misses, but the bald man coils his line for another try.

Once again, the line and gleaming bait climb in the bright blue air; and the albatross turns, its calm and mighty wings outspread, and snatches the hook in its beak.

The sailors roar and shout. The bald man hauls in with grim intensity of purpose, skinny body crouched in its tight blue jacket, long arms furiously working, like a figure in a medieval skeleton dance. And the great bird at the end of the line has lost all dignity; all its lovely grace. Frantic, it flaps and flutters like a broken kite, its huge angelic wings beating uselessly; and when it's pulled across the deck, it screams and screams again, the harsh and pathetic sounds mingling with the laughter and shouts of the men.

Now the bald man has his victim at his feet. Its wings, with their twelve-foot span, have become flapping, ruined sails. For the first time, the bald man smiles, toothless mouth opening with the glee of an ugly infant. He dances lightly about the great, ruined white bird, seeking an opening; then he seizes it by the neck with both bony hands and strangles it, still grinning blankly as he does so.

If I had a gun, I believe I would shoot this human skeleton where he stands.

Instead, I can do nothing but turn away, my eyes blinded by tears. Glanced at by a passing soldier, I stumble down the companionway towards the quarter-deck, and my cabin. There, seated at the table, my head in my arms, I weep as I have wept only once since my arrest, *The Ancient Mariner* chiming in my head again:

> *Ah wretch! said they, the bird to slay,*
> *That made the breeze to blow!*

What is the matter with me? Is my mind breaking down? I'm weeping for a slain bird, and can't stop.

September 30th

For the past twelve days, we've been lying in Simon's Bay, at the Cape of Good Hope.

On the morning of September 18th, soon after we anchored here, the Simon's Bay harbour master appeared on deck. Doctor Richards beckoned me over with a kindly air, and handed me a large packet of letters from home, which the official had brought on board.

Shuffling through them, I looked for only one hand. It was there. Yet even as my heart leaped, I wondered at the fact that her writing appeared on only one envelope; and a fugitive dread began to take shape, at the very core of elation.

I was anxious to get away to my hutch; but Doctor Richards and the harbour master held me in conversation. The harbour master had news of particular interest for me, he said. Eight days ago, a fast man-of-war brig, the *Revenge*, had touched here for provisions – and my Young Ireland comrades had been on board. Alas, I'd just missed them: the *Revenge* had lain here for only two days, and was already on her way to Van Diemen's Land.

This was enormously tantalising; but I doubted that we would have been allowed to meet. Having asked after their health, and been told by the harbour master that all of them had seemed well and in good spirits, I made my escape.

Reaching the cabin at last, I tore open Catherine's letter, scanning the neat round hand I had so long waited for, so long loved.

Within seconds, I knew all was lost. My mouth went dry, and a remorseless, freezing sensation crept through me. What I'd dreaded most in fancy had now become fact.

But what's the point of writing all this down? I've refrained from doing so for these past twelve days; why do so now? What will it serve, to put a red hot iron on a wound that ceaselessly aches? I won't preserve her letter; there's no need to do so. For as long as I live, I'll recall every word. Am I to examine in this journal – as I've done a thousand times in my mind – how she's justified her decision? How she's made my pain more vivid by convincing herself that this decision is actually in my best interests?

No. Enough. Anger will merely be my destroyer, not hers or Terence Butler's; and to hate them both is base.

Over these twelve days, I've even come to see that her feelings and her action might be viewed as justified. More was being asked of this respectable young woman than I had any right to do; more was being asked than she had the character to give. But dear God, even as I try to reproach her in this way, her beauty and delicacy and lost tenderness rise up in front of me, and I know that my efforts to dismiss her are doomed to fail. Let me instead show myself no mercy.

Was it reasonable to ask this gently-reared, refined and intelligent girl to come on my account to the most dreaded of all penal colonies, at the final, savage edge of the world? Was she to set up house with me in some cottage in primeval woods, surrounded by English murderers and thieves? And was she to share with me – perhaps for many years – what she and her family see as my disgrace?

171

No; clearly no: not this young lady.

Catherine!

I will write no more tonight.

⋆ *Dublin,*
June 10th, 1849

Dear Robert,

I have written and rewritten this letter many times, always tearing it up, and always wetting it with my tears. Now it must be sent.

I am glad to hear that you will be given some form of freedom on Van Diemen's Land, but I cannot join you there. I cannot marry you, and must ask you to release me. I have spoken of this many times with my parents, and they agree that my decision is best for us both. They have often begged me to see that your wish that I should make a life with you in a convict colony asks too much of me.

My parents and I have read what we can about Van Diemen's Land, and we learn that most of its population are felons of the lowest kind. We also learn that it is a place of crime and public depravity, with no decent woman safe in the towns, and bandits raiding farms in the countryside. My father is beside himself at the idea of my living there, and I must say to you that I could not imagine our having children in such a place – nor being separated from those dearest to me by half the world. You will think me weak, but I really could not bear it.

You are strong, Robert, and I believe you will even half enjoy such an adventure. Eventually, I'm sure, you'll find a partner in life made of stronger stuff than I; and in the end, I believe you will see that this decision of mine is the right one. We could not have been suited, given your aims and beliefs.

You already know my feelings about your politics. However noble and patriotic your aims may be, it is my view – and that of my family – that you have gone much too far, alarming most moderate and reasonable people, and that you are now paying a price which you cannot in fairness ask me to share with you. Your actions have lost you your home, your rank in society, and your life in this very country you say you love. You can bear all this, since you are a great man, and the world knows it. You'll despise me, I know, for not bearing it with you, and will probably never forgive me. And this thought causes me great pain, since I have truly loved you.

But Robert, I cannot really understand you, or go with you. I can only ask you to forgive me, and accept that what I want from life is something much less noble than the things that you strive for. I want quiet happiness, and safety, and things that are familiar.

And now I must tell you that, for all these reasons, I am considering a marriage proposal from Terence Butler. He is not a hero, as you are, and what I feel for him is simply fondness, not passion. In the end though, this may be best, and

* EDITOR'S NOTE: Despite his stated intention to destroy this letter, Devereux retained two pages of it, which survived in his writing-slope. At this point, it breaks off.

R.B.

October 2nd

We've at last set sail for Van Diemen's Land.

The *Raffles* is moving slowly out from Simon's Bay, headed into a strong, gusty wind. Fourteen weary days we've lain here, twenty miles from Cape Town, surrounded by mountains. The great Table Mountain is visible to the north; soon, like the small colonial town that lies at the head of this bay, it will fade from reality: a thing merely glimpsed, and then gone.

I'm glad now to be alone. I've kept to my cabin, for the most part, and have no more wish for human company. Now and again Doctor Richards makes attempts at conversation on deck; but I answer only briefly. Thank God that at present I can live as a hermit.

Richards brought me English newspapers, two months old. Prussia has stamped out revolution in Germany, and confronts Austria. Distant thunder; mighty events in a dream.

What do I care?

October 10th

At sea.

Our second week out from the Cape, on this grey Southern Ocean, with no sight of land. We go straight before the wind, along the parallel of 46 degrees, south latitude.

I've had no heart to write in this log. A week after sailing, my asthma assailed me again. Doctor Richards is concerned, but can do little to help me. I must place my hope of recovery on our safely reaching Van Diemen's Land, he says, and the beneficial effects of dry land.

Let it be soon. Let me be anywhere but on this sea.

October 18th

At sea; always at sea.

In between bouts with the enemy, I read books on Van Diemen's Land, lent to me by Doctor Richards. Some give accounts of its geography, and contain detailed advice for intending settlers on methods needed for farming there. Others have been written by journalists and travellers to turn a penny, and feature lurid accounts of encounters with blacks and bushrangers.

I learn that this heart-shaped island lies between the parallels of 41 and 43 degrees, and that its extent from north to south is 210 miles, and from east to west 150 miles: an area similar to Ireland. The climate is said to be healthy, without the extremes of heat endured in New South Wales.

I might as well read of Lilliput – which Swift located in this latitude. Does Van Diemen's Land exist? I begin at times to doubt it, though the convicts and soldiers continue to believe so. I've heard them talking: they say that another week should bring us to our island gaol.

I doubt it. I doubt the existence of anything but these huge, long-rolling, Antarctic seas.

October 30th

Very ill and weak.

I grow sick to my soul of this accursed ship, in which I've now lived seven months, and which seems to carry us through eternity.

Very ill now. At night I fight to breathe, and Doctor Richards fears for my life.

They say we are nearing Van Diemen's Land.

November 10th

Landfall: final landfall! I can scarcely believe that I write these words.

Seven weeks after leaving Cape Town, we're lying off the mountainous southern coast of Van Diemen's Land. And this dread penal island is actually beautiful. Nothing had prepared me for its stern, outlandish beauty.

I write this having just come down from the quarter-deck, to which I'll soon return. It's two in the afternoon. We're lying almost becalmed in a broad, serene inlet called the D'Entrecasteaux Channel, which runs between the mainland of Van Diemen's Land on the west, and an island called Bruni – named, like the Channel, after an early French explorer, Rear-Admiral Bruni D'Entrecasteaux. Doctor Richards has been pointing out landmarks to me: he's become a good deal more friendly now that we've reached our journey's end, apparently assuming that the ban on our association has been lifted.

To the north of Bruni, he tells me, we will enter the wide expanse of Storm Bay, and so reach the estuary of a river called the Derwent, running many miles inland, where the harbour of Hobart Town lies. On the eastern side of Storm Bay is the Tasman Peninsula, site of the penal settlement of Port Arthur, where incorrigible convicts are sent: those, that is, who commit further crimes in the colony. That the place is greatly feared I already know; and when Doctor Richards explained the nature of its location, I could only admire the genius of the British penal administrators.

To escape from Port Arthur is almost impossible. Should any poor wretch flee northwards, he comes to a slender neck of land joining the Tasman Peninsula to yet another peninsula, across which vicious dogs have been chained at distances of six feet apart. And if he goes south, he comes to the coast at Cape Raoul, where the seas of the chill Southern Ocean boil up the rocks to draw him down. This extraordinary headland, which I've seen in an engraving in one of the Doctor's books on the island, is a phenomenon that the artist clearly found grand. But to me it looked nothing but grim: a structure from nightmare, consisting entirely of perpendicular columns of black basalt rock, rising some thousand feet above the sea. It resembles the work of man, rather than of nature: a temple, perhaps, built by some race of Antipodean Titans. But this is a cruel deception: there are no civilized structures on that stony coast, and never have been. There is nothing there at all; and nothing lies beyond it but the wastes of Antarctica. I'm told by Doctor Richards that one poor soul did try to escape in the direction of Cape Raoul, and left his bones on the rocks.

Approaching Van Diemen's Land from the west this morning, through seas notorious for their destruction of ships, under tall, fast-moving clouds that eternally brew storms, we sighted a coast as forbidding in its way as the engraving of Cape Raoul. This was the island's south-western tip.

I went out and stood with Doctor Richards on the slippery quarter-deck, clinging to the rail as the ship tacked eastwards under close-reefed topsails, through mountainous, dark blue billows of a size I found terrifying. They bore down on the ship as though to engulf her; they broke across her decks, which leaned at an angle of some forty degrees; we plunged into valleys between them from which it seemed impossible to escape, and then climbed groaning to their crests – at which point I believed that I would never be a prisoner on Van Diemen's Land, but would find my grave off her coast; but Langford had been right about the qualities of the *Raffles*, and she heeled and plunged on without harm. We passed a headland called South West Cape, and I viewed the coast through the Doctor's glass. Light rain was falling – as it apparently falls on this side of the island for most of the year, carried by the Westerlies from Cape Horn. No attempt has been made to settle the region, and I have never seen a landscape more desolate. The nearest resemblance I could think of was the far north of Scotland, near Skye. In the distance were dark blue peaks, one of them topped with snow, while close at hand were low, round hills of green and brown heath, gleaming with quartzite, and empty of any sign of life. On the stony shore, the waves exploded in white violence. Albatrosses wheeled, and rode on the waves.

Wild! Wild! Here was the world's end, on this rim of the Roaring Forties. Here were the walls that would pen me in – together with all the other felons who'd been carried here, sixteen thousand miles from their wives, children and parents; from their sweethearts and their trollops; from their reeking, reassuring taverns and their friends; from their dog fights and their poaching; from huddled alleyways and fragrant country lanes; from everything that was known, normal or consoling. Many of the convicts must weep on seeing this coast – which irresistibly suggests a prison. When forests appeared along the shore, these too were like a prison, resembling dark olive ramparts. Opaque, sulking and monotonous, they instantly induced despair.

I called out in jest to Doctor Richards, above the shrieking wind. If this was the door to Van Diemen's Land, I said, then surely all hope must be abandoned.

But he smiled his tight smile, and told me there were better scenes to come. In this, thank God, he's proved to be right.

An hour later: three in the afternoon. Back in the cabin, having been on deck again. Writing here helps me to contain my excitement, and my huge impatience to be ashore.

We're still becalmed in the Channel. November is Spring, here in the Antipodes, and the air is clear and bracing as the air of home. I've just returned from the quarter-deck, where simply to breathe has been intoxicating.

The landscape here is very different from that of the empty south-western coast. It's of an almost pastoral beauty – though strange. The water of this channel, glassy as a lake, reflects the promontories that come down to it. The afternoon is clear and still, and the mild sun of this inverted temperate zone has a precious quality, like some rare, golden liquor distilled over time, every drop of which should be savoured. Intoxicating smells float across the water: a pot-pourri of the alien and familiar.

Land! The beloved, rank yet subtle odour of Gaea herself, for whose great body I've yearned so long: an odour overlaid with sharp, unfamiliar scents. The evergreen trees, which are eucalypts, are near enough to be discerned, on one of the virgin headlands. Apparently they shed not their leaves, but their bark, which hangs in long strips like torn and tattered clothing – giving them the look of a crowd of shabby, disreputable giants. As I stood on deck, dark green, densely wooded hills and headlands confronted me like a mask, their foliage not soft, like the foliage of Europe, but oddly hard and polished, glinting like the surface of a pool. Everywhere were hills and peaks, green and then dark blue: for this is one of the most mountainous islands on earth.

The *Raffles* moved by inches through flat, silver-blue water, as though the island were entranced, and we had sailed into that trance. Over the few hundred yards between us and the shore, the calls of the forest birds came, breaking the prehistoric silence. These were harsh, somewhat jarring calls, with little melody in them; when they died, a silent harmony was resumed.

So still was it here that even the idling and curious convicts down on the main deck had grown quiet, and leaned on the rails in a spell, in their arrowed shirts, staring at the wooded shore of their new home as though to decipher its secrets. I did the same.

We were about to enter the Derwent's broad estuary. For now, there was no sign of life on either shore. We'd passed some fragmentary, distant huts on Bruni Island at one stage, with a few small boats anchored off-shore; but these hints of civilization were now out of sight. It was all as virgin as the day that D'Entrecasteux sailed here – and probably more silent, since that eighteenth-century admiral would have seen on the beaches some of the island's dark, diminutive aboriginal race: a race who fought the later British settlers fiercely at first, according to Doctor Richards' books, but who have now been hunted nearly to extinction. Only a handful are left, the surgeon tells me – kept on a settlement here in the Channel, dressed in the white man's clothing, their hunting grounds lost for ever. Merciless Empire!

I'm eager to be up on deck again. Within hours, perhaps, I'll be free of this rocking wooden prison.

Four-thirty. Have just come down again from the quarter-deck, where I was engaged in conversation with Doctor Richards.

We'd come to the head of the Channel when I made my way above, and had dropped anchor to take a pilot on board. The whole wide, milky-blue expanse of the estuary had opened up before us, under a sky of tall white clouds. On our right, and to the north-east, were distances of hills: soft, blue and tender as any in Ireland, and seemingly going off to infinity. Were I not in exile, I could almost fall in love with these hills. The pilot's timber cottage, on the steep western shore, was neat and homely. White-painted, with two storeys, and a green lawn in front, bordered with a sweetbriar hedge, it could have been in Cork. Doctor Richards pointed out the figure of the blue-clad pilot, who was making his way down some steps to a boat-pier at the bottom of the garden.

– He will take us up to Hobart Town, Richards said.

It was almost as though he spoke reassuringly to a sick child, whose ordeal was nearly over; and I was reminded that my appearance, although I'm lately feeling better, has become somewhat alarming. I'm once again very weak, and have lost nearly two stone in weight: when I appear on deck, the officers look at me as though I'm an apparition. Doctor Richards, for his part, contemplates me with a scarcely-veiled anxiety, and I believe he'll be very relieved to see me safe on shore, and off his hands. Indeed, in my inmost heart, I know that I've reached this island just in time to cheat death.

– You mustn't count on going ashore for at least another day, Doctor Richards said. Much official business has to be done before you'll know your fate. Much red tape. A special despatch must go to the Governor.

He gestured towards the convicts milling about the main deck.

– Your case isn't as simple as that of *those* villains, he said.

The felons below were an extraordinary sight. Soon, they'd be granted the freedom of their Tickets-of-Leave, and a simmering excitement was brewing. Given leave to do so, a good many had now discarded prison garb, and had donned their finery: clothes obtained at Bermuda, and hoarded until now. I seemed to be looking at a main thoroughfare in Whitechapel or Seven Dials, on a Saturday night. Villainous, toothless faces laughed from under tall round hats and raffish caps; dwarfish figures strutted in fustian and corduroy, and even in frock coats. Some of the coats and hats were more expensive than anything in my own wardrobe. Cravats and neck-ties of wonderful colours abounded. One hulking fellow with a broken nose wore a plum-coloured tail coat with a velvet collar and white trousers, and carried a bamboo cane which he twirled, to the applauding laughter of his mates. Even the watching soldiers grinned tolerantly. It was becoming a sort of carnival; voices rose in yelps of dog-like excitement. But here and there one detected quiet, self-respecting men in plain, sober dress, who stood apart from the revelry.

One of these was Langford – who'd no longer been sent to wait on me since we left Pernambuco, and whom I'd scarcely seen for months.

His appearance startled me: not because of any ostentation, but the reverse. He wore a dark, plain suit of good cut and quality, and he looked – how shall I put it? – like a gentleman. A self-made gentleman, perhaps, but nevertheless a man one would respect. He stood alone at the rail, his eyes narrowed, looking towards the shore; and I wondered what he was thinking. I wanted very much to see him again when we got ashore, and wondered if I'd find him. Rather sadly, I reflected that by the time I was released, Langford would probably have disappeared into whatever life it was he sought in Van Diemen's Land. We would find our different levels, and society would separate us, in spite of what he'd said when we left Bermuda.

Doctor Richards was continuing to talk about the convicts.

– Most will be at liberty tonight, he said, and drunk in Hobart Town's dockside taverns. Did you know that many of the strongest of them will be recruited as police constables before they even leave the ship? It's the practice here.

A faintly ironical, contemptuous note had crept into his voice.

– Yes, he said, in a few days, the worst of our *Raffles* ruffians will be dressed in blue, carrying carbines, and lording it over *you*, Mr Devereux.

He pointed.

– We're almost there. You could not be more southerly than this town – and whaling makes it a rough and noisy one. All the whalers come here now: Yankees and Norwegians as well as our own. It rivals New Bedford, and its whalers and merchants grow rich. I dare say you'll find it colourful – if a little raw.

We had rounded a point, and I almost exclaimed at the scene that opened up: whether because of its exotic grandeur or its contradictory familiarity I couldn't have said.

Ahead, at the western culmination of the broad estuary, loomed a dark blue mountain we had seen in the distance for some time, with a curious fluted peak that was surely the cone of an extinct volcano. At its feet were the ascending smokes of what looked like a well-established, decent little port city in Ireland or England, its houses climbing a set of tall foothills. A battery stood on a point; a red windmill and a stone church tower rose behind. Distantly, on the quays, I made out a reassuring and familiar frieze taken from any sea-port at home: stone warehouses, ordnance stores and taverns, with draught horses drawing laden wagons up to their doors. Behind the city, further up the Derwent in the deepening afternoon light, the rounded, mysterious hills of the still-virginal island rolled into a blue, illimitable distance where I instantly longed to fly. The harbour was crowded with shipping, both sail and steam; and an imperial frigate, the *Meander*, lay in mid-stream. It all had the air of being utterly secure and civilized, and snugly at the centre of things.

Yet this was the last port in the Empire: civilization's outermost limit. I was looking at that college of crime and abominations, Hobart Town.

A red-coated soldier stood guard by the door of the captain's quarters, where Doctor Richards led me at a little after six o'clock. Here, it seemed, my future would be decided.

The *Raffles* was now berthed at Hobart Town's New Wharf. The gaol colony had received its prisoners, the roll having been called on the main deck by officials of the penal government. Only I was left unaccounted for.

The surgeon opened the door and ushered me into the day cabin. There was no-one here but an individual in a sober grey suit, seated at a polished table in front of the sweeping stern windows. This was Mr Laird, the Assistant Comptroller-General of Convicts. Doctor Richards presented me, and it was indicated that I should sit on a chair in front of the table. This I did, blinking through the windows at the estuary in the sunset, with ships riding at anchor as far as the eye could see, and a steamer moving by like a beetle. The surgeon remained standing, hands behind his back.

Mr Laird was studying a document. He frowned at it, as though digesting grave news. Finally he looked up again and spoke.

– Doctor Richards tells me you've been ill, Mr Devereux. I must say you do look ill. Do you think yourself well enough to take up a life ashore here?

– Certainly, I said. Once I'm able to leave this coffin-ship, I expect my health to recover.

His frown returned. The fellow was the perfect public official, and the frown was in keeping. His suit and waistcoat were of excellent cloth, and in the latest cut; he wore a gleaming white choker collar on which his small chin rested, and a tasteful, green-striped cravat, so beautifully knotted that it was difficult to believe that it had been tied by mere mortal fingers. But his own fingers seemed well suited to the task, being white and delicate, like a musician's. His curling brown hair was combed forward over a narrow white brow, and his eyes were so exquisitely cautious and sensitive that they could never remain on one's face for long; they made me feel gross for trying to hold his gaze. This is a characteristic I've noticed in other government officials. He turned now to Doctor Richards.

– And you agree, Doctor?

– I do, Doctor Richards said. When he leaves the confinement of this ship, I expect Mr Devereux's asthma to improve.

Mr Laird turned back to me, and his voice became officially reassuring.

– As a prisoner of state, your case is a special one, he said. Instructions concerning you and the other Irish state prisoners have been forwarded to the Governor of Van Diemen's Land from London. They come from the Secretary of State for the Colonies, Lord Grey. I have them here.

His fingers touched the document with reverence, and his eyes now asked me to be impressed.

– Sir William Denison has passed these instructions on to my superior, the Comptroller-General of Convicts, he said. I am now to acquaint you with them, and to obtain your response.

– Do, I said, and a response will be forthcoming.

His sensitive eyelids fluttered. He glanced at Doctor Richards, who gazed through the stern windows; then he sighed faintly, and continued.

– The Secretary has decided, as he's done in the cases of your fellow-revolutionaries, that your banishment to this colony, and the loss of your station in life, is sufficient punishment in itself for the crime of which you are convicted. Therefore, the conditions of a common convict will not be imposed on you, and a Ticket-of-Leave is to be offered to you.

He watched my face again for a response; failing to see one, he went on.

– This is usually only earned by a prisoner after many years of good behaviour, he said. It means that you will have comparative liberty here, living within the rules imposed by the Ticket. You may purchase land, or seek any honourable employment you wish. You may bring out members of your family. But you may not leave the island.

He paused to see the effect of this, toying with the document, his eyes less evasive now. He was enjoying his moment of power.

– There are certain other restrictions, he said. Firstly: should you prove refractory, or create any disturbance, the Governor may revoke the Ticket, and have you confined in prison. Secondly: this colony being divided into police districts, you must live in a district of your choice – and may not move outside it without the Governor's permission.

He paused again; when he continued, his voice was soft and bland.

– And you may not choose a police district where another Irish state prisoner resides.

I took a deep breath.

– I see. So your Government wishes to keep us from meeting one another.

– I understand it's thought not desirable, he said. But I merely transmit these instructions, Mr Devereux. I make no comment. And what I must tell you finally is that you are perfectly free to accept this offer or reject it.

He spread his fingers on the document, and looked at me directly.

– If you reject it, you must live confined to prison. And if you accept it, you must do so on condition that you provide the Comptroller-General with a letter addressed to the Governor, in which you give your word as a gentleman that *you will not attempt escape from the Colony*. Are you prepared to do that?

I sat absolutely still, thinking. I had little choice, I decided; and I had no intention of keeping the agreement for ever. I told him that I was prepared to write the letter.

Mr Laird smiled; then he asked me to sit down and draft something immediately. He would take it back to the Comptroller of Convicts, he said, and I would be informed of my fate tomorrow morning – when I would probably be able to disembark.

After I'd performed my task with Mr Laird's steel-nibbed pen, he gathered up his documents and left the cabin. Doctor Richards turned to me, his long face serious yet friendly.

– Despite your good fortune, I believe you're disappointed, he said. I imagine you'd hoped to see your comrades.

– Yes, I said. I had hoped so. What do they imagine we'll do, if we meet? Foment a rebellion on Van Diemen's Land?

– The supposition isn't unnatural, he said, given your histories. But take heart, Mr Devereux. I think I can assure you that within a few weeks, despite the official restriction, you'll be joining your friend Mr O'Neill, in the police district of Bothwell. I've written to Sir William Denison requesting it. A few more weeks on this vessel, and I think you might have died. I've pointed this out to the Governor, and am recommending that you remain for a few weeks in Hobart Town, where Doctor Howard is expecting to see you. He can further assess your condition, and you will then almost certainly be placed in the care of your friend O'Neill – who's leasing a cottage in the highlands. There you should stay until such time as your health returns, and you're ready to choose your own district.

My heart was leaping, but I strove to remain impassive. I stood and bowed.

– Thank you, Doctor, I said. I'm much obliged to you.

He waved a dismissive hand.

– Not at all. I simply don't want your death on my conscience. Nor, of course, do the authorities. And now I must leave you, and wish you good afternoon. Before you return to your cabin, you have another official interview, I'm afraid.

He walked to the open door, spoke to the soldier outside, and then disappeared from view.

Instantly, a new figure appeared: a small, very thin man with wiry black hair, a high brow and a sallow, skull-like face, neatly dressed in a blue, tight frock coat that made him appear almost tubular. He must have been lurking there in waiting; when he came in, he carefully closed the door behind him and advanced across the cabin with a scuttling and ingratiating rapidity, his shoulders stooped like those of an old man – though he could not have been out of his thirties. He carried under his arm a large green portfolio, which he laid on the table as though it were made of glass. Then he smiled, and bowed to me with an air of great humility.

– Good afternoon to you, sir, he said. I'm Mr Vincent, Assistant Registrar of Convicts. I shan't trouble you for long. It's my duty to obtain the details of your background. Also your *physical* particulars.

He had a quick, eager voice that ran little above a whisper – as though he brought secret and momentous news. But his parchment-like face with its philosopher's brow, long jaw and dark, sunken eyes put me more and more in mind of a death's head, and the only tidings that I could imagine him bringing would be drear and mournful ones, from the kingdom of the shades. I bowed in return.

– In other words, you wish to compose a prison record for me.

The sunken eyes grew alarmed. They had the naked intensity of a poet's – or perhaps of a man with guilty secrets.

– That is the case, Mr Devereux, yes, he whispered. Be assured that I shall carry out my duties as courteously and discreetly as possible, bearing in mind your position in society. But it's required

185

of me to be extremely accurate. I do hope you'll understand.

I said I'd try, and he gestured towards the chair I'd previously occupied, deferentially asking me to sit down. He then took his place on the other side of the table, opened his portfolio, delicately picked up the steel-nibbed pen, dipped it in the inkwell on the table, and prepared to write.

He began by taking down my biographical particulars: my place of birth, age, profession and religion. Then he produced a tape-measure and discovered my height, requiring me to stand in my stockinged feet against a wall of the cabin: he pronounced me to be five feet eleven inches. Once I was sitting down again, he sat gazing at my face with pen poised, like a painter before his subject. His voice now was so thin and conciliatory that I could only just hear it.

– You'll excuse me sir, he said. I shall get through this as soon as I can, but I really must study you with care. My task is a delicate one – a very delicate one, as I'm sure you'll appreciate.

I said I did, and sat looking out the windows while his whisper informed me of what he saw, and his pen dipped and scratched – painting my portrait in words for the benefit of the Comptroller-General of Convicts, and Britannic tyranny's archives.

– Complexion pale, the whisper said. You are not well, Mr Devereux, and I'm sure you're not always pale – but I must record what I see. Head oval, I think. Hair, brown. Chin, medium. Nose – I think I must say long, Mr Devereux. Your nose is a fine one, but we're limited in the categories we're allowed. Long, then. Eyes, grey. Or should I rather say blue?

I told him to make his own decision, it was all one with me, and he settled on blue. Then he blotted his page, slid it reverently into the portfolio, and stood. Begging my pardon once again for his intrusion, and wishing me good afternoon, he moved backwards to the door like a crab, bowing to me twice as he went.

Now I was recorded. Now I had a ghostly life on paper, in the kingdom of Dis.

PART TWO

CITY OF WOE

Through me you pass into the city of woe:
Through me you pass into eternal pain:
Through me among the people lost for aye.

DANTE ALIGHIERI, 'Inferno', *Canto III,*
translated by Henry Cary

It's often when I slumber
I have a pleasant dream;
With my sweetheart I've been sitting down
Beside a crystal stream.
Through Ireland I've gone roaming
With my sweetheart by the hand;
Then I wake, quite broken-hearted,
Upon Van Diemen's Land.

VAN DIEMEN'S LAND *(old convict song)*

1. EXILES

Hobart Town, Van Diemen's Land
November 11th, 1849

I stand on the New Wharf, waiting for Liam Kinane.

Two of the seamen from the *Raffles* rowed me across here, together with my trunk and portmanteau. Skirting a long line of whaling ships, whose masts and spars receded like winter trees, they named the nationality of each one, glancing benevolently at me from under their wide-brimmed canvas hats. It was as though I were a boy being conducted on a treat: no doubt they were aware that they ferried me to 'comparative freedom'.

After they'd carried my luggage up a set of wooden stairs on to the wharf, and had bidden me goodbye, I stood quite still, staring. I continue to do so, as time congeals around me.

The day is cool and cloudy, with a thin sun breaking through; a brilliant cap of snow has appeared overnight on the mountain. It's exactly like the weather of home; and I begin to be seized by a powerful anticipation. I've been a prisoner for close on seventeen months, never once setting foot on dry land (unless I count the breakwater at Bermuda), and everything I see is remarkable: endearingly familiar, yet new. Re-entering the world, I've become a full-grown infant: a sensation made complete by the sad state of feebleness in which asthma has left me.

On the far side of the roadway are the warehouses and ordnance buildings that I saw from the ship. Drays unload there, bales are hoisted to their lofts by block and tackle, and I watch these activities with mindless delight, standing motionless beside my portmanteau.

In a few more minutes, I'll be moving into the town – going wherever I wish, unsupervised and unwatched – and this simple fact makes me tipsy. My smile must betray it: a merchant in a low-crowned hat glances at me dubiously as he passes.

Land! I've been so long at sea that the ground sways under me like a deck. I want to go down on my knees and kiss it; tears prick my eyes. I love every stone and weed on the roadway, and gaze with fascination at the whale-oil barrels standing on the wharf, and the huge iron try-pots used for melting blubber. Land, and its noises and smells! Hammering, shouts, and the grinding of wheels are sounds from a long-lost life, and I inhale with uncritical delight a pungent brew of odours: fresh-sawn planks, tar, horse-dung, and the stench of whale blubber. The blubber-smell rises over all, like the scent of some monstrously fecund plant: clinging to the rigging of the ships; absorbed into every crevice of the port.

Ten minutes have gone by by, and there's no sign of Kinane; but I find this doesn't concern me. I'm curious about him, and look forward to meeting him, but I'm in no hurry: I inhabit a different scale of time from the world that hurries past me.

Liam Kinane is a comrade, but one I scarcely know. He's a man of the people, and a Catholic. The son of a poor tenant farmer, he gained an education through his own efforts. He once worked as a printer, and was employed as a clerk in a legal firm in Dublin when I encountered him in Young Ireland. I seem to remember his telling me that he had ambitions to become a solicitor, and was studying at night, and I'd been told by others that he was a great reader of philosophy. But his duties at the office and his family responsibilities had left him little time for his studies, it seemed.

I'd not even known that he was in Van Diemen's Land. I learned of it only an hour ago, from Doctor Richards.

The surgeon had appeared in my cabin just after breakfast, to inform me that my Ticket-of-Leave had been granted by the Governor. He was also carrying a letter from Neville Howard – who had asked that he deliver it to me personally. Doctor Howard was leaving Hobart Town this morning, Richards told me, on a visit to the north of the island. Otherwise, he would have come down to the ship to greet me.

– The Colonial Surgeon is a very good friend to you, Richards said. And a powerful one, as well. He was entirely sympathetic to the idea of your joining O'Neill at Bothwell. He and I last night attended a dinner given by the Governor – and we spoke with Sir William afterwards about this proposal. Sir William gave his consent immediately, since he holds Doctor Howard in high esteem.

He cleared his throat, and his tone became delicate.

– Do you have money in the colony?

I said I did. A letter from home at Cape Town had confirmed that a letter of credit, providing me with ample funds, had been forwarded some time ago from my bank in Dublin to the Bank of Van Diemen's Land, and was being held here pending my arrival.

– Good, the surgeon said, and nodded approvingly. That should make your life here quite tolerable. Doctor Howard tells me that he's personally arranged lodgings for you. The address will be in his letter. As I expected, you're given leave to remain in Hobart Town until you can move to Bothwell. This is also a favour from the Governor – since in this town, you'll be temporarily in the same police district as another state prisoner.

I asked him who this was – hoping against hope that it would prove to be Paul Barry.

– Your friend Mr Liam Kinane, he said.

At this I was both surprised and disappointed.

– Kinane is hardly a friend, I said. An acquaintance, merely.

– But he's a fellow-rebel, is he not? A member of your movement?

– He's a member of Young Ireland, yes – and a friend of Mr Fitzgibbon's.

– Yes. And I understand he assisted Mr Fitzgibbon in his acts of rebellion – for which he was recently tried and sentenced, and transported with Mr Fitzgibbon and the others on the *Revenge*.

– I wasn't aware of that. Well, I honour him for it.

Doctor Richards took refuge then, as he often did, in a study of the backs of his hands.

– Yes, he said, I'm sure. At any rate, Mr Kinane seems to feel a friendly responsibility towards you. He'll be waiting on the quay when you disembark, and has sent messages to the ship that he wishes to convey you to your lodgings, and get you settled in here. We see no objection to that. He'll also take you to the Police Office, where your Ticket-of-Leave will be waiting for you. It's important that you keep this on your person, to be shown to the police on demand.

– I'm well looked after, I said.

– I hope you may continue to be, he said. And I hope that eventually you'll be pardoned, Mr Devereux, and find your way home. Your exile here will be comfortable, I'm sure – but no man would wish for exile. Goodbye to you.

I've not had time to open Doctor Howard's letter until now. It carries yesterday's date, and is headed: *Bay House, New Town*. It's brief but cordial. Howard is pleased and relieved, he says, that the *Raffles* has arrived safely. He understands from Doctor Richards that I've arrived not a day too soon, and that my life has been in some danger. He'll now do all he can to see that I'm permitted to recover my health, in the bracing air of the highlands. He's sorry, he says, not to have come to the ship to greet me, but he thinks it best to remain in the background until my official position is decided. Meanwhile, he's arranged 'respectable' lodgings for me – and gives the address. Despite the fact that I've come here unwillingly, Howard says, he hopes I'll find the island as beautiful as he does. He's acquired a house that's 'much too spacious for a bachelor', and he trusts that when he returns to town, I'll visit him there. Will Sunday be suitable? Perhaps we'll resume our stimulating debates. He's found himself missing them.

It seems that Doctor Howard is determined to stay in my life, and to act as my guardian angel. And I find myself wondering, as I did on Bermuda, whether this interest is entirely unambiguous. Its immediate effect on my situation as a prisoner is certainly agreeable. I'll no doubt discover in good time whether it has a price.

I hear a sudden shout to my right: someone is calling my name.

A four-wheeled open cab is rattling along the quay from the direction of the city, its two passengers waving to me. One I recognise as Liam Kinane: he's a big man, and his size and his florid face make him unmistakable. But the bearded cab-driver on his perch in front is half-obscuring the other passenger, so that at first, I can't identify him. Then the landau halts beside me, creaking and jingling. The driver leans back to rein in his pair of horses, and the passengers smile down on me.

One is Kinane, sure enough. The other is Matthew Casey.

For a few seconds, none of us speaks. The noises of the wharf recede, giving way to silence. I gape at Casey, not quite believing what I see. He's far better dressed than when he came to me on Spike Island, and wears a grey, low-crowned round hat of fine quality. Grinning, he raises one hand to the brim in salutation, the fingers loose; but the pose has an awkwardness about it as though it's imitated, and not quite mastered.

I draw breath to greet him; but I'm given no time. Kinane leaps from the cab and advances on me, huge red hand outstretched.

– Devereux! Welcome, man, welcome! 'Tis a joy and a delight to see you!

He has a strong Wicklow accent, and says 'deloight'. Well over six feet tall, he stoops a little to peer at me, grasping my hand. His tall black beaver hat with its narrow brim is also a reminder of his origins, being of the type that's favoured by men of the peasantry at home: battered and dented, it balances precariously on his mass of curling dark hair. The rest of his outfit is not unlike a collection of garments picked up off old clothes stalls, and put together incongruously: a rusty brown tail coat, somewhat the worse for wear, green neckerchief, check waistcoat, and light summer trousers. Altogether, a somewhat raffish figure; but his smile is joyous and boyishly unaffected, his florid face glows, and his enthusiasm is plainly genuine – despite the fact that he and I have only met two or three times, at meetings of the Confederation in Dublin. He holds my hand in both of his, pumping it up and down repeatedly, and gazing into my face. Meanwhile, Casey watches us, still seated in the cab, his eyes behind their spectacles searching out mine with a sly, ironical intimacy, as much as to say: *Here I am again. You knew I'd be here, didn't you?*

I'm impatient to greet and question him; but Kinane prevents me, continuing to hold my hand and to make his speech of welcome. He speaks so rapidly that he stammers, telling me how glad he is that I've survived the voyage, and how glad all Ireland will be. Although he's somewhere in his late thirties, he has a boy's eagerness and enthusiasm. I believe I smell brandy on his breath, which perhaps accounts for his vivacity; but it would be churlish not to respond with the same warmth. So I curb my impatience to speak to Casey, and tell Kinane it does me good to see him, and how pleased I am that he's come here to meet me.

– No need to thank me, he says. No need, no need. An honour, Devereux.

Then he frowns, leaning backwards to study me better.

– But Jesus and Mary, what have those English buggers done to you? God rot the sons of bitches! We knew you'd been ill, but this is bloody monstrous. You're wasted to a shadow, man! Did they starve you, on that God-damned hulk?

I tell him that my asthma has been bad, but that I expect to recover my appetite now that I'm on dry land. He's about to begin another speech, but I turn now to Casey, who has climbed down from the cab and is extending his hand.

– My dear Casey, I say. What can this mean? Surely you've not been transported?

My words instantly sound fatuous to me, and perhaps to him too; his smile widens as we shake hands. But something flashes in his eyes that I can't read, and which I put down to embarrassment.

– No, sir, he says. I don't share that distinction with you and your comrades. I paid my own passage.

– You came of your own volition? To *this* place? You do amaze me. In the last letter that reached me on Bermuda, you said nothing of such a plan. Have you been in some trouble at home?

– Not trouble of the kind *you've* suffered, Devereux.

He pauses, looking at me with a pleasant but enigmatic expression, twirling the watch-chain on his waistcoat. It's a fine, double-breasted waistcoat, very much in fashion, like his hat, and swelled by his small paunch. His black tie is also fashionable, being extremely narrow and tied in a bow; so are his dark green tail coat and grey nankeen trousers. He really does look very different from the man I remember; yet somehow, he still isn't stylish: although these fine clothes fit him quite well, he appears like a man who's been lent someone else's.

– I decided to emigrate, he says. At first I considered America – but then I thought: what better place than this colony, where so many of our circle have been forced to come? I've secured a post on an excellent newspaper here: the *Hobart Town Independent*. The editor, Mr Davis, is very sympathetic to the Irish cause, having family connections in Dublin. He's given Kinane here employment as well, working as a printer.

– And very glad of it I was, Kinane says. It's lucky I learned the trade as a boy – otherwise I'd have had to remain in the Campbell Street Penitentiary, since I've no money at all.

– Davis has been very generous, Casey says. The *Independent* pays me far better than my journal at home did. And they want me to write a piece about you, Devereux. But we'll talk of that later. Now we must get a dray for your luggage. It can go straight up to your lodgings – we'll follow after in the cab, when we've made our calls.

– Sure. I'll find a drayman, Kinane says quickly. You gentlemen wait here – you'll have much to talk about.

He hurries away across the quay towards the warehouses, ponderous in his heavy boots, head extended downwards and forwards, like that of a charging bull. The stovepipe hat tilts precariously; he snatches it off and carries it, freeing his bouncing dark curls.

Casey and I look at each other, standing by a wheel of the carriage in the bright, peaceful air. Above us on his box, the grey-bearded cabman sits staring into space, smoking a short pipe.

– Well now, Casey, I say. Won't you be frank with me?

He raises his eyebrows.

– Frank, sir? What do you mean?

– I mean that I find it hard to believe that you chose this place over America in order to contemplate the fate of Young Ireland, I say. And as to a career in journalism – you're hardly at the centre of events in Van Diemen's Land, are you? For God's sake, man, we're almost off the bloody map here.

He pulls at his lower lip.

– Astute and direct as always, sir – I should have remembered, there's no other way to be with you but frank. How can I explain? When the sentences were carried out on our friends, I grew curious about this colony. I read, and I made enquiries, and I began to understand that its fearsome reputation is exaggerated, and only half of the truth. And the fact that it was chosen as your place of exile *did* have an influence on me – believe me, Devereux. Your friendship – and that of O'Neill and Barry and Kinane as well – means much to me. I hope it will grow stronger here. I also hope that in some small way, I can use my freedom and my position to serve you all, and to act on your behalf.

He gazes at me now with an expression that appears genuinely moved, his eyes a little red. He takes out a handkerchief, blows his nose, and his voice sinks to a melancholy murmur.

– But of course, Robert, what made me decide on this course in the first place was something much more personal. It had to do with my great unhappiness over a certain lady. I'd hoped to marry her – but my hopes were shattered. So I needed a fresh start, in another world.

He is looking away over the roadway; in front of one of the warehouses, Kinane can be seen talking to a man beside a horse-drawn dray.

– Yes, another world, Casey repeats softly. I believe you'll understand this better than most men, since our situations are similar. May I say, my dear Devereux, how deeply sad I was to hear of your broken engagement? And permit me to say too that the lady proved not to have the strength of character to be worthy of you.

– I prefer not to discuss it, I say.

– I understand, Casey says. Our grief is the same.

To this I say nothing. We stay silent for some moments, eyes bent to the ground. Then Casey looks up again, his face brightening. He removes his hat, which he waves in a general gesture at the estuary, the city on its hills, and the blue, looming mountain with its cap of snow.

– Look at it sir, he says. Hobart Town. Isn't it fine? I've been here now for over four months, and Van Diemen's Land has exceeded my expectations. The climate is superb: bracing yet temperate. A wretched penal colony it may be for the creatures from Britain's gaols, but for those who come here free, and who have sufficient funds – I tell you, it's a little Paradise. And that will be *your* position, Devereux. Let me assure you, you'll be received on terms of absolute equality by the best people in the colony, and will not be seen in any way as a criminal – except of course by servants of the Government.

I laugh.

– To be received on terms of equality by Van Diemen's Land society! What a dazzling prospect you offer me, Matthew.

His face falls, and I lay a hand on his shoulder.

– I'm sorry, my dear fellow – you mean well, and I appreciate it. And certainly life here sounds tolerable – for the time being.

He glances at me sideways.

– For the time being, sir? Do you still hope for a quick pardon? I'm afraid it may take time.

– They can keep their humbug of a damned British pardon, I say. If I must, I'll leave without it.

He frowns.

– But you've given your written word not to escape – have you not?

I look at him in surprise.

– I have. But how did you know that?

– You wouldn't be standing here had you not done so, sir. I know because it was demanded of the others, three weeks ago. Barry and O'Neill agreed, and are free. Martin Fitzgibbon would not, and is confined at Port Arthur.

I stare at him.

– At Port Arthur! Jesus Christ, Matthew – why? Why would Fitzgibbon refuse their damned Ticket?

– Let Kinane tell you about that, he says. He's very close to Martin Fitzgibbon, as you'll realise. Here he comes now. He's eager

197

to speak to you about Fitzgibbon, and much else besides. He's a man of much eagerness, is Liam.

The three of us climb into the cab, which rattles and jingles away along the wharf, and out on to a broad, well-made roadway. Flanked by warehouses and timber yards, this road winds up a low rise, leading to the centre of the town. There, Kinane tells me, we must call at the Police Office, and I'll be able to collect that sacred document, my Ticket-of-Leave.

Casey and I sit side by side, facing forward. Kinane hunches opposite, on a single seat that seems too small for him, his back to the driver. Bright, clear sun has come out, delicious on my face. It's wonderful to smell horses again, and to breathe the land's dry air, and to hear the land-sounds it carries, above the grinding wheels of the cab. But I'm unable to give myself up to these sensations for long, because Kinane is talking to me. He talks almost constantly, and certainly there's brandy on his breath, despite the early hour. I smell it when he leans towards me, as he's doing now.

– So you wrote to the bloody tyrant Denison, and you promised not to abscond – just as Barry, O'Neill and I have done.

This is a rhetorical statement: I've already confirmed it for him, and he nods.

– Good! he says. Good! Sure, it gives you freedom to move until you can make your plans. I see nothing dishonourable in that. Would to God that Martin Fitzgibbon could see it the same way. But he won't. Proud and honourable man that he is – he won't! And so he rots down there at Port Arthur, a prisoner in a bloody little cottage with a few feet of garden, spied on by bloody guards.

He shakes his head, compressing his lips, his eyes fixed insistently on mine. They seem to implore me to find some answer to Fitzgibbon's plight.

– At least he's not confined in the penitentiary, I say. But in God's name, why has Martin put himself in this position? He has only to write the letter they require to be out of there immediately. Has he told you his reasons for not doing so? Is he allowed to correspond with you?

Kinane looks grave and judicious.

– They do let him receive mail, he says. They open his letters, though, the long-nosed English bastards – so you must remember that everything you write to him yourself will be read by spies of the Government. Yes, I've had a letter, giving me his reasons. Those reasons make me proud of him – but they also make me sad. Ah, sure, Martin Fitzgibbon's made of finer stuff than most of us – as well you'll know! But I can't help feeling that he's mistaken.

I interrupt his flow.

– Can you tell me then, in simple terms, what his reasons are?

Hands on knees, straightening his back, Kinane throws back his head to survey me – endangering the balance of his beaver in doing so. He seems to draw about himself a cloak of nobility on his hero's behalf, and his rhetorical tone grows more heightened: almost bardic. He raises a forefinger.

– I can, he says. I can, and history should record them. Fitzgibbon says he'll give no assurance that he'll not attempt escape, since he has every intention of doing so. What he has told the tyrants is this – and I remember his words well, since he put them in his letter to me: 'I cannot, in honour, enter into an engagement with you that I intend to break. You are my unlawful captors, and I will therefore make no agreement with you whatsoever.'

He smiles; but then tears spring to his eyes. He takes out a handkerchief and blows his nose hard.

– May God and all the saints protect him, he says, in a muffled voice. He sits in that God-damned hut, in that savage place, surrounded by the worst of English criminals and their cruel, buggering gaolers – badly fed, and not allowed enough exercise to keep up his health. A man of *his* quality! He's not been there two weeks, but in the letter he's written he sounds very low in his spirits. Sure, he's in my mind constantly. You must do something, Devereux! He'll listen to you.

– I'm not sure that he will, I say. I admire Martin greatly; I admire his courage. But he and I never did agree over tactics. He was always a stiff-necked man, and I think in this case he's giving himself grief for nothing. He's allowing the British to confine and

199

torment him to no good purpose – and it's the purpose we wish to achieve that we must constantly think of, Kinane. We're engaged in a war, remember, with no quarter given. We must use any tactic we can, in order to give ourselves freedom to act.

Kinane slaps his knee, his eyes now shining with enthusiasm, and his deep voice rises.

– Just what *I* say! And this was the way that Barry and O'Neill saw it too. Ah, Devereux, I'm so glad you're here – it does me good to listen to you! You and Barry and Fitzgibbon are our greatest leaders – the ones Young Ireland looks to, and whom all Ireland waits on. But although Fitzgibbon is a great patriot, he's almost too fine for this world – I've always said it. He's never a coward, he's shown that – yet he hates the thought of bloodshed and struggle. But *you*, Devereux! You're our fighting captain! It's you who called us to arms! You'll give these bastards no quarter!

He's gazing at me with open admiration – but I fail to respond with the pleasure he might wish for. Flattery of this kind – however well-meant – tends to make me stiffen and close up. I also find his rhetoric overblown; and catching Matthew Casey's glance, in which I detect a gleam of indulgent amusement, I suspect that Casey does too.

– I scarcely know Martin Fitzgibbon, Casey puts in. I met him only once – and then very briefly. Of course I respect his nobility of character. But I believe you're right, Devereux: he's placed himself in a hopeless situation, to no avail – and he's seen in some quarters as deliberately trying to make himself into a martyr. Sir William Denison detests him for it, I'm told. So I'm very glad, sir, that *you* didn't take that course.

He looks at Kinane.

– For the time being, at least, Devereux must do nothing to annoy the authorities. He needs time to recover from his trials and his illness.

– Of course, of course, Kinane says.

The cab jolts over a rut, and he claps a hand to his hat.

– But once he's better – then we'll see the sparks fly. Eh, Devereux?

He winks at me, and waits expectantly.

– I have no plans at present, I say. I'm waiting to talk to O'Neill – and Barry too, I hope.

– Aye, Kinane says. A council of war. I understand.

He licks his lips, leaning forward eagerly, and another gust of brandy reaches me.

– You're the ones to decide what's best, of course: I'm just a foot soldier, I know. But anything you want me to do, I'll do – whatever the risk, at any time. You'll not forget that, will you?

– Of course not, Kinane, I say. I know we can depend on you.

– You can, and it's an honour and a joy to me, Kinane says. It's all for Ireland, and freedom! All for the Holy Ground.

Chin tilted, he seems to await applause; but I merely nod, and he goes on.

– I've not been idle, Devereux, in these two weeks I've been here: I've a scheme I can't wait to tell you about. Something *you* might undertake here – and that I could help you with. Something that will make the bloody British sit up.

He's leaning even closer, in the landau's cramped quarters, his face mere inches from mine. It has a coarse, masculine handsomeness, this large, plebeian face with its broad forehead, broad nose, and soulful blue eyes, with their slanting lids: he puts me in mind of the typical Irish police detective, except that his face has much more intelligence. He's clean-shaven, but his strong chin is blue with the shadow of a heavy beard, and there's a pouchiness about the eyes and a redness in the nose that betray a weakness for the bottle. I know him to be passionately idealistic – his support of Fitzgibbon in the hopeless rising at Ballingarry proves that – but he's beginning to make me uneasy. He's too big, too loud, too ingenuous, and clearly half drunk. I try not to show my feelings, however, and ask him what his scheme might be.

– A newspaper! he says, and sits back in his seat with a look of triumph. He snatches off his insecure hat and nurses it on his knees, his dark curls moving in the wind of our passage.

I look at him stupidly.

– A newspaper?

– Sure, a newspaper, he says. A newspaper to be the voice of the Irish people, here in Van Diemen's Land! A weekly newspaper that *you* would edit, Devereux! *The Irish Exile*, I thought we might call it. I'd be the printer – and contribute articles too, if you'd let me. I'd hope to see Barry and O'Neill contribute – and maybe Matthew Casey here as well. What do you think, now?

I glance at Casey, whose face in profile tells nothing; he's watching Kinane. I would laugh, were I not appalled. The thing is grotesque: an absurdity.

– And who would finance this paper?

– Mr Davis at the *Independent* would put some money into it, he says. I have a promise from him. But it'd soon pay for itself, I swear. There's a big enough Irish population to support it – and we'd be bound to get advertising. People are starved for reading here. Sure, it's a great place for newspapers.

Wordless, I look at Casey again, who gives me an enigmatic smile.

– That's true, he says. There are five of them running at present. You must remember that any English journals we read here are up to three months out of date – so the local ones do well. And a fairly wide range of views is tolerated – including criticism of the Government.

He says no more, and I turn back to Kinane.

– And what would be the purpose of this newspaper?

He gapes at me.

– The purpose? Why –

But I let him get no further.

– You say it would be the voice of the Irish in this penal colony. With what aim in view? Do you seriously imagine that we could call for Irish freedom *here*, or protest the wrongs that have been done to us? Are you asking me to believe that the convict authorities would permit such a thing for a moment? That they wouldn't immediately close such a paper down?

He thrusts out his lips, like a boy reproved.

– I don't say that we can openly call for rebellion, no, he says. But if we keep within limits, there are many things we can discuss that will give heart to our people here, and acquaint them with issues that affect us. We could report on the situation of Fitzgibbon, for instance. We could act as a watch dog.

– I see. Well, I'm sorry, Kinane, but I must tell you that I see no use in such a thing whatsoever.

He stares at me, and for once he seems at a loss for words. I lean towards him, and attempt to keep my tone kindly; but I doubt that I entirely succeed. Out of the corner of my eye, I see Casey watching me intently.

– We're here as prisoners, for demanding Irish freedom, I say. And my resolve is never to forget that. This island is our gaol, whatever little pantomime of liberty may be allowed us by the English – and in my view, we must hope and plan constantly for our return to Europe, where the true fight will be carried forward. If we lose sight of that, the English will have achieved their aim – don't you *see*, Kinane? We'll have become like Ulysses and his men, on the isle of the lotus-eaters – drugged with an illusion of ease and freedom, playing the game they want, and content never to return.

I take a deep breath, and sit back.

– Well, be damned to that, I say. I understand your good intentions, my dear fellow, but I have no interest at all in running a newspaper in a gaol, by courtesy of my gaolers.

He sets his mouth stubbornly, staring.

– I see what you're saying, he says. I respect the power of your purpose, Devereux, and I know you look always at the highest goals. But as long as you're here, could you not do good with such a paper, and give us a voice? As you did with the *New Nation*?

I shake my head.

– I ran the *New Nation* to educate the people of Ireland in preparation for nationhood, I say. To show them exactly how the English are maintaining their tyranny, and to call on them to resist –

Kinane's eyes, fixed on my face, light up again, and he interrupts me.

– And we all know how gloriously you did it, he says. I still have the best of your articles: I've kept them, and brought them with me. They've inspired me as nothing else has – as they've inspired so many others. Ah, Devereux, will you not publish for us

203

here? Will you really let yourself be silenced? Maybe you'll change your mind.

– No, I say. We have no such audience here as we have in Ireland – and no such purposes could be pursued as those of the *New Nation*. It would do no good, Kinane, and could even threaten our position – I beg you to realise that.

But I see from his wistful gaze that my speech has failed to convince him. He's loath to give up his toy: he needs it to sustain his hopes in this place, and my heart sinks a little. But there's no use pursuing the matter now; we're already approaching the Police Office.

It has taken us only a few minutes to get here, so close is the centre of the city to the masts and spars of the docks. We sway north up a road called Murray Street, which I examine in some surprise.

I don't know what I've expected, in a town on the edge of nothingness – but certainly not the permanence I now see. The Police Office, on our right, is one of a group of solid public buildings constructed of pale yellow sandstone – the others being the Criminal Court and the Treasury. Their style is a sort of simple colonial Regency, with classical porticoes and pilastered windows, and they don't lift the spirits. This is the colony's administrative heart; and since the colony's main business is punishment, Murray Street has a sombre air. Even the Roman cypresses that stand by the portals of the Court have a dark, oppressive look, like mercenary guards from the other hemisphere; and the Court stares across the street at the Hobart Town Gaol. This is a massive structure with a high, red brick wall, topped by iron spikes. Beside its wooden gates, hooded hansom cabs stand waiting for trade: copies of the hansoms of London, with tall-hatted Cockney drivers. Above the wall, a set of gibbets can be seen, and Kinane points at them.

– This is where they do the hangings, he tells me. Sometimes they string the bushrangers up in rows, poor devils, like tassels on a blind. And the bloody gentry sit and view the show, from the Court and Treasury windows.

Our cab draws up outside the Police Office. Here we're

watched by a small crowd, standing on the footpath in front of the entrance. As we halt, they begin to surge forward: perhaps a score of men and women. They gaze at us directly, smiling and gesticulating, and I begin to see from their faces that most of them are Irish. The men are waving their headgear: a mixture of beavers and the local palm-leaf hats. Some of the women are in flower-trimmed bonnets, but others have shawls over their heads, in the peasant manner. They all cheer – and to my amazement, they seem to be cheering us.

To my greater amazement, Kinane now stands up in the carriage and waves his hat back at them. Then he begins to shout, in his hoarse yet powerful voice.

– Aye, he's here! Robert Devereux's here! Three cheers for Ireland's greatest son! Three cheers for the leader of Young Ireland! *Erin-go-bragh!*

I reach up and grip his arm, remaining in my seat.

– Christ, man, I say. What are you doing? Are you trying to get us all arrested?

He turns, his ruddy face exultant, and smiles down on me.

– No, no, you don't understand, Devereux, he says. They're here for *you!* These are some of Hobart Town's Irish – and they're waiting to welcome you!

– Here? Outside the Police Office?

I'm half-laughing, and half-angry. By the portico, I can see two police constables in dark blue uniforms, thumbs hooked in their belts, watching the scene. But they make no move towards the crowd. Instead, to my surprise, they merely stare, with placid curiosity. Kinane remains standing, while the group surrounds the cab.

– Don't concern yourself, Devereux, he says. There'll be no trouble. They'll not cause a riot – they just want to greet you. The bloody police can't stop them doing that.

Now I hear the crowd call my name, and see their shining eyes fixed on me. I glance enquiringly at Casey. He's watching me with the same self-contained smile that he's worn for some time, and I have the impression he's enjoying some joke at my expense.

– The price of fame, sir, he says.

At this moment, the crowd begins to sing. A number of them –
those able to read, I suppose – are squinting at tattered broadsheets,
on which the words of their song are printed; and one of these is
thrust into my hand. I hadn't known I was already figuring in street
ballads. The well-meant words and sentiments are even more
embarrassing on the printed page than they sound bellowed out in
the street, since the brogue of my followers makes a good many of
the words incomprehensible. I copy out a sample here:

BOLD DEVEREUX
Pray give attention to what I will mention,
Concerning bold Devereux, that patriotic man,
Who spoke so endearing of the state of old Erin,
But who's exiled now from his dear native land.
To cruelty resorting, fourteen years they're transporting
Bold Devereux the hero, that patriotic man!
From Dublin to Newry, all classes blame the Jury,
Who had him transported from his dear native land.
A Jury was packed to try bold Bob Devereux,
Determined upon him their vengeance to wreak,
And when they had tried him, and justice denied him,
Fearless Devereux the patriot to the Jury did speak:
Saying, 'Unjustly you try me, and justice you deny me,
And make me a victim of tyrannical law;
But I nothing am fearing for the rights of old Erin,
And am doomed to be banished – poor Erin-go-bragh!'

When they've done, and have given another cheer, and I've
waved and smiled until my cheeks ache, I turn back to Kinane.
   – This is your doing, isn't it? I say.
   – Sure, I thought you'd be pleased, he says. They've waited for
months –
   Seeing his apologetic smile, I feel suddenly ashamed.
   – Well then, I *am* pleased, I say. And God bless them.
   I get out of the carriage, and begin to shake outstretched hands.
The crowd presses around me, patting my shoulder and badgering

me with questions, their faces alight with a simple pleasure which touches me despite my unease, and which causes a surge of affection to run through me.

– Jesus and Mary, how thin he is! one woman croons; and her dark eyes examine me with motherly concern.

Others address me in Gaelic, and I can only shake my head until Kinane translates: he spoke Irish as his childhood tongue, it seems. Finally I farewell them, while hands continue to grasp at my sleeves.

I pass into the Police Office, to receive the certificate that will allow me to walk free.

I've written this entry late at night, in my sitting room in Mrs Turner's lodging-house: a villa built of the local yellow sandstone, with a slate roof and a long front verandah. It stands on a ridge on the north-western side of the city, in a street called Bathurst Street.

After my hutch on the *Raffles*, the simple, middle-class comforts of this house overwhelm me like luxuries in a fairy tale. I'm to pay Mrs Turner two pounds a week for my board, which will include plain but nourishing meals – the first of which was brought to me this evening by a stubby little convict housemaid, tongue-tied and somewhat clumsy, who spilled some of the soup as she carried it up the hall.

Mrs Turner – who is the first member of her sex with whom I've held converse in seventeen months – is a thin, small-mouthed woman in a lace cap, her greying hair severely pinned back. The widow of a Hobart Town draper, she lets out rooms to support herself. She informed me immediately that Bathurst Street is 'one of the most select in the town'; and certainly it seems airy and congenial. She was also concerned to let me know that she'd 'come out free', and that she lets her rooms only to the most gentlemanly lodgers.

One is either 'bond' or 'free' here: this is the primary truth to be learned about Van Diemen's Land. The 'free' are the free settlers, who are headed by the colony's dual aristocracy: the Government's administrators, and a small elite of merchants, lawyers and clerics. The rest of the population consists of various categories of the unfree – or those who were once unfree, are now conditionally pardoned, and are called 'emancipists'. Few of the convicts on this island are actually put in prison, it seems. Instead, the island itself is their prison: and the British administration has created for them both Inferno and Purgatorio.

I learned much about this system from Doctor Richards; now I learn more from Mrs Turner.

Inferno is imprisonment in the penal stations at Port Arthur or Maria Island; but a felon is only sent to those dreaded outposts if he commits fresh crimes here. The majority inhabit Purgatorio – whose other name is Probation. It's a system composed of three main circles, through which the felon is able to make his way to the remote Paradiso of a pardon – to be earned by repentance and diligence. The circle at the centre is the Hobart Town Penitentiary in Campbell Street – known to the felon population as 'the Tench' – where many male convicts are housed on arrival, to labour in the town by day in Government probation gangs. Also at the centre of Purgatorio lies the *Anson* – a prison ship for female convicts, anchored in the Derwent near the town. From these two starting points, both sexes may make their way through Purgatorio's two outer circles, arriving finally at a sort of freedom.

In the second circle, convicts put aside their prison dress to become passholders. These passes enable them to move about freely and to work as servants for wages – either in the household of a free citizen, or for the Government. But they are always under surveillance, and may not be abroad after eight o'clock at night. One false step, one complaint, and they go back to Purgatorio's centre. In the third circle (the one which I now inhabit), they have more privileges: they are granted the coveted Ticket-of-Leave. A few favoured convicts like our *Raffles* consignment, who served their sentences elsewhere, are granted this privilege immediately on arrival, and are therefore free to move about the whole island unhindered – a liberty that's expressly denied to me, despite my Ticket. Another special provision made on my Ticket is that I must personally report myself to a police office every month – while the virtuous ex-burglar or footpad only needs to do so twice a year. Otherwise, I share the same privileges; and as the Assistant-Comptroller of Convicts explained to me, Ticket-of-Leave holders may sell their services to whom they please, and even set up in business; and I'm told by Mrs Turner that there are wealthy ex-convicts in Van Diemen's Land. But all must be in after curfew – which is at ten o'clock at night. This is our 'comparative freedom'. If we offend, we can slip back to the second circle, or even to detention at the centre – to begin all over again. We too are 'bond' – and between the two classes, bond and free, an invisible gulf stretches.

The worthy Mrs Turner must be aware from Doctor Howard that *I* haven't 'come out free' – but she seems quite unable to regard me as she would an English burglar or forger, and to view me instead as the victim of some incomprehensible tragedy.

I have two of the villa's front rooms: this sitting-room, and a connecting bedroom to the right of the front door. The verandah is very elevated – the house being built on a slope – and the French windows of my sitting room open on to it. From this eyrie, I look south over the town, and enjoy a fine view of the port and the estuary – seen tonight as glimmering lights. The sitting-room is no doubt furnished to suit Mrs Turner's idea of elegance, with heavily-patterned red wallpaper, small cedar chairs, a sofa covered in green chintz, and a little round table for writing and dining on, at which I sit now. There are a number of English watercolours on the walls: insipid romantic landscapes, of the type which assure the timid that the world is safe. Fussy but pleasant: a refuge. And the bedroom seems enormous. Ah, the bed, with its fine, clean linen! I can scarcely wait to sink into it.

Strangely enough, after my long isolation, I find I'm quite happy to be alone here this evening. I was glad of the meeting with Casey and Kinane, but the enemy has greatly reduced my stamina, and their company – not to speak of the encounter with our followers at the Police Office – has left me exhausted.

These two men have never been among my close friends, and both of them, in their different ways, had begun in some way to make me feel crowded. It's as though – I know of no other way of putting it, and it's probably my exhaustion speaking – *they wish to take me over.*

Casey, for example, wants to conduct a discussion with me concerning his piece for the *Independent.* He suggested as he took his leave that we might begin this dialogue within the next twenty-four hours. But I begged to postpone it. I was feeling too debilitated, I said, to be able to use my wits. The truth is, I've no wish for immediate public notoriety, and I intend to avoid this interview until I'm much more clear about my situation here. Or I may not sanction the piece at all, since my instincts warn me that it can do little good. In a place like this, it can scarcely advance our cause; to the British authorities, it will at best be an irritant, and at worst a word-picture of an enemy rendered impotent: something to smile over. Of what use is this to me?

I find, in fact, that I want to keep Casey at arm's length – at least for the present. I'm not quite sure why, except that there's something oddly *persistent* about him, which troubles me in a way I can't define. This, and his detached watchfulness, combine to make me cautious. I'm pretty sure the feeling is without foundation; but he seems – how can I put it? – to tread closely on my heels. And his being in Van Diemen's Land at all is very strange. Yet he plainly wishes to be a good friend, and his manner towards me is always tactful and considerate. I'm probably being suspicious without reason: he's a journalist, after all, with a journalist's congenital curiosity.

Liam Kinane is another matter.

Before he took his leave on the verandah here, he produced from his pocket some handwritten sheets.

– I'd be obliged and honoured if you'd read this, Devereux, he said. It's an essay I want to publish in the first edition of *The Irish Exile* – should the paper ever come about.

Saying this, he looked at me from under his brows, smiling with a sort of dogged defiance.

– It's about yourself, he said. I'm hoping it'll meet with your approval. It's a poor effort, entirely, but I put my heart into it. Maybe you'll feel some of it's worthwhile.

I've now laboured through this essay, and it appals me. It deals with my activities as a patriot, and my trial and transportation as a felon – and ends with a passionate and histrionic plea that I should be pardoned! It will never be published, if I have any say in it. Yet how am I to stop him – any more than I can stop him launching his damned newspaper? His inflated, hackneyed rhetoric makes my flesh cringe, and his prayer to our British overlords – carefully refraining, as it must, from any direct criticism of them – makes me fume.

'This great and noble patriot . . . Devereux the voice of Ireland's soul . . . The conscience of our people . . . Surely not deserving of so savage a punishment . . .'

God preserve me from well-meaning fools! What I'm presented with here is something far more damaging than anything that Matthew Casey might produce. I'm the subject of unconscious caricature, paraded before the public of this penal colony by a drunken, enthusiastic windbag. But what's far worse is his presumption in petitioning the British on my behalf. This could do damage to whatever strategy I may decide to adopt in this place.

Kinane's kind of adulation makes its object into a puppet: a reflection of the worshipper's dreams. And this, far from being genuine support, amounts to a blind, paradoxical threat. I hope I'm wrong, but I fear that his clumsy enthusiasm may end by endangering us all.

November 12th

The chiming of a clock floats up from the city below. Nine in the morning: my first as a citizen here.

Somewhere in the house, the voice of Mrs Turner rebukes the convict maid. Sounds of wheels and hooves rise through bright air, like noises merely imagined. But these vehicles do exist. Hobart Town exists, though my senses sometimes doubt it, and though I've yet to explore its byways.

I've set up my writing-slope on the little round table in the sitting-room, and here I sit by the open French windows, looking out over the verandah. A day of clear sunshine, already growing warm. The sky is of a deep, gentian blue: a blue never seen in Europe. Red blooms nod against this blue: geraniums, climbing from the garden. Transported to Van Diemen's Land, they grow with amazing luxuriance, reaching sizes unknown at home.

Hobart Town, capital of this gaol colony, is framed like a picture by my doors, and by the posts of the verandah.

Miniature metropolis: London built for dwarfs! City on the frontier of Void! It lies spread out below me, with the Derwent's blue estuary behind. Perverse British genius has erected a whole toy city above Antarctica, with a population of some 20,000 souls; and though I take no joy in being here, I'm compelled to acknowledge the grandeur of its setting. Its streets and buildings climb half-a-dozen hills; the estuary is flecked with a multitude of sails; the gold-grassed hills on the Derwent's eastern shore recede into depthless mauve distance, and the brooding, extinct volcano looms 4,000 feet above the town. Its name is Mount Wellington, and its frowning crater of basalt columns is flanked by blue, wooded ranges, hiding wilderness beyond. Some of the city's streets – including this one – run towards this mountain in the west, climbing its foothills. Where these streets run out, distant green patches of cultivated fields can be seen, and crude wooden huts: the last bounds of settlement, where civilized society straggles and finally dies out. Beyond those stony escarpments, savagery begins. Yet from here, they seem only half real: a drawing in the Gothic manner, like Cape Raoul.

Half an hour ago, Mrs Turner paid me a visit, coming along the verandah. She pointed out the city's landmarks – at the same time discoursing on its wickedness, and warning me of districts to avoid. Two pincers can be seen to enclose the town: the Old Wharf on the east, and the New Wharf on the west. The great fleet of whaling ships crowds the New Wharf; and I see that the *Raffles* still lies there. Above, on Battery Point, with its windmill and church spire, stands the flagstaff which signals ships' arrivals. The day before yesterday, in honour of the *Raffles*, the flag that it flew was red, meaning: *prison ship*. Towards the east of the frame, among dark native trees, are the roofs of Government House – a rustic-looking rookery which harbours Lieutenant-Governor Sir William Denison:

petty colonial tyrant and controller of my fate. In the centre of the frame is the tiny, pepperpot tower of St David's Cathedral, the striking of whose clock I've just heard.

Listening to those chimes a few minutes ago, I was briefly gripped by despair. Their sound transported me to the right side of the earth, where a host of such clocks are marking out the hours, on Europe's recollection-laden air. Then I recalled where I was, and that the chimes of this colonial cathedral were rising into an ether that was innocent of history; empty of memories; blank. *I may be deceiving myself*, I said: *I may never escape from this prison.* Instead, sonorous and tedious – above all, tedious! – the chimes of that stuccoed yellow tower would mark off all the hours of my days, through the whole of the next twelve years.

What sad nonsense! I have no intention of submitting to such a future. The town is a picture, and unreal: it induces unreal fears. Late this afternoon I'll go down into the picture, and take my first walk in freedom.

November 13th

I crossed this prison colony's Acheron, last night: its river of sadness.

The Infernal Regions lie very close to the surface here; and Hobart Town, I find, is their receiving depot. This, after all, is the Antipodes: the extremity of Earth, beyond vast Ocean: the region which Circe told Odysseus was the entrance to the kingdom of Hades.

But my excursion doesn't begin in these regions of darkness. It opens in Spring sunshine, and in the pleasure of release.

I walk, and the flagstones sway under my feet, like the deck of the *Raffles.*

I stroll through crowds, and find I've almost forgotten what crowds are like. I smile, and the odd, curious glance falls on me. But for the most part I walk like anybody else: unwatched, unsupervised, unchallenged. I roam without supervision, and without any boundaries to my roaming. I'm free; or rather, as my captors so delicately put it, *comparatively free.*

Hobart Town! A fine afternoon, in a colony not fifty years old.

I might almost be in a provincial town in England, were it not for little blue-winged parrots that are everywhere, darting in the poplars and locust trees planted along the streets. Even the temperate air seems English. Landaus and broughams and gigs carry sheltered young women in ribboned bonnets, and gentlemen in low-crowned round hats. The centre of the city has a favoured set of streets called the Block; and here, according to my guide Mrs Turner, is where the leaders of Van Diemen's Land society promenade: on Elizabeth, Liverpool, Murray and Collins Streets. And so I walk the Block, observing the colony's elite.

At half-past four, I pause on Wellington Bridge, under the canvas awning of a bookshop. Here, at the junction of Elizabeth and Liverpool Streets, is the town's favourite meeting place. The bridge is scarcely in evidence, being signified by a stone parapet wall a few yards south of the bookshop: one of many such bridges that occur throughout the city, carrying its streets across the Hobart Rivulet. Once no doubt a pure mountain brook, the Rivulet runs from the wilderness in the west down to the harbour, and is over-whelmed and overlaid by Hobart Town – for which it supplies drinking water and mill races. From the odour that drifts above the parapet, I suspect that it's also become a sewer. Yet Hobart Town's gentry greet each other here with small cries of pleasure. Hats are raised; parasols twirl; they make me feel shabby, in my old blue cap with its glazed peak, and my worn grey frock coat. The tail coats and riding coats and buckskin trousers of Hobart Town would look elegant even in Bond Street – though the gaudy cravats and waist-coats would perhaps be seen as vulgar. The ladies are equally gay, in brightly-coloured day-dresses of silk and muslin and taffeta; and here, in this sunny, bright blue air, their display of colour seems natural, like the colours of the brilliant little parrots in the trees.

I step from the footpath and cross Elizabeth Street, avoiding a hansom cab and a brougham. As I near the kerb on the far side, I'm aware of an ominous jingling: the old familiar sound that used to fill my ears on Bermuda.

I turn to see a cart going by filled with road metal, drawn by two convicts. They strain between the shafts like horses, while three

214

more push from behind. All except one, who's clad in a prison uniform of plain grey, are wearing 'cross-irons': bars locked between their ankles, from which chains go to belts around their loins, setting up a constant, mournful music. They're sweating in heavy woollen costumes of an ugliness that sickens the heart: a magpie pattern of mustard-yellow and dark grey, the arms and legs differing, like the suit of a clown, and branded on the back with a prison number. They wear sinister leather caps, making them look like demons in some medieval painting of Hell.

I avert my gaze and walk on, entering Liverpool Street. I walk west, towards the mountain; and now I begin to move towards the strange misadventures of the night.

The opposite side of Liverpool Street has well-paved footpaths and handsome stone buildings; but this southern side is clearly less respectable, with rows of little buildings of brick and weatherboard, and open-fronted stalls of medieval crudity. I find myself on paving stones that are crazily undulating; the gutter is overgrown with marsh weed. Like all such sections, in every city, it has an air of harbouring disreputable mysteries. I greatly prefer it, in my present mood.

I walk.

The noise and the odours make me giddy, after months of monastic silence. Here is the world again: earth-strong fruit and vegetable smells, and the knife-edged tang of ocean fish; the fragrance of bread, carried by in baskets; the shouts of fishmongers, butchers and old clothes men, standing at their stalls. With a child's uncritical interest, I read every signboard; I study every advertisement in every fly-specked window. *Prime Colonial Hams; Fluid Magnesia; Sperm and Tallow Candles; Preserves and Rare Condiments; Ladies' and Gentlemen's Visiting Cards*: the silent chattering of commerce, strange to me now as runes.

Here is the open door of a grog-shop: a crude little weatherboard shanty. Crowded at the counter, men and women in the greasy caps and broken straw bonnets of the London streets. They're singing together: loudly, sentimentally, and very flat, in Cockney accents. No doubt they're mostly emancipated or pass-holding convicts. Something like half the people around me must belong to these same categories, since half the population of the colony has been transported.

The notion's disturbing. Although it may appear otherwise, and although I may not wear the magpie garb and leather cap, am I not one of their number? I'm their brother in captivity, and a Ticket-of-Leave man, after all. Even though I walk these streets as I wish, with money in my pockets drawn on the Bank of Van Diemen's Land, I am 'bond', and ordered indoors by ten o'clock. I'm no longer myself, but a creature who walks free on sufferance, at the Colonial Government's pleasure – and who may not pass the limits of the town without express permission. British official ingeniousness has ensured that I move in an invisible snare. The hills beyond the town are the walls of my prison; the Southern Ocean is its moat.

I walk.

Nearly at the corner of Murray Street, I've come to a Jewish section. Pawnbrokers; small retailers and wholesalers; warehouses and workshops. A sign reads: *MESSRS. NATHAN & MOSES, Warehousemen and Importers of English and Continental Goods*. I pause here. This business occupies a long wooden shop-building of one storey. In the window, dressing cases, jars of snuff, toilet bottles, fine china and Bohemian glass. Down a cobbled lane at the side, a big stone warehouse of two storeys. A horse and dray laden with boxes trundles by, and I glimpse at the lane's end the sinister, degraded Hobart Rivulet, running fast and furtive behind the backs of the buildings, between grim retaining walls of green-slimed stone. Piles of broken rubbish on its banks; thin stray dogs scavenging.

The Rivulet both repels and interests me, in my idleness. I begin to suspect that it's a subterranean corridor, leading to Hobart Town's most squalid secrets. Tumbledown hovels of grey weatherboard can be seen down there, behind the main shop-buildings; and I guess that the lane and others like it have subsidiaries that run into hidden mazes: a town-behind-the-town, far less respectable than the miniature colonial metropolis I've been walking through.

I begin to move on. But now I'm arrested by the sight of a bookshop.

It stands on the opposite corner of the lane – the next shop after that of Nathan and Moses. It's in a long, narrow little building of rough orange brick – single-storeyed, with an odd, hat-shaped gable in front which looks quaintly Chinese. The display window on the street, with its many little panes, is filled with shelves of books – some of them in French, their paper covers yellowed by Antipodean time. On the topmost shelf a corpse-white bust of Napoleon stares from under a half-lowered blind that screens the top of his head and bicorn hat, so that the Emperor appears to be spying on Liverpool Street. No entrance doorway here at the front: instead it's at the side, opening on to the lane. Above this door, which stands open, there's a signboard with the legend: *J. LENOIR, DEALER IN OLD AND ANTIQUE BOOKS*. And on the rough orange bricks above the display window, the name *J. Lenoir* appears again – but very much faded and ghostly, so that the shop appears to exist in a dimension that's neither past nor present: a shop in Limbo.

I walk through the door – pausing for a moment to adjust my eyes to dimness. A dry, sterile odour here that's sweeter to me than perfume: that of many books, with an added element that could only be met within a shop devoted to the antique: the serious, mystical effluvium of volumes that are aged, and of bindings that have begun to moulder.

I find I'm the sole customer here, standing in what I suspect is a permanent twilight.

The place consists of a long, single room with walls of horizontal boards painted apple-green, dim with age and grime. Up near the high wooden ceiling, a few of the bluebottle flies which seem to be ubiquitous in Hobart Town can be heard droning and buzzing; a fly-paper dangles from a beam, black with their corpses. The shop's only windows are the large one on Liverpool Street with its half-drawn blind, and a smaller one by the door to the lane. These, though dusty, give reasonable light to the top end of the room. But the other end – further down the lane towards the Rivulet – is in semi-darkness. A ladder there goes up to a sort of platform under the ceiling which is supported by wooden pillars: boxes and books are piled on it. In the area under this platform, a man in a green Russian cap is sitting at a roll-top desk with his back to me, bent over some papers by the light of an oil lamp. This is presumably Mr Lenoir; but he doesn't turn around when I come in, and I pay him no more heed, giving my attention to the books.

They're arranged in no sort of order that I can see. They seem, in fact, to be in chaos: piled in jumbled heaps on tables; leaning like rotting tenements in shelves along the walls; tottering in piles about the floor. Some very large volumes are in a big metal press by the far wall. But what books! And what joy to be among their multitudes again! At a glance, I see that there are many fine editions of the classical authors, as well as of those of our day: both English and foreign. A good many are in French, unbound in their paper covers. Most of the English poets are here, with the Romantics well represented, all in excellent calfskin and morocco bindings; and a beautiful edition of Dryden's translations of Virgil, bound in green morocco, arouses my lust for possession. So does an equally splendid edition of Dante's *Divina Commedia* in Henry Cary's translation, which I pick up and ponder over, sampling its passages as though for the first time. Surely, I say, the Florentine genius envisioned future Hells of man's creation; and who can doubt that this chill-breathed city of prisoners is one of them?

But after a time I forget that I'm in Van Diemen's Land. I put the Dante aside and move among the tables, turning over book after book: breathing the dry, still air of civilization; attending to its many soundless voices. The buzzing of the flies recedes, and the silent figure at the desk is forgotten. But then I come across something that causes me to recall him to mind.

It's an edition of Cicero in the Latin, which I see to my considerable surprise is printed by Elzevir. I can't imagine its likely price, but it's surely of great value. That it's found its way here to Hobart Town seems to me extraordinary. I turn and address the man in the cap, who's still bent over his papers, writing with a quill pen, his face entirely hidden.

– Tell me, sir – how did you acquire this Elzevir?

For a moment, he makes no sign that he's heard – and at this distance, it seems possible that he hasn't. But then he carefully stands the pen in an inkwell and turns to peer at me over his shoulder, looking over the tops of a pair of steel-framed spectacles. The effect is disconcerting, since he still doesn't speak. He has a full grey beard and gaunt, hawk-like features, and his expression in the light of the lamp appears surprisingly unpleasant: he seems almost to sneer.

He slowly stands up, taking off the spectacles and laying them on the desk, and shuffles between the tables towards me.

I see that he's old – probably over seventy. His clothing, including the cap, brings to mind the haphazard garments of a vagabond. A dark blue pilot coat; a thick green neckerchief, loosely knotted; an ancient, rusty waistcoat, once black, and a pair of crumpled cotton trousers – over which he wears a shopman's apron with a large hole in it. A very decrepit old bookshop man indeed, of a type one finds in the back streets of many great cities. He halts in front of me, still in silence, and glittering greenish-blue eyes in deep sockets peer into my face. He's certainly not English: French, presumably; and perhaps Jewish. He studies me insolently, from head to foot. When he speaks, his voice is hoarse yet distinct; there's no discernible foreign accent, yet somehow it's not quite English.

– Are you an interested buyer, sir – or are you just idly prying?

I stiffen.

– I may well buy one or two of your books, I say. Not necessarily this one. But if you offer me rudeness, sir, I'll buy nothing.

This rebuke appears to leave him quite unaffected. Instead, it seems to amuse him, since he smiles with a hint of mockery.

– Come now, not so hasty, he says. Are you a book-lover, sir?

I tell him that I am. My stiffness becomes faintly ridiculous, under his gaze; I begin to feel like a boy standing on his dignity.

– Then to walk out of my shop would be a mistake, he says. In this town, I can assure you, you'll not find another like it. And then where will you be for books? I have a lot of fools coming in here asking idle questions, who have no intention of buying anything. Are you fond of Cicero?

His rude familiarity, as well as his eccentric changes of tack, have begun to divert rather than irritate me. And what he says may be true: there may not be another source of books like his in the colony. I decide not to take offence, and instead to humour him.

– Cicero? The greatest of orators, I say. But won't you tell me the origin of this edition?

His smile becomes less forbidding; almost ingenuous.

– He still has something to say to us, does he not? *'Dolebam, dolebam, patres conscripti, rempublicam uestris quondam meisque consiliis conseruatam, breui tempore esse perituram.'*

I gaze at him in surprise: rude and shabby he may be, but he's an educated man, it seems.

– *Recte dicis,* I say. *Aptissimum temporibus his quod olim a Marco Tullio accepimus: facillime nempe honestatem, libertatem, immo ipsam rem publicam venum dari, semel autem venditam nunquam redimi posse.*

He applauds, clapping softly with his long, wrinkled hands – whose nails, I see, are black-rimmed.

– *Doctus es, domine. Facunde loqueris!*

– You flatter me, I say. But still you haven't told me the origin of this rare and valuable book.

He returns my gaze with his head on one side, squinting cunningly and pulling at his beard.

– Ah. Then you realise its value. You are no fool, sir. You wish to buy it?

– I very much doubt that my pocket would run to it. I may well buy your handsome Virgil over there – but I'm simply curious to know how an Elzevir found its way to this brutal penal colony.

He studies me even more intently, his head cocked further to the side, making him resemble a bedraggled crow.

– You are a stranger in the colony, he says. I thought so. How long have you been here, may I ask?

I tell him, and he nods.

– Many new arrivals of gentle birth make your mistake. They imagine themselves in some primitive outpost – which in many ways they are. We're surrounded by violent barbarians and ignorant blockheads here, there's no denying it. But then they discover that the leaders of society are many of them quite cultivated, and that the arts and sciences flourish. Why, the previous Governor and his lady had dreams of making this an Athens in the Southern Seas.

220

He chuckles – a short, wheezing sound – and continues to watch my face.

– Well, well: a trifle grandiose, perhaps. Sir John was a dullard: no wonder he lost his way in the North-West Passage. But Lady Franklin was a highly cultivated lady. So Hobart Town now is not entirely uncivilized. Some even call it the Dublin of Australia. That might be more accurate.

He smiles again, and looks past my shoulder, still pulling at his beard. Then he continues.

– Our present Governor is also a dullish man: an engineer, and you know what engineers are – mechanical, with mechanical minds. Yet I must admit that Sir William's a great enthusiast for the sciences. And the Colonial Secretary, who is one of my customers, is a real bookman: a jolly fellow, and a man of refined literary taste. We also have a very active Royal Society, to which I have the honour to belong. So you see, sir, you're not entirely among barbarians, even though much here is barbarous.

He looks down at the Cicero, and strokes its cover.

– You ask about this Elzevir. It was published in Holland in 1642 – the year that the Dutchman Abel Tasman discovered this island. A nice coincidence, no? Many gentlemen in the colony have fine libraries – and sometimes they have things they wish to sell. The man who sold me this is very mean, and rather ignorant – and he let me have it among some other books for a song. When I sell it, I shall make a thousand per cent profit; and I shall tell him, and it will break his heart.

Seeing me laugh, he joins in, with a high, prolonged giggling that makes his old eyes become slitted in their caverns, glinting there like the sea. The laughter ends abruptly; he wipes his mouth with the back of his hand.

– I can let you have the Virgil for a florin, he says.

– Done, I say. That seems a fair price.

– A very generous price, he says. But I make no doubt you're a book-lover, and that you'll be back. You are staying long in the colony?

– I fear so, I say. I have no choice.

And I hand him a florin. He takes it without looking at me, his face gone empty, and shuffles to a low chest of drawers that apparently serves him as a cash desk. The coin disappears into one of the drawers, and he begins to wrap my Virgil in brown paper from a roll. Without looking up, he says softly:

– You are bond, then?

– I believe that's how you put it in Van Diemen's Land, I say. Your enlightened administrators have granted me a Ticket-of-Leave.

Now he looks up swiftly, his expression shrewd and serious, his gaze coldly bright. He holds the wrapped book with both hands, not yet giving it to me.

– We have many gentlemen here who are in your situation, he says. Few people despise them for it, except our greatest snobs. I certainly don't do so.

He raises his eyebrows, narrows his eyes at me, and delicately licks his lips.

– Perhaps yours was what we call the gentleman's crime? But of course, this is not my business.

– The gentleman's crime?

– Why, forgery, he says, and smiles sweetly.

– No. My crime was political, I say. Sedition, to be precise.

The smile vanishes, perhaps because my tone has been cold. Still he remains in a fixed position: bent, the book suspended in front of his chest like a dish.

– Ah, he says slowly, and his voice has gone still softer. Political: I see. Yes, of course. So. That is a horse of another colour. I took you at first sight for a man of honour – and now I see I was right. I am usually right about my fellow human beings.

– But I think you may have contradicted yourself, I say. Had I been a forger, Monsieur Lenoir, you would not have despised me, you said. Now it seems that perhaps you would have done.

At first he says nothing, his gaze still fixed on me. Then he speaks as though to himself.

– A fiery young man. And you will be Mr Robert Devereux, perhaps?

I bow. Then I say:

– You surprise me. Did your patrons in the Government provide you with a description?

Smiling and shaking his head, he holds out the book like a peace offering, his arm at full length.

– No, no, no, Mr Devereux. I read about your arrival in the *Hobart Town Courier* yesterday morning – did you not see the piece?

I take the book.

– No, I say. I've not yet had time to read all the newspapers – but I can imagine the type of article it would be.

– It did tend to lecture you on your good fortune in being set at liberty, he says. You and your comrades who arrived recently. The *Courier* is often sanctimonious. But take heart, Mr Devereux – it's very critical of the Government, and so are many of our leading settlers. You may find more sympathy among them than you imagine. They grow quite hostile to London.

– Indeed? Thank you for the information, monsieur; it's encouraging and interesting. I hope to call on you again: you have a wonderful stock of books. *Vous êtes français?*

– *J'étais français, autrefois. Mais il y a longtemps que je suis anglais.* I shall look forward to another talk, Mr Devereux. So many of my customers are fools – one cannot have intelligent conversation with them. I welcome those who are otherwise.

He makes a low bow, and there's a touch of the *ancien régime* about it, giving to his shabby garments and Russian cap a ghostly hint of style.

I walk to the door with my parcel under my arm. As I reach it, he calls my name, his voice thin, like the buzzing of the flies near the ceiling.

I turn. He's leaning forward with both hands resting on his cash desk, his gem-bright old eyes staring across the dusty space between us.

– You will have heard of the duck-billed platypus, Mr Devereux? A grotesque furred mammal with the webbed feet and bill of a duck. It lives in the streams here.

– I believe so.

I wait, puzzled.

– We have a drawing of it on the title page of our Minute Book, at our modest branch of the Royal Society, he says. Underneath is the legend: *All things are queer and opposite.* And they are, Mr Devereux. They are, out here. All things are queer and opposite.

– I have no doubt of it, I say. Good day to you, monsieur.

Outside the shop, I find that sunset's coming down. I walk on westwards: further uphill, in the direction of the mountain. The sun inches lower, glowing on the peak and dark-green foothills; and I notice how the light in this far southern latitude makes everything uncannily distinct.

I turn right into a cross street, intending to make my way to my lodgings up in Bathurst Street. But in between the two lies Goulburn Street; and Goulburn Street draws me in.

Like Liverpool Street, it runs straight uphill to the town's western limits: an area of taverns and mean lodging houses, set hard against the footpath. No smart shoppers stroll beside these oozing gutters. Instead, there are crowds of passholders here, both male and female, more brutal-looking than any I've yet seen, who stare at me hard as I pass. And now I recall my landlady telling me that Goulburn Street is the centre of a thieves' rookery named St Giles, after the one in London: violent and unsafe after dark, if Mrs Turner is to be believed. Yet I begin to ascend its hill – drawn, I suppose, by morbid curiosity. The principal vice of St Giles would seem to be drink: I've never seen so many taverns in a single street. They recede uphill into ultimate, red-hued distance, their signboards clamouring for attention: the Black Bull; the Man at the Wheel; the Waterman's Arms; the Whale Fishery.

The Whale Fishery is a mustard-coloured, two-storeyed house whose signboard depicts a great whale surfacing, with a whaleboat in pursuit. Through the doorway comes laughter, singing, and sudden, dangerous shouts. On a sudden impulse, I go in. I'm not normally fond of districts or public houses like this one; but suddenly, like any simple sailor who's been long months at sea, I crave strong, crude diversion. Anything seems better than a return to my genteel lodgings.

I have entered a long tap-room with a dirty timber floor and many small tables. Lamps hang from its low timber ceiling: they burn whale oil in their lamps here, and its strange marine stink mingles with the odours of spirits, tobacco-smoke and unwashed bodies. The voices break on me in a wave; the place is crowded to suffocation. Faces briefly turn to me, through a blue and yellow haze: most of them those of whalemen. All are costumed alike – low-crowned hat; blue jacket; wide duck trousers – but the faces are from all over the earth. A number of soldiers are in here, and a sprinkling of passholders, and more than a sprinkling of Hobart Town's nymphs of the pavement, in coal-scuttle bonnets and indecently low-cut gowns, singing and laughing and waving their mugs of grog.

I sit down at one of the tables, placing my parcel on its sticky surface. A pale, hurrying potboy in an apron brings me a bottle of ale and a dented pewter mug. As I begin to pour, a sonorous and cultivated voice addresses me, coming from my right.

– Pardon me, sir: may I take the liberty of engaging you in conversation?

I turn to find myself being closely studied by a very thin man of about forty, alone at the next table, a mug of grog in front of him. He's an odd figure to find in here, since from his manner of speech he's apparently a gentleman: but a gentleman in very poor circumstances. He wears a narrow-brimmed round hat of dirty grey plush with a crown of flower-pot shape, tall to a degree that has long ceased to be fashionable. His rusty brown suit is shiny and threadbare, and his yellowish old neckerchief is pinned up in a way that conceals the state of his shirt – or perhaps the lack of one.

– Why not, sir? I say. We're both here to idle away time, I take it.

– Well, that's true, the thin man says. Sad, ain't it?

His face is care-worn and undernourished, with an uptilted nose and prominent cheekbones: a face sadly at odds with his resonant and confident-seeming voice. He stands, holding his mug.

– May I join you, sir? My name is Mark Handley-Smythe.

I gesture in assent, and introduce myself; and he moves to my table with a look of happy eagerness that makes my heart sink. But

225

I resolve to be pleasant with him; twilight's gathering outside the tavern's open door, and any company's better than none.

– It's a pleasure to make your acquaintance. I imagine you're newly arrived in the town, he says. One gets to know faces, and to recognise new ones, after eight years.

– You've been in the colony so long?

– So long, he says. Seven years being the length of my sentence. And condemned entirely unjustly.

– Come now, I say, you're a fortunate man compared to me, Mr Handley-Smythe – since my sentence is twice as long.

– You? Fourteen years? A gentleman like you?

He gives a sudden whinny of laughter, his hand going quickly to cover his mouth – but not before I've seen what he wishes to hide: a set of horridly blackened and decayed teeth. Then he leans forward, inviting confidences.

– May one ask what misfortune brought you to this, Mr Devereux?

– One may not, I say.

– Of course not, he says. Of course not. I merely –

– Nor do I ask what crime has brought you here, I say. It's none of my business, and I don't condemn you for it.

I signal to the pale, hurrying pot-boy.

– Allow me to buy us more drinks, Mr Handley-Smythe. I find I'm quite thirsty, from walking about the town.

His face brightens.

– You're very kind, sir. I was about to leave, before meeting you – but one more rum would be very heartening. May I suggest that you try it? A good Jamaican.

I order two rums, hoping that he'll not return to the topic of his injustice; but as soon as the drinks are set before us, and he's swallowed a good portion of his mug, he does so.

What follows is a long and complicated tale which I find difficult to follow. I order further rums for us as he talks, in the end scarcely pretending to understand him. But I gather that he comes of good family, that his father had a banking business in Norwich, and that when the father died, he left the business to Handley-Smythe's uncle. The uncle was to have paid Handley-Smythe an annuity, but apparently failed to do so.

– And so I took justice into my own hands, Handley-Smythe says.

– Indeed? I say. How so?

– I was accused of putting my name to certain bills, he says. Well sir, I did so, and don't deny it. I, a man of liberal education, was robbed of my inheritance, denied all justice, and forced to work in menial and degrading positions. How else could I obtain what was rightly mine?

– I do see the difficulty of your position, I say. But perhaps you were unwise.

The pot-boy has brought two more rums. As I pay for them, Mr Handley-Smythe sits with a distracted air; but his hand closes quickly on his mug.

– Unwise? Oh yes, I was unwise, since I had nowhere to turn. And what's the consequence? I sit here as you now see me. My wife and children, who followed me to this vile colony, are at home close by in the hovel we must live in, with nothing to eat. Two of the children are ill – and I was forced recently to dispose of some of our furniture to get medicine for them. What was over I've spent on drink. Oh yes, on drink: every penny.

He gazes at me directly, seeming to invite me to express my contempt for him.

– I see what you think of me: a worthless wretch – eh? Well, I *admit* it! I admit it, but I tell you: only drink allows me to forget what's been done to me – and also the horror of *where I actually am*.

– And where is that?

At first he doesn't answer me directly. Instead, he sneers.

– Hobart Town's charming, ain't it? he says. A very pretty town. But only look *behind*, Mr Devereux! We're *here*, on Van Diemen's Land, at the end of the God-damned world. Do you comprehend that? How much do you really know of this place? Have you walked in our lovely St Giles before?

I say I haven't. He nods, and continues to sneer.

– Of all the cities and towns in all these blasted colonies, Hobart

227

Town is the wickedest, he says. And of all the thieves' kitchens in the Empire, ours are the bloody vilest. For sheer *depravity*, sir, nowhere else can rival Hobart Town. The place is a Sodom.

He leans to place a familiar hand on my shoulder; he's quite drunk now.

– You and I are gentlemen, are we not? Yet here we are, pent up with these bloody ex-pickpockets and whores.

He gestures at the room: at a group of drunken ex-felons by the counter, engaged in noisy argument; at a crowd of laughing prostitutes in smeared silk dresses. His resonant voice rises; his face becomes twisted with rage.

– Damn them! Damn their eyes! They ought all have been transported to Hell!

He slumps back; and now his rage gives way to hopeless melancholy. At the same time, he becomes foul-mouthed.

– We're marooned, he says, on this fucking wretched island, and nothing to the south of us but the Pole. One can never be at *home* here: do you see? One is always – *lonely*.

I'm trying not to show my distaste for this sad, garrulous creature; but I've resolved, as soon as my rum is drunk, to get up and take my leave.

– But surely, I say, you could do a little more to repair your life here – could you not?

At this, the face that stares back at me becomes that of a stricken child. The tall, grubby hat has become a child's fancy dress, and tears well up in his eyes.

– Oh, Christ Jesus, he says. *Look* at me! Look at what I've *become*! Do you really think I've any life left to repair?

I stand up, and find myself swaying; the rum's affected me, and I want to get away.

– I'm afraid I must leave you now, I say. I'm sorry to hear of your troubles, Mr Handley-Smythe – but perhaps you should go home to your family.

He shakes his head, and the tears roll down his cheeks, and his mouth remains open in woe. Then he holds his hand out, palm upwards.

– Please, he says, in a small voice. For my family. Spare me a few shillings.

I take out a sovereign and push it into his hand; when mine comes away, I find with distaste that his tears have wet it. Picking up my parcel, I turn and make quickly for the door.

I pause on the broken pavement. Out here in the air, my head begins to swim: I'm more drunk than I imagined.

Darkness has descended on Van Diemen's Land. Darkness fills the long, shouting channel of Goulburn Street, and the street lamps have been lit: dim flares fuelled by whale oil, adding to the general marine stench. Receding on crude wooden standards, glowing like gloomy stars, they march uphill through an air gone icy cold, and through softly falling rain.

I turn without thought and begin to follow them, resuming my pilgrimage towards the city's western heights. I walk: cap pulled low over my eyes, collar turned up, my paper-wrapped Virgil under my arm. Occasionally, as the weakness that's asthma's legacy overtakes me, I stop and pant for breath. On one of these halts, I find myself at the entrance to a lane. I turn and step into it, passing between a cottage on one side and a tall, noisy tavern on the other. And so I enter the town's Third Circle.

Why do I do this? I'm drawn by curiosity, I suppose, and am too intoxicated to be cautious. I'm also drawn by a sound. Confused and obscurely thrilling, it comes out of the lane's dim tunnel like some essence of human excitement made audible, and suggests that the lane may lead to that town whose existence I've surmised: the town-within-the-town that I glimpsed by the city's sluggish Acheron.

The lane is empty for the first few yards, its wet, greasy cobbles reflecting the lights that stream from the tavern. But as I go on, it grows darker. The darkness stinks of decaying vegetable matter, and of canine and human ordure. Then an enormous barking breaks out, echoing in the tunnel. I'm confronted by a black mongrel dog, standing in my path to challenge me. It looks starved, yet seems of great size. Its eyes shine green in the dark, and its barking's so loud

229

that it stuns me. I halt, and consider turning back. But now two sailors appear, lurching towards me and singing. One of them throws an empty ale bottle at the beast, striking it directly in the muzzle.

It yelps, cowers, and runs away. The sailors shout with laughter, and call out after me:

– Good night, mate. Don't lose that parcel in Black Lion Square.

– No, nor your ticker neither.

Then they stagger on.

I continue towards a brownish glow that shows at the lane's end, while the sound that led me in here grows steadily more distinct, coming from some invisible source, and seeming to be made by fierce and riotous voices. I emerge from the lane into the square the sailors spoke of – and just as I expected, I find that I've penetrated the secret town of vice.

Many people wander here: seamen, soldiers, children, bedraggled and tattered women of the night, and the lowest stratum of Hobart Town's poor – whose home this place appears to be. The square lies entirely hidden behind the backs of Goulburn Street's buildings on this side, and the backs of those of Liverpool Street on the other, down the slope of the hill. The Rivulet can be glimpsed between two warehouses, its surface dully flashing in the moon. Over the back door of one of the taverns down there, a sign reads: *The Black Lion*.

Black Lion Square is of Lilliputian size. It has no official existence, I feel sure, and will not be on any street map. Around its perimeter stand rotting, broken-down, weatherboard tenements, cottages and cribs – all of them so small that it's difficult to believe that they're inhabited. Most have broken windows, patched with rags and paper; and these are the source of the glow, created by smoky lamps. A gutter runs at the square's edges, blocked with every kind of filth; its odour, and the odour of cess-pits, hangs over everything. I move forward, looking about me. The rain has now ceased, and things drip.

In windows and doorways, people are shouting, laughing, drinking from bottles, gnawing on scraps of food, quarrelling and cursing.

Many of them – even the women – are half-clad, despite the cold. Others wear clothing that's falling into rags. In the middle of the square, whose only paving is earth, someone has lit a fire with old boxes and rubbish. I can make out a crowd beyond this fire, and it's from there that the calling voices come; but I can't make out the cause of their excitement.

As I pass by, I'm stared at by the people in front of the houses. A gross, fat brute of a man in a broken round hat and under-vest is gnawing greedily on a chicken bone. He licks his fingers and laughs, and calls out to me.

– Looking for a friend, your honour?

A young woman smiles at me from the window of a tumble-down wooden crib, a lamp burning on a table behind her. She's clad only in a thin white chemise, without any bodice, and has a fine, full bosom: but when she smiles, she has no front teeth.

– Won't you spare a penny, sir?

In my path, a blind, white-haired beggar in a filthy brown frock coat and blue-tinted glasses, led by a mongrel dog. I hand him a coin, and move on. And now a tribe of children follows me: bare-foot boys in shirts and ragged trousers, rolled to the knee; little girls with dirty, matted hair, clad only in petticoats. All call out, and nag me.

– Give us a penny, sir! Give us a shilling! Where are yer going, sir? What do yer want in Black Lion? What you got in the parcel?

How little they ask, to satisfy their avarice! Small, dirty hands take my pennies; then I wave them away.

But one child remains at my heels. She's a thin little girl of eleven or twelve, with tangled, mousy hair and a heart-shaped face that would be pretty, were it not so sallow and starved. There's a cut on her lower lip, and her wretched pink petticoat has been so torn about that it hangs in strips, leaving one shoulder and her fish-white chest mostly bare. Her grey eyes are icy and empty; yet they stare at me with the knowing directness of an adult woman's, and seem to ask for something. Two paces behind her comes a bent old woman in a rusty black gown, a shawl over her head. She mutters, and I stop and look at them.

The old woman puts a hand on the girl's shoulder. Then she mutters louder.

– You like her, your honour? Pretty, ain't she? Pretty, and never been touched. She's yours for a sovereign, sir.

The child's cold eyes turn on me; she runs her tongue over her cut lip, and speaks in a piping whisper.

– Won't you take me home with you?

– Come now, the old woman says. A sov sir, an' it's done. Take her with you – or there's a nice crib near, and none the wiser. What do you say?

– I say that I ought to get the police to you.

I am filled with rage; but this is the rage of helplessness, and the old woman knows it. I turn away, and her cracked voice follows me, raised in jeering contempt.

– And who might you be? A sneaking, tuppenny ha'penny cove with no fucking money – that's what *you* are. Get the bloody traps? They don't bleeding dare come in Black Lion! Call 'em! See how far you get, your bloody lordship!

I walk on, with despair in my guts. And now I've come to the bonfire, and its fierce, exultant voices. The crowd on the far side of the fire is so dense that it's impossible to see what it is that absorbs its attention: but whatever it is, it causes the mob to surge about like a dark, tethered animal, and to cry out in sudden bursts. Under the excitement and pleasure of these cries, a counterpoint can be heard: a bestial, growling fury that agitates the nerves.

It isn't easy to get through the ring of spectators, most of whom are men: soldiers, whalers, ordinary seamen, and a sprinkling of British man-of-war's men, spruce in low-crowned hats, high-heeled boots and black neckerchiefs. One of them turns to look hard at me; but he speaks in an amiable manner, his voice raised above the shouting.

– Come to see the cat-fight have you, sir? Come on: it's Double-jointed Sal and Slippery Molly, going at it like men.

He stands sideways in the press of bodies to allow me entry. Clutching my parcel, I find myself squeezed between the sailor and a very tiny creature wearing a huge green tail coat that enfolds him like a blanket: a dwarf with bushy black hair, no bigger than a child, but with an old face. He's shouting and giggling, and the sailor turns away now and begins to shout too, miming with his fists.

– Ho! Yes! Pitch into her, Sal! A crown says you can do it! Lay her out, my beauty!

In the centre of a ring formed by the crowd, two women fight with their fists, stripped to the waist like bruisers. One of them is aged in her twenties, the other much older. Hands raised, they circle each other, long skirts and naked torsos spattered with mud and blood, while the roaring surges and wanes and surges again.

The older of the two is a tall woman in her thirties in a dirty calico cap, dark hair straggling like weed over her thick white shoulders, face bloated with drink, and coarse as a man's. This – from the shouts – is Double-jointed Sal. One eye is swollen and closed, the skin around it plum-coloured; the remaining eye glares at her opponent: a bright and surprisingly beautiful sky-blue. Blood is running from her nose and from a corner of her panting mouth. Her long, swaying breasts are marked with angry pink splotches, and with the parallel weals left by fingernails. Angrier still, and more gross and pitiable than her wounds, are the circles of her nipples.

Her younger opponent circles her, making gestures like those of a cat scratching. Slippery Molly is very thin and agile: long-waisted and almost boy-like, her ribs showing clearly through her scratched and heaving flanks. Her wide lips snarl; her narrow eyes gleam. I guess her to be Irish. She wears no head-covering, her coarse fair hair tied back with a green scarf; the same coarse hair is like tufts of grass in her armpits. Now she lashes out, and there's a shriek. She has punched Double-jointed Sal between the breasts, which shudder and tremble and swing: zones of maternal tenderness monstrously invaded. Nausea fills me, and I close my eyes.

But I can't close my ears. Shouts go up around the circle: foul exhortations fill the air. The crowd calls eagerly for hurt; they shout detailed instructions as to what these women might do to each other's bodies; some of them seem almost to weep in the fervency of their lust. On my right, the British tar is shouting with the rest; on my left, the dwarf is sniggering, and making high carolling noises. His body is pressed snugly against mine; he seems to fidget, and I try to draw away;

but this proves impossible, the press of the crowd being so great.

Molly is now hammering Sal's swollen face with both fists, opening a cut in one eyebrow so that the blood courses down. Then she strikes a blow into Sal's belly. The grunting cry which results rises above all the shouts and passionate suggestions of the mob. The older woman's single, bright blue eye grows filmed and emptied of sentience; she falls on her hands and knees, and Molly begins to strike more blows at her face. But Double-jointed Sal grasps her by the hair and pulls her down into the mud – where they strike at each other now with their heads as well as their hands, and bite each other's faces. They roll, wrapped in each other's arms, their sullied flesh alone still human: miraculous and tragic in its whiteness.

I can bear no more, and struggle to escape; to be gone from Black Lion Square. Bodies press against me from all sides; but I thrust the giggling dwarf out of the way, and get free.

I retreat at a jog across the square, making for the lane through which I entered, still carrying my paper-wrapped Virgil. Passing down the dark, narrow tunnel, I half-expect to be obstructed or attacked. Figures lurch in my path, but always give way; someone shouts after me. Unscathed, I emerge into Goulburn Street again.

Now I remember my curfew. Is it ten o'clock yet? I look for the watch in my waistcoat pocket, and find it gone.

The dwarf, I say. *The damned fidgeting dwarf: he's picked my pocket.*

Two redcoats loom up in front of me. One is carrying his shako, his hair standing on end. He has the brick-red face of the addicted drinker; someone has given him a swollen lip, and his eyes bulge with wondering resentment.

– *Here's* a game, he says. A gentleman, been in Black Lion. Visiting gay women, squire?

He's clearly looking for another fight, and drink has made him both dangerous and childish. But his companion is more cautious.

– Come on William, he says. Come on, do. You don't want this gentleman reporting on you to the Barracks.

But the first redcoat stares stupidly at my parcel.

– His honour's got a book, he says. He's come to Black Lion to read. He thinks it's a bleeding library.

He snatches the Virgil from my hand, tears off the wrapping and opens it, squinting at the Latin.

– What's this, then? he says. A fucking foreign language. You a bloody foreigner, then?

– Yes, I'm a foreigner, I say. And your cretinous English face makes me glad of it.

His eyes bulge further; he drops the book on the pavement and raises his fists, cursing me. His companion takes hold of his sleeve, begging him to desist and come away; but I raise my own hands and face him. I've not fought since my schooldays, I'll probably be thrashed, but I plan a blow to his brick-coloured nose with a fierce and dreamy joy.

But a body thrusts itself between mine and his. A voice speaks to me quietly: a voice I don't at first recognise.

– All right, sir. I'll take care of this cove.

Smartly clad in a blue riding coat, the man is just recognisable as James Langford. He wears a white, wide-brimmed felt hat of a type that I've noticed is favoured by the colony's gentry; this he carefully hands to me to hold. He moves after that with confusing swiftness. A fist in the redcoat's stomach doubles him up; then, with a methodical precision that almost makes me cry out for him to stop, Langford delivers a series of repeated blows to the head, left-and right-handed, the sound like meat being chopped. The soldier wanders about like a crab under this, still bent double, leaking blood; after which, he falls to the pavement unconscious.

Chest rising and falling, hands opening and closing in front of him, my former convict servant looks at the other soldier, cat's eyes empty of mercy.

– Do you want trouble too, corporal?

– No, mate. Not me. And I don't want our CO to know about it, neither.

– He won't, Langford says, if you just piss off.

He stoops and picks up my book; then his fingers lock on my arm and draw me away.

❧

We walk downhill towards the town. Langford continues to hold my arm, and I find I'm laughing.

– I'm very glad to see you, Langford. I suppose I owe you thanks, I say. What a fighter you are.

– St Giles is no place for you, Mr Devereux, Langford says. Especially as weak and thin as you look just now.

I ask him how he comes to be here himself.

– Well sir, I've been looking for *you*. I went to your lodgings up in Bathurst Street, and since you wasn't to be found there, I prowled about the district. Doctor Howard's orders, sir. He's away in the country just now, but he told me before he went to see how you was settling in.

– Really? You're Howard's servant again, Langford? I thought you had bigger plans, now that you're free.

– Maybe I do, sir. All in good time. But the Doctor sent a servant with a note to the *Raffles* offering me the job of running his property – and I jumped at the chance. It's a beautiful place the Doctor has: only two miles from the city. A fine house, with a neat little farm attached.

– I look forward to seeing it this Sunday, I say. Meanwhile, Langford, you can report to Doctor Howard that you found me well, but somewhat drunk. As drunk as a whaler, in fact.

– No need for me to tell him that – even though it may be true, Langford says. And it's not like you to be drunk, is it, sir? In all our time on Bermuda and the *Raffles,* I never even seen you tipsy. I'd say you've earned a little spree: you kept yourself on an uncommon tight rein for a long time: or that's been my observation. But you ought to be getting home now, sir – else you'll be nabbed by some bloody constable. We both will. It's curfew, in less than an hour.

And he winks. He's telling me, I believe, that he and I are now on an equal footing.

2. ARCADY

November 16th

The main street of Hobart Town climbs out of the city to the north, by way of Lord's Hill. Once it has crossed this low hill, it ceases to be Elizabeth Street and becomes Main Road: the chief coaching road of the colony, running through the centre of Van Diemen's Land from south to north, to reach the second city of Launceston. The first place that it brings you to, on the other side of Lord's Hill, is the semi-rural district of New Town, where Doctor Howard has his house and farm. But until you arrive at the summit of the hill, both New Town and the island's interior lie hidden.

Langford was my coachman yesterday, and took me to the edge of that land.

He arrived at Mrs Turner's lodging-house in Doctor Howard's gig, a little after half-past five, to drive me to Bay House for dinner. He was even more spruce than he'd been the other night, his flat, broad-brimmed hat set at a confident and swaggering angle, making him look rather like an American. His tail coat was of excellent cut, and his white buckskin trousers were drawn over gleaming top boots: an equestrian touch that was no doubt intended to signify his present role. He sat with military erectness, holding the reins loosely in both hands – looking as though he'd been driving about the colony for years, instead of a mere four days. One would never have taken him for an emancipated felon.

Coming out of Bathurst into Elizabeth Street, the gig joined a busy procession of traffic: barouches, broughams and the lumbering spring carts of farmers, all moving north out of the city. Langford drove with expert ease, and I began to admire and covet this smart little gig of Howard's: a new English Stanhope with sweeping, red-painted shafts, its two low wheels made for town use. It would have had trouble on a rough road, but to my surprise, this convict-built highway was very good indeed: macadamised so perfectly that there was seldom a jolt. We followed a long, steep curve. Behind us, in the south, lay the city and its harbour and blue estuary. Then Langford brought the gig to a halt, on the summit of Lord's Hill. The vista to the south was gone behind our backs, and the heartland of the island lay spread out below us to the north.

– There we are, sir, Langford said, and waved his hand. New Town – and a lot more besides.

There was a wonderful stillness up here. Muted and far, the barking of dogs and the lowing of cattle rose to us through fathoms of mild air. The leather of the seat was warm where my hand rested on it, and I gazed at what Langford had brought me to with pleasure and amazement.

Here in Van Diemen's Land was a near-perfect replica of England. The native bush had largely been cleared; in its place, rolling off for miles, was a sweet, gentle countryside of villas and farmlets, open, green and park-like, dotted with the gold of gorse. Roses, geraniums and hollyhocks grew around the doors of shingle-roofed cottages; substantial stone villas crouched behind oaks and cedars. In the middle distance, through a blue film of wood-smoke, a tiny stone church-spire rose, honeyed and ancient in the prelude to the Sabbath sunset: a painting by Constable. Imperial magic! England in a looking glass! The illusion was complete – until one's glance went further, to the distant horizon in the north.

There, everything altered, and I saw that this English pastoral was contained in a larger picture: the true, virgin landscape of the island. Out there, the numberless hills of Van Diemen's Land receded in waves: peaked like witches' hats, blue and then violet, ending in a region almost beyond vision, where a long line of clouds stretched above their tops, touched with the gold of sunset. A country lay out there like that of fable: one that was largely unsettled; much of it scarcely explored.

– Good Lord, Langford, I said. Doctor Howard is living in Arcadia.

He shot me a puzzled glance.

– I'm sorry, sir. Where?

– In the land of all good things, I said. The one the ancient Greeks wrote of.

– I wouldn't know about that, sir. All I ever saw of Greece was the Bay of Navarino. But it's choice land, true enough. A man might settle here and be happy.

– I can understand your thinking so, I said.

– Mind you, this is for the gentry, he said. New Town's expensive, being only two miles from the city. And Bay House is one of the prettiest properties here. It's a pleasure to manage it for the Doctor. There's only five and a half acres, and I've got a general farmhand and a gardener working for me – both passholders, but behaving reasonably steady, now I'm here. They were pretty bloody idle before I came, and giving the Doctor some headaches, he being too busy at the hospital to watch them.

– You sound as though you've found a berth that suits you, Langford.

– It's a place that suits me for now – but not for long, he said. The Doctor knows that. I've got plans of my own.

I glanced at him curiously. What sort of future here would satisfy this ruthless ex-soldier and train-robber?

– Tell me about these plans of yours, I said.

– Why sir, he said, what I want is a farm.

– Really? But is that possible? It would cost a good deal – not just the property, but the equipment. Can you afford it, so soon?

He grinned at me.

– Well now, I believe I can, he said. Within two months or so. It's only a matter of how good a farm I want to buy.

His gaze, pleasant but hard, now seemed to challenge me.

– I'll tell you what you're thinking, sir, shall I? You're asking yourself how I might get the money for a farm so prompt. Am I right? But being pretty shrewd, you've already got a notion, I should think. Yes, I've got the money for a farm, I promise you, and there won't be a bloody thing the traps can do about it.

– What became of your loot is no concern of mine, I said. But I must confess, Langford, I've always wondered how you managed such a thing. How on earth was it possible to rob a train?

At this he laughed outright, throwing back his head.

– Well now, Mr Devereux, you're asking me to tell you what the British Government couldn't find out. And *they* wanted to know very bad, I promise you.

– Well then, Langford, you mustn't tell me.

– Oh, but I've informed them *now*. How else do I come to be sitting here, free as a bird?

– I don't follow you, Langford.

– You really don't know, sir? I somehow had the notion the Doctor would have put you in the picture. At first, I was sentenced to be hanged, do you see? Then they changed it to fourteen years, and sent me to Bermuda. But after I got there, the Prime Minister himself had a private communication sent to me.

He rubbed his chin and paused, squinting at me.

– It offered to remit my whole sentence, he said, if only I told them the secret.

– The Prime Minister offered that? Good God. And what secret was it that he wanted so badly?

– Why, I mean my *method*, sir – how it was done. It had never been done before, you see – and the Government was desperate eager to guard against it happening again, on other train lines. But at first, I couldn't tell. There was two coves in it with me, see, who was still walking free. I wouldn't grass on them. But a year ago I learned that they'd skipped out of England – so I was able to come to an agreement.

– You're an amazing fellow, I said. However, I've no wish to pillage your secrets, like that bastard Jack Russell.

– But I *want* to tell you, he said. I'll tell you because I trust you, sir – and I want you to trust *me*.

He wasn't the sort of rogue who was given to idle boasting, I knew. If he wanted to favour me with such a vital confidence, he had a definite motive. It was one I couldn't guess; nor did I intend to try. Instead, I sat back and drew out my pipe and tobacco-pouch. We had plenty of time to get to Doctor Howard's for dinner, and I was filled with a mood of luxurious consent. Let Langford delay us, here in the Sabbath calm on Lord's Hill, and make whatever outlandish disclosures he wished.

– Very well, I said. But understand that you tell me this of your own volition.

He smiled, and turned his narrowed eyes on the traffic of Main Road, and the hills in the north.

– There was three of us, he said.

There were three of them, and they robbed the London–Folkestone train, on the newly-opened South Eastern Railway. Langford was the master-mind. The scheme and the 'method' were of his devising. He'd discovered that the train carried regular consignments of gold bullion, bound for Paris. At Folkestone harbour, the bullion was transferred to the Boulogne steam packet. The consignments, in gold coin and ingots, were carried in the guard's van, in sealed, iron-bound boxes which were locked in steel safes. The officials of the South Eastern Railway must have felt that their arrangements were impregnable; that the gold lay at the heart of a fortified labyrinth. But Langford devised a way to penetrate the labyrinth.

It wasn't easy or simple; the whole scheme had about it the tactical skill, daring and ruthlessness of a brilliant military campaign. More; it displayed the implacable patience without which such an enterprise – like so many others, in so many fields of endeavour – could never have succeeded. It's patience that distinguishes the great man from the merely gifted one. Impatient over trivial things, such a man has the patience of the ant over the detail of the task in hand. Patience makes the great leader and the great artist; a sort of remorseless patience must have characterised both Beethoven and Napoleon. Patience, I believe, must always accompany genius, if success is to be found – and patience of this kind is what our leaders in Ireland have so often lacked. As I listened to Langford, a part of me couldn't help admiring him – while another part grew appalled at his cold criminality.

241

– At first it wasn't serious, he said. Something I thought about to amuse myself. A game, you might say, to take my mind off the bloody miserable life that Bess and I was leading.

This was over five years ago, in the February of 1844. He was living in a hovel in Camden Town at the time, with his wife and only son – a boy then aged thirteen. Langford was thirty-eight years old, and they were very poor. After his wounded knee had put him out of the Marines as a young man, he'd gone to sea again in the merchant service, serving as an ordinary seaman, and making many voyages to America and the East. But then, in his early middle age, he began to find that his damaged knee was growing worse, and making the work on sailing ships not only more and more trying, but dangerous. Once, going aloft in a storm, the leg caused him to slip and nearly fall from a yardarm; rather than court death any further, he decided on a life ashore. This did not prove easy. He worked in a variety of menial occupations, while his wife took in washing and mending to help support them. Then, drinking in a tavern one night, he fell into conversation with a poor clerk: an undersized, wistful young man named Bennett, who worked in the South Eastern Railway's traffic department.

– He seemed out for a bit of excitement, but didn't know how to get it, Langford said. He'd led a boring life, lived with his widowed mother, and dreamed about adventures. You know the sort of cove, sir.

I knew. I could see them together, in a tavern in Camden Town, drinking their glasses of gin in the crowded, malodorous tap room: the tiger-eyed, limping ex-seaman and the thin-faced, wistful clerk – who no doubt scented in Langford the very essence of wildness; of escapades, risk, violence, and the rumour of foreign places, rising about him like the odour of his clothes; his body. Outside the tavern would be the grim and thrilling cold, and all London's mazes of blackened brick and stone – mazes containing not a vestige of pity for Langford's maiming, or for Bennett's wistful dreams.

– It was him that told me about the gold, Langford said. He did it to impress me. Well, I *was* impressed, I tell you. We began to joke about what a lark it would be to lay hands on it. We met regular, drinking together. He knew every detail about how it was moved, see – and I began to get ideas. That made young Bennett more and more excited. As I say, just a joke, at that stage: not meant to be real. But then I thought: why not *make* it real?

He turned to look at me, his eyes as cold as they'd been when he'd beaten the soldier in Goulburn Street.

– Yes, I know what you'll say, Mr Devereux – it was wrong – and I don't expect you'll agree with the path I took. But I'll tell you this: I don't regret it. And I'll tell you what my thinking was. I'd served my country and been wounded, and my country didn't give a fucking tinker's damn, if you'll pardon my French. As far as dear old England was concerned, I could beg in the bloody streets, or take work that scarcely kept us from starvation. But what really decided me was when Hugh died – my young son.

He paused for a moment; his big fists still held the reins, and I saw them tighten. He was gazing into the far distance, and tears had started to his eyes. He blinked them away, cleared his throat, and began to speak again, continuing to study the hills, his voice grown harsher.

– We never understood what was wrong with him, he said. He caught a fever, and couldn't eat. We got a doctor – not much of a bloody doctor, since we couldn't afford one of your fancy specialists – and *he* didn't seem to know what was wrong either. Hugh died very quick. He was the only one we had or ever will have – since Bess can't have no more.

– I'm truly sorry, I said.

He cleared his throat again, and turned to look at me now with a menacing intentness.

– That's when I decided to do it, he said. I thought: bugger their bloody eyes, I'll do something to make them sit up, and make me rich! I knew the risk – but I'd taken bigger risks in the Marines. And if I was caught, it wouldn't be much worse than the life I was living. So I set about the planning, and I found a screwsman.

So now there were three of them: the screwsman, whose name was Mobbs, Bennett, and himself. Langford dealt with them as though they were mercenary soldiers under his command; he impressed on them the importance of obeying his orders without question, and following his plans to the letter. To this, they apparently agreed.

The difficulties were formidable, and the preparations took many months. Langford had learned from Bennett that the safes containing the bullion travelled in the guard's van, under the guard's eye, together with other luggage – the new South Eastern Railway having just begun to carry passengers. The safes had double locks, needing two keys to open them; and a set of these was kept in the traffic office in London where Bennett worked. This, Langford said, was where he saw his great opportunity. Once Bennett was recruited, everything else could follow.

Bennett waited many weeks for his chance. Finally it came: when no other clerk was in the office, he was able to briefly purloin the two keys, taking them to Mobbs in a lane outside, where the screwsman made quick wax impressions. But Mobbs knew that rough copies like these wouldn't be good enough for safes of this calibre: they'd need to be fine-tuned. It was now essential to find a dishonest guard. After many months, through Bennett's delicate enquiries and approaches, this was achieved – the guard being promised a substantial share of the bullion. His first task was to allow Mobbs to make a run in the guard's van, in order for the screwsman to adjust his copied keys. Mobbs boarded the train with a greyhound, requesting that he be allowed to travel in the van with his pet – an irregular but not unusual procedure when an animal was involved. On the journey, travelling with the dishonest guard, he was able to file and adjust his keys at leisure, until they fitted the locks perfectly.

Now, in April, the plan was ready to go into operation. On a day when the bribed guard was on duty, and when three safes loaded with bullion were on board, Langford and Bennett boarded the train in London as first class passengers, bound for Folkestone. Between them they carried three courier's bags, in which were stowed large amounts of lead shot – and these they sent by porter to the guard's van. Bennett took his seat in one of the carriages; but Langford slipped unobserved into the van at the end of the train, and immediately got to work under the eyes of the dishonest guard. He unlocked one of the safes, carefully unsealed a bullion box, removed the gold, substituted the lead shot from one of the bags, resealed the box, relocked the safe, and loaded the bullion into the bag. This procedure was to be followed with the other two safes – Langford having calculated that their weight would then seem normal on unloading at Folkestone, and that they'd go onto the steamer for France without attracting suspicion.

At a station not far out of London, Mobbs the safebreaker was waiting on the platform. Langford got out and handed him the first bag of bullion, and Mobbs very quickly disappeared – to make his way back to London on another train. Meanwhile, Bennett had emerged from his compartment, walking down the platform to join Langford in the guard's van. As the train journeyed on, the two of them removed most of the contents of the other two safes, filling the two remaining bags. Then, on arrival at Folkestone, their moment of greatest danger came.

– Here the safes was unloaded, Langford said. And Bennett and I had to hide, in a nice dark corner of the van. But nobody saw us, and we was soon away, each carrying his own bag. We gave the guard his share a few days later. We was all very honest with each other, divvying it up fair: it's most important to be honest, in my view. If you're not – someone will grass. I made no mistakes like that.

He hadn't looked at me for some time; now he gave me a swift glance, smiling in a ruminative sort of way, like a man who contemplates an old love, or the happiness of youth. Meanwhile, I sat staring at him, the pipe in my mouth gone out.

– So you got clean away? Nothing was discovered?

– Clean away, sir, he said.

He shook the reins, and clicked his tongue twice to Doctor Howard's horse: a dainty brown mare called Topsy. She flicked her ears, and began to move.

– Clean away, Langford repeated. And we'd realised five thousand pounds. The safes went off to France, and nothing was known until they opened the boxes in Paris. I like to imagine the looks on the faces of the Frogs. Eh, sir? Nothing in there but shot!

Topsy broke into a trot; soon we were spinning down the slope of Main Road, joining the stream of other traffic. As we went, I broke into laughter: a laughter that took possession of me.

– Nothing but shot, I repeated, and laughed until I grew weak, slapping my knee while Langford accompanied me with a low, continuous chuckling, sending sly glances as he drove.

– You should have seen the stories in the newspapers, he said. They was *very* impressed: the South Eastern Railway Gold Affair, they called it. Bess bought a nice little dress shop in Maidstone two years ago, which has kept her nicely – and the rest of our money's safe.

– My God, Langford, I said. I don't condone what you did, but I'm compelled to say that you're a brilliant villain. If only you'd turned your talents to some noble struggle! Christ! If I had some followers like you–

I broke off, partly because I was laughing again, and partly because he'd greatly increased speed, encouraging Topsy with low cries. And now I breathed in the wind of our passage with a mindless, mirthful exultancy, and Langford's chuckling turned into frank laughter. He threw back his head and guffawed with me, urging Topsy faster on the downhill slope – taking us towards New Town, and the unplumbed land in the north.

The road levelled out; we'd come to a toll gate, where New Town proper began. Langford halted the gig beside the road, and pointed.

– No trains to rob *here*, he said. They don't have any, on this island. They're still in the bloody coaching days.

Beyond the small white turnpike house, a yellow coach-and-four was just resuming its journey: the stage for Launceston, with six passengers on top and more inside, driven by a grossly fat coachman in broad-brimmed hat and top coat. A guard in a dirty scarlet uniform clung to its side, playing on a bugle to signal their departure: a Negro melody from America, its notes soon lost in this calm English prospect, among these alien hills.

Langford and I sat on in silence, watching the coach disappear into Main Road's level distance: a phantom from a lost, unhurried era, preserved in the Antipodes. The waning western sun was on our faces, pleasantly dazing us, and time seemed suddenly suspended. Langford showed no inclination to urge Topsy forward towards the bars of the toll-gate, and I had no great wish for him to do so. The highway was enveloped by a warm and sleepy quiet: a quiet broken only by the rumbling of a red and blue farm-wagon, coming the other way towards Hobart Town, toy-small and far, seeming to advance by inches between Main Road's garden fences and long rows of poplars, a lean brown dog trotting beside it, its old wooden frame and ungreased axles sending groans and cracks like gunshots across the miles, profound and significant as sounds in a reverie. And now a deep peace stole into me, like the product of some process of exquisite fermentation. It remains with me today: a calm I've not felt since my arrest in Dublin.

Finally, I broke the silence.

– I have one more question, Langford – if you care to answer it. Since your plan was so perfect, and since your accomplices are still free, how is it *you* were taken?

A small, tolerant smile touched his lips.

– Well, sir, he said, it was the guard. They questioned him pretty fierce, as you might imagine – but he wouldn't admit to anything. Claimed he'd seen no-one in the van, and that the switch must have been made at Folkestone, or Boulogne. There wasn't much they could do about that – and for a few months, all went quiet. But then the silly bugger quit his job, and he and his wife went to Brighton, and bought a nice little house. That was much too soon. It made the traps very interested – and they came back to questioning him again, wanting to know how he'd got so prosperous. It was the wife who blabbed – she got frightened, and thought if they turned the three of us in, her old man would be shown clemency. Well, he was – his sentence was only seven years. They questioned my Bess, o' course, but got nowhere – nothing frightens Bess. So although they caught *me*, they never got the money – and they never caught Bennett or Mobbs. They went to ground – and as it turned out, they had the sense in the end to slip off to the Continent. So I was all the traps had; and the guard swore blind he'd no idea how we got into the safes. They believed him – and that left *me* as their only hope of finding out. Which has turned out fortunate for me, you might say.

– And the money? I asked. Was any of it recovered?

– From the guard sir, of course – but his cut was nothing like the size of ours. Mobbs and Bennett are safe, with *their* share of the loot. They'll never be taken. And mine's with Bess, who I'd trust with my life, and who's now on a ship bound for Sydney.

He grinned at me sideways, while I stared. Then he shook the reins and urged Topsy forward, holding out pennies to the toll-keeper. The old man swung back the creaking cross-bars, admitting us to New Town, and the highway to the north.

Langford drove east, going off Main Road up a small hill. Then he turned downhill again, and we entered the district's innermost valley, by way of a thoroughfare called Bay Road. This road descended in a long, gentle run to an inlet of the Derwent called New Town Bay, which gleamed silver and broad below us, between dark, native eucalypts and the distant roofs of a village. In the east, beyond the river, rose a double-humped mountain called Mount Direction: lighter and more friendly than Gothic Mount Wellington, and a deep, inviting mauve in the sunset. At the bottom of the hill, Langford told me, we'd come to Bay House: Doctor Howard's villa.

The gig swayed on down the slope; and again I found myself silenced by the peace that surrounded us. Here in this valley by the river, Britannia's empire had been able to establish perfectly that pattern of domestic intimacy so dear to the English soul. Reassuring smoke rose from Bay Road's tall brick chimneys; respectful farm labourers in smocks passed us on foot, touching the brims of their hats, and the fragrance of sweetbriar and hawthorn hedges reached us in the gig – mingling queerly with the tang of native eucalyptus. We drove through long shadows cast by the trees, passing ordered orchards of apple, plum and cherry, where the blue-winged native parrots darted like creatures of fancy. There were shadow-barred nut-walks here, and neat green fields dotted with fat cattle, and gravelled driveways and lawns, and many-coloured beds of immigrant flowers, and handsome stone villas in the Regency manner.

The gentlefolk of New Town were living in a picture book – whose coach-houses, mellow stone barns and drowsing garden walls, with drowsing English cats on top of them, made a barrier of protection against those presences they deplored: the drunken emancipists of the town, and the magpie-suited convicts who menaced them in byways. And underneath everything, low yet audible above the gig's wheels, came the drawling, languorous complaints of English pigeons and doves: near as memory, yet magically far.

I sighed with a sort of nostalgia.

– I can understand your wanting to take up land in this island, I told Langford. I might almost wish it myself.

He turned his head to me quickly.

– That's what you *should* do, Mr Devereux – in my opinion.

– Perhaps, I said lightly. Perhaps I should go partners with you, Langford.

I told myself that I spoke in jest; but Langford's response disconcerted me. He leaned back, pulling on the reins, and brought the gig to a halt.

– Now that's exactly what I've been hoping, he said. I'm glad you was the one who said it first, Mr Devereux – and I'd like to take you up on your offer.

I looked at him in astonishment, and laughed.

– My dear Langford, I said. I spoke lightly – with no sort of seriousness at all. I won't deny that the idea appeals to me, but it was merely a fancy. I was moved by the beauty of this place – that's all.

His eyes remained fixed on me. He seemed to be inwardly revolving something of great importance to him, while striving to remain composed.

– We'll reach Bay House in two more minutes, he said. But before we do, Mr Devereux, will you give me the favour of a hearing? You've only to say no, and I'll drive on. I ask it in memory of our times on the *Medway*.

– I do you no favour by talking to you, Langford. I owe you a debt of gratitude, for your kindness to me on that filthy hulk. I'll happily listen to anything you have to say – and if there's any sort of help that I can give you, I will.

– Then, sir, he said, I'd like to discuss your offer. Maybe you meant it as a joke – but I take it serious. I need a partner, and you're the partner I'm wanting. I'd be truly obliged if you'd give it consideration: I mean equal shares in a farm, and taking equal shares on whatever it returns us. It's been on my mind since Bermuda. I wasn't going to speak just yet a while; but now I hear you say you might like to go farming – why, I'm encouraged to do it.

– I appreciate your offer, I said, and I do wish you well. But you scarcely need me. I'm no farmer.

He'd set his big jaw on a slant that was almost truculent, as though about to challenge me; and his next words confirmed this impression.

– *Do* entertain it, sir. Don't shut your mind to it.

– Listen to me, Langford, I said. You, more than most men, should understand my position. I'm forced into exile here against my will – and I've no intention of accepting this fate for ever. I'll not become a Van Diemen's Land colonist.

His eyes narrowed.

– *I* don't ask you to remain a prisoner here, he said. You *are* one, just like me. But unlike me, and unlike a lot of other poor bloody bastards on Van Diemen's Land, you've *chosen* your situation.

Somewhat theatrically, he lifted his hand, holding it with the palm turned towards me.

– I know, sir, I know: you've chosen it for patriotic reasons. But I simply say in passing that I never saw the buggers beaten by going at them at head-on; you've got to come at them from behind, in my experience.

No man of Langford's station had ever presumed to speak to me with such familiarity; and yet, since I'd come to be fond of him, it neither angered nor disturbed me. I waited for him to go on, saying nothing. He'd dropped his head now, hands fidgeting with the reins. He seemed to search for further words, at the same time examining the reins with an awkwardness that was quite unlike him – almost approaching shyness. Then he looked up at me again, and spoke with a new abruptness.

– Be that as it may, you ain't white-livered; I saw that on

Bermuda. I can see why you're taken as the leader of that bloody cause of yours, and why the traps hate you. There was nothing they could do that would break you – not even if they'd sent you to the quarries; not even if that bloody asthma killed you. And you never whined, or crawled to them. I admire that in a man – even if he may be wrong-headed.

Again he showed me his palm, elevating it quickly with a sudden, placatory grin.

– I don't say you *are* wrong-headed, sir – I just say that I don't twig at all to what you and them other Irish gentlemen think you're doing. They've got you penned up like sheep, sixteen thousand miles from home, for twelve or more years – come now, that's the long and short of it, ain't it? And as I understand it from the Doctor, you've given your written word to them not to scarper. What will you *do* here? Twiddle your thumbs? You're not that kind of man. So why *not* take up land? Why not farm? There's some bloody fine country here, you admit that. So will you listen to what I'm proposing? Won't you simply listen?

I sat back in my seat.

– I'll listen, Langford. But what exactly do you propose? That we grub out a living in the bush, keeping pigs? I don't know how much money you still have left from your railway affair – but I have only a small amount of capital. I doubt that we'd afford a wealthy sheep property.

– No, he said. The gentry with friends in the Government have got all the best grazing land picked off: I've found that out already. But I've got a better idea – and one that won't cost us too much.

He leaned towards me, pointing a finger at my chest.

– I'm talking about hops, he said. I'm a Kentish man, and hops is something I know about. You don't need many acres for a hop garden. And this is a place that's perfect for hops. They're the coming crop here.

– Are you sure of this, Langford? After all, you've been here little more than a week.

He pointed to the north: to the hills at the limit of vision, touched now with sunset's rose and bronze.

251

– Twenty or so miles up the Derwent, there's a district called New Norfolk, he said. There's hop gardens there – and they're doing amazing well: as good as anything you'll see in Kent. I've taken a trip on the river steamer, and seen for myself. Everything's right for hops there: good climate, good deep river soil, and transport to Hobart Town by barge for your crops. And the market's good too. Hops are four shillings a pound, at present. The biggest grower up there is a very wealthy man – and how can he not be? They like their beer, in Van Diemen's Land.

– That I'll grant you, Langford.

– I found a property for sale, he said. Five miles south-east of the town of New Norfolk: fifty acres. He's a stupid cove, and knows very little about growing hops – so he ain't doing as well as the other growers, and he's anxious to sell and go home. The property's not on the Derwent, which is where the choicest farms are – it's on a little tributary called Sorell Creek. That's why it's cheap. But it's a sweet little place, and I know we can do a lot with it. The land's at a pound an acre – a lot of it uncleared bush. But there's five acres at present under hops, a kiln, stables, and a handsome brick house. He wants five hundred pounds for the lot. It's cheap at the price, sir. I tell you, New Norfolk's one of the best situations in the colony.

He paused, watching my face like a bird-dog waiting for the report of the gun.

– You go on very fast, I said. Stop saying 'we', Langford.

But his absolute confidence, and the smile he now gave me – a smile which was quaintly at odds with the truculent thrust of his jaw – were diverting me so much that I began to smile back. And in that instant, I realised that I was genuinely tempted.

To be a landowner here – why not? It might well be years before I gained a pardon, or effected an escape. The idea offered me something that had been denied me since my arrest: contentment, in a pastoral retreat from the world. Hope had never deserted me – but contentment had. To be content! The thought of it was like the promise of something so long denied that I'd ceased to believe in it, or to recognise its face. Still Langford watched me:

and I saw the urgency of his need to persuade me. Like any sign of vulnerability in a strong man, it was touching and disturbing. I had no wish to trifle with his hopes, and I chose my words carefully.

– So what you're proposing to me is that we put up two hundred and fifty pounds each, and that I – who know nothing about farming – should become a hop-grower with you. Is that it?

– Better than that, Mr Devereux.

His voice became throaty and persuasive, and his smile broadened; he looked cunning, as though tempting a child with sweets.

– We put up half each, and we split the profits equal, fair and square. But you don't have to share the work. You can be a gentleman farmer, if you want. Practise the law here – carry on with your writing; whatever you like. *I'll* take care of the farm.

– And why should you offer such an unequal bargain?

He answered without hesitation.

– I need the extra money. I need to buy equipment, and expand the hop grounds in the way I want. I could buy a poorer property – or I could start to grow from scratch. But I want *this* property. And I want the advantage of being partners with a gentleman like you. I can't put it plainer.

– Come, I think you can, Langford. Why me?

He took off his handsome white hat, and scratched his head.

– I could tell you sweet lies, but I won't, he said. I ain't wanting to share my fortunes with some tricky ex-burglar or forger – and I can't see any gentleman settler wanting a partnership with a man like me.

– Whereas I'm a gentleman fallen from grace, I said.

– No, he said. I can't see the sense in what you done, and if I was still a soldier, and they ordered me to shoot you, I would. But you ain't a criminal, Mr Devereux. Excuse me, but I must speak plain. I don't believe you know how to swindle, or be tricky. We was together a long time on Bermuda – I got to know you, waiting on you, and I've made my judgment of you. And you'll have made one of me, I suppose. It may be cheek to ask a gentleman like you to go partners with a villain like me – but I'm asking it. And I tell you – I'll work hard, and by Christ, I'll make us rich. Well?

– I'm glad of your good opinion, I said. And I believe you'll succeed in anything you do. I won't deny that your proposal's attractive. But I don't want to encourage you to think that I'll make any decision now. All I'll say to you is that I'll think about it.

He nodded without speaking. Then he picked up the reins again.

– That's all I ask sir, he said. Think about it. But do give me your answer soon – for that farm won't wait. Then we'll talk serious.

Another man would have said more; but not Langford. Instead he shook the reins, and started Topsy off. Rolling down Bay Road again, we sat in perfect silence, facing ahead. We must have looked rather comical.

– I'm delighted – absolutely delighted – that you agreed to give your *parole*, Doctor Howard said. I was damnably afraid you might refuse – like Mr Fitzgibbon. *That* was unexpected – and pretty aggravatin' to the Governor.

Knife and fork suspended, he glanced over his shoulder, perhaps to assure himself that the housemaid wasn't just now entering the room. She came in only to bring food to the sideboard and remove dishes; we had the room to ourselves, and Howard had been carving the roast for us, and pouring our wine. This was the first time I'd seen him out of naval uniform, and his dress matched his new prosperity: a beautifully-cut grey tail coat, a gleaming choker collar, an elegant satin cravat.

Clearly, he was far more comfortably off than I'd imagined, even taking into account his salary as Colonial Surgeon; I might have been in the home of one of my more wealthy friends in Dublin. Before I came here, I would not have imagined discovering such a room in Van Diemen's Land. The high-backed mahogany chairs we sat in were beautifully carved, and all the other furniture was of similar quality. A fire burned in the grate under a mantelpiece of white Carrara marble. The room was illuminated by the flames, and by many other soft lights, yet its dimensions were spacious enough for its corners to remain mysterious. An Argand lamp hung suspended by chains from the ceiling, and a silver candelabrum stood between us on the big oval dining-table, its flames reflected in the polished surface, and reflected again, like a cluster of stars, in the gilt-framed mirror above the sideboard. Tall windows looked out onto the garden, where dusk was finally consuming the tender English green of the trees.

– Mr Fitzgibbon's action is of course very annoyin' and inconvenient to the authorities, Howard was saying. I don't mind tellin' you, Sir William's furious about it. He seems to feel that Fitzgibbon's done it purely to create annoyance for him personally – and perhaps to cause him difficulties with London.

He smiled regretfully, and re-filled my glass with an 1835 Chateau Haut Brion that I was finding exquisite.

Everything else on the table was as good. The beef we were eating was tender, and the fresh peas, carrots and potatoes accompanying it were from Bay House's garden. I'd not had a meal to compare with it since my removal from Ireland, and a glow of well-being filled me, despite the topic of our conversation. But my physical pleasure was small in comparison to that of being reunited with Howard himself. I found I liked the man as much as ever; and I had consciously to remind myself, as I'd done at Bermuda, that our friendship was ambiguous.

– However, from what I know of Mr Fitzgibbon, Howard said, he acts purely out of his own notions of honour and patriotism. That's not to be doubted.

He shook his head, and took another mouthful of beef.

– Idealistic, but misguided, he said. An *earnest* sort of man, Mr Fitzgibbon – or so I've heard. I've not had the pleasure of meetin' him – but there's not a lot of flexibility in him, I gather. Not mercurial, like you, Devereux. Fixed: even a little obtuse. Eh? But perhaps I'm goin' too far.

This was said in a tone that came delicately close to being mocking. Doctor Howard had lost none of his taste for gossip, I saw. It was as though our conversations on Bermuda were being resumed without a break, their enigmatic colouring and humour intact – as was our underlying situation. True, I now had freedom of movement: but in fact I remained a captive, and he an exalted servant of the system that held me. His receiving me as a guest was therefore somewhat unusual – just as his attentiveness to me on the hulk had been. Doctor Howard was no longer a mere surgeon, but an important official in this gaol colony: a leading figure, in fact, in the Civil Establishment. The Colonial Surgeon – as Doctor Richards had made clear to me – was one of the inner circle of civil servants who ran Van Diemen's Land; and I wondered how Howard had gained such an appointment. He must have had powerful family connections at home; his career as a naval surgeon would not have been enough.

– Yes, I said, Fitzgibbon is earnest, I suppose – and I don't imagine he finds much that's humorous in his situation at Port Arthur. He's a serious man, a great patriot, and not to be bought or bullied.

Chewing, Howard stared at me, raising his brows.

– I don't doubt it, he said. Admirable, I'm sure. But such people can often be a nuisance – to themselves as well as others. At all events, Devereux, I'm certainly glad that *you* did nothing so wrong-headed, and are able to sit here at my table. Like old times on the *Medway* – but a little more comfortable, wouldn't you agree?

– Well now, I don't know, I said. I sometimes miss my cosy little kennel.

Howard laughed, and I saw him scan my appearance – no doubt registering the fact that I was clad tonight in far different attire from the few essential garments I'd had sent to me at Spike Island, and in which I'd been forced to live for this past year and a half. I'd had no time yet to equip myself with a complete new wardrobe, but on Thursday I'd gone to a tailor in Liverpool Street and had been measured for a suit of clothes to wear this evening. He'd finished the outfit yesterday, and his work had proved surprisingly competent – so now I appeared in a well-cut grey dress coat, with matching waistcoat and trousers, and a narrow bow tie and low collar, in the new fashion. To be prevented from keeping up a civilized standard in one's dress insidiously reduces one's confidence – however one may tell oneself that clothing is merely surface – and I enjoyed the fact that I now met Howard dressed as I would have been at home. I raised my glass.

– Your new Antipodean house is exceptionally fine, I said. I'm heartily pleased for you. Your very good health, Howard.

– And yours, Devereux. And yours. I really am amazingly glad to see you again.

He raised his glass to his lips with the sensuous yet delicate enjoyment I remembered, and drank off his wine. Then he put down the glass and threw himself back in his chair, studying me in the way I also recalled, as though making a diagnosis: head tilted back, tanned, bald forehead reflecting the candlelight, enlarged green eyes behind their spectacles pleasant yet searching.

– At the same time, he said, I remain concerned about you. When Langford brought you to the door, I was worried by your appearance. You're lookin' not much better than when I last saw you at Bermuda. You've lost a great deal of weight.

– Come, Howard, I'm feeling better every day, and wheeze very little. My asthma is gone, since I landed. I realise my death would have been very inconvenient for the authorities, but put your mind at rest. You were right – the climate of this place really does agree with me. And thanks to your generous help in sending me to stay with Thomas O'Neill, I expect to recover completely.

He waved a dismissive hand.

– I only did what I saw as my duty – so did Doctor Richards. But I'm very glad that Sir William Denison accepted our recommendation. Was you to be alone and uncared for, I believe your condition might get worse. The climate of the highlands in this place is superb: that should set you on your feet, if anythin' can. Then you can decide what you'll do here, and in which police district you'll finally settle.

– The thought of settling in any police district rather chills my blood, I said. I'd rather think of this island as a temporary residence.

– Dear me. I'd hoped you'd resigned yourself, Devereux, he said. You really will be here for many years – why not enjoy your exile, as far as possible? The place has many advantages – which is why I've come here.

– I agree the island is very beautiful. One might indeed enjoy it, had one come here voluntarily. But forgive me, Howard: your situation is a little different from mine.

He fell silent, pouring us more wine, and continued to frown at the tilted decanter as he did so, the candle-light glinting on his spectacles. Then he looked up at me.

– I don't forget that, of course, he said. But I wonder if you understand the reception you might enjoy in society here. Outside of official circles, you and your comrades are not seen as felons at all. In fact, I'm told that many of our leading colonists see you as prisoners of war – who've in no way lost your honour. You'd find yourself well-received by them; and some are not uncultivated people.

He leaned forward, holding my gaze.

– Don't make your life miserable, as Fitzgibbon's doin'. Enjoy what there is to enjoy. You'll always be welcome in my house, I assure you – I'll value your acquaintanceship more than ever, now that our situation's different. Conversation with a man like yourself is a pleasure I don't often find.

– I'm gratified to hear you say so, I said. And the pleasure in our talks is mutual. I'll be glad of your company – and of any other civilised companionship that may offer itself here.

He sat back, his smile returning.

– Good, he said. Good. Now my advice is this: make a new life here, in this new world. Why not take up Langford's offer? Why not buy a little farm?

Seeing the surprise in my face, he laughed.

– Oh yes, I know about it – and I must say I approve. Langford has my backin' in anything he wants to do. He's an excellent man, my James – a most unusual man, as I think you know. I'd be delighted to see you go partners with him. He may have been a robber on the grand scale, but I don't believe he'd fail you in any way. He's so damned capable, I believe he'd make you both wealthy.

– But wouldn't you be sorry to lose him as your steward?

– I would indeed – but I know I can't hope to hold him for

long. He's been quite open about it. James is free now, and ambitious – and I see his goin' in with you as an ideal solution.

I laughed, but refrained from asking him what solution that might be. A solution to my wish to regain my freedom, perhaps? I guessed that Howard had discussed Langford's scheme with him at some length; perhaps had even influenced him in arriving at it. It begins to seem that everyone I meet in this colony is trying to persuade me to take up a life of his own devising for me.

I'd certainly be thinking over Langford's offer, I told Howard. In some ways I found it attractive; but in the end, I must decide my future for myself – if indeed I had a future here at all.

Howard became sober again at this, gazing at me as though trying to read my mind; then I saw him decide not to press me. He nodded quickly, and said:

– Of course. You'll be the one to decide this, Devereux, and no-one will influence you. I know you too well to imagine otherwise.

At this moment, the housemaid crept in again, carrying towards the sideboard a tray laden with bowls for our dessert, a large apple pie and a jug of cream. I'd scarcely noticed her before; but now an incident occurred that caused me to do so. As she set the tray down, she somehow managed to upset the two empty bowls, which fell to the floor and shattered.

– Ah, *mo bhrón*! she said. Jesus, Mary and Joseph.

She was Irish, and I looked at her now with mingled amusement and pity, knowing what disaster she felt had descended on her. Frozen at the sideboard among the shards of crockery, her head in its white muslin cap bowed and thrust forward, she'd raised one hand to her mouth, while the other clutched her apron. Small in stature, half-submerged in her lilac print dress with its bell-shaped skirt – from under which small black slippers peeped, like those of a child that had donned its mother's gown – she remained with her back to us. But we were able to see her face, reflected in the mirror above the sideboard as the flames of the candles were, which danced about her image like fireflies; and this white, counterfeit visage in the looking-glass, its lips parted in panic, its pale eyes flaring, looking back at Howard and at me (or rather, looking back at our reflections), had a briefly uncanny appearance: we seemed for these moments to be presented with a face which was no convict housemaid's at all, but that of some water-sprite from legend, staring from the depths of a pool.

Then she turned around and became herself, facing Doctor Howard in silent, anguished appeal. He wiped his lips with his napkin, regarding her with a regretful expression.

– Oh dear, he said. Another accident, Kathleen.

– I'm so sorry, your honour. They just seemed to leap from my hands.

It was an accent from the West, I thought: from Mayo, perhaps, or Galway. Her voice was soft, not unpleasing, with a piping, pleading note like a girl's. She was certainly no longer a girl – I judged her to be somewhere in her twenties – but she had something of the look of an undernourished child. This was suggested by the narrowness of her waist, and especially by the gauntness of her face, with its high, round cheekbones, hollow cheeks, and small, narrow chin: a physiognomy typical of our peasantry, and hardly novel to me. Why then, as she turned, had there been a constriction in my throat?

I found her attractive, I suppose, this little Irish passholder. Her face retained traces of its double in the mirror: a strangeness expressed most vividly by her eyes. Set wide apart, and of a light, sky-blue, they had that slanting, Slavonic cast which sometimes occurs among our Celtic people: a cast that's exotic and almost wolf-like. Unreadable, even cold, going from one to the other of us and finally back to Howard, they remained remote from her present trouble, and invulnerable to anything that Doctor Howard might say or do – even though her body shrank, waiting for reprimand; even though her small white fist went on nervously twisting her apron.

– I'll go and get the broom, your honour. And I'll have fresh bowls in a moment, she said.

Howard smiled, and his voice grew kindly.

– Good, he said. Don't fret about it, child – but try not to break many more, or there'll be no dishes left for us to eat from.

Her face lightened, and anxiety left it. She hurried away for her broom and pan and fresh bowls, returned in moments, cleaned up the broken crockery, and served us our apple pie. When she'd gone again, Howard looked across at me with mock-resignation, helping himself to the cream.

– Kathleen's a willin' girl, he said, but like a lot of passholders, she's inclined to be clumsy. Everyone has stories of disaster with convict servants here, so I shouldn't really complain. A friend of mine hired one who was an ex-ploughboy, and the fellow destroyed an entire dinner set. You can send them back to the Government hiring depot – but the next one you pick may be just as bad. They pretend they've had experience as servants in order to get hired, but quite often they're lyin'. Well well, a free servant's wages would cost me five times as much.

– And what of Kathleen? Will you send her back?

– Oh, no. She's been with me about eight months, and she's pleasant and obligin' – nothin' like so hardened or depraved as a lot of the London women. I find her rather appealin', and want to help her.

He cleared his throat here, and pursed his lips.

– She's a fairly tragic case: been in and out of trouble ever since gettin' to Van Diemen's Land. It happens to so many convict women: they fall foul of the system and start on a downward spiral, instead of an upward one. This girl was originally given her pass quite quickly, but was hired by a master and mistress she didn't get on with; they laid a complaint with a Magistrate in order to be rid of her, and she went off to the prison they call the Female Factory, doin' hard labour at the wash tubs. She's been there twice: the second time, she was pregnant, and bore an illegitimate child. It caught a fever, apparently, and died at about three months. That was last February. She was granted a pass again, after that, and I hired her from the Brickfields depot.

– God help her, I said. The poor creature. No wonder she appears sad. And who was the father of the child?

– She won't say – but I gather it was another convict servant. It happens all too frequently, y' know. And she's a pretty thing, wouldn't you agree? The more vicious sort of men among the convict servants prey on young women like that – and it's hard to stop them. She'd be temptin' to the wrong sort of master, too; and there are one or two of those, I'm afraid. The wives often turn a blind eye – or refuse to believe it.

– And what was her crime in Ireland?

– Transported from Limerick for larceny, about two years ago. I've no other details.

– From the West, I said. I thought so. And a peasant girl. The Famine was very bad there. It would have reduced her family to starvation. To me, she's no criminal at all – unlike your English pickpockets.

Howard held up both hands, placatory and smiling.

– You won't get me to disagree with you, Devereux. I try to treat her kindly; and my housekeeper does too. Mrs Bates makes no complaints about her – and Mrs Bates makes my household respectable. A very upright woman who came out free, and is married to my pass-holding gardener. Under the regulations, without a married woman here, I couldn't have female passholders assigned to me – my bein' a bachelor. Our authorities do try and protect the women in that way. Those who are given permission to hire them are supposed to be assistin' in their reform.

As he made this statement, his expression remained neutral. Then he pushed his bowl aside and smiled at me with a whimsical expression, his chin tilted higher.

– But I must confess I've taken advantage of Kathleen in one way, he said. I persuaded her to model for her portrait. That's a little beyond what her duties require – but she has an interestin' physiognomy, and I'm quite pleased with the result. I become more and more devoted to portraiture lately, and look for models everywhere. Langford's obliged me, and so has William Bates the gardener. Let me show you my latest efforts, Devereux. I thought we might have coffee in my studio.

Bay House is in the Regency style, and built of the local, tawny freestone. Single-storeyed, with green-shuttered windows, and green trellis columns of wrought iron that run along the verandah in front, it's set on a rise, facing east across the reaches of the Derwent. Some distance below on its northern side lies a small hamlet, huddled on the banks of a rivulet which runs into New Town Bay. Doctor Howard's studio is at this northern end of the house, with French windows looking on to the garden. They stood open this evening, since the weather was mild, framing the distant lights of the village.

As we took coffee and brandy here, reclining in Genoa velvet armchairs, I decided that the studio probably reflected the second aspect of the Doctor's nature. And clearly, Doctor Howard does have two aspects. The more public one – that of surgeon and colonial official – is suited by his formal dining room, where he no doubt entertains other eminent servants of the convict Government. The second aspect – that of amateur artist – is at home in the studio; and the studio, I suspect, expresses that part of himself that's nearest to his core.

This had once been a music room, Howard told me. It was large, and highly individual in its fittings. It seemed to me a blend of painter's studio and some curious apartment in the Orient – since most of the furniture here, other than our armchairs, was Chinese. All of it was black-lacquered, and painted with Chinese birds and flowers: a tall, odd-looking cabinet, two large chests, a screen in front of the nearby fireplace, and the low, round table between us. Howard had acquired these pieces on his voyages to Canton, he told me: they'd followed him to Bermuda, and now here. Instead of a carpet, coarse fibre India matting covered the floor. In the centre of the room stood a large, cloth-covered kitchen table, piled with portfolios of drawings. An easel stood nearby, and many of Howard's paintings and drawings hung about the walls – some of them watercolours of scenes on the China Coast and at Bermuda, others pastel and oil studies of the heads of convicts, guards, and the Negro inhabitants of Bermuda.

On the far side of the room stood a strikingly beautiful marble sculpture, almost life-size: a nude youth and maiden embracing, whom Howard identified as Eros and Psyche. The piece was a copy of an antique, he informed me – the original being in a museum in Rome. He treasured it, and was delighted that it had survived the voyage here unbroken.

– I've found a good deal of contentment here, Devereux, he said.

He waved his hand vaguely at the room. Like me, he was perhaps a little tipsy, since we'd drunk two bottles of wine.

– Bay House suits me, he said. Van Diemen's Land suits me. Which is why I'm urgin' you to sink roots here yourself.

– You don't miss Europe, Howard? You don't miss home, and civilization?

– Civilization? It's become a good deal too fast for me, in the last few years. I think it has somethin' to do with the comin' of the railways – and so many other God-damned machines. Everyone's in a constant hurry now, at home: everythin's at high pressure, like these bloody steam boilers. Everythin's about speed. I don't like speed. Have you noticed somethin' about Van Diemen's Land, Devereux? No steam trains – and no damned rush. It's the world as it was thirty years ago – even older. Slow, sleepy wagons in the lanes; slow, friendly pedlars comin' to your door. Even spinnin' wheels, still. And I'm almost self-sufficient. This little estate of mine grows most of what we eat: our hens give us eggs, our cows give us milk, and Mrs Bates bakes our bread. It's the world of Virgil's *Georgics,* Devereux – and there are worse worlds to live in, wouldn't you say? I feel at times I'm almost livin' in the Golden Age.

– Very tempting, Doctor: and like Virgil and the other Roman gentry, you have your slaves.

– The passholders? Come now, that's a bit harsh. They do earn wages – and eventually their freedom. It's a quite enlightened system, with all its faults. And it's endin' – did you know that? The colonists here don't want it any more: they want a new country, free of the offerin's from our prisons – and London's almost given in. The ship that brought you from Bermuda may well be the last convict transport that will ever come to Van Diemen's Land. It's a free society that's comin' into bein' here. They want it re-named Tasmania. The Australian colonies are a new America, in their view.

– I won't deny that you tempt me, I said, with these bucolic

264

visions of yours. I don't like the new bustle, either – even though I love the new political freedoms. Do you read Thomas Carlyle, Howard? I'm a great admirer of his. He wrote nearly twenty years ago that the Old had passed away, but that the New had yet to appear. It's here now with a vengeance, in Europe – and its face isn't always attractive. So I see what you mean. One could happily vegetate on Van Diemen's Land: pretend that the New isn't here; recover lost Boeotia, in the southern hemisphere.

Swirling the brandy in his glass, sitting quite still, Howard was watching me with narrowed eyes as I spoke – his expression mingling benevolence and shrewd calculation, as it had so often done in the past.

– Then perhaps you'll answer Langford's prayers, he said, and start that farm with him. Find your own Boeotia.

He put down the glass and stood up.

– And now let me show you my paintin's, he said. Come and look at my study of our forthright James Langford.

He crossed to the big table, and I followed him. Rummaging among his portfolios, he drew out a watercolour drawing which he propped up on the easel. A striking likeness of Langford, clad in a rough blue blouse for farm work, stared at me with tiger's eyes. The artistic penetration that Howard had demonstrated in his oil painting of Commander Moffatt at Bermuda was even more evident here: he'd depicted both Langford's good-humoured surface and the underlying warning of a savage yet disciplined violence. It lurked in the eyes, as it did in life, and in the set of the chin.

– It's Langford to the life, I said. What a talent you have, Howard. You capture the man entirely: upright servant and secret rogue, all in one.

– You're very kind, Howard said, and his smile showed the frank, childlike pleasure of an artist praised. You've understood exactly how I see him. But you know, I really do believe that the rogue in Langford has been put aside for ever, and that all he wants now is to be a law-abidin' Van Diemen's Land farmer.

– I believe so too, I said. But rogue he is at the core, and rogue he remains, does he not?

265

– That may be, he said. But does it really matter, here in far-away Boeotia?

As I stared at him, he turned and rummaged in his portfolio again, pulling out another watercolour drawing, which he placed on top of the likeness of Langford.

– Here's our little convict maid, he said. What do you think?

She looked not at the viewer, but slightly downwards and to one side, with her tragically cold eyes. Again, the likeness was so skilful that it was as though she'd reappeared in front of us. It was a full-length study. She stood holding a pail, clad in a servant's long, tight-waisted jacket, a full skirt, and a white linen cap like a milk-maid's. Long copper hair fell from beneath this cap, to hang to her shoulders. There was an odd delicacy about her, almost as though she were a girl of gentle birth who had put on these humble gar-ments as fancy dress; but this impression was ambiguous. Hers wasn't the face of a young woman of the gentry, yet neither did it have a bucolic coarseness. What was unambiguous was its beauty: she was as beautiful in Howard's picture as she'd been in reality.

A little shiver went through me – partly in response to this beauty, and partly in sudden homesickness. Hardly knowing that I spoke, I said:

– My God, how Irish she is.

– I'm thinkin' of workin' it up into an oil, Howard said. She's such a good subject. I'd call it 'The Milkmaid'.

– I look forward to seeing it, I said. She's delightful – and you've captured her sadness, Howard. As you say, it's an unusual physi-ognomy: yet it's really very typical of our peasantry in the West of Ireland.

As I spoke, still looking at the drawing, I experienced a pang of shame that at first I could scarcely account for. Then I realised why. A peasant from Limerick Kathleen might be – but was she not one of my own, on whose behalf I struggled? Closer to me and of more importance to me than any well-bred Englishman? And yet I'd discussed her with this servant of British tyranny as though she were a butterfly. That I liked Doctor Howard made no difference to this fact.

As though he half-read my thoughts, Howard said:

– She's somethin' of a mystery to me, this little Kathleen. They're still pretty wild in the West of Ireland – ain't that so? This young woman's first language is Irish, I believe – but her English is really very good. She's had some sort of education. And yet she's quite superstitious. She believes in the banshee, I've discovered that.

Chuckling, he gathered up his paintings. Then he said suddenly:

– Will *you* sit for me, Devereux? I'd be honoured if you would. You've an interestin' face: full of the contradictions of your nature, if you don't mind my sayin' so. I'd like to try and capture it, as far as my limited skill will allow. I mean an oil – so you'd have to give me quite a few sittin's.

I told him I'd be happy to do so. But I asked him how such sittings would be possible, once I went up to the Bothwell police district.

– Don't worry, I can arrange permission for you to travel to the Hobart Town district as often as need be, he said. So you see, sittin' for me could have some attractions for you – it would get you down to town every so often. A damned nuisance, these restrictions on your movements. I'll be glad to alleviate them, in the interests of art.

He drew out a watch from his waistcoat.

– Talkin' of which, if you're to get back to town before your curfew, I'd better go and ask Langford to get the gig ready. I hate to end our evenin' so soon, Devereux, but there'll be many more, I hope. Will you excuse me a moment? Have a look through my drawin's, if you'd care to.

I stood leafing through his portfolios for a time; then I wandered across to the northern side of the room and stood beside the French windows, studying the figures of Eros and Psyche. It really was a lovely thing, this prized piece of sculpture of Howard's. The lips of the youthful, antique couple were less than an inch apart, on the verge of a kiss that eternity would not see consummated. Their marble eyes were blind to this room; blind to this barbarous, alien hemisphere; blind to anything but themselves, as their bodies twisted towards each other. The love-god's right hand caressed the earthly face whose beauty had enchanted all men, and which had now enthralled him too – he whose usual sport was to arouse such passion in others. His left hand grasped and imprisoned the back of her head, pulling her hair away to expose her exquisite ear. But he had no need to detain her: both her arms about him, she strained to be closer – yet would never be closer than this. The youth was entirely nude; the little Hellenic princess almost so. Her gown had fallen to well below her navel, exposing not only her sweetly-carved belly, but the final, exquisite plumpness of her Mount of Venus. Only the mystery of her delta was insecurely hidden – as were her breasts, behind her reaching arm.

It had now been a year and a half since I'd embraced a woman. It would be foolish to conceal from this journal that I gazed with envy at the son of Aphrodite, and at Psyche with a longing that verged on adoration: this full-bodied yet exquisite human maid who would end by becoming a goddess. Tantalised by the swing of her waist and hip, by the gown which slipped low yet would never slip lower, I stood for a period that had no measure, the fumes of the brandy still in my head.

Finally, the sound of whispering footsteps in the room made me turn.

I expected to see Doctor Howard back; instead I found that Kathleen had come in with a tray, and was crossing towards the small round table by the fire, where the coffee pot and brandy flask stood. She moved quickly, not looking at me, her head a little bent, as though in anticipation of a blow.

– Pardon me, your honour, she said.

She bent over the table, carefully putting our glasses and cups on the tray. As she'd spoken, she'd glanced across at me quickly, with a curious mixture of timidity and eagerness. There'd been the same eagerness in her glance when it had rested on me in the dining room, and I was at something of a loss to account for it. It was neither the bold glance of a loose woman, nor the frankly curious stare of a stupid one. It was almost as though she'd had some previous acquaintance with me, yet didn't quite dare claim it; or as though she were trying to send me some signal. This puzzled me, and I stood with my hands behind my back, watching her. She had now begun to hum under her breath, in a small, high, musical voice. This surprised me, given her timidity. I also seemed to recognise the tune, but couldn't place it.

– That's a pretty tune, Kathleen, I said. Will you tell me what it is?

Her head came up abruptly; she straightened, holding the brandy flask in both hands, and her eyes looked into mine. Her lips hung open, but at first she said nothing: it was as though she gazed in some sort of shock, and something stirred in me, as it had done in the dining-room. Then she smiled; and the smile transformed her face, so that all its sadness seemed to disappear.

– An' please your honour, I thought that you might know it, she said.

– Know it? How should I know it?

She glanced over her shoulder at the door, clearly nervous of Howard's return. Then she faced me again, a flush appearing on both pale cheeks, hectic and unnatural; and to my amazement, she sang two lines of the song, in the same high, true voice.

> – *Pray give attention to what I will mention,*
> *Concerning bold Devereux that patriotic man . . .*

Then she broke off, and the smile left her face.

– Oh sir, she whispered, I know who you are. My father so admired you, we had your picture on the wall in our house, cut from a magazine: you and Wolfe Tone and Daniel O'Connell. You were our hero. I know what you've done for Ireland, and what the English have done to you. I know that you're their prisoner. And I want to say: God bless you, and I pray for you. Forgive me for speaking like this, and please not to tell the Doctor.

Hardly knowing what I did, I swiftly crossed the room to her, and took both her hands in mine. They were small but rough: rather like a boy's. As I held them, her head went back so that she could gaze up at me, and her expression now was one that mingled elation with alarm. Out through the open French windows an unknown native bird made a muted, frog-like call: a sort of owl, perhaps. My heart was racing; I was intoxicated now by much more than the brandy, and I spoke to her quickly, and very low.

– Forgive you? No, Kathleen, you shouldn't ask my forgiveness. It's I who should ask for yours – and I thank you for your dear words. It's you and yours that I've fought for, but I've not fought hard enough. I promise you, I'll fight on – and so will all my comrades. I promise you that; and I bless you.

Her eyes never left mine. Her uptilted face was drained of blood, pale as the marble face of Psyche, and fixed in an expression that was devout, fervent, fanatical – as though what she'd heard from me had been a revelation for which she'd waited years; perhaps a lifetime. When she spoke, it was in a whisper that I could only just hear.

– Sir – will you come again?

I could hear Howard's footsteps in the hall. But Kathleen was so rapt that she heard nothing; her head remained tilted far back, and her sky-coloured eyes searched mine, waiting for their answer.

– I'll come again, I said, and dropped the small, rough hands.

In bed two hours later, I lay sleepless in the dark.

A formless, giant expectancy had risen in me; had caused my throat to swell. I saw again that country rolling north from New Town, its stillness broken only by a wagon's drowsy rumbling. I saw again those hills that went away in waves, dissolving at the edge of fable.

No doubt this island was a Hades for lost felons; but Boeotia was here as well, I said.

Boeotia! It lay somewhere in the island's heartland: the country of the *Works and Days*. Boeotia! Ancient, rural world where tyranny and power-seeking were unknown; where the nobles and the kings of Metropolis had yet to make their entrances, to hold good men to ransom. It lay waiting to be found: here, after thousands of years; alive once more in these virgin hills and forests, under these strange constellations.

What had been Hesiod's prescription for the life of virtuous completeness? *A house, a wife, and an ox to plough with.* I trembled with absurd elation, and the little passholder's face was tilted up to mine: timid and yet eager. Her cold eyes were tragic in the dark, and wouldn't let me sleep; her white face was near, and yet would come no nearer; her full lower lip was parted from the top one, and her mouth waited to be kissed.

A peasant from Limerick, I said. *A felon; her virtue lost.* But was she not also stricken Ireland – a woman of the fairy hosts? Was she not the woman in the *aisling* song? I lay sleepless, my body tingling, and Langford smiled beside me in the gig.

Why not sink into a valley in Boeotia? Why not return to the plough? To hard and simple bodily labour; to the harvest, fertility and contentment? To that land where neighbours were equal; where no man was king, and the just man was honoured? Why not turn my back on Metropolis and the New, and the struggles of frantic, bitter Europe? Why not rediscover the land of gods and cattle? The country of Artemis: nymph of pools and rivers?

Her white face stared from the depths. I trembled, and my heart and loins yearned: yearned for the ordinary, and yet for nothing real.

3. WILD STARS

November 19th

At last: contact with one of my fellow-exiles! A letter from Thomas O'Neill was waiting for me at the Post Office this morning.

He writes from Bothwell, his police district in the highlands. I read and re-read these pages, the soothing, familiar voice sounding in my head as though he's in the room: that voice which I've known since boyhood, and our schooldays together in Ennis. His letter tells me that I'll soon be re-united not only with him, but with Paul Barry as well — despite the decree that's supposed to keep us apart.

I pace my sitting-room: how am I to contain myself until then?

> ⋆ *Glengarry Cottage,*
> *Nant Lane, Bothwell*
> *Nov. 16th, 1849*

Devereux, my dear, dear fellow!

I almost despaired of seeing you again. How glad I am that you're safe and well, I won't attempt to describe. So you're coming here to recuperate! I'll play the nurse, and the air of this place will cure you of your asthma, I promise you.

We have much to celebrate, you and Paul Barry and I. After all, my dear, we've escaped a sentence to be dragged on a hurdle to a place of execution; hanged; then chopped into pieces. I must confess that this medieval formula put a chill through me, as the vulturous old Judge mumbled it out in the court. So now I give thanks to God — but not, of course, to the English hypocrites who commuted our sentences — that we find ourselves instead in this island gaol. (What a suitable name it has! I've decided that Demon's Land is the title by which it will be known henceforth.) Soon, I promise you, we'll all raise a glass together at the Lakes – in a high, hidden land of beauty and comradeship, far beyond the eyes of English spies. You'll learn more of this place when you come here.

Barry's been banished to the Campbell Town police district, a good way to the north, and lives in a village called Ross. I've written post haste, telling him of your arrival. In spite of Sir William's cunning arrangements, Barry and I have already met twice – through an oversight on the part of officialdom of which you'll also learn more when I see you. I assure you, it won't be long before you'll shake Paul's hand.

Though Hobart Town is but 45 miles away, very few roads link Bothwell to places of settlement; all must be brought here by wagon, over rough tracks. There's a mail coach, but no passenger vehicles; so when you come, you must take the Launceston coach up the Main Road to the village of Green Ponds. I will lead a horse down there and meet you at the inn, and we'll ride up here together, by way of Den Hill. You'll like it here, I feel sure. The Bothwell police district may be my prison, but it's an attractive place of confinement. This part of the Highlands is fertile, beautiful and bracing – yet also utterly strange. It's been colonised for the most part by free Scots settlers – who've given it Scottish names, and grow prosperous through sheep and cattle grazing. An Antipodean Scotland! One could do worse.

I've already been invited as a visitor into their houses. These are homes where no member of the convict class is ever received; but the settlers up here refuse to see me as a felon. In their eyes, dear boy, I'm a romantic exile, pure and simple. I've been treated with particular kindness by an English family called Morton – the richest landed proprietors in Bothwell, whose pastures are those that come to the edge of Nant Lane, where my cottage stands. Their property is called 'Grasmere': Mrs Morton is a lover of Wordsworth, and she and her husband no doubt see their domain as another Westmorland, lying beneath these southern constellations. At their request, I've begun to tutor their two young sons in Latin and Greek, for a nominal fee.

Bothwell village is in a sheltered and extensive valley at the foot of the Highlands, on the little River Clyde: a mountain stream that flows down from regions higher up – from a vast, empty tableland that rises in the centre

273

of the island, where it snows even in the summer. Up there, the country of the Lakes lies: lakes as large as inland seas, which lie in the craters of the mountains. Lakes on the tops of mountains! It's true, I swear to you, and certainly not one of my fancies; and it's there that we'll meet our comrade.

I eagerly await you. Meanwhile, I walk, and read, and sketch the peculiar trees and wildlife: the stringybark gum and the she-oak; the brush kangaroos and opossums; the gem-like little parrots; the wattle birds. I glimpse other, more peculiar shapes at night, at the edges of the bush: spirits of the Antipodes, perhaps.

Come! Come as soon as possible to Glengarry Cottage, and we'll ride through these primeval woods, and hunt the weird kangaroo! At night we'll smoke our pipes and drink brandy, as we did in our student days; we'll read poetry, and philosophise, and plot! Yes, Robert, all those things that are dear to our hearts can be done here too — under these strange, wild stars.

Write quickly.

Your affectionate friend,

THOMAS O'NEILL

PS: When you come, would you, like a dear creature, be so kind as to bring me some articles from Hobart Town? These are things that cannot be obtained in our wilderness village, and I shall be deeply grateful. I enclose one pound, which should pay for all. I need:

Some first-rate cigars, since the God-damned awful cheroots obtainable up here are fit only for the convict shepherds who dote on them.

A school atlas.

Three quires of note paper, and envelopes.

Bless you.

T. O'N.

★ *EDITOR'S NOTE: Letter found in Devereux's writing-slope.*

R.B.

Glengarry Cottage, Bothwell
November 24th
No wonder we call Thomas 'Father' O'Neill — despite his being a Protestant. He does put one in mind of a monk, with his benevolent

expression, high, balding forehead, and the strands of dry brown hair that lie across it. Tonight, in shirtsleeves and rough corduroy trousers, he looked more monk-like than ever. Sitting on the other side of the fire, he teetered back and forth in a red American rocking chair, his mild, near-sighted eyes blinking behind their spectacles. For perhaps the third time this evening, he said:

– It's so good to see you, Robert.

– Likewise, I said. How good it is I can scarcely convey to you, Thomas.

– I do hope you'll be content here. Will your restless nature allow it?

– I'm sure of it. To be here is delicious. But tell me, do you never get bored, in this wilderness?

– Never. My landed proprietors entertain me frequently, and my notebooks and sketchbooks are filled with weird creatures and plants. What more can I ask – except to be sent back to Ireland?

– You were always able to create your own happiness, I said. I believe you'd do so anywhere.

We'd eaten an excellent dinner, exchanged our news, talked of Ireland and our imprisonment, and laughed as we'd done as boys. O'Neill is my oldest friend, so that to fall back into boy-like habits, especially when we're jubilant, is easy for us to do. His family estate – which he and his two sisters recently inherited – is near Clarecastle, just outside Ennis, only a few miles from Sixmilebridge and 'Deerpark'. He and I began our schooling together at Ennis College, and roamed the countryside in our holidays, and fished in the streams, and talked together endlessly. Then we went on to Trinity. His father, unlike mine, was successful in managing his estates, and Thomas and his sisters live modestly but comfortably on rents – despite the fact that they supported their poorer tenants through the Famine. O'Neill has many scholarly interests, but little ambition, it seems: in this, he is also somewhat monk-like. Only the plight of our country seems to rouse him to genuine indignation; otherwise, nothing disturbs him. His reading in literature and philosophy is wide, but he gives most of his energies to the study of botany, which absorbs him deeply. He had many women friends,

275

at home, but seemed little inclined for romantic attachments; he seemed content to be a bachelor, living with his sisters – both of whom are spinsters. I doubt that he'll ever marry.

He and I had been drinking port, and smoking the cigars I'd brought here with me. The port bottle stood on a sea-chest which did duty as a table: it had carried O'Neill's belongings here on the *Revenge*. We fell now into a comfortable silence, lulled by the warmth of the gum-log fire, and by the odours of the tiny parlour: oil of eucalyptus from the spitting, burning logs, and a faint, under-lying scent that resembled that of hay. My coach trip from Hobart Town had been followed by the two-hour ride on horseback that O'Neill had warned me of, coming up from Green Ponds through a rough, empty country of marshes, high hills and deep valleys; and I was now deeply tired. I stretched my legs in front of me, revelling in the warmth, and in the calm I unfailingly enjoy in O'Neill's company. He always introduces into his surroundings a meditative peace: he'd achieved this at Trinity, I recalled, as well as in his study at home; now he managed to do so in this cottage in the wilds of Van Diemen's Land.

A wind moaned outside, and draughts found their way into the room, seeping under the door from the passageway. Even in Spring, it grows cold enough up here for a fire to be needed at night – and the nights are very dark, since O'Neill's little cottage stands beside open pasture land at the edge of Bothwell village. Here on Nant Lane, the last small lights of settlement die out, and the blackness rushes off into yawning zones of Chaos: the unexplored wilderness and mountains of the west. Glengarry Cottage is rudimentary, but O'Neill has made it relatively comfortable. It's owned by the local grocer, who lets it out to supplement his income, and charges O'Neill what he no doubt regards as a vast sum of money. For this, the grocer's wife also cleans the house, and prepares the evening meal. The place has a main bedroom for O'Neill at the front, a second bedroom at the side for me, and a kitchen. Here in the parlour there was the luxury of wallpaper, with a pattern of roses. Built into the wall on each side of the fireplace were sets of shelves for our books.

O'Neill roused himself, and poked the fire. Then, lighting another cigar, he looked across at me again.

– I've had a letter from Fitzgibbon at Port Arthur, he said. The first he's written to me.

– Ah. And how well is he bearing up?

O'Neill frowned at the end of his cigar, and shook his head.

– He's reading Virgil's *Aeneid*, but desperately needs more books. He has a tooth-ache, and fears that some prison doctor will have to draw the tooth. The cottage they've confined him in has a few feet of garden, where he walks under the eye of a constable. It's not enough to provide sufficient exercise, he says – and he begins to have chest pains.

– All this sounds bad, I said. But Fitzgibbon's conditions are surely pretty lenient, for a place like Port Arthur. He's housed in a furnished cottage, however mean, is fed well enough, and is still treated as a gentleman – and he's been there only three weeks.

– Yes, quite true, O'Neill said. But what sounds tolerable as bald fact is very different in reality, Devereux. Think: a man of his sensibilities and former station in life, crouching in that squalid little hut! He describes it as resembling a bathing booth. And outside, that awful settlement. The prisoners there are some of the most depraved convicts on this island. Yes, he's kept separate from them – but the life of the settlement is *there,* a few hundred yards away. And he fears that Governor Denison may eventually find a way to put him among them – in chains, with those murderers and thieves. He's become very melancholy, Robert, very downcast. At the end of the letter, he says: 'I am no longer in the world. I squat on the world's edge, surrounded by brutes. For me, civilization is lost. My whole reality is this hut.'

– He does sound low, poor fellow.

– And worse is to come. If Fitzgibbon continues to refuse the Ticket, they will alter his easy conditions. Bars will be put on the windows, a permanent guard will be stationed in the house, and his presence will be checked every four hours, day and night. He will eat strict convict rations, and no-one but the Superintendent will be permitted to speak to him.

– Most unpleasant, I said. I know. I endured treatment very similar on Bermuda, and at sea – for a good deal longer than three weeks. I certainly don't envy him. But it can be endured, you know.

– No. Not by *him*, Robert. He hasn't your will, your determination to survive. Men have died from sinking so low in their spirits as he seems to be. And I believe his heart is not sound. Remember, he's a good deal older than we are. He *must* come out and live healthy, and be among his own kind, and take proper exercise!

– That certainly seems desirable. If he's breaking down, then his continuing to refuse the Ticket is simply folly. He has only to reverse his stand, and be as free as we are. He's obviously not cut out for martyrdom. But will he do so? He seems very stubborn about it.

– We must change his mind, O'Neill said, and leaned forward. We must write to him, and urge him to give his *parole*. Will *you* write, Devereux?

– Martin and I have never agreed on very much, as you know – and I doubt that he'll pay much heed to me. But yes, I'll write, if you think it will help.

– I'm very glad – very glad indeed, O'Neill said. Whatever your differences, he has a high regard for you. He may heed you.

Throwing his cigar into the fire, he rocked back in his chair again, narrowing his eyes in the way that he did when he wished to explore an idea. He steepled his fingers.

– You know, what the British have created on this island is a *Panopticon*, he said. Do you realise that, Devereux?

– The term's unfamiliar to me, I said. Expound, my boy.

– I'm referring to the penal theories of Jeremy Bentham. He recommended that a prison be built in such a way that every section radiated out from a central observation room, or tower. In this monstrous 'Panopticon' of his, the prisoners would thus be spied on at all times, do you see. 'A machine for grinding rogues honest,' Bentham called it. Such a penitentiary has yet to be constructed – but what I put to you is this. Van Diemen's Land is itself a Panopticon!

He pointed his finger at me.

– This is a colony infested everywhere by spies – you must have learned that already. So I ask you: is not every felon and ex-felon watched and accounted for at all times? And doesn't our Grand Turnkey Denison sit at the centre of the machine like a spider – kept informed of everything through his many official agents and convict informers? You see? The entire bloody colony is a Panopticon!

– Very ingenious, I said, and laughed. I believe you're right, O'Neill. But sitting here cosy like this, it's hard to be uneasy.

– True – and now we must go to bed. But before we sleep, let me show you where it is we're bound tomorrow.

He jumped up and went over to the table that served him as a desk, his tall, stoop-shouldered shadow in the candle-light resembling some wading bird's. He bent, and spread out a map of Van Diemen's Land on the sea-chest. It was marked with the various police districts, and I stood beside him to study it.

– Here's the tableland where the Lakes are, he said, and pointed. A thousand feet higher than where we are now. A cold, barren, lonely land – good only for running sheep. It extends to regions of forest in the west that are quite unexplored and impenetrable. As you'll observe, our police district of Bothwell extends well on to the plateau, and includes two of the biggest lakes, which lie side by side: Crescent and Sorell.

He traced the Bothwell border; then his finger moved along the eastern shore of Lake Sorell.

– Now observe: here's the border of the police district of Campbell Town – Paul Barry's district. *And it touches ours at Lake Sorell.* You see?

– And this is where he comes? This is where you meet? What do you do, Thomas? Shake hands across the border in the wilderness? Each with his feet in his own dungeon district?

– Well now, we don't get too nice about observing where the line might be. Barry's compelled to come just a few hundred yards into the zone of Bothwell, of course – or else I must go into his Campbell Town dungeon. But who's to know, up there in that wilderness? Who's to *see*, Devereux?

I began to laugh, and so did he. It ended with falsetto notes and helpless coughing: a mirth disproportionate to its subject. This had occurred all the evening, over even the most trivial things: an overflow from the glee of our reunion. But then I asked:

– Look here, though: do you propose to make these meetings a regular thing?

– Of course. We arrange the time of rendezvous by letter. We even have accommodation, so that we can stay overnight or longer: the hut of an old, Ticket-holding shepherd. He tends sheep for Mr Morton – who owns a good deal of land up there – and we pay the old fellow for his trouble.

– But you know the terms of the Ticket-of-Leave, I said. If we're caught out of our districts, then surely Denison will have his excuse to send us in irons to Port Arthur.

– Don't be concerned: I've gone to the local authorities and discussed it with them. You must understand, old fellow – the small officials here don't *care* what we do, provided there's no flouting of the law. Denison and his Comptroller-General in Hobart Town care – and to be found out of your district down there would be serious. But up here, since we're almost within the letter of the law, they turn a blind eye. I went to Captain Anderson, the magistrate here in Bothwell, and discussed the question; he made it plain that we needn't be too concerned about the line's exact position, and that if Barry and I met quietly, it didn't trouble him. 'There's no-one up there for you to raise in revolution,' he said, 'unless it's the black swans.'

He straightened up as we laughed again, and put a hand on my shoulder.

– Tomorrow, the Lakes, he said. That's if you're well enough to ride in rough country. The first time I went, I paid a local bushman to be my guide. Now I can find the way myself. I'll lead you to Paradise, my dear.

November 25th

At nine o'clock in the morning, we ride through dense fog.

O'Neill is only a few yards in front of me, yet I can barely make him out: he and his mare have become a shadow horse and rider. The fog comes and goes, eddying and lifting and descending again with baffling speed. Sometimes it screens everything in front of us, and our horses stumble through a white universe, where only the horses themselves and the ground under their hoofs are real. In these intervals, I'm riding alone, and my little bay horse moves as best as he can around the shapes of fallen trees. At other times, the fog opens doorways into the landscape, and we ride out of blindness into colour.

It does this now, and begins to dissolve. It retreats among bushes, leaving mere wisps about our horses' flanks, to reveal that we're jogging through an open, level country, under a low grey sky. Despite the weather, I'm filled with joyous expectancy. O'Neill has been worried that I might not be strong enough to make the journey; but I feel confident that I am. Although I remain somewhat weak from the enemy's attacks, he's still not visited me since my arrival into Van Diemen's Land, and I managed yesterday's ride to Bothwell quite well.

We're riding north-east – having just set out from O'Neill's cottage – and are still in the valley of Bothwell. There's no sign of life here except for small green parrots: brilliant, swift little creatures that swoop and dart about us. It's a place of dry yellow grass and scattered trees – many of which O'Neill has already identified for me, being a passionate amateur botanist. Most prominent are the tall, wide-spreading eucalypts, or gums, as everyone calls them here. Their fragrance fills the sharp, pure air. Numbers of wattle trees – a kind of mimosa – are out in blossom, making bright yellow splashes in the sunless landscape; and a native honeysuckle called banksia is everywhere: a weird, spiky little tree with cork-like bark, whose flowers are not flowers, but hairy cream spools, like blooms from another planet. The hulks of fallen gums lie in the grass: some felled by settlers, others by age. They are not long-lived, it seems.

In front of us, in the north, looms the country we must reach: immense, thickly-wooded hills, rising above the valley like an olive-green wall. These are the approaches to that plateau of which O'Neill spoke to me: the island's roof, formed by mountains called the Western Tiers. To get there, O'Neill tells me, we must ride for some twenty-four miles, through a dense and difficult wilderness. Once on the tableland, we'll arrive at the long-awaited Lakes – and Paul Barry will join us there at around three in the afternoon, having ridden over the other side of the Tiers from Ross, in the Midlands.

O'Neill turns in the saddle now and waves, as though to encourage me. I smile and wave back, diverted by the outlandish figure he's become, on his big roan mare. O'Neill, the dreamy scholar – always seen in Dublin in sober and tasteful dress – has fitted himself out this morning with the clothing of a rough Van Diemen's Land settler: dark blue donkey jacket, moleskin trousers, heavy blucher boots, medieval leather leggings secured to his belt by straps, and a wide-brimmed, shapeless, grey felt hat – a brigand's wideawake, which on him becomes the hat of a vagabond poet. Despite my amusement at this transformation, a deepening chill in the air reminds me of the fact that it may snow in the high country even in summer; and I begin to think that I should have brought similar garments for myself. I've tried to be practical, wearing drab cloth trousers, top boots, and my old peaked cap; but I suspect that my riding coat won't be adequate to keep me warm.

We're now about four miles out from Bothwell. Behind and below us, far across miles of air to the south, is a scene of prehistoric grandeur, worthy of the brush of some German Romantic: range after range of grey-blue mountains, some of them capped with snow, receding into distances which I'm told the Empire's colonists have yet to penetrate. O'Neill and I ride side by side now, crossing a wide green paddock where sheep are grazing. On its far side is the well-built stone mansion of a prosperous Scottish settler named Cameron, surrounded by outbuildings for his convict farm workers – a number of whom can be seen toiling over there, in blue blouses and moleskins and leggings like those that O'Neill's wearing. Behind it, coming abruptly out of the flatland, stands a strange, cone-shaped hill, or small mountain, composed of grey-green pillars of upthrust rock. It's known as the Quoin, and it marks the point where the wilderness begins.

The Quoin puts me in mind of the fairy hills of Ireland. I remark on this to Thomas, and put the idea to him that Antipodean elementals, of which we can have no notion, may inhabit a place like this. His face lights with calm enthusiasm, under the brim of his big hat; he's tempted to believe in fairies, as I am, and has always been fond of the youthful work I published on Celtic fairy tales and fairy lore. Yes, such a fancy's compelling, he says now; he's often entertained it, riding in these hills, and he believes he's already sensed such presences here. No doubt the unknown nature spirits of Van Diemen's Land were familiar to the vanished blacks – of whom, he tells me, the settlers of Bothwell lived in fear until quite recently. O'Neill sometimes senses the presence of the Aborigines themselves, he says: ghosts in the bush of that small, sad people so recently driven from their country.

We continue this discussion at some length, renewing, as we did at the fireside last night, all our old pleasure in like-minded talk. Fellow spirits! Life without them is only half a life. As we've talked – passing on somehow to the poetry of William Wordsworth, and then to Emanuel Swedenborg's *Arcana coelestia*, and his ideas on the correspondences between the natural and spiritual worlds – we've ridden around the base of the Quoin. Now we enter a gorge behind it. Still absorbed in Swedenborg, we leave the open places behind, and dense, wild bush closes around us.

There are no more distances now; we can see only a few yards in front of us. The giant gum trees, growing close together, are dominant. Their naked, yellowish trunks, from which the shaggy grey bark hangs in strips, are pillars receding into regions of primeval gloom. They have little foliage low down; they're dense only at their tops, where a canopy cuts off much of the day's muted light. Down here are smells of eucalyptus and damp earth, and the bush is entirely silent, except for the jingling of our harness and the abrupt shrieking and warbling of parrots and magpies. There's a good deal of undergrowth, and the ground is scattered with stones, so that our horses must move cautiously. They begin to plod up a steeper and steeper incline: our climb to the Lakes has begun.

At the same time, rain begins. It's a light rain, but the air grows freezing. After we've gone perhaps another half mile, white flakes begin to come down through the eucalyptus canopy, faster and faster. Soon, it's snowing heavily.

O'Neill turns to me as his horse plods between two gums, his mouth open in a laugh, and waves his hat like the manager of a theatre. His lips move, but he's too far off for me to hear anything, and the snow seems to be muffling all sound. I wave my cap in response, and he turns and rides on. Sally, his big mare, is stronger than Dan, my bay pony, and begins to leave us behind. Dan was hired from the grocer in the village, and hasn't been up to the Lakes before; he stumbles over the stones, and sometimes halts at fallen logs; but he's a good, patient little horse, and suits me in my weakened condition. This weakness – asthma's accursed legacy – hasn't troubled me until now. But the snow grows thicker and a high wind comes up, hissing and whistling through the waving heads and limbs of the gums overhead; we find ourselves riding through a blizzard, and a dizziness overtakes me. It grows intensely cold, and I begin to shiver in spasms.

O'Neill in his brigand's hat is always in front of me. We ride for what seems hours through the roaring and fluting wind and whirling whiteness – but when I consult my new pocket watch, I find that it's only ten o'clock. Not half an hour has passed. The wet reins are slippery in my hands; the peak of my cap does little to protect my eyes from the sleet, which lashes into my face, half-blinding me. A white coating gathers on the sleeves of my coat, on Dan's mane, and between his ears. He stumbles on a boulder, and shies: I pull hard on the reins, and bring him to a halt. I squint through the dazzling snowflakes to find that O'Neill's no longer visible; he's vanished into the whiteness among the hissing and groaning trees.

I shout to Dan, and spur him into a stumbling trot. I tear off a thin branch to lash him forward, suddenly aware that if I lose sight of O'Neill, I may well be lost entirely in this wilderness. Then, with a surge of relief, I see him. He's halted his horse under a banksia tree, and is waiting for me. His scholar's face peers at me from under his dripping hat – the long, patrician nose and feminine mouth divertingly at odds with his bushman's rough garb. What are we doing here, in this place of primeval fury? How has a man like O'Neill come to such a pass, wearing this rough fancy dress? Are we both dreaming? Yet even as I ask myself this question, I'm impressed with his unexpected hardiness.

I ride up to him, and he raises his voice against the shrilling of the wind.

– I'm sorry, Devereux – this is probably too much for you, in your present condition. I hadn't anticipated such weather. Shall we turn back? Barry will understand.

– Nonsense, I shout. I can go on. Just don't lose me, Thomas.

We laugh again, as we did last night. It does me good, and we set out once more through the blizzard.

I've learned now that the distance from Cameron's property to the top of the plateau is some fifteen miles. Not a very long ride, under normal conditions; but in that weather, and over that terrain, it seemed like fifty.

Finally, however, the ground began to level out. At the same time, the wind eased, and the snow fell less thickly. Within minutes, the blizzard had ceased. Stones, grass, white-dusted trees and a crude log fence appeared, and we found ourselves riding out of the forest onto an open plain. We had come to the tableland: the plateau of the Lakes.

It was one o'clock in the afternoon, and there was a vast stillness. The sky was covered in high, moving cloud, which one sensed might soon break up. Both of us cheered; and on a mutual impulse, spurred our horses into a gallop. My weakness ceased to matter, and my head cleared instantly; I'd seldom known such a sense of freedom. The plain extended for something like two miles, patched here and there with snow left by the blizzard, and dotted with giant, spreading gum trees. It looked almost like a park in Ireland; and this made it no less strange. Urging Dan forward so that O'Neill and I were neck and neck, both of us shouting like savages, I experienced an exhilaration in riding such as I'd never known before: we were riding as our ancestors must have ridden, across the grasslands of earliest history.

From here we went on through another tract of bush; but soon we came into open country again, breathing an air so pure that it seemed like ether. Every detail of the landscape extending in front of us showed with an extraordinary distinctness, making it more than real. We had reached our goal, O'Neill said.

Before us lay the two lakes. Their full extent could not yet be seen, since low wooded promontories jutted into them like fingers: but one sensed they were of great size. Lake Crescent, whose hidden shoreline we'd been following, lay close by on our right, with marshy banks, and reeds appearing far out on its surface. Of a brilliant silver, it reflected the gums along its far shore – whose heads stood olive-black against crystal sky. Lake Sorell, which O'Neill had told me was by far the larger of the two, showed only as a long silver streak to our north – perhaps a mile away.

We rode towards it, over a marsh-like neck of land which lay between the two bodies of water. A sluggish little stream ran across this neck, no bigger than a canal, carrying the waters of Sorell to Lake Crescent. Lake Sorell began to look vast, like an inland sea; and O'Neill told me that what we saw was only one of its southern arms. He pointed.

– Carter's hut, he said.

There was no sign of life there except for scattered sheep, grazing among prickly green bushes, and two large hounds chained to a banksia tree. The shepherd's dwelling was built of perpendicular gum logs with the bark left on them; it had a shingle roof, a rough stone chimney from which smoke was climbing, and a number of small square windows, unglazed, with crude wooden shutters. The carcass of a sheep hung from a wattle bough, just out of reach of the dogs, and a post-and-rail fence marked out an enclosure for animals, next to the house. We dismounted and began to lead our horses there, while the dogs barked at us.

A man emerged from the open doorway, shouting at the dogs to lie down. He carried under his arm a double-barrelled shotgun, which was pointed in our direction. He was a lean, wiry-looking old fellow of about sixty, with close-cropped white hair that stood up in a brush. He was clad in a blue serge blouse fastened by a belt, a black rag of a neckerchief, and filthy moleskin trousers. A London villain of the most hardened kind, I thought; and I found his pointing the gun at us less than reassuring. But now he lowered it, and grinned in a manner that seemed to be welcoming.

– Why, it's Mister O'Neill, he said. You'll pardon the firearm, sir, but it's a habit from the old days. You two gen'lm'n look mortal cold – go inside to the fire, won't you? I'll see to the feed for your horses. After which I'll carve you some prime mutton chops, which is waiting over there.

He pointed to the carcass hanging in the wattle tree.

– Carter is famous for his chop cookery, O'Neill said. He also smokes like a furnace, as we do.

And he handed the hermit a number of tins of tobacco which he'd taken from his saddle bag.

– Bless you sir, you remembered, Carter said. Barrett's Twist! I dote on this tobacker.

The conditions in which the shepherd lived proved to be of the most primitive kind. The room we entered through the open door was a combined kitchen and sitting room, whose floor was of hardened earth. The hut consisted only of this, and an adjoining store-room. There were smells of stale mutton-fat, smoke and eucalyptus. The gum-logs from which the hut was made had been split into slabs, and the walls in here were the flat sides of these slabs, the crevices between them being roughly stopped up with mud. Carter had decorated them with torn-out pages from the *Illustrated London News*, as well as with more useful articles, hanging from pegs: horse-hobbles, pannikins, a stock-whip, and another gun: this one an old-fashioned flintlock. The ceiling was unlined, and glimpses of sky could be seen through breaks in the shingles. A crude slab table stood in the centre of the room – obviously a work of bush carpentry – and for seating there was a huge gum stump covered with a sheepskin, a canvas chair, a couple of slab benches and a few small stools, also bush-made. It was the hospitality of a bandit's den; yet I'd seldom known such sheer physical bliss as now enfolded me.

Simply to be warm and dry seemed the greatest luxury I'd ever known. We'd quickly removed our sodden outer garments and boots, and had changed into spare trousers that O'Neill produced from his saddle bag. Now we sat in our shirt-sleeves in front of a fire of gum logs that Carter had built into a blaze. The stone fireplace was of medieval proportions, large enough to walk into, and the warmth of the flames went into my bones. I felt myself reviving; my breathing became even, and O'Neill and I sat blinking in mindless contentment. Mugs of hot tea in our hands, we watched Carter cook the mutton chops. He did this by spitting them on a length of wire, suspending them above the fire. He was also cooking what he called 'damper', or bushman's bread: a flat cake made simply of flour and water, and baked in the coals. Chops and damper were what he lived on, it seemed, morning, noon and evening.

When we began to eat, sitting at the big slab table, I decided that he was in no way to be pitied for this diet. The journey and the cold had made me ravenous, as it had O'Neill; the chops, flavoured with eucalyptus smoke, seemed the finest meat I'd ever eaten, and the humble damper was manna. Carter provided salt in an old round container that had once held soap, and had managed to produce some chipped willow-pattern plates for us. But he had very little in the way of cutlery; we ate the chops in our fingers, civilized manners discarded, gnawing eagerly at the bones.

When we'd finished eating, the old man disappeared outside, and O'Neill and I sat smoking our pipes in front of the fire. We said little, but we were filled with a mutual expectancy. It was now after two o'clock, and I frequently consulted my watch. Paul Barry was due here in approximately an hour, and we intended to ride out to meet him.

We went out and saddled up again just before three o'clock.

The sky was now quite blue, and a perfect stillness held the tableland, disturbed only by the lightest of breezes. We rode through mild, thin sun across the tussock grass, towards the southern shore of Lake Sorell. Barry would most likely ride around the southern side, O'Neill said, coming from the east; so with luck, we should soon encounter him. I took deep breaths as I rode. The air was elastic, exhilarating, setting the blood racing. It was air to rival that of the mountains of Connemara, or my longed-for coast Clare.

And now we'd come to the lake. We reined in our horses, while I exclaimed in delight, and O'Neill smiled and nodded: a complacent parent who'd delivered a promised treat.

But this was a Como, I said, here in the Antarctic forests. A Windermere!

On the western shore, dense, blue-shadowed forest came down to the water. The eastern side had many promontories and rocky little headlands, going off into remote distance. O'Neill informed me that the shores of Lake Sorell ran for thirty-five miles; that it was half a dozen miles in length, and something like the same in breadth. But in that moment, such facts had no meaning. The lake seemed to me much larger than this: almost limitless. On its silver surface, there was a soundless dancing and glittering, like the lights of a spectral city; and far in the north, where the blue peaks of the Tiers lay on the horizon, long silver highways of air seemed to extend, signalling the nearby presence not of wilderness, but of some province of marvel.

And all things were queer and opposite, as old Lenoir had said. Out on the surface of the water two swans sailed side by side, exactly like those of Europe – except that these were jet black. There were ducks here too: a group of teal rose from beyond the reeds, with a whirr of wings and harsh cries. Then silence came back, while O'Neill and I sat listening.

Both of us have loved nature from our youth, and had no need to speak further; by mutual consent, we were listening to the silence. At first, I thought it complete, except for the sounds of the birds; but then I found that it wasn't. There was a mysterious, all-pervading sound here: a long, enormous hushing which I couldn't at first account for; which was neither the lapping of the water on the shore, nor the movement of the breeze on the lake. In the end I decided that it was the whole vast movement of the water, in the mountain-top crater that contained it.

Searching for Barry, we now rode on around the southern shore.

We jogged through weird, tawny spaces: through a parkland

littered everywhere with stones, and with mysterious, lichen-covered boulders. The green, hairy lichen coated the trunks of the wattle trees as well, in a place that seemed to drone of barbaric memories. We shouted, calling Barry by name.

– *Paul! Paul! Paul Barry!*

We thought we heard an answer, after a time: very distant, so that it had no words. My heart leapt, and we both called back at the top of our lungs. No further answer came, but we went on calling the name of our comrade: an Irish gentleman in exile. *Barry. Barry. Barry.* His name echoed here in a manner that was infinitely mournful, dying among the empty, dry-grassed spaces, among the lichened stones. And a shaft of desolation went through me. *We're lost*, I thought. *Are not all three of us lost here?*

We rode on, moving away from the lake. Again we thought we heard someone call, and spurred our horses forward. Then it came clear: a falsetto, two-note call this time, like that of a bird.

O'Neill cupped his hands around his mouth, and made the same sound: a signal used by the settlers here, he said, when searching for someone who was lost in the forests. We pushed through a belt of green bushes; we stooped as our horses came under some wattle boughs, and rode out into a clearing.

He was here.

He waited for us, seated on a fine black horse; and at first, although the slight, boy-like figure was familiar, I could scarcely credit that this was Barry. Red-faced from the sun, he looked even more like a brigand than O'Neill did – or rather, like a revolutionary soldier. On his head was one of those broad-brimmed, low-crowned straw hats that are made in New South Wales from the cabbage-tree palm; a shotgun hung from his saddle, and a bandolier was fastened across his red serge overblouse, which was belted at the waist over a bright blue shirt. His rough cord trousers were tucked into top boots, and a mackintosh cloak was slung across his pommel. He took off the cabbage-tree hat and waved it – and now, with his thick blond hair uncovered and his eyes shining with humour, he became the Barry I knew.

We flung ourselves down from our horses, and took the few

fast paces that would bring us face to face. And strange to record, in those first few moments not a word was spoken. Instead, we threw back our heads and laughed. We laughed full-throatedly; uproariously. We laughed until the tears came, bending almost double, pointing at each other. Then, wiping our eyes, we embraced one another in turn.

– So *here* we are, gentlemen, Barry said.

He pulled a droll face, head on one side, blue eyes gone sly and narrow. Spoken in this place, his words were bizarre, setting off our laughter once again. Here we were, in this land of alien trees and lichen-coated boulders. Here we were, in a wilderness on the Empire's farthest frontier, for no worse crime than demanding our country's freedom; and our laughter was joyous, yet perhaps not far from weeping. Its youthful shouts echoed from the sullen hills of bush, and died away over the lake.

– To Ireland, Barry said. To Dark Rosaleen!

He raised his tin mug of brandy and water, and O'Neill and I did the same. Then, in his sweet tenor voice, Barry sang a single verse of *Róisín Dubh*, the anthem of our movement: the heartbreaking *aisling* by Owen Roe MacWard about the woman who is Ireland – and which our comrade James Clarence Mangan has translated as *Dark Rosaleen*.

> – *O! the Erne shall run red*
> *With redundance of blood,*
> *The earth shall rock beneath our tread,*
> *And the flames wrap hill and wood,*
> *And gun-peal, and slogan-cry*
> *Wake many a glen serene,*
> *Ere you shall fade, ere you shall die,*
> *My dark Rosaleen!*

When he'd done, Barry drank off his brandy, his narrow white face lit orange by the flames, a sheaf of pale, childish hair fallen across his brow. O'Neill and I had tears in our eyes, and Barry saw this and smiled: that smile of his which says that nothing in life is finally tragic, which draws others to him wherever he goes, and which makes him so attractive to women. Certainly it has always drawn me: of all my Young Ireland comrades, I am most fond of Barry; and he and I have most in common, both in regard to temperament and our thinking. Just to see him again, after my long isolation, had filled me with an elation more heady than the fumes of the brandy.

We were sitting by the fire in the hut, and it was now ten o'clock at night. The only light in here, other than that of the fire, came from a very dim slush lamp on the table which old Carter had fashioned from a cup filled with tallow, a twist of corduroy serving as a wick. O'Neill sat on a eucalyptus bench that was provided with an ancient, greasy cushion; Barry occupied what he'd dubbed 'Carter's throne': the sheepskin-covered gum-stump on which the shepherd was accustomed to dine; I sprawled in comparative ease in the single canvas chair here, my stockinged feet stretched to the blaze. We'd feasted once again on mutton chops. As we'd eaten, the old shepherd had told us tales of his early days here, when any unexplained sound outside could mean the arrival of marauding Aborigines, and when an isolated stockman like himself lived in fear of being speared at his door. Now he'd retired to the store-room which served him tonight as a bedroom, and snored. Outside, it was crisp and still: the night not so cold as I'd feared it would be, though surely not far from freezing, and the sky very clear. Looking up at the hut's unlined ceiling, I could see a bright star, twinkling through a gap in the shingles.

Our talk had been flowing without cease: in my case, a pent-up flood that had waited a year and a half for the ears of my true companions. Gazing from one to the other of them, what a sense of liberation I had! I'd come home to myself, as well as to them. The time that we'd been separated seemed immense: far longer than it had actually been. They were still only half real to me, and I noted with pleasure all their little tricks of speech and manner, each of which confirmed their reality.

Our mugs were re-charged from bottle and water-jug; and now I raised mine in a mock toast.

– God rot our Governor, I said. Our little colonial despot, Sir William Denison. What have you two gentlemen discovered of him, in these busy first weeks of yours?

– That the son of a bitch hates all Irishman, Barry said, and Young Ireland in particular. An officer on the *Revenge* with whom I grew friendly had a conversation with the Comptroller of Convicts after we docked. He was good enough to pass on the news to me that if Sir William and the Comptroller had their way, we'd all be labouring in chains, in suits of canary and grey. 'Wearing the motley' is how they charmingly put it.

– Never fear, O'Neill said, he won't dare do it. He's forced to obey London's orders: we're to be dealt with as gentlemen, whether he likes it or no.

– Only so long as the bastard don't find an excuse to do other-wise, Barry said. He's filled with furious vexation that London have tied his hands, you can be sure. Our being at liberty in this convict domain of his is an affront to his power. All he needs for an excuse to have us breaking stones – side by side in chains with English thieves and buggers – is that we break our *parole*. Which is what we're doing now.

He pointed a finger at me, and his voice took on the drawling insolence of British authority.

– Devereux, my good fellow! Have you read all the rules set out on your Ticket-of-Leave? You must report to your local Police Magistrate once a month! You must not enter a theatre or a billiard room! You must not be absent from your registered place of resi-dence after ten o'clock at night! So how is it that at this very moment, ten o'clock having struck, you and Thomas O'Neill are absent from your appointed cottage in Bothwell?

He made a sudden craven face and hugged himself, looking fearfully about him.

– As for me – I should be in Ross, tucked up in my little bed at the inn. How in Jesus' name do I come to be *here*?

While we laughed, he lit his pipe from a twig plucked from the fire. His habitually ironical tone and drawling delivery had been produced by Stoneyhurst: the Jesuit college in Lancashire where he'd completed his education, in the company of young English gentlemen. The son of a wealthy Catholic merchant in Waterford, Barry's always led a life of enviable ease and pleasure. He has many talents, in particular his gift for music. He's composed and published a number of ballads which stand comparison with those of Thomas Moore, and which were published and grow popular among the people. But he refuses to pursue his music with any seriousness. He is, I suppose, a dilettante, and is only completely dedicated when it comes to our cause. Because of his dandified air and his usually fastidious taste in dress, he's sometimes taken for a fop – and I thought him one myself, when we first met. But this is misleading – just as his compact, elfin slightness is. What one fails to take in at first is his wiry physical toughness, and the nature of his gaze. He treats life mostly as a joke; but when his feelings are aroused, or when he speaks of our cause in public, his light blue eyes lose their usual glint of humour. Then they suggest regions of aerial emptiness, high and far and cold, and warn of the possibility of fury. Martin Fitzgibbon, I remember, once described Barry's eyes as 'strange in their expression'. This is because Paul makes Fitzgibbon uncomfortable, I believe. At bottom, Barry is a warrior, and his eyes are the eyes of a fighter; and Fitzgibbon is no fighter.

– Well, it ain't so bad in Ross, Barry said now. I'm surrounded by wealthy sheep farmers, who are dim but friendly enough. The town's a military post, ruled from the barracks and the Police Office: a pretty enough place, attempting to convince the subjects of Britannia's empire that they're living in dear old England. But only if one doesn't look too closely. At the end of the village there's a female convict station, which they call here the Female Factory. It's a depot for female prisoners who've not yet been hired out as servants – or who've committed new pieces of naughtiness in the colony, and are undergoing correction. But they do have their pleasures, it seems. Despite their nun-like situation, they're mysteriously able to produce babies, those women. Yes, babies! Large numbers of 'em have an infant at the breast or on the hip.

– Virgin birth, perhaps, suggested O'Neill.

– Some of our poor Irish women there are quiet, gentle

creatures, Barry said. Often with a sad, sensual beauty: it's those I feel sorry for. But most of the London women are pretty tough customers: thieves and whores from the rookeries. Yet even some of *them* looked quite tempting, I may tell you, when I first arrived. After a year without female company, I could even have yearned after one of those English doxies.

O'Neill shook his head with resigned disapproval, and Barry laughed.

– Fear not, Father O'Neill – I've been saved from such folly by my lovely landlady, at the Man O' Ross Inn. She's a widow – a very decent and charming woman – and Irish, if you please. Mary McCormack welcomed me here with open arms – I speak figuratively, of course – and it's many a night now, after the inn is closed, that we've sat in front of a blazing fire in the parlour, and consoled ourselves with a glass of wine, and walked together in our dreams through the valleys of Cork and Waterford, and grown sentimental, and sung a song or two together at the piano. I've written a new song just for her.

He broke off suddenly, and looked at me.

– I was very sorry indeed, Robert, to hear that your engagement with Miss Edgeworth was broken. May you find someone else who's more worthy of you, dear boy.

– Thank you, I said. It will be a very special lady, I suspect, who'll be prepared to share the trials of *my* life.

We fell silent for a time; then O'Neill said:

– We three are pretty comfortable, all things being considered. But we should be thinking of what's to be done about Martin Fitzgibbon. His letter from Port Arthur gives details of the most insolent petty tyranny and annoyance.

He was looking at Barry, eyebrows tragically raised. His eyes grew larger, taking on the care-worn expression they often show when his thoughts go to the sufferings of others, and his chin was set at an angle of outrage. But it's such a small chin that it doesn't do well at conveying warlike threat. O'Neill's a caring, tender-hearted man – much more so than Barry and I are, I fear – and he'll fight injustice fearlessly, with a stubborn insistence on principle;

he'll never be cowed. But the rage that we two harbour is not in his character. I smiled inwardly, remembering a description of Thomas that was made to me once by a member of the '82 Club in Dublin: 'A lamb in a passion.' It's true; he's a lamb, not a lion, and I love him all the more for it.

Barry finally answered him, his drawl pronounced, his eyes fixed sleepily on the flames.

– But this has been Martin's situation for less than a month, dear boy. How can he have succumbed to despair so soon?

– Come, that's not charitable, Paul, O'Neill said.

He turned to me.

– He'd already grown melancholy and cast down on the *Revenge*, he said. And our year in Kilmainham Gaol didn't agree with him. Remember that Fitzgibbon's a married man, and has been separated from his wife and daughters now for well over a year. He misses them sadly – and being at Port Arthur gives him nothing to take his mind off his unhappiness.

I suddenly became impatient.

– For God's sake, O'Neill, the poor wrong-headed fellow has placed *himself* in this position! Yes, I know: he will not recognise the validity of his trial, or his sentence, or anything that has been done to him. So he won't sign agreements with his captors. Very noble, I'm sure: but does he think that the God-damned British will change their minds? Or that it will all go away, like some dream of kidnap by hobgoblins?

– I suspect this is exactly what he *does* think, Barry said softly. Perhaps the struggle has become a bad dream for him: one he can't wake up from – much though he may wish to.

O'Neill turned his long white nose from the fire towards Barry, and the look he gave him now was reproving.

– Fitzgibbon's a gallant and noble man, he said. He's proved his bravery and his faithfulness to the cause as few others have. He's faced English bullets, which we've not done – and it's the affair in Tipperary that has done so much to weigh his spirits down, as you well know. The poor old fellow even told me once that he wished he'd been shot there.

Barry and I looked back into the fire for a moment – I suspect to hide our embarrassment. Then I asked the question I'd been saving for some time.

– Why did the rising fail? The only accounts I've read were written by malicious jackals, pouring out their poison in the bloody English press. They certainly made mock of Fitzgibbon – but that was to be expected. I've waited for the truth for a year and a half. So tell me: spare me no detail – unless you're wishing to go to bed.

We'd all sleep tonight in this main room of the hut, on beds set around the walls: rudimentary constructions of poles and stakes, on which were laid straw mattresses and opossum-skin rugs. But we agreed that none of us was inclined to sleep yet, and that now was the time for me to be told about our lost revolution. Barry leaned over and poured us fresh brandies, sighing as he did so. Then he sat back on his gum-stump, and looked at me.

– Oh dear, Devereux, he said. It was a sad bloody business. The greatest chance we ever had to rally the people – lost. Ireland's opportunity to throw off tyranny, along with the other new nations – lost. A great attempt, ending in a set of God-damned blunders! It must have given glee to Dublin Castle, and to that bloody little shit Clarendon. Yet it *could* have succeeded, Robert – and next time, it will.

– It will, I said. But it couldn't have done so this time, in my opinion. The fault wasn't yours, Barry. The time was wrong, and the place was wrong as well. It should not have been attempted in the countryside.

O'Neill spoke now.

– You always did maintain that, Devereux, and of course you were proved right. But events overtook us. Ah, you should have been with us, my boy, in those twelve days, and all might have been different!

– All *would* have been different, Barry said.

He was looking at me, and the fervour in his gaze and in his smile was like a bright light turned on me.

– Ah Christ, he said, if only it had been *you* that led, and not Fitzgibbon! If only you'd been on the War Council! If only you'd been with us in Tipperary! But there you were on Bermuda – lost to us!

The telling of it took until one in the morning. As I listened, much of my anger focused not on the English, but on Martin Fitzgibbon.

The rising had almost certainly been doomed. Yet Barry was right, I felt sure: had Fitzgibbon not been in charge, the end might have been glorious – even had it still been a defeat. It might have been the first real battle in our war of revolution, and cost the English much: in blood, prestige and treasure.

Instead, it had been no battle at all: it had been nothing but a farce; a poor aborted thing. The reports of the Grub Street hacks and jackals of the Government had been correct in that – even though they'd stirred into their broth every lie and half-truth they could find, to diminish what had happened. They'd distorted the incident at Ballingarry grotesquely, to please their official masters, and to reassure the English public; and they'd depicted Fitzgibbon as a coward and a clown. He is neither; he'd clearly behaved with dignity, and with a certain amount of courage. But essentially, the scribblers had been right: it had been a sad comedy in the end, and not much else. Dear God, what a gift the episode had been to *The Times*, and to *Punch*, and to every sneering English journal that seeks to convince the world that our cause is hopeless! As always – as in the Famine – England has the world's ear; she can whisper into it whatever tale she wishes, and the world will listen.

Can all this really be blamed on Fitzgibbon? Were there not elements in the situation that made it a lost cause from the start?

No. To think so is to deny the vital, transforming effect that a truly great leader may have in history – if only fate places him at the heart of events. How does my mentor Carlyle describe such a man? 'The truest-hearted, the justest, the noblest man' – one who sees, in a crisis, 'the wisest, fittest thing' to be done. Such a man needed to be there last year, in that marvellous, tragic July. A true leader would have taken the elements at hand in those brief twelve days, and would have dragged them into a new shape, against all the odds. He would have rallied the people, and had them storming behind him; he would have struck the first real blow for Irish freedom – and had he and his followers gone down under Albion's guns, they would have gone down leaving the first great breach in the wall, and everything changed!

Writing these words, I almost choke. *I was not there*, with Barry at my side. Martin Fitzgibbon was there instead, and his loyal jester Kinane.

It's hard for me to be dispassionate about Fitzgibbon. I must try to be, nevertheless. Now that we share the same fate, and now that he shows to our captors such stoical, wrong-headed firmness, my heart can't help but go out to him – though it does so even now in an abstract sort of way. So let me be as honest as I can, for the unknown reader of this journal: a reader who may never exist.

I know Martin Fitzgibbon to be one of the most upright, honourable men I've met: a man of the highest ideals, scrupulous in the extreme, incapable of baseness, and unshakable once he has taken up a position. God knows he's often demonstrated that to a fault – and is doing so again, to the point of perversity, crouched in that cottage at Port Arthur. A man to respect – and yet I can't like him. Perhaps it's his tediously stiff-necked manner: his fixed aloofness. More likely it's his lack of humour; and surely there's no humour in the man at all. One grows tired of his wooden gravity: even of his uprightness. He's boring. As Barry once remarked, even his idealism is boring. Barry has always failed to like him – although he's seldom until now made any direct criticism of his character. As for O'Neill, he seldom speaks ill of anyone, and has never belittled Fitzgibbon as a man. But I know very well he shares our lack of warmth towards him.

Fitzgibbon has always stood outside our circle and our lives. In some ways this is natural – we three being in our early thirties, while he is a man in middle age. He was never at Trinity; he was educated in England, at Harrow and Cambridge. (It is one of the ironies of his situation that Lord Grey, who has laid down the conditions of his exile, was a fellow-undergraduate.) So we share no past together: no youthful enthusiasms or follies. Yet he's a native of Clare, like O'Neill and myself, living with his wife and children on his aged father's estate near Newmarket, which he will soon no doubt inherit. He used to travel quite often to the Continent, and has spent a good deal of time in Italy and Greece. As a result of these journeys, he has published a small work on classical antiquity. Otherwise, he manages the estate, and interests himself in various charities, as well as in public life.

His father, Sir Richard, has always led a quiet, obscure, farming life, and is comfortable but not particularly wealthy; but another branch of the family is both wealthy and powerful. Sir Richard's late great-uncle was that notorious John Fitzgibbon who became Earl of Clare and Lord Chancellor of Ireland: hater of Catholics despite his Catholic ancestry, and ruthless opponent of the 1798 rebellion. Martin is not proud of Lord Clare, who did more than anybody else to push through the Act of Union which Martin and all of us oppose, and which robbed the Ascendancy of its independent parliament.

This connection of Martin's with the more illustrious branch of the Fitzgibbon family, and his acquaintance with Lord Grey, is known to our English captors very well. It must add to Governor Denison's caution in dealing with him – and it may yet see him given a pardon. Much though his noble relatives must detest him, they could well bring their influence to bear in London, were they so inclined. After all, were he to repent, he could so easily be forgiven; he was born to be a servant of English rule.

His defection began some six years ago, when he turned his face against the Union, and joined Daniel O'Connell's Repeal Association. This was where my comrades and I first met him, before we left to form Young Ireland. Fitzgibbon had made O'Connell his hero and mentor, and was liked and trusted by the Liberator. He began to make his reputation as a patriot then, just before the Famine – especially in those circles that believed as O'Connell did in 'peaceful means'. Through his speeches and articles, and O'Connell's good opinion, Fitzgibbon grew moderately famous – and he never ceased to believe in O'Connell's political philosophy. But after O'Connell died, and when the Famine had racked the people for nearly three years, Fitzgibbon joined Young Ireland: the movement which O'Connell in his dotage had come to hate, dismissing us as a crowd of 'juvenile orators'. Fitzgibbon remained a champion of 'peaceful means', and found others in Young Ireland of like mind.

My conviction, which also became Paul Barry's – that only force of arms would break the British grasp – was one that Fitzgibbon still rejected. Soon he had his faction and I mine – though we mostly kept polite, and strove to avoid a rift. Our factions quarrelled more openly than we did, and we were seen as opposed figureheads, standing for different philosophies in the struggle for freedom. At the time of my arrest, Fitzgibbon was still maintaining his pathetic belief that a form of self-government would be peacefully granted in the end by our English masters – masters whom I believe he still respects, in his heart. Were we given this limited self-government, there would be no more loyal subject of Queen Victoria. And this is the man who accepted the call to be leader of an armed rebellion!

Did he really wish for the role? Or was it thrust upon him? The man was an enigma – and I said this now to my comrades.

– A boring enigma, Barry agreed languidly. A nut not worth the cracking. The kernel would be as tedious as the husk.

Even O'Neill laughed at that. I threw another log on the fire and we all drew closer, warming our hands. We had lit fresh pipes, and puffed in silence for a time. Then I said:

– And yet, for all that, he stood at the centre of events in July last year. You must have expected great things of him.

– Great things were expected of everyone, Barry said.

He took the pipe from his mouth and turned to me. The slush lamp on the table had gone out; our only light now came from the fire, and his face was tinted by the flames on one side only. His lips were parted like those of a man who studies the face of his love.

– Great things, he repeated.

Then he quoted from Wordsworth: that passage which we had doted on in our student days:

> – *Bliss was it in that dawn to be alive,*
> *But to be young was very Heaven! O times,*
> *In which the meagre, stale, forbidding ways*

301

> *Of custom, law, and statute, took at once*
> *The attraction of a country in romance!*

He sighed; then he said:

– And that was how it was in Tipperary, in the fine summer weather, near Cashel of the Kings.

He fell silent. It was O'Neill who now went on to tell me of the first of those fatal twelve days: July 18th, when Young Ireland summoned a mass meeting.

The gathering was to be held on Slievenamon, the mountain that rises twenty miles from the rock of Cashel, in the plain of Tipperary. I know it well, that blue, spellbound, softly-rounded hill: the Mountain of Women, home of Finn MacCool and the fifty beautiful maidens, visible from half a dozen counties. Barry rode there from his home in Waterford; O'Neill travelled through the night from Dublin. Both men were to speak.

At first, on that hot July morning, they thought that all would go well, O'Neill said: some fifty thousand people were toiling up the slope. But the numbers did not increase, and they discovered that the authorities had put it about that they and other Young Ireland leaders had been arrested, and would not be there to address the people. They had also been branded as infidels, and enemies of the Catholic Church. Great numbers from Waterford, Cork and Wexford who had been making their way to Slievenamon had been filled with these lies by Protestant clergymen and by servants of the Government, and had halted in discouragement at Carrick-on-Suir, to come no further.

When they learned of this, Barry and O'Neill decided to ride back to Carrick. Instead of speaking at Slievenamon, they would rally the crowd that was gathered on the border of Barry's native county.

– Ah, Robert, O'Neill said, if you had been with us! You know what an orator Barry is – but I tell you, the speech at Carrick was inspired: the best he ever gave. The effect on the crowd was like nothing I've ever seen. Because of that speech, he's now known to the nation as Barry of the Sword. Of course it was reported by pimping damned detectives and Dublin Castle spies – and this was the speech, more than anything else, that did for him with the Castle. Aye, it was the Sword speech that put him here, in this southern wilderness.

Puffing on his pipe, Barry looked at neither of us, and made no comment. Legs extended, he stared into the fire as though mesmerised, a faint smile on his lips. It was not a smile of self-satisfaction – Barry has never been vain – rather, it was the smile of one who remembers a vast and fabulous event which can never be repeated, and barely even recalled in its totality. He has always been by far our greatest orator – and clearly this had been his finest flight, on the crest of what must have seemed the first great wave of revolution.

– He stood on a cart in that main street of Carrick in the late afternoon, with the mass of people around, O'Neill said. They were confused, angry and uncertain – but he hushed and he wooed them, and at first there wasn't a sound. Then they began to roar. I remember whole passages in that speech: we published it as a pamphlet, and now I can recite it by heart.

He raised a long white finger.

– 'Listen to no British lies. Our cause is sustained by the truth, and by our love of Ireland. We are here to change the fortunes of the Irish race; we are here to build a new nation from the genius of the Irish soil. British imperial rule is *not* the rule of law – it is a tyranny, backed only by armed might. Such rule merely steals the name of Government – and we say that false Government must now be overthrown. The nations in Europe have risen against tyranny, in this great and glorious year: now it is Ireland's turn! And to undertake this struggle is to enter a holy war.'

He turned to Barry.

– I hope I quote you more or less correctly?

Barry merely nodded, grave now, staring fixedly at the fire, his legs extended to the blaze; and O'Neill continued.

– 'None of us loves bloodshed. But is a tyranny open to persuasion? Will a tyranny listen to pleas? Daniel O'Connell said that Young Ireland was wrong to call for the sword: to call on the men of Ireland to fight. But great man though he was, we say that old Daniel was wrong.'

Our gentle O'Neill had grown excited by the echo of Barry's oratory, and by the phantom of that evening in the faraway streets of Carrick. He stood up now from his bench, his back to the fire, eyes fixed on Barry, and pointed his pipe stem at him.

– Come, Paul, he said, don't let me mangle your words. Recite the rest of it for Devereux: recite the passage of the sword!

Barry shook his head as though in dismissal; but then he began to speak, still looking into the fire, his mug of brandy in his hand. His voice was soft; but it's a deep, rich voice, and it gathered in strength.

– 'Men of peace abhor and reject the sword,' he said. 'They ask instead for reason and fair argument. And I understand their scruples; I respect and honour their delicacy. But they fail to face the fact that tyrants can't be reasoned with: that the only argument tyranny fears is the sword in the hands of the brave.'

He drank down his brandy, and smiled at us.

– 'Abhor and reject the sword? No: not when heartless despots rule our land! Abhor and reject the sword? No: not when their troops tear down Irish homes, and drive our people on the roads to starve! Abhor and reject the sword? But the sword ended Austria's tyranny; the sword brought mighty America into being! They say that God blesses the meek: but I say God blesses the oppressed. And I say too that He'll bless our flag of freedom – and bless the patriot sword!'

He broke off. He had straightened, and had raised both fists in front of him as he spoke; now he let his hands fall loosely to his thighs and sat back.

– Well, well, enough, he said. It doesn't have quite the same ring to it, here in this hut in the wilderness.

But I had stood up from my chair, my heart hammering, and had taken his right hand.

– Ah, my dear boy, I said. Such a speech! I would give this hand to have written it – and much more than that to have been there with you.

– And would to God you had been, Barry said. But not for my

poor speech, Robert. No: for what came next. What came next was amazing and magnificent, and I'll recall it until I die. The excitement was so great, you see, that the people were well-nigh uncontrollable. So we decided to lead them out of Carrick, and to march through the countryside to the town of Waterford.

– With what aim? I asked.

Barry paused, staring at me. O'Neill looked at him, waiting like me for his answer.

– With what aim? It's very hard to tell you, Devereux, he said. We've come to the heart of the question, I suppose. We led them because they wanted to be led. I know, I know: we were unprepared for struggle; there was no proper organization; events had overtaken us. But at the same time, I knew that others in the Confederation beside ourselves were bound to come out, and that the people would gather behind them like a wave, just as they were doing with us – and then, just possibly, all over the country, the police and the military would be driven to capitulate. Towns could be taken; and I had the wild notion that night that we might take Waterford. You simply can't imagine what it was like, my dear, unless you were there.

But they tried to help me picture it, the two of them; and they very largely succeeded. I could *see*, and my pulses raced as they spoke.

They were followed through the streets and lanes of Carrick by a human river. A great, tumbling mass of humanity hurried and struggled and pressed forward in tens of thousands, all of them crying: *Erin-go-bragh!* More kept pouring out of doorways and lanes: clenched fists raised, faces grimacing with mingled joy and rage. From out of this wild confusion, rising above the flood, came male roars of purpose and the chilling shrieks of the women. They shouted their passionate defiance of England, their support for Paul Barry and Young Ireland, their hope-filled invocations; their voices roared and shrilled like voices in a storm. It was as though, Barry said, all the misery they had suffered in the Famine had now found a way to show itself, and to seek both relief and revenge. It was like the bursting of a dam, and he and O'Neill rode on the crowd-flood's crest. He could steer it wherever he wished, he said: it was the greatest moment of his life.

The police were not to be seen; they had hidden. The mob surged on, following where Barry led, yet threatening at any moment to go beyond, to some high, delirious territory of orgiastic violence. He could only just control it. The eyes of the men were bloodshot with excitement; the eyes of the women rolled in the frenzy of possession. Oaths were shouted at the invisible British; the men cried out that they were ready to die. As they reached the countryside, it came on dark, and rain began to fall. But they surged on unheeding, and sang songs of rebellion in Gaelic, passing among peaceful green fields, watched by the dim, tawny hills.

Torches were lit. In the flares, the faces became gargoyles, distorted by shouting. White fists waved and shook above the tossing crowd-mass; pikes and even pistols could be seen. Some of the women were screaming in an anger like madness; others wailed and prayed, appealing to God and His intercessors. *Jesus, Mary and Joseph defend us! Mary and all the saints be with us!* I saw them, these barefoot women in their eternal red cloaks: most had the hoods over their heads, but some were bareheaded, their long hair drenched by the rain: disordered, tangled and wild. Their piercing wails were terrifying; they were Maenads, Barry said: had he been a British soldier he would have feared them, gun or no. It was they, more than the men, who seemed to expect him to take them to the uplands of freedom; and Barry told me solemnly that their laughing and weeping mouths did most to urge him on.

– I tell you, Devereux, he said, it was the Revolution put into our hands, if we wanted it. We had only to accept.

– Then why? I asked. Why did it not come into bloom?

He and O'Neill looked at me in the firelight, their deeply-shadowed faces becoming sober masks. It was Barry who answered, in a low, flat voice.

– That I cannot clearly explain. Not even to myself.

O'Neill turned to me.

– Perhaps I might try to do so, he said.

He re-lit his pipe with a shred of flaming bark, frowning over his thoughts.

– It took us all night to get to Waterford, he said. The crowd was so slow-moving. We arrived exhausted, at three in the morning, with the whole town asleep. Our following had thinned by now, and had lost a lot of its passion – except for a faction of empty-headed idlers, who were simply out for a brawl. We didn't trust those people; and Barry and I now had time to discuss the situation. Were we to make an attempt on the military barracks here? On the police stations? The chances of success seemed poor: the men at our disposal were neither disciplined nor properly armed. You see, Robert, it had been to avert such a situation that our original meeting had been called on Slievenamon. We had aimed at gaining promises of support; at assessing what strength we had; at discussing our strategy for a future rising – not mounting a rising that day. We had also called the meeting on the mountain to be far from senseless brawlers and troublemakers – as well as from Her Majesty's troops, and from spies and detectives. We simply hadn't anticipated what was now happening; and we weren't prepared to throw away men's lives in an attempt that could scarcely succeed. We told the crowd this; we asked that they continue to organize, and we promised them the rising would come soon – and so they dispersed.

He fell silent for a moment; then he put into words a thought I've often had myself, but have never voiced to my comrades.

– What hope did we have, Devereux, at such short notice? We needed to enlist the support of the people all through the country. But the people didn't *know* us, as they knew and loved Daniel O'Connell. The peasantry knows little of us at all – and it's very hard to know the peasantry. I remember thinking so, as they pressed around us in the march. They might have been Hottentots, for all I really knew of them. And it's true of both of *you*, if you're honest.

Barry had begun to laugh.

– I can't dispute that, O'Neill. Sure, we may *love* the Irish people – but none of us in the Confederation really *knows* the people, if the truth be told.

– I don't dispute it either, I said. But surely it need not prevent us from defending them, and raising them up.

Barry merely smiled at me ruefully, and shook his head; and O'Neill went on with his account.

The march on Waterford had far greater effects than they anticipated, he said – and their hands were forced after all. The rioting, as well as Barry's speech, had thoroughly alarmed both Dublin Castle and London: two days afterwards, on July the 20th, the Government issued a proclamation calling for the surrender of all arms in a set of proclaimed districts.

Young Ireland's answer was to hold a hurried meeting of the War Council in Dublin, on that same day.

There were four of them on the War Council's executive: Barry, Fitzgibbon, O'Neill and Kinane. There was nothing for them to do now, Barry told the meeting, but to *go out*. At the same time, he admitted to being filled with misgivings. The people might be willing, but they were weakened by the Famine: many of them were half-starved. If only things could have been delayed until the harvest! And the Catholic priests – so many of whom favoured the movement – were warning the people that the time was not ripe, and that the bloody British ruthlessness of 1798 could well be repeated. Young Ireland had not yet done enough to succeed, Barry said; but it had also gone too far to turn back. So the rising must be now, whether they wished it or not.

Only Martin Fitzgibbon disagreed: he was still rejecting force of arms. The others over-ruled him, and he agreed to their decision; but he urged that the rebellion not take place in Dublin. There were too many troops in the city; it would have to be in the countryside, he said. The Council agreed to this; but their plans were otherwise quite daring.

Barry was to take a fortress, steal the weapons it held, and convey them to Waterford to arm the people. Fitzgibbon was to go to France, there to recruit officers to drill a volunteer army from the peasantry. O'Neill was to take Cashel, and Barry to take Waterford. Fitzgibbon and Kinane were then to move at large through the countryside, enlisting support. Eventually all parties would converge, and march on Dublin.

But events overtook them again. Two days later, on Saturday

the 22nd, the Westminster Parliament suspended *habeas corpus*. At the same time, writs were issued for the arrests of Barry, O'Neill and Fitzgibbon. No planned campaign could now take place: instead, they fled into the countryside as wanted men.

On the night of the 22nd and on Sunday 23rd, they and other members of the Federation lay low in the houses of trusted associates. Barry and O'Neill took refuge with an old friend of Barry's – a doctor named Sheridan – whose house was near the base of Slievenamon Mountain. Fitzgibbon and Kinane went to ground nearby in the town of Cashel, in the home of a friend of Fitzgibbon's. This region in the plain of Tipperary, near the seat of Ireland's ancient royal city, seems to have drawn all four like a magnet. Perhaps – pathetic though this seems, considering the circumstances – Cashel of the Kings and Tipperary's Golden Vale were a source of hope and strength.

Here, in outrage and despair at the suspension of *habeas corpus* – a thing that had shocked him profoundly – Martin Fitzgibbon at last decided that he must lead an armed resistance. That he *must* be the one to lead, and to appeal to the people, was agreed to without dissent. His illustrious name, his powerful connections, his friendship with the great O'Connell and the work he'd done in the Repeal Association all made him known to large numbers of the population – and this, it was agreed, would be essential in gaining their support. But what followed in Tipperary, as Barry and O'Neill told it between them, was a dismal story: one which made me groan in rage and pain, and sometimes curse aloud as they spoke, beating my hand on my knee.

It was a story of wretched and inconclusive wanderings: of surgings to and fro from village to village within a few, petty square miles, like the impotent progress in a nightmare. It was a search for heroic battle whose fulfilment never came: a sad children's game. And always at its centre was the noble, righteous, utterly ineffective Martin Fitzgibbon, on whom so many hopes had been placed – a sort of Don Quixote, filled with scruples and ideals, his Sancho Panza Kinane at his side.

It began on Monday the 24th, when Barry and O'Neill came in from Slievenamon to Cashel, to meet Fitzgibbon and Kinane.

From there, the four warriors set out together on a tour of the Tipperary villages, riding in two gigs. All of them, it seems, were armed with pistols.

But Fitzgibbon, although prepared to call for a rising, had declared that he must 'first test the will of the people'. This he did in the main street of the village of Mullinahone. He stood up in his gig and announced himself, and the crowd quickly grew. A police barracks stood opposite – and Fitzgibbon asked the people if they would save him from arrest. They shouted that they would, and grew very excited; but there was no clash, since the constables, all of them Irish, were looking on without taking action – and when Fitzgibbon began to speak, they smiled with approval at his words. He addressed the people on the sufferings of Ireland, and the necessity for a rising. Would they follow him?

– The enthusiasm was extraordinary, O'Neill said. It was as though they'd been waiting for us – and in that moment I felt that the rebellion might actually succeed. The people cried out that they'd follow Fitzgibbon anywhere, and drive the English out. Some of them went and tolled the chapel bell, and more came in to town to hear him speak. But then the parish priest appeared: a hulking, red-faced fellow called Father Malone. One of the people: a peasant. He asked to be heard; and as soon as he spoke, I knew we'd met with an enemy to our enterprise. He was all soft soap, of course. He declared that his heart was with Fitzgibbon and the rest of us, and that he wept for the condition of the people – but he warned that a rising would be premature. The harvest wasn't ripe; the people were starved; they would be crushed by the English military. We should wait for the harvest, he said. It was the line all the priests were taking: and you know what sway they have over the peasantry. Some began to waver now; but most cried out that they were starved already, they had nothing to lose, and would follow Martin Fitzgibbon. The priest withdrew; but we hadn't heard the last of Father Malone.

– A pox on him, Barry said. The sly black cockroach. He made me ashamed of my Church.

He sighed, and drank off his latest mug of brandy and water.

– We spent that day and the next drilling the men of the village in the use of pikes and guns, he said, and in hedge and street fighting. The police were no longer to be seen. Our idea now, you see, was to go through the countryside collecting followers, and to lead them to Slievenamon Mountain, where we'd begin to build and train an army – just as the War Council had planned. It seemed possible at that stage, God help us.

Early on Wednesday morning, Martin Fitzgibbon decided that he should lead the nucleus of his ragtag army up six miles of road to the mountain district village of Ballingarry, to recruit more men. The procession was at least six hundred strong, Barry said. The men had sworn that they would ultimately follow the Young Irelanders to Slievenamon, and were filled with a sort of joy: singing and roaring, brandishing pikes, pitchforks and guns. And in Ballingarry, in the bright summer sunshine, where they were joined by an even larger crowd, Fitzgibbon had his great moment – as Barry had done in Waterford.

He stood on a stone wall, clad in a dark frock coat and peaked cap, a pair of pistols pushed into his belt, and looked down on the crowd with an air of solemnity and warning. On Fitzgibbon's person, the pistols were decidedly incongruous, O'Neill said; he looked like an armed preacher. But the country people called blessings on him: they hailed him as their deliverer, and the hope of Ireland. Then he began to speak.

– And that was when he began to lose them, Barry said.

His tone and expression were savage; he drove a fist into the palm of his hand.

– They were ready to be *his*, that morning, he said. They'd have followed him anywhere; they were with him wherever we wanted to take them. But as he spoke, you could see the confusion coming into their faces. First confusion; then disappointment; then the beginnings of despair. And although we didn't know it at the time, the rising had already begun to be lost.

He poured himself more brandy, while we waited. The fire spat a spark in the silence, and we heard a tough snore from old Carter. Barry drank, and wiped his mouth.

– He asked at first that they rise against the British, he said. Well and good. He asked that they follow us, when we marched in a few days to Slievenamon, with the men from other villages. For now, he wanted only twenty men, to guard him against arrest: a personal bodyguard. Good. But then his tune changed. He began to warn the people that *they must do no damage to property*. The rights of private property must above all be respected, he said. He warned; he hectored; he grew very high-flown: it became the main gist of his address. This, to men who were ready to make revolution! But Fitzgibbon's a land-owner; and protecting it's bred into him, isn't it? The thought that any estate such as his might come under threat was appalling to him.

Suddenly, Barry began to laugh. I did the same, while he and I looked at each other. But there was now little humour in our laughter: it was a mere exhalation of bitterness.

– My God, I said. So *that* was his theme.

– That was his theme, Barry said. And in every God-damned village we went on to, he harped on it. At first, they'd gather around him in delight. Here they had O'Connell's successor: a captain who'd lead them out of misery; who'd take them down the road to revenge for every bloody wrong the English ever did them. They were full of passion; they were riding on a wind of fury; they were ready to plunder and destroy! It was *revolution* that was being proposed; and these are the things of which revolution's made, are they not? Revenge was what they hungered for: revenge and the spoils of rebellion. Yet here stood this dull, careful preacher, ordering them *not* to take revenge – and to touch nothing belonging to those masters who sold grain and butter to England while our people starved! How could they reconcile *this* with revolution? At first they were puzzled; then they were dismayed; then they were disgusted, and began to turn away. Even Liam Kinane, who'll hear no word against Martin, would stand frowning beside him as he spoke, looking down at his bloody big boots. Fitzgibbon *lost* them, Devereux – he lost them! And so the rising was lost.

– Jesus, I said. Jesus. That pious, God-damned fool! Well, blood will tell, Paul. He's a true Fitzgibbon, in the end.

Barry and I sat staring at each other in silence; and O'Neill turned a wide, troubled gaze on us both.

– Come, my dears, he said, this is a bit too strong: I really must protest. Are you not a Devereux, Robert? Do you forget what *your* Norman ancestors did? And Paul: has the Barry family been innocent – any more than mine has – in its dealings with the people? Martin Fitzgibbon is true to our cause; he has sacrificed himself for it. Doesn't he sit now in that foul penal station for his bravery and idealism? If he has a fault, it's that there's too much virtue in him; he has a conscience that will never allow him to pander to the vicious. Oh, yes: a leader without conscience or decency could have led those mobs on a fine career of pillage and rape: but Fitzgibbon was not that sort of leader. If success must depend on rapine and sack, then Martin scorns success. And I honour him for it.

Barry closed his eyes as though in pain.

– Yes, yes, O'Neill – all true, no doubt. I don't deny that he's upright, and of course he must be respected for it.

He opened his eyes again, and looked at O'Neill in the flickering firelight with a sad and empty stare.

– But the truth is that wildness and savagery, much though you may deplore them, are the things that are needed for revolution – and the people at that time were filled with wildness and savagery. *Those* were the passions that were begging to be released – aye, and to be channelled. And to see Fitzgibbon failing to do so – *refusing* to do so – was a pitiable sight. Even Kinane felt that – he has said so to us in so many words. Those poor, half-starved wretches would have followed Martin Fitzgibbon to the death. And a ruthless man – a vicious man, to use your term – who carried Fitzgibbon's name and Fitzgibbon's reputation, could have taken them with him to break English rule in Ireland. *That* was the man that was needed: one who would say *yes* to pillage, destruction, and death. A ruthless man? Yes, I suppose so. I suppose Napoleon was ruthless.

That Fitzgibbon had few Napoleonic qualities became painfully evident over the final three days. At times I seemed to be listening to a tragedy; at others, to a grotesque comedy.

Fitzgibbon had made Ballingarry his base: he and the others

lodged with a sympathetic farmer, just outside the village. On the Thursday, Fitzgibbon reviewed and drilled his troops there, with the help of O'Neill and Barry; they also erected barricades on the road. They had slept very little, taking turns to watch through the night, since they constantly expected an attempt to arrest them. Fitzgibbon, it seems, was particularly nervous about this. Now, with his volunteer bodyguard, he approached the small police barracks, and asked the five Irish constables there to surrender their weapons. But the constables begged to be allowed to keep them: they'd be dismissed if they lost their guns, they said, and their families ruined. They swore they'd make no attempt at arrest, and would join the rising themselves, when the time was ripe. Fitzgibbon acceded to their request: a fact that not only tells me much about his gullibility, but to what degree the enterprise had descended into farce.

On the Friday morning, he decided to begin the march to Slievenamon. They would first pass through Mullinahone again, to enable the volunteers there to join them. They had a band of three hundred or so behind them, armed with every kind of weapon: spades, axes, pitchforks, guns. Fitzgibbon rode in state in a hired cart, his faithful Kinane by his side. When they arrived in Mullinahone, hundreds more joined them, swearing they would follow to Slievenamon that night.

– But during the day, Barry said, while we were gathering weapons and buying bread to feed the troops, that bastard priest Malone was sneaking about among them, repeating his warnings. We knew nothing of this until the damage was done. We might have countered it even then, I believe – but Fitzgibbon had already put confusion and uncertainty into the people's minds, with his warnings against revenge and his orders to touch no private property. So when Father Malone began to sow doubt and fear, and their resolution was put to the test, they hadn't the fire in their bellies: Fitzgibbon had put it out. And sure enough, just after the march began that evening, a third of the men deserted us, only a mile down the road. As we went on, the rest of them melted away. In the end, only twenty were left.

– And to add to the misery of all this, O'Neill put in, it had begun to rain.

I put my head in my hands, while they brought the dismal story to its climax.

Fitzgibbon now dismissed his last few followers, and seems to have fallen into a trance: or more likely, despair. He lay down in a field beside the road, sheltering from the rain behind a haystack, and refused to speak to anyone for half an hour. The others tried to discuss the crisis; but he only shook his head, and would make no response. It was Kinane who finally managed to rouse him. The faithful squire suggested that if they were to try and raise another army, they should first rob a bank. A revolutionary force needed food, and therefore money, Kinane said – and he, Kinane, was prepared to go and hold up a bank in Carrick.

But Fitzgibbon was horrified, and forbade him even to suggest such a thing again. The real question was, Fitzgibbon said, whether they should continue with the rising at all. He had begun to feel now that all hope was over, he said; and he began to talk of escape. He would probably go back to his estate in Clare, and hope that his tenants might defend him against arrest. And he asked where his comrades would fly to.

But Barry refused to think in this way. Hope was not over, he said: the rising had only just begun, and they must now seek elsewhere for volunteers. He suggested that they go to the inn at Ballingarry, and have a proper discussion of their plans.

At the inn, they sat around the table in the parlour over chops and glasses of whiskey. The talk was protracted; but eventually it became clear that there could be no unanimity.

– So that was the end, Barry said. That was when we flew in different directions. I tried to save things – useless. I told Fitzgibbon that we should fall back on Cashel, occupy a house there, make it our fortress, issue a proclamation, and rally the people again near Slievenamon. Others in Young Ireland could be summoned from Dublin to join us. But to this Martin wouldn't agree – and I told him that if he couldn't offer leadership, he should cease trying to lead. He became quite heated – I won't say angry, since he doesn't have enough blood in him for that – and said that had it not been for my urging – and *yours*, Devereux – he would never have considered taking up

315

arms. He seemed to blame you and your published articles in particular for what we'd now come to – instead of the British suspension of *habeas corpus*! I told him that had you been there, we wouldn't have been sitting in this sorry plight, with our band of followers lost.

O'Neill now spoke gently, his gaze looking back to that sad inn parlour.

– In the end, we agreed to disagree like gentlemen, he said, and to go our different ways – coming together later, if circumstances made it possible. Barry and I would leave immediately, travelling to take shelter again with our friend Doctor Sheridan near Slievenamon. Fitzgibbon and Kinane would stay here in Ballingarry overnight – where his bodyguard would probably continue to protect him – and would then attempt a return to County Clare, to take shelter on Fitzgibbon's estate.

– So Thomas and I said goodbye to them, Barry said. And as it turned out, it was Fitzgibbon, poor devil, with Kinane beside him, who faced police guns the next day.

He winked at me, leaning back on his gum-stump throne; the bitterness had gone from his face, and the mischievous, humorous light that's more natural to it had come back.

– Fitzgibbon fought the Battle of the Cabbage Patch, he said. Not much of a battle to be sure, with the loss of only one life – but the only battle that our rising has to record.

Their account of this sorry affair was secondhand. Their only witness – apart from Fitzgibbon – was Liam Kinane; and it was Kinane's version of events that I was now given.

Kinane and Fitzgibbon stayed at the inn that night, sleeping very little, and taking turns to watch. But there was still no sign of the police. Fitzgibbon, it seems, spent a good deal of the night composing a letter to the newspapers, defending Young Ireland's actions. When they rose on the Saturday, Kinane said, his chief had swung back to more optimistic spirits – and during the morning, Fitzgibbon actually began to consider continuing the rising.

Two things seem to have encouraged this: the arrival from Dublin of another Young Irelander – a young man named Patrick Mahoney – and the discovery that a good number of the men in the village were still awaiting Fitzgibbon's orders, and ready to follow him again. So Don Quixote and his squire, together with Mahoney, embarked on a fresh course of action. Fitzgibbon was attired once more in his sober frock coat and military-style peaked cap; his two pistols gleamed in his belt. Mahoney, a fresh-faced, boisterous young man, full of optimism and eagerness for battle, had brought a pistol, and wore a bandolier for cartridges. He and Kinane assisted Fitzgibbon in putting their followers through some drill; and they ordered some rude pikes to be forged at the blacksmith's. Their force in the end consisted of about forty, only half of whom had guns or pistols.

Just after noon, this ragged, ill-equipped army gathered on the outskirts of the village and prepared to march towards Urlingford – where Fitzgibbon hoped to raise more men. Many people thronged about him, offering him advice and delaying the march; all was confusion, with the usual lack of order and discipline. And then a cry went up. A detachment of some fifty police could be seen coming down the white road towards them, about half a mile off. Here at last were the Empire's mercenaries, marching in a body in their tall black helmets, carbines at their shoulders.

Fitzgibbon now seems to have gained resolve: even to have shown a certain quiet bravery. He ordered his troops into a hollow square, to prepare for battle. But at this the police turned aside, going off the road up a side lane. They were seen to be making for a solitary stone farmhouse on top of a low hill: the home of a widow named MacManus, who lived there with her five children. The troops raised a shout at this, and ran after the police; a group of idlers followed excitedly, and Fitzgibbon and his two comrades could only try and take control as best they might. Running, the band entered a field behind the house where cabbages grew, to find that the police were now inside, with the lower windows shut and barricaded with mattresses. From the upper windows, a dozen or more carbines projected, levelled at the crowd.

Confronted with this, Kinane expressed the opinion that their foe had made themselves impregnable. But Fitzgibbon insisted that the constabulary would surrender if an attack were made. He'd become strangely stubborn, apparently, and his nervousness seems to have left him. Because he wished the police to surrender, they *would* surrender: this was his thinking. First, however, he was determined to make a last attempt at 'peaceful means'.

Braving the downward-pointing carbines, he walked straight up to the house, Kinane following. The florid, fleshy face of the Widow MacManus could be seen at a ground floor window, which was open at the top: she was standing on a chair and crying out to the crowd to ask them to spare her children. The two men went up to this window, and Fitzgibbon stood on the sill. The widow retreated from him; but he pushed his hand through, offering to shake hands with one of the policemen who stood there, and make peace. The policeman actually took Fitzgibbon's hand; but at that moment, the gang of idlers in the garden began to throw stones at the house, breaking some of the windows.

Instantly, the police at the upper windows opened fire with their carbines. The noise was terrific, Kinane said.

Fitzgibbon fell back from the window, and he and Kinane ran towards the cabbage patch, where they crouched behind some casks to take what cover they could. Nearby, a man with a shock of black hair, his tattered felt hat beside him, lay still among the cabbages: the only death in the whole affair. Another held his shoulder and cried out. Kinane found that he too was wounded, bleeding from the calf of his left leg. He fired his pistol at the windows, as did many others in the makeshift army: most had taken cover behind the garden's long stone wall. Young Mahoney now joined his two comrades, firing at the windows too. But there were no visible targets, and all their efforts were useless.

Kinane never saw Fitzgibbon discharge his pistol, he said, and he doubted whether his leader ever did so. But despite the bullets whistling around them, Fitzgibbon would not retreat. Instead, he got up, showing no regard for his safety, and stood with folded arms, staring at the house. Kinane and Mahoney tried to draw him away, but he would not come. Meanwhile, the crowd behind the wall were screaming and crying; many were disappearing, and soon only a dozen or so men were left. Then Kinane saw the reason. A black-clad figure was moving among them and talking to them: the red-faced priest, Father Malone. Within minutes, he had persuaded the rest to retreat; they followed him away down the lane.

It was all over; and only now, Kinane said, were he and Mahoney able to persuade Fitzgibbon to leave. He was still reluctant; but both of them took his arms, drawing him away. The three walked slowly down the hill, occasional bullets whistling after them.

The aftermath was mostly known to me already. Fitzgibbon, Kinane and Mahoney made their way back to the farmer's house outside Ballingarry, where Kinane had the flesh wound in his leg dressed, and where they hid until dark. Then they set out for different destinations. Fitzgibbon made for Kilkenny, and was arrested there two days later as he boarded a coach, attempting to get back to Clare. Mahoney went in stages to Cork, was sheltered there by friends, and made his escape by ship to America. Kinane set off on foot for Slievenamon Mountain, to reach there next day and take refuge with Barry and O'Neill, in Doctor Sheridan's house.

Warrants were soon out for all of them, and Barry, O'Neill and Kinane now left the doctor's house to hide on the mountain itself, sleeping out at night. Eventually, they decided to make for Cork as Mahoney had done, and to try and find a ship for America; but they got no farther than Cashel when they were recognised in a public house and arrested. They met Fitzgibbon again when they were taken to Kilmainham Gaol in Dublin, where all of them were incarcerated. Barry, O'Neill and Kinane had kept their spirits up; but they found Fitzgibbon deeply depressed.

– He carries a deep hurt, O'Neill said. How is he to live down the way he's been pictured by the press? *The Times* and other British papers mocked him as 'the King of Tipperary'. The lies of those vulgar London scribblers have done him great damage. They said he was seen weeping, and crawling among the cabbages on all fours. They said he was of unsound mind. All untrue. He was almost foolishly brave, exposing himself to fire from the beginning – and many of the people were just as brave. The truth has been concealed about Ballingarry. It was useless, but we were not dishonoured – and some day Ireland will know it.

His small chin was set, and I saw that he was moved and indignant. I therefore refrained from comment.

Barry was meditating on the fire, eyes half closed. When he spoke, his voice was soft and regretful, all its anger gone.

– Fitzgibbon had been moving like a man in a dream, he said. That's the truth of it. All of it was a dream to him: all of those twelve days. He never came out of it – and I doubt that he has now.

Moving like a man in a dream: the words summed it all up, I thought – and a good deal else besides. None of us spoke again, but sat staring into the coals. Soon we'd go and sleep on our rough bush beds, under our opossum-skin rugs. Our mood was not happy, yet neither was it sad; it was a melancholy beyond melancholy, vast as space, yet somehow not dispiriting: probably the state in which all men contemplate tragedy which is larger than their own lives. We knew only that we were glad to be together, and that despite all the blows we'd been dealt, we were not done with fortune, nor fortune with us.

As for Fitzgibbon, I had ceased to feel anger about him, and had begun to feel pity. There are always casualties in war; and Fitzgibbon, I suspected, was one of them.

A little later, just before going to bed, I went out to ease my bladder. I walked away from the hut, among spaces of pale dry tussock grass.

A line of gum trees rose at a distance, in the direction of the lake: tall, bare, wraith-like forms, with black, swaying foliage at their tops. Level emptiness here. Lichen-covered rocks and prickly green bushes. Fathomless dark beyond them, with a half moon above. I came to a halt by some banksias: crooked black spirits.

The air was thrillingly cold: the sky clear, a breeze rushing steadily from the west, its breath filling the land. One of the bushes was tossed about suddenly, so that I swung to look with my heart in my throat. I had a sense of some presence behind me – but there was nothing. Occasional noises: the croak of a water bird by the lake, and the stamping of our horses in the enclosure. One of Carter's dogs barked twice; I heard the sound snatched up by the wind, and flung away for miles.

My head swimming with brandy, I passed water in the grass. Then I looked up.

The sky was so near, I grew giddy. The stars! Buttoning up my trousers, I reeled, and almost fell over. The Milky Way's white river arched so close above me that I exclaimed: its source might have been just behind the eucalypts. Vast, this blue-black sky: vast but not distant. No sky in Europe came so low. Here in this thin, untainted air, I stood on the brink of space; and I looked at a different firmament. Some constellations were standing in unfamiliar positions; others were lost; a few were entirely strange.

Low in the south was the native Southern Cross, with its pointers. Polaris of course was gone, and nor could I see Charles's Wain. But there was the belt of Orion, flung down here in the north-east, with the Dog Star brilliant at his heels. Here on the bottom of the world, O'Neill had pointed out to me, the hunter is no longer the herald of winter, but of summer. *Wild stars*, he'd called them: looking up at them now, I found that the disaster at Ballingarry and the troubles of Ireland had ceased to have importance. All that had ever happened in the hemisphere which gave me birth was becoming unreal. And I suddenly understood that terror of infinite space which had gripped Pascal. This made my brain swim as much as the brandy was doing; I took hold of the rough, corky limb of a banksia to steady myself, and began to converse in whispers with my double-goer – as I often do, in times of turmoil or dilemma.

Self: – What is the true nature of this wilderness? Are Plato's immortal Forms behind its mask? To put it another way: does this southern emptiness contain those ideal presences which give meaning and solace to the North? *Are they universal truths after all?* Is Beauty really *here*? Truth? Goodness? Justice? Here, where no human minds have ever conjured up such things?

Doppelgänger: – Perhaps not. Perhaps Chaos alone is sitting behind the mask: mother of Erebus and Night.

This proposition created a sort of vertigo, and I began to lose my hold on existence. I wished to reject such a notion out of hand – and yet it was wickedly convincing, here among the rocks and banksia trees.

Doppelgänger: – Let me put this to you. What thoughts would Jean Jacques Rousseau have had in this hemisphere? Would nature and its forms have brought his spirit joy as those of the North did – filling it with the impulse to worship? And suppose your William Wordsworth had wandered on this roof of Van Diemen's Land – among mountains whose dead craters are like entrances to Hades? Would he have found *here* those 'huge and mighty forms' that gave him such consolation at Grasmere? *Is* Lake Sorell another Windermere?

No: clearly not; I could only acknowledge the force of my double-goer's case, and fell silent. The wind from the west that strode tall through the tussocks had come from the wastes near Cape Horn, crossing territories from which the soul recoiled: miles of freezing ocean, and the island's western forests, where the rain never ceased, and where no men had been. It passed nowhere that was softened by human skill; nowhere offering haven to the soul. These rocks were rocks that had never been part of our story; these stars inhabited alien legends.

The rank smell of terror rose about me, and the grass turned white as nightmare. I turned, and started back to the hut.

But as I went, a sudden piping broke out overhead: the cries of plover, infinitely lonely yet exalted. I stopped again, and listened. Long-drawn-out, fainter and fainter, they dwindled away and then vanished, like voices of phantom lovers, calling across distances never to be bridged.

November 26th
This evening, I have spent many hours writing up the above account under yesterday's date.

O'Neill and I parted from Barry at noon today – he setting off for Ross, while we rode back here to Bothwell. Just before we separated, a brief but crucial discussion took place on the question of escape.

Throughout the morning, not a serious word had passed between us. After the sombre talk of the previous night, we'd turned by mutual consent to physical activity, and to mindless jests and foolery; neither

322

Ireland nor any other matter of consequence was mentioned.

We were early out of the hut. The day had dawned perfect, almost cloudless, with a thin, dancing sun that melted the last few patches of snow on the grass. We saddled up and rode off to the shore of Lake Sorell – Barry leading the way on his gleaming black horse. Spurring him into a gallop, he careered across the soft yellow grass at breakneck speed. Furious bush-riding followed, with calls and whoops and near-accidents: we raced between the gums and under low-hanging wattle boughs, while the lakes gleamed always nearby: great Sorell, and smaller, silver Lake Crescent.

The Lakes! Like my friends, I believe I'll grow addicted to them; their virginal enchantment is already working on me. Sorell's blue-grey mirror, steadily inviolate as we three rode and shouted, seemed always to contain a mystery, just beyond vision, somewhere on the edge of unvisited space. Sitting here tonight in the parlour of Glengarry Cottage, I still see its expanse in my mind, and already yearn to be back there. Up on that tableland, my comrades and I have a freedom that's real, and not 'comparative': a freedom where we can't be spied upon.

On a rise among some boulders, I saw my first kangaroo – or Brush Wallaby, as this particular type is called – and laughed in amazement. It sprang away, grotesquely propelled on its huge back legs, and Barry fired at it with the double-barrelled shotgun he's purchased. He missed, and regretted the lack of a 'kangaroo dog' – a greyhound that's used here for hunting. (O'Neill has acquired two of these dogs, and has promised me a kangaroo hunt soon. The flesh is good, he says, tasting like hare.)

At noon, our excess of spirits somewhat reduced, we tethered our horses and sat by the lake, on the trunk of a fallen gum. A flock of Carter's sheep wandered by a grove of banksia; except for their bleating, nothing broke the silence here. Lighting our pipes, we stared for a time at the low blue line of mountains on the far-off eastern shore. Then Barry said suddenly:

– So what are we going to do?

– You're thinking of escape, I said. Is escape possible?

He nodded, and grinned at me.

– Of course. Anything's possible, you know that. It's difficult and risky, and those poor devils of convicts who steal boats and attempt it are always caught. But I'm told it can be done if you've money – and can find a ship's captain to bribe. A good deal of money's needed, of course.

– It would have to be America, I said.

– Naturally, America, Barry said. The haven of so many Young Irelanders since last year. I long to go there. We'd not want for Irish company in New York – nor support for the cause from the Irish community, political and financial. Letters have already reached me: I'll bring them next time. Your faction there is very strong, Robert: they'd greet you with joy. Think: we could go on working in New York for a future rising – backed by American money!

We smiled at each other, daring to hope. But O'Neill was shaking his head.

– It can't be done, he said. We can't, as gentlemen, break the conditions the authorities exacted from us when we gave our *parole*. We've given our written word. If we break it, our honour's gone – and what have we left, if we lose our honour? The British, and every knave and villain in the British press, would sneer at us for ever. Worst of all, we'd lose the respect of those who look to us for leadership.

– My dear Thomas, I said, of course there's no question of breaking our *parole*. I for one have never even considered it.

– Nor I, Barry said. When the time comes, we must simply return our Tickets-of-Leave.

– Exactly, I said. Why Martin Fitzgibbon hasn't thought of the same thing, and spared himself his incarceration, I can't imagine.

But still O'Neill shook his head.

– Perhaps he *has* thought of it, he said, and has realised its hope-lessness. Perhaps that's why he's given them no promise not to attempt escape. If he *does* make his escape from that penal settle-ment – not having given his *parole*, or accepted their Ticket – he does so without losing his honour.

He took off his spectacles and polished them on his neckerchief, looking from one to the other of us with his solemn hazel eyes.

– Think, he said. If you return your Tickets, you are saying to

324

the authorities: 'put me in prison' – which the Governor will delight in doing. He's been very cunning, this colonial jack-in-office. London ordered him to give us the privilege of a Ticket-of-Leave – and the British newspapers complained of the leniency shown us. But Denison undermined that leniency with the special conditions he imposed on us. Consider: a common British burglar with his Ticket may go anywhere he likes in this island – provided he obtains a pass – and need only report himself to the authorities in person twice a year. Under *those* conditions, we might write returning our Tickets and escape very easily, long before they knew what we were doing. But since we must report personally to our local Police Magistrate each month – and since we have given our written word to Denison not to escape – we are placed quite differently, as I see it. Honour requires that we resign our *parole* personally at our local police office – while also writing to the Governor cancelling our agreements. And how much time would we then have to get away? Clearly our gaolers would guess our intentions instantly, and would lose no time in seizing us, and putting us on a prison settlement.

Barry frowned.

– By God, O'Neill, you have a very stringent idea of honour.

– Is there any other? Can you see a flaw? And have you considered the way in which the matter would be analysed in print, by both friends and foes?

Barry looked down at his feet, and kicked with his heel at a tuft of grass. Then he looked up and sighed.

– You're right, he said. But what a damned inconvenient voice of conscience you are, Father.

– Of course he's right, I told Barry. Then I turned to O'Neill.

– It would have to be done as you say, Thomas – but given favourable circumstances, I believe it could still succeed.

– Forgive me, but I doubt it, O'Neill said. Should they remove those conditions from our Tickets, then in my view we might hope to abscond. Otherwise, no. I shall therefore continue to hope for a pardon, through the efforts of our friends at home. Meanwhile, I'll make a life here. It does have its compensations. Look about you.

He gestured at the lake, where a distant black swan and her

cygnets were sailing in a line through a glittering path of light. Then he turned back to Barry.

– Come, Paul, it could be worse. After all, you're enjoying the friendship of your widow – and you've purchased a dog and a gun. You're almost becoming a bushman.

Barry smiled faintly, and reached out beside him to one of the prickly green bushes that grew everywhere up here; he pulled off one of its pink berries, and rolled it between finger and thumb.

– I can't dispute your logic, dear boy. An opportunity to escape may not come for some time. But if it does, and I can escape with honour, I'll take it. What do *you* say, Devereux?

– I say the same, I said. And let us hope an opportunity does come that can be grasped. Otherwise, we'll be here at the end of the world for the next twelve years.

A silence fell. We looked out over the lake, sitting on our gum log. Barry knocked out his pipe, and O'Neill turned up the collar of his pilot coat. My words had struck a greater chill than I intended. The sun was still out and the water still glittered, but a cold, invisible wave had crossed the lake, gathering on the soft, matted grass and the lichen-patterned rocks. It entered my bowels – and those of my comrades too, I believe. Soon we would mount our horses, and ride to our separate districts down below. Meanwhile, for a few more minutes, we gazed at the low blue line of mountains across the water. They seemed like a barrier, hiding the country of our wishes.

4. DIS

December 11th

– I fear today's surgery will be drastic, I said. Use the knife gently, Howard, won't you?

Doctor Howard smiled, seeming to look through me rather than at me, eyes glassily blank behind their spectacles. His diagnostic stare: similar to the one he'd bent on me when I was ill.

– Never fret, Devereux, he said. The only knife I'll use will be the palette knife. And this is your final ordeal, you'll be pleased to hear. Today you should be finished.

He looked down at the portrait on the easel and frowned, head on one side. He had placed me, as always, in a chair directly facing him. He required me to wear the same grey frock coat for each sitting, and a green satin cravat. This was the third sitting, but he'd never allowed me to peep at the work in progress, keeping it covered with a cloth whenever he went out of the studio. He said that it brought bad luck for the sitter to view his portrait before completion – and hearing the subject's opinion on his own image would only be distracting.

All was as usual: the big work-table in the centre of the room, littered with his folios and drawings; the black-lacquered Chinese furniture; the figures of Eros and Psyche by the open French windows. Howard had set up his easel close by, with his back to these glass doors; smoke-blue Mount Direction was framed there, hazy with summer, seeming to muse on the horizon. Howard now loaded his brush from the palette on the table beside him, and began to work on the canvas. He always looked very much the artist on these occasions, in his paint-stained white smock; but his trousers were of excellent, dove-grey nankeen, and his shoes were well polished: he was too fastidious a man to indulge in artistic disarray.

We fell silent. I took pleasure in the studio's Saturday peace, and in the warmth of the summer afternoon. Nothing broke the stillness but the lowing of cows, the whisper of Howard's brush, and the music of New Town's dream: the mysterious cooing of pigeons and doves, exiled and lost in Time. But I knew that we'd soon talk again. The sittings had become a series of conversations, since Howard seemed able to talk and paint simultaneously – only breaking off when he encountered a difficult patch.

I sometimes wondered whether painting my portrait was a way of making certain that I'd visit him here regularly. He'd arranged for me to do so by dealing with the authorities, just as he'd promised; so I was able to come down from Bothwell and stay here as his guest for two or three days at a time. This was achieved by riding Dan down to Green Ponds, leaving him stabled at the inn there, and catching the stage coach as far as New Town, where Langford met me at the toll gates. The visits have been made possible through a somewhat remarkable favour Howard has obtained for me. I've been granted a 'pass', which carries my description, and which enables me to travel from one police district to another at any time I wish. All that I have to do is to present it at the police office of the district I visit. This puts me on the same footing as a genuine British convict who holds a Ticket-of-Leave – a privilege that has not been granted my fellow-exiles, who must apply to their local Police Magistrate for permission if they ever wish to leave their districts. It's surely a measure of Doctor Howard's influence with the Governor and the Convict Department that this pass has been granted to me.

He claims to have done this because he values my company; but I'm inclined to wonder whether he has other reasons.

Thomas O'Neill believes that Howard reports on me to his colleagues in the Colonial Government. He points out that the Hobart General Hospital, of which Howard is in charge, is under the control of the Convict Department, whose tentacles grip most things in Van Diemen's Land. And Howard, as Colonial Surgeon, has as one of his colleagues the Comptroller-General of Convicts – who, together with the Governor, officially holds my fate in his hands. Most of the Hospital's patients are convicts – so the management of felons remains Howard's business, on a large scale. His citadel of suffering is a grim stone building at the bottom of Liverpool Street, just around the corner from the long stone walls and staring windows of the 'Tench': the Penitentiary in Campbell Street. Here, removed by only a few miles from the elegance and peace of New Town, Doctor Howard spends his days; and in caring for his diseased and dying felons, he no doubt has frequent official contact with the Comptroller-General – and probably social contact as well, since the world in which the colony's officials have their being is a small one.

Well, Howard may report away, I told Thomas; it's a matter of indifference to me. But sometimes the thought is unpleasant, since I'd like to believe that his motives are otherwise. I don't wish to see him as a Government spy. I continue to like the man.

Now he stepped back from the easel, head cocked, paint-brush and eyebrows raised, staring at his work.

– Interestin', he said softly. As I come to completion, I see that you have two faces.

– Very likely, I said. Most men do.

Howard tilted his chin up in that particular way he had, half closing his eyes and gazing across at me.

– But the second self isn't so strikin'ly apparent in most faces as it is in yours, Devereux. The two faces constantly shift and merge into each other, like water. This is what I've tried to capture – and I think I may have done so. One of them's the face of the political rebel, and has anger to be found in it. That's the face of the man who wrote that rather terrifyin' and notorious piece callin' for insurrection in the Irish countryside, and for the tearin' up of railway lines.

His eyes went back to his canvas, and he addressed the invisible man there.

– But then I see the other face. The face of a dreamer: of a man capable of compassion. This is the face of the Robert Devereux who wrote those pieces on the Famine, which are filled with such pity – and who published that little book on Irish myth, re-telling some of the stories in a way that was pure poetry.

I told him I was pleased that he liked my writing.

– The question is, he said, which of the two faces predominates? And how can a man in whom I see such gentleness advocate bloody insurrection?

– The answer's simple, I said. If the gentlest man is confronted with atrocity, as my comrades and I have been, he will harden his heart.

Another swift glance.

– You were bound to say that. But in my opinion, Devereux – if you'll forgive my bein' personal – the dreamer and man of peace will eventually prevail. I hope you may write beautiful things, while you're here in Van Diemen's Land, and forget the need to hate.

I said nothing, and he stepped back to the canvas and resumed his work. I had let myself lean back in the chair as we spoke; now, straightening up again to resume my pose, I found myself studying a row of Howard's unframed drawings, propped up on a chest of drawers against the wall. All were pictures of elegantly-dressed young ladies, executed mainly in pastel, but sometimes in water-colour.

– You've found some attractive subjects, I said, and pointed.

– Ah, he said. Yes. The daughters of Van Diemen's Land's rulin' class. I persuade their parents to allow them to sit for me – and I'm beginnin' to get commissions. They're mostly empty-headed little creatures – but pretty, ain't they? They mature unusually quickly, in this climate. Mere nubile girls appear like ripe women – and their interest in the opposite sex is remarkable: bold and frank to a degree that no young lady would display at home. Their parents have some difficulty in controllin' them. You must have noticed our local beauties, Devereux. If you've not done, you have the nature of a monk.

I studied the sheltered Anglo-Saxon faces. Happily oblivious of this island of despair, they might have been living in Surrey, these young ladies. They were protected entirely from the horrors of Van

Diemen's Land; its sullen and brutal prisoners existed merely to serve them. One picture drew my gaze back: a pastel of two very pretty girls, of sixteen and seventeen years, perhaps – clearly sisters, with long, highly-bred faces. Their braided, light brown tresses streamed over their filmy muslin gowns; one rested her hand on the other's arm. Closeted from the Antipodean heat in an airy summer room like this one, far removed from such places as Goulburn Street or Black Lion Square, they gazed out of the picture with identical, sleepy-lidded grey eyes: eyes which seemed to enjoy some secret joke, and which held the terrible, distant amusement of those to whom misery and pain are things only suffered by the tedious. Fortunate colonial princesses! Howard had excelled himself with this study.

When I expressed my admiration, he said:

– The Montgomery girls? Yes, they are rather fetchin'. You'll meet them tonight at dinner – they and their parents are comin' to dine with us. You may care to look for a wife here, Devereux, among well-bred young colonials like these.

I said I had no intention of it.

– I see. So you'll remain a bachelor, like me. But for a man such as yourself – young, vigorous and attractive – deprivation of the company of the fair sex for so long a time must surely have been a trial. For a man of my age, bachelorhood's not so bad: one becomes resigned to one's condition.

He looked at me over his glasses.

– Don't misunderstand me. I love the company of women – and don't lack for it, as you've been doin'. Women and paintin' are my greatest pleasures, and I combine those two pleasures by paintin' their portraits. What more can a man ask than a pleasure that's both artistic and sensual?

He worked for a time; then shot me another glance.

– I've another picture here that may interest you. You'll know the subject.

He walked over to the chest of drawers, picked up a watercolour drawing that lay flat, propped it up, and came back to his canvas again, smiling with an oddly complacent expression.

A new likeness of his servant Kathleen looked out at us: so uncannily lifelike that she might have entered the room. But it wasn't this illusion of reality that cause my heart to jump: it was the fact that Howard had portrayed her in a state of semi-undress.

She was carrying a little basket of herbs – sage, thyme and rosemary – and had halted to look directly at the viewer, the large, oblique eyes both questioning and changelessly melancholy. Her coarse, dove-coloured skirt was of the usual type worn by servants; but above the waist, her jacket bodice had been discarded, and her only covering was her chemise.

This wasn't the plain cotton undergarment that might have been expected. It was the sort of dainty chemise a lady might wear – made of fine white cambric, a draw-string around the neck, its short sleeves prettily edged with lace. Howard had lavished particular skill on it, painting it in such a way that one glimpsed the flesh's hues beneath. It quite concealed the upper part of her body; but it out-lined her breasts with an exactness that was nudity's twin. Howard's previous drawing of Kathleen had been chastely rendered, I thought; but the man who'd painted this new portrait had done so with manifest sensuality.

My heart continued to beat unevenly, and I thought: how dare he paint her like this?

– Kathleen took a bit of persuadin', to pose with her bodice off, Howard said. Surprisin'ly puritanical, your Irish women. I'd bought that chemise for her: I told her it would look very flatterin' in the picture. Nothin' like appealin' to female vanity.

I looked at him, and he smiled.

– No, no, Devereux, I'm not seducin' my servants. But a pedlar came to the back door sellin' ribbons and women's clothes, and I came upon Kathleen in the courtyard there goin' through them. I saw how much she wanted the chemise – but all she could afford was a few ribbons. So I bought it for her, and told her it was a reward for good work.

– It's true that our Irish women are very modest, I said. They must face their priests in Confession. It's a wonderful study, Howard – but I'm surprised that she'd pose like that.

He gave me a bantering, sideways look.

– Come, he said. She looks decent enough, does she not? I've seen other servant girls here take off their bodices on a hot day.

– I don't mean to sound censorious, I said. I do admire the picture.

Howard went back to his painting again, and I sat with my thoughts in confusion, stealing an occasional glance at Kathleen's likeness.

Here I should disclose to this journal that on every visit to Bay House, as I came down the highway on the coach, my thoughts would turn to Howard's Irish passholder. I always hoped to speak with her again; but the opportunity had never arisen. I saw her only in the dining room, when she waited on us at table; and sometimes she would bring coffee to the studio. On these occasions, our eyes would meet; and when no-one was looking, she would give me a smile that made my pulses quicken. But usually, her look was grave, her long upper lip drawn down; and sometimes I thought that her fathomless blue eyes implored me in some way. At meals, I would sit waiting for Kathleen to appear; and absurd though it is, I'd find myself trembling inwardly at such times, in the way one only does in anticipation of the extraordinary – or something much longed for by the spirit.

Doctor Howard cleared his throat, leaning to peer closely at his work.

– I need just a few more minutes of your time, he said. All that's wanted is a few finishin' touches. You've been very patient, Devereux – bear with me, and I'll prepare to face your judgment at last.

A few minutes later he stepped back, threw down the brush, and pulled off his painter's smock to reveal an immaculate white shirt and checked waistcoat. He smiled at me, his expression combining both triumph and diffidence.

– Done, he said, and thrust his hands deep into his trousers pockets. One always feels one can do more, but there comes a time to stop. Knowin' when to stop: that's probably the greatest trick in art. Well, now – tell me what you think.

And he carefully turned the easel around, so that the painting faced me.

That the likeness was remarkable was immediately apparent to me; yet its effect was very strange and disconcerting. I had never had my portrait painted in oils before; the only likenesses I'd seen of myself until now had been crude black-and-white drawings done by newspaper artists – the last one appearing at the time of my trial. I was now confronted by a magic mirror: one that not only showed my outward appearance, but gave me a glimpse of the inner self which no mirror can show us clearly. Howard had somehow re-invented me.

The man who confronted me (not looking at me directly, but somewhere to my right), certainly had my features – though I wondered whether my nose was quite so long and narrow. He wore a faint smile, which made him not disagreeable, at first glance. But on closer examination, there seemed to be something derisive – almost mordant – in his expression. Yes: there was something inside this man that put him at odds with the world.

– It's remarkable, I said.

– You really think so?

Doctor Howard's tone was both pleased and anxious: the tone, I suppose, of every creator exhibiting his work.

– A wonderful likeness, I said. You see beneath the skin: I've often thought that it must be your medical training.

– You flatter me. I'm merely an amateur.

– Far more than that, Howard, surely. I wonder that you never gave up medicine, and became an artist outright.

– I often wished to, he said.

He pulled up the other small armchair and threw himself back in it, gazing out the door into the garden, his thumbs hooked in his waistcoat. He sighed, and I seemed to read sadness in his face.

– But that would have been foolish, he said. One can only do that if one *knows* that one's an artist. There are fools who persuade themselves that they are artists or poets, who are not – they merely wish to be, and clutter up the world with their rubbish. Sometimes I wish it were otherwise. I wish it when I go in to the Hospital, and find myself surrounded with the stenches of my diseased and dyin' felons, and by the whinin' incompetents and pass-holdin' thieves I must put up with as medical assistants and wardsmen. I wish it when the stink of that foul Rivulet comes through the windows on the breeze, now that summer's here. Most of the Hospital refuse goes into it, you know, despite my protests. Then I can't wait to be back here in Bay House, with these flower scents comin' in, while I work with a brush instead of an amputatin' knife. But I know what I am, Devereux – a somewhat gifted amateur. That's all. Knowin' that, I'm able to enjoy what I do: and it's a great solace to me after a day of dealin' with the pox and amputations. I enjoy the pleasures of art, without the torment.

I offered him a cigar, and we both lit up. When he had blown a long plume of smoke, he went on.

– I've glimpsed that torment, and want none of it. I glimpsed it as a boy, when I began to spend most of my time drawin'. I neglected my studies; I neglected everythin' else. In the holidays, home from St Peter's, I drew everythin'. I lusted to capture birds and animals in my sketchbook the way other boys lusted to trap them in their snares. Not far from Brotherton we have the Dales – and I would wander alone through those valleys for hours, always with my sketchbook. My parents grew deeply worried. They were right to be. Even then, at sixteen or so, I was in love with the female form, and began to draw it from the imagination. There were stables at the back of my father's house, with a loft –

He broke off, still smiling, staring at distant Mount Direction. Then he chuckled, and went on.

– My father came up there eventually, and surprised me. He found my nude studies. Can you picture the effect of them on a respectable clergyman? I'll never forget that moment. He said that through my drawin', Satan was puttin' me in bondage. He beat me, and forbade me to draw any more. And you know, Devereux, it was a good thing he did; it cured me of the disease, and I went back to my studies. I might otherwise have ruined my life, moonin' over images – and all to no good purpose.

– But you did draw again, I said.

He smiled and adjusted his spectacles, looking at me briefly. Because of the way he was confiding in me, there was a new feeling of intimacy between us: one that had not existed before.

– Now and then I had a lapse, he said, and hid the drawin's in an old drystone wall behind the stables. I wonder if they're still there? But for the most part, I did give it up. I only began to paint after I became a surgeon. Only when it was safe. You see, Robert? I'm not an artist.

It was the first time he'd ever used my Christian name. His face was controlled, as usual; and yet I sensed infinite regret, and a wish to discreetly show me that regret. From the easel, my other self looked sardonically past us both, and I said:

– I still reject that, Neville. I think your father deprived the world of an important painter.

He shook his head.

– No, no. A true artist would have gone on drawin', no matter how many beatin's he was given. Don't you see?

– Well, I won't argue with you, I said. But I believe I know the sort of dreams you had, roaming your Dales. Such visions we have, at sixteen!

– Yes, yes. And then we lose sight of them.

– Everybody does. Except true artists, perhaps.

He stood up, brushing ash from his waistcoat, his cigar jutting from his teeth. I followed suit.

– I must leave you for a short time, he said. I promised Langford I'd look at an ailin' cow. I shan't be long – meanwhile, see what you think of the drawin's in that portfolio over on the table. Some of them are nude studies – will that shock you?

– Not at all. But surely, Howard, you didn't persuade the daughters of the colonial gentry to pose for you *sans habillement*?

He shook his head.

– No, no, no – I'd probably be horse-whipped if I did, and certainly lose my situation. But emancipated convict women in the town can sometimes be persuaded, for a fee. My bein' a surgeon helps. It gives them confidence in me, and stops them bein' frightened. I hope you don't disapprove, Devereux.

I'd grown faintly uneasy; but I did my best not to show it.

– Why should I? I said. If the artists of ancient Greece and the Renaissance could portray the naked female form, surely the artists of our time ought to be free to do so. Yet the middle-class prudes in both England and Ireland frown on it, these days. Unless, of course, the woman is disguised as a figure from classical antiquity. I find that absurd.

Howard was nodding vigorously in agreement.

– Absurd, he echoed. I'm glad you think so. But this is becomin' an age of prohibitions – and we're governed by middle-class prudery. The Evangelical revival has been a stiflin' thing, in my view. Mrs Grundy rules.

– But not in France, I said. When I was last in Paris, I particularly admired some paintings by Ingres. His women had a quite wonderful voluptuousness, I thought.

Doctor Howard regarded me now with an expression of frank delight, his full lips open and slightly wet.

– Ingres! The contemporary painter I most admire! I had no idea that you were a man of such enlightened artistic taste, Devereux – but then, I might have expected it. Ingres!

He rubbed his bald, walnut-coloured forehead in an access of enthusiasm, and gestured with his lean hands.

– A master of the portrayal of flesh, and of female beauty! What I most admire is the way he shows the body's vulnerability – its *tenderness*, if you understand me – contrastin' with opposite surfaces, such as stone and darkness . . .

He went on, but I was only half listening. The way he'd pronounced the word *tenderness* – his pink mouth savouring it like some rare sweetmeat – had told me more about Doctor Howard than I'd hitherto suspected. Despite his correct and even ascetic official exterior, I decided, the love of women probably governed his life to a degree I'd not imagined.

– But now I must see to Langford's cow, he said.

He moved to the doorway into the hall. As he opened it, he turned to me.

– By the way – the portrait's yours, Devereux.

I began to protest. I could not accept such a fine piece of work for nothing, I said. He must allow me to pay him.

He raised both hands in protest.

– Certainly not. It's a gift, my dear fellow. A token of our friendship.

He smiled, and was gone out the door.

Left alone, I stood at the table, opened the portfolio he'd pointed to, and soon began to come upon the 'nude studies' he'd referred to, executed in black and white and watercolour. That his models were girls and women of the convict servant class wasn't immediately evident, since he'd posed them in ways that suggested the nymphs and fays of legend. He was too good a draughtsman, though, not to render them with a fair degree of accuracy, and their faces, though winsome, could be seen to be somewhat plebeian. The attitudes they struck were tasteful and modest: most of them stood holding draperies that half-concealed their bodies.

But as I went on, I came upon pictures of a different kind. Masterly in their execution, they were disturbing in their content, and resembled no other pictures I'd seen. They seemed to me like medical drawings, rather than works of art – since only a medical purpose seemed to justify the way in which these bodies had been depicted. Here were convict women of all sizes and ages, from starved-looking girlhood to gross middle age – all of them entirely naked, and drawn with remorseless exactness. A few had some physical beauty; others were grotesquely ugly. No detail of their bodies was spared. There were faces bloated and coarsened by drink, and faces made severe by unhappiness; some had over-ripe bodies, with gross, deep-navelled bellies; others had the limbs and torsos of undernourished children, their ribs standing out like cages. Finally, there was a watercolour over which I paused for some time. It seemed to be inspired by a classical theme, since the title *Andromeda* was scribbled in pencil underneath.

A naked woman hung in chains. Her modesty was entirely unprotected, either by drapery or shadow. She was perhaps in her thirties, and had a forbidding air of suffering. She faced the viewer in semi-darkness, raised a little on her toes, her arms stretched above her head, the fetters clamped about her wrists. And although the painting was allegorical in its intent, and the chains were no doubt a fiction, there was nevertheless something cruel about this fiction, since fetters could hardly have been new to the woman who was Howard's model. Tangled black hair fell across her shoulders; her head was half-turned to one side, and her sad eyes looked sideways into the dark. She resembled those mythical women by Ingres, in the pictures that Howard so admired; but her body had none of their idealised quality. Her breasts, lifted by her straining, back-flung arms, had a tragic heaviness, and the over-abundant hair of her armpits was pitilessly disclosed. So too was the dark, secret thicket of her Mount of Venus, and the grotto's cleft beneath.

I closed the portfolio in a state of considerable unease. The quiet of the studio took on an ominous quality; and I asked myself a question. *Was Neville Howard cruel?* Suddenly, I found myself recalling his calm supervision of the flogging of Long Lane. Did this cultivated, talented man enjoy seeing bodies tormented?

And how would he paint Kathleen next? Naked, and in chains?

What occurred at the dinner party that evening was not, I'm sure, something that Doctor Howard could have anticipated. Whether it gave him the degree of discomfiture it did me is another matter. On the whole, I think not.

To be fair to the Doctor, he's always been at pains until now to introduce me to people who are compatible and sympathetic, and who'll neither disapprove of me nor cause me to be discountenanced. He's held a number of such dinner parties since my visits to Bay House began – and they've gone off pleasantly enough. He's never invited military officers, or members of the ruling coterie of public servants who are his colleagues, but has always drawn his guests from those circles in Hobart Town society which don't directly serve the Government: people such as lawyers, senior clerics, and prosperous merchants and bankers. Mr Montgomery was a banker, with a house in New Town not far from Howard's.

Neither my status as a Ticket-of-Leave man nor my political exile had so far been touched on at these dinners. This has made the situation pleasant, if somewhat artificial, since everything about me is well known – and since finding themselves seated at table with anyone who was 'Ticket-of-Leave' wouldn't normally have been tolerated for a moment by people of the type whom Howard has to dine. For this tiny upper stratum of gentry – as for the slave-owners of Virginia – there are only two categories of human being: the bond and the free. This makes my position all the more strange. It really does seem to be true, as Howard has claimed, and as Thomas O'Neill has discovered in Bothwell, that we Irish state prisoners are considered by many here to retain our social rank, and are seen as 'prisoners of war' – thus being free from the taint that a Ticket would normally bring.

The Montgomerys appeared to be of this opinion, since their demeanour was cordial and easy – even if an underlying vein of curiosity was detectable in their glances. Mr Montgomery and his wife and two daughters had been in the colony for only about a year, and were apparently 'well-connected at home', as Hobart Town puts it. Being 'well connected at home' places one on a social pinnacle here; and this no doubt was why the Montgomerys had a serene certainty of manner which hovered on the edge of complacency.

In their daughters, Lucy and Jane, this tranquillity had been trans-muted by youth into that aura of mysterious bliss which Howard had captured so perfectly in his pastel. His drawing come to life, the two girls sat across the table from me, in tight-waisted, lace-trimmed taffeta dresses, eating with a perfect daintiness. When I glanced at them, I would usually find the sleepy-lidded grey gaze of one of them resting on me in enigmatic speculation. Mrs Montgomery sat on my left; on her other side was Doctor Howard, at the head of the table, while Mr Montgomery was placed at the foot. As always, candles were lit in the silver candelabrum in the centre, to be reflected in the table's polished surface; the rest of the room was in twilight. We ate roast pork, and our knives and forks tinkled on bone china. We were waited on this evening by the housekeeper Mrs Bates: a plump, dignified woman with grey hair drawn back in a bun, whose face preserved a wondering blankness. Of Kathleen there had been no sign: she was presumably kept busy in the kitchen.

The talk was of Hobart Town and its pretensions – as it very often is, at Howard's table.

– I find it amusin', Howard said, that people in society here pose as bein' so absolutely virtuous. It's as though they fear bein' infected by the vices of their convict servants. And some of our passholders get up to quite a bit of naughtiness, as you'll know – particularly on the estates in the country. In the stables; even in the kitchens. No controllin' some of 'em.

– Alas, too true, said Mr Montgomery. And you're right, Howard – people do seem desperate here to assert their respectability and importance. One poor lady we know of, received everywhere in society, and of very good family back home, had a tale told against her concerning some scandal in her life in England: now nobody invites her anywhere. Well, it's the nature of a colony so remote, I suppose. Even after a year, it takes getting used to.

He gave a tolerant chuckle, and cut into his pork. He was a blond, ruddy, healthy-looking fellow of middle age, with a shrewd, frank, unimaginative gaze.

– And the summit of everyone's social ambition, Mrs Montgomery put in, is to be frequently received at Government House.

Brows arched high, knife and fork poised, she smiled at us all with an air of sweet tolerance. But her drawling voice contained a note of mischief, and her attractive grey eyes – eyes which her daughters had inherited – were bright with mocking amusement. She was a tall, lean, animated woman in a gown of rich green satin, worn with a white fichu. Her greying, ash-blonde hair was elaborately sculptured about her ears, and her long, narrow chin and patrician, high-bridged nose, suggestive of old Danish blood, had a jaunty yet cautionary arrogance.

– And will you be goin' to the Governor's Ball? Howard asked.

– I suppose we shall have to, Mrs Montgomery said. We have an invitation – and most people here seem willing to kill for these invitations. If they fail to get one, their hearts are quite broken, poor things.

Her daughter Lucy spoke now, smiling at me as she did so.

341

– Mr Devereux should come with *us*. Have you an invitation, Mr Devereux?

The younger daughter Jane joined in, her face filled with childish animation.

– Oh yes, Mr Devereux. *Do* come!

There was a sudden, embarrassed silence around the table.

– Well now, I said, I'd like to join you young ladies, I'm sure. But I doubt that the Governor would want to have me.

Mrs Montgomery released a small, regretful laugh.

– Forgive me, Mr Devereux, she said. My daughters are somewhat forward – and they're ignorant of your situation. Not another word, girls, if you please.

She frowned at them with mock severity, and their heads bent over their plates; but they continued to dart curious glances. Mrs Montgomery turned back to me, picking up her glass of claret.

– Sir William Denison really does *hate* you, it seems – you and Mr Fitzgibbon and Mr Barry. He spoke about the three of you at a dinner we attended. An upright but somewhat rigid sort of man, our Governor.

– Now, my dear, Mr Montgomery said.

His voice sounded a note of mild warning; but she smiled at him quickly and went on, turning her head to look at me again. Her expression was now one of flirtatious provocation, and her amused, bright gaze held mine.

– Lady Denison is the same – and seems always at one with her husband's views. Their hatred of you appears quite – *personal*. Extraordinary, I thought.

– I can't imagine why it should be personal, I said. I've not had the pleasure of meeting the Governor and his lady.

I glanced at Doctor Howard; he was watching Mrs Montgomery without expression, cutting into his pork.

– I'm sure you have not, she said. Yet Sir William seems *obsessed*. He worked himself into quite a passion, speaking of your undeserved good fortune in being exempt from hard labour in chains – and of how you all failed to appreciate it. He mocked Mr Fitzgibbon for trying to be a martyr, in his cottage at Port Arthur.

He even made mock of the legion of female admirers you and Mr Barry have in Ireland, and compared you to stage actors. He joked about finding a way of getting you both into a gang at some penal station, sawing logs in the bush. Some of the convicts there might 'spoil your pretty faces', he said, if you annoyed them.

Watching me sideways, she sipped her wine with a mischievous air, as though she'd passed on a harmless piece of gossip. Before she could say more, her husband cleared his throat loudly, and addressed Doctor Howard.

– We have servant problems again, Howard. Our cook has absconded.

– Indeed? Very provokin', Howard said quickly. You got a wrong 'un, I suppose. It's very important, when one goes to the hiring depot, to make the right choice.

– Oh, most of them are quite convincing about their abilities when one sees them at the depot, Montgomery said. But then they transform themselves, once they're hired.

Mrs Montgomery had put down her knife and fork, and was dabbing at her mouth with her napkin.

– And a most extraordinary transformation it is, she told Howard. This delightful cook of ours would lie dead drunk on my kitchen floor and subject me to language I'd never heard in my *life*. Now she's simply disappeared – taking with her two of my best gowns. Well, it's back to hard labour at the wash tubs in the Factory, when they catch her. Or so one devoutly hopes.

She adjusted the fichu that covered her shoulders, as though it too might be snatched away. Mr Montgomery addressed Howard again.

– You seem not to be troubled by these difficulties, Doctor Howard. Your housekeeper appears an excellent woman. Is she free or Government?

Mrs Bates had recently re-entered the room, bringing further dishes to the sideboard. She moved about the table, offering fresh helpings of baked potatoes; but Montgomery made no sign of knowing that she was here. Nor did Mrs Bates look at him.

– Oh, Mrs Bates is free, Howard said; and he smiled in her direction. And yes – I could scarcely do without her. But I do have

343

a housemaid who's a passholder. She's very willin'. An Irish girl.

– Really? said Mrs Montgomery. You're fortunate if you've had no trouble from *her*, Doctor. Our drunken cook was Irish. But what else can one expect of them? They're little better than apes.

Then she looked quickly at me, her hand going to her mouth. But still she smiled.

– O dear. I meant no offence, Mr Devereux: I spoke without thinking. I was referring of course only to your peasantry. And you are *not* native Irish, are you? Yours is an Ascendancy family, I understand.

I was now very angry, and found I was mainly so because of Kathleen. But I kept my voice low and even.

– We of the Ascendancy have been long enough in Ireland to be Irish, I said. We are Irish in our affections, our loyalty and our pride, I do assure you, madame. And our common people are no more apes than yours, I believe – and a good deal more attractive.

Mrs Montgomery had suspended her knife and fork above her plate, her smile fixed. Her daughters too were staring at me, as though I were a curiosity on display. But before his wife could reply, Mr Montgomery leaned towards her.

– Come, my dear. Mr Devereux is a patriot, as we know, and cannot agree with such a view of his people.

Doctor Howard spoke now, his tone soothing and urbane.

– You see, Mrs Montgomery, Mr Devereux is also somethin' of a romantic. He fights for a people who are divided, and so enfeebled by the Famine that they are almost broken. Little of their blood flows in his veins; he doesn't speak their language, but he sees himself as one of them in his heart – am I not right, Devereux? I admire him for that – but I think he seeks to rid himself of an ancient guilt. Mr Devereux's Anglo-Norman ancestors were sent to tame Ireland, and carried out much slaughter there, in the service of Queen Elizabeth. The case is similar with a number of his colleagues in rebellion. I believe these youthful gentlemen wish to atone for the sins of their forbears.

– There are many ancient sins to atone for, I said. But much greater sins to oppose today.

Everyone except Mrs Montgomery looked serious at this, and became busy over their food. Her gaze remained unchangingly humorous; but she said no more, and the conversation turned to less troubling topics.

As soon as sweets had been eaten, and before the ladies had left the table, I begged to be excused from joining Howard and Montgomery over the port and cigars. My journey down from Bothwell had wearied me, I said, and I wished to retire. I had enjoyed the dinner very much, and was delighted to have met Mr and Mrs Montgomery and the two young ladies.

The Montgomerys assured me that meeting me had been delightful, and that they were sorry I must go so soon. I stood and bowed, while Doctor Howard explained that asthma attacks had greatly weakened me, and that he'd advised me to rest.

When I reached the door into the hall, I turned and bade the company a final good night. Howard responded, watching me speculatively, while Mr Montgomery's smile was pleasantly neutral. On the other side of the table, his wife and their two exquisite daughters observed my exit in silence. In their faces, nothing could be seen but an unquenched curiosity.

The bedroom that Howard had given me was a small but pleasant one, in a wing at the back of the house. Its old-fashioned tester bedstead had curtains of dark green velvet, giving the chamber a secretive air. The window, which was open, looked on to a courtyard and a herb garden, whose scents came into the room. A vase of lavender stood on the mantel shelf, adding its scent to those of the herbs; I breathed in the fragrance, which did much to quieten the anger that still tingled in my blood.

I had lit the candlestick on the chest of drawers and was preparing to undress, when a tapping sounded at the door.

I opened it to find Kathleen, standing in the darkness of the hallway outside. She was holding a tall white jug covered with a towel.

– I brought you hot water, she said. In case you might like to wash, your honour, before going to bed.

She spoke in a quick, nervous whisper, and looked up at me with an anxious expression, as though fearing a rebuff. She was probably uneasy about coming to my bedroom at night, however innocent the purpose. She had never done so before; and this visit seemed somewhat curious. Had she been sent by Mrs Bates? I'd taken a hot bath before dinner, and had expected simply to wash in cold water before retiring, as I usually did. So why should Kathleen be sent here now? Or had she decided to come on her own account?

I stood aside and thanked her. She moved to the basin-stand by the fireplace, and poured the steaming water into the basin. Then, cradling the jug, she turned to me.

– Will your honour be wanting fresh towels? Or extra candles?

I told her no, that I had everything I wanted. But even as I spoke, I was searching for an excuse to detain her. The single candle on the chest of drawers did little to illuminate the room, and we stood caged in shadows. The candle flickered, its flame reflected in her eyes, whose blue was more brilliant than I recalled; more vivid, I thought, than any I had seen. Dark, profound shadows were under her cheekbones, and her face was the face of a *spéir bhean*. But then I looked again, and saw that this was no sky woman, but a convict girl from Limerick, in a cheap print gown of mauve and white, with thick copper hair spilling to her shoulders from under her frilled muslin cap, a faintly turned-up nose, and the long upper lip and delicate small chin of a woman of the people. Yet just to stand near her caused a thickening in my throat.

She turned to go, the empty jug dangling from her hand. As she did so, she gave me a sideways glance. Her face told me nothing, and the meaning of the glance was impossible to read; but it gave me the courage to delay her.

– Are you happy here, Kathleen?

The question was awkward and clumsy; but it caused her to pause.

– To be sure I am, sir. I'm treated well, and Mrs Bates is very kind.

Her voice was flat, seeming to belie her words. Her brogue, I noticed, was not so thick as it is with many of the peasantry, and she had few of those quaint tricks of speech which can make them difficult to follow.

– But sometimes I am afraid, she added.

– Oh? Why should you be afraid?

She looked away, searching the darkness out the window, where the lights from a servants' cottage glowed beyond the courtyard. Her lips were slightly parted. Doctor Howard had rendered these lips with loving fidelity, capturing almost perfectly their vulnerable, generous fullness. It was a mouth too wide for conventional beauty, yet compellingly attractive. Finally she said:

– There's much to be afraid of everywhere in this place. This Van Diemen's Land.

But what could harm her here, I asked, at Bay House?

– Ah, you never know what will happen next, she said, in this colony. For the least thing, you can be sent back to the Factory.

As she pronounced the word *factory*, she frowned at the floor.

– You'll not be sent back there, I told her. Not by Doctor Howard, I'm sure.

Her stare took on a sceptical canniness. She was silent for a moment; then she said:

– You have told me before, sir, that you are fighting for *me*. Was it the truth?

– It's the truth, I said. I struggle for all our people – and you and I are both Irish prisoners. Our loyalty is to each other, Kathleen – and our secrets are safe from the English. Especially from people such as those who are now at Doctor Howard's table. Even from Doctor Howard himself. Do you understand me?

She examined my face closely at this, and a cold and ancient knowledge showed in her eyes: a knowledge that would always be absent from those of Mrs Montgomery and her daughters. When she spoke, her voice had no tone.

– Your honour and I are both of Ireland, surely. But you are of the quality.

– Listen to me, Kathleen, I said. I love the people of Ireland above all else. I disown my English blood.

She put her head on one side.

– That's a queer thing to say. Can blood be disowned?

– It can, I said, and I do so. You and I are the same.

Without warning, she smiled, her white front teeth emerging on to her full lower lip, her eyes narrowing, the points of light from the candles glimmering there like stars. The smile transformed her, as it had done in Howard's studio: there was nothing in her face now but gladness, and something turned over in my throat, as it had done when I first saw her. She glanced at the half-open door, raising the jug to hold it with both hands.

– I should be gone, she said.

– Stay a little, I said. I want to know you, Kathleen.

She looked at me, the smile fading, and I imagined I saw a new quickness in the rise and fall of her breast, in the mauve cotton gown. Then she spoke in a rush, as though knowing that she wouldn't dare release the words unless it were done quickly.

– You are kind, she said. Your face is sometimes stern, but I'm thinking your mouth is kind. I was dreaming of you last night. They told me that Robert Devereux was coming here today, and I dreamed of you. And in the dream I told you many things, and you listened, and never grew angry.

– Your dream was true, I said.

She continued to look up at me, her face becoming grave. It was so pale now that it seemed in the dimness to be luminous. I put my hand on her shoulder, and felt its small roundness and warmth through the cotton gown. Except when I'd taken her hands in the studio, it was the first time I'd touched a woman since my imprisonment, and my head swam. She looked down at my hand with what might have been apprehension; but she didn't draw away.

– Tell me all you wish to, I said, and dropped my hand. But perhaps Mrs Bates will be looking for you? I don't want to cause you trouble, Kathleen.

– Mrs Bates does not know I'm here, she said. She told me I might go to bed, since I've worked from very early. She'll be clearing away after them in the dining room when they go – and then she'll be locking up the shutters and doors in the front of the house. She always takes a great time about it.

She glanced across at the basin of cooling water on the stand.

– But your water will be getting cold, sir.

– The water doesn't matter, I said. We both know that, Kathleen.

We smiled at each other, guarded yet ingenuous as children; then I said:

– Tell me all you wish to. I know that you were in the Factory, not long ago.

Her smile disappeared. She frowned again, as though at a stab of pain; then she set the jug on a chair, and sighed: a sound so soft, I only just caught it.

– I was sent to the Factory to have my baby, she said. That is what they do here when a probation servant falls pregnant – which they say is a crime. I had been working on the farm of Mr Pearce, at O'Brien's Bridge, along the highway out here. Mr Pearce sent me to the Magistrate and I was charged, and then I was taken to the Cascades Factory. And my baby was put in a room with seventy others, four in a crib, top and tail, like fishes. They die in scores there, and so did little Brigid. She died of a fever, last February. She was three months old.

She broke off, looking away, and suddenly began to cough, holding her apron over her mouth. The cough was deep in her chest, but it was only a brief spasm.

Speaking as gently as I knew how, I told her I was sorry. Then I asked her why the father had not been able to help her in any way.

– The father was the man who forced me, she said. The man who destroyed me.

I asked her who the man was, but she shook her head. In a muffled voice, she said:

– I cannot speak about that man. He is a passholder like me, and Irish, and working for Mr Pearce. But he was not punished. Instead, Mr Pearce had me sent to the Factory.

Her voice didn't rise, but now grew sharp with anger.

– Sure I'd rather sleep on straw, or die in a ditch in Limerick, than be in that place again. We were thirty in a ward, and some wicked whore was always trying to steal my bedding, or do something filthy to me – for some of the women go with women there. One of the creatures I beat about the head with a broom, and was punished for it. And the air is so foul in those rooms that the turnkeys would stand back when they opened the doors in the morning. I thought that I would choke. May the Blessed Virgin protect me from being taken there again.

She broke off, hands clasped tightly together. Then she said:

– I'm sorry. Forgive me for speaking to you so.

For a time, I had no words. Then I said:

– I don't even know your family name, Kathleen. Or where it is you come from.

– My name is O'Rahilly, she said, and I am from near Adare, in County Limerick. But my family are all dead: my parents, my two sisters and my little brother. May God and his saints give them rest.

And she made the sign of the Cross, looking towards the flickering candle on the chest of drawers.

As gently as I could, I asked her to tell me what had happened to her people.

– My father was destroyed by the Famine, she said. Three years past. The potatoes were all that we had. The whole crop was bad, and we had nothing to sell or to eat. We were told that the landlord wished us to leave – but my father refused to go.

– Brave fellow, I said. There should be a million more of his kind.

But she shook her head.

– Being brave was no use, she said. He could do nothing in the end against the sheriff and the police. They tore our house down, and we watching. You would have liked my father, sir. He would sometimes read your writings to us, sitting by the fire at night.

She paused, and when she went on, her voice sank lower than before. Yet it stubbornly persisted, and the things it told me now made me clench my teeth. Kathleen's voice had high, piping notes, like that of a very young girl; but sometimes it would sink to a hoarse and troubling deepness: the voice of woman of blind and

350

extraordinary strength, who had endured the torments of a fate that few could have borne without going mad. Reciting its history, her voice told me nothing new: I had heard this story all too many times, and had dwelt on it in my essays. But I had always heard it at second-hand, through written report or observation: never like this.

They had nowhere to go, she said, in that bitter winter of 1846, and the north-east wind blew every day. At first they survived in a sod hut on the seashore; but then they began to walk the roads. They walked for many months, begging food and sleeping in *scalpeens*: the pits where houses had been dragged down. Then they went to Limerick city, to the depot where food was given out. But there was never enough; there were thousands like them, wandering the streets. Many had the fever, she said. The workhouses were full, and there was nowhere to get out of the cold. Her mother died first, and then her two sisters and her brother – all from the fever.

– So then my father and I were alone, she said. We went on the Works, near Limerick city. They paid my father ten pence a day to break stones, and myself four pence. It was oatmeal and turnips mostly that we ate. We had waited a long time for tickets to work: such great crowds of people were there, and not enough work. We slept in ditches and in doorways, and our clothes were nothing but rags, and we were now nearly destroyed by the cold. My father had grown very thin – and he a man who'd always been big and strong – and so he caught the fever. He begged me not to let them take him to the fever hospital: they say that no-one came out from those places alive. So then it was that I began to steal. I went into Limerick city, and got into the houses of the rich people, and stole clothes and blankets to cover us, and also food. But one night when I came back to the Works, they told me my father had died, and been taken away.

She broke off; and her eyes at last filled with tears. I was about to speak, but she coughed again, wiped her eyes with her apron, and recovered herself.

– I went back into Limerick city, she said, and made friends with other girls and women as poor as myself. Some of them were selling themselves to men – but let you not think that I did so. I slept where I could, and stole what I could. Then one night I was caught by the police in the yard of a big house, and taken away to the gaol. And I was put on trial, and transported out here on that ship called the *Midlothian*. I am not ashamed of having stolen. I would do it again, if it could save my father. But it could not, I know that now. There was nothing that could save him.

She ceased to speak, and looked back to me. Then, without warning, she began to weep. She clutched her apron, drew it to her face, and turned away.

My throat swelled, and my own eyes filled with tears. I took her by both shoulders and turned her towards me, speaking her name.

You are Ireland, I said. But I didn't say it aloud; instead, I said:

– Ah, my dear, I'm so sorry. If ever I can make the English pay for all that's been done to you, I will.

But these fine words sounded empty; and it was then that I made a decision.

– Don't fear being sent to the Factory again, I said. I promise you, it will never happen.

She sniffed back hard, and gave her eyes a hard wipe with her apron. She had done with crying, and looked at me with an expression that attempted dignity, but instead was utterly bereft.

– But how can you promise such a thing?

– I'll tell you when next I visit here, I said. Depend on it.

She shook her head.

– I don't understand. But may God attend you – and I'll wait to see you again. And now I must go. I must – or I'll be found here.

But still I held her shoulders; and now I drew her hard against me. Should the housekeeper or Howard discover us, I could scarcely imagine the consequences; I was abusing Howard's hospitality, and endangering Kathleen's situation. But I was now beyond caring; I was filled with the greatest hunger I've ever known, and I kissed her on the lips. They were warm, wet and strangely large under mine: faintly coarse, yet thrilling. They made me aware that I kissed no careful, demure, tight-lipped young lady, but a woman of the people.

For a moment she stood rigid; but she did not attempt to escape me. Then I felt her body relax, and her mouth open like a flower. Her arms went about me, and clung with an urgency like despair.

I released her, and touched her cheek.

– Forgive me, I said. I had not meant to do that – but all that I love and miss is in your face.

She studied me, head thrown back. Her voice when she spoke was no more than a breath.

– I have waited every week to see you. I came here to this room with the water because I hoped we might speak again. You'll not do me harm, will you?

– I will never do you harm, I said.

When she'd gone, I lay awake in bed for some time, the curtains of the bed drawn back. Through the window, I could see the servants' cottage: a light glowed in one of the windows, and I wondered whether this was Kathleen's bedroom. I pictured her there, in her narrow bed, and a slow amazement filled me.

I was in love, and couldn't doubt it. I was in love with a convict girl: a peasant from Limerick.

December 13th

My decision is now firm: that decision I reached two nights ago, as I spoke with Kathleen O'Rahilly.

I shall buy the farm with James Langford, and go partners with him – subject to a satisfactory legal agreement being concluded between us. Today I've written to my bank in Dublin to request that a letter of credit for the necessary two hundred and fifty pounds be sent to the Bank of Van Diemen's Land. This is a significant deduction from my inheritance: the money that came to me as my share from the sale of 'Deerpark'.

But I believe that the decision is a sound one. The idea of farming with Langford, on the terms that he's suggested, has grown increasingly attractive: certainly more attractive than any other occupation I can think of to fill the time I may spend here. That I'm very likely trapped in this colony for some years is something I've faced squarely since the discussion with my comrades at the Lakes. O'Neill's bleak analysis has convinced me that to escape is near-impossible – and since this is so, I shall need to establish an agreeable mode of life. I've no wish to practise as a lawyer, no intention of writing for any local newspaper, and certainly no intention of joining Liam Kinane in his folly of running an exile's journal. This means that farming, and the purchase of property at the favourable terms available in this colony, is the very best option available to me – especially since Langford will take the brunt of the planning and management of the farm, leaving me largely free to pursue my own interests. I have great confidence in his qualities: his skill, shrewdness and ruthless determination. I have little doubt that the enterprise will succeed.

Let me come now to the other reason for my decision: the one that has actually done most to nerve me to take the leap. I intend to ask Doctor Howard to release Kathleen O'Rahilly to Langford and me – allowing her to come and work for us on the farm as a maidservant.

In this way, I shall deliver her from Howard's attentions, and bring her under my own protection. Perhaps I'm doing the Doctor an injustice, but I'm inclined to doubt now that that those attentions will remain purely artistic. And even if they do, I believe that he will end by outraging Kathleen's modesty – if he has not already done so. I have thought a good deal about this. Suppose he should ask her to model for him naked, like his other convict women – how could she refuse a man so powerful, without fearing to lose a situation in which she has found some ease and security? True, Doctor Howard would run a risk of being charged with abuse of his position, should such irregular use of a female probationer ever be exposed. But to whom would Kathleen go with such a charge – and who would believe her? Her fear, I feel sure, is that should she refuse what Howard wants, she would find herself declared unsatisfactory on some other grounds, and returned to the hiring depot as before.

I don't imagine that Howard will be happy about releasing her. But to justify asking him to do so, I intend to point out that an Irishwoman will surely be most happy working for a fellow-countryman, and that I have a special interest in rehabilitating her, as one of my own. I shall beg this as a special favour from him, declaring that I'll be deeply grateful to gain a servant for the farm whom Howard knows to be trustworthy. And I'll add that Kathleen will be given the proper female supervision, since Langford's wife Bess – who will arrive here as a free settler – will be in charge of her. More: I'll make the point that, out there in the country, Kathleen will be far removed from the dangers and temptations of Hobart Town, with a better chance of reform.

I must pray that these arguments succeed.

A house, a wife, and an ox to plough with . . .

If I have whispered old Hesiod's formula for contentment once, I've done so a dozen times. I smile at myself as I do so; I tell myself that it's folly; the most unreal of fancies. Yet doing so only gives the fancy greater sharpness; and the thought of having Kathleen near me every day fills me with a wave of mindless joy.

I weigh no consequences; I make no enquiries about the future. I shall be in Boeotia, where a love like this will be natural as breathing. I ponder the possibilities no further, and scarcely even analyse my own intentions.

December 14th

Today a letter from Matthew Casey arrived at the Bothwell Post Office. I have made no attempt to see Casey or Liam Kinane again since my arrival; so I opened the letter with a certain degree of guilt.

Casey wishes me the compliments of the season, and reproaches me with neglecting Kinane and himself. He asks that I meet them both in Hobart Town next Saturday, in the coffee room of an inn on the Old Wharf. He says that they wish to discuss an important topic with me – but mysteriously gives no detail. I've written back agreeing to his proposal. I shall use the new freedom granted by my pass to travel to the Hobart Town district, and stay at an inn in the city. O'Neill doesn't wish to go through the tiresome process of applying to the local magistrate to do the same – so I shall go down alone.

My portrait having been completed (and brought back with me here to Bothwell), I shall not be calling at Bay House on this trip. But Doctor Howard still insists that he wants me to visit him regularly, and has suggested that I come the following Saturday: Boxing Day. This I shall do – and will then inform James Langford of my decision over the farm.

Hobart Town
December 18th
Thirty or so customers are here when I come in: all male, sitting at small polished tables. A number of them are reading newspapers – piles of which, from Britain and the various colonies, are laid out on a table by the fireplace. I pause and look about me, searching for Casey and Kinane.

The coffee room is on the second floor of the Diamond of India Tavern: one of a set of sandstone buildings running like fortifications along the back of the Old Wharf, on the eastern side of the port. A green and silver elephant is painted on the inn's signboard, conjuring up the Empire's Oriental possessions. A good many trading ships bring luxuries from India to Van Diemen's Land, and their captains apparently favour this coffee room, which is where they do business with the city's merchants. So there are many blue coats and brass buttons in here, as well as much good-quality broadcloth.

My name is called, piercing the sober hum. I turn and see Liam Kinane, sitting with Casey at a table by one of the tall windows. Huge and florid, grinning with delight, he heaves himself to his feet, hand outstretched. He seems to be wearing exactly the same assembly of cast-off garments as before – the worn brown frock coat and light summer trousers, sadly creased – and looks more than ever like an ill-clad police detective.

– Devereux! he cries. Praise be to God, man, I'd almost despaired of seeing you again!

Casey has also risen, and waits for Kinane's noisy greetings to

356

be done. He watches me, with his usual knowing smile; then he too shakes my hand, and we all sit down at the table, the port and its masts and rigging framed in the window beside us. This long, well-carpeted room, with its dark wainscoting and its prints of historic naval engagements around the walls, is preserved from the England of forty years ago, like so much else in Van Diemen's Land; it imitates a gentlemen's club, and Kinane looks somewhat disreputable in here. But Casey, in a fine grey frock coat and shining black satin cravat, seems perfectly at home. He and Kinane are drinking sherry; I order coffee, which is poured for me by a clean, plump waiter with snowy white hair and a snowy white apron. He's a perfect replica of a waiter in the sort of London establishment this wishes to be; though no doubt in reality he's a passholder.

– How very well you're looking, Casey says to me. A different man entirely, Devereux, from the one who stepped off the *Raffles*. But of course, you've had a good long time to recuperate.

– A good long time indeed, Kinane says. Over a month. Sure, we thought you'd forgotten us.

He gives me a mock-reproving look, tosses off his sherry, and wipes his mouth on the back of his hand. Then, gazing at me significantly, he reaches into the pocket of his coat and draws out a folded newspaper, which he hands across the table.

– But never mind, Devereux. Now we've *this* to celebrate, he says. Just off the press this week! I would have posted you a copy – but it's a pleasure to present it in person.

Opening the paper, I sit staring at it with a consternation I try to hide. The title on the front page reads: THE IRISH EXILE. Beneath this banner is a harp; and the rest of the page is filled with advertisements from prominent Hobart Town traders – as is the next.

– So you did it, I say.

Kinane laughs with pleasure and leans towards me, bulging eyes shining with triumph.

– Aye – I did it! We're using a little printery in Collins Street, and I help to set up the type myself. A voice for the Irish in

Australia, that will be read and heeded throughout these colonies! Sure, the bloody authorities did everything they could to stop us, God rot them, once I issued a prospectus. Their creatures spread every sort of rumour, including the idea that we'd preach insurrection on behalf of the Irish state prisoners. But the buggers hadn't the power to stop publication, as I've pointed out in my editorial. One in the eye for Sir William bloody Denison, eh, Devereux?

– No doubt. Where did you get the capital?

– Some came from subscriptions. The Irish community has been loyal – even the poorest of them. And Mr Davis at the *Independent* has invested in it. So has Matthew here – who's a kind of sleeping partner. He's a very persuasive fellow: he's sold a wonderful amount of advertising.

I turn to Casey, who is letting Kinane do the talking as usual. Eyebrows raised in guarded amusement, he seems to wait to see what my response will be.

– Have you, indeed? I say to him. And do you really think this a good idea, Matthew?

His grin widens, perhaps in embarrassment. He adjusts his spectacles, at the same time running his fingers through the spiky, rusty hair which remains as unruly as ever.

– I do, he says. I know your objections, Robert, and I don't dismiss them. But Liam has convinced me that it's a paper that's truly needed – and the response would seem to prove it. I know you fear that it will provoke the authorities – but believe me, that will not be the *Exile*'s policy, will it Liam? It will simply be a voice for the Irish community.

– Just leaf through it, Kinane says eagerly. My article on yourself is there, Devereux, as well as a statement of the paper's aims: to fight for every civil and religious freedom. The Catholic bishop himself approves of it. Sure, I know you didn't want the article on yourself published, and nor did you approve of the *Exile* at all, but –

– That's true, I say. I don't approve – and you know my reasons.

There's a silence. Kinane sits back with an expression that's at once crestfallen and defiant, rubbing his big blue chin. Then he bursts out:

– But if you'll only *read* it, Devereux! You'll see that I deny that the paper speaks for you, or Barry, or for any of my fellow-exiles. And the dear knows I'm careful not to challenge their poxy bloody Government directly. What I *have* done, though – with Martin Fitzgibbon's permission – is to write a short article about *his* situation. I reveal the fact that his health is rapidly failing down there at Port Arthur, and that the cruel confinement he suffers may bring about his death. The world will take notice of *that*, by Christ – and all eyes will turn on that tight-arsed bugger of a Governor.

– The Governor will close you down, I say.

I look again at Casey; but Casey twirls the stem of his glass of sherry, and says nothing.

– Denison will never stand this public defiance of his rule, I say. He can't afford to. He'll seek London's backing to destroy you. How can you ever imagine he will not? I admire your bravery and fervour, Liam – even though I believe the paper does no good to our cause. But I beg you to consider: Denison may well use this as an excuse to send you in irons to Port Arthur, as a common felon. He can't do that to Casey, of course, since Matthew is a free man. It will be *you* who will pay the price. Do you want to find yourself labouring in chains, with the worst villains on earth?

It's Casey who answers me now; and his tone is both certain and complacent.

– No: the Governor will not do that, Robert. Not unless the paper preaches sedition.

– You sound very confident, Casey. How can you be so sure? And what do you think they will make of an attempt to preach to them about their treatment of Fitzgibbon?

He smiles like a man with a secret, in a way that I begin to find irritating.

– It will all depend on such an article being written with restraint – as a plea, not as a rebuke to the authorities. You must understand, Devereux, that I have dealings with most of the leading officials here, through my work at the *Independent*. Recently, I was writing a story on the anti-transportation movement – you'll know that the free settlers here are up in arms about taking further convicts – and I was granted an interview with the Comptroller-General of Convicts, Doctor John Cramp. I found him quite courteous – even sympathetic.

– Really? You'll be telling me next that our Grand Turnkey is an enlightened reformer, who keeps my comrades and me incarcerated for our own good.

My tone is heavily sardonic, and Casey's expression grows wary. Kinane watches us both in silence now, one elbow propped on the table, his hand supporting his big chin, like a man following a chess game.

– No, Casey says. Of course not. I merely comment on the sort of man I found him to be. Know your enemies – don't you agree? I realised that meeting him gave me a splendid opportunity to ask after my fellow-countryman in exile – and I took the opportunity to beg to be allowed to visit Martin Fitzgibbon at Port Arthur. I asked on compassionate grounds: I said I wanted to take a few books and other comforts to him. And Doctor Cramp has agreed – on the condition that nothing I carry there is of a political nature. I go next week.

– That seems rather extraordinary, I say. Their policy has been to isolate Fitzgibbon from just this kind of contact. You must be very persuasive, Matthew.

– It *is* extraordinary, Kinane breaks in. And this is where *you* come in, Devereux.

He leans forward in his excitement, and takes hold of my forearm. I look at him; but it's Casey who goes on.

– There was another reason the consent was given, he says. It wasn't merely compassion.

His voice has dropped to a conspiratorial murmur; he leans forward, glancing over his shoulder. But there are no eavesdroppers. A fat, red-faced merchant at the next table has begun to slumber, hands clasped on the newspaper in front of him, spectacles slipping down his nose. As I watch, he licks his lips with a tongue as fat and pink as a sausage, and belches loudly. Colonial manners.

– What the Comptroller wishes me to do, Casey says, is to try and persuade Fitzgibbon to take his Ticket-of-Leave.

– I see. And will you?

– Of course. You know what annoyance Fitzgibbon's refusal to accept the Ticket causes the Governor. Sir William sees it as a deliberate attempt to attract public sympathy. And he only waits for the opportunity to make Fitzgibbon a common convict – as he does with all of you. He craves to do it.

– I have no doubt, I say. Nevertheless, I must applaud Fitzgibbon – even though I see his suffering as fruitless. What Lord Grey wished to do when he transported us was to consign us to comfortable, gentlemanly oblivion. No chains, no prison walls, and therefore no pity – no martyrdom. This is what taking the Ticket means. The public and the newspapers, here and in Britain, will simply forget us: that's the thinking, and it's largely right. Well, we others have let him succeed – for the moment. But Fitzgibbon's stand is a slap in the face for the Colonial Office. By refusing the Ticket, Martin stands outside the situation.

– Indeed he does. He's begun to attract just the sort of attention that the Governor and London detest. There have been newspaper articles, both in Britain and here in the colonies, protesting at the harshness of his treatment. And Fitzgibbon has written a large number of letters of protest to people of influence, both here in Van Diemen's Land and in Britain. They include some of his powerful relatives – one of whom is a member of Parliament at Westminster – and a number of prominent churchmen. The main complaint in these letters is that he's being kept illegally in solitary confinement. All this is very brave – but it's also great folly, and can only make his situation worse.

– I agree. But what do you expect *me* to do?

– I simply ask that you write a letter to him that I can carry with me when I go, urging him to change his mind.

– I've already written to him once, I say. I'll do so again, if you wish – but I think you over-estimate my influence with him, Matthew.

– You under-estimate his respect for you, Casey says. You could well sway him, since he's already beginning to fear for his future. Thank you, sir. I'm delighted.

He smiles like a man who's been granted some highly valuable favour, and signals to the waiter. He's no close friend of Fitz-gibbon's, and I wonder why he cares so much – and why I feel that he's playing some complex game, little of which is revealed.

December 19th

I spoke of this today to Thomas O'Neill. His response was very disturbing.

During the week, he and I are always pleasantly occupied. We wander through the bush on foot, gathering strange wildflowers for his collection; or we ride our horses out among the hills, guns over our shoulders, followed by O'Neill's newly-acquired pair of hounds, hunting kangaroo for the table. At night, with the dogs slumbering at our feet, we sit by the fire in Glengarry Cottage: talking, smoking, reading, and writing our articles and letters. In spite of our isolation, this simple frontier life gives us a certain contentment. Sometimes, we tell each other, it even grows difficult to preserve our anger at being here. And it has brought back my health completely: the enemy has gone.

At noon today, after attending Sunday service in the little Angli-can church in the village, we took one of our walks together, climb-ing to the top of the hill on the hamlet's western side, where we sat on the trunk of a fallen tree.

Below us in its valley, Bothwell lay in a doze, as peaceful as a village at home: neat stone church; small military barracks and gaol; four inns, and the shingled roofs of fifty or so cottages. But summer had made the surrounding landscape tawny, removing any illusion that we were living in an inverted Britain. For all the abundance of water up in these mountains, the streams of Van Diemen's Land in summer don't have the flow of those in Europe, and the Clyde has become a mere trickle. Below us the well-watered meadows of 'Grasmere' made a green oasis, on the levels north-east of the town.

– So what do you think? I asked.

O'Neill took his spectacles off, pushing them into a pocket of his pilot coat. He rubbed his eyes and stared at me, strands of hair blowing in the faint, warm breeze.

– I think he may be a spy, he said.

– My dear Thomas: a *spy*? What kind of a spy? And for whom?

– For Dublin Castle, perhaps.

– Casey? A Dublin Castle spy? You're not serious, I said.

– And a spy now for Denison, and his Convict Department. A Government agent, in fact. This is my theory, listening to what you tell me. I may of course be wrong.

His light, high voice was both careless and matter-of-fact; he looked at me calmly, drawing on his pipe. But I knew this tone: had known it since boyhood. It meant that he was entirely serious.

– It's a monstrous idea, I said. Casey's concern for Fitzgibbon and for all of us may be absolutely genuine. How on earth do you justify such a notion?

– I don't. I merely suspect – as *you* do, or you would not have spoken as you've done. And suspicion, surely, must be our stock in trade. You're growing slack, my dear, if you forget that. I haven't mentioned these suspicions before, because they hadn't taken shape in my mind – and Matthew Casey scarcely seemed worth thinking about. Forgive me, Robert – I recall you were friendly with him at Trinity – but the man has always seemed to me a tedious nonentity.

– I won't argue against that. Please be as frank as you please.

– I have few facts to point to – but those I do have worry me. Consider Casey's history. At first, it seems innocent enough. Years ago – seven years ago at least – he was a member of the Repeal Association. He attended many public meetings, never saying very much, that I recall. Did you ever hear him speak out? No. But he was always there: a loyal face in the crowd. And he was there at the meeting in July, 1846, when we took Young Ireland out of the Association. He then became a member of our cause – though not a very active one. From time to time I'd see him in the council rooms of the Irish Confederation in Dolier Street – as you must have done. Then, after that, he seemed to fade away.

– He moved to Cork, I said. He took a post on a newspaper there.

– Yes, O'Neill said. But he'd still turn up in Dublin from time to time. I remember seeing him about, although I scarcely gave him a thought. And I've remembered something else, you see, which I'd forgotten until now.

He knocked out his pipe on the log, and then began to examine it, as though for flaws in the wood.

– Some of the members of the '82 Club spoke to me about him once, and said some peculiar things. Do you remember a tavern in Dolier Street, opposite our Council Rooms? It was called the London Tavern, and was a haunt of police detectives, who were no doubt keeping us under watch. I was told that Casey was sometimes seen in their company. It occurs to me now that he might have been acting even then as a spy for the Castle.

– But surely his work as a journalist could have been the reason for his associating with detectives, I said. It isn't proof.

– No, it isn't proof, O'Neill said. But I put it together with the fact that he maintains an extraordinary interest in *you*, Robert: an interest sufficient to have caused him to visit you at Spike Island when you were first imprisoned. He achieved this despite the isolation in which you were supposed to be kept, did he not?

– Yes. I thought it rather remarkable at the time.

– Yes. And now he's come out here to be in our proximity – at the same time enjoying a cordial relationship with our gaoler, the Comptroller-General of Convicts. This will enable him to visit Fitzgibbon at Port Arthur: again, a man who's meant to be kept entirely isolated – especially from the press. You tell me his mission is to urge Fitzgibbon to take his Ticket-of-Leave; and he'll take a letter with him adding your voice to his. Very good. But for whose benefit is he actually doing this? Fitzgibbon's? Or Sir William Denison's?

I stared at him. He raised a finger, as he'd done in philosophical argument in our student days.

– If Fitzgibbon will take his Ticket, he said, and stop being a public martyr, no-one will be more delighted than the Governor. Sir William would be very grateful to Casey for such a service – don't you agree?

I shook my head, and laughed. It was outrageous; but it was also plausible. It grew more plausible as I thought about it.

– If this is true, I said, and Casey is an agent for Denison and his turnkeys, then something must be done.

– I disagree, O'Neill said. We have no proof – and I may still be doing Casey an injustice. My theory may be wrong. For the present, my dear, we can only wait and watch.

– You're right. But you've convinced me of your other theory, O'Neill: this island is truly a Panopticon. Everyone must watch everyone else.

December 28th

On Boxing Day, as arranged, I went down to New Town to stay at Doctor Howard's. It proved an eventful visit. I've made my commitment to the hop farm with Langford; and he and I have been embroiled in a most bizarre episode together.

I arrived at the toll gates at five o'clock, and Langford was waiting in the gig. As we drove down Bay Road, he informed me that Doctor Howard had been called in to the Hospital on urgent business: it was possible that he'd not be back in time for dinner, and he'd sent his apologies. Mrs Bates would serve me dinner in his absence, Howard had said. I was to make myself comfortable until he came, and enjoy a bottle of wine he'd left for my approval.

My impulse was to tell Langford immediately of my decision about the farm; but I decided to wait until we reached Bay House. With admirable tact, he had not raised the subject again; but whenever he looked at me, on these visits, his expression told me that he waited.

We climbed out of the gig in front of the stables: a pretty, gabled brick building behind the servants' cottage, reached by a cobbled drive. It was a hot afternoon, and very still. English starlings and sparrows twittered in Doctor Howard's walnut trees, which cast cool English shadows on the drive.

– Well now, Langford, I said, Doctor Howard's absence is actually rather convenient. It gives us time to talk.

He swung around and looked at me, holding Topsy's reins, his expression becoming almost stern. Today he was clad in the belted blue blouse of a labourer; but even in this he looked military.

I told him, without any unnecessary preamble, that I wished to go partners with him. Instantly, he dropped the reins and smiled: a smile so broad that the gap between his top teeth seemed exaggerated.

– By God, how happy you make me! he said. Shall we shake hands on it, sir?

We did so, clasping hands for the first time in our acquaintance. His grip was very strong, his hand so roughened from outdoor work that it felt like tree bark. He gave a low chuckle, and his gaze held a conspiratorial glee – as though he and I had agreed on an enterprise which was in some way illicit. I would soon find out that it was.

– I'm glad you're pleased, I said.

– I'm a sight better than pleased, he said. Now I can start the life I've wanted for so bloody long! You won't regret it, sir – I'll make us both rich.

– *You* can be rich, Langford. All I ask is to be contented.

– Well now, I dare say you will be, on a pretty little property like this one. But you'll have to come out and see it, won't you, Mr Devereux? You won't buy it unseen, I'm sure.

– I'll need to inspect it, of course, I said. But you needn't worry, James. I'm sure I'll be satisfied.

A farmhand led Topsy and the gig into the stables, and Langford and I sat down on a bench in the sun. He immediately began to speak about his plans for the farm, picking up a stick and drawing designs in the dust. His talk was all of hops, as it had been before: of how well they did here, and of the new varieties he was going to plant.

– O' course, he said, we won't be able to put in new crops straight away – the time for planting here is August. But this cove Harrison as owns the place has five acres under hops at present, and we should be able to harvest them – that's at the end of February. I'll write to Harrison tomorrow, and tell him we're ready to buy. He's that bloody anxious to get out, I reckon he'll let us occupy in a few weeks. Maybe the third week in January, if we pay him cash on the nail. He ain't found another buyer, and he wants to get home to England as soon as he can.

But I held up my hand.

– Not so fast, I said. I've only just written to my bank in Dublin, and we're so devilishly far away, in this colony. You know that it will take three or more months for my letter to get to them, and the same at least for a letter of credit to come back. So it will be six months or more before we can buy, James.

He shook his head with a complacent air. Mrs Langford had already reached Sydney, he said, and had boarded a ship for Hobart Town two days ago. When she landed here, in three days' time, money would no longer be a problem: he would be able to pay Harrison in full.

I stared at him.

– If you and your wife can pay the money in full, Langford, why on earth do you need me?

At first he didn't answer; he looked down and seemed to ponder, tracing a circle in the dust with his stick. Then he took a deep breath, as though nerving himself for something.

– Why, as I told you before, he said, I'll need your money to expand and improve the place. And I want to ask a favour, sir. I'd like to tell Harrison's lawyer that most of the money we put up is yours – and when we draw up an agreement, it's Bess as you'll be partners with on paper, not me. Can you agree to that?

– Bess? I'm to be partners with your wife? Why on earth would you want that, James?

He had lit a cigar, which was clenched between his teeth; lips drawn back, he squinted at me through the smoke. It gave him a dangerous appearance.

– *You* know why, he said. Think, sir.

I gazed; then I laughed. Of course: this was why he needed my involvement – more than he needed my money. He didn't want the all-seeing convict authorities to inform London of the fact that he'd been able to buy a farm. Nor did he wish them to know that his wife had much money, either. I would be seen as the Langfords' benefactor; and to achieve this end, he was prepared to take a gamble on my honesty – making me a partner in the farm before I'd put up a sovereign.

I sat thinking, conscious of his hungry stare. Then I said softly:

– You want me to enter into a deception, James. To deceive the lawyers, and this colony's officials.

– It ain't such a big deception, he said. Bess will be true joint owner – and *she* ain't been convicted of any crime.

He said no more; he made no further plea or excuse; he waited. I was forced to admire that, even as I digested his brazen bid to make use of me.

– Very well, I said. I must hope I don't hang for it.

His wide, triumphant smile came back, and he threw the stick across the drive into a flower bed.

– *You* won't sir, I promise you. I'm deeply obliged.

– Make the farm pay, James, and you won't be obliged at all. And stop calling me 'sir'. We're partners, now – in truth, if not on paper. You'd better call me Devereux.

– If it's all the same to you, sir, and since you've been calling me James, I'd sooner call you Robert.

This was more familiar than I'd bargained for. I'd not have accepted it, at home; yet here, in this upside-down colony, it seemed almost natural.

– Why not? I said. I believe we've become friends, James.

– We have, he said. We have.

On a sudden impulse we shook hands again, smiling at each other. After that, we sat silent for a time, contemplating our future. It was pleasant on the bench in the hot sun, our backs against the stable's warm brick wall. In the courtyard at the back of the house Mrs Bates could be seen, hanging out sheets on a line. I wondered where Kathleen was, and when she'd appear; and I decided that the time had come to tell Langford of my plan concerning her. He listened attentively. When I'd concluded, I added:

– I have a particular sympathy for Kathleen, and not just because she's Irish. She has a very sad history, James.

– Well, they all do, Langford said. There's not a convict woman here as hasn't got a sad history. O' course I've no objection to taking her on – provided the Doctor will let her go. She's a good girl, and no doubt Bess will be glad of her in the house. But she's a girl who's attracted some trouble, Robert. We'll have to hope she don't attract more.

– I understand she was forced by another servant, I said, on the property where she worked.

– There's more, Langford said. The Doctor won't have told you about it, because the Doctor don't know. She ain't got rid of that passholder: O'Donnell, his name is. He got transported from Ireland for burning down the farmhouses of the gentry, and killing their stock. A pretty dangerous villain – and he won't seem to go away.

– But the matter's over, surely? He's well removed from here.

– No. Pearce's property is only a few miles up the Main Road, Langford said. A bit of a tosspot, old Pearce is, and slack about controlling his servants. O'Donnell's his farm overseer, and Pearce favours him, Kathleen tells me – which is why the son of a bitch was never charged with what he done to her. Pearce sends him on errands about the district, and gives him a fair bit of rope. And that's why he can turn up *here* as he does.

– He calls at Bay House? How is that possible?

– I don't mean that he comes up and rings the doorbell. No, he's been seen hanging about – trespassing. The first time, only Kathleen saw him, behind the servants' cottage, and ran in to tell Mrs Bates, very frightened. Then Mrs Bates saw him on the drive one day, and called one of the farmhands. And the last time, *I* saw him, up behind the stables here. I ordered him off the property, and he cursed me. A nasty sod he looked, and big. I picked up a shovel and moved after him, and he went off pretty fast after that.

He smiled faintly.

– He's trying to get to Kathleen. It seems like he won't give her up. Some coves is like that over a woman.

– But hasn't this been reported to Doctor Howard? He should deal with the master, Pearce, and have the fellow charged.

– No, Langford said. Kathleen begged us not to – me and Mrs Bates. She's afraid of the trouble it'll cause. Old Pearce protected the dirty bastard – and she thinks it'd be that way again. She could even be right. So maybe coming to us at New Norfolk is the best thing that could happen to her.

I grew thoughtful, sitting beside my new partner in the sun. I began to see now why Kathleen never felt safe. Had she seen me as a saviour, before I saw myself in this way?

– And where is Kathleen today? I asked.

I attempted to sound casual; but I saw Langford glance sideways at me, a hint of speculation in his face.

– Why, she has a holiday, he said, for Boxing Day. She's gone in to Hobart Town with the Wilsons. They work on the property next to this one. Sam Wilson has the use of a spring cart, so he and his wife and Kathleen have all gone shopping together.

I asked him when she was expected back. I wanted to tell her of our offer to employ her on the farm, I said.

– Well now, curfew's at eight o'clock, he said. The Wilsons won't be later than that, being passholders. She's in good hands, don't worry.

He grinned; and I could have sworn that he guessed at my feeling. Am I so transparent?

I ate my dinner alone in the dining room, served by Mrs Bates. At a little after eight o'clock, as she was clearing away the dishes, I asked her whether Kathleen had returned from the city.

She paused by the door, holding some plates in both hands, and turned back to me.

– No sir, she's not come back, and it's after curfew. I never thought that Kathleen was the sort of servant that couldn't be trusted in the town. And this the very first time she's gone in there.

The housekeeper was clearly distressed, in the way of dutiful people who feel they may be blamed for failing in their responsibilities. As I questioned her, she grew more agitated still, and her face became flushed.

Sam Wilson had just called in, she told me, and had spoken to James Langford. Wilson was alarmed, and concerned that some blame would fall on him. It seemed that Kathleen had parted from him and his wife on the Old Wharf, having met some Irish women with whom she'd come out on the *Midlothian*. The Wilsons had arranged to meet her again on Wellington Bridge at six – but they'd waited for nearly an hour, and she'd not appeared. So then they'd come on back to New Town, fearing to be caught out after curfew themselves.

I asked Mrs Bates what was being done. She'd discussed the situation with Langford, she said, and he was going into town to look for Kathleen directly. I asked her to tell Langford to come in and see me.

When he appeared, he was dressed in rough clothing: drab, broad-brimmed hat, dark pea jacket, and corduroy trousers. He intended to search for Kathleen at the New Wharf, he said. The Doctor had taken the Stanhope to the Hospital, but there was a second gig in the stables.

– I'll come with you, I said.

He raised his eyebrows.

– But the Doctor's expecting to join you here, ain't he? Better leave this to me.

– I'll come with you, I said.

He raised his eyebrows higher, but said no more.

He drove fast along the Main Road, whipping the horse up the slope of Lord's Hill. The summer nights here are generally cool and refreshing, no matter how hot the day; but tonight remained hot and breathless. Early stars burned in a sky like deep water, and the dipping, glowing lamps of spring carts and broughams came towards us on the road. We jogged through baleful blue spaces filled above and below with lights, and I wiped my forehead with my hand-kerchief. I was sweating more than the night's heat warranted.

Langford and I spoke little; but as we wheeled downhill towards the city, I turned to him. We surely had little hope of finding Kath-leen, I said. She could be anywhere in the town. Did he have some plan in mind?

– I have a bit of a notion, he said. There's a tavern where a lot of the Irish drink, on the Old Wharf. I sometimes go in there, and I'm known to them. I'll ask after her there, to start with.

– You think that she went drinking with those women? That she's drunk in some tavern in the port?

– Well, Robert, she's Irish, ain't she?

I felt swift irritation at this English assumption that our people are all drunkards. Nevertheless, my hopes rose a little. Langford made many mysterious expeditions to the city in his hours off, and no doubt knew a variety of people there.

But then he said:

– O'Donnell drinks in that tavern. He's what I'm concerned about.

O'Donnell. The name was beginning to make an echo in my head.

That night, I discovered another section of the town-behind-the-town. Langford was to conduct me through the portals of Dis, which lie on the south-eastern side of the city.

First, however, we rattled in the gig over the cobbles of the Old Wharf, passing in front of its wall of sandstone buildings. Flares of ships at their moorings tossed in reflection on black water. There were boat-builders here, and sail-makers and coopers, and a brewery whose odour hung pungent in the darkness. Blameless enough trades, these; but hidden behind the backs of the buildings was the small, foul estuary where the Hobart Rivulet discharged into the port, on the borders of a slum called Wapping – whose warren of drinking shops, dance rooms and bawdyhouses catered to sailors ashore. The whalers had a name of their own for this district, Langford told me: in tribute to its perils, they called it South West Cape.

We passed the Diamond of India, and came to a halt at the carriage entrance of the Sailor's Delight. This was a tall, narrow tavern whose signboard depicted an anchor and a physically unlikely mermaid. Here, Langford said, we could put the gig safe inside for a few pence. We needed to be on foot from now on.

I followed him into the bar parlour. It was a long, large, noisy room with wood-panelled walls, its ceiling black from the smoke of oil lamps. At least a hundred people were drinking in here: some at tables, others crowded around the bar counter. Most were sailors, but a good many were local men and women of the servant class. Langford shouldered his way towards an Irish couple standing at the counter. The man was a big, brown-haired fellow with a full beard, wearing a red serge blouse. The woman was plump and middle-aged, with a cheerful, inebriated smile; like many of the female passholders in here, she was dressed as richly as any of the ladies on the Block, in a bright silk dress and a summer bonnet trimmed with flowers, worn somewhat askew.

As Langford greeted this pair, I hung back. They hailed him with enthusiasm: he seemed to be regarded as a friend. He began immediately to question them, his expression serious and intent.

Listening, the Irishman fingered his beard and looked doubtful. James turned and beckoned to me. I had brought no rough clothing with me to Bay House, and felt somewhat conspicuous in here, in a dress coat and light buckskin trousers. I took off the low-crowned, white felt hat that was the latest addition to my colonial wardrobe.

– This here gentleman is my business partner, Langford told the couple. He's a friend of Doctor Howard's, and he knows what a value the Doctor puts on Kathleen as a servant. He's anxious to find her on the Doctor's behalf, and he'll be grateful for any information you can give us.

He nodded at me quickly, and touched his nose. I felt in my pocket for some money. As I did so, Langford said to me:

– My friends tell me she was in here – and she was with Dan O'Donnell.

I passed the Irishman a sovereign. He raised his eyebrows with a swift look of joy, and thrust it into his pocket.

– Please tell us anything you can, I said.

– Concerning Dan O'Donnell? I know him, sure, the man said. He's often in here with his mates, sir. He's just got his Ticket, do you see, and has left the farm where he worked – so he goes where he pleases, now.

– Does he now? said Langford.

– And he's a bad bugger to cross, sure, the Irishman said. I've seen Dan destroy a man in a fight entirely. But a true Irish patriot, I'm thinking: a Ribbonman, I believe he was. And by God, how he hates the English!

He grinned; then, suddenly abashed, he put his hand on Langford's shoulder.

373

– Begging your pardon, James, but that's the truth, now.

– Please tell us what else you know, I said.

– Sure, there's not much to tell. I saw a pretty little Irish girl similar to the one that James describes – but I don't know for certain that this was your Kathleen. She was drinking with her friends, and O'Donnell and his boys came up to them, and bought drinks for them all. And what I noticed later was this: that the girl was so drunk she couldn't stand.

The woman spoke now.

– And that was queer, your honour, because I swear to God, she'd not been in here long enough to be so destroyed by the drink.

– And then O'Donnell and one of his friends were helping her out the door, the man said, because she couldn't walk on her own feet. I can tell you nothing more, sir.

– Where can we find O'Donnell? Langford asked.

– He lives nearby, I'm told: somewhere in Wapping. But I can tell you no more than that.

Langford looked at me, and jerked his head.

– We'll have a look about in Wapping, he said.

He led me into the inn's central hallway, and took us to a doorway at the back. He swung it open, and we stood on a tumbledown boat landing, looking out over the narrow, secret estuary of the Rivulet.

There was no moon, and it was very dark, except for the light from the windows of the Old Wharf's line of buildings, rising behind us like ramparts. As my eyes grew accustomed to the night, I found that the estuary resembled a marsh rather than a stream – and the foulest marsh in my experience.

Here, it seemed, was Hobart Town's cloaca. The black, oily water was stagnant and almost motionless, and every sort of filth floated in it. An overwhelming stench hung here, at which I exclaimed in disgust, taking out my handkerchief and putting it to my nose. This, I would discover, was the final destination of the soakage from the cess-pits at the Female Factory, far up-stream at the Cascades; of many another cess-pit on the way; of wastes from factories along the banks; of refuse from the Government Hospital, and of any other nastiness that people saw fit to drop into this Antipodean Styx. To the stenches of the creek were added those of a slaughter-house, crouched on the opposite bank.

Langford spat in the water, and grinned at my use of the handkerchief.

– I know, Robert, it don't smell like roses. But I want us to pay a visit here to someone who was with us on Bermuda – and who come out with us on the *Raffles*. I'm talking about Lane – Arthur Lane.

He peered at me in the darkness.

– I don't believe you liked the bugger, and neither did I. But if anyone knows where O'Donnell's to be found, Arthur will. He deals in second-hand goods – a fence, if you want to know the truth, and already doing amazing well. We can reach him from here by boat. There's a boatman will ferry us over to Wapping for sixpence or so.

– Then let's go there, I said. The faster the better.

All my thoughts were of Kathleen; I was now filled with deep anxiety for her, and felt only faint surprise at the prospect of meeting Long Lane again. The city was so small that I'd expected to catch sight of my old servant sooner or later; though hardly in circumstances where I'd be asking for his help.

Langford put two fingers in his mouth and whistled. A few moments later a figure appeared, climbing up the ladder from below: a bulky, silent man with a stubbled grey head like a pinecone, clad in a blue flannel shirt. He had only one bright grey eye: the other was an empty socket. Langford addressed him as 'Ralph', and gave him money and instructions. The man grunted, and we followed him back down the ladder and entered a skiff that was moored there.

Langford and I sat down in the stern, and the boat glided off on the Stygian lake. Here in our miniature London was a miniature Fleet Ditch: on its far side, miniature Wapping could be seen, its dim lamps glowing like marsh-lights. As he rowed, Ralph regarded me fixedly with his single eye. Excrement and other filth fell from the blades of his oars, and the stench grew overpowering. Finally he addressed himself to Langford.

– Now why would this fine gentlemen want to come to Wapping?

– Never you mind, cully, Langford said. Just row us up to Long Lane's, and earn your bloody fee.

Our ferryman fell silent, growling to himself, and the boat went on through the slimy water. The night remained still and stifling; my face became oily with perspiration, and I struggled against the idea that the foul miasma of the place was settling on my flesh: the fetor of Dis. We moved level with some mud-flats now, where a number of figures moved: men and women of every age, and children as young as eight years old. All of them appeared to be fashioned out of the mud itself. Their skin and ragged clothing were plastered with it, so that they were mainly a blackish-grey in appearance; some were almost naked, and their deathly flesh showed through, like the flesh of corpses. They stooped to pick up any discarded materials they might sell: pieces of wood, rope, iron or copper. Some fought over this treasure-trove: as I watched, two men wrestled each other into the mud, contesting some object – lunging and snarling like dogs, eyes rolling in blackened faces, lost to every feeling but anger.

– Mudlarks, Langford said. Now we know we're in Wapping.

We went further up the narrow stream in silence, passing dim shapes of ketches and other small sailing craft, and moving into thicker, light-pricked darkness. A crude, single-arched brick bridge appeared, close to which squatted small, misshapen houses. I asked Langford for our bearings.

– Why, this is the bridge at Campbell Street, he said. The Palladio, the jokers of the town call it. You wouldn't know it, but we're not far from the Hospital here, and the Royal Victoria Theatre. And here's Lane's crib.

He pointed towards a two-storeyed brick house standing just before the bridge, which seemed to lean sideways. A long weatherboard structure like a cabin projected from the ground floor, supported on piles above the evil creek. This, it would turn out, was Lane's receiving depot – the rest of his establishment being a rooming-house. A light burned in a window there, and Ralph turned us towards a boat-landing which was the depot's back entrance.

As we left the skiff and began to climb the ladder to the platform above, I saw a strange, white object in the muddy bank below. To my disgust, it appeared to be a human arm – the hand clawing upwards, as though still connected to an owner who strained to escape. But peering at it more closely, I decided it was merely driftwood.

Coming in through the door, we found ourselves in what looked partly like the kitchen of a very crowded lodging house, and partly like a second-hand shop.

It was a dim, ill-ventilated room some thirty feet long and fifteen in breadth, full of shadows and dark corners. It appeared to have no windows. Despite the evening's warmth, a fire blazed in a grate at the far end, making the place stifling. Two large boilers of hot water sat on either side of the hearth. Clothing hung to dry on lines stretched between the rafters, which were blackened by fumes. After the stench of the creek outside, the odours in this place were not entirely unpleasant: frying bacon, coffee, tobacco-smoke. Deal tables stood along the walls, piled with a great array of objects: crockery, silverware, men's coats of all kinds, trousers, women's dresses, and hats and bonnets.

A remarkable number of people sat and stood about here: men, women and children. Some were drinking tea or coffee; others played cards, or simply smoked pipes and idled. But not all were idle: one man was sorting shirts into piles; another was cobbling a pair of shoes; a woman sat mending a shawl. By the fire, a boy in a tartan cap was eating a plate of bacon and eggs. At first, I didn't see Lane. Then he stood up from an obscure position near the fire, and advanced down the room towards us.

This Long Lane (I was unable to think of him as Arthur), was very much different from the convict I'd known on the *Medway*. Stoop-shouldered, soberly dressed, his hands clasped together in

377

front of him, he wore a politely enquiring, deferential expression, like a verger coming down the aisle of a church to usher in new members of the congregation. As he came, his eyes rested on Langford and me, and became somewhat fixed; but there was no other sign of recognition. His sombre, clerical appearance was assisted by a tail coat of superfine black cloth, dark trousers, and a gleaming white shirt of excellent quality. Only his silk neckerchief struck an incongruous note: it was a loud, gypsy scarlet. The hair I remembered as mere stubble was now worn very long, and gleamed with pomade. He halted in front of us and smiled, greeting Langford first.

– If it ain't my flash friend James Langford. It's always good to see you, mate.

He turned to me, with a widening of his well-remembered horse's eyes. I was briefly and strangely back on the hulk, in my wretched little hutch, and I wondered whether he hated me. But he was all politeness.

– And Mr Devereux: what a great surprise to meet you again, sir, in this little nest of mine! You're as handsome as ever, I see: they ain't done *you* no harm. I knew you was in town, of course: I read about it in the newspapers.

– No doubt, Lane, I say. How do you do?

– Oh, I do very well, sir – as you see.

He jerked his head at the room behind him. His smile, though affable enough, had a mechanical quality, and a nerve jumped in his cheek: a phenomenon I didn't recall seeing there before. I remembered hearing it said that a man never fully recovers from the sort of flogging Lane endured.

– But you ain't come here for nothing, he said, I'm sure. Won't you gents tell me how I can be of service? Have you brought some items you're anxious to sell?

Before either of us could answer, a tow-haired boy of about sixteen appeared at Lane's elbow, tugging at his sleeve. He wore a vast yellow waistcoat which must have belonged previously to a much larger owner; his trousers hung by one brace, and his white, puffy face had the hardness and cunning of a middle-aged man's.

– Mr Lane? You was going to pay me for them potatoes. I want my money.

Lane laid his hand on the boy's head. His voice took on a throaty, reassuring note, and he delved at the same time in his waistcoat pocket.

– O' course, my covey. All serene: I've got two cartwheels for you. Here.

But the boy shied away, staring indignantly at the extended coins.

– Two bloody crowns! Them potatoes was worth five times that! They're in terrible short supply!

– Maybe, young 'un, maybe. But look at the risk I run. I have to be paid for that, don't I? Bring me a lot more, and I'll pay you in sovereigns, depend on it.

Muttering, the boy retreated with the money, and Lane turned back to us, sighing and shaking his head: a great man pressed for time, granting us an interview. He gestured at the figures about the long, shadowy room, with its flickering firelight.

– How they'd live without me, I just don't know. There's *none* of 'em here would manage it, I swear – young or old. But no matter what their cut is, it's never enough. The buggers forget that I give them a home as well. Eh? Ain't that true, James?

– True enough, said Langford. They'd be lost without you, Arthur. They'd all be back in the Tench.

If Lane heard the irony in Langford's tone, he gave no sign of it. His smile grew humorously sly, suggesting some past complicity between the three of us; then he looked directly at me.

– Yes, I've done very well here, Mr Devereux. You looked down your nose at me, on the *Medway* – don't deny it now, you did – but I forgive you that, now. We're all Ticket-of-Leave now, ain't we? You and me and Jim here. So in one way, we stand on the same footing, ain't that so? And Van Diemen's Land has turned out to be just the place for a man like me. A bleeding *wicked* place, it is – but I ain't complaining. It's making me rich, I tell you.

He gestured at his depot in an expansive manner.

– Just *look* at these people. They all do my bidding. I've got experts in every field. Sneaks; magsmen; dwarfs – no-one like a dwarf for gaining entry to the trickier places – blind fiddlers; nigger minstrels; cripples to go out and beg. A marvellous lot they are, and no mistake. I could almost start a bleeding theatre. I could also start a workhouse, the number of poor useless old buggers I'm support- ing. But there, I don't complain.

As he spoke, I looked around more closely in the half-light, and found that his claims were true. There were indeed a number of dwarfs here – little men no more than four feet high – as well as three blind men of the type I'd seen in St Giles, wearing their blue glasses, their dogs at their feet, fiddles laid close by. There were also some nymphs of the pavement, in varying degrees of drunkenness and disarray, and a number of shabby and pitiful old men and women whose usefulness to Lane or to anyone else was difficult to see.

Setting down these details, I see that I'm in danger of making Long Lane's troupe sound quaint: but they were anything but that. Some – mostly the young – were jaunty enough; but others were sunk down in depths beyond despair. A very old woman in a filthy white shawl sat as close as she could to the fire, mumbling to herself, picking at an ulcer on her ankle of a size and loathsomeness that made me avert my eyes; and I began to scent disease in here, among the smells of coffee, smoke and bacon. One of the blind beggars stood helplessly while two boy pickpockets teased his dog with a poker, laughing at his pleas to them to stop. A young prostitute on a bench embraced herself in some sort of anguish, arms crossed, rocking to and fro and weeping, her face blue and green with bruises. We had penetrated Dis, where tears and empty laughter mingled: these were Albion's lost children. Criminals, perhaps, are all lost children.

– Yes, they all get a berth here, Lane was saying. But you're wondering why I'm so open with you, Mr Devereux. Am I right?

He moved closer, smiling intimately into my face.

– I'm telling you because I want you to *know*, Mr Devereux. I'm telling you because I always *admired* you, sir, no matter what you thought of me. A noble and patriotic hero, that's what you are.

That's why I tried to look after you, on the *Medway*. As for James Langford here, he's one of the great men among robbers – and I honour him for it.

Langford screwed up his mouth, as though at a bad taste.

– I don't want your bloody honour, Arthur. Let's get to the point.

But Lane went on, ignoring this.

– I ain't got a thing to fear, you see? There ain't anyone can touch me. The traps? The traps here are all old lags – and they're in my pay, the bastards.

His expression suddenly altered: his dark eyes glared, like an animal's looking from a trap.

– Those bloody sods at Bermuda thought they'd finish me off, didn't they? Well, they didn't. God rot the fucking sons of bitches – they didn't. Here in this colony I do as I bloody well please. So who laughed last? Eh?

As though to confirm his words, he gave vent to a sudden sniggering; but the sound was like something caused by pain rather than mirth. Then he rubbed his hands.

– But come, we'll get down to business. What can I do for you, gentlemen?

While Langford explained, Lane looked from one to the other of us.

– And that's all? That's all you come here about?

– That's all, I said, and drew a five-pound note from my pocket book. This is for you, Lane, if you can tell us where O'Donnell is now.

– Well, well, Lane said. A flimsy. You must want her bad.

He turned, and called across the room.

– Charlie! Charlie Porter!

One of the dwarf burglars in the room descended from the chair he was sitting in – doing so by gripping the arms and swinging himself to the floor. He hurried across to us, moving with a rocking gait. He had a shock of black hair that stood up like a brush; he was no taller than a child of seven, but his large, yellowish face was middle-aged. He wore a green tail coat, whose tails dragged along the floor – and the coat caused me to recognise him. This, I was almost certain, was the creature who had stolen my watch in Black Lion Square. But Long Lane's depot was like a room in a dream; and as in a dream, the theft seemed now to have no importance.

– These gentlemen require your help, Charlie, Lane said. And so do I. I'd like you to take them round to Dan O'Donnell's place.

The dwarf surveyed Langford and me with intelligent, wide-spaced eyes. If he recognised me, he gave no sign. He spoke in a high, cracked voice.

– Yes? For what sort of fee?

– The gentlemen are friends of mine, Charlie. I'm sure they'll give you a crown.

Lane turned to us.

– It's quite close. Just around in Sackville Street. I'll show you out the front door, gentlemen. Are you still handy with your mauleys, James? I do hope so, because O'Donnell can be ugly, you know. I've seen him beat men something cruel.

– We're not looking for trouble, Langford told him. Just the girl.

Lane put his hand on my arm.

– I'll take my leave of you now, Mr Devereux. I do hope to see you again, sir. And if you don't mind, I'd rather my name wasn't mentioned to Dan O'Donnell. I'm glad to have been of assistance, but I'm sure you understand: not *mentioned*.

His smile now had a certain nervousness. It was an emotion that O'Donnell seemed to inspire everywhere. Not for the first time, I felt grateful that Langford was with me.

Now, by secret lanes, led by the rocking dwarf, we made our way deeper into Wapping.

We were somewhere behind Campbell Street, near the back of the Royal Victoria: the city's principal theatre. But I soon lost my bearings in a maze of alleys. All was miniature: tiny, crumbling cottages set dead on the pavement; crowded timber groggeries no bigger than the booths at a fair. Fiddle music danced in the thick, warm air, and women of the demi-monde called to us from cottage doorways, feathers nodding in elaborate bonnets. We entered Sackville Street, which was also narrow, but lined with somewhat larger houses. At the door of one of these – a tall brick structure of two storeys – Charlie stopped, and put out his hand to me.

– This is O'Donnell's crib, he said. I'll take that cartwheel, if you please, and be on my way. I don't want nothing to do with Dan at this time of night. He'll be fighting drunk by now, and looking for trouble.

He disappeared, the coin I'd given him clutched in his fist, and Langford and I were left on the front door-step. The door was ajar, but there were no sounds from inside. I rapped with the iron knocker. We waited for a few minutes, and then moved cautiously into the passageway, which was dark. Langford called out; but there was no answer. The passageway led to a flight of stairs, which we cautiously ascended.

Still no sign of life when we reached the landing. No lamp was lit here, but a faint illumination came from a street lamp outside, shining though a window in the stair-well. There were two doors here, both closed. I looked at Langford, and he nodded.

I tried the first door. It wasn't locked, and I cautiously pushed it open and went in, with Langford close behind.

A small, bare room, its sole illumination a candle on the mantel shelf. Sickly yellow half-light; tall shadows. No ventilation: the window shut, the air intolerably close. A bed in the centre, on which lay a dim form: a woman. In these first seconds, her posture seemed somehow unnatural.

– Just like I thought, Langford said. Damn O'Donnell's bloody eyes.

Kathleen O'Rahilly lay on her back, her arms extended behind her, her hair in disarray on the dirty pillow. Her wrists were tied by ropes to the black iron bedstead. She was awake, and looked at us; but her eyelids drooped, and I could not be sure that she actually saw us. Her eyes seemed dazed, and almost blind. Her lips were parted and swollen-looking: her top teeth glinted in the candlelight. She said nothing. She was clad in a skirt and the white chemise familiar to me from Neville Howard's painting. Her jacket bodice lay on a chair.

I bent over her, and spoke her name. I asked her who had done this. There was a smell of spirits, and of perspiration; there were large damp patches under the arms of the short-sleeved chemise. Her eyes narrowed, looking into mine as those of the sick do. She licked her lips and moved them; when she finally spoke, her voice was slurred.

– Is it you, sir?

Before I could answer, Langford had pushed me aside, and had drawn a clasp knife from a pocket in his pea jacket. Carefully and methodically, he began to cut the rope that fastened her left wrist.

– We don't have time to waste, he muttered.

– Christ, James, I said. What has this villainous bastard done to her?

Her left arm was free, and fell to her side; Langford hurried to the other side of the bed and began to cut the rope that secured her right wrist, glancing at me as he did so.

– Why, Robert, she's drunk. And my guess is, from what my friends told us, they dropped laudanum into her gin.

He sniffed, wrinkling up his nose as Kathleen's right hand fell to the bed. He picked the hand up in both his own, and began to chafe the wrist. She gave a little cry.

– It would help if you was to rub her other wrist, Robert, he said.

I did so, while Langford leaned close and spoke to her, his voice reassuring.

– Now, Kathleen, we need to get you on your feet. But tell us: where's O'Donnell?

Again she licked her lips, looking bewildered.

– I don't know – but he'll be near.

Langford handed her the jacket bodice from the chair.

– Put this on, he said. Waste not a minute, my dear, and we'll be gone from here.

She stood, swaying, and drew on the jacket while Langford and I turned our backs, facing the door.

– Will you take her back to New Town, Robert? I'd be much obliged if you would, Langford said. We don't know how many friends this shit has with him, so we need to get her away very prompt. You'll soon find a cab in Campbell Street. I must pick up the gig.

My arm about her shoulders, I led Kathleen down the stairs of her prison. We moved along the street, past the pygmy grog shops and cottages of ill fame, her feet stumbling on the cobbles. After many wrong turnings, I brought her at last out of Wapping's mazes, emerging in front of the brightly-lit entrance of the Royal Victoria Theatre. Here was civilization, of a sort: a little portico with a classical pediment and Tuscan columns; hoardings announcing the latest play from London; well-dressed ladies and gentlemen waiting about the doors to go in, laughing and talking as though no Citadel of Dis lay in the lanes behind.

Under the black leather hood of an ancient cab, drawn by a single old horse, Kathleen and I sat side by side. The cabby, a skinny fellow in a tall black beaver, erect on his perch in front of us, never turned around.

Kathleen sat silent, staring into the night, her hands locked tightly in her lap. She was a sad sight. There were stains on the jacket bodice, and on her grey cotton skirt: the finery in which she'd gone to town. If there had been ribbons in her hair, they were gone now. So was her bonnet.

Many conjectures revolved in my head. Had I been wrong about her? Was she no different from any other convict servant, taking advantage of a few hours' liberty to drink herself senseless in a tap room? Had O'Donnell succeeded in raping her, before Langford and I came? I was startled by the pain these questions gave me, and resolved to have answers to them.

– Did you lose your bonnet, Kathleen?

Her look was still dazed.

– Yes. I lost it – I don't know where.

Her voice was indistinct above the grumbling of the wheels. I put my arm about her shoulders again, and her head turned towards me with great speed, like that of a startled bird.

– You came for me, she said.

– I came for you. Somebody had to do so.

With a sudden, convulsive movement, she twisted entirely towards me, putting her arms about me and burying her face in my neck. I held her, as the cab ground on. She smelled of gin and sweat; she was in great need of a bath; from her thick, tangled hair came the reek of tobacco smoke. Yet I found, with the warmth of her body creeping into me, that my desire for her had not lessened: if anything, I desired her more. I could never have imagined such feelings, until now. Was I becoming gross?

– Why did you go drinking?

Her face remained pressed against my shoulder; she was silent for a moment. When she answered, her voice had a defensive note.

– The Wilsons took me to the tavern on the Wharf, just to take a drop together. And I met some Irish women there. They were some of them very good friends to me on the prison ship. When the Wilsons were leaving to go shopping, my friends asked me to stop and take another small drink with them – and I could not say no. So the Wilsons said they would meet me in an hour, on Wellington Bridge.

She raised her head, peering at me in the dark.

– Sure, it was meeting those women that made me want to drink more than I should have, she said. I was unhappy, and they were from home: from Limerick and Galway. Ah, it was good to be with them, sir – you cannot know! But I had not drunk very much when Dan O'Donnell and his friends came in. They knew some of the women, and bought everybody drinks. I was afraid; I wanted nothing to do with Dan, and tried to leave. But all my friends asked me to stay and have one more drink, and I did. When Dan came up next to me at the counter, I would not speak to him. But then, when I had drunk that one glass of gin, I felt queer. Everything went away – it went black entirely, and I remember nothing. I woke on that bed tied up, and Dan not there. But I remember having horrible dreams, and there were people touching me.

– He put something into your drink, I said. You made a great mistake in not leaving. Perhaps you should not have gone into that tavern at all.

She looked at me with a challenge that surprised me, her eyes becoming pale and fixed. She was still a little drunk.

– Should I not? I will tell you something. After two gins with my friends from the prison ship, I felt I might not go back to Bay House at all.

– But why? Surely Doctor Howard has been good to you?

– Good to me? Let me tell you, Robert Devereux, what it means when a gentleman like Doctor Howard is good to a pass-holder like me. He wants to take her into his bed. The Doctor has not tried to do that yet – but he will, I'm thinking.

– You can't mean that, Kathleen. I believe Doctor Howard to be an honourable man.

But she looked down stubbornly into her lap. Then she muttered:

– He must always be making drawings of me.

– I've seen them. They're very fine.

– I cannot like them. When I must pose for him, he is always touching me.

We'd passed over the summit of Lord's Hill. The cabby flicked his whip, and the old horse trotted down the slope of the Main Road, harness jauntily jingling. Kathleen's fingers now gripped my upper arm, as though she sought to keep her balance. The night had grown cooler; the few little lights of New Town twinkled for miles off in the darkness, and scents of flowers and hay came into the cab.

– Listen to me, Kathleen, I said. Doctor Howard will do you no harm, and you'll not go back to the Factory. You're coming to me.

And now I began to explain, while her eyes never left my face. It was as though my words were telling her whether she was to live or die.

I felt a sort of shame, mingled with elation.

Doctor Howard poured more brandy into my glass. He rubbed the side of his nose with his index finger, smiling at me obliquely.

– Most grateful to you, Devereux. You and Langford both, he said. Considerin' the number of taverns there are in the city, restorin' Kathleen to me was quite a feat.

It was after eleven o'clock. Alone in his studio, we sat on either side of the small round table by the fireplace, enjoying our usual nightcap.

– It's Langford who most deserves your thanks, I said. The question is, what's to be done about this villain O'Donnell?

– We can certainly draw him to the attention of the Comptroller, Howard said. And perhaps we may bring him before a magistrate. But I warn you, it may be difficult to make any charges stick.

– Difficult? How so? Langford and I are witnesses to what was done to the girl. I want to see this brute put on trial for kidnap and possible rape, and sent to Port Arthur.

Howard smiled faintly.

– I'm glad to find you so zealous for British justice, Devereux, even when its punitive hand may fall on one of your own country-men. Forgive me – I'm bein' a little frivolous. But you must admit there's a certain incongruity in the situation – especially since O'Donnell appears to have been one of those rebels of yours who burn barns. What do they call them? Ribbonmen?

– I admit no such thing. O'Donnell is no patriot, but a common criminal.

– Of course, Howard said. I was jokin' – and I understand your feelin's. But it may not be that simple, Robert. You see, I've spoken to Mrs Bates, who's discussed with Kathleen what happened to her – and it seems that Kathleen herself is not wantin' to press charges against O'Donnell.

– She's afraid of him, I said. She must be made to change her mind, or she'll never be safe.

– I doubt that she'll do so. And remember there are no actual witnesses to what happened. O'Donnell wasn't there when you arrived. That house is probably a nest of thieves, and is unlikely to belong to O'Donnell. So if he claimed that it wasn't he who tied Kathleen up, but some other rogue or rogues, it might be difficult to prove otherwise. Also, I find it hard to believe that Kathleen was conveyed there against her will, or in a state of unconsciousness, as she claims.

I stared at him in outrage; but he continued to smile. I asked him what he implied.

– Merely that her passionate and feckless Irish nature may have made Kathleen careless, he said. I don't say this as a criticism – I find it appealin', to tell you the truth. But once such a girl has a few drinks – and we know how your women of the peasantry love the bottle – then unforeseen things may happen.

I said nothing for a moment, sitting with one arm dangling over the arm of my chair, fist clenched. Keeping my temper was costing me a considerable effort; but I reminded myself how important it was to do so. I picked up my box of cigars and offered one to Howard, who accepted it with a murmur of thanks. Removing one for myself and putting it between my lips, I leaned to the candle on the table to light up, feeling him watch me as I did so. When he followed suit, I leaned back and blew a long stream of smoke, composing myself.

– I have a higher opinion of Kathleen than you do, I said. But even if you're right, Neville, there's now urgent reason to take her out of the Hobart Town district, to a place where she'll be safe from O'Donnell's attentions. And this brings me to something I've been wanting to discuss with you. Kathleen touches me deeply – representing as she does the plight of so many of my people. Should she be willing, I'm asking whether you might release her to come to Langford and me when we take up our farm next month. Mrs Langford would be directly in charge of her – and out in the Derwent Valley she'd be far from the evil influences of Hobart Town, and from the attentions of O'Donnell. I'm assuming that it will be not too difficult for you to replace her, holding the position that you do. I'd be infinitely obliged if you could do me this favour.

Howard had been watching me carefully as I spoke. He put down his cigar and picked up his brandy glass, swirling the liquor gently as though testing it in some way.

– Well, now, he said. This is a surprisin' request. Kathleen does seem to be in demand. I can understand why, of course – she's an attractive little creature, as we both know.

He smiled at me slyly, but I didn't respond. He grew serious, and put down the brandy glass. He drew on his cigar, and looked at me directly through his spectacles.

– Of course, Devereux, I understand both your need for a good servant, and your sentimental feeling about Kathleen. And I do want to help you in any way I can – you and Langford both. But the fact is, I've grown quite fond of havin' her about, and would hate to part with her. And she's such a wonderful model: I was lookin' forward to doin' some more studies of her.

– Will you at least consider it?

He frowned and began to grow restless; he put down his cigar in the ash tray, and avoided my eye.

– I may do eventually – certainly not at present, I'm sorry. And you know, Devereux, we're not allowed under the regulations to hand passholders over to one another as though they were slaves. It would have to be her decision to agree to the change of employer. What are her feelin's in the matter? Have you asked her?

– I think she would be glad to come, I said.

– I see.

He looked at me now with a coldness I'd not seen before; and it seems to me now that the ease which he and I had known for so long began to disappear in that moment. Perhaps it had been destined to end with the completion of my portrait.

– There's somethin' else I must point out, he said. The Convict Department might not look sympathetically on Mrs Langford as a protector for Kathleen. She is, after all, the wife of a notorious train robber, despite bein' a free settler, and may very well have concealed his ill-gotten gains. I merely point out the facts as they might see them.

He leaned forward.

– Look here, Robert: I'm sure you and Langford would easily find another deservin' young Irishwoman among the passholders at the Brickfields hirin' depot. Have you considered that?

– No, I said. I have a particular interest in Kathleen.

– Yes, he said, and nodded a number of times. Perhaps it's too particular: that's my concern.

So now things were out in the open. Meeting the enlarged green eyes – whose old geniality was now entirely absent, being replaced by a glassy hardness – I felt my heart jump. There's nothing so unpleasant as the appearance of direct antagonism in one who has always been well-disposed, and I straightened myself in my chair. Open strife, I knew, would be disastrous, since I was comparatively powerless, and held no cards except one. That card was so dangerous that to play it could bring disaster: and yet I knew that I'd do so, if given no alternative.

– My dear Howard, I said. What can you be suggesting?

– Come, Devereux, we've known each other long enough to be frank, he said.

He drew on his cigar, looking at me, his eyebrows raised in a parody of tolerance.

– You're saying –

– I'm sayin' that you're in love with her – or rather, that you lust after her. Your extraordinary behaviour tonight, in rushin' out to look for her with Langford, leaves me in little doubt of that. Well, it's a common enough phenomenon, in this colony: lustin' after convict servants.

He held up his hand, as though to prevent my interrupting; but I said nothing.

– I'm sorry to have to classify your feelin' as lust, rather than some more honourable sentiment. But I'm forced to that conclusion. It's not as though you're deprived of more suitable and more conventionally attractive female company. A good many eligible young ladies in society here would be only too happy to fall in love with you, as I've told you often enough. Instead, you wish to pursue a little peasant – and one who's borne an illegitimate child. Most people might find that rather puzzlin'. *I* don't find it so, of course – but I'm not typical. I do see it as folly – but I can also see why Kathleen would arouse passion, in a man given to fancies such as yours.

He bent to ash his cigar and then leaned back again, looking me full in the face. He smiled, with something of his old affection, and with a curious intimacy.

– She has the beauty of a dryad, he said. Don't you agree? But a true dryad, as dryads must have been in actual antiquity: not in the pretty drawin's made by old maids of either sex. A daughter of the earth and a mother as well, with all the earth's coarseness, as well as its beauty; with a body that smells of soil and vegetation; of sweat and of milk. One may lust after such a creature as she is, Devereux – but one may not be romantic about her. You should think about that.

For many moments I was quite unable to answer, while the smoke of my cigar went straight upwards, in the studio's still and secret air. My gaze went across to the open French windows, and the figures of Eros and Psyche; I saw Kathleen posed beside them, as naked as they were, while Howard grinned at her from his easel. How had he understood so much? Because, I thought, he was held in thrall by Kathleen just as I was; he saw her as I did, in his secret imagination, which uncannily resembled my own. The thought was intolerable, and I roused myself to speak.

– Let me answer you, Howard. I deny that what I feel for Kathleen is lust, and I resent the implication that I seek to take advantage of her. That I love her, I won't deny – but it isn't the sort of love you're speaking of. I see in her the soul of my people, and in her sufferings, the sufferings of my people. I seek to protect her from more suffering – and the sentiment I feel most strongly is compassion.

I saw Howard's brows go higher above his spectacles; and now, with deliberate recklessness, I played my card. I had little left to lose.

– You question whether the household that the Langfords and I will establish would be seen by the Convict Department as suitable for the employment of a female passholder. But would it be any less suitable than one where she's asked to be an artist's model, and to pose for her master naked?

Howard stared at me. Through the doorway, the call of the nameless native owl floated: two low notes, muffled and secret. I put my cigar to my lips, and attempted to draw on it. It had gone out, and Howard saw this. I put it in the ash tray. Finally, Howard said:

— Are you threatenin' me, Devereux?

— Of course not, I said. I respect you far too much, Howard, and am in no position to make threats. I merely compare our situations. Perhaps they are rather similar.

— Perhaps they are, he said, and sat back. Perhaps they are.

He stubbed out his cigar, and sat looking at it. Then he looked up at me again.

— Take her, he said briskly. You are clearly more infatuated with her beauty than I am, Robert. I suspect you'll regret it — but take her. As a passholder of the second class, she must write to the Comptroller-General for permission to seek another employer. I shall make the process smooth.

He stood up, brushing cigar ash from his waistcoat with the backs of both long hands.

— And now let us away to our beds, before we say worse than we've done.

He smiled at me, with a return of something like warmth. I could not but admire him for that.

PART THREE

BOEOTIA

I have learnt that there can be no remedy for love,
No special herb or ointment to soothe the heart
Except the Muses. It is light and quick, their drug,
And works for all, but it is very hard to find.

THEOCRITUS, 'The Cyclops', *from* The Idylls,
translated by Robert Wells

By that hidden way
My guide and I did enter, to return
To the fair world . . .

DANTE ALIGHIERI: 'Inferno', *Canto XXXIV,*
translated by Henry Cary

1. THE TIME OF GLARE

At 'Clare', in the Derwent Valley
January 28th, 1850

Evening: the end of my first day on the farm. Supper over, I write this in the room I've taken as my study. All my muscles ache from physical labour; but I'm filled with a novel contentment. It flows through my body and mind: a strange opiate, native to this countryside.

Let me describe our property – which I've named, with Langford's agreement, after my native county.

The valley of the Derwent at New Norfolk harbours myriad smaller valleys. Ours is one of these, encircled by bush-covered hills. To the west, these hills become tall and forbidding, leading to those regions of mountains and rain where the British have attempted no settlement. But the hills to the east of our valley are smaller and more domestic, with cultivated fields lying at their feet, and a dusty white road running between them. This road joins the highway that links Hobart Town with New Norfolk – the town five miles away which gives its name to this police district.

Most of our property, including the house, is on the western side of the road. The hop gardens are on the eastern side, on level land between the road and Sorell Creek. Beyond this little brook, a high, forest-clad hill rises like an olive-green bulwark.

Lombardy poplars have been planted along the road as a wind-break, and there are English willows along the creek. The bright, singing green of these immigrant trees is the green of Europe: a colour which is nowhere to be found in the native vegetation. Elms, oaks, pines and cedars were planted on the farm as well, when its first owner settled it twenty years ago; peach and apple and plum trees bear fruit in the kitchen garden. The farm might be in Tuscany or the Loire, if one ignores the looming hills.

Thirty of our fifty acres are still covered with bush. Fifteen more, on a hillslope on the western side, have been cleared as pasture land, and we paid Mr Harrison a little extra to purchase a small herd of cows that grazes there, as well as some farm equipment. It isn't very good equipment; but the house is a fine one, as colonial farmhouses go.

It stands on a low rise about thirty or forty yards from the road. Spacious and rambling, it has only one storey, and is constructed of rough orange bricks, no doubt made locally by convict labour. A driveway, lined on each side with young English oaks, runs uphill from the front gate, passing along the eastern side of the house and so entering the farmyard at the back. The steep, hipped roof is of silver-grey shingles cut from eucalypt, and its four brick chimneys have handsome corbelled tops. A good-sized sitting-room opens through French windows on to the front verandah, which has white-painted wooden columns in the Doric manner, giving to an otherwise rustic homestead a touch of formality. The verandah is enclosed at each end by a section of the house projecting beyond the main wall: the one on the eastern end contains my study, and the other, on the western side, is for Langford's use as an office. There's a large dining-room at the back, and the house has five bedrooms in all. I've had fine cedar furniture brought by wagon from Hobart Town, and a mahogany desk for my study, on which I write now.

If the front of the house is for formality, the back – looking on to the farmyard – is for rural simplicity and work. A central hallway links the two spheres. During the week, we eat in a small second dining-room adjacent to the kitchen: the territory presided over by Bess Langford. The windows here overlook the back verandah, along which run rough, green-painted posts of undressed cypress, like trees that have strayed inside.

There's a maid's room on this verandah's western corner, which has been assigned to Kathleen.

∾

Early this morning, as we walked down the drive to the hop gardens, Langford explained our exact situation to me. He and Bess and Kathleen moved here ten days ahead of me, and he seems already to have a grasp of everything.

The hops we inherited from Harrison had begun to blossom, he told me. The ripening process was proceeding, and he was watching very carefully over our crop. What we had to fear most was wind and rain: despite the fine, hot weather that January had brought in, Van Diemen's Land was notoriously changeable, and hops did not like wind. But our valley was well sheltered by its hills, and everything had been done for the plants that could be done. At the end of February, the harvest would begin. Dressings of manure – fortunately in good supply from our cows – had been applied in just the right proportions. But the ground must now be continually broken up between the rows of hops, to ventilate the soil and clear it of weeds. We had no horse-drawn harrow, and this work was being done with hoes, wielded by two passholding servants we'd inherited from Harrison: a farm overseer called William Richardson, and a general farmhand called Patrick O'Leary.

These men – both living in huts on the property – seemed good, reliable hands, Langford said. But they were all the male servants we had. We couldn't afford wages for more, he said, and soon we'd have to pay the pickers. So he did a good deal of the hoeing himself, as well as the more expert work of stripping the lower branches of the hop-bines to allow the air to circulate, and to encourage richer growth at their tops.

– Well then, James, I said, you'd better give me a hoe, as well.

He squinted at me in the sun, pushing back the broad-brimmed straw hat he now wore with his blue serge blouse and moleskin trousers. He'd grown the rusty moustache whose ghost had always been there: it reinforced his look of military authority.

– That's handsome of you, Robert, he said. But don't you want to be at your books? I told you there was no call for you to do farm work.

– My books can wait, I said. The hops clearly can't.

He grinned, opening the gate into the hop fields, and handed me the hoe he was carrying.

– Don't chop too deep, he said. At this time of year, we daren't damage the fibres of the hops, which are just below ground. They're mortal delicate.

We walked among the rows, which he surveyed with a frown, like a proud, anxious father. He pointed.

– We've got to get rid of them weeds, he said. Your hop is a gross feeder, and wants all the soil to itself. *Then* it can grow: up to six inches in twenty-four hours. You can almost see them bines moving.

And so it was, wearing the broad-brimmed, drab felt hat of a farmhand, and clad in a red cotton shirt, black neckerchief and moleskin trousers, that I began to wield a hoe. I worked in a row next to Langford's, and watched what he did: it didn't take long to grasp his method. The sun was now high, and the heat was very great; the sweat ran down my face as I hoed, and my muscles began to ache from the unaccustomed effort. For the first time in my life, I worked like a peasant; now I have painful blisters on my hands, making it difficult to use this pen.

Yet it was not unpleasant. I even began to enjoy the toil's unthinking rhythm, as the sweat soaked my neckerchief and shirt; I chopped with a will into the rich brown earth which was now our own, gouging out the enemy weeds. I began to test my body's strength, and to know a sort of happiness that was new to me: yet one which I'd truly foreseen, when I decided to become a colonial farmer. This indeed, I said, was the world that old Hesiod knew, where monotony and toil did not mean unhappiness, but contentment; where cities and kings and leaders and struggles for earthly power were all far away; where the bond between man and man is not based on blood or station, but on their common tie with the soil, and their common effort. This was how it was between myself and Langford.

This is our soil, I said: *mine and James Langford's*. And I brought down my hoe in a steady rhythm, tenderly careful of the underground hop fibres, exulting as the earth crumbled and broke up.

The hop glades, with their long, straight corridors of deep green

Kentish foliage, were deliciously cool. The bines of each hop plant were entwined about a pyramidal structure, some fifteen to twenty feet high, made from three thin poles of tea-tree, pitched to meet each other at an angle of some ten degrees. These pyramids stood on hillocks, in rows seven feet wide, over the whole five-acre garden. This gave us about twelve hundred plants to the acre, Langford said. The hop bines, after reaching a height of four feet, had been lovingly encouraged up the poles where necessary, and tied with rushes by Richardson and O'Leary. They had guided them by hand, turning them from the sun – and this, Langford told me, was the reverse direction of the turn employed in the northern hemisphere.

– The bloody world's upside down here, right enough, he said.

The bines had now reached the tops of their pyramids, and were close to the peak of their luxuriance, their pale-green blooms nodding in the faint, hot breeze. And here in the aisles between the dark green vegetable towers, hidden in coolness from the sun's vast glare, we were back in the climate and colour of our native hemisphere. Outside, through doorways in the foliage, the other hemisphere was glimpsed, in blazing fragments: the hemisphere of exile, whirring and throbbing. Seen so, from within these glades, it looked suddenly intolerable: bleached yellow bush grass, metallic eucalypts, and hills whose olive-drab undertone became like the colour of desolation. The throbbing was the voice of this land, conveying no messages that we could possibly decipher; and a pain went through my heart for the green of Clare, so that I almost cried out. But I went on swinging my hoe, and the moment passed.

We paused to rest, Langford and I, and shared a bottle of water. I could smell his sweat, which had darkened the under-arms of his blouse as mine had done. I plucked one of the heart-shaped leaves and put it to my nose, inhaling the sharp, quick, beer-like odour.

– So what do you predict? I asked him. Will the harvest be good, James?

– Well now, it might just do, he said, and narrowed his eyes. But it won't be all that it could be, Robert. I suspect that our Mr Harrison stinted on the food for his plants – and you can't do that with hops. But I'll do my best by them, and we must hope. We'll know in a month's time. Next year will be another thing. I'm going to put in irrigation. That creek's got enough flow for it.

His eyes shone; he paused, looking towards the creek, and I saw him dream, my reformed bandit. I admired his optimism more and more: his resourcefulness seemed limitless. To apply his Kentish knowledge of hop cultivation to the Antipodes, with its upside down cycle of the seasons, he'd read articles on the subject in local periodicals which Harrison had left behind, and had sought out other growers in New Norfolk, charming them into sharing their hard-won knowledge.

– But Harrison hasn't irrigated, I said. He claimed the climate of this valley was perfect without it, and that his hops didn't need irrigation.

– Wrong, Langford said. That's why he never done as well as he could have. We don't irrigate at home in Kent because the soil's moist enough. But here in New Norfolk the soil's very dry. I've just begun to twig that there's not enough rain in this main part of the island: the Westerlies drop it all on the west coast, in the flaming wilderness. There's a hop-grower started on the Derwent who's irrigating: pumping water up from the river. And his hops are bloody marvellous, I'm told – better than the English. Harrison wasn't lying about this valley – it's more sheltered than on the Derwent, and it does get more moisture. So you *can* grow hops without irrigating – but only just. The soil still needs more water, Robert. When I bring it in, we'll have the best hops of the lot.

– It will cost money, James.

– We'll make the money, he said. Then I'll get a steam pump.

I laughed; but somehow I didn't doubt him. There seemed to be nothing he couldn't do, and I have no doubt at all that our farm will succeed.

February 2nd
Two-thirty in the afternoon. At my desk: a place where I'm not often found these days. Not needed in the fields just at present, I decided to return to my translation of Aeschylus; but my attention has soon wandered.

My desk is placed next to the open window, which looks out on to the drive. I finger my newly-grown moustache; unlike Langford's, it looks sinister rather than martial. Scents of hollyhocks and roses float in to distract me, and a scattering of pollen lies on the desk's polished surface, next to my books. Richardson just passed with a horse-drawn cart, going from the farmyard down to the hop-gardens; I had an impulse to get up and follow him.

Boeotia has claimed me. My hands grow too clumsy for pen and paper, and their cracked, dirt-engrained roughness, which no amount of washing will now smooth, seems to sully the polished wood of the desk top. They are like foreign objects, lying here in front of me: they belong to someone else. Yet I'm foolishly pleased with them, as I am with the new-found muscles in my calves and forearms. My body not only submits to daily physical labour, but has grown to welcome it, as a well-loved horse welcomes the harness and bridle.

I've come to need this labour and its rhythms, as I need food and drink. To sit here in this study during the hours of daylight has grown unnatural to me. I'm summoned outside by the hot, dry acres of the soil to which Langford and I have pledged ourselves; by the bright green glades of the hops; by the chattering of the creek, and by the tall, olive hills that ring our valley in, making a soundless humming.

I laid down my pen a moment ago. Kathleen had passed my window.

She came walking down the drive towards the gate, carrying a basket covered with a white cloth: bread and cheese and bottles of beer for Langford and the farm hands. She was dressed much as I saw her in the first sketch that Doctor Howard made. On her head, the white linen cap with its wide frill in front, like the upturned brim of a hat, framing her small-chinned face: her long, thick, copper-brown hair streaming down her back, the sun putting russet lights in it. The close-fitting, hip-length jacket-bodice, buttoned down the front, emphasised the narrowness of her waist. It's a garment I find curiously charming: there's something medieval about it, and I never tire of seeing her in it. Its flat, spreading collar left her thin neck exposed, and the loose, full sleeves were rolled back to bare her arms to the elbows. She went barefoot, and her narrow white feet appeared in quick rhythm from under the hem of her skirt. The Langfords have warned her about the deadly snakes here, but she likes to discard her shoes whenever she can, as she no doubt did in Limerick.

Level with the window, and a little below me, she looked up sideways and smiled. The sky-blue eyes with their Celtic slant looked long into mine, her head turning a little as she passed, in order to hold my gaze. But she didn't pause; she went on down the drive, looking to the front again, bent a little to one side from the weight of the basket, her small figure moving with a slightly rocking gait.

For many moments after she'd gone I sat fixed here at my desk, both hands spread on its surface, continuing to smile, my pulses racing. No doubt I looked rather foolish.

Two-thirty, then, in this time of drumming heat – which has now reached eighty-five degrees. The strange, still, breathless time of pause, when the sun of Antipodean February seeps and probes into every crevice, and even birds and insects are struck silent. The time of glare, when day is at its height; when the long descent towards evening's mystery has yet to begin. Everything outside seems to wait; and I wait too. The pause has an eternal quality: at its heart, a terrible emptiness. It drones; it promises everything and nothing. Here in the Antipodes, one waits on events that will never come, since history takes place elsewhere. Far; so very far!

I wait; and I'm held in the arms of an extraordinary happiness. But is happiness the right word?

Perhaps not; my present feelings have none of the calm associated with that word. *Joy* might be a truer term: a joy whose source is a frantic, consuming restlessness. Boeotia! Antipodean pastoral! The earth-rhythms that Hesiod and Virgil knew sound sweetly in my head, here in this island in the world's utmost South, filling me with an impulse to invoke the gods of plenty – or whatever strange deities are lurking in these hills of bush.

Ye deities, who fields and plains protect,
Who rule the seasons, and the year direct,
Bacchus and fostering Ceres, powers divine,
Who gave us corn for mast, for water, wine;
Ye Fauns, propitious to the rural swains,
Ye nymphs, that haunt the mountains and the plains,
Join in my work, and to my numbers bring
Your needful succour; for your gifts I sing.

Beside me on the desk lies the Virgil translated by John Dryden that I bought from Monsieur Lenoir, and which survived my evening in Black Lion Square: now I read and re-read Dryden's masterly rendering of the *Georgics*. Monsieur Lenoir is adding steadily to the library that now lines a wall of this room, its pine shelves built for me by the able William Richardson. My latest purchase from the book-shop on Hobart Town's Acheron is a volume containing the source of all pastoral: the *Idylls* of the divine Theocritus. I've begun to translate the *Idylls*, and my brain is filled with the sighing of little pines and drilling of cicadas on the dry-grassed hills of Sicily – which these dry-grassed slopes of Van Diemen's Land, with their eucalypts and weeping casuarinas, must very closely resemble.

Neville Howard was right: it's possible to persuade oneself here that one has re-entered the world of rustic antiquity. I grow obsessed with the bucolic, here at 'Clare'; I yearn to discover a southern Mount Helicon, and there to meet the Muses of the Antipodes, and learn their songs. Everywhere about me I see shadows of the vales of Attica, and the woods of the Peloponnese: the territories of Artemis. Here in the valley of the Derwent, I croon the songs of Dorian herdsmen. And working in the fields of noon, or wandering the hillslopes of evening, I glimpse the figure of that Nereid who was 'whiter than goat's cheese, and firmer than a ripening grape'. She wears a linen cap, and a serge jacket-bodice; she carries a brimming bucket from the well in the farmyard, the upper part of her body bent to one side, her head bowed. She looks up briefly and smiles, and my heart falters, and I whisper the lament of Theocritus: '*There can be no cure for love!*'

༄

Kathleen!

Simply to write her name (this name that's carried by so many thousands of women of the people), is both sweet and hopelessly tantalising, since the Kathleen whom I see every day – in the kitchen, in the farmyard, in the hop glades – is as far from me as the lovely Galatea ever was from the sad Cyclops; as remote as any altar-girl in the grove of Artemis.

This state of longing for a convict servant girl is one that can only seem unworthy – even ridiculous – in the eyes of others; even those of my friends. Every day, I'm swung between frustration and joy: that joy whose accompaniment is a restless and frantic unease. That, of course, has always been the state of those whose love is unrequited. But in fact, this is not my situation. My Nereid is not indifferent; she'd probably not deny me. Instead, I've decided to deny her to myself.

It was Thomas O'Neill who brought me to this decision. He was ideally suited to the task. When we're bent on folly, the opinion of an enemy or a scoffer may harden our resolve to press forward; but that of a concerned and loving friend is less easy to ignore. So on the night before leaving Bothwell for New Norfolk, I decided to tell him of my feelings and intentions.

He sat in silence, pipe in one hand, the other scratching the ear of the hound that lay by his chair. When I'd done, he asked:

– And you are truly in love with her, Robert?

– I'm in love with her, I said.

I saw him blink, and felt somehow proud and relieved. I had wanted to make this declaration.

He put his pipe down on the sea-chest; then he sat back, lacing his fingers together over his waistcoat.

– You're in love, he said flatly. With a peasant girl. A convict. Do you really speak seriously?

– Yes, I do. And yes, she is one of the people: the people we struggle for, O'Neill. Do you despise them? Have we not said that from the genius of the Irish people, we will build a new nation? Kathleen embodies for me the spirit and soul of the people. And she is far lovelier, and far closer to my heart, than that young lady whom you know of, who discarded me at the behest of her God-damned parents, when my struggle had me branded as a felon. Like so many of our friends of good birth, she had no stomach for that struggle, when the blows began to fall. Well, I don't complain of that; I know her limitations, and those of so many like her. But now that I intend to be a farmer in Van Diemen's Land, why should I not love Kathleen, and all that she is?

O'Neill was shaking his head, staring at me.

– You have been a very long time without female company, he said softly. And you are the kind of man who needs a woman's love. I understand. But this is a sort of madness.

Seeing my expression, he leaned forward and touched my shoulder.

– Don't be angry with me, my dear. I *don't* despise the people – I care for them as much as you do, or I would not be sitting here: a guest of Sir William Denison. But you forget the vast gap that society and fate have placed between you and this young woman. I'm partly thinking of *her* welfare, do you see. I take it that you don't intend simply to enjoy her body – as so many of the colonists here do with their female passholders? As her former master did? As Doctor Howard, according to you, might well have done?

I sat confounded. No, I said, I had no such plan. But even as I spoke, I knew that this was not quite true. Whatever my intentions had been concerning Kathleen – and I had kept them pleasantly vague – they bore a disturbing resemblance to just what O'Neill had described, if looked at too closely. The fact was that I had deliberately refrained from thinking about them in any concrete way at all. I suppose I had seen her (in some of my fancies), as a semi-mythical being, whom I would make love to outside space and time. In other fancies, with more honesty, I had seen her as my loved and respected mistress, and co-mistress of the farm, together with Bess Langford – so long as I remained in Van Diemen's Land. But I had not seen her as my wife.

As though reading my thoughts, O'Neill asked bluntly:

– There's only one question that matters. Do you intend to marry her?

– No, I said slowly. I hadn't thought of that.

O'Neill nodded slowly: a habit of his. He re-lit his pipe, which had gone out.

– Well, then, he said, if you don't, you must treat her honourably, must you not? So – forgive me, Devereux – your love for her must remain a charitable love. Love for an unfortunate young Irishwoman given into your care – and nothing more. But be careful of compassion: you may make it into a mask for something else.

My silence was the silence of defeat. Finally, I laughed under my breath, and shook my head.

O'Neill puffed sedately on his pipe, smiling at me fondly.

After my arrival at the farm from Bothwell, two days went by before I found an opportunity to speak with Kathleen.

It was close to four o'clock in the afternoon; I'd come up from the fields, and was sitting here in the study. I'd completed a number of letters to supporters in America; now I sat musing over an article I'm writing, for submission to an Irish newspaper in New York. I'd ceased to be conscious of the sounds of the farm outside; when I compose, I hear little of what goes on around me. So it was some time before I became conscious of a knocking on one of my study doors.

The study, as I've described, is in one of those sections of the house which extend to enclose the front verandah; so in addition to a door that leads into my bedroom, in the house's interior, there is another, in the same wall, that opens on to the verandah. That was where the knocking came from; assuming that it was Langford, I called to him to come in.

Instead, it was Kathleen who appeared, carrying a tray with a coffee pot, cup and milk-jug. There was a new lightness and happiness about her, expressed in the trusting, open way her glance rested on me. Even her printed cotton dress, of pale green and white, seemed new and fresh, like a morning leaf. I rose, facing her as she crossed the room.

– Mrs Langford was thinking you'd like some coffee, sir, she said.

She set the tray down on a vacant space on the desk; then she straightened, her hands folded over her apron.

– Do sit down, sir, she said. You should not be standing.

– I'm glad to stand, I said. I've been sitting too long at this desk.

– You have, sure, she said. I have seen you there through the window. You are thinking, and see nothing. You sit winding your hair around your finger, so.

And she raised her right index finger to her hair, and imitated my action.

I stared at her, somewhat startled by the intimacy of these observations. But what had I expected? How could we two continue to remain within the limits that separate servant from master? When last we'd been together, hadn't I held her in my arms, and felt her breath on my neck? And yet so little had been said to acknowledge intimacy, or to make it possible; we scarcely knew each other.

– It's a habit I've had since boyhood, I said. My sister Margaret used to say I was 'twirling the lock'.

I had picked up the coffee pot, intending to pour; I held it suspended as I spoke. She tilted back her head to meet my gaze, her eyes glinting with amusement.

– 'Twirling the lock', so you are, she said. And so far away in your thoughts that you see nothing. Do you think about Ireland, then? And is it Ireland that you write about?

– Mostly it is, I said. Even this far away, there is much that can be done for our country through words.

– Through *your* words, yes, she said. You are the one whose words the English fear – I know that.

Her light, dazzling eyes, holding mine, had the look of someone in a trance. But then, as though with an effort of will, she took her gaze away, surveying the books that filled the wall beyond the desk.

– Jesus, so many books, she said.

I laughed, pouring my coffee. Then I asked:

– Can you read, Kathleen?

She turned back to frown at me.

– Of course I can read. I went to a school in Adare, until I was twelve. The master was a stupid old man, and beat the boys a lot with his great bush of hazel – but we learned our reading and writing, and mathematics. I am not so ignorant as you may think.

– I have never thought you ignorant. I must lend you one of my essays to read – would you be interested?

– I'd be honoured to read it, sir – but would I understand it?

– I'm sure you'd understand anything you wished to, Kathleen.

A silence fell, in which we continued to look at each other. I saw that she was nervous, but it was not a painful nervousness: a smile played all the time about her mouth. It was time for her to go, but she did not. I should have picked up my coffee cup to signal this; but I did not. Bird calls and the lowing of cows outside became suddenly distinct, and I heard myself ask:

– Are you glad to be here, Kathleen?

– Glad? I am very glad, she said. And much more. You have saved me from all that's bad. And Mr and Mrs Langford are so kind to me.

She coughed briefly, putting her hand to her mouth; then she looked up at me again, and her expression was fervent.

– It's you I've to thank. I pray for you every night, and yours is the last face I see before I sleep.

I took her by the shoulders; her face turned up to mine expectantly; but I kissed her only on the cheek.

– Your face too is the last I see at night, I said, and you know how beautiful you are to me. But that is the last time I'll kiss you.

She frowned, and her eyes searched mine. Under that stare, the phrases I thought of were pompous or worse. Finally I said:

– I will not behave to you as your previous master did. I have sworn that to myself.

– You could never do that, sir.

– But should I make love to you, I said, I would be misusing you just as he did. I won't allow myself to do that – I care for you too much. My whole wish is to protect you. Do you see?

Still she frowned in puzzlement, searching my face, her eyes narrowed as though against strong light. When she answered, it was barely above a whisper.

– Yes. I see. But you need not have spoken so. I know that you would never hurt me. There is nothing you could ever do to me that would hurt me.

Before I could answer, she had turned, and had hurried from the room by the door that led to the verandah.

I stood by the window, holding my coffee untasted, gazing between the oak trees down the drive to a distant corner of the hop-garden. In that moment, instead of feeling virtuous, I detested both myself and Thomas O'Neill.

March 3rd

We are bringing in the harvest.

The hop-smell fills our days, and I see I've neglected this diary for some time. I write this after twelve hours of labour: weary but fulfilled.

Hops! When I lie in bed in the dark they dance before my eyes – scaly, evanescent cones, light and insubstantial as paper, pale green-gold against the sky's hard blue. There is something almost magical about them, like fruits from a land of Faery. They make a papery, rustling sound when touched, and their bracts are sticky with the yellowish substance called lupulin – whose bitter, aromatic resins are so highly valued for brewing, as well as for nostrums and opiates. The sharp, weird reek, resembling no other I've known, hangs everywhere in the valley's drowsy air; it permeates all our waking hours, and my sleep at night. This is the hop-smell, inducer of dreams and intoxication, which for Langford is the smell of money.

He now commands an army of pickers: forty-odd men and women we recruited in New Norfolk. Most of them are Ticket-of-Leave; some are free settlers of a vagabond type. They are a gypsy-like tribe, moving from district to district to pick whatever crop is in season. Some come on foot, some in crazy wagons drawn by long-suffering horses. Their children come with them, the older ones working beside them, the infants wailing in improvised box-cradles under the hop leaves. On the hillslope on the western side of the farmyard, just below the cow pasture, there are four long slab huts, without separate rooms and without fireplaces, their only furnishings a few rough-hewn tables and benches, with wide shelves set around the walls for sleeping-berths. These are the pickers' huts, left empty until they come again each year. They have all crammed into them, God knows how, and make no complaint. They must carry water up the hill from our well, and at night they cook their food on fires lit outside, among the rocks on the hillslope. From the farmyard, looking up, I see their troll-like figures in silhouette, moving in front of the flames. Later, their voices will be heard singing – the London street ballads echoing off these steep black hills with a brave, poignant jauntiness. Ah, they are so far from home! Yet the pickers are a tribe who seem to laugh, joke and sing continually, despite their hard life. They do so even as they pick; but their fingers seldom pause.

I go down to the gardens each day, to help where I can.

The glades now look as though a great wind has blown through them: scores of the tea-tree towers lie fallen. At intervals, armed with long, iron-hooked poles called 'dogs', Langford, Richardson and O'Leary cut the bines, and pull more of the hop-poles to the ground. These are then laid over wood-framed hessian bins, for the pickers to strip the hops. The exposed alleyways bake in the still, dry heat, and dance with foreign colours: bright print dresses and aprons and bonnets; gaudy neckerchiefs and many-hued shirts. Mothers and grandmothers work beside little girls of nine or so; women predominate, since it's the fingers of the women that move most nimbly. They slap at stinging March flies, and their brown arms, if they bare them, are marked with bites, and with weals from the stinging bines. The pickers work at great speed, the papery hops showering gold into the bins, and from time to time they plunge their arms in to the bottom, to clean out leaves and stalks. They work in 'sets', and are supervised by Paddy O'Leary – a short, cheerful man from Wexford, with tangled brown curls – and by Richardson the overseer: lean and morose in a green peaked cap, his pole held in his hand like a badge of office. As 'pole-pullers', these two have great authority over the pickers – the ultimate commander being Langford.

– Clean picking, Langford says to me. We've got to have clean picking – so we have to watch them constant. Some of these buggers leave too many leaves in the bins, to get the weight up. The crafty ones even drop stones in.

His narrowed eyes move everywhere, as we walk down the aisles together. It's rather like walking through a fair, in the once-quiet glades. Festive, chattering voices – most of them from London's East End – sound among the leaves; invisible women give sudden shrieks of laughter, like wild birds; some sing snatches of their street ballads. Names are called from glade to glade; jokes are made using the London thieves' cant which is a mystery to me, but which Langford understands, and chuckles at. Hilarity is always in the air, like the reek of the hop cones. Yet at bottom, this is a serious business. From under straw bonnets and the peaks of cloth caps, many eyes follow Langford, commander of the garden. It's he who measures the bins when they're full, to record the tallies. At these times, accompanied by his pole-pullers, he carries a measure and a notebook with him; he leans over each full bin, ramming the hops into the measure, and enters the tally in his book. When he finds a dirty bin, he reprimands the pickers; sometimes there are sullen mutterings, but his level, tiger gaze soon quells them.

Meanwhile, a big, four-wheeled spring wagon, drawn by two aged draught horses, comes and goes at intervals between the gardens and the farmyard on the other side of the road, laden with hops for the kiln. Once picked, they must go there very quickly for drying, Langford tells me; if left too long, they'll sweat and be spoiled. He gnaws his new moustache; he has so many hazards to guard against if our crop is to go safe down the river to Hobart Town and fetch its price. Watching him, I feel like a boy without responsibilities, trusting to a resourceful father to guard against all misfortune.

The wagon is managed by one of the farm-hands whom Langford has hired for the season: Luke, an amiable young man from New Norfolk, who loads it with the bags of hops he calls 'pokes'. We need more help up at the kiln, Langford says; so I offer my labour, and ride on the wagon with Luke.

We lumber into the farmyard which lies at the back of the house. An ash tree, out in pale green leaf, stands in the centre; the well is just beside it. Hens scratch about, in the warm dust. Behind the tree are weatherboard stables, and on the western side of the yard stands a building like a medieval tower. This is the hop kiln.

Langford, using the Kentish term, refers to it as the oast-house. It's connected to a long, two-storeyed storage building, and its tower is of the same ochre brick as the house, rising to a height of some thirty-five feet. Six-sided, with a grey-shingled hexagonal spire, strange in this countryside as a building in a dream, the tower has only a few small windows: high up under the spire, and at ground level. The spire is topped by a miniature structure which repeats the form of the main steeple: a six-sided turret whose own spire is completed by a weather-cock, its walls consisting of wooden louvres. This, Langford has told me, is the cowl, which lets out steam and sulphurous vapours when the hops are being dried. Dusky brick tunnels enter the tower at ground level: fire-holes, letting in air to cool the furnace-room.

Luke and I are met by two more hired hands. They are lifting the bags into the storage building – hoisting them up on a block and tackle, whose beam projects from a little wooden balcony in the upper storey. It becomes my job to help to receive them there, in a passageway that runs the length of the building, and to carry them into a storeroom – where they wait to be taken to the drying-room in the tower.

In this circular brick chamber, the heat is intense, and the sweet-sour hop-smell overpowering. The floor, supported by joists, consists of wooden slats, across which haircloth has been stretched, and a golden carpet of hops covers it to the depth of about a foot, tended by a serious, barefoot old man wielding a medieval wooden rake. The heat comes up from the furnace-room, fifteen feet below. A door leads into a cooling-room, where the hops are shovelled when they're dried.

I find the cooling-room a curiously attractive place. Silent, without windows, its only furnishing a black iron press, its dry air dim and secret, it seems in my fancy like a chamber in some pagan temple. Sometimes, when it's deserted, I go in there and linger among our harvest. A place to meditate, where the resinous aroma is like incense.

Langford comes up to the kiln from the fields many times throughout the day; and I can understand this. The kiln is the heart of our enterprise: so many things could undo us here, and he can't trust the hands to watch it unsupervised. The hops must not be over-heated, or else they'll be scorched, and their flavour ruined; while under-drying could make them sweat in their bags, and so become useless to the brewer. He lies awake at night, I believe, worrying about such things; and so, I suppose, should I, since I'm his partner. Yet I don't; I have such confidence in his abilities that I'm perfectly relaxed, and happy to work as a simple labourer.

Perhaps I become too rustic altogether, here in Van Diemen's Land; perhaps my mind sleeps, while my body thrives. As I swing the bags through the doorway from the balcony, and carry them along to the storeroom, I wonder what my followers in Dublin and New York would make of me now. Yet something in me welcomes this incarnation, and tells me it's right – at least, for the present.

And as always, when I affirm this to myself, I whisper a name, and see in front of me a pale, delicate face whose cheekbones are high and rounded, and whose mouth now fills me with empty longing. Standing by the block and tackle, looking down on the sunlit farmyard below, I catch sight of her moving from the well to the kitchen, carrying her bucket of water. Bent slightly to one side, she moves with that faintly rocking gait which causes me to smile, and which also catches at my heart.

I bite my lip, and turn back to my bags of hops.

March 25th

Everything has changed. Yesterday, Sunday, I was freed into the world of joy. I am trembling as I write this.

These confessional notebooks of mine are unlikely ever to be read by anybody – let alone to be published. And so, since they will not invade the sanctity of those middle-class English homes where Evangelical sensibilities shrink back at the mere suggestion of the sensual, I intend to set down all that took place, with nothing held back.

On Sundays, like good citizens, we all go to church in New Norfolk. The authorities expect landed proprietors to ensure that convict servants attend church, and we comply. Richardson drives Paddy O'Leary and Kathleen into town in the spring wagon; I go on horseback, while the Langfords take our new gig.

The Langfords, Richardson and I attend the Anglican service at St Matthew's, a handsome little church in the centre of the township, while Kathleen and Paddy O'Leary go to Mass at a tiny Catholic church called St Peter's. I don't believe the Langfords are particularly religious, but James sees social and even commercial advantages in becoming a member of the congregation here, and is already on good terms with a number of leading farmers as a result. When we come back to 'Clare', the servants have their day off. The Langfords and I eat a lunch of cold meats; then James and Bess retire for an afternoon sleep.

Yesterday at this time, I read for perhaps half an hour in my study; then I grew oddly restless. I had a new batch of newspapers from London and Dublin, ordered through Monsieur Lenoir; but I tired of the one I was trying to read, and threw it aside. I decided to go out for a walk.

Three in the afternoon, and the farm slept. I set off down the drive, crossed the road, and went along the edge of the hop fields. I was going towards the creek, lured by the thought of its coolness. I was not in my usual rough bush dress: to attend the church service, I had put on a white cambric shirt, frock coat and nankeen trousers. For my walk, I discarded the frock coat and went in my waistcoat and low-crowned felt hat. March is a milder month than February, and the warmth wasn't extreme; but there was a curious closeness and breathlessness which made me perspire. The land lay in sullen stillness under a white, cloud-masked sky, and I longed for the coolness of the hop glades.

But alas, the hop glades were gone. The fields were empty and devastated, like the theatre of some recent battle. The picking had ended: our harvest lay in sacks up at the kiln, ready to go down to Hobart Town by barge, and the hop poles stood stacked upright like skeletal tents, waiting for use next season. This woke melancholy in me, and the tedious complaints of the crows sounded like some dirge for the dead. I walked through white glare across the dry brown earth, slapping at the March flies we have all come to hate, and making for the line of willows. Their pale northern green had consoled me until now for the loss of the hop glades; but today they looked wan. Reality, with the hop garden gone, was that tall, bush-covered hill that rose steeply in the east beyond the creek, and whose sombre, olive-green wall seemed now to loom much closer, adding to my sense of oppression. I tore off my neckerchief, and opened the collar of my shirt.

Once inside the line of willows I breathed easier. I was in a little tunnel of coolness, where Sorell Creek ran bubbling and chattering over its round grey stones. Its water glinted silver where the sun came through branches overhead; then, in the shadow of the banks, it ran green and profound. A little further upstream there was a miniature waterfall, over which hung one of the weeping native casuarinas called she-oaks, with long, grey-green fronds and blackish bark. Special, water-sharp odours rose around me: damp earth, and rotting willow leaves.

I sat down on a flat, warm stone and lost myself. How I love all streams and rivers! And the streams and rivers here are very like those of home. Of little else in this alien land can that be said: even the leaves on the trees make a different sound in the wind – being too metallic to sigh, as beech or sycamore or elm will sigh. Ah, lovely, lovely Ireland! Ah, Europe, and the trees of Europe! Homesickness gripped me, like a vivid flash of pain. Sitting by this creek, staring at the water, I could imagine it one of the streams of Clare; but the fact remained that I was *here*, in this half-wild countryside in the valley of the Antipodean Derwent.

There was a stillness over the whole valley now which began to seem unnatural. I was conscious occasionally of flies buzzing, and of the far-off barking of a dog; otherwise, the hush was absolute. Even the birds had been silenced. How long I sat there, I don't know; but eventually I became conscious that I was no longer solitary. Looking upstream to my right, I saw her almost instantly.

She was standing some eight yards off, by the little waterfall, in the shadow of the she-oak. The stillness of the day seemed to have imposed itself on her; she made no move when I saw her, but merely looked at me. But it was useless to speak at this distance, since the bubble and rush of the creek would have drowned our words. She wore a peaked, close-fitting straw hat, trimmed with a dark green ribbon, its brim entirely enclosing her face, as a bonnet's might do. The way in which she looked out from this frame I found utterly charming. Her cotton gown was of a faded lilac, prettified for Sunday with an embroidered white collar, and a brooch that had been given her by Bess Langford. She was holding a bunch of wildflowers. I gazed at her as one gazes at a picture; then I recalled myself, and stood up.

As I approached her, I took off my hat, and greeted her. She smiled; but the smile was fleeting and uncertain.

– I hope I don't disturb you, she said. I have been walking, and picking these.

She held up the wild flowers, whose pale pink petals were so tiny as barely to be flowers at all; but I told her they were pretty. Did she know their names, these flowers of Van Diemen's Land?

– I do not know many, she said. But one of the women among the pickers told me the name of this one: they call it Dolly Bush.

– They are very small, the wildflowers here, I said. And they seem to have little scent.

– But they are still pretty, she said. They hide, as violets do – you have to look carefully for them. I have come to like them.

– You are learning more about this land than I am, Kathleen. Do you not grow homesick, as I do?

– I do not; not now. I am happy on this farm – and what have I to miss?

– I understand you, I said. But Ireland is still our home; the place whose hills and streams nurtured our spirits from childhood. Our motherland.

– All that is poetry, she said. But poetry is for the quality, like yourself – and a cruel mother Ireland was to me. I'm thinking sometimes that I may find more kindness here, in this wild place, where we are told that humble folk may begin again.

She looked suddenly anxious.

– I do not mean to be rude, Mr Devereux. And I know how

you dream of home. I think you were doing so as you sat on the stone over there. But I think you are sometimes content on this farm, are you not? When I saw you hoeing in the fields like a farmhand, it was a strange and wonderful thing. It gave you joy, I'm thinking, and it made you look well and handsome. And James Langford says the crop is good, and should fetch a good price. Are you not pleased with that, now?

I laughed. Her remarks made it difficult for me to maintain my resolve that we conduct ourselves strictly as servant and master. Somehow, here by the creek, it seemed natural that she should talk in this manner, and I had no wish to discourage her. Meanwhile, I was conscious of the vast, oppressive hush that seemed increasingly to smother the world, broken only by the creek's ceaseless bubbling. The sky pressed down over us like a lid, its white tinged with a strange, dirty yellow; it had now subdued all the small noises of life that the land usually harboured, and seemed to be preparing us for some vast, unknowable change. Yet our words were not muffled; they fell on the air with great distinctness, like words on the frontiers of sleep.

– Yes, I said, you are right. I am pleased with the farm altogether – and we owe its success to James Langford. I have much to be thankful for; I know it. But I am still a prisoner as you are – landowner though I am. My true life is elsewhere. This farm is the future for Mr and Mrs Langford – but not for me. Some day, I must escape this island.

She looked back at me for a moment without answering, revolving the bunch of wildflowers in her hands. Then she spoke, in a low, earnest voice.

– Do not go.

I stared at her, uncertain that I had heard correctly.

– Don't go? Why do you say that, Kathleen?

– You know why, sir. It would make me very sad.

My pulses quickened. The density of the heat seemed to have increased: I saw a dew of perspiration on Kathleen's upper lip, and felt my own face perspire. At that moment, as I searched for a reply, I became conscious of a sound in the air.

It was a kind of huge rushing, not far off, and I could find no way to account for it, since the air remained still. I turned to look back across the hop fields for its source: to the line of poplars, to the white road, to our grey-roofed house on its rise, and to the mottled hills beyond. And then I noticed a strange phenomenon: on the top of a nearby hill to the north, the green-black tops of the trees were in violent, tormented struggle, lashing to and fro – though no wind appeared to stir them lower down, and no wind blew here in the valley. I found also that the sky was turning from yellow to a weird, coppery brown. Then it changed to a sombre shade that was like no colour at all, and which grew darker as I watched.

Light was vanishing from the air; I turned back to Kathleen, and saw as I did so that the grasses and ferns at our feet were beginning to stir – as were the willows behind us, and the trees across the creek. I was about to remark on this to Kathleen – whose expression had grown uneasy, and who began to look about her – when the rushing grew in volume. It approached from the north, from the direction of New Norfolk. It became a roaring blast, and entered the valley.

Within instants, we were clinging to each other, striving to keep our feet, hats in our hands, hair whipping our faces, engulfed by a phenomenon new in my experience, and which I can only describe as a hurricane – despite the fact that hurricanes are not supposed to occur in this far southern zone. That knowledge made it all the more alarming; even supernatural. It brought with it from the north a vast cloud of dust; and it burned. It was hot as the vapour from a furnace, and now engulfed the world. It bent the willows double, and tore up a young eucalypt that stood near us, flinging it through the air. Whole big branches whirled past, ripped from the trees. Then I saw little more, since most of the light of day was obscured by the dust, as though by a dense London fog. We were lost in a fiery, copper-brown infinity which rushed and whistled and roared; in which only nearby shapes could be discerned. It was as though we were experiencing the end of all natural order. My arm was tightly about Kathleen's waist; she clung to me, and I could see through the coppery veil that her white, vague face looked up at me in horrified appeal. Perhaps she spoke; but I heard nothing.

I pointed across the fields in the direction of the farm. Still gripping her waist, I began to lead her away along a furrow, crossing the hop field.

As we went forward, bent in a crouching position, our right sides received the battering of the gale, and we were forced to lean sideways against it. I put Kathleen on my left, and shielded her as best I could; sometimes we almost lost our footing, but we continued very slowly to advance. The wind made new and fearsome noises now, booming and whistling – and once, I heard the ghostly neighing of horses. We reached the road, where the poplars were bending almost to the ground, crossed to the open gate of the farm, and struggled up the drive. Even the dignified oak trees here were swaying and bowing: forced to abase themselves before this outrageous, barbaric force. The house, as we passed it, was a mere phantom shape: all its windows shut; no sign of life. Nor was there anyone in the farmyard at the back.

I should now have taken Kathleen along the verandah, and so to the shelter of her room – afterwards seeking my own. Instead (my arm still about her waist, as hers was about mine), I trudged on through the roaring air as though through the universe of a nightmare, leaving the verandah behind. I was making across the yard towards the hop kiln, whose steeple rose in eerie silhouette through the copper-grey veil. Why did I do so? I have asked myself this a number of times. I weighed up no consequences in that moment: I simply intended that we should take shelter together, while the hot wind persisted. I wanted to continue to protect her; and I was not prepared to leave her in that small housemaid's room – where she would be physically safe, no doubt, but isolated and fearful.

The blast was as strong as ever, and there was no possibility of discussion. Seeing the direction in which I was moving, Kathleen looked up at me in enquiry; but she made no attempt to resist. Instead, her fingers tightened about my waist. I had an errand to perform, on the way: I was concerned about the safety of our horses.

I wanted to see that they were secure, in their stables behind the ash tree. I found the doors shut and barred – and a muffled stamping and whinnying assured me that they were safe inside. I should have known that James would make sure of that. So now we went on towards the kiln, and came to the foot of the tower. Taking Kathleen's hand, I guided her through the door into the furnace-room.

In an instant, the roar of the gale was diminished; our bodies were no longer buffeted, and the motionless, sweet-sour air of the kiln closed around us like the air of a tomb. But I didn't pause. Still holding her hand, I led her on up the steep wooden stairs to the drying-room.

Emerging into its blind, circular brick chamber, we halted at last. The place was in semi-darkness, and we could only just see each other's faces. We were trembling, our chests heaving from our exertions, and our panting filled the silent air; we slapped at our clothing, which was filmed with the fine red dust. The hops were all gone, though their odour was everywhere; all that remained were a few scattered cones, lying on the haircloth floor. The booming and whistling of the dust-storm could still be heard, but very much muffled by the tower's brick walls: our castle was proof against the enemy. And although the air in here was close, it was surprisingly temperate: the only furnace now was the one that roared outside.

– Come, I said.

I took her hand again, to lead her through the door into the cooling-room.

The devotional quiet of this dim, windowless, wooden-walled chamber was what I'd been struggling to reach; here, we were utterly shut away. In the darkness that had fallen on the world, the cooling-room seemed more than ever like the inner sanctum of some ancient religion: one that worshipped deities of the earth. The board floor was bare; a pile of empty sacks had been left against a wall. The black iron press still stood in a corner, with some baskets and wooden spades nearby. Seen through the open door to the passageway outside, the window above the yard framed patches of copper-grey sky, and trembled in the gale; but its panes remained unbroken.

We stood with our hands hanging at our sides, our breathing loud in the silence, inhaling the phantom pungency of the vanished hops. Kathleen dropped her hat to the floor; her bunch of Dolly Bush was lost. When she spoke, it was in a whisper.

– Holy Mary and all the saints. Will we be safe in here?

Quite safe, I told her. I was whispering too, since the cooling-room made any sort of loudness seem like a violation. My hair had fallen over my forehead; I pushed it back, dropping my hat to the floor as she had done.

– Jesus protect us, she said. Where can such a terrible great gale be coming from?

I could not account for it, I told her: a hurricane surely wasn't natural in this latitude. In this I was right; but I have learned today that some of the older residents in the district remember a similar gale when they were young: a hot wind coming from the continent in the north.

– It is like the end of the world, she said. I'm thankful that you're with me.

She plucked at the embroidered white collar of her Sunday dress. Her hair was in great disarray, falling in tangled masses on her shoulders, one strand pasted across her damp forehead.

– Ah, it's so hot, she said. And my clothes are full of that dust. I feel it on my skin.

– Perhaps I should have taken you to your room, I said. But I thought you might not want to be alone.

– I do not, she said. I want to be with you until it stops. I am glad you have brought me here. I'm wishing all the time to be with you – though I know you will say I should not.

Her face, in the chamber's dimness, was a pallid, heart-shaped blur, its expression unclear; but her eyes gleamed pale and brilliant, fixed on mine.

– I can make myself say that no longer, I said. Every time I see you by day, I'm filled with happiness; and you wander in my dreams at night.

– How can I not be in your dreams, since I think of you all the time? I've tried not to, since you've told me I have nothing to hope

423

for. But I see you at breakfast in the kitchen, I see you in the fields, I see you 'twirling the lock' at your desk, and I cannot help it.

– I am glad, I said.

We looked at each other in silence; we heard each other's breathing; then she spoke in a whisper.

– Glad? What is it you are saying, sir?

– Never call me 'sir' again, I said.

– I will not, then, she said. What is it you are saying, Robert Devereux?

– I am saying that I love you, I said.

When I kissed her, she clung to me with a wild and desperate strength. Her lips against my ear, she whispered as though praying:

– *Beautiful man. Beautiful man. Ah Robert, how I love you.*

My heart hammered violently at this, since my heart knew that by bringing her here, and by saying what I'd done, I'd discarded all my scruples: discarded my resolution never to begin anything that could end by bringing her pain. At last we drew away to stare at each other again, as though searching for the answer to a problem.

– There is nowhere to sit down, she said. Nothing but the bare boards.

I gestured towards the corner. We would have to make do with the hop-sacks, I said, and we laughed. It was the first time we had laughed together. I picked her up in my arms, and carried her through the dimness towards the corner, the sound of my boots echoing from the floor. She seemed very small; a hint of her body's moist odour came to me, and made my head swim.

The lilac gown, made of the same cheap cotton as all her dresses, fastened down the front. Undone, pulled away, it disclosed that bulky chrysalis of undergarments that women must wear for decency: even here in the balmy Antipodes; even in a Summer as hot as this. Kathleen wore less than a gentlewoman would have done; but she was still encased in a white, short-sleeved linen chemise, a coarse stuff petticoat, and a second petticoat of flannel – both of them infested by the red dust, as my waistcoat and shirt were. But at last her whiteness was exposed: deathly in the chamber's deep twilight. She gleamed like a fish in water, her beauty discovered in glimpses; and these glimpses did not always match. She had seemingly become two women: one just out of girlhood, the other of a daunting maturity. Her face was that of the ethereal sprite in the mirror in Doctor Howard's dining room; but some of her body's aspects were at odds with this face, creating a thrilling shock. Affecting and maidenly, the rounded slimness of her arms, the frail perfection of her shoulders, her narrow, tender waist. But this waist supported breasts of a melancholy fullness, and the grotto of her womanhood was dim and veiled and frightening as the air.

Naked, she frowned, with what seemed severity. But this was the frown of desire: her arms went around my neck, and drew me down.

And now the lingering reek of the hop-plants, whose resins induce sleep and intoxication, was joined in the dimness by the odours of bodily passion: indelicate, pungent and innocent as the odours of the vegetable world. When I recall our frenzy, I recall the mingling of those essences, vegetable and human: distillations I might once have called gross, but which now I see are nothing of the kind, any more than Kathleen herself is gross. Or if she is, I am in love with her very grossness, which is the grossness of life.

I have ventured into life's heartland, where the sacred groves lie – and where I never dared venture before. The Eleusinian mysteries and the ecstasies of Demeter have been closed to me until now – or rather, I've closed myself against them. This is because I've thought of beauty as something which must always be refined. I have failed to understand that those who seek Demeter, and the ancient, sacred mysteries of Harvest, must accept carnality as beauty's other face. Then they will delight not only in flower-scents, but in the odours of bodily toil, and the female serum of love.

We lay drifting on the hop-sacks, indifferent to their roughness, indifferent to time, and cocooned in a warmth that had now become mild and bemusing. The gale had dropped as suddenly as it had come; there was silence outside, as well as in the kiln. But the dust, seen through the windows, still hung in the air, making a permanent evening out there – so that whether true evening had come was impossible to judge. At last – reaching to where my waistcoat lay on the boards – I drew out my watch, and found that it was six o'clock.

Kathleen smiled up at me, heavy hair spread on the sacking.

– I must now be going back to the house, she said. Mrs Langford will be wondering where I am. They will be wondering where we both are, and whether we have come to harm.

– No, I said. Not yet.

– I'll be getting into trouble with Bess Langford, she said. There's supper to prepare.

– You will not get into trouble, I said. I am your master, and I forbid you to go.

She laughed with me, but then became serious. Her naked arms shot up quickly to embrace me, and her lips were against my ear again, breathing a fervent message:

– *Yes. Yes. I am yours, and you will not let me go.*

2. DARK ROSALEEN

April 13th

Two in the afternoon in the Midlands hamlet of Tunbridge, eight miles south of the garrison town of Ross.

A hawk, passing high overhead, might well miss sighting Tunbridge. It lies on the coaching road that links the island's north with its south, and consists of perhaps a dozen houses, the inevitable stone convict station, two inns, and some outlying farms. The Main Road is empty of traffic just now, and the hamlet lies contained in a vast silence, broken only by bird-calls and the intermittent bleating of sheep. Two old men are standing outside a cottage in conversation, one of them holding a horse. A maidservant in a white mob-cap hangs out washing in a garden.

These Midlands at the centre of Van Diemen's Land are said to be a set of ancient lake floors, long ago dried up: the only part of the island which is open and low-lying. They have been occupied for grazing by the colonists, with long miles of paddocks fenced off. The effect is one of liberation: after the confinement of the valleys, the eye drinks in these gold-grassed distances, and the spirit stretches out its hands. In the clear air of autumn, the low blue hills and mountains that stand on the flatland's edges are far-off yet distinct; and above them, as always in low country, there rises an enormous sky. Vast white clouds sail here, with thin, thrilling filaments stretched out behind: static yet seeming to flutter, like signals of some Elysian event.

A small stone bridge stands just outside the hamlet at its northern end, taking the road over a meandering little stream – grandly named the Blackman River. Halfway across, against a stone parapet on the bridge's eastern side, a table has been set up, covered with a starched white cloth, and set with a lavish dinner. Seated here, on straight-backed oak dining chairs, with white linen napkins on our laps, are Martin Fitzgibbon, Paul Barry and myself.

– Martin, Barry is saying, let me offer you a leg of this excellent bird. You are partial to the leg, I hope?

At the moment that I'm recording, Barry is standing up; he has just removed the cover from a heavy silver dish, and is setting about carving a roast chicken. The big, matching soup tureen has already yielded a hearty pease soup, and we have just finished our fish course: some tolerable local trout. Covered dishes of vegetables and a jug of gravy are waiting at Barry's elbow, and he serves us with jovial *élan*, presiding over our meal like a benevolent host.

The reason for this singular outdoor feast, and for its odd location?

It's a reunion with Martin Fitzgibbon, who has at last responded to the pleas in our letters: he's given his written *parole* to Governor Denison, and has been granted his Ticket-of-Leave. Ten days ago he emerged from Port Arthur, and was advised by the authorities to take up residence in Oatlands – another garrison town, fifteen miles down the highway to the south of Tunbridge. And at this point on the bridge (according to Paul Barry's calculations), the invisible border runs which divides Fitzgibbon's police district of Oatlands from Barry's district of Campbell Town. So our feast, Paul declares, cannot be objected to by the authorities.

Barry and I are on the northern side of the table, looking towards Tunbridge. Thus, we sit obediently within the Campbell Town district. Martin Fitzgibbon sits facing us on the southern side – his back turned to the hamlet – and so is within his district of Oatlands. The horses we have ridden here are tethered beside the stream below the bridge. We have all dressed in some style for the occasion. Barry is easily the most colourful of us, in a bottle-green riding coat, a checked waistcoat, and a green neckerchief. Over this, when he and I rode here from Ross – where I'm staying with him at the inn – he wore a dark, dramatic mantle, now draped over the parapet. A quaint Austrian military cap hangs from the back of his chair.

It was he who made the arrangements for the dinner, which has been provided by one of the local hostelries – an establishment called the Tunbridge Wells Inn. To do so, Paul admits, he had to trespass yesterday for five hundred yards into the Oatlands district, entering Tunbridge to speak with the innkeeper. The inn can be seen from where we sit: an aged, salmon-coloured, weatherboard building that must have been here since the early days of settlement. It offers refreshment to the stage-coach passengers who stop here on the way to Launceston, and its standards are surprisingly high. The innkeeper, it seems, is a man with both a sense of humour and a sense of occasion; he proved susceptible to Barry's persuasiveness, as well as to the generosity of his purse. The Tunbridge police magistrate was informed of our coming by an envoy from Barry's friendly magistrate in Ross (in order that no local constable might legitimately challenge us), and the innkeeper declared to Barry that he would be proud to oblige such distinguished visitors to the town. The luncheon, together with the necessary furniture, was delivered to the bridge by cart.

We cut into our chicken, Barry having served us all. He chews reflectively, head on one side.

– Very good, he says. A tender bird, no doubt slain in our honour. But I think perhaps that the gravy has not fared well on its journey through the open air from the Tunbridge side. Somewhat *solid*, don't you think, gentlemen?

– One can hardly complain of that, I say. Mine host had no control over it during its passage. My dear Fitzgibbon – may I trouble you to move the potatoes over from the Oatlands district?

At this, Barry begins to laugh, and I join in. What I've said has hardly been the height of wit, and is by no means the first joke that's been made referring to the geography of our situation – so it's somewhat difficult to justify our degree of mirth. It reaches a point where we must put down our knives and forks and gasp for breath, while Fitzgibbon, wearing a constrained smile, sits watching us. We are behaving like schoolboys, this smile says. It's true; and perhaps this very judgment in his expression is what makes us laugh all the harder. We are highly delighted with our table on the bridge, and at the way that Sir William Denison and his minions are thus mocked – with the happy cooperation of his own local officers.

We are drinking an excellent Van Diemen's Land bottled ale; I raise my glass.

– Here's to our reunion, I say. And confusion to our enemies, here and across the globe. And welcome again, Fitzgibbon – I give you joy of your new freedom, with all my heart.

Fitzgibbon dabs his lips with his napkin. He holds out his glass to touch mine and then Barry's, his smile still uncomfortable.

– To our reunion, he says. It does me good to see you – I am still so little used to good company, it is all a little unreal to me. My dear Devereux; my dear Barry; your health, both of you.

As we drink, I glance at him again. When he first rode onto the bridge, I was shocked by his appearance, not having seen him for over two years. Dismounting from his horse, he had advanced towards us stiffly, like someone whose body had been affected by illness. He had always been a trimly-built, healthy-looking man who carried himself well, head thrown back: now, although he retained his austere dignity, his shoulders were stooped; and although only forty-seven, he looked closer to sixty. His thick, waving hair, formerly of a vivid reddish-bronze, had faded to a dull, copper-brown, and was streaked with a good deal of grey, both at the temples and in front. He'd always worn a slight frown, which completed his aloof, judicial air; this frown's vertical line had now deepened, and his wide-set, narrow brown eyes, instead of expressing the keen, scholarly seriousness I remembered, had in them an expression of wounded bafflement. He remained clean-shaven, and his well-cut mouth was vulnerable yet firm, while his cleft chin was determined. It was a face whose patrician authority still commanded respect. But the unhappy eyes worried me.

The chicken disposed of, we have now come to the dessert – a gooseberry tart with clotted cream. Barry and I consume this with enthusiasm, making admiring comments on the pastry; but I notice that Fitzgibbon only toys with his. When we push our plates away,

Barry produces a bottle of Spanish sherry he's brought here in his saddlebag, and reaches for fresh glasses. With these in our hands, we sit back, gazing at the eastern view: the shingled roof of a farmhouse; the levels of tufted grass; the scattered green bushes and warm brown stones. The bleating of sheep rises and is lost there, and the stillness of the land is uncanny. It's Barry who breaks the silence.

– Tell me, Fitzgibbon: did your gaolers ever allow you to read the colony's newspapers, down at Port Arthur? There was a good deal of local press support for you, you know.

Fitzgibbon raises his eyebrows. Instead of replying immediately, he seems to gather his thoughts. It's this sort of self-important ponderousness that makes it so difficult to like the man; but I strive to maintain a mood of sympathy. His head is tilted back, making him perhaps look more haughty than he is: he can scarcely avoid this posture, since his choker collar's points are so high. His dress, although perfectly respectable, and of excellent quality, adds to his look of venerability. Not for him the shooting coats, low collars, and loosely knotted neckcloths that Barry and I now wear; with his sober, dark grey tail coat, double-breasted waistcoat and stiffened black cravat, he looks like a banker. He dressed like this at home, appearing perfectly normal; but here in tiny Tunbridge, in these alien, empty plains, he's transformed into something of an oddity. I have the feeling that he's refusing to acknowledge the scenes through which he moves: that he believes they'll soon dissolve around him, allowing him to wake as though from sleep, and to find himself at home in bed.

When he finally answers Barry's question, it's with the deliberation of one addressing an official enquiry.

– The newspapers were always denied me, he says. That was one of the hardest things to bear.

He has a deep, pleasant, precise voice, somewhat monotonous when heard for too long, its accent and delivery that of the English ruling caste which moulded him at Harrow, finished him at Cambridge, and which now holds him prisoner.

– As you know, he says, all my mail was censored, and letters informing me about newspapers which had commented on my situation were carefully kept back. But one letter did get through that quoted the *Hobart Town Guardian*.

Raising his eyebrows higher, he quotes from memory.

– 'Tyrannical and arbitrary coercion is being exercised in the case of Martin Fitzgibbon.' Those were their words, and they did not exaggerate. They gave me some comfort at the time. You know what my situation was, on Denison's direct orders: absolute confinement, and petty persecution.

We murmur assent; we do know these things. But he seems not to hear us. Head tilted back, addressing the fields and the river, he goes on; and a plaintive note enters his voice.

– I had no money – did you know that? The funds that my wife sent from Ireland were held back, only to be given to me if I took my Ticket. I needed shirts – the ones I had were falling to pieces. I needed a hat. I wanted tobacco. *But they would not enable me to buy these things.*

He clenches his fist beside his plate, his narrow, outraged stare returning to us.

– Finally, on Denison's orders, I was reduced from hospital rations to convict rations. Dry bread; tea; a pound of potatoes; a pound of meat. Nothing else. The meat so tough that I could not eat it fried. I asked that it be boiled, merely adding a leek. *This was forbidden.*

The fist clenches and unclenches, and his gaze now holds mine, beginning to make me uneasy.

– I tell you, he says, I used sometimes to lie on my bed for hours, gnawing my hands. For how long can one divert oneself with reading, or writing one's diary, without friends or a loving wife? I felt I would truly go mad. You cannot conceive of the atmosphere of that place. It sits on a pretty blue bay, among virgin wilderness: but they have filled the air with melancholy; with dread. I seldom saw a convict, of course – except when I went to church on Sundays, which the poor wretches were obliged to attend. But I was always aware of them; their misery hung over the settlement like a stench. And one of those damned, smirking redcoats who supervised my exercise used to disobey his orders and talk to me – telling me about the brutal and barbaric punishments the felons endure. He did it to torment me, of course; to make me afraid that these things might soon become *my* lot. What is done down there ought to be made known to the public – and some day I shall do so.

He gnaws at his lip, staring down the road.

– And this is the fate that Denison has eventually in store for *us*, he says.

Barry laughs.

– Come, now, he says. I think not.

– Oh yes! Certainly! If we are caught outside our districts, if we attempt escape – then he will be able to disregard Lord Grey's instructions, and deliver us into that hell, wearing the yellow and grey, with the worst villains on earth set over us, free to practise what atrocities they wish. This is what the folly of '48 has brought us to.

– Well now, it's true that this William Denison is a dreary and spiteful sod, Barry drawls. And all of us have truly appreciated the unpleasantness of your situation, Martin.

He frowns, looking down at the tip of his cigar; I sense that he's growing as uneasy with Fitzgibbon's recitation as I am, and that he has not liked the use of the word 'folly'.

– You spent five months in this isolation, did you not? It seems to have worn you down, old fellow – you're not looking hearty, he says. But you'll recover, depend on it. When Devereux first arrived, I wouldn't have given you twopence for him. A wheezing, shuffling wreck. And now look: a rudely healthy farmer!

He punches my upper arm, and winks.

– And of course, he tells Fitzgibbon, his isolation was a good deal longer than yours.

To this, Fitzgibbon says nothing. He is twisting his empty sherry glass in his fingers. I pick up the bottle and pour him another measure; he seems not to notice it.

– At least we were not put into convict dress, I say, or made to work in chains. We do have that to be thankful for.

He sighs.

– I know what you both are thinking, he says. Five months in a cottage of my own, with my meals brought to me and my wants attended to, isn't such torture. And yes, Devereux, you were cooped up alone on ships for far longer than I spent in that cottage. I don't know how you stood it; you must be made of unbreakable stuff. But we are not all made in the same way; and you are much younger than I.

His words prompt me to notice again how greatly he's aged.

– You two gentlemen are not yet married, he goes on. But you may perhaps imagine how I miss my wife and children. It's twenty months since I last saw them. Dear God, nearly two years!

He stares beyond the parapet, whose rusty iron staples are stamped with the dread broad arrow of the Convict Department. His expression is filled with yearning, his mouth tight with pain. Then he turns back to Barry.

– When you and I and our other comrades were in Kilmainham Gaol, Paul, we had each other's company, and were visited by our families. That was quite supportable, wasn't it? Eh? Even jolly, at times. So was our voyage on the *Revenge*, with those happy hours spent reading aloud and debating with each other. But complete isolation is something I find intolerable. To isolate a man is inhuman. It's done at Port Arthur only with the most intractable and violent convicts, and then for no more than thirty days – did you know that? They are put in pitch-dark cells, on nothing but bread and water, and so are worse off than I was: some of them come out raving. Yet *I* was just as isolated as *they* were – and had I not taken the Ticket-of-Leave, I should have remained alone not for thirty days, but indefinitely. *Indefinitely!* Is that not outrageous?

His voice has risen again, and his face twitches. Then he seems to recollect himself, and goes on in a quieter tone.

– I spent some days in Hobart Town before being posted to Oatlands. I've made some influential friends there – including the Anglican Bishop, who is most sympathetic. He told me in confidence that Denison hates me in a quite personal way, and wishes to break me. It was my letter refusing the Ticket that seems to have most incensed the creature.

Barry claps his hands.

– Bravo, Fitzgibbon, he says. I'm sure that's true. This and the fact that you are his social superior.

Fitzgibbon shakes his head.

– But I *have* taken the Ticket, in the end, he says. And that gave the damned tyrant his victory. Oh yes, I know how many supporters thought it sensible that I give my *parole*. Many letters came to me besides yours, pleading that I do so. But still I resisted the temptation while I could. Meanwhile, I was mocked in the London *Times* – did you know that? Did you see the piece, may I ask?

We have not, we say, and he fumbles in a pocket of his coat and draws out a newspaper clipping – at the same time putting on a pair of spectacles. He then reads aloud.

– 'Martin Fitzgibbon is refusing his Ticket simply to make himself a martyr. He is a poor, foolish fanatic, of the kind that enjoys torturing himself. The English people will view him as they view those misguided creatures in India, who lie on beds of nails, or hang themselves from hooks. An excessively vain and childish man, Fitzgibbon enjoys the attention all this brings. And he deludes himself with the notion that he represents that rebellion which has now so totally failed. He represents nothing.'

He puts away the clipping, takes off the glasses and gazes at us, waiting for comment.

– Come, we've all endured this rubbish, I say. What do you care for the ravings of some Fleet Street jackal? Throw the thing away, Martin. If I may be crude: wipe your arse with it. Why torment yourself?

– Why *torment* myself?

He glares at me, the twitching in his face more pronounced – and I begin to realise that he is truly unwell, and not the man he was: something has broken in him, at Port Arthur.

– Because my honour and my character have been impugned, he says. And in taking the Ticket, I have allowed these creatures to crow over me; to triumph over me.

– Well then, Barry says suddenly, why did you give your *parole*, since this is how you feel?

At this, Fitzgibbon spreads both hands on the table in front of him; he expels a long breath, leaning forward and staring at Barry without speaking. Then he takes a grip on himself: when he answers, his voice is low and resigned.

– I had begun to have chest pains, he says. It seems I may now have a weak heart.

He raises his hand to his chest, holding it under his coat. He appears to listen, his eyes wandering off to the distances beyond the parapet.

– The doctor on the settlement formed this opinion, and warned me against giving myself strain, he says. So it was either give my *parole*, or risk losing my life. Or at the very least, my sanity.

– I'm very sorry to hear this, Barry says.

– And I. You have nothing to be ashamed of, I say. You would have achieved nothing by losing your health or your life. I made the same decision myself, Martin, when I chose to leave Bermuda. And I greatly admire the brilliance with which you turned the situation to the advantage of our cause. Look at what you achieved, my dear fellow! A thousand Irishmen gathered in Tammany Hall in New York, to protest your ill treatment – and to declare that a hundred thousand Irishmen in America were ready to take up arms for you. Groups in Cork and Limerick petitioning the Queen; and the letters you sent out exposing your ill-treatment quoted by your friends and supporters in articles in the press around the world. You've greatly embarrassed your old undergraduate friend Lord Grey – and his dog Governor Denison will surely have been reprimanded. No, you have nothing to regret.

But Fitzgibbon is looking beyond the parapet again, his face drawn with sadness.

– I was insulted, at Port Arthur, he says. Insulted and demeaned in a way that I have never in my life had to tolerate.

– Insulted? By whom? I ask.

For a time, it seems that he won't answer. When he does speak, it is without looking at us, his voice only just audible.

– The Commandant of Port Arthur came to see me. A military bully by the name of Captain Sinclair. He brought the chief of the colony's Medical Department with him: a Doctor Gibson, an oily, patronising, vulgar creature. Gibson had come down to the settlement from Hobart Town: Sinclair said he wished him to check my heart, and to confirm the diagnosis of the prison surgeon. Of course, the real purpose was to ask me to take the Ticket, and to report on me to Denison. When Gibson had examined me, he claimed that my problems were nervous – that there was nothing wrong with my heart. I was, however, very debilitated, he said – and in no state to play the hero. I had not the constitution for it, and should leave it to a hardier type of man. Those were his words. Then he took it on himself to tell me that Denison found me 'sulky and obstinate', and that I could only harm myself by pursuing my present course.

– Insolent bugger, Barry says.

– He went far beyond himself, of course; and it grew worse. He flagrantly disregarded my station: he attempted to rebuke me as though I were a schoolboy. But of course, there were no witnesses except Captain Sinclair, who stood grinning. I told the man I wanted none of his advice, and that I had no intention of changing my decision. Then Sinclair also became familiar, encouraged by his colleague. 'I would take the Ticket, if I were you, Mr Fitzgibbon; I would pay heed to Doctor Gibson,' he said, 'or you really will get very ill indeed. You Irish gentlemen haven't much sense of proportion, that's your trouble. But then, your people never have absorbed civilized moderation, have they? Perhaps they haven't the capacity.' And off they both went, having insulted me.

All of a sudden, Fitzgibbon's eyes fill with tears. He bites his lip, attempting to control himself; but he fails. Turning away towards the parapet, he covers his eyes with one hand, the other gripping his glass. His shoulders heave, but he makes no sound beyond a shuddering intake of breath.

Barry and I look at each other, frowning and horrified. His collapse appals us both; but we quickly seek to comfort him.

– Forget this absurd medical official, Fitzgibbon, I say. He's not worth your distress – and surely he couldn't touch your honour. Nor could your gaoler, Sinclair.

But he ignores this, sitting with his face hidden by his hand, elbow propped on the table. Barry stands up, walks around the table (illegally crossing into Oatlands), and places a hand on his shoulder.

– Look here, Fitzgibbon, he begins.

– Let me be.

Fitzgibbon has spoken in a muffled voice; his face remains hidden. A magpie warbles loudly nearby, with sudden, heartless gaiety.

– Only listen to me, Martin. They have gained no advantage, Barry says. The victory has been yours. Yours! This is why they hate you. Consider all the support you have won – even here in Van Diemen's Land, and in the other Australian colonies. Why, the Launceston *Examiner* only last week called your motives 'pure and patriotic'. And it went on to say that we have only to be patient, and we shall all obtain conditional pardons.

Fitzgibbon draws out a large handkerchief, blows his nose loudly, and dries his sadly reddened eyes.

– Forgive me, he says. I have not been myself for some time.

He puts the handkerchief away, his expression composed and disdainful – as though he's just learned of some regrettable behaviour on the part of someone else: someone with whom he's barely acquainted. There is a greater pathos in this, I find, than any expression of woe.

We tell him there's nothing to forgive. Barry sits down again, after patting Fitzgibbon's shoulder, and Martin sits looking up the road, his hands locked in front of him.

– As to our pardons, he says suddenly, neither London nor Denison will listen to such opinions. We will serve out our full fourteen years. It will therefore be that long before I see my wife and children again – for I will never bring them to such a place as this. And I am almost as alone in that wretched village of Oatlands as I was at Port Arthur.

– You are wrong, Barry says. I believe pardons are possible – but if not, I mean to escape, when it suits. I may have given my *parole*, but I can also withdraw it.

Fitzgibbon shakes his head, and turns to me.

– And you, Devereux? Do you entertain such ideas?

I do, I tell him – but if I can't escape, I intend to enjoy my life here, for as long as need be. At present, it makes me content.

I then go on to tell him about the farm, and of the success we've had with the harvest. But I tell him nothing about Kathleen O'Rahilly, who stands in my mind as I speak: the spirit and secret of my contentment.

His frown deepens, as he listens. Finally he gestures at Tunbridge, and the empty miles of grass.

– You are content with this? *You*, Devereux? Is all your brilliance and passion to be given to a life beyond the edge of civilization? I cannot believe it.

I am about to reply, when we all become aware of the sound of hoofs, coming from the direction of Tunbridge. Looking along the road, we see a group of horsemen: the only traffic to appear here since we sat down at our table.

Within moments, the riders have passed through the hamlet and are bearing down on us, whooping and yelling like Red Indians. There are perhaps half a dozen of them: young men in their twenties, of the type known as 'currency lads': the native-born. They are easy to identify: they are taller and better-made than the stunted little felons who fathered them. They are stockmen and kangaroo hunters: I've seen their counterparts at Bothwell. The stockmen wear serge shirts, red and yellow neckerchiefs, and a variety of wide-brimmed hats; some are waving these over their heads, while others swing heavy riding whips. The hunters have shotguns slung from their saddles; their jackets are trimmed with kangaroo fur. All of them resemble the pictures I've seen of their counterparts in the American West; and no doubt they have much in common. Now they are upon us, thundering on to the bridge. They point at our table and yell with laughter; but their faces, seen close to, are open and good-natured, and their mirth is neither mocking nor vicious. Barry and I stand up and raise our glasses to them.

– *Good health, your honour*, one calls; and then they are past, turning in the saddle to look back at us, whooping and doffing their headgear in salute. They gallop up the road to the north, leaving a pale cloud of dust in their wake, and the sound of their hoofs grows faint in the dreaming silence.

Barry and I are still laughing; they have pleased and exhilarated us.

– Good hearty fellows, he says. God, what soldiers they'd make! One can see them as cavalry.

– Their fathers fought the native blacks, Fitzgibbon says. Now, not a dozen of those poor creatures are left. They and their hunting grounds are gone.

We had half forgotten him. He remains seated, his expression severe, recalling us to a duty to be unhappy, and to make moral judgments; and this is not our mood. But we sit down opposite him again, and pick up our glasses.

Nobody speaks, and my thoughts are free to roam – made vague and disordered by the effects of the ale and sherry. Very distantly, I can still hear the hoofs, and the exultant, calling voices. Where do they ride, these young colonials? To what great adventure? In the northern hemisphere, I reflect, they might well be on the way to some high and significant event: to war or revolution, or some deadly feud. But what adventure is there here, in this far, silent island of the South – in this colony which is also a gaol? Must they turn bushranger for excitement? And I'm aware once again of the *weirdness* of this place, and of the weirdness of our position: a world away from where we should be, at our dinner table on the bridge. The joke wears thin; we seem to me reduced, sitting in these silent, tawny spaces. And an odd, foolish thought dismays me, before I dismiss it.

In the northern hemisphere, we are giants; in the southern hemisphere, dwarfs.

Catching Barry's eye, I smile: but the smile is wry.

– Ah well, at least he didn't read us any of his poetry, Barry says.

– Is he inclined to do that?

– Very inclined – I listened to a good deal of it on the *Revenge*. And it's such damned *dull* poetry.

Barry and I look at each other from either side of the fire, and burst out laughing. Then, just as quickly, we become sober. We feel guilty, speaking of Fitzgibbon in this way; and yet our very guilt tempts us to more laughter.

It's after ten o'clock at night. We're alone in the small, down-stairs parlour of the Man o' Ross Hotel, drinking tea. We lie back in brocade-upholstered armchairs, our waistcoats unbuttoned. A pretty French clock ticks on the marble mantelpiece above the fire. Green-figured muslin curtains are drawn across the windows. A picture of Saint Patrick hangs near the door, to leave visitors in no doubt of the loyalties within these walls.

Barry still makes the inn his home, and declares himself very comfortable. It's a handsome, well-run establishment, built of the local freestone; coming into its hallway, one is welcomed by clean country odours as poignant as childhood memories: baking bread, furniture polish, and fresh flowers in vases. They signal the fact that the Man o' Ross is in the charge of a woman – the widow Mary McCormack. Her presence does much to add to Paul's comfort, it seems: he's now confessed to me that their friendship has deepened to a point that can no longer be called Platonic. This scarcely sur-prises me; Paul is a great philanderer, and can never be without a woman for long.

We continue to discuss Fitzgibbon, as we've done off and on since farewelling him at Tunbridge.

– We shouldn't be too harsh, Barry says. The poor old fellow is in deep despair, that's plain. He's changed: usually, he exerts great control over himself. I have only seen him weep once before – when we were together in Kilmainham Gaol, on the eve of being transported. His wife and children came to farewell him: his face was like a mask while he spoke to them. But when the door of the cell closed, I saw tears stream down his cheeks.

– Exile is hard for a married man, I say. Harder than it is for us. And he shouldn't be alone in Oatlands: this is only adding to his depressed state. I've decided to approach Doctor Howard, putting the case that Fitzgibbon has a weak heart, and asking Howard to recommend that he be moved to Bothwell as I was, on compassionate grounds, to lodge with Thomas O'Neill.

– Excellent idea, Barry says. Father O'Neill is saintly enough to indulge and defer to Fitzgibbon.

His drawl becomes sardonic and pronounced.

– Jesus! How weary I grew of the poor dear man, coming out on the *Revenge*! He still condemns us, you know, for urging force of arms. And he sees you in particular, Devereux, as being the author of our situation – since you were so influential in urging rebellion. At times, cooped up for months as we were, the differences grew very trying. It was his bloody conceit and *solemnity* I couldn't bear: sometimes I wanted to pitch him overboard.

He chuckles, glancing at me.

– Although he doesn't dare say it, I believe he actually blames *us* for his being transported here.

– Really? Good God.

– Oh yes. He sees himself as having been caught up in a process of violence against his better judgment – and against his precious principles.

– Principles! Martin lives in a book. He thinks revolution can be made through gentle conversation and compromise. With the God-damned English!

Barry laughs.

– It's as well you and he weren't sharing a cell: you never did suffer fools gladly, Robert. But I confess he stirs the same irritation in me. And when he becomes so low, he makes *me* low.

– *You* low, Paul? I've never seen you low – that's what I love in you. Come: you find a beauty in this island, just as I do, and enjoy your riding and hunting in the bush – and you have your pretty widow to console you. I thought you found your situation quite tolerable. You've said so.

Barry picks up the poker and leans to stoke the fire, stabbing at it hard many times, causing sparks to rise, and his hair to fall over his forehead. Then, looking at me over his shoulder, he says:

– Yes, I find it tolerable – for much of the time. It's true that the island is beautiful – and so is Mary.

His expression, even when his emotions are as equivocal as they seem to be now, hovers always on the edge of a smile. He and I are said to be alike: similar in our views and our temperaments. But in some ways he's quite different from myself; quite other. With his narrow, roguish face and elusiveness of spirit, he brings to mind those

442

beliefs among our people of an ancient race of fairy folk – and of occasional fairy intercourse with humans. Sometimes, in my fancy, I see him as the descendant of a long-ago union with one of that otherworld tribe which is eternally light, ethereal and happy: untouched by the sorrows and wretchedess of heart that afflict the human race. There is another difference, of course: one more mundane. He is a Catholic, and has more Irish blood than I do, being descended from the Barrys of Cork, who were thoroughly Gaelicised.

– So I'm not going to weep, as Fitzgibbon does, he says. I have much to be thankful for, and I know it. Mary has saved me from going mad, or worse. You know me, Robert, and will forgive and understand what I say next, I hope. When I first came here, after being so long pent up in male company, I was mad for a woman. I was ready to drag some convict wench into a field, like a beast in rut. Well, I regret to say that I did so – although I didn't tell this to our dear O'Neill, when we spoke at the Lakes. I got myself into a somewhat unsavoury situation with a girl from the Factory here. It cost me some money to be rid of her.

– Oh dear, I say.

– Yes. Well, Mary has saved me from any further adventures like that. She's a strong and decent woman, and a friend: warm and discreet and understanding. We both know that we're sinning, but we don't believe our happiness is sinful. We even go to Mass together.

– Is she in love with you?

He glances at me.

– Yes – I suppose so. In a manner of speaking.

– And you with her?

– I can't afford to be. I'm sincerely fond of her, of course.

His tone dismisses the topic. Looking into the fire, he goes on in a near-whisper.

– I have strange dreams, lately, Robert: dreams that repeat themselves, and from which I wake up in a state of enormous regret. Always I'm in the same place: a house set in a great park, somewhere near Waterford – but it's not a house I recognise. It has hundreds of high, big rooms, all of them sad, and I search

443

through them endlessly, going down corridors, going through doors –

He breaks off, still looking at the fire, his eyes narrowed.

– I know such dreams, I say. What is it you search for?

– For *her,* he says. For someone I loved deeply, who is now lost to me. I don't wish to say her name. She was very beautiful, Robert – but she had no understanding of the things I believed in. Do you take my meaning? But of course you do – forgive me, my dear. This is the price we both pay for treading the path of rebellion. I was right to break it off, we would not have suited; and when I'm awake, I don't regret it. But in the dream –

He pauses, and breathes in deeply.

– In the dream, I long for her as I used to do. Sometimes, I actually see her, at the end of a corridor. But then she goes through a door and is gone, lost – and the knowledge goes through me like a sword. I wake, and I long to go in search of her. You know what that longing is like?

He looks at me sideways now, raising his brows; I nod, and he smiles without mirth.

– But then I hear the screeching of those bloody little parrots of Van Diemen's Land out the window, and the cawing of crows, and the voices of the convict servants. And I know myself *here*, in this tiny, dusty little gaol-town, at the bottom of the world. And I say to myself: 'You can never ever search for her – and nor can you pursue anything else that you long for. You are trapped here, in the Antipodes. You are lost to the world.'

He sits bolt upright, staring into the fire, both hands gripping the arms of the chair. When he speaks again, his voice vibrates with a frustration I have never before heard in it, and which startles me.

– Fitzgibbon is cut off from his wife and family – very well, that is what torments *him*, in his middle age. But we are *young,* Robert, you and I! These are our best years, and we are caged! Oh yes, this island has a wild sort of beauty; but it palls; dear God, it palls! Our situation here is so deadly monotonous, in the end. Riding, hunting, reading: very well, my boy, these are enjoyable diversions. But for how long can we pursue them, without dying of boredom? For how long? *Years?* No, by Christ, I won't think of it!

He jumps up, laughing as he often does to dismiss too much seriousness, and begins to pace the room.

– I need always to throw myself into the heart of great events, he says. More – to turn them around. *You* know that, Robert – it's true of you too. And by God, we've both done so – have we not? But now! Now, we're removed by half the globe from the stage where that action proceeds. They've done their work well, our bloody imperial gaolers: here, we can do *nothing!* Nothing for our country; nothing that matters!

He stops by my chair, looking down at me.

– Yesterday, he says, I rode up on to a hill behind Ross here, and sat looking at the view below. It was beautiful, to be sure. Yet suddenly, I longed for the true, lovely green of home, instead of that strange, dry, olive hue that is underneath everything here – like a hint of death. When I was a boy in Waterford, I used to climb a hill not far from our house, and look down on the Suir Estuary, and the sea. And I wanted with all my being to be *there*, in the gorse, with the curlews wheeling. But there was more, much more that I was missing. I was remembering Ardmore's old Round Tower, which I would often walk to: Ardmore, like a great stone bottle, that was built by the Gaelic monks. And I thought: *that* is what I miss, and will never see here! You understand me, Devereux? Of course you do. To live in a country *without history*: my spirit grows heavy at that prospect.

– And mine, I say. And mine.

– But this is supposed to be our fate! To languish in a land whose monuments are convict stations; whose society consists of wool-brained farmers and their felonious servants: burglars, forgers and murderers. So here we sit, you and I, while the world rolls on without us.

He throws himself into his chair again.

– As to our cause, he says, *that* goes on without us too! It's now in the hands of toadies who ask for compromise. Have you seen recent editions of your own newspaper? Have you seen what has become of the *New Nation*, in Fitzgerald's hands?

Seeing my expression, he nods.

– I read the newspapers from Dublin and London, and it's sometimes more than I can bear. I curse and trample on them! And then I read letters from my comrades in Ireland and New York – and I feel I really will go mad. God help me, sometimes I want to go out with a shotgun, and to mow down a few of their bloody redcoats, just to relieve my feelings.

This time, he laughs quite heartily, throwing back his head; but his pale eyes grow paler, and look mad.

– Paul, I say. Paul. This is what you must never do.

– Of course not, he says. I may be a lunatic, Devereux, but I'm not a fool.

He relaxes visibly, leaning back in his chair, hands hanging loose. When he goes on, his voice has softened, and has returned to its usual languid drawl.

– Forgive me, I'm beating my breast like Fitzgibbon. These moments pass. I know we will both escape when the opportunity comes – but it's sometimes hard to believe. I'm not made for inactivity. And sometimes, like a child afraid of the dark, I see my youth being lost here – lost like the lady in my dream.

– I do understand. When I listen to you, it might be myself speaking.

He smiles at me quickly, sideways: a smile like a flash of light. Both of us fall silent, and sit looking into the fire for a time. Then he says softly:

– Shall I tell you what else I miss? Sometimes, I have a sentimental wish to turn the clock back, and to find myself sitting in the smoking room of the County and City Club in Waterford. Of course, they were nearly all Tories in there: the fashionable men of the city, like Lord Carew and the Marquis of Waterford – as well as attorneys, and military men, and people like the proprietor of the *Waterford Chronicle*. But do you know, I was very fond of them all: they were good, jovial fellows, and utterly honest. They loved Queen Victoria, and were loyalists to their boot-heels – but *sincerely* so. I could never dislike them. Very few there were Repealers like me – but nobody cared a rap. Politics were left at the door: that was an iron rule. A club for Irish gentlemen – a social club, where we went for merry evenings. They knew I was a rebel, but they knew I also loved the Club, and they were fond of me, I believe. I would toast the brotherhood of all Irishmen, and they would cheer, and drink my health.

He sighs, smiling into the fire.

– That is another dream I have. I dream that I'm back there, coming into the smoking room in the evening – that snug, dusky room that looks out over the river. When I come in, the circle of chairs around the fire shifts to make room for me; they greet me with cries of welcome, smoking their cigars and clay pipes. There was always a chair for me, in that circle around the fire; they always made room, despite their disapproval of their rebel's desperate views. I hear their laughter, and their voices telling stories, and gossiping about the day's events. I'll eat anchovy toast again, and drink whiskey, and sit in great clouds of smoke, and talk until midnight with my quaint Tory friends. Good, generous, self-indulgent fellows, for whom my idealism was folly!

– Perhaps you've begun to think so yourself, I say.

My tone is both jesting and sympathetic; but he turns to me quickly, his face growing hard.

– Never, he says. Never. But one does grow homesick, Devereux, and I'm sad, I suppose, that I'll never again walk into that Club. They were talented, well-read, well-travelled men – but they wished to take life easy, and that is not for me.

He gives me a sudden shrewd look, steepling his fingers under his chin.

– But what of your own case? It seems to me that you yearn less than I do for home. You have an air of satisfaction about you, Robert. Explain.

I see that I must tell him about Kathleen. I do so, reciting only the bare facts of my involvement with her, and of her past. He listens intently, saying nothing, frowning into the fire.

– And you truly love her?

– I truly love her. In fact, I may marry her.

– My dear Devereux! I thought *I* was the one for romantic

madness. But you outdo me. You are not in earnest, surely?

In reply to this, I say to him what I said to O'Neill: that Kathleen is of the people we struggle for; that she has suffered every outrage and privation that British rule has brought to Ireland; that she is a casualty in the war that we fight, and she has my respect and my honour. So why should I not be in earnest?

He reaches over and touches my hand.

– My dear man, she has my respect too – have no doubt of it. I'm sure your Kathleen is very beautiful, and if I made you feel that I in any way despise her, I apologise. Of course I agree with you – she is what we fight for. But I wouldn't be your friend unless I asked you to consider what you are doing, when you speak of marriage. Your compassion for her is a noble feeling. Yes. But she is a woman of the people; a woman presumably without education –

– She can read and write.

– Good – but I don't imagine she reads Chateaubriand or Shelley. I am not trying to be cruel. I am asking you: what will you two talk about, once passion becomes affection?

He smiles; but reading my expression, becomes serious again.

– Robert, Robert – there's no condescension in what I say. I'm not the one to lecture you against passion – I *live* for passion. And if your passion for this young woman sweeps aside everything else, then I envy you, dear boy, and good luck to you. I mean it sincerely, and I long to meet her, and God bless your union.

– I'm glad to hear you say so, Barry.

– Yes, Devereux, joy to you. You have never lived by other people's rules. But we are out of the world here, and I wonder if you picture the future when you go back to it – that world? The tiresome problems that it always throws up: the difficulties such a marriage would make for you in society, should you finally return to Ireland. The likely grief of your parents; the unease of many of your friends and associates. That sort of thing.

– Be damned to all of it.

– Very well, be damned to it, he says, and laughs under his breath.

We are silent for a moment; then he says:

– Our positions are very similar in this regard. That is why I told you I can't fall in love with Mary. I'm not quite as noble as you, my boy. Mary's a fine woman – but in the long run, a union between us wouldn't work. There are too few things we could share; too few things we could talk about – and this puts a limit on my feelings. That is what counts in the long run, my dear – what a man and a woman talk about together. What they share in their souls.

He stands, smiling.

– It's time I went to bed.

I stand too, facing him.

– None of what you say matters, I say. None of it. I don't dismiss the truth of it – but I'm in love with a woman who transforms the world for me.

He claps me on the shoulder.

– Then by God, Devereux, don't let go of your Kathleen. I tell you, you have my blessing – but this won't prevent your escaping, surely? You must bring her *with* you, of course.

I stare at him, startled at the fact that I've simply never considered this idea.

April 28th

I lie awake in the dark, waiting for her.

My bedroom's French windows open on to the front verandah: they stand slightly ajar now, in readiness for her coming. She won't use the room's main door, in the house's central hallway, for fear of encountering the Langfords. I point out that they're long ago in bed, by this time; but still she refuses to take the risk. So she comes to me each night by creeping out into the darkness from her room on the back verandah, going down the driveway past my study, and so up the steps on to the verandah.

Watching the glass doors, I contemplate ragged silver clouds, and the black, tossing heads of the trees. A moon that's almost full fills the garden with frigid light. There's a cold, north-west wind blowing: a wind of autumn, moaning down the valley of the

Derwent from the highlands and the Lakes; from those wild mountain valleys beyond Bothwell, empty of any human traces. I shiver, under the blankets. Is O'Neill lying awake up there, listening to the wind as I do? And poor, tormented Fitzgibbon – recently installed there at Glengarry Cottage, through Doctor Howard's influence – does he listen to it too? I pity the loneliness of his exile.

She's here. Small and insubstantial, wrapped in a petticoat and shawl, she stands framed against the glass like a spirit: one fist raised, pantomiming knocking so that no actual knocking is heard. Kathleen, yet not: her face a Celtic mask, the prominence of the cheekbones exaggerated. She sees me sit up, and smiles: a white flash.

She's in my arms, in the bed, shivering and laughing.

– It's so *cold*, she says. Will you warm me?

Her face, close to, is lit by simple affection; yet its beauty is always strange.

You are of the Danaans, I say.

In the midst of love, I whisper such things to myself, and sometimes to her, while she narrows her eyes and smiles. Her hands, with their small, blunt nails, are rough from their work; and the soles of her feet (so often unshod), are as hard as flint. But I care nothing for these things. This is the woman I've sought in my blood, and false fastidiousness is banished. I am changed, greatly changed. I'm possessed by this woman of the people, by this daughter of the soil of Limerick, whose neck and limbs are delicate as a child's, yet whose body is touched by coarseness: by maturity come too soon. Moist, bitter hollows of her armpits; long, daunting valley of her breasts; deep-navelled belly, its flesh gone faintly loose: I do homage to them all. Coarseness and beauty are one. I'm lifted and borne upwards as though by the wind outside; I look down from a height, as her flesh sways and shudders, and her cries come up to me; I see her bite her lips, and her head toss to and fro. *Who is she? Ah, who is she?* She is far from me; far: not just in space, but in time. It's another, long-lost face I see below me: a white, haunted face I remember in my blood.

You are Ireland, I say; but she is too far off to hear.

❧

450

And so it's the end of April – and the end of our time of deception. Over the past three weeks, while this journal has been silent, Kathleen and I have led a secret life. This is now over, and I'm glad of it.

During those weeks, we imagined that we concealed our feelings and our liaisons; but Bess Langford has now made clear to me how little we actually hid. Being furtive about my intrigue with Kathleen made me uneasy in my dealings with James, and particularly with Bess; but I didn't feel ready to confide in them. As for Kathleen, she was deeply afraid of what they might think or do, and begged me to postpone saying anything to them at all. It didn't matter how often I told her that neither Bess nor James Langford would question my actions, or whatever wishes I might have; Kathleen thinks as a passholder, and her mind is full of fears: the special fears bred by Van Diemen's Land's system.

What made her most fearful was the fact that Mrs Langford is the only one of us here at 'Clare' who is free, and not Ticket-of-Leave. Bess Langford is Kathleen's mistress, in the eyes of the Convict Department; it's Bess who can legally decide her fate, while James and I can have no say in the matter. Bess can keep her at 'Clare', or return her to the Brickfields Depot – or worse, to the Cascades Factory. Kathleen likes and respects Bess, but she's also in awe of her; and this I can understand. Bess Langford is a formidable woman.

During the week, Kathleen and I could only be together when she crept to my room at night. Her Sundays off were our best time. Then, in the afternoons, we could disappear on walks into the bush – meeting well away from the farm, on the forest-covered hill that rises in the west beyond the pickers' huts.

The time of heat was gone; April's air was crisp, and made more so by the tang of eucalyptus. Although soft rains had begun, there were still many days that were fine, with a golden, delicate sun. Colours grew darker and more dense: the blue of the hills in the east, and the brown of the soil in the hop fields below us – which were presently being ploughed, in readiness for next season's planting. Distinct as an etching, each white-trunked gum tree, fence post and lichen-coated rock. The valley was held in a cold, glassy light: a light that resembled Europe's. When I picked up a stick and snapped it, the sound was sharp. Sharp as well came the warbling of the magpies, and the screams of the little parrots. Nothing was muffled or vague any more, now that the heat was gone; almost, I felt at home.

Taking deep breaths, I would find myself striding fast up the slope, leaving Kathleen behind. Short-legged, unable to keep up, she toiled behind me as best she could, through flax-yellow bush grass lit with gold; and I would stop and turn and see her wave to me, in her peaked straw hat. At a distance, in this large hat, she looked childlike: a girl of perhaps twelve years old. She was never ill-humoured about being left; her smile was free of reproach. But the jaunty tilt of her head, and the humorous light in her wide-set eyes, seen across the clear, gold space between us, would touch me with regret at my thoughtlessness.

Once, though, I was in the mood to walk fast for miles, and grew impatient. I did not slow down or wait. Then she called after me, her high, thin voice rising in the land like one of its bird-calls, and carrying a plaintive note. Turning, looking back at the diminutive figure in its straw hat, I was pierced by guilt; and as well, by an irrational fear. It was as though she was farewelling me – as though I was losing her for ever. She had come to a halt, down the slope, and as I watched, she began to cough, her hand over her chest. She went on coughing for some time, stooping a little and frowning; and I saw that she was in distress.

I hurried back down the hill to her. When I reached her, she looked up at me, still holding her chest, and tried to smile; but she was drawing in air with difficulty, making wheezing noises that were only too familiar. I held her, my arm about her shoulders, until the attack was over; then we sat down on a fallen tree.

– That was very bad, I said. Do you know what is the matter with you, dear?

– Sure, it's just a cough.

– No. I believe you have my complaint: asthma. I should have known before.

– I know nothing about it, this asthma. It is nothing but a cough.

– It is asthma, and must be treated. I'll find a doctor in New Norfolk, who will come and see you.

But now she grew alarmed, and fearful.

– I want no doctor. If he finds something wrong, Bess may not want me to work here.

I told her this was nonsense, and that Bess would not think of opposing my wishes – in this, or in anything else. But she only grew more agitated, and I agreed to do nothing for the present. But she must take Stramonium, I said; and should she have a bad attack, I would insist on bringing a doctor to the farm.

Like all human beings coming to know each other, we have exchanged the stories of our lives, walking hand in hand through the bush, or lying in the grass on the top of our hill.

Between these lives, there stretches a gap of such dimensions that I sometimes wonder how it can be bridged. It is like that distance at home between the cabins of the peasantry and what Kathleen calls 'the Big Houses'. Fitzgibbon and O'Neill came from such houses, I told her – but in my case, the estate was lost. She grew sorrowful over this on my behalf, as though I had been reduced to a poverty like her own. She has no bitterness towards those more fortunate than herself – only towards the English.

Her story was soon told – the story, that is, of her life before the Famine destroyed everything. The joys of sitting around the table in the cabin in the evenings, before a turf fire, eating hot potatoes from the common bowl, and drinking sweet milk. Weekly visits to the town of Adare, with all her family, to attend Mass. A priest who made her frightened when she went to Confession. A pig she grew fond of, and how she was heartbroken when her father finally slaughtered it. But of the Famine, and what had happened to her family, she would not speak again, although she would sometimes speak sadly of her parents as they once had been.

Knowing that I speak almost no Irish, she seldom breaks into

453

the language, except for a few words – and these I always ask her to explain. One she uses frequently is *a-ghrá* – which means 'darling'. 'Robert, *a-ghrá*,' she will say; and in English, she calls me 'my honey'. She is comfortable in English, this being the language she was taught in at her hedge school, and the language used by the Catholic priests. Like all our people, she is deeply religious, and deeply superstitious. God and the Virgin and the saints are always on her lips, invoked with a sort of artless familiarity which is nevertheless deeply reverent. When I told her that my Old English ancestors were Catholics, but that my family had later become Protestant, she stared at me in deep concern.

– Ah, then, you must come back to the Church, she said.

I laughed.

– And why should I come back to the Church of Rome?

She frowned, looking at me, and I saw her hesitate, not knowing what to say for fear that she might offend me.

– Because it is the true Church, she said, whatever the English may say. And if you are a Catholic, our Blessed Mother and all the saints will protect you in all that you do.

– Don't they protect a poor Protestant?

– They do – but only because I am praying for you, she said. Every night I ask God and the Blessed Virgin to attend you.

Her gaze was fixed on me with a mixture of humour and devotion, and I checked an impulse to laugh. She is not easily hurt; but sometimes an unintended slight will wound her deeply.

Close to the western side of the house – a side that's little frequented – there's a small gully, which we skirt on the way up the slope towards the pickers' huts, and the pasture where the dairy cows graze. Last Sunday evening, returning from our walk, we wandered down into this gully, in order to exchange final kisses in a spot that was hidden from the house. I found the place gloomy, in the twilight: empty of trees except for a few spiky bushes and some dark-haired she-oaks, and with a somewhat eerie stillness in its air that brought on sombre conjectures. Something had once happened here, I thought: something grim and sad. Perhaps the vanished Aboriginal people had used it for their ceremonies; or more likely, some of them had been slain here by the valley's first settlers.

As though reading my thoughts, Kathleen said suddenly:

– I do not like this place. It's a place where ghosts might be. My bedroom is not far away from here, and sometimes at night I hear a sort of howling which comes from this hollow. And queer voices.

She had heard nothing but native bush animals, I told her; all the creatures here were nocturnal, and made strange noises at night. She had probably heard possums, or the ugly native dogs called devils.

We lingered; but it was not a place where one wanted to stay long. Clumps of European stinging-nettles – no doubt introduced here by accident – showed deep green among the blanched grey bush grass, and Kathleen pointed to them.

– These are going to waste, she said. I should take a bunch in to Bess Langford.

When I asked her why, she told me that the nettles could be cooked, and eaten as greens with our meals.

I laughed.

– Eat nettles? I don't think Bess will thank you for that, my dear. Nettles are poverty food – and we are not so poor as that.

She stared at me in silence, with an expression of dismay. Then her eyes filled with tears.

– I am not so grand that I know about these things. At home we would boil nettles to keep us alive.

And she turned away, one hand pressed to her mouth.

I took her in my arms, begging her forgiveness for having caused her hurt. But she wept; and it was not about the nettles that she wept. Pressing her face into my shoulder, speaking in a muffled voice, she said:

– You will grow ashamed of me soon, Robert. You will grow tired of me.

I took her face between my hands, and turned it upwards to look at me, and murmured my ardent reassurances. Soon, she was able to smile at me again. She has a natural cheerfulness that seldom leaves her for long, and she is easily mollified – perhaps because she wishes to be. Or perhaps because her hopes are constructed out of air, and she wilfully ignores those English official shackles that are coiled about our lives.

Both probation passholders and Ticket-of-Leave-holders may marry, if they humbly petition the Governor for permission. But the thought of having to do such a thing in order to marry Kathleen fills me with revulsion.

When I mentioned the idea to Thomas O'Neill, he was horrified. In going to Denison as a convict supplicant, he said, and asking his permission to marry – and to marry a fellow-convict into the bargain – I would demean myself in a way that was not to be contemplated. Could I not see that?

He became quite passionate on the subject, begging me to consider the use that would be made of such a step by our enemies in the English press, and asking me to postpone any such decision; to give myself time to consider.

I agreed, which was not hard to do; and I am still considering. I need to think deeply about entering into so momentous and unusual a bond.

On one of our walks on the hillside, coming back towards the house, I began to ask Kathleen about O'Donnell: the brute who had violated her.

I hadn't mentioned the subject before, since I hadn't wished to revive what she'd suffered, on that farm at O'Brien's Bridge. Nor had I wanted to bring back to her the memory of the loss of her baby: a loss which I suspected was often in her thoughts. But there were certain unanswered questions that had been revolving in my mind for some time, and which troubled me.

Had she had much to do with O'Donnell, I asked, in the time before he attacked her?

She glanced at me quickly, as we walked between the shadows of the gum trees. At first, she didn't reply. She wore a grey velvet bonnet today, and a shawl about her shoulders, the clothing of Summer no longer being adequate. The sun was setting, and the air was blue and still: it had begun to grow cold, with a first, icy thread of Winter running through it. Yes, she said finally, O'Donnell had talked to her sometimes, when they met about the farm.

This surprised me; I had somehow imagined that very little contact had existed. I had pictured O'Donnell descending on her without warning or encouragement: a convict satyr. But no; he had actually been quite kind at first, she said.

She told me more, speaking in brief, jerky sentences. Their both being Irish made it natural for Dan O'Donnell to take an interest in her; and since he was farm overseer, she had wanted to please him, and show herself a willing worker. He was not in direct authority over her – but he sometimes gave her little tasks to do, such as carrying provisions to the fields. O'Donnell was a favourite with their master, Mr Pearce, who permitted him to take charge of most things – while Mrs Pearce was a timid woman, with very little control over the servants, who questioned nothing that her husband did.

– Old Pearce loved the brandy bottle, she said. He enjoyed his pleasures, and left most of the work to others. So he was letting Dan do anything he wished.

– Was there a time, perhaps, when you saw O'Donnell as a friend? Or when you allowed him to feel that he might hope for something more?

She frowned.

– No. I am telling you I was friendly with him: that is all. And why would I not be? I had come to this place a prisoner, with no-one to stand by me anywhere. And here was one of our own, who seemed to be kind to me. I did not understand then that he wanted only one thing from me – like Mr Pearce.

– What are you telling me? That Pearce –

– Yes. Pearce, she said; and now her voice grew fiercely angry. He took hold of me one evening in the passageway, he being filthy drunk, the red-faced pig. He tore my dress, but I fought him and got away. So now he hated me – and that is why he sent me to the Factory after Dan had done what he did, and made no complaint against Dan.

I stopped, causing her to stop too.

– My dear, I'm sorry, I said.

The words were inadequate, and both of us knew it. It was growing dark quickly, and we had come without noticing into the gloomy little gully. She looked at me in silence, and her face had grown obscure; but I saw that its expression now was hard in a way that was new to me, and her eyes cold.

– The truth of it is, she said, that I liked Dan well enough at first, but not as a man I could love – never. He is horrible in his ways, and frightens me. And he ruined me, just as I told you: he came upon me near the stables and forced me. He is very big, with great strength in his arms, and I could not stop him: when I cried out, he hit me in the jaw to make me dizzy. I went to Mrs Pearce to complain, and to ask that Mr Pearce defend me, and punish Dan O'Donnell. But instead, they said that I must have caused it; that I must have lured Dan on. And later I was found to be pregnant.

She paused, looking off into the dark between the trees.

– Before I was sent off to the Factory, I stayed well away from Dan. But when he heard that I was pregnant, he came up to me and told me that he would marry me, and make the child his. I refused; I told him never to come near me, for I hated him. After-wards, when I had lost little Brigid, and had gone to Doctor Howard's, Dan came there looking for me, still wanting to marry. But I would never agree, and would not speak with him.

– But you spoke with him in that hotel on the Old Wharf.

She looked at me, her face a white blur in the dark. Yes, she said: when O'Donnell and his friends had surrounded her there, he had begged her again to forgive him, and to marry him. He had seemed sincere, and she had felt half sorry for him now; but she had liked him no better. She remained afraid of him, and told him so; nothing could make her love him, and she told him that too. But she had accepted a glass of gin from him, hoping to leave soon after.

It was now so dark that I could no longer make out her expression. But her voice remained bitter.

– I was foolish to do so, she said. And now I think you despise me, Robert.

458

I kissed and reassured her with all the conviction I could summon. No, I said, no. I would never despise her; she must put such a thought from her mind.

And now I truly hated this gully, with its doomed, unknown spirits moving like smoke among the trees. I led her away up the slope, making for the lights of the house, which glowed like certainty.

This morning, Bess Langford brought our deception to an end.

I found her alone in the kitchen, setting out cups on the long pine table in the centre of the room. A cup of tea in the kitchen, with a snack such as pancakes or apple pudding, is a daily ritual at eleven o'clock. Langford and I come up from the fields for it, and Richardson and O'Leary are asked to join us – the only meal that they ever take in the house. Today, however, I'd not been in the fields; I'd been working at my desk, and had walked down the hallway about ten minutes early. I came in and sat down at the table, and at first Bess and I talked of inconsequential things. Kathleen, who was usually about at this time, was absent.

To sit here like a field hand gave me pleasure. Less well-finished than the rest of the house, the kitchen was that of a pioneer home-stead, with no pretensions to being anything else. The floor was of stone flags, and its windows looked out on to the verandah, framing the farmyard and the kiln. A straw bonnet of Bess's, which I'd never seen her wear, hung on a peg by the door; James's long percussion rifle was slung on two pegs above the stove. There was a dark, heavy beam across the ceiling, from which hung sides of bacon, some pots, and a laden fly-paper. The fly-paper seemed not to deter new invaders: their low, sleepy buzz was always to be heard here. Hens ran in from the verandah at odd times, through the open door; one cheerfully accepted these bucolic irruptions, in Bess's kitchen. It was her pivot of command: the house's heart, whose odours of baking made it soothing to the spirit. It was warmed by a fire that never went out, burning in the black iron range at the room's far end.

Using a dishcloth, Bess picked up the steaming black kettle that stood on top of the range. She carried it across to the table, and poured the water into a giant teapot. As she did so, she said:

– Now do wait for it to brew, Mr Devereux, before you pour yourself a cup. Give it three minutes, won't you?

She always employed my title in addressing me – despite an invitation I once made to her to use my Christian name, as James does. She could not feel comfortable, she said, being so familiar with me. She said it firmly, not humbly. Humility is not Bess's style; nor, I think, is it in her nature.

My official partner in the farm is an energetic woman, some forty years of age, who gives an impression of remorseless physical power. Large, with a handsome figure, she carries no extra flesh. Despite her habitual good humour and frequent, hearty laughter, there's a certain severity about her – even, I sometimes think, an air of concealed threat, ready to be unveiled if needed. But I may imagine this. In no way slatternly, she appears nevertheless to have little concern for her appearance – not, that is, of a feminine or frivolous kind. Her thick brown hair, beginning to be streaked with grey, is always pulled back in a bun. She has a long, lean face and a strong jaw – often set hard when she concentrates on something. Her large, dark blue eyes have a cold, insistent stare, the whites strikingly clear. When they remain on one's face, they tend to make one draw oneself upright mentally. I would like to call this stare honest, but I'm not sure that it is.

Perhaps I'm unduly influenced here by thoughts of her past – of which I know little. Bess is so forthright and direct that it's difficult to see her as Langford's accomplice in crime; yet this, of course, was what she was. Whether honest or dishonest, however, she gives the impression of having a very strong will, of knowing exactly what she wants, and of being unlikely to submit to anybody. Yet she is no shrew, and treats James with affection and respect. I suspect that he is one of the few men who could win this deference from her. She is, I believe, a woman who has seen the worst of the world, and yet is prepared to treat the world tolerantly – provided it offers her no trouble. When she drinks her ale or porter in the evenings – which she and Langford love to do – she never grows visibly tipsy. But her heavy eyelids droop, then, and her stare seems to contemplate a past of unimaginable enormities; of chasms of risk. Then I glimpse the woman who was her husband's associate, helping him to hide the profits of his fantastic episode of banditry.

I have learned that Bess comes originally from a village in Essex, but spent many years in London, where she worked as a seamstress, and where she first met Langford. Whether she ever did rural work is something I've not discovered, since she doesn't encourage personal questions. But she's taken to being a farm wife as though she's done this work all her life; and in any task that's needed – even milking cows – she shows herself formidably capable. She's clearly happy to be mistress of 'Clare', and is entirely committed – as Langford is – to their new colonial life.

This morning, as on most mornings, she wore a loose, grey-blue print dress with an embroidered collar fastened by a brooch, and a coarse sacking apron to protect her from kitchen stains. The dress's long sleeves were pinned above the elbows, baring her big, shapely arms. Having carried the kettle back to the stove, she turned to face me again.

– I suppose you'll be wondering where our Kathleen is, she said. She's out collecting eggs. She'll be here in a moment, I've no doubt. So you can set your mind at rest.

– Really, Bess? Why should Kathleen's whereabouts give me concern?

– Come, Mr Devereux. Don't you think I see your eyes follow her, whenever you sit down at this table? Don't you think I see the way she smiles on you at breakfast, when she puts down your bacon and eggs in front of you? Can you deny it? More: can you deny that you and she are in love with each other?

She held up one hand, palm outwards, in a gesture that James often used.

– I know I've no right to speak to you like this.

– Well, Bess, you and I are business partners, and you may speak to me as you please, I suppose. But this is all very personal.

– I don't deny it is. I don't deny I'm being personal, and perhaps I ain't got the right to be. But the girl is my responsibility, you know, with that blasted Convict Department looking over my shoulder. And I worry about her.

A hen strutted through the door. Bess broke off, grim-faced, and ran down the room, clapping her hands; there was a flurry and a squawk, and the hen was gone. Returning, Bess sat down, and began to pour tea for us both.

– James worries too, she said. Look here: we both know how it is between you – do you think we don't? And we wonder where it's leading.

She pushed my cup across to me, glancing from under her brows.

– You're a gentleman, and she's what she is, poor little Irish creature: so what has she to hope for? Excuse me, but that's what we ask ourselves, you see.

I poured milk into my tea and leaned back in my chair, postponing my reply. Then a sort of happy madness took hold of me – induced, perhaps by the embrace of the kitchen, with its beneficent dry odours of baking, and the range's welcoming warmth. Why should I ever leave 'Clare'? Why should I go back to the struggles and treacheries of that other, northern world?

– Well then, Bess, I said, I'll answer you very simply. She has marriage to hope for.

She put down her cup and looked at me. Her brows were raised, her expression blankly sceptical.

– And you're serious about this? No gammon?

– No gammon, I said.

Bess frowned, and her eyes continued to assess me. She sniffed – a habit with her, accompanied by a sideways twist of her nose and upper lip. Then, apparently satisfied with whatever it was she had seen, she smiled.

– Well now, she said. Well now. You do surprise me – but I'm sure you know your own mind. I'm happy for you. And I'm happy for her: she's a good, warm-hearted little thing, and a game one.

She stood up from the table, leaning on it with one hand.

– They'll all be coming in, at any moment, she said. But I've this to say, Mr Devereux, before they do. If Kathleen's to be your wife, she can't go on as our serving maid, now can she? Not in the family. She'll help me with the work, I hope, just as she does now – but I don't suppose you'll be wanting her to go on serving us at table, and then eating her meals on her own: will you, now? She should join us when we eat – wouldn't that be fitting?

Why yes, I said. That was certainly my wish, and would make me happy.

Bess nodded, looking at me directly. Her eyes, always cold, even when she smiled, were difficult to read.

– And there's something else, she said. There's no need for that poor girl to go sneaking out at night to you, now that the cold weather's here. She'll catch her death. Take her into your bed, and have done with it. Won't that be easier for us all?

At the Ship Inn, Hobart Town
May 4th

Ten o'clock at night, in this penal capital: curfew time. Tolling of St David's clock, the sound's solemn circles widening in the dark above the town. Sitting before the fire in my room, I find that the day's events have made me disinclined for sleep.

I came down by coach from New Norfolk this morning, on one of my regular trips to the city. Since Doctor Howard surrendered Kathleen to me, I no longer stay overnight at Bay House. Howard still urges me to visit him, which I do; and we continue to be cordial, and to enjoy our conversations. But there's a subtle constraint between us, and I feel easier being his guest for a shorter duration. So I stay now at this comfortable hotel in Collins Street: the terminus for public coaches, in the middle of the town.

I had some shopping to do today, and some calls to make: on Howard this afternoon, and this evening on Liam Kinane. But my first call, as always, was at Lenoir's antique bookshop. The old man had written to inform me that a number of books and newspapers had arrived for me from London.

I have come to rely on Monsieur Lenoir not only for new and old books, but for good conversation. He seems always to be pleased to see me, and will talk with me for an hour at a time – breaking off to serve customers with a sigh and a show of reluctance. If I make a move to go, he will usually detain me longer by introducing some new and interesting topic. His rudeness, it seems, is only visited on customers whom he despises as crass, and has not been directed at me again – although he's always inclined to be frank. He's a strange, complex old fellow, the range of whose interests has proved to be surprising. I've discovered that he's not only a bibliopole, but a devoted bibliophile whose knowledge of his subject is extraordinary, and whose chaotic hoard of books is richer and more vast than at first I realised. He corresponds constantly with other collectors and bibliopoles around the world.

He issues no catalogues; he employs no assistants. People who come looking for rarities must go through his dusty book-mountains for themselves, and I'm told that some of the book-buying colonial gentry dislike him intensely, regarding him as a rude, shabby, grasping old bookman who forces them to pay exorbitant amounts for books that they can't otherwise obtain. People whom he likes, however, and who respect his knowledge, see him quite differently – and these are sold books at very reasonable rates. One day I saw him ask an amount for a volume which the customer said was too much. The man was a pompous official, and Lenoir eyed him sourly, and told him to take it or leave it. A short time later, he sold it to a man who came in whom he liked – for half the price.

Most of his customers – those outside the Royal Society, at least – are quite unaware of his worldwide reputation; and they would be startled to discover what circles he once moved in. He doesn't boast of these things; I've extracted them from him in tantalising glimpses. He let drop once that he'd been a friend of Leigh Hunt's, for example, in the years when Hunt edited the *Tatler* and the *London Journal*. He also knew Charles Lamb quite well, whom he refers to as 'poor, gentle Lamb'. All this keeps me intrigued by him, and makes me greatly look forward to my visits to his shabby, narrow little shop in the Jewish section, with its odd, hat-shaped gable. When I pass the windows of Nathan and Moses, and catch sight of Lenoir's ghostly sign, fading above the doorway in the lane,

I seem in some strange way to enter Europe. It's a dingy, shabby Europe; a Europe of those narrow and dubious streets in Paris near Montmartre, or of the dirty lanes and courts in London off the Tottenham Court Road – but Europe nevertheless. I enter it when I come to Lenoir's many-paned display window, where the bitter white face of the Emperor peeps out from his Limbo on Hobart Town, from under the half-drawn blind: trapped in an exile more terrible in its tedium than that of Saint Helena. (*Reduced to this! Reduced to this!*) And there are times when I hurry towards this window with a strange sense of yearning. These are times when that mood has come upon me which makes me physically ache to be out of Van Diemen's Land: an ache that's considerably eased through my rambling conversations with the old bookshop man.

Few of his customers and acquaintances know anything much of his origins. He is seen as a mystery, and discourages prying questions. He's known to be French, of course – but even in this, he's puzzling to his fellow-citizens, since his English has very few French sounds in it, and is well-nigh faultless. However, he's been willing to divulge more to me than he does to most people. Perhaps this is a sign of some regard for me – although one can never be sure, with so caustic and inward a man. And they are details that leave me unsatisfied, being given quite impersonally, as though about someone else. Perhaps, in a sense, they *are* about someone else: another self left in Europe, long ago.

He was born in Paris, ten years before the Revolution; and I'm fascinated to reflect that those ancient, deep-set, greenish-blue eyes must have witnessed in their childhood (however disjointedly, however uncomprehendingly), the greatest drama of that century: the scenes of the birth of the Republic, and afterwards of the Terror. In adulthood, he saw Napoleon ride through the streets in triumph; and I suspect that even now he nurses some sort of sad regard for his lost Emperor. Why else does the one-time master of Europe sit on that little shelf in the window, staring out at Liverpool Street? He is not for sale.

Lenoir seems to have no formal religious beliefs – but his parents were Jewish, and his father had some sort of shop or small business in Paris. He's not forthcoming about its exact nature, beyond saying that it was humble enough to attract no unfriendly attention from the authorities – or from the *sans-culottes* – through the years of upheaval. The Lenoirs remained equally undisturbed during the reign of Napoleon, and Jacob seems to have joined his father in the business. But for some reason he doesn't discuss, he and his wife moved to London in their middle age, in about 1820, where he set up in business as a dealer in curios and antique books, and became a British citizen. He seems to have maintained a connection with Paris, and to have divided his time between the two capitals. Then, when he was in his mid-fifties, with his children grown up, his wife died. He emigrated soon after to Van Diemen's Land, in 1836.

He discourages any questions about his reasons for this, beyond saying that he was growing old, and wanted a change. Perhaps his wife's death caused him shattering grief. Perhaps he lost his money. I cannot know.

This morning, when I arrived, the shop was empty of customers. Lenoir was hunched at his roll-top desk under the platform he uses for storage at the dim, far end of the shop – his usual situation when there is no-one to serve. His green Russian cap was on, and he was huddled in a voluminous grey top coat and cape. He feels the cold, and yet there's no fire in the shop. The oil lamp was burning on his desk, and I found when I came up that he was examining a sea-shell under a magnifying glass.

As well as being a bibliopole, Monsieur Lenoir has a worldwide reputation as a conchologist. So he corresponds not only with his network of book dealers and book-lovers, but with fellow-conchologists, and with the British Museum. He has published a monograph on the land shells of Van Diemen's Land, and wanders about the countryside and shorelines looking for his molluscs, as well as paying others to bring them to him. One that he discovered has been named after him – an honour of which he seems quite proud, and which has brought him much respect at the Royal Society here. His own collection of shells is said to be one of the largest in the Australian colonies.

Half-turned away from me, he did not look around, as I approached; yet I knew that he was aware that I was here. There would have been a quick, sideways glance: this being his usual way. As I came up to the desk, he spoke to me, still peering at the shell.

– What do you think, Devereux, is there a God?

I unbuttoned my greatcoat, took off my hat, and sat down on a straight-backed chair that stood beside his desk: my usual place. I have learned not to be surprised by any of Lenoir's conversational gambits, and I told him that I was still prepared to consider God's existence possible – despite my puzzlement over the evils He tolerated, and the scepticism of free-thinkers I admired, such as Shelley and Tom Paine.

– As for you though, monsieur, I said, would I not be right in assuming you to be a rationalist, and a non-believer?

He frowned, and turned in his chair.

– You would assume wrongly, he said, and held out the shell to me.

– I am a believer in mysteries, he said. And the greatest mystery of all is how something like *this* – so delicate and exquisitely made – could be thrown up by blind chance. Study it through the glass, my dear young man, and you will see the hand of God at work. It is not the *precision* of this pattern that convinces me, but its beauty: a quite *unnecessary* beauty. One might almost see it as frivolous – eh? So: is it possible that a blind mechanical universe would give birth to a beauty that is frivolous – other than to delight our hearts? Or perhaps they delight the heart of the Supreme Being – what do you think?

I laughed, and said that I was inclined to agree with him. I admired the blue and green whorls through the glass; he told me his sea-creature's name, but I've forgotten it already, having no interest in molluscs.

Lenoir now pulled open a drawer of his desk, dragging out a bundle of newspapers and periodicals.

– Here are your latest London papers, some as late as January, he said. And a copy of *Punch* to enrage you. I took the liberty of looking through them. Europe seems to have been quiet, in January. No wars, no revolutions to stir your blood. No great news from Ireland.

467

I picked up the papers hungrily, sighing as I scanned them.

– January! I said. An age ago. In these last three months, who knows what may have happened in the world? We are as far away here as though we sit on the moon.

He glanced at me, putting on his spectacles.

– You grow restless, he said. You pretend to be a contented Vandemonian land-owner, but I think this pretence is already wearing thin. How much longer will you stay here, Devereux, while your followers wait for you to return?

I reminded him that I was not in a situation where I had much choice, and could certainly not return to Ireland. Why did he ask such a thing?

He grinned, and stood up.

– I believe you may escape, he said, when you are ready. The world is large – there are many places that you could go. Come – I will make us some coffee. It is so damned cold, this morning: I feel it, when snow is on the mountain.

He shuffled away, leading me into the long back room of the shop. This is a storehouse for more books, and is also his kitchen and sitting-room. At the far end, a fire burned on top of an iron colonial oven that had been fitted into the grate; a kettle boiled on two iron bars suspended across the flames. There was a kitchen cupboard, some chairs, and a Turkish rug on the floor. This room opens into a smaller one containing a narrow bed and Lenoir's shell collection, which is housed in glass cases. A crude wooden bath-house stands in a yard behind, close to the noisome Rivulet. This is his whole accommodation. His shop is his home, and he seems entirely content with it. Lenoir is a survivor of the age of perfume, and of indifference to cleanliness and bathing: an eighteenth-century man.

He made coffee now in a wickedly dirty iron pot. As I watched, I told him that I had no immediate intention of escaping. But he shook his head, and grinned at me again.

– The Governor thinks that you will, he said. You and at least one of your comrades. He waits for it to happen. He *longs* for it to happen, so that he may put you in Port Arthur.

I asked him how he knew this. He picked up two grimy cups

and carefully poured our coffees, watching always through the far door for customers.

– As you know, he said, I have friends in the Royal Society, and also among my customers, who are highly placed in the Government – and who dine quite often with Sir William and Lady Denison. In particular Mr Bicheno, the Colonial Secretary, who is a jolly, well-read, conversable fellow, and who comes to me for all his books. These men know nothing of our friendship, and they gossip rather freely. It's the chief amusement here. They tell me that Denison despises Mr Fitzgibbon, who tries to be a martyr, and is confident he can crush him. But *you* he actually hates, my dear. He has reports on you from London, and has read your articles, where you called for the de-railing of trains and the taking up of arms and such things. These reports horrify him – he calls you arrogant, dangerous, and a terrorist. He also hates Mr Barry, and Mr Kinane. You three seem in some way to fascinate him – and he wishes to put you all in chains. He writes to his masters in London, asking that they free his hands to do so. So be careful. There are ways in which he might trap you.

We carried our coffees back into the shop. When we'd resumed our former places, I asked him what he meant. Bending to sip at his coffee, holding the cup in both hands to get warmth from it, he spoke without looking at me.

– I mean that you should be careful of spies, Devereux. You are watched.

– Really? By whom?

– But you already know, I think. By Doctor Neville Howard, of course – but also by your compatriot, Mr Casey. You will not of course tell him that I said so. I would deny it.

I asked him how he knew Casey, and he told me that Casey bought books from him.

– His is not a face that I would trust, he said. But that is neither here nor there. I cannot reveal where I learned what I am going to tell you, Devereux, but will simply remind you again that I know many public officials. Eh? You understand?

He glanced about the shop, as though a hidden customer might be eavesdropping. But there was only one lone gentleman here, turning over books at a table, too far away to hear. Lenoir leaned towards me, lowering his voice.

– Well, then: Mr Casey plays a double game for the English, and has done so for years. He will be well rewarded for it. That is all I will say.

– Some of us have suspected this, I said. Yet it's still difficult to believe. Casey is even helping Kinane to produce the *Exile*. Now why should he do that, if he's an enemy?

Lenoir spread his hands – one of his few gestures that seemed French – and pushed out his lips.

– Think, Devereux: you are not very good at intrigue, are you? That paper is very reckless, you agree? I am acquainted with your Mr Kinane also, you know – he buys many books from me, and we talk. You stare: but this town is so small; what do you expect? He talks often about you and Mr Barry – you are heroes to him. Very dangerous, is it not, to be a hero for someone? He may end by hating you as much as he loves you.

He sipped his coffee, and shot a crafty glance at me.

– He is always eager to talk about 1789, and the great years under Bonaparte. When I tell him that Napoleon betrayed the Revolution, he's not happy.

He chuckled wheezily, and went on.

– A great reader, your Mr Kinane. He is a revolutionary from the people, no? One of the kind we knew in France, who is clawing his way out of ignorance and poverty, who is hungry for knowledge because knowledge will give him power. Forgive me, Devereux, but this kind of man is driven in a way that you of gentle birth are not.

I opened my mouth to object, but he held up his hand.

– You are driven by idealism: and you are the ones who actually *make* revolutions; not Kinane. Robespierre and Saint-Just were of your kind. But Kinane is driven by a rage and desire of a different kind from yours. These are the men who are revolution's soldiers: I know them.

He sighed, looking past my shoulder: looking, I imagined, to those days which were over before I was born, and which resound

470

in my fancy like a dark and thrilling dream, turning always into nightmare, and the Terror.

Then he came back to himself. He opened a drawer and drew out a newspaper, which he opened and spread out on the desk.

– Here is the latest copy of the *Exile*, he said. You have seen it? No? Then you may not know how close to the wind your friend is running. I understand that when he set up this paper, he was told that direct criticism of the Government would not be tolerated. And he has told me himself that after his editorial criticising the treatment of your comrade Martin Fitzgibbon, the Comptroller-General of Convicts gave him written notification that he would not be permitted to comment again on any measures taken by the Government. Well, he has mostly been clever enough to avoid doing so directly, since then. But now listen to *this* effort, which he signs. It deals with the paper's independence, and answers some Irish letter-writer who questions that independence.

He lifted the paper and coughed, peering at it through his spectacles.

– 'The Lieutenant-Governor is not invested with any Prerogative, by which he could prevent our publication. And we say perish all earthly hopes, and welcome death along with exile, before we consent to be the tool of the British Government or any of its dependencies.'

He threw the paper across the table and leaned forward, his voice sinking now to a harsh whisper.

– The fellow loves trouble, does he not? He's worse than *you*, Devereux. And what do you think will come of his thumbing his nose at Denison like this? I will tell you, my dear. The Governor will have the evidence he needs to close his paper down – and also to ask London to allow him to do with Mr Kinane what he wishes. He is doomed, I believe, your Mr Kinane. So *now* do you see why Mr Casey encourages him to be so daring in print?

I swore, and the old man nodded many times.

– Yes: on behalf of his masters, Mr Casey is giving your passionate comrade the rope with which to hang himself. Be sure that he does not do the same with *you*.

471

I thanked him for the warning – and asked him why he'd given it to me.

He looked at me severely, as though I had insulted him, and slowly shook his head.

– Perhaps because you make my life more interesting than most of the blockheads who come in here, he said. Perhaps because you like authors such as Victor Hugo. Perhaps because you are a *romantic* revolutionary. The other kind depress me – the fanatics, I mean. Yes, I like romantic revolutionaries – even though I know now that the games they play and the poems they write can change nothing – since most human beings will always be of two kinds: the bad, and the stupid; and the stupid are mostly led by the bad. The good are very rare, and quite outnumbered. It is for this reason that I agree with Benjamin Constant: democracy will probably bring us despotism in the end, and a new oppression by the masses, instead of by kings and nobles.

I smiled. My liking for Hugo and other French authors was what had made Lenoir warm to me; and a 'romantic revolutionary' is how he likes to see me. He came to his middle age in the period of the Restoration in France, after 1815, when Socialism and workers' movements had flowered there; and he seems to have been an enthusiast for these things. Despite his being resident in England at the time, he had given me to understand that he was somehow caught up in the Paris Revolution of 1830 – the 'good revolution', he called it – when the Romantics had given their support to the cause of liberty, to the notion of the rule of the common man, and to the cause of the poor and humble. But something had made him disillusioned.

– You are very pessimistic today, monsieur, I said. Remember that Constant also believed in the natural rights of man. And he said that man was a temple, containing the divine.

– I too once wanted to believe those things, Lenoir said.

He stared into his coffee cup, holding it suspended in a way that was incongruously elegant, as though he sat in a drawing room; and his eyes, in their deep hollows, held a sudden, infinite sadness I'd not seen there before.

472

– But I seldom see evidence, he said. So I no longer study men, or seek their company: I prefer to study my molluscs. They give me no disappointments.

He gave me a cynical smile, dismissing his mood as quickly as it had come.

– With you, I make an exception, young fellow. Can you guess why? Because we have something in common. Your nature as an Irishman and a rebel has made you an outcast among those of your own class. Even when you do nothing – as is now the case – you make them uneasy. I think you are an exile in more ways than you know: I believe you are misplaced in the world. And this of course is my own position.

– How so, monsieur?

Lenoir's glance at me now was shrewd and almost suspicious; he seemed to doubt the sincerity of my question.

– Because I am a Jew, he said softly.

For a moment, I could only look at him blankly.

– But surely, I said, nobody in this colony has troubled or insulted you on that account? And you are held in high regard here for your scholarship.

He waved a blue-veined old hand impatiently, on the third finger of which he wore a large ruby ring; he wrinkled up his face as though at a bad odour.

– Yes, yes, yes, he said. I am tolerated as an intellectual jester – and they call me a dirty old Hebrew behind my back. I know this; I have always lived with it, and no longer care.

– But monsieur, I can assure you, in my own case, this is not something that I think about.

– I know this, Devereux, he said, and avoided my eye, his tone brusque and dismissive. There is a freemasonry of the intellect, fortunately, to which you and I belong.

He drained the dregs of his coffee, and set the cup down with a click.

– So tell me, Robert Devereux, where do you stand yourself, in regard to the common man and woman? I have heard you say things that are not complimentary to them. Can you tell me honestly, although you say you fight for them, that you do not also despise them?

I sat in thought for a moment.

– Once I might have almost said yes, I said. But since being transported my opinions are more complicated. I scarcely knew the people, before.

He looked amused; almost mocking.

– And now you *do*, my dear?

In response to this, I was compelled to speak to him of Kathleen – being at that fond stage of love where to speak of her gives me joy, and where I look for excuses to do so. I had fallen in love with a woman of the people, I told him; and I went on to describe our situation.

Now he grinned openly. He has very few teeth: this and his sceptical expression made him look almost villainous. Had I not known him better, I might have taken offence; as it was, I merely broke off.

– So, he said. And are you going to do what men of your class so frequently do with women of the people? Enjoy her, exploit her, and discard her?

I told him quite hotly that I would not. I intended to marry her, I said.

He raised his brows, his head on one side. For some moments he said nothing, but merely rubbed his chin, looking at me.

– You are serious, he said. You are actually serious. Bravo, Devereux – bravo. I see that you really *are* a romantic revolutionary.

A fat man in a beaver hat came in the door: another customer. We both stood up, and I gathered my papers and books together, telling Lenoir that I must go. He continued to squint narrowly into my face, as though studying one of his shells. Then he took my arm and guided me to the door, his bony fingers gripping quite hard. As we went, he murmured in my ear, too low to be heard by the customer:

– You are very impulsive, Devereux, and I think you have no head for plotting. Remember what I say, and beware of those who do.

∽

At three in the afternoon, as I rode in a cab to New Town, my thoughts dwelt on Liam Kinane. Lenoir was right in his predictions, I felt sure: unless our over-zealous comrade could be persuaded to give up his recklessness in print, he'd very soon find himself dragged off to a penal station. So far, he'd disregarded every warning my comrades and I had uttered – and his foolishness made me angry. But it was the anger one feels towards a rash yet gifted child. After all, he was one of us, and I resolved to do everything I could to make him see his danger when we spoke together this evening.

Matthew Casey was another matter. What I felt towards Casey was something more than anger and less than anger; and it was mingled with a deep perplexity. A traitor is a monster, and one loathes and despises a monster; but he's unworthy of being the subject of an emotion so passionate as anger. One wishes to destroy him, simply; and one cannot understand him, since his humanity is lost. Why had Casey done it? Why had he betrayed his own? Driven simply by greed for money? Or driven by hatred? Perhaps by both; but if so, what was the source of Casey's hatred? And how had he hidden it so well?

I had no answers to these questions; and even now I asked myself whether some mistake was possible, and whether we somehow did him an injustice. So unbelievable was his treachery that I toyed with the notion that the double game he played was for *us,* not the British: that he merely pretended to be their spy. But I wasn't really able to convince myself of this. In a subterranean part of my mind to which I hadn't listened, I'd known Matthew was treacherous before his treachery began to be seen; had known it without knowing it, as it were – even in the yard of the prison at Spike Island. I simply had not listened to that small, uneasy voice.

Doctor Howard and I sat over tea and cakes. Although still crisp, the weather had turned bright, still and sunny, and a table and two chairs had been placed beside the fish pond, on the lawn at the front of the house. At the edge of this lawn, Howard's garden sloped away quite steeply, so that he and I seemed almost to be sitting on an elevated platform. Below us, beyond the garden's bronze autumn trees, empty yellow slopes rolled towards Mount Direction, and the ranges of hills in the east. A broad stretch of the Derwent shone in the sun. It was a wide and lovely landscape, and my gaze kept returning to it as we spoke.

We had talked for over an hour on neutral subjects: the progress of the hop farm, and Langford's success with it; the news from Europe; books that had lately diverted us. Now things took another turn.

It began with Howard's asking a question, put in a deceptively casual manner.

– And shall you be seeing your friend Mr Kinane on this visit?

I said that I would; I intended to call on him this evening.

– Hm, said Howard.

He had bitten into a seed cake, and chewed for a moment, his eyes behind their spectacles narrowed against the sun's late rays. Then, brushing crumbs from his waistcoat, he said:

– I'm glad to hear it – because I'd like to ask a favour of you, Devereux. I recall that you don't approve of Liam Kinane's newspaper, and I'm wonderin' how you'd feel about suggestin' that he'd do well to cease publication.

– Really? And why should I do that?

He looked out on the view for a moment, apparently gathering his thoughts. The barking of a dog rose out of New Town's bowl of peace, and a man's distant voice, shouting.

– One hears little sounds for miles here, Howard said softly. I grow very fond of this spot.

Then he turned back to me, his voice growing businesslike.

– I'm sure you'll have noticed that Kinane's attacks on the Government grow more and more blatant, he said. He's a headstrong and intemperate fellow, and he lacks commonsense. He's givin' Sir William Denison a good deal of annoyance, just between ourselves. I believe the Governor may withdraw Kinane's Ticket, if this continues. He may even go further.

He sipped his tea and looked at me.

– I agree that it's an absurd situation, I said. It's absurd that a man who's a convicted felon – at least, in your Government's eyes – should be indulged to run a newspaper at all. *That* is why I oppose it,

476

Howard – not because I disagree with any of Kinane's opinions. But he'll not listen to me – nor to my comrades. So why should I seek to persuade him again on your Government's behalf? And why does the Governor simply not close the paper down out of hand?

– Well, now, said Howard, I'll try to answer you. Firstly, the Governor doesn't want to cause a public outcry – and I speak to you very confidentially, Robert. Secondly, should *you* get Kinane to give up his hobby horse, you'd be doin' it for the man's own good. You might well be savin' him from incarceration at Port Arthur, to be frank.

He leaned to pour more tea into our cups, glancing up over his spectacles as he did so.

– But what's more important is the good it might do *you*, my dear fellow. I was about to tell you that I would hope for a *quid pro quo* from the authorities. Should you succeed in stoppin' this nuisance, it would bring you a good deal of credit, do you see – and we might start buildin' a case for your pardon.

I sat silent, looking at him. Suddenly, I had a wish to bring things out into the open: to be done with this polite, stealthy game. When I answered, I spoke as mildly as possible.

– You mustn't try to buy me, Neville. I thought you had more regard for me than that. Nor must you take me for a fool. I have little doubt that you act at your Governor's behest – and at the behest of your masters in London. Why not be plain about it with me?

His eyes grew suddenly cold: a look that now seemed natural to them. He put down his bone china cup.

– I have never taken you for a fool, Devereux. I'm not tryin' to buy you, and I'm infinitely distressed that you think so. I'm merely tryin' to help you. And what is this talk of 'masters'? What are you tryin' to say to me?

– That you act as a spy for your Government – and always have done.

He half-closed his eyes, drew in breath through his nose, and sighed. Then he said:

– Very well. From time to time, in the past, I served the Royal Navy's intelligence service. I no longer do. I'm bein' quite open with you, Robert, since I've come to esteem you highly. I'm excessively sorry that you should regard me as treacherous – or as hostile to your best interests. I only wish you well.

– Is that what you said in your reports on me?

He threw back his head in that way he has, and looked down his nose at me from under his lowered lids.

– For a man whose business is intrigue, there are times when you do seem naive, he said. I assumed all the time, on the *Medway*, that you'd realise I was reportin' on your situation to London. That was my duty. I was also foolish enough, as our friendship grew, to assume that you would guess my reports were sympathetic. And they *were*, damn it.

– You were wrong in your assumptions, I said. My business is *not* intrigue, as I believe I have often made plain. I hide nothing. I despise intrigue. What I give my life to can always bear the light. It doesn't need to skulk in the dark.

He blinked at me, his mouth tightening. I saw that I had offended him, and felt a certain shame. But I pressed my advantage; and my tone, I'm afraid, grew sardonic.

– And what of your current reports? Are *they* sympathetic too?

– God damn it, there *are* no regular reports! But of course, since I associate with you, I'm compelled to keep my superiors informed – including the Governor. Again, I assumed you'd know this, Devereux, and would know too, since we're friends, that I do all I can to present you in a favourable light. However –

He broke off, and suddenly stood up. He took a few paces to the edge of the lawn, where the land sloped away. Here he stood with his back to me, hands in trouser pockets, rocking on his heels – apparently surveying the view of hills and river that his garden commanded. After some moments, he turned and walked back, and I rose from my chair. I was startled to see in his face an extraordinary tautness and pallor, and was startled still more when he reached out and gripped my shoulders. I'd always seen Howard as changelessly sanguine, no matter what the circumstances; but now, when he spoke, his voice vibrated with vehement chords of pain.

– Jesus *Christ*, Devereux! Has it not become apparent that I like and admire you, whatever I may think of your politics? Yet you sit there glowerin', as though you've been given some injury! You Irishmen are *children* – all of you!

He dropped his hands and stood back; then he thrust them into his pockets again, and gave a sharp sigh.

– Well, perhaps that childlike aspect of your nature is one of the very things I've liked about you: it goes so strangely with your understandin' of so much else. But what you cannot know is how I've protected you: how many times I saved you from unwelcome attention by the authorities. Even, on one occasion, I may say, from being sent to hard labour. I *struggled* for you, damn it! I even struggled to save your life, in gettin' you off Bermuda. You are my country's enemy, and I had my duty to perform; but you know that I've understood your misguided devotion to your cause, and even your refusal to compromise – which my colleagues call stubborn pig-headedness. *You* call it livin' for the truth, I imagine. But I have to live with reality, Devereux, while you –

His mouth worked. Then he went on:

– You, if you'll pardon me, are living in a child's dream, Robert. Even your revolution is a dream, and will probably remain one.

He pointed a long finger at my chest.

– But don't see *me* as some cunnin', skulkin' spy who seeks to damage you – that is not the way of it. I'm not the first naval surgeon – nor the first intelligence agent either – to come to respect and like a man whom he's forced to keep under observation. Is this beyond your understandin'?

It was I who now turned away, and walked to the brink of the lawn. I needed to collect myself: my heart was beating hard, so surprising had been the force of Howard's outburst. It was difficult to doubt his sincerity; and I began to feel regret for the way in which I'd spoken. I gazed out at the eastern prospect. Mount Direction had turned a deep mauve, as sunset came on, with indigo in its bosom. Nearer, in the middle distance, a low, empty grass-rise was being flooded with gold. When I turned back, I said:

– I do most sincerely apologise, Howard, for any discourtesy I may have offered you.

479

– Accepted, Howard said, and watched me without expression.

A shadow from the fountain that rose in the centre of the fish pond lay across the grass between us; it was beginning to grow cold on the lawn.

– But you must understand, I said, that I still have to regard you as one of my captors. I'd be foolish to forget that, would I not?

He sighed.

– In my case, Devereux, I wish that you'd make an exception.

– I sincerely wish that I could. You often saved my sanity on Bermuda: I know that, and I'm deeply thankful to you. And I've greatly valued your company, Howard. But life has placed us in contrary positions, and there's no help for it.

He put out his hand. His expression was profoundly sober, and possibly touched with grief.

– Then let us at least shake hands as friends. We can do little more, it seems.

We did so, and I left.

I'll not see Doctor Howard again, I believe. Both of us knew it. We had spoken together for the last time, on the edge of his beautiful lawn. Raised above that landscape in the east, we had been like travellers going nowhere.

At seven-thirty, having eaten a chop at the Ship, I walked up the hill of Goulburn Street, where Kinane had taken lodgings.

The air was dark and icy now, and there was beginning to be a fog. Blurred candles trembled in windows; phantom-like broughams and cabs rumbled by. The sign-boards and lamps of the taverns receded with the street lights into a dirty white vacancy, and I stepped off the kerb to avoid bands of shouting whalers. Soldiers and whores, arms linked, loomed and dissolved in the mist; one redcoat bent vomiting by a fence.

Kinane had been pressing me to call on him for some time, in letters written to me at New Norfolk. I searched for his cottage, while laughter and curses and fiddle music followed me through the fog. Why Liam lived in St Giles, I couldn't imagine. He had very little money, of course; yet I wondered why he hadn't looked for cheap accommodation somewhere else, rather than in this warren of criminals and the lost.

His lodging proved to be a mean weatherboard cottage with an attic window, a tiny front door, and a few miserable feet of weedy garden. It was close to the entrance of the lane that had led me into Black Lion Square. The fog had become so thick now that I stood enveloped by whiteness, peering at the number on the gate. Figures passed me in silhouette, their steps muffled. I put my hand on the gate and pushed it back.

As I did so, a voice said:

– You won't find him at home, sir.

I turned, and found that Matthew Casey had materialised behind me. He'd appeared out of the fog as though he had dropped from nowhere, clad in a low-crowned hat and greatcoat – yet somehow I wasn't surprised. He leaned lightly on a blackthorn cane, propping it at an elegant angle; his amber eyes peered at me through their spectacles, and he grinned.

– Good evening, Devereux. I came after you to tell you that Kinane is not in the house, he said. We're drinking in the Concert Room of the Bull, and I just now saw you go by. Won't you come and join us?

He pointed into the whiteness with his cane, indicating the dully glowing lights of a tavern I'd just passed.

– I told Liam I'd come and fetch you, he said. Excuse me if I gave you a start.

– Not at all, I said. But this is very odd, Casey. Kinane was expecting me to call on him here at this time; it was arranged between us.

Now Casey looked embarrassed – or affected to be so.

– Ah, he said. Well you see, Devereux, to be quite truthful, Liam is not reliable when he's in drink. And that's the case at the moment, I'm afraid.

– Is it, indeed?

– Yes, that's how it is, sir. He's really very drunk.

He looked quickly down at his feet, digging between the flagstones with his cane.

– He's been drinking since yesterday, he said. Yes, since yesterday, without going to bed, as far as I know – and scarcely even eating, I'd imagine. I know how he is at such times. He told me some days ago that he was expecting you. He was so delighted, Robert! Full of joy and pleasure.

He looked up at me brightly: the bearer of good news. Then he became solemn again.

– He feels a little neglected, you know, by you and your comrades. They write to him only rarely – and he hears of your meetings at the Lakes, and he longs to join you there. I'd like to join you myself, Robert – I can picture the jollity and excitement, when you meet out there in the wilderness.

His grin was odiously ingratiating. If he expected an invitation, none was forthcoming; instead, I stayed silent, clenching the fist that I'd thrust into a pocket of my greatcoat. I wanted to challenge him; to tell him that I knew what he was. But this would simply have been foolish. Like him, I must wear a mask until I could find out more: until I had proof. Creatures who wear masks force others to do the same, it seems.

– So poor Kinane feels himself cut off, Casey was saying. Cut off from those stirring meetings of yours, where he imagines your talk is all of Young Ireland. He's thwarted and maddened by his confinement to this city, and your coming meant a great deal to him. But then –

– But then he began to drink, I cut in. Damn him: how long has he been doing this? I mean drinking like a sot?

The anger in my voice, ostensibly directed at Kinane, was the anger I felt towards Casey. He blinked at me, his face becoming sober and wary.

– Come, he is not really a sot, Robert. No, I wouldn't call him that. There are times when he won't touch a glass – not for weeks. He tries very hard not to give in to the drink – he knows it's his enemy. But he often has great unhappiness. He misses his wife and children; he fears what the authorities may do to him; and then he begins to drink. And when he does, when he joins his cronies in one of the taverns, he simply can't seem to stop.

He soars away, then – soars into the clouds, as it were, and won't come down.

– How oddly you put it, Matthew. You seem to understand him very well.

– I believe I do, Robert. And I try to help him. Kinane is a man with a great deal of heart. A man who overflows with fervour, and wants to fly free of the earth. He has *too* much ardour, perhaps. His feelings often overwhelm him, and he pays no heed to consequences. That, of course, is a dangerous way to be.

He lifted his blackthorn slightly, sighting down its length as though it were a sword, and seeming to cogitate.

– His feelings are too near the surface – and he's never a careful man. Like so many of our poor Irish people, he doesn't know how to be careful.

– But *you* do, Matthew – you are a very careful man, I'm sure.

– I hope so, sir. And I try to counsel brother Liam to be cautious too – in the hope that I'll keep him from falling from the sky.

His smiling glance was so self-satisfied that it set my teeth on edge.

– Commendable, I said. But I understand that you also assist him with this God-damned newspaper of his. Would you call *that* a wise and cautious venture? Are you not concerned about the consequences of such foolishness?

– I'm sorry that you and Barry and O'Neill still think the *Exile* foolish – although no doubt your point of view is consistent with your views and ultimate aims. But the paper means a lot to the Irish settlers here – and it stabs Liam to the heart that you are set against it. As for me, I do very little, sir. The paper is all his; he even writes most of the articles. But I help on the practical side – and I like to think that I keep Kinane from going too far, and thus giving the Governor the excuse to close him down.

– I see. Your concern goes beyond normal friendship, I'm sure. But he has other friends who fail to keep him as restrained as you do, it seems. And he's with them now, you say? And you suggest that we join them?

– If you want to see Kinane, sir, I regret it's the only way. I'm not fond of the Bull, myself: it's a dangerous and disreputable place. But there'll be no getting him out of there now, until he drinks himself insensible. Or else is thrown out.

The Black Bull was a grim, two-storeyed structure resembling a giant packing case, being built of dim grey weatherboard. The sign over its lamplit main doorway was plain and direct: BLACK BULL. TAP. But we didn't enter there; instead Casey led me to a smaller doorway, further down the street.

Here, an ornate signboard was propped against the wall, reading: MELAPHONIC CONCERT ROOM: *Ethiopian Serenaders*. In order to go in, we were obliged to pay a shilling to a hulking ex-felon seated at a table.

We sighted Kinane at once. He was leaning against a bar counter, in a big, resounding room that was crowded to its dirty green walls. Sailors and their women danced in a space in the middle. Others sprawled at tables – most of them half insensible. At the far end, on a low stage, sat the performers whose music rose above the din: five black-faced men in huge bow ties and bedraggled silk costumes of many colours, who appeared at first to be Africans. But they were merely nigger minstrels – their faces blackened with burnt cork, their pale eyes staring from out of these masks like those of comic demons. On their hands they wore black gloves. These were the Ethiopian Serenaders. They played banjoes, fiddles, and bone castanets, and I found them grotesque and dispiriting; but the lively American ditty they sang was clearly pleasing to their audience, who jigged and shouted the words:

> – *De Camptown ladies sing dis song,*
> *Doo-dah, doo-dah . . .*

This is all I remember of it; but I do so with horrid clarity, since it repeated itself in my head for the rest of the evening, and would not be dislodged.

Kinane slowly turned to me, swaying as he did so. He stared at me without recognition, his eyelids drooping. Casey grasped his arm, murmuring into his ear like a courtier, and Kinane's wet lips then curved into a sheepish smile.

– Devereux, he said. You're here. You mus' – mus' *forgive* me.

He gestured around him.

– Got caught up here with associates, and –

He broke off and frowned, apparently losing his thread; he looked at Casey, and back at me.

– But Matthew found you, so all's well. Yes? All's well. You're here!

He smiled again, holding out both huge hands in his usual manner. I took them with some reluctance. He would not let me go; he squeezed my hands with an urgent and painful grip, leaning to peer into my face, his bulging, bloodshot blue eyes alight with befuddled joy, while his 'associates' watched and smiled too. But then he wrinkled up his forehead in anxiety.

– You're not – not *offended*?

No, I said, I was not offended, I was glad to see him.

I'm not sure that I managed to sound convincing. In fact, I was shocked at his appearance, which had deteriorated considerably since last I'd seen him. His dark blue frock coat was hopelessly stained and creased, as was his neckerchief; his shirt was filthy, his shoes broken. He had clearly not shaved for some days, and his sooty black beard, showing up against the pallor of his skin, as it does with dark-haired Irishmen, made him look as much of a villain as any ex-felon here.

He called for rums all round, and we drank together – he and I and Casey and Kinane's band of cronies. One of these was the unfortunate gentleman I'd met on my first walk in the town: Mark Handley-Smythe, in his tall flower-pot hat, who smirked at me like a long-lost friend, his fingers across his lips to hide his ruined teeth. He was clearly quite speechless with liquor, and I was glad of it. Next to Kinane stood a tipsy young prostitute with crooked eyes, in a smeared satin gown and a coal-scuttle bonnet trimmed with flowers; Liam put his arm about her, introducing her as 'Alice', and stared at me with faint belligerence, defying me to disapprove.

– Alice is my friend, he said; and the young woman turned her crooked gaze on him in simulated adoration. She stroked his cheek, and crooned to him:

– Liam's my sweet man: my honey.

The rest of the 'associates' – some half-dozen men – were of the poorest class of Irish, all of them as drunk as Kinane. It was clear that they all revered him, and attended him like a chorus – or perhaps a set of protectors. One of them stood out from the rest, and could scarcely be ignored: a straw-haired giant called O'Hegarty, well over six feet in height, who seemed to be known to one and all as 'Ballybunion Tim from County Kerry'. He was quite amazingly hideous, with a vast jaw, a broken nose, and a mouth that lacked many of its teeth; he wore a wrecked straw hat and a pilot coat which appeared to be his bedding. He had a sullen and dangerous air, staring at most things around him as though he meditated assault. This, it seemed, was no false impression, since one of the cronies, speaking in my ear, assured me that Tim got into many fights, all of which ended in his opponents being destroyed. He had a grudge against the world, having been flogged many times as a convict. Only when he looked at Kinane did Tim's gaze soften; he was Liam's faithful lieutenant – or saw himself as such.

I could scarcely believe that a man of Kinane's abilities and education came to this place out of choice, and could wish to surround himself with such people. Perhaps he only did it when he was drunk; but even so, I now saw a deadly flaw in the man, which was likely to bring him to some sort of ruin. I resolved to leave the Bull as soon as possible; but I knew all too well that Kinane would do everything to prevent me.

At the outset, he gave me exquisite embarrassment by shouting to his followers that I was 'Ireland's greatest hero' – whereupon they cheered, and toasted me with their pewters of rum, and peered at me in frank and inebriated awe, some of them even clutching at my arm, or squeezing my shoulder. Many more rums were drunk – and then, in an interval when the Ethiopian Serenaders had fallen silent, Kinane insisted on reciting a passage from my speech from the dock after my trial, which he'd faithfully committed to memory. He did so at the top of his booming voice, jumping on a chair to command attention.

He made me inwardly cringe, as he roared out my pleas for Irish freedom, and my list of England's crimes against our land; but there was nothing I could do to stop him. He was drunker than ever, and his voice was slurred; yet he rendered the passage accurately. His memory is remarkable. An interested crowd gathered, and a whaler dared to laugh, and to call out some sort of insult.

He was a big fellow in a red shirt, who looked ready for any trouble. But Ballybunion Tim turned, stared once, and punched him in the mouth. The force of the blow was shocking. The whaler staggered, and then went down on the floor, his mouth a bloody hole, his front teeth smashed. I felt sickened; but the 'associates' were roaring with laughter, slapping Ballybunion Tim on the back.

– That shut his fucking mouth, sure, said Tim, and picked up his pewter again.

– *Doo-dah,* crooned the Ethiopians, commencing the favourite song again. *Doo-dah.*

I decided now to quit the Concert Room, which had become a chamber in a nightmare. I turned to look for Casey, to tell him so. But Casey had slipped away, in the same furtive manner in which he'd appeared. I would have to take my leave of Kinane, but there was no hope of doing so immediately; when the Ethiopians completed their recital, he sprang on the chair again, finger upheld for attention.

– Now we shall sing the loveliest of songs about Ireland, he cried, and much of the slur had gone from his voice. Ireland, our mother and our queen! Stripped naked by her enemies; left without husband or son; the homes of her people wasted! This was written by my comrade, the dear Clarence Mangan – who died but six months ago of the cholera, and may God rest his soul.

Then he began to sing 'Dark Rosaleen'.

I had not imagined that he would sing it as well as Paul Barry did, or even sing it well at all. Instead, I discovered that I was listening to a genuine artist. Despite his drunken state, he sang flawlessly, and I was startled at the richness of his voice. One of his Irish friends accompanied him on a cheap tin whistle, the sound thin and plaintive, and surprisingly poignant.

Poor, eccentric Mangan! This was the loveliest thing he ever wrote, and will surely never die. And the passionate, yearning tenderness, the naked yet delicate intensity of Liam's rendering of the words, is not to be described; all of his love of country and all his bitter grief at the loss of her was in it.

> – Over hills, and through dales
> Have I roamed for your sake;
> All yesterday I sailed with sails
> On river and on lake.
> The Erne, at its highest flood,
> I dashed across unseen,
> For there was lightning in my blood,
> My dark Rosaleen!

If Ireland was a woman, then Liam Kinane was truly in love with her, I thought; and now I regretted every scornful opinion I'd ever held about him. I looked at his flushed, singing, blue-bearded face with a wondering affection: an affection which was extended as well to the upturned faces of his ragged and violent 'associates' – exiles all, as Kinane and I were, and harbouring the same love of Erin. That much of this feeling would fade with the music, I had little doubt; but surely a core would remain. And I resolved now to stay, and to talk to Kinane alone, whatever inconvenience it cost me.

It wasn't easy to get him out of the Concert Room. I was forced to drink a good deal more rum with him before he'd listen to me. Cross-eyed Alice had vanished; so had Handley-Smythe, and most of Kinane's other followers. But still he ordered fresh pewters from the barmaid behind the counter.

Finally, I gained his attention by placing my hand on his shoulder, and bringing my face close to his.

– Listen to me, I said. You are very far gone in drink, Kinane, and should be in your bed. Let me get you home – I want to talk to you.

– Talk, he said. That's right, we must talk, Devereux. Talk here.

No, I said. I had something serious to tell him, and would do so at his lodgings or nowhere. If he refused, I'd not trouble to visit him again.

His large eyes grew larger with surprise; he frowned, and appeared to be on the verge of taking offence. But when I frowned back at him without wavering, he saw that I meant what I said, and seemed to sober a little. He ran a finger through his tangled black curls and looked about him, as though seeking a memory that eluded him; then he quietly agreed to come back to his lodging.

Getting up the hill with him to his cottage, although not far, proved to be something of a trial. He wove uncertainly on the broken, slimy flagstones, tripping in the cracks and cursing. I took his arm to steady him, and now he put a heavy hand on my shoulder, supporting himself as he went along. He peered sideways into my face.

– Devereux, he said. Bold Devereux.

Ponderous and drawling and sentimental, its brogue grown much thicker, his voice dwelt on the fatuous title inflicted on me by the street ballad, and I looked to see whether he mocked me. What I saw instead was a drunken, unrealistic reverence that might have pleased a more vain or foolish man than I am, but which produced in me instead an embarrassment mingled with foreboding. Jacob Lenoir's remark to me this morning was very likely true, I thought: Kinane's hero-worship could prove dangerous, in ways I had yet to discover. There was something in his over-sized, over-zealous, over-passionate presence that made this seem inevitable.

– You have been an in – inspiration to me, he said. Do you know that, Devereux?

He was now having difficulty in finding and pronouncing his words; one had to wait while he did so. I have always found this the most tedious characteristic of drunkards, and the affection I'd felt for him while he sang began to be eroded. I told him that he did me too much honour – employing a caustic note that I hoped would stop his flow. But it quite failed to penetrate his fuddled wits, and instead, he took me literally.

489

– Ah no, joy, he said. I could never do you too much honour.
And it's honour you did me by coming here – and now I'm
ashamed.

His mouth turned down, and his hand tightened on my
shoulder.

– You came to me here, into this filthy stew – into this nest of
low-life scum where I'm forced to live – and I was not even there
to greet you. I'm sorry for that: will you please accept my apology?
It's the drink, you see, Devereux – the drink has destroyed me,
today.

– It had better not do so tomorrow, I said.

He stared, and his gaze seemed to clear for a moment; he had
registered my rebuke.

– It will not, he said. I promise you. But sometimes it grows
hard here. Sometimes the drink is all that stops me from going mad.

I asked him why he was compelled to live in St Giles.

– What else can I afford? At least I have a cottage to myself
here, where it's possible to work on my articles for the paper. Sure,
I haven't the money to do better.

And now I felt ashamed, and fell silent. As we stumbled forward,
Kinane began to sing under his breath, in broken snatches:

– *The heart in my bosom faints*
To think of you, my Queen,
My life of life, my saint of saints,
My dark Rosaleen . . .

He took all the usual trouble of a drunken man in unlocking
the door of his cottage. Inside, it was pitch dark, cold, and intolerably close, and smelled of unwashed clothing and stale food. He
took an equally long time in lighting a candle pushed into a beer
bottle. This he held aloft, illuminating a tiny, box-like room with
a table covered in galley proofs, some kitchen chairs, an armchair
in the last stages of dilapidation, and a sofa covered by a blanket.
The ceiling was so low that our heads almost touched it; Kinane
was like a giant in here. He had made some bookshelves out of

boxes, and these were crammed with works on politics and philosophy. A framed engraving of the Blessed Virgin hung on one wall, together with a crucifix. The front page of the first edition of the *Irish Exile* was tacked up on another. Through a door was a pitch-dark closet I guessed to be a kitchen. There was no evidence of a bedroom.

He swayed, casting a huge shadow on the wall in the candle-light, and put the candle down on the table. He waved his hand.

– My home, he said. My bloody little pigsty. Welcome. Excuse me, but I must –

He suddenly collapsed on the sofa, smiling at me weakly, his head sinking back on to a greasy cushion.

– Have to lie down, he said. Sorry. Pull – pull up a chair.

I did so, and sat down beside him. He struggled to remove his boots, and I helped him; his socks were full of holes, and a toe stuck out in a comical manner. He thanked me, his smile grown childlike; then his big frame sank back into the couch. He had not slept for some time, he said, and was feeling a little tired. I told him that I would not keep him from sleep for long, but that I must speak of certain things to him.

– Aye, he said, do. *Want* you to speak to me, Robert.

It was the first time he had addressed me in the familiar. Reflecting the light of the candle, his strong blue eyes looked up at me, from under their slanted lids: wondering, doubtful yet trusting. Despite their bloodshot whites and the pouches under them, they were arresting eyes: eyes that shone with a force which only death would extinguish. What a power of life flows through some of our men of the people! And how terribly such talented men as Kinane abuse it! Spurred by this thought, I began:

– You are a man of intelligence and capacity, Kinane –

– Liam. Call me Liam. We are friends. Friends.

His look became both truculent and imploring: a drunkard's reversion to puerility.

– Liam, then. Listen to me. Despite your talents, you are dreadfully abusing yourself. I ask you out of concern as a comrade – can you not stop?

491

He closed his eyes.

– Intend to do so, Robert. There's nothing you can say that I don't say to myself. I am sinking into beastliness, I know. Missing my family, missing my true comrades: yourself; Fitzgibbon; Barry and O'Neill –

He broke off, and opened his eyes; they were filled with tears. He reached out and seized my hand.

– I try to flee from the pain. But that's no excuse. Promise you – I will give up the bloody drink. I've beaten it before.

– Good, I said. It can only give advantage to our enemies. To Denison, and all these other colonial jacks-in-office.

– You are right. Yes. Ah, Robert – *you* can save me, sure!

The hand tightened painfully, and I said:

– I can save no-one. I am as isolated here as you are. I can only offer my comradeship and support.

But still he held my hand, gripping it as though he sank into a swamp, from which I must draw him out.

– But you do *not* give me your support, he cried. None of you do. Forgive me saying so – but it's true. I'm alone here, in this vile bloody town. Alone!

– Come now, we're all penned up in our different ways, I said. You know that. We –

But he interrupted, his voice hoarse with feeling.

– I need to *meet* you all, he said. Why – why can I not join you when you go to the Lakes?

I leaned forward.

– You know that's impossible, Liam: your district doesn't touch any of ours. *And you must not leave this police district.* If you do, that bastard Denison will take the opportunity to imprison you. I beg you not to think of it.

– Sure, I can do it and not be seen, he said.

His speech became more coherent, his befuddlement seeming to lift. His chin thrust out stubbornly, blue and wedge-like.

– There's a good, strong little horse that a friend will let me have – I can slip through the hills behind New Norfolk, and so up to the Bothwell district. Always keeping among the hills – never entering a town. See? It's wild country. I'd not be spied.

He smiled, begging me to agree. But I shook my head. Their police were everywhere, I said; and he must not attempt it. He dropped my hand, but still his gaze searched mine.

– You say I'm your comrade. But I'm not truly *with* you, am I? I never bloody was.

His voice had lost all its eagerness; his lower lip crept out, and a sudden, truculent bitterness entered his face.

– Sure, you're all still gentry together, you and Barry and O'Neill – and my kind are outside the door! That's the truth of it, I'm thinking, when it all boils down.

That was nonsense, I exclaimed. Utter nonsense. We all admired his bravery and devotion; we all respected his qualities and his intellect. He was our comrade, and we would welcome him wholeheartedly at the Lakes – if it could only be done without such a risk to his freedom.

His deep blue stare remained accusing on my face; he shook his head, and I knew that my protests rang hollow. In a sort of exasperation at being forced to dissemble, I said:

– But the fact is, Kinane, we disapprove of the *Exile*. You know that, and you know our reasons.

– The *Exile* is a success, he said stubbornly. It pays its way – it sells. Sells very well.

He reared himself up on the couch, propped on one elbow, and looked at me in sorrowful accusation. His voice remained slurred, but he seemed through sheer will to rise out of his drunkenness.

– It's valued – valued by the Irish, not just here, but all around Australia! I give them a voice, do you hear? I speak for freedom, here in these bloody prison colonies! Not just Irish freedom: freedom for all men – even those poor bastards of felons who want to begin life here again. In spite of all the God-damned slander and lies told against the paper, have I not *beaten* the English? Have I not beaten Sir William bloody Denison? And didn't they go on spreading every sort of rumour and false report to destroy me? By Jesus, they did. That I planned to preach revolution against the Government! That I was a *tool* of the Government! Well, they founder in

493

their own shit: I've beaten them, sure! I still bring out the *Exile*, and I win respect. Do you *begrudge* me that success, Devereux? Do you know what you ask, if you want me to give it up?

When I remained silent, he went on; and his voice had now dropped to a throaty, fervid whisper.

– Unlike you fortunate gentlemen, I have no private means. I'm penniless, do you understand? Yes, you do: have I not borrowed money from Paul Barry? And I hated to do it. But I'm now earning a living from this newspaper, and am not ashamed of it. I'm able to send money home to my wife and children – who are living on the charity of relatives. I earn a living from doing what I believe in – do you know what that means to me? And the only help I have is from Matthew Casey, God bless him. From you I have only disapproval.

He pointed a finger at me.

– But what is it that *you* are doing, Devereux? What are you doing for Ireland? It's a black shame that you are here: but have you not turned colonial landowner, and turned aside from the struggle?

Cold rage gripped me.

– What are you saying to me, Kinane? How dare you speak to me like that?

What he saw in my face seemed to quell him; he sank back, and looked away from me. His voice sank.

– Ah, sorry. Forgive me, Robert. I am drunk, and should not have spoken so. Christ help us – you and I should not quarrel. None of us should quarrel. But you strike me to the heart when you condemn the *Exile* – you, whom I most admire. And I cannot understand you, that you wish to do nothing in this place to carry on our struggle. I cannot understand Barry or O'Neill, either.

He closed his eyes, and his face became like stone. With this last speech, all of his energy had apparently been expended, and the drink's heavy stupor seemed to close around him. Perhaps he wished it to.

I leaned over him.

– Listen, I said. You may not like what I say, Liam, but I beg you to hear me, before I go. Only one thing matters for all of us:

to escape. And that time will come. But instead of waiting for that moment, you are letting yourself be used – and are placing yourself in great danger. Denison only tolerates your running this paper because he has you under his eye. What he most wants is to put you in chains at Port Arthur – and he waits every week for the *Exile* to give him that excuse. And meanwhile, his spy sits at your elbow, and urges you on. Do you hear me? His spy!

He looked at me dully. His senses were betraying him; he was sinking towards oblivion.

– Spy? What spy?

– Why, Casey, I said.

He frowned; with an effort, he reared up on his elbow again.

– Casey! Sure, were anyone but you to say so, Devereux –

– Wait, I said.

Speaking very slowly, I outlined the evidence for him. But now he was losing his grip on consciousness. His eyelids drooped, and his upward gaze was only half-comprehending. Sullenly, he shook his big head, and sank back on the greasy pillow.

– No, he said. No, no, no. Not Casey: he's a comrade. Know him better than you do. Not true. You're wrong – all of you. You do him – injustice.

He closed his eyes, and I took him by the shoulder.

– *Listen* to me, I said.

But it was too late: unconsciousness had taken him. His head rolled to one side, and he began to snore.

I am on the coach to Ennis, going home.

I sit on the roof beside a number of other passengers, whose faces I can't quite see. The glad air of Summer flows past us, and all is bright. We are rattling along a narrow little road sunk between steep green banks; brambles grow on top of these, and small white cabins can be seen beyond. Ahead are the mountains, violet and purple. I know this road, and am full of gladness. Oh, how glad I am! I'm free, and at home in Clare!

But then I see with dismay that this is a yellow coach-and-four, driven by a florid, grossly fat coachman in a broad-brimmed hat and green top coat, with a guard in a dirty scarlet uniform clinging to its side, blowing on his bugle. I'm being carried on a Van Diemen's Land stage coach: how has it come here? I grow inwardly cold: I'm seized by the suspicion that I'm not free at all; that I will not be taken to Ennis. I ask the passengers next to me where we are, addressing them urgently: but they seem not to hear. They sit bolt upright, unmoving, and their faces are those of statues.

We turn a bend, coming around the side of a hill – and now I cry out in amazement. We've come into a country that has no resemblance to anything I've ever seen before.

It is certainly not in Clare, nor even in Ireland. The colours here are so bright as to be quite unnatural, and the entire region is suffused with an uncanny yellow glow: a light never seen in this world, bathing the steep green valleys, the flowers beside the road, and the occasional pretty houses – which are rather like the chalets of Switzerland. No people are to be seen. And this landscape has a strange and contradictory effect on me: it floods me with sensual delight, but also with a profound apprehension. I may be irrevocably lost, I say; the coach may be taking me into a land from which it will prove impossible to get back.

No! I'll not submit to this! I turn to ask the other passengers where we are; but they are gone. I'm alone on top of the coach: the driver and the guard have also vanished, and yet the vehicle goes forward, swaying along a road that runs above a very steep valley, the horses trotting on as though their reins are held by invisible hands. And now I'm seized with panic: I fear that we'll topple down the slope.

We come around another bend; the vehicle sways dangerously, sideways above the ravine, and indeed begins to capsize.

As it does so, I leap off, reaching the ground unhurt. I don't turn to see what has happened to the coach, but make my way down the valley. Here, in a quiet, deserted landscape, in a pocket of late green gloom, I come upon a railway line, and a little station. There's no-one on the platform: I'm quite alone here, and the emptiness and silence depress me. I decide to buy a ticket for Ennis, even though I fear that no line runs there; but there's no-one to sell me a ticket. There's a signboard on the platform, beside the stationmaster's house: now, I say, I will discover the name of this place.

The sign reads: PATIENCE.

I cannot describe the horror with which this fills me. PATIENCE. I know now that I am truly lost, and must at all costs escape from this region, and from its morbid, threatening silence. A steam train comes in, and the station is filled with the smell of coal smoke. I board a carriage, and am carried through pallid, empty fields where night is coming on. I'm alone in the compartment, and my fear is still with me: but as the train speeds on its way, the fear becomes icily thrilling, like the fierce anticipation of some dangerous pleasure. We enter a tunnel, and travel through darkness; at the other end, the train stops, and I get out.

But I find myself in a vacuum: in a darkness as black as death. Am I in my coffin?

I hear St David's clock begin to strike the hour, and I lie and count the strokes. Four in the morning, and I'm not lost after all: I'm flooded with relief. The fire in this bedroom in the Ship has burned itself out, and has begun to smoke. There's a fierce, thrilling smell of coal dust.

3. FORESTS OF THE SOUTH

At Glengarry Cottage, Bothwell
July 24th

A frosty mid-winter night. The fire of spitting gum logs in Thomas O'Neill's parlour burns bright and high as always.

He and Martin Fitzgibbon and I sit close to it, with O'Neill's kangaroo hounds dozing at our feet. I'm here to spend a few days as O'Neill's guest, and to see how Fitzgibbon is faring in his new situation. The night of Bothwell is cold and diamond-hard; the mountains move closer in the blackness. Outside the cottage, there's ice in the water-barrel, and in the puddles on Nant Lane.

Fitzgibbon, his spectacles on his nose, a sheet of paper held out in front of him, is reading aloud: a poem of his own composition. O'Neill and I, pipes in mouths, look carefully into the fire, our faces inscrutable.

The poem lies in front of me as I write; Fitzgibbon gave copies to us both, and so I transcribe it here:

> I wandered in a foreign land,
> Through hoary grass and moping hills,
> And wept, lamenting for that band
> Of comrades crushed by Albion's mills.
>
> But then I raised my head and saw
> A fairy child, between two trees

That bent above her like a door.
She smiled, and brought my spirit ease.

Child or fairy? Maid or child?
I scarcely knew; my gaze was dimmed.
Her face was elfin, sweet and wild;
She'd sped here on the teeming wind.

O sweet the smile that touched your mouth,
Thou sprite transported from the North!
You've come to bring back hope to me,
And charm these forests of the South!

Finished reading, Fitzgibbon puts the sheet down on O'Neill's sea-chest. He clears his throat and takes off his spectacles, looking from one to the other of us: half apologetic, half proud, like all determined amateurs who insist on offering their creations to an audience. In his tail coat and white cravat, he looks more than ever like a banker: a poetic banker.

– I call it: 'A Van Diemen's Land Fay', he says.

I draw on my pipe, neckerchief pulled off, toasting my stockinged feet at the coals, and appear to ponder; I don't want to make the first comment on this insipid little broth, brewed from elements of Wordsworth and Alfred Tennyson. Fitzgibbon has enough technical ability to be a passable versifier – but I dread hearing his efforts, since he quite lacks genius.

– Delightful, says O'Neill.

Ever kind and tactful, he lightly claps his hands, his large eyes resting warmly on his friend.

– Yes, delightful, I echo. Quite delightful.

As though reading my thoughts, O'Neill says:

– It reminds me somewhat of Tennyson's 'Rosalind' – always a favourite of mine.

Then, seeing Fitzgibbon's permanent little frown grow deeper, he adds hastily:

– Not that it *imitates*, Martin – no. But there is a faint echo: possibly coincidence.

Fitzgibbon allows him a small smile. Yes, he concedes, there may be an echo, since that poem is one he's fond of too. But it was not in his mind when he wove these verses about his subject.

– And who is that subject? I ask. A fairy of your own imagining – or some delightful daughter of Bothwell, seen in the woods?

Fitzgibbon pauses before answering, looking at me cautiously and rubbing his chin. He has the ability to make one feel that almost any direct question is crudely inquisitive: an invasion of his privacy. In this he resembles a stiff-necked Englishman; he lacks Irish warmth, and easy Irish frankness.

– No, she is not imagined, he says. Although I doubt that she could be described as 'a daughter of Bothwell' – if by that you mean a daughter of the people. She has for her model a gently-bred young lady: my pupil, Edith Morton. I believe you saw her for a moment, Devereux, when you and O'Neill came visiting yesterday afternoon.

Here I should set down the fact that Fitzgibbon no longer lives in O'Neill's humble cottage, but is merely visiting. He has moved to nearby 'Grasmere' – where the Mortons have made him very comfortable. He wanted some employment to occupy his mind, and has therefore replaced O'Neill as tutor to the Morton children: the two boys, Ralph and John, who are aged eight and ten, and the girl Edith, who is eleven years old. She came into the parlour and curt-seyed to us yesterday: a typical little Anglo-Saxon, with long, pale blonde hair and transparent skin. For his schoolmaster's duties, Fitz-gibbon is paid sixty pounds per annum, together with his board and lodging. He instructs the boys in English, Mathematics, Geography, History, Natural Science and Latin, while Edith is taught English, a little Mathematics, Geography, French and drawing – Fitzgibbon being quite skilled at watercolour. He undertook this tutorship at O'Neill's urging. O'Neill declared that he had tired of being school-master to the Morton children; he was much more happily occupied with his botanical pursuits. This is partly true; but I suspect that he also recommended the occupation to Fitzgibbon in the hope that it might cure the poor fellow of his melancholy, and relieve his loneliness. And in this, our generous O'Neill seems to have been successful. Fitzgibbon now has an appearance of contented calm, in striking contrast to the miserable figure he presented when we met at Tunbridge. The climate suits him too: he is growing quite ruddy.

– Why, yes, I say to him now. I recall the child. A delightfully pretty girl. Excellent manners. They bloom here, these children of the English settlers – I've noticed it frequently.

– I dedicated my poem to her, Fitzgibbon says. Her mind is mercurial: she loves stories, and her fancy takes flight in a way that's a delight to see. She eases the pain I feel when I think of my own daughter, and of how old Jane may be before I see her again.

His face grows deeply sad for a moment; a silence falls, and he reaches down to scratch the ear of Brian, one of the hounds.

– Edith sometimes makes me forget that I am here, in this wild outpost – and so do her parents. The Mortons are kindly people – as I'm sure you'll agree, Devereux. At 'Grasmere' I have a life that's possible to bear, for the first time since being flung into this accursed island. There are times when I find myself almost happy.

– I'm truly glad to hear it, I say. I have found the same happiness at 'Clare', as you know. But where is this taking us, Fitzgibbon? Shall we sink roots in this southern soil? Shall we forget where we belong?

Leaning back in his chair, his newly ruddy face becoming serene and philosophical once more, Fitzgibbon raises his eyebrows.

– What are you asking me, Devereux? No, we'll not forget – but what can we do?

– Will you not think of escape?

He shakes his head.

– I have accepted their wretched Ticket – as all of you urged me to do. I have given my *parole*. I can't now escape with honour. No – I must wait for a pardon, as Thomas here is doing. And as you must do.

O'Neill sets down his brandy glass, stands up, and yawns. Then he says:

– Let us not talk of escape tonight. Let us accept our lot, and have peace of mind. This fire and the brandy have made me unusually sleepy – I'm off to my bed, gentlemen, if you'll excuse me.

Fitzgibbon begins to rise, but O'Neill holds up his hand.

– No need for you to go yet, Fitzgibbon. Fortify yourself with another brandy and water, before you ride out over the cold paddocks. Devereux is a night owl, like you – he'll sit up and take a nightcap with you. You still have much to talk about, I'm sure.

– A good idea, Fitzgibbon says. Our factions would expect it of us, Devereux.

His smile is both cautious and ironical.

But our talk, as it turned out, didn't concern our factions, and wasn't political at all; instead, it was entirely personal.

Tonight, for the first time, Fitzgibbon and I achieved a measure of mutual ease – as far as ease is ever possible with Fitzgibbon. He and I had never before found ourselves alone together; we had always conversed with other comrades present. Now, enjoying the comfort of O'Neill's fire, with the pleasant, civilized litter of his books and papers about us, and only his kangaroo dogs for witnesses, we were both encouraged to unbend – and took pleasure as well in the uniqueness of our position. Here we sat, in this far, Antarctic region – contained, as it were, in a small, warm pod, and surrounded by black, icy air whose piercing and terrible purity was like the ether beyond the earth: leaders with no-one to lead; martyrs whose martyrdom the world was half-forgetting. It was true what Fitzgibbon had said: we still had our factions, he and I. The newspapers from Dublin and New York told us that our rival followers continued to invoke our names, and conducted their feuds by stridently declaring that Fitzgibbon would have approved of this, or that Devereux would never have tolerated that. But it was all unreal; it could have no substance for us, and we seemed to be reading about figures who were no longer ourselves.

We discussed none of this. Instead, in a mutual, unspoken decision to avoid those topics that would raise the spectre of political conflict, we talked only of our present situation, and of what was tolerable in it. I spoke of 'Clare', and of Langford's success with our

502

first harvest; and I hinted at my fondness for Kathleen, and of how she brought me solace.

His narrow brown eyes watched me curiously; he drew on his cheroot, and blew a long stream of smoke.

– Ah, said he, and pondered the fire. Then he turned back to me, and said:

– Such a liaison would be impossible at home. But I'll not judge the wisdom of it. Better that you should care for a woman from the Irish people than for some false and haughty young lady from Van Diemen's Land society. And do you know, Robert, sometimes it seems to me that we are not only outside normal custom here, but outside the everyday world altogether. Certainly Bothwell seems so. Many things seem possible that would not be possible at home.

– I often feel so myself, said I.

We nodded at each other; and a genuine, uncharacteristic warmth came into Fitzgibbon's sober face. It was one of those moments when more is understood than the bare words seem to convey.

The highlands delighted Fitzgibbon, after the wretchedness of his imprisonment in the cottage at Port Arthur, and the tedium of Oatlands, in the plains. They had brought him exhilaration, he told me: an illusion of freedom. In these rolling, parklike, virginal spaces, he felt almost as though he'd been liberated from his sentence; and he'd found the first ease he'd known since he was carried to Van Diemen's Land.

'Grasmere' had enfolded him in a thoughtless, child-like peace; and I could see that it offered him more. His painfully sensitive nature had been given its self-respect back, after his humiliation by the Commandant and the medical officer at Port Arthur. Mr and Mrs Morton treated him with both kindliness and deference: they respected him as a distinguished patriot, condemning as cruel and unreasonable the sentence of exile imposed on him. So he sat in their parlour and at their dining table as an exiled hero, and was introduced as such to other landed proprietors in the district. All this had clearly been balm to his wounded pride. He had found asylum here, and a sort of tentative happiness.

Charles Morton was the most important proprietor in Bothwell, and his sheep and cattle grazed over many miles of this system of high valleys and plains. Extensive and self-enclosed, with a bucolic self-sufficiency that Virgil would have admired, 'Grasmere' was like a small country, with its many convict servants and green, transplanted English pastures: one which Fitzgibbon scarcely needed to leave, except to ride the mile or so into the village to borrow books from its library, or to visit O'Neill, or to go to church on Sundays with the Mortons. And the contrast between the pastoral intimacy around him and that mountainous wilderness which stood on the horizon was something he never ceased to find strange. Strange too, in this frontier landscape, was the handsome Morton homestead, where Fitzgibbon had been given a snug pair of rooms: an extensive, single-storeyed stone house whose long front verandah was completed by a line of handsome Ionic columns.

This classical gesture in the wilderness had been added to please Mrs Morton, when the place was built. She is a cultivated woman, wistfully determined that the styles of civilization will be planted in barbaric Bothwell. Yesterday, when O'Neill and I visited them, she and her husband proved to be a very amiable couple. They are in robust middle-age; they came here from Sussex, and have that reassuring quality which some people gain when they have found what they want in the world. He is a lean, quiet, grey-haired gentleman with a weatherbeaten face, whose squinting blue eyes, bleached as though from the sun, are amused and shrewd without being cunning. She is slim and pink-cheeked and youthful, her fair hair tinged with grey; her sympathetic gaze rests on one's face with a direct, unflirtatious yet flattering interest that is no doubt very pleasant to Fitzgibbon. Colonial life suits the Mortons – even though they say they sometimes miss the pleasures of life at home, such as good theatre and good conversation. I had mingled pangs of pleasure and nostalgia, sitting at high tea in that parlour, with its Nottingham lace curtains, Persian carpet, brocade-upholstered chairs and grand piano. There, Mrs Morton and Fitzgibbon spend many hours talking poetry together, and reading their favourite excerpts aloud; she also listens to his own verses, and praises them, apparently – which has done much to make him devoted to her. So he has both soothing company, and a number of diversions to keep him from melancholy, in the vale of Bothwell.

One of his solitary pleasures is to walk by the River Clyde – a bend of which lies not far from the back of the house, where his rooms are. This little stream, carrying down its torrents from Lake Crescent, on that high central tableland where we rendezvous, winds through 'Grasmere' on its journey to the lowlands. English willows grow along its banks, and are presently bare – but the native, ever-green gum and wattle and banksia grow there too. Queer though these trees are, Fitzgibbon has come to like them, he says: he wanders in their groves, and meditates. It was here that his 'fairy child' made her appearance.

She emerged from between two wattles, he said, as though through a doorway. She wore a green taffeta dress, with a sash about the waist; its long skirt streamed after her in the breeze like one of those gowns that fairies are shown to wear, and her hair streamed behind her too. In her hand, she carried a willow twig, which she pointed and waved as though with some cryptic purpose, her gaze directed far away, her lips moving. Her expression was rapt, almost devout, as is often the case when children talk to themselves. Her feet were bare, and she carried her shoes in her other hand. She glimmered, he said; and she seemed, in that strange southern twilight, scarcely to be real.

– You smile, Devereux, he said. But her beauty was so extraordinary that it really did seem that I'd seen a sprite of some kind: an Antipodean dryad, perhaps.

I made no comment; but I think that Fitzgibbon exaggerates his fancies, and is inclined to woo the fantastic deliberately. No doubt he thinks it proof of his poet-nature.

Mrs Morton had made her sewing-room at the back of the house into a classroom, Fitzgibbon told me, with desks and a globe of the world. He taught Edith separately from Ralph and John. She spent little time with her brothers, he said, and seldom saw other children. She lived much in a world of her own.

505

It was a world she was soon prepared to share with him, as she grew to like and trust him. And he delighted in encouraging her interest in fairies and fairy stories – which was quite unusually fervent, he found, even for a girl of her age.

He would take her, with Mrs Morton's approval, on sketching expeditions about the property. She had a talent for drawing landscape, and had rapidly improved. Often they roamed by the Clyde, seeking out his favourite grove of trees, where they sat on a fallen gum when their sketches were done, before she went in for tea. He pictured her for me, sketching: crouched on a little stool in her greatcoat, a Scottish tam-o'-shanter on her head that her mother made her wear against the cold, its bobble swinging and jumping as her head turned and moved. Charming, he said: he had made a small pencil drawing of her wearing it. This he presented to her parents, and they were so delighted with it that they had it framed, and it now hangs in their drawing room.

Edith asked him about his home in Ireland, he said, and his family. So he talked to her freely of all that he missed.

Poor Mr Fitzgibbon, she said, and put her hand over his.

As part of her English lessons, he read fairy tales to her. Some of these stories were from the works of the brothers Grimm, but most were by that odd but gifted Dane, Hans Andersen – whom Fitzgibbon deeply admires. She responded with an excitement and fascination that gave him great pleasure; she even loved best the story that was his own favourite: 'The Snow Queen.'

– Such a wonderfully quick, subtle imagination, he said. Imagine, Devereux: she understood at once the story's deepest meanings, and spoke passionately against the falsity of the Snow Queen, and was fearful for little Kay. She's so wonderfully unspoiled. But eventually she'll be sent to a school in Hobart Town, with the empty-headed daughters of merchants and army men: I dread to think of it.

As the weeks went by, early snow began to fall on the great central plateau, so close to them in the north. The air grew freezing: flurries of snow fell in Bothwell, and distant Table Mountain was capped with white. Edith pointed through the window, as they sat at their books. The halls of the Snow Queen must lie there, she said.

– So delightful, he said. She is so delightful – and full of un-spoiled affection. She brings some sweetness back into my life; just to see her appear is a joy. The child and I have similar souls. But there are times when I realise that I cannot know her further.

– Should you wish to do so? I asked.

He looked at me quickly, but said nothing. There is a deep strain of childishness in Fitzgibbon, I believe. Well, there is in all of us; but in him it is more pronounced; and sometimes I think that it dominates his nature. I don't doubt for a moment that his interest in his 'fairy child' is blameless, and that he is filled with only the finest and purest of feelings. There would never be anything base in his feeling for her, I am absolutely sure – and he would be incapable of letting sentiment lead him into any sort of improper affection. He is a devoted father, he misses his own children, and Edith is like a daughter to him – and one who responds in ways that are a consolation to him. And it's apparent from what he tells me that the Mortons are gratified by his attention to her, and pleased by her progress with him.

So why do I feel faint misgivings? I cannot really know, and probably they have no justification at all.

At 'Clare'
August 2nd

A weekly newspaper lies on my desk: the *Hobart Town Advertiser,* dated last Saturday, and collected from the New Norfolk post office this morning. There is a startling and disturbing article in it, which I clip and affix in this journal.

BUSHRANGERS RAID HOMESTEAD
AT GREEN PONDS ⋆

We had thought that bushranging had lately been eliminated. Since Martin Cash and his gang were captured some seven years ago, the community has felt itself safe from organised bands of outlaws. But now it seems that earlier days have returned: the days of desperadoes such as Cash, Mike Howe and Matthew Brady. A ruthless gang of bushrangers is out in the Brighton and New Norfolk police districts, where a number of farms have been raided. The gang is led by an Irish felon named Daniel O'Donnell – until recently a Ticket-of-Leave holder.

Last Wednesday, the bandits descended on 'Glendale', at Green Ponds, the home of Mr George Tucker. Five men, all of them armed, with O'Donnell as their leader, rode on to the farm late in the afternoon, where they surprised Mr Tucker's 22-year-old son David tending some sheep. A double-barrelled shotgun was pointed at Mr Tucker's head by O'Donnell, and the young man was ordered to lead the bushrangers to the house. Here they tied up the servants and plundered the homestead, taking Mrs Tucker's jewellery, a silver watch, ammunition, spirits, and a bag of over one hundred sovereigns kept under his bed by Mr Tucker senior. Mr Tucker's prize hack was also taken – ridden away by O'Donnell. Before the gang left, O'Donnell warned the Tuckers against raising an alarm, or trying to follow them. Should they do so, he said, he and his gang would return, and burn their house and their barns.

These 'gentlemen of the bush' next went on to the Royal Oak Hotel on the Main Road, where they boldly occupied the bar parlour, forcing the landlord to supply all his customers with free drinks. It appears that O'Donnell – who is known to his followers as 'Captain' O'Donnell – deludes himself that he is some sort of Irish patriot. He was in fact a Ribbonman: a member of one of those vicious secret societies of Catholic tenant farmers who burn and destroy the farms and livestock of their landlords. It was for activities such as these that O'Donnell was transported. He apparently made a speech to his captive audience in the hotel, informing those present that he and his men hated British rule in Van Diemen's Land, and that they would set up what he called 'a territory of Irish freedom' in the mountains, where those who agreed with them might come and join them.

O'Donnell's career of bushranging began some two months ago, in June. He had assaulted a man outside a tavern in Campbell Street, beating him so badly that it is said that his victim may never fully recover. Constables were sent to O'Donnell's dwelling in

Wapping to apprehend him. They did not return, and were found in O'Donnell's house many hours later, having been overpowered and tied to two chairs. An insolent note, addressed to the Governor, was pinned to the chest of one of the constables, in which O'Donnell swore never to be confined as a convict again. He had fled into the bush with some cronies – most of them passholders, or absconders from probation gangs.

Their raids began soon after that, valuables being taken from properties as far north as Oatlands. The gang is rumoured to have its depot in the ranges somewhere behind Bothwell, but police search parties so far have failed to discover them in that wild and difficult country. Although no murders have yet been committed by O'Donnell's gang, two constables have sustained gunshot wounds in trying to arrest them. 'Captain' O'Donnell is regarded as a dangerous man, and a reward of one hundred and fifty pounds is offered by the Government for his capture.

* *This article has survived, folded into the journal, and I reproduce it here in full.*

R.B.

Just after lunch today, I gave this item to Langford to peruse.

He and I sat side by side in a pair of cane chairs that stand on the back verandah, close to the kitchen door. Reading, he held the pages of the *Advertiser* open in front of him like a pair of shutters, frowning and breathing heavily through his nose. He'd been in the hop fields before lunch, digging ditches with his men for our new irrigation system; his boots stood beside his chair, covered with moist soil, and his battered felt hat lay beside them. We have taken to sitting in these chairs whenever we want to discuss business: the back verandah is Langford's quarter-deck, where he can keep a watchful eye on farmyard, barn and kiln. Now, waiting for him to finish reading, I sat savouring the thin Winter sun, and listening to the voices of Bess and Kathleen, murmuring to each other in the kitchen. Once, Kathleen laughed. I had not yet told her about O'Donnell, and wondered whether I should do so.

Langford closed the paper and folded it over once, handing it back to me with his brows raised in sober surprise.

– We'll need to keep them guns of ours loaded, and ready by the door, he said.

I stared at him.

– You think he'll come here?

– Oh, he'll come here all right. He'll be looking for *her*. Do you doubt it, Robert?

– I suppose not. And it would seem that his nest is not far away.

– Not far. Somewhere at the back of Bothwell, it says. Less than a day's ride.

– I'll inform the police in New Norfolk.

Langford smiled.

– And what use would *those* buggers be, if O'Donnell and his mates arrived unexpected? Think: the police barracks is five miles from here, and by the time we got word to them – even if we was able – O'Donnell would have done his worst. And most of them bloody constables don't have much stomach for a fight. Sitting in front of a fire suits them better, with a mug of ale in their fists.

I felt my mouth go dry. What Langford was saying seemed unreal.

– For Heaven's sake, James, I said. Are you claiming that the law can give us no protection?

– Not much, if the gang arrives sudden. And excuse me, Robert, but since when did *you* set so much store by British law? I thought you'd no great opinion of it.

He grinned, and gave me a mocking wink. At first, I glared in annoyance; but then I was forced to grin back.

– Very well, James, you make your point. But I shall still alert the police. Aren't you concerned? There seem to be half a dozen of these bandits at least – and all armed.

His eyes went hard and took on their feline blankness, looking across to the kiln.

– Oh yes, I'm concerned. Do you think I want that scum on our property? But it ain't much use to be *concerned*, is it? We'll just have to lock the house up well at all times, and make Richardson and O'Leary keep a sharp look out. I'll give you some lessons in shooting with that nice Holland's sporting gun of yours. If you don't mind me saying so, Robert, you're no great shot − I noticed that when we went after kangaroo.

− Thank you. I seldom had much to do with guns, before coming here.

His grin widened, and when he spoke next, he sounded almost jaunty.

− Well, you'll need to get friendly with one now. Don't worry, we'll make a crack shot of you in no time. We'll deal with that bunch of bloody lags military-style.

− You seem very confident, James. I wish I felt the same.

Bending, he'd begun to pull on his boots. He paused and looked up at me, seeming to savour something.

− I'll see to this bugger O'Donnell, he said. I'll appreciate collecting that hundred-and-fifty-pound reward that's on his head. It'll pay for my irrigation scheme.

He laughed and stood up, his eyes gleaming; and I saw to my surprise that he was half enjoying the prospect. I should not have been surprised, I suppose: the violent and lawless part of Langford has not been banished altogether; it has merely lain dormant.

When he'd gone, I sat quite still. The sun's faint warmth seemed to have faded, and a chill ran through me. Surely Langford was wrong, I said, and O'Donnell and his villains would simply not appear. But I knew in my heart that they would, sooner or later. O'Donnell had always been going to appear: this had been inevitable from the time that I chose to take Kathleen under my protection. And I began to see what it meant to inhabit a frontier society like this one: a place where one's life could be threatened by barbarous louts, and where the servants of the law − once outside Hobart Town − could do little to prevent it.

I laughed under my breath, and shook my head. The situation was medieval, I said: grotesque. But grotesque or not, it would eventually have to be dealt with. My only comfort came from the thought that in such a society, men like Langford emerge as dominant.

At Lake Sorell
September 28th

Evening over Sorell's great water, which gleams like a mirror in an unlit room. The edge of Spring now, piercingly cold but fine. Lights glow in the windows of Paul Barry's new cottage; smoke rises from his chimney, and our laughter fills his little crimson parlour.

Built of weatherboard, the cottage is humble but well-made. It has a shingled roof, glazed windows and a verandah, and stands on a promontory called Dog's Head, on the eastern side of the lake: a finger of land extending for a mile into the water, clothed in dense gum forest. Barry has moved up from the Midlands to make his home here – just inside the border of his police district. He completed the cottage two months ago, having leased a plot of land from a wealthy Scottish sheep-farmer named Ingles, who owns most of the lake shore on this side. Barry brought tradesmen from Ross to carry out the work; and with his usual impulsive lavishness, he has also built a jetty here, and acquired a six-oared boat to sail on Lake Sorell.

A boat! We are amazed and hilarious. It was hauled up from Hobart Town via Bothwell, for seventy-five miles, using half a dozen bullocks. It has been converted to a yacht, flies the American flag, and is named *Young Ireland*. It takes Paul out to an island in the lake – also leased from Mr Ingles. There, a hired man ploughs Barry's fields, and plants his oats and potatoes. Another hired passholder – an English ex-sailor called Brown – includes in his duties the occasional navigation of the boat, and cooking. In his hermit-like situation up here, Paul is no doubt glad of the company of these servants, since he only sees Mary McCormack once a week now, when he rides down to Ross. But I have the impression that the arrangement suits him.

There are six of us here, filling the parlour from wall to wall: Martin Fitzgibbon; Thomas O'Neill; Liam Kinane, who has made his way here at last; a priest from Hobart Town called Father Brennan, who is a friend of Barry's; Barry himself, and me. Barry has an aesthete's ability to make any space he occupies attractive, and his parlour, with its red-painted walls, makes one cheerful immediately one enters it. He did the same (Thomas O'Neill once told me), with his cell in Kilmainham Gaol, which he furnished with a sofa and a rich, warm carpet, and hung with attractive French prints. Presents from his female admirers (watch-chains, cigars and purses), lay piled on a table. Here, before his trial, he cheerfully entertained his friends, while a nervous turnkey warned them against the noise of their jollity, and the prison Governor would finally come down to reprimand them. The same group of comrades was waiting to receive him on the night he was condemned to death: most were weeping, but Barry – though white and tense – was as cheerful as ever. There should be no weeping, he said; they would all have a night's fun and drollery, and be damned to the Governor. This they proceeded to do, with toasts drunk, and stories told, and the songs of Davis and Mangan sung, until the Governor (an indulgent soul), finally arrived to stop them.

This parlour, I've no doubt, is in much the same taste as that cell of his in Kilmainham. There are crowded bookshelves, easy chairs, vases of native flowers, and a piano – also conveyed here by bullock wagon. Barry is an accomplished pianist, and brought with him on the *Revenge* a good deal of sheet music. Now, seated at the keyboard in his shirtsleeves and loose red neckerchief, a cigar between his teeth, eyes half-closed, he nods as he plays a medley of Irish airs. Strange to hear such music here, on the edge of primeval forest, where no such sounds have ever been known! He has sung *The Last Rose of Summer*, by Tom Moore, and then one of his own songs, recently composed: a haunting ballad of exile he calls *Ireland Lost*. Father Brennan has sung *The Bells of Shandon*, in a fine tenor, Fitzgibbon has given us one of his poems, and O'Neill has recited from memory the poem by our lost Thomas Davis which is the prayer of our movement: *A Nation Once Again*. Unashamed tears sprang to our eyes as he did so, and O'Neill loudly blew his nose.

Barry pauses in his playing now, and turns to Liam Kinane.

– Sing for us, Liam, he says. You have a far better voice than I.

At first Kinane protests; he is no match for Barry, he says. But all of us insist. And so, in his deep, rich voice, he sings *Aileen Aroon*: an *aisling* of unearthly beauty.

— Youth will in time decay,
Aileen Aroon;
Beauty must fade away,
Aileen Aroon.
Castles are sacked in war,
Chieftains are scattered far;
Truth is a fixéd star,
Aileen Aroon.

When he's done, our applause is surely heard across the lake — if anyone is there to hear. O'Neill shakes his head, and says:

— What a darling Irish boy you are, Kinane! Ah, to be able to sing like that!

And Barry jumps up from the piano.

— By God, Kinane, what a voice you have! What lyric feeling! You shall sing it again, before you go, or you'll not get a skerrick of lamb, or a single glass of whiskey!

The two embrace, laughing. Kinane, looking at me over Barry's shoulder, nods once, his face like a boy's. I have never seen him look so happy. His large eyes gleaming, he appears like someone who has at last come home, and is now in the bosom of his family. Disregarding all our warnings, he broke his *parole* to come here, travelling secretly on horseback, and taking the route he spoke of on my visit to him. He rode first through the hills behind Hobart Town and New Norfolk, and then to the country near Hamilton, where he spent the night in a barn. Next morning he rode up to Bothwell, avoiding the township. By prior arrangement, O'Neill and Fitzgibbon met him at noon in the bush just north of the town, and the three came up to the Lakes together. Kinane had encountered no mounted constables — which he easily could have done — but all of us took him to task for the risk he'd taken. Now he says:

— Did I not do right to come, Devereux?

It's not in my heart to deny him.

— You did, I say. It was worth all your rashness to hear you sing, Liam.

514

He answers me in Irish, gesturing at the fire in Barry's rough stone fireplace.

– *Níl aon tinteán mar do thinteán féin.* There's no hearth like your own hearth, Devereux.

– At this, Barry leaps up on the table, and raises his glass. His pale face is flushed, and alight with jubilation.

– To the Lakes! he cries. *This* is our hearth, my boys! And is it not a joy, this place? Here at Dog's Head, we're two thousand feet nearer to the stars than the felons and their gaolers down below. Here we breathe an air untainted by the breath of murderers and spies. To the Lakes, where convict civilization holds no sway! To all us comrades – together here at last!

Standing in a circle around the table, we raise our glasses and cheer him; then we toast our comradeship. In this brief, fond and foolish moment, we are one.

Dinner is eaten outside, where Barry and his servant Brown have built a bonfire, and where Brown has roasted a lamb on a spit. Superbly tender, it's garnished with rosemary and onions, and with potatoes roasted in the coals; it's accompanied by ale and porter, and by Barry's excellent Islay whiskey. The blue-black sky of the island's roof is above us as we eat: the vast sky of wilderness. The air grows colder, but is absolutely still. Sparks from the bonfire whirl straight up, as though striving to join those other sparks that are pulsing overhead; and sparks of exultation tingle in our blood.

Finally replete, we sit about the fire on gum stumps and rough wooden benches. Nearby, pinned to one of the verandah posts, is a large black-and-white portrait of the Governor, copied by Barry from a picture in the *Illustrated London News*: he uses it for target practice. The stern and humourless face watches us in the dark, marred by two bullet-holes in its teeth.

– When English rule is ended, Kinane says, what Ireland will need will be Socialism. Then our people will truly be free and equal.

Paul Barry leans forward, seated on his gum stump on my left; he pokes at the fire with a stick.

– Really, Kinane? A strange thing to wish, for an Ireland made free. But I remember your expressing the notion on our voyage out. You were reading Saint-Simon, I recall, and God knows what other theorising creatures.

– Sure, and still am, Kinane says. And Proudhon and Blanc too.

Sitting between Fitzibbon and O'Neill on the other side of the fire, he looks across at Barry with a hint of challenge, his forehead lit bronze by the flames.

– I admire Louis Blanc entirely, he says. A patriot driven out of his country by the tyrants and bloodsuckers of 1848, when the workers' revolt failed. Exiled in England, God help him! Sure, his fate has been the same as ours: should we not regard him as a brother? *Organisation du Travail* is a great essay, I'm thinking.

Despite his brogue, Kinane's French accent is very good, I notice. What a strange mixture he is: brawling and drink-sodden man of the people, and serious, self-educated scholar, steeped in French revolutionary theory!

Barry rubs his nose.

– A brother? Come now, I'm not sure of *that*, Kinane. Louis Blanc may be a patriot, but he's also an authoritarian, like your beloved Saint-Simon – and you know, dear boy, authoritarians *worry* me. What was it all about, that 'assembly of workers' of Blanc's? It would have totally controlled society, would it not – instructing the population in Socialist principles? No wonder freedom-loving Frenchmen became alarmed. And doesn't Blanc say that the state should have absolute supremacy?

Kinane's face has grown flushed; he is shaking his big head, and running his fingers through his tangled curls.

– He does: but you don't *understand*, joy! Through being supreme, the state would bring us *real* freedom!

– Oh? Something of a paradox, surely.

– It is not. Blanc believes in the Rights of Man. And he's saying that those rights can only be assured by the state: a Socialist state, expressing the people's will, through a national assembly. No more capitalist competition, with its exploitation of the weak – instead, all men working for the common good, and equal wages for all!

He raises an instructing finger.

– The democratic will of the nation – not rule by a God-damned aristocracy. Nor by those grasping capitalists who destroy the people in their horrible factories! You see? Blanc carries on the great ideals of the French Revolution. Sure, you must have respect for *that*, Barry. I know you do – a leader with your ideals!

Barry softly laughs, both hands flat on his gum-trunk seat, head on one side. When he speaks, his drawl becomes more languid: always a sign that he is in disagreement.

– Ah yes, the Revolution, he says. The Jacobins also put their faith in an all-powerful National Assembly – do you remember? And look what they gave us. The Terror.

He leans forward, no longer smiling.

– They gave us Robespierre. Now *there* was a fellow who sincerely believed in virtue, and the Rights of Man, and the idea that all private interest should be sacrificed to the interests of the State. Robespierre, the blood-soaked Inquisitor! They gave us Fouché, a destroyer without pity. They gave us that bloody young monster Saint-Just, with his terrible lists: heretics and traitors, all for the guillotine – all chosen by *him*! And the lists kept growing, didn't they? 'You have to punish not only traitors but also the indifferent.' I'm quoting from Saint-Just himself, Liam. 'The indifferent!' Ain't that charming? So one couldn't even stand aside – it was enthusiasm or death. By Jesus, they were terribly sincere, those Jacobins: I'll grant them that.

Kinane is attempting to speak; but Barry holds up his hand.

– They believed in social equality sure enough, my boy – but *not* in individual liberty! That is what happens when men take absolute power in the name of the State. Human beings have a tendency to naughtiness – have you noticed that, Liam? You're a good Catholic: it's called Original Sin, as you must know. And it always rears its head when men are given total power. Ah, what a brew that is! No-one can be trusted to drink it!

He lights a cigar, cocked head lowered to a twig plucked from the fire, glancing with impish amusement at his friend Father Brennan, who is nodding on his left.

– Those mistakes would not have been made again, Kinane says.

That is not what would have happened had Blanc's co-operative society been allowed. It would have meant fraternity, and justice for the common people. Won't you want justice for *our* people, Barry, when the Republic is achieved?

But Barry shakes his head.

– Your faith in Socialism is touching, my boy. You would give the same sorts of leaders the same sorts of weapons – and you'd trust that *this* time, they wouldn't use them.

Kinane turns his gaze to me, his shadowed face both challenging and imploring.

– And you, Devereux? Would you not want a Socialist state for our people, bringing freedom from exploitation, and equality for all?

– Thank you, no, I say. I would not want to pay the price.

He takes a deep swallow of whiskey, and looks at me from under his brows.

– Price? What price?

– It sounds all very fine, Liam; but you'd exchange the tyranny of the British for the tyranny of an authoritarian government. And there'd be no appeal against such a government, would there? I prefer Benjamin Constant, among French thinkers. He has an opinion as to what absolute equality would mean. It would mean the oppression of each man by his neighbour, he says. Vulgar despotism, in fact.

– I have no time for Constant, Kinane says. A defender of property-owners. An enthusiast for the English system. Piss on him!

He's becoming drunk, I see; but I ignore his lapse into crudity.

– Yet Alexis de Tocqueville found that much of what Constant predicted was actually happening in America, I say. He saw true individualism and refinement in danger, under Democracy. And *he* was a believer in the Revolution – and an enthusiast for America's great experiment. Think, Liam: what would your all-powerful State really bring us? A new set of Jacobin fanatics, I believe, setting out dogmas against which no-one could dissent – unless he wished to lose his head. An army of tyrannical clerks, drafting more and more regulations to oppress us. A new Committee of Public Safety to guard

518

against heresy, and another Bureau of Police, to arrest us should we voice heretical notions. This benevolent State of yours would grow bigger and bigger, while the individual would shrink. And freedoms would shrink as well. Religious freedom; freedom of opinion; freedom to own property. And selfish materialism would grow. Levelling, in other words – with many equal pigs struggling at the trough. Are you *sure* you believe in freedom, Liam? Or simply in levelling?

Barry gives a single bark of laughter, throwing back his head. But Kinane is staring across at me as though he has seen something shocking; his expression is one of outrage, and he appears to search for words. Before he can answer, Martin Fitzgibbon's dry, precise voice carries suddenly and clearly across the fire.

– Come now, Devereux. That goes too far.

Seated on a bench on Kinane's right, imposing in a voluminous grey cloak, he looks rather as though he's been spirited here from a public meeting in Dublin. He clears his throat, like a barrister beginning his defence.

– Liam's idealism is surely to be respected, he says. I have a good deal of sympathy with his ideas. I've had much time to think, here in exile. I've been reading the works of Jean Jacques Rousseau, and find much to agree with in his notions on human equality.

And he looks around our circle of firelit faces, as though to impress on each one of us the importance of his revelation.

– Too much inequality surely sets man against man, as Rousseau says, and prevents us from being happy. And surely, as he claims, men are not naturally bad, but are made so by society. So I'm not sure that I can agree with Barry about Original Sin. I do respect your Catholic faith, Paul – and yours too, Father Brennan – but like Rousseau, I would rather reject such a belief.

He bows his head respectfully towards Barry and Father Brennan, clears his throat again, and with ponderous deliberateness, resumes.

– It seems to me that when national freedom is won, we must give some thought to equality, and to the state of the common people. Liam is right: in France and England, the poor suffer from the cruelty of the factory owners as much as ours do from the

Famine, and from bad landlords. Such things must be remedied, surely.

Thomas O'Neill is listening to him intently, his eyes widening in sympathy.

– They must, he says. They must. You are right, Martin. We have fought for the people. We should also care about them.

And Father Kevin Brennan is nodding in agreement. Wrapped in a heavy black top coat that seems too large for him, he is a stocky little man from Kerry, with a bald head, turned-up nose and luxuriant brown side-whiskers. His cheerful, round, gnomish face is one of those that seem naturally to smile most of the time; but now he's holding this smile in check.

– True, he says. No Christian can contemplate such things and wish them to continue. Liam and Martin have generous hearts, surely.

But Barry is shaking his head.

– The heart is not enough, he says. The mind must also come into play. And my dear Fitzgibbon, I wonder if you are using yours? When he speaks of human nature, your Rousseau reasons like a child. He speaks of what *ought* to be – not what is. Reforms must be made; yes. The condition of the people must be improved; yes. But do you really wish for Socialism? For levelling of the kind that Devereux has just referred to? I'm reminded of what Doctor Johnson once said: levellers wish to level down as far as themselves – but they cannot bear levelling *up* to themselves.

He laughs; but Fitzgibbon doesn't smile.

– I don't believe that is my position, he says stiffly. I would wish to see our Irish peasants given every advantage possible – and more land of their own, on which they could be secure.

– Really? But there is not enough land to go around – that has been one of the problems, hasn't it? And if they are to gain more land, someone must give it to them – or else it must be taken away from its owners by force. Would you give them *your* estate, old man? Perhaps you agree with Proudhon – that property is theft.

– Something in that, too, Kinane growls suddenly.

He is looking at the fire, and drinks off his latest glass of whiskey.

520

Fitzgibbon turns to him, and frowns.

– Now *that* I can't agree with, Liam. And I doubt that you mean what you say.

Kinane makes no response; he's pouring another whiskey.

Barry looks sideways at me and winks, drawing on his cigar. Then he turns back to Fitzgibbon.

– There speaks the Protestant landowner. I'm reassured, Martin. After all, had you wished to see the people seize land, you had your opportunity at Ballingarry. But you behaved as a member of your class, and persuaded them not to touch property. And this at the one time when such action might have been justified: when the Revolution might have been won, and the British pushed to the wall! But of course, my dear boy, your *own* estate might have been at risk. Wasn't that the difficulty?

I see that the liquor has taken hold, even though he gives little outward sign of it – except for a look that I recognise, in his strangely pale eyes: one that seems languidly amused, but which warns of the unpredictable.

For a moment Fitzgibbon stares at him across the fire, chin tilting upwards. Then he draws his cloak together and rises to his feet. When he speaks, it's in a thin, measured voice that betrays the effort needed to control his anger.

– I followed my principles, Barry, as I have always done. I take full responsibility for the way in which I led the 1848 insurrection – and I did not believe pillage justified. I did not believe that we would achieve an honourable victory by using the methods of banditry. I still do not. You will withdraw that remark, which insults my honour. If not, you must give me satisfaction.

There's a silence. We all sit quite still, and I'm conscious of the larger silence here: that of the lake and the black wall of gum forest, out beyond the circle of our fire. I can scarcely believe what Fitzgibbon has said. No reasonable man fights duels, if it can possibly be avoided: it's surely the greatest folly that we of the Ascendancy are given to, and begins to be outmoded. But his expression is grimly determined, and his face has gone chalk-white. Barry gazes back at him with a look of deep interest, and actually seems to smile;

but he doesn't immediately respond. A spark is spat from the coals.

It's Father Brennan who finally breaks the silence.

– Gentlemen, he says soothingly. Gentlemen. Don't quarrel in this way, I beg you! What hope is there for the cause if its leaders fall out? And Martin, you cannot be in earnest. For the love of Jesus, you'll not seek violence as a way of dealing with this matter. Come. I'm sure our friend Barry regrets what he has said.

But Barry's eyes remain fixed on Fitzgibbon. At last he answers, speaking almost gently.

– I shall be very happy, Martin. Pistols, I presume? I have an excellent pair of Colts.

His smile seems to savour the situation, and his gaze, by contrast, has become entirely cold. I'm appalled to realise that he's actually enjoying what's happening: that he welcomes it. I shall have to intervene, in a moment; but for now I sit watching the two in fascination. I begin to see just how much Barry has resented Fitz-gibbon's misguided scrupulousness in Tipperary – that lack of heart and lack of will which did so much to contribute to the rout and ridicule of 1848. Paul is drunk, of course, and not entirely in his right mind; if he were, he would not even entertain the idea of this gamble with Fitzgibbon's life and his own – nor would he have originally said what he did. But drunk he is, and his pent-up ener-gies and frustrated longing for action are so great that he is actually ready to seize on Fitzgibbon's challenge as an outlet. 'Barry of the Sword'! I understand now how badly he wants to wield one; and I reflect once again that he was born to be a fighting man, and that his body and his spirit are longing for the release of battle.

Before Fitzgibbon can answer, O'Neill jumps up from his bench, nervously smoothing the sparse strands of hair across his head.

– Really, this is absurd. Childish! None of us has ever questioned Fitzgibbon's high motives – whether or not we have always agreed with his judgment. I'm sure you don't wish to do so either, my dear Barry. Come: I believe you should apologise.

I rise and add my voice to his.

– I am in agreement with O'Neill. I've never for one moment

doubted Fitzgibbon's sincerity: he is a man of honour, and has suffered for it. I'm sure you don't wish to give him hurt, Paul: I must also ask you to withdraw what you've said.

Barry stands up from his gum stump, holding his glass and swaying slightly. He drinks it off, glancing at me, and his smile broadens, as though he merely plays a game. But it is not a game: I know that he is capable of going through with this business. Here in the remoteness of our exile, far from the stage of the world, he is more and more tormented. Despite his light-hearted nature, he is less able to bear his banishment than any of us; even his new house and his boat will not divert him for long. Deprived of action, deprived of engagement with the genuine enemy, he is no doubt beginning to feel that any sort of enemy will do: even a substitute, perhaps.

– Since you say so, Devereux, he says. You are my truest friend, and the one true leader here – and I have never doubted *your* judgment.

He throws his cigar into the fire, and bows in Fitzgibbon's direction.

– I sincerely apologise, Fitzgibbon. I've never thought you base, and did not wish to imply it.

Fitzgibbon, his hands beneath his cloak, looks fixedly across at him, holding himself at attention like a soldier. Then he nods.

– Accepted, he says coldly. We would be foolish to give comfort to our enemies, Barry; and I'm sure a quarrel between us two would delight our gaolers here – and delight many others, as well.

– No doubt, Barry says. And no doubt the death of one of us would enchant them even more. But you know, Martin, there is one thing you need not take responsibility for. You were never the true leader of the July rebellion: you merely joined it.

There is another, disconcerted silence. Does he intend fresh insult?

This time it's Kinane who speaks first. He's been looking from face to face around our circle with an expression of wondering outrage. Now it seems he can contain himself no longer: he too jumps to his feet.

– Ah, Barry, man, how can you be saying such a thing? Were you not there with us, in Tipperary? And do you not remember the people, how they followed after Martin Fitzgibbon in great crowds, and said that they would follow him anywhere? He not the leader? Then who *was*, for Jesus' sake?

Without replying, Barry walks around the fire to Kinane, and holds out his hand for the bottle. He pours whiskey into his glass, while all of us watch him. Only when a measure is poured and he has drunk it does he answer Kinane.

– The *people* saw him as their leader, he says. Yes. But Fitzgibbon was not responsible for the rebellion – since he never approved of it. It was Robert Devereux who changed the policy of Young Ireland to the adoption of revolutionary tactics. *He* was the true leader for such a revolt; but he wasn't there.

He walks back around the fire, and places his hand on my shoulder, facing the others.

– Wasn't it my comrade here who first had the courage to publish articles calling on the people to rise? Wasn't it Devereux who first spoke out in public to urge rebellion through force of arms – knowing the bloody police spies were listening, and knowing what that would mean for him? And wasn't it he who first made us agree to this in the Confederation? Do you remember his words? 'The only argument for freedom the British will ever understand is a gun in the hands of an Irishman!' Yes, by God: he was the first of us to defy Dublin Castle – knowing that arrest would follow, and likely execution! Have you forgotten all this, Kinane? And when July came – although Devereux was already taken from us, and penned on a hulk in Bermuda – O'Neill and I and others saw that the time for that rising had come.

He looks directly at Fitzgibbon.

– But *you* opposed it even then, he says.

Fitzgibbon nods sadly, still standing at attention.

– I opposed it, yes, he says. I believed in peaceful means as the only way that would succeed, without bringing ruin on the people – and I still do. I believe that the great O'Connell was right. But since I accept majority rule, I abided by the decision of the

War Council. So what is it you are saying? What do you accuse me of now?

– Gentlemen, gentlemen, pleads Father Brennan.

But no-one pays him heed.

– Nothing, Barry tells Fitzgibbon. I accuse you of nothing, Martin; I mean no offence. I absolve you of guilt, in fact. By your own admission, you answered the call to arms against your will, and therefore were not the true leader of 1848. That could well be grounds for a pardon, when you think about it. The true leader – absent in the flesh when we went into Tipperary, but with us in spirit – stands *here*.

And he gestures theatrically at me, staggering a little, his smile brilliant and mad.

– Come, Paul, I say. We've all made enough speeches, and there's only the wilderness to listen. How Governor Denison would laugh at us! Yes, I was with you in spirit – and I thank you for saying so. But 1848 is gone, and its opportunities lost. *Lost*, do you understand? So let us all sit down, and talk like friends again.

And I smile across at Fitzgibbon. But his face is pinched, and his look betrays a bitterness that plainly won't be healed.

– I'm glad that you acknowledge your own responsibility, he says. Barry is right, of course. It was *your* policy of violence that set us on the road that has brought us here: your lust for blood and destruction – though you yourself never fired a shot, did you?

I look at him in amazement. I have had no idea, until this moment, how deeply he resents me.

– Barry was your worthy lieutenant, he says, and carries equal responsibility for the folly of what took place. Damn you both! There was never any hope of success. We had no army, as Young Italy did: we were recruiting from peasants who were demoralised and starving. Thank God no proper war ensued: the British would have butchered the poor wretches. So it was all done for nothing – and now here we are. Yes, here we are.

One arm emerges from his cloak: he gestures at the forest of stringybark gums behind us, its high, dark hallways leading into wilderness. Then he turns back to us, speaking in a voice gone dry with resignation.

– Because of you, Devereux – and you too, Barry – my life is ruined. I am torn from my family for another twelve years: and what have I become? A broken-down gentleman, in a colony of broken-down gentlemen and thieves! A nursery governor! And you? Colonial farmers – with convicts for your workers!

He laughs, and the sound is painful. O'Neill steps quickly beside him, and places a hand on his shoulder.

– You don't mean these things, Martin, he says. You are not yourself.

But Fitzgibbon shakes him off.

– You'll excuse me, gentlemen. It may well be that I am not myself, and will never be myself again. I am going to bed. Good night.

He turns and walks out of the firelight, shoulders hunched under his cloak, moving towards the house. As he does so, there is a sudden outcry in the upper air: the wild, tragic piping of plover, passing over Barry's roof.

Nobody speaks, for a moment. Then Kinane raises both fists, in the dark and windless air. Throwing back his head to look up at those pulsing white lights that burn so unnaturally near, he releases a howling exclamation.

– Ah, *Jesus!*

We turn to him in astonishment. Clad in the same shabby pea jacket and mud-stained moleskin trousers in which, at the risk of his freedom, he rode up here from Hobart Town, on unmade roads and tracks and through hills and flooded marshland, he resembles a giant scarecrow. He points after Fitzgibbon, his long arm fully extended.

– What is it you have done to that man, Barry? He has sacrificed his life for Ireland; and little joy he's had from it! Sure, and he did his *best*, at Ballingarry! I know that to be true: didn't I stand at his side? He ignored the police bullets; no man could have been braver. Maybe he wasn't saying the things that the people expected; maybe his ideas were too high-minded. But that's the sort of man he is – and he said what he believed. He was my leader, as *you* are,

Devereux, and I gave him my loyalty, as I give it to you, and to Barry. Father Brennan speaks truly: if our leaders quarrel, what hope do we have? And what hope is there for Eire?

– Liam, says Father Brennan. Listen to me, now. You are a good man, and right in what you say. But we've all had too many whiskeys, and it's time to be getting to bed. We've had a grand night – let us not fall out. All this will be forgotten in the morning.

The priest's round face is screwed up into an expression of gnomish concern and reassurance, and his white, clerical hands are clasped prayerfully in front of him. But Kinane is not to be consoled – even by one of his clergy. Like a great, disappointed boy, he clenches and unclenches his fists, his face distorted with grief. He looks wildly about him as though in search of help: at the moon-calm lake, at the tops of the gums, and at the shape of Barry's cottage, whose glowing parlour window is the one human sign in the land's unending darkness. Then he points at the four of us – Father Brennan, Barry, O'Neill, and myself.

– Yes, we were beaten, he cries, and his voice has risen to a hoarse, drawn-out shout, echoing off the lake and the trees. We were beaten because of traitors and deserters, and because the people were too starved to rise. But there were many of them brave enough to follow, and I say there was *glory* at Ballingarry! It was not for nothing! And I'll not forget marching beside Fitzgibbon as long as I live, with the guns and pikes behind us. Our names will go down in history, I tell you! We showed those buggers of English that the people would fight – and will fight again! They have seen that revolution will come from the people – and everything was *changed*, at Ballingarry!

His wet lips work and his wide eyes stare, their whites flashing in the moonlight; his blue chin juts in defiance. His own rhetoric has made him more drunk than the whiskey can do; and suddenly he represents all that I have to overcome, if our cause is ever to succeed.

– Now listen, Kinane, I say. You maunder on about glory; you cling to it to comfort you against disappointment, as so many Irishmen do who defend Irish defeat. You see Ballingarry as a kind of

527

upside-down victory. You probably hope that songs and poems will commemorate it – don't you? Well, I tell you, Ballingarry is not worth a song by a beggar!

He opens his mouth to speak, but I raise my voice and go on. I do so half against my better judgment, since I long ago resolved to waste no time on speeches or disputes like this in Van Diemen's Land. They are the kind of pathetic indulgence that can only make fools of us in our exile, as Kinane's newspaper is doing. I have avoided such sad silliness until now, as Barry and O'Neill have; but Fitzgibbon's attack has affected me, and so has the whiskey. I feel my blood rise, as it used to do when I took flight at Conciliation Hall.

– Will you never understand, Kinane? It's this sort of sentimental nonsense which causes us to fail, and which means that the English can go on squatting on our country without a single care. They laughed at the Ballingarry affair– and they were right to laugh. Ballingarry has no glory: Ballingarry shames and disgraces us! Learn something now, if you're ever to learn it. Successful rebellion does not come from the people. *Nothing* in a struggle such as ours comes from the people. It comes through leadership; through leaders of a ruthless tenacity. Then the people can respond, and follow. The people must be instructed and led – and if leaders bungle their chances, as they did in that accursed July, then the people die for nothing.

Thomas O'Neill speaks suddenly.

– Spoken like a true Norman, Robert. The blood of the terrible Essex is strong in you.

I turn to him, and examine his gentle smile.

– Am I now to have my ancestry held against me? And where would Ireland have been, without the Normans? We would have no towns. We would have no civilized arts. And no understanding of politics either.

Barry laughs.

– And no 'ruthless tenacity' either, he says. God bless the Normans.

O'Neill laughs, and I laugh too. We look at each other with a return to good humour, and I imagine we will now turn our backs on dissent. Father Brennan, who has been watching us anxiously, allows himself a hopeful smile.

But Kinane is still glaring at me as though this exchange has not taken place, ignoring the others, his chest rising and falling.

– Bungled? You say Ballingarry was bungled?

I sigh.

– Of course it was bungled. What I wrote in the *New Nation* many times, and urged in our meetings again and again, was disregarded: that when the time for the rising came, it must *not* be carried out in the country. It should have been carried out in the Dublin streets: *that* was where we'd have got results. We could have inflicted destruction on the enemy at the centre of his power, and then gone underground. Instead, you wandered about the countryside at the head of a rabble. Christ, how Lord Clarendon must have laughed! Pardon my blasphemy, Father Brennan.

Kinane turns to Barry.

– And you agree with this, Barry?

– With every word, Barry says. Once I might not have done; now I do. I've refrained from saying so to Fitzgibbon, since I'd no wish to hurt him. But we must learn from our mistakes, Liam.

Kinane makes a noise in his throat: a sort of bubbling growl. He walks over to the bench where the whiskey has been left, and this time doesn't trouble to use a glass: he up-ends the bottle and drinks from it directly. Then he staggers back to us, clearly as drunk now as he was when I met him in St Giles. His hooded and reddened eyes accuse all three of us, Barry, O'Neill and me – avoiding Father Brennan, to whom he gives unfailing respect.

– And this is what you think of the common people, is it? You despise them, so.

– I do not despise them, I say. But they must be led; and they are not always easy to lead. They need to be educated – and I have tried to do that too. Even Wolfe Tone spoke of the cowards and bigots with whom he had to deal.

– And Daniel O'Connell said worse, Barry puts in. 'Animals', he called some of them. 'Crawling slaves', as well.

Kinane knits his brows, and his bloodshot glare is dangerous.

– I am one of them, he says. *I* am of the people. Is it as a slave you see *me* – you fastidious gentlemen?

– Nonsense, old fellow, begins Barry; but Kinane interrupts him.

– Aye, blood will tell, he says. I believe you see the common people as those English bastards do, in their God-damned *Punch* cartoons. 'Paddy', is it not, who looks like an ape in a hat! Is it this that makes you all stay away from me – leaving me to rot, in that town of thieves? Is it this that made you tell me not to come up here and join you?

– Liam, Liam, says Father Brennan. You do not mean what you say. You have had a drop too much. Go and get some sleep, my boy.

Kinane sways, staring stupidly at the priest. His voice grows more slurred, and his brogue more coarse – as though he now bitterly mocks himself, and discards his education. Turning back to us, he says:

– Aye, it's perfectly plain. This is why you all despise the *Exile*. A paper produced by an ape, is it?

– Go to bed, Liam, O'Neill says softly. You are badly misjudging us. We admire you; we are proud of your courage; you are our comrade. You'll see it all differently tomorrow.

He tries to take Kinane's arm, but is shaken off.

– But all you fine gentlemen now do *nothing*, he says. Since you have come here – *nothing*! Sure, Daniel O'Donnell the bushranger does more than you! I used to raise a glass with him in town, before he took to the bush – and I tell you, he's a fighter and a patriot! He may have done wrong – but at least he thumbs his nose at the Government, in the name of Irish freedom! And doesn't he put the fear of God into those bloody English settlers and police – he and his bold Irish boys!

– O'Donnell? Barry says. That murderous criminal? You cannot be serious, Liam.

But Kinane laughs in his face.

– Aye, O'Donnell, he says. I'd be better off joining his bush-rangers, I'm thinking. He's here, in these hills. Sure, I may just do so!

He is clearly beyond reaching: drunk, childish and deranged. He turns from us now, and jogs towards the lake-shore, stumbling through whey-faced bush-grass towards the neat little jetty that Barry has built, some fifty yards from the house. A dinghy is tied there; a little way out, on levels of phantom radiance, the yacht lies at anchor. Wordless, we watch Kinane's confused figure weave on to the jetty, black against the moon's gentle shine.

He stops, reeling precariously, and raises his arms. Then he begins to shout, in his deep, singer's voice, lapsing partly into Gaelic.

– O'Donnell! Dan O'Donnell! Are ye there? *An bhfuil tú ansin, a Chaptaen?*

Resounding, sorrowful and impotent, his words go out into these virgin spaces. They echo from the trees, and rebound across the water from that far shore of wilderness which lies hidden in the night. We listen to the echoes, and O'Neill shakes his head and laughs.

– Oh dear, he says. Can we get him into bed?

But Kinane's voice rises again.

– I'm ready to join ye, Captain! *Mise an fear agat!* We'll eat a dish of *cál ceannann* together, and drink *uisce beatha!* Do ye hear? I'm your man: I'm not needed here! I'll turn bushranger! *Éire go brách!*

Nothing answers him but the boundless sighing of the lake, beyond which lies no city; no town; no-one at all to hear. He sways; he mutters to himself and gesticulates; he turns, and misses his footing. He cries out, and falls like a tower.

With a splash, he enters Lake Sorell.

The echo of the splash is far more profound than his voice has been, and goes on for much longer. So do the sudden voices of wild duck, disturbed among the reeds. Meanwhile, all of us are running towards the jetty, and the silver, expanding ripples where Liam has disappeared.

As we run, his head comes up, and then his chest: he begins to make swimming motions with his arms. It's not very deep there; by the time we reach the jetty he is wading out. Barry curses; O'Neill laughs, and soon we all are laughing.

– I'll see to him, poor fellow, Father Brennan says. He must be quickly got inside. He'll catch his death, in this cold.

– Do, Father, says Barry. I'll be grateful. He's a poor, dear man, but I can bear no more of him tonight. I'd recommend a brandy, in any other case but his, after a dip in that water.

– A hot tea, perhaps, says Thomas O'Neill. He has no other clothes, of course. I'll have to let him have some of mine – though I doubt that they'll fit him very well.

– Sure, I'll look after him, says the priest.

And so it's Father Brennan who leads our difficult comrade up to the house, murmuring reassuringly and guiding him by the arm. Barry, O'Neill and I follow close behind. Kinane is quite silent now, and seems barely conscious. Head low, sodden clothing clinging, feet dragging and stumbling in the tussock-grass, he looks at no-one. He is shivering in violent spasms: the cold, away from the fire, is probing. A breeze is springing up, making the trees and bushes toss and sway.

As we pass the dying embers of the bonfire, Kinane turns and looks back at us, while Father Brennan grips his arm to keep him upright. In the moonlight, his black curls plastered on his forehead, he appears uncannily corpse-like. He mutters; then we hear him say:

– Forgive them, Father, for they know not what they do.

– Come, Liam, Father Brennan says briskly. Don't be blaspheming, now. You've said enough, tonight.

They go up the steps on to the miniature verandah, and so through the front door of the cottage. O'Neill follows, clearly too tired and fuddled to wish for anything now but bed. But as I begin to do the same, Paul Barry grips my shoulder, coming up behind me.

– Devereux: wait.

I turn and look at him. Swaying, his blanched hair fallen over his forehead, he's still a little drunk; but his expression in the dark is confiding, and conveys a private elation more momentous than any tipsiness.

– You and I are going to have to talk, he says.

– My dear old fellow, there's been enough talk tonight – has there not?

– There has, Devereux: there has indeed. No; not tonight. But there's something we must discuss in the morning. We'll go out in the boat: just you and I and O'Neill. There we can speak undisturbed.

I ask him what the topic might be. He draws closer, and his sudden smile is joyful.

– Escape, he says. I have had word from New York.

Nine o'clock in the morning: sunny yet cold, with blinding pathways of light glittering on the lake, whose surface is milky blue glass. *Young Ireland* tacks into a faint breeze, the American flag fluttering from her masthead. Barry sits in the stern, one hand on the tiller: he's dispensed with the help of his passholding sailor today. O'Neill and I sit side by side on a bench provided with a possumskin rug, facing our helmsman. Our task is to attend to the single sail, when he orders us to do so; but this is seldom necessary. We glide, moving by inches, in the centre of the lake.

Apparently unaffected by his night of carousal, Barry roused us both at eight o'clock. Fitzgibbon, he told us, had ridden off for Bothwell alone, leaving very early, with the briefest of farewells. Kinane was still unconscious in his bed; so was Father Brennan. So the three of us breakfasted together on coffee, damper, and sweet black trout from the lake, caught and prepared by Brown. Now we feel our energies returning: the air out here is an elixir, entering the nostrils in twin, icy streams, clearing last night's fumes from our brains.

So far, by silent consent, we've spoken very little. Of the incident with Fitzgibbon, nothing has been said. Behind us, on the Dog's Head promontory, a thin spire of smoke rises from Barry's chimney: the only sign of life anywhere in this landscape, except for the passholder's hut on the island. Six miles up the lake, the north-west wilderness begins, coming down to the shore in a dark olive band. Beyond, the snow-covered crater of Cradle Mountain stands against the sky; behind us in the south is Table Mountain, and all the other peaks of the great Western Tier. We drift, cupped by mountains, and I sigh in absolute well-being, reaching for my pipe and pouch of Cavendish.

O'Neill trails his hand in the water, his wide-brimmed brigand's hat pulled low over his eyes. He's wearing his rough bushman's dress: donkey jacket, moleskin trousers, heavy boots.

– Such beauty, he says. Nowhere on earth could be more beautiful.

– There's no denying that, Barry says. These lakes are the most beautiful region in this sad, strange land – and I've almost come to love them. Yet even under this beauty, I still sense a sadness.

– The sadness of vacancy, I say. One looks at this landscape, and one senses the void. Stare at its loveliness straight: it neither entices nor repels. The land wears a mask; and the mask frowns.

– How strangely you talk, you two over-civilized souls, O'Neill says. I find here the beauty of a world unspoiled. The world as it was, before we humans filled it with our greed and our crimes.

– Be careful not to love this island too much, I tell him. Or you may never escape it, Thomas.

Barry sits forward, pushing his green military cap far back on his head, as though to see us both better. He moves the tiller slightly to starboard; the sail flaps once, the yacht leans, and the water rattles at our bows. He looks from one to the other of us, the collar of his pilot coat turned up against the sharpness of the morning.

– True, he says. And escape is what I want to discuss, gentlemen.

He pauses, smiling, making sure of our attention.

– I've had a letter of considerable interest from the Irish Directory in New York.

New York! How strange the name of that American metropolis sounds, falling on this bright, empty air! How unlikely its very existence, here on Lake Sorell! One might as well say: *Camelot*. Yet a shiver runs through me, as though at the sound of a stirring musical phrase.

– I've been in correspondence with Michael Callaghan, Barry says. I don't believe you met him, Devereux – though you did once, O'Neill. He's a native of Waterford, and I've known him since boyhood. We were at Clongowes together. His father's a well-to-do merchant: Michael went to America young, with his father's backing. He was always a great man with the horses: now he has a farm in Kentucky, breeding thoroughbreds. But he often visits New

York, and is active in the Directory. They call him Kentucky Callaghan.

We laugh; then I say:

– And what does Kentucky Callaghan have to offer?

– Escape, Barry says.

The light that now dances in his eyes reflects the dance of sunbeams on the lake. Gripping the tiller, he leans closer, and begins to explain.

The Irish Directory – that organisation founded in New York to support us in 1848 – is making funds available for escape on an American ship. Any of us who wish to make the attempt will be supported, he tells us. More: the Directory will commission Michael Callaghan to travel to Australia to help put our flight into effect. He has considerable funds at his disposal, it seems, since the New York Irish are very generous. And considerable funds will be needed. An American ship must be found with a captain who is willing – for a price – to transport us from Sydney to San Francisco. And another ship's captain must be found who is prepared to smuggle us out of Hobart Town to Sydney. Callaghan, when he reaches Australia, will organise this first stage from Sydney, Barry says – since Hobart Town is far too dangerous a situation in which to put out feelers. But Callaghan has little doubt that, with careful organisation, everything can be achieved. He is prepared to sail for Sydney or Melbourne as soon as we write to the Directory – and asks which of us will make the attempt.

– And that is the question, Barry says cheerfully. Which of us *will* make the attempt? *I* will, I can assure you. And surely you will, Devereux. O'Neill, you have said that you won't – but I hope to change your mind, dear boy. As for Fitzgibbon – he's declared that he won't, and I believe he's too dispirited and tamed to change his mind.

– And Kinane? I ask.

Barry looks at me and shrugs.

– Liam is dangerous, he says. He talks too much in his cups, and he continues to associate with Casey – who I agree is almost certainly a spy. It's simply not worth the risk, to inform him of this at present. So I vote that for the present, nothing be said to him. Later, if we're successful, something can be done for him too. Remember, even if I write immediately, we must contemplate a seven-month wait at the least: three months for my letter to reach New York, and some four months more for Callaghan to make the voyage out here. So the time, if we're fortunate, will be April or May next year. Now tell me, gentlemen – are you with me? What shall I say to the Directory?

There's silence for a moment, broken only by the rippling of the water, and the distant cries of birds around the shore. O'Neill and I look at each other, and then at Barry again.

– Yes, I say. I'm with you.

Barry laughs in delight, and leans to slap me on the shoulder.

– My dear fellow! Good! Good! I'll write tonight, and you can post it for me in Hobart Town. Callaghan and other members of the Directorate are especially anxious to hear of your decision. Callaghan is one of your great admirers, you know – and your following in New York grows larger all the time. They are all for force of arms there – and *you* are seen as the leader of the future, if you can only reach America. And I have a modest following of my own. We'll work for Irish freedom in America, Devereux. Jesus, what a welcome we'll be given!

– There's something else, I tell him. I must bring Kathleen with me.

For a second, his eyes narrow. Then he raises his brows and smiles again, throwing his cigar over the side.

– But of course, he says. Yes, bring her to New York, if she's game. Will she come as your wife?

– She will. Or else I'll marry her in New York.

– Do. Then you'll need no permission from our esteemed Sir William Denison.

We both begin to laugh, in pure exhilaration.

– You are like a pair of boys.

– O'Neill has spoken for the first time since Barry made his announcement. He leans with one elbow on the gunwale of the boat, looking at us.

536

– No doubt we are, I say. And with reason – surely you'd agree? Now Thomas, tell us you'll come too.

– I will not.

– For God's sake, why? Is not the risk worth taking, with the help that's now being offered?

For a moment he stares at the water. Then he looks at us both, and says:

– I must say to you first that I don't relish the thought of working under the lash at Port Arthur, and living with English murderers. Which is what you both face if you fail, of course – and failure is quite likely. Perhaps I've become a coward.

– No, Barry says. You've never been a coward, O'Neill. What are your real reasons?

O'Neill sighs, taking off his hat. He smoothes his sparse strands, not looking at us.

– America may be a great and wonderful nation, he says. And this is merely a convict colony. But you will still be in exile, in America, and will not be able to return to Ireland. I could not bear that. I miss Ireland dearly. I shall wait for a pardon – and then I shall be able to go home. It may be that you never will.

Barry frowns.

– That may be true, he says. But are you truly prepared to lose your youth here – to grow middle-aged at the end of the world?

– Perhaps, O'Neill says. I've come to quite like it here, you see.

– To *like* it? Are you losing your wits? America may not be Ireland – but America is the *world,* O'Neill! The world where we belong – the *right* side of the world! A free nation – a place where we may join our own, and carry on the fight! What will you do *here*? Have you forgotten what it's like, down below in the lowlands? No free nation, but a pox-ridden gaol colony? A society without ideals or nobility, whose leaders think of nothing but money?

O'Neill sighs.

– In Bothwell, I can ignore most of that. There are good people here as well, and the woods and wild places of this island hold a great fascination for me. To study a new flora and fauna gives me much satisfaction; and to tell you the truth, political passions grow less and less attractive. That will shock you both, I'm sure. But what has 'the right side of the world' given us? The endless bitter feuds of the great, and the oppression of the small: the old, repeated tragedies of Europe. I am tired of all that. I want to experience the world unsullied.

We stare at him in silence. He turns away from us, looking up the lake into the glittering tracks of light. Then he gestures to the north, and the white, gleaming turret of Cradle Mountain. His voice grows musing and mild.

– Out there is a world that is only half inside reality. That interests me deeply, you see. This landscape is still waiting for something. It will have its poets, some day.

Barry is looking at him now with an expression of unfeigned sadness.

– Very well, Father, he says. You were always a little unworldly – and I see that you've become even more so. We'll lose a good comrade. What will you do, in this place? How will you occupy yourself?

– I'm quite advanced with my book on the island's flora. That will keep me busy.

Barry shakes his head, and smiles as though at a harmless madman. He begins to put the boat about, and tells me to shorten sail.

4. THE RIBBONMAN

At 'Clare'
October 4th

The latest copy of the Hobart Town *Advertiser* lies open in front of me. It brings news of a fresh raid by 'Captain' Daniel O'Donnell and his gang of bushrangers.

Since the report in this newspaper two months ago, no more was heard of O'Donnell until now, and I had allowed myself to forget him – or at least, to put him to the back of my mind. I had even begun to tell myself that he'd not actually dare to invade us here. Now, I can no longer afford to be so complacent.

He has struck in country only a few miles away: in the vicinity of the Dromedary. And it emerges that this small mountain has actually been his stronghold.

The Dromedary lies in the north-east, on the other side of the Derwent: one of those local mountains whose top is an ancient crater, forming a double peak. Riding through the hills beyond the farm, I have sometimes gazed across at that distant blue shape, which stands in a profound serenity. O'Donnell and his gang have fled from it now, according to the *Advertiser*, since their raid in the vicinity ended badly; but in my mind's eye, the Dromedary has taken on a sinister look. And this morning, riding into New Norfolk on my regular visit to the Post Office, I found that the hills around the township wore the same forbidding aspect.

The town of New Norfolk poses as a village by Gainsborough, with its meadows and hop gardens, English hedgerows (white until recently with Spring blossom), handsome riverside villas mirrored in the broad, calm Derwent, and the small stone tower of St Matthew's correctly in place at its centre. Now, its peace and certainty have proved merely to be properties of that painting it has been made to resemble. Reality is otherwise, it seems; and the talk in its Post Office and shops is all of 'Captain' O'Donnell.

O'Donnell's bushrangers, according to the *Advertiser*, raided a farm in the district of Broad Marsh, close to the Dromedary: the property of a family named Shaw. There were five of them, and they came onto the property in the late afternoon. They captured and tied up the convict servants and held Mr and Mrs Shaw at gunpoint, while they looted the house. Then O'Donnell recognised one of the servants. He had been in Port Arthur with the man, and knew him to be an informer. According to Mr Shaw, O'Donnell shouted abuse at this unfortunate creature, filling him with terror. Then, as the man begged for his life, O'Donnell shot him through the head. After this, with sacks filled with booty, the gang rode off towards the hills.

But then their luck began to turn. Mr Shaw knew that a party of mounted constables was quartered less than a mile away, and rode to inform them. They followed in O'Donnell's tracks and by twilight had tracked him to the Dromedary. His headquarters was on the very top of the mountain, where he could survey the whole countryside, and see his pursuers coming. A desperate and foolhardy position to take up, in these days of percussion rifles! But I suspect that O'Donnell was following an ancient Irish tradition: one that goes back to the early *dúns* – those round stone forts in which our ancestors held off the Danes. He no doubt relished the idea of a stand in his mountain fortress, outnumbered by his enemies, if necessary going down fighting. He is clearly acting out the part of an Irish hero – or rather, debasing it.

As the police advanced up the hill, O'Donnell and his cronies fired on them. One constable was shot, and mortally wounded: so a second killing was added to the first. A pitched gun battle now took place, with the constables using the bush for cover, and coming on up the mountain. They outnumbered the bushrangers, and quickly closed in: one of O'Donnell's men was killed, and another seriously wounded. But now full darkness had fallen. Under its cover, O'Donnell and his two remaining rogues escaped, fleeing through the bush down the other side of the mountain.

That was a week ago; and there have been no more sightings. But Langford believes that the three are not far away, and will arrive here at any time.

No doubt they will: and I continue to find this prospect outlandish and unreal. O'Donnell and his bushrangers are an anachronism, even in a colony like Van Diemen's Land. They belong to the world of twenty and thirty years ago – as the *Advertiser* is fond of pointing out. An article on the subject reminds its Vandemonian readers of those far-off, lawless days when escaped convicts gone wild, clad in suits of kangaroo-skin, raided cattle and farms with impunity – feared by the respectable, but supported and revered by many of the colony's ex-felons. The legendary names are recalled: Brown, Lemon and Scanlan; Mike Howe, 'Governor of the Ranges'; Matt Brady and Martin Cash, who were gallant with women. In the early days, men such as Howe raided with impunity over a good deal of the island: robber barons of the hinterland. But all this belongs to the disreputable past, the *Advertiser* says. Now, with closer settlement, in this increasingly civilized colony whose new name is to be Tasmania, there is no place for bushrangers any more, and no decent settler will give them aid. There are fewer wild regions for outlaws to hide in – unless they retreat to that stormy western wilderness where nobody wishes to live. Their day is done, the sermonising writer informs us. O'Donnell and his men will be hunted down, and all of them hanged in Hobart Town.

No doubt they will be, in time. But they'll come here first.

October 6th

I have acquired a pistol. It lies on my desk as I write: of a sinister, dull blue, its varnished walnut grip polished to the gleam of fine furniture. Accompanied by Langford, I bought it yesterday from a gunsmith in Hobart Town, who eagerly extolled its virtues. It's a 'gentleman's pocket pistol': one of the very latest revolvers produced by the American Samuel Colt. This Pocket Colt has a revolving chamber holding six bullets; all that has to be done between shots is to re-cock the hammer. As its name indicates, it's intended for concealment on the person, in order to surprise an attacker. To underline this, a picture is engraved on its cylinder depicting the hold-up of a stage coach.

– A remarkable weapon, the gunsmith said, smiling like a barber who sells you a new pomade. The first of its kind to be seen in this colony, and the very latest weapon for a gentleman such as yourself, sir. Your assailant has no warning: you can conceal it in your jacket so that he don't even guess that you're armed. They need these in America, with all those ruffians they have there.

Well, we need them here too, it seems; and I view my Colt with a mixture of complacency and misgiving. Paul Barry is fond of guns, and has a pair of Colt Dragoon revolvers, which are very large and heavy weapons indeed. But I've never owned a pistol before, or even fired one. Despite my fame as an advocate of armed resistance, guns have little attraction for me – and my acquaintance with weapons has been limited to the occasional use of a shotgun for hunting.

I sit thinking about this. The revolver has made me take stock of myself.

Ironically enough, although I'm described by the British as a terrorist and a man of violence, I do not like the idea of violence. Nor do I wish to turn to it unless it can't be avoided. If my blood were up, and I faced an enemy who had to be dealt with, then I believe I would fight, and fight giving no quarter. Had I been with my comrades in that fatal July of 1848, I would not have hesitated to carry out armed insurrection, with all the taking and losing of life that would have been involved. How brave a warrior I would have been, I cannot know; no man can know, until the time comes. But brave or not, I would have taken no pleasure in blood being spilled. I have meant it – truly meant it – when I have said that the British have given Ireland no choice: armed resistance is a final, desperate necessity, if we are to gain what we so greatly yearn for. But it is also a terrible and hateful necessity, in my eyes; and Fitzgibbon wronged me, up at Lake Sorell, when he accused me of 'a lust for blood and destruction'. I have brooded on this, and am surprised at how greatly it has offended me.

Soft Spring darkness falls out the window of my study, and I go on contemplating my Colt. This is no shotgun or rifle, for use in hunting fowl. The Colt is an entirely different sort of creature, specifically intended for use on human beings. As such, it seems like a portent of a new, unthought-of life of bloodletting and fury. It may even portend my own death.

These are morbid thoughts, and I cannot afford to dwell on them.

James Langford is determined to make sure that I'll be ready when O'Donnell comes. He's been doing all that he can to improve my marksmanship.

The pistol, of course, is merely a weapon for use in emergency, and at close quarters. Our main means of defending ourselves will be our guns: those guns which we use to hunt kangaroo and duck, and which hang in Bess's kitchen – looking no more ominous than her pots and pans.

Mine, which hangs by the door, is a Manton double-barrelled percussion shotgun, for use at reasonably short range. Langford's, which hangs above the mantel-shelf over the stove, is an American gun: a Kentucky percussion rifle. During his period of service at Doctor Howard's, he won it from the captain of an American whaling ship, in a card game in some gambling den on the New Wharf. He often refers gleefully to this; the captain had run out of cash, and asked Langford to his ship to persuade him to pick out some object of value as payment. The captain grieved at losing his Kentucky rifle: it was a prized possession, used for shooting goats on islands in the Pacific, where he put in for supplies. Langford is extremely proud if it; and certainly it's a handsome weapon. Very long and heavy, with a forty-two-inch barrel, it has a beautiful maplewood stock with a wavy, blond and brown pattern that Langford calls 'tiger striping'. Firing only a single small ball, it's the most accurate long-distance rifle in the world, he says; in its earlier incarnation as a flintlock, it enabled the Americans to win the Battle of New Orleans. He's proved his claims for it: he's a deadly shot – no doubt as a result of his years as a Marine – and brings down kangaroo at extraordinary distances, scarcely ever missing.

In mid-afternoon, he and I carry these guns up the slope behind the pickers' huts, where Langford supervises target practice. We have done this for some days now, shooting at beer bottles on fence posts, and I watch in admiration as my partner unfailingly picks them off, with his single ball. My own accuracy is improving under his guidance, and his instruction is both encouraging and chilling.

– Come, you're shooting a whole lot straighter, Robert. Don't worry – you can hit a bloody barn door with that Manton, at medium range. If your man was reasonable close, you'd blow a hole in him two feet wide, with all that shot you're scattering. Once I get off my single shot, I'm out of the game for nearly two minutes while I reload – which is quite a while, in a fight. But you've got your two barrels, which means a second chance – and that could prove mighty important to us. But remember: if you're not careful, you can still miss, when things get ugly. Some men don't remember that, in battle – the buggers rush; I've seen it. They aim the gun in the general direction of the enemy, and hope for the best. That won't do, Robert – you'll die that way. Remember what I'm saying, partner, as our lives might depend on it.

I assure him that I will, but he continues with great earnestness.

– It's the same with that revolver of yours. Don't just pull it out and fire in his general direction. You'll have a few seconds up your sleeve, because of surprise. Use them – and make bloody sure you aim for the heart.

I look about me: at the silent gum trees and wattle; at the roofs of the pickers' huts down the hill. I grow cold, despite the mildness of the afternoon.

– It may not come to this, James.

– It may not – the police may get them first. But if it does, we ain't going to make any mistakes. I want that reward.

– Sometimes I think that's your main consideration, James.

– Well, it's one of 'em.

He smiles at me from under his wide-brimmed felt hat, his pale eyes narrowed in the sun, and briefly rubs his moustache with his forefinger: a habit of his. In his belted, blue serge blouse and grimy corduroy trousers, he should look like a typical colonial farmer; yet he doesn't. Perhaps it's the effect of the prized Kentucky rifle, tucked under his arm with its immensely long barrel drooping to the ground: it gives him the look of a renegade soldier or back-woodsman. And I remember now that he was once a far more formidable and successful bandit than those we may have to face. The ludicrousness of this causes me to laugh; and he laughs with me. His smile lingers as he says:

– You ain't got a taste for this sort of thing, have you, Robert? But you're not going to shirk it, and I'm glad of that.

I feel absurdly gratified by this, but say nothing. Guns under our arms, we begin to walk back down the hill.

– Tell me, Langford says, if that revo-*lushion* of yours hadn't been nipped in the bud, would you have picked up a gun yourself, to help it along?

– I would have had to, James. But I wouldn't have had much liking for it. I don't relish the idea of taking life; but I would have fought English troops, just as the Americans did who used that rifle of yours.

– I see. Well, now.

We walk on through the pale yellow tussock grass, looking down at the sloping ground as we go. Then, as we pass the long grey pickers' huts, Langford glances at me, eyebrows cocked, and grins.

– If you'll pardon me saying so, Robert: this revo-*lushion* has been mostly in your head, it seems to me. Affairs of that kind are inclined to be different from what you think, when the guns are firing. Everything changes, when you start smelling gunpowder. I reckon you'll find that out if we come to deal with O'Donnell and his mates. Instructive for you, you might say.

– No doubt. We all find reality different from the plans we make for it. Do you ever regret robbing that train, James?

He turns his head again, squinting at me severely, his eyes narrowed to slits. I have never asked him this before, and wonder if he'll grow angry. But his voice, when he answers, is very quiet and toneless.

– I'm sorry I did it, in one way, he says. It makes me no better than them bushrangers, I suppose. But I don't *regret* it. There's a difference, if you see what I mean. It brought me all this, didn't it? And I'll tell you, Robert, I ain't giving it back.

He waves his hand at the twittering Spring landscape around us: at the lush green meadow on our left, with our small herd of dairy cows grazing on it; at the roof of the house below, with its smoking kitchen chimney and its grove of blossoming plum trees at the back; at the hop fields across the road, where the poles for the new season's crop have already been erected in their rows, the green bines curling about them. He chuckles, deep in his throat. Then he repeats:

– No. I ain't about to give it back.

October 7th

The seat stands inside the gate to the hop garden, underneath one of the poplars that line the road. It's been crudely constructed from eucalyptus wood by William Richardson: at noonday, he and O'Leary sit there to eat their bread and cheese, and to drink their hop beer. Now that the Spring weather has arrived, Kathleen and I go there after supper when the field is deserted. We did so this evening.

– They'll be hanged now, she said. May God have mercy on them.

She was speaking of O'Donnell and his gang. Her voice was sober and regretful; and I found this disconcerting.

– You pity them? You pity a man like O'Donnell? After what he did to you?

She looked at me sideways, sitting with head slightly bent, her hands folded in the lap of her dress. She wore no bonnet, and her hair fell forward to partly hide her face. At first she made no answer; then she said:

– We are asked to forgive our enemies. I don't find it easy to forgive Dan O'Donnell, but I believe I pity him, now. He has become a murderer, and so is almost surely damned. That is a terrible thing: I can't bear to think of it.

– If damnation exists, I said, then O'Donnell richly deserves it.

She looked off down the rows of tent-like hop poles. Their

546

new, spiralling shoots were a brilliant green in the evening light, which glinted in Langford's new network of irrigation channels.

– I am not so sure of that, she said. He has killed two men, it's true. But one was a dirty informer – and the other was a constable serving this English Government. And at least Dan O'Donnell stood up and fought them.

I returned her gaze in amazement.

– I'm astounded to hear you say so. He and his henchmen are nothing but thieves and murderers. He is no Irish hero – he disgraces Ireland, and disgraces our struggle. His kind enable the English to brand us as a nation of ruffians. How on earth can you think otherwise, Kathleen?

My heat had shocked her. Her eyes widened as I spoke, and when she answered, her voice dropped to a murmur. Yet her face held a sort of blank stubbornness.

– I'm sorry, Robert. I'll not speak of him so again. I did not mean to compare Dan O'Donnell with men such as yourself or Mr Barry, or Mr Kinane.

– I scarcely thought that you did. But –

– I am afraid of him, she said, and I hate him for what he did to me. Dan is entirely mad, that's the truth of it. But supposing he had not been put in gaol and flogged, he might have been a better man – and one who might have fought for you, since he fears nothing. Being flogged by the English made him mad. It also put an anger in him that cannot be cured. Now, his soul may be lost.

I reached out and took her hand. It clasped mine instantly, and the light in her eyes, which continued to search my face, became softer, and at the same time anxious. Their brilliant blue melted my unease, and a wave of love surged up in me again. We had never before come so close to quarrelling.

– I did not intend to scold you, I said. Forgive me. But I hate the thought of this lout who once forced you. Let us put him out of our minds.

– Yes, let us do so, she said.

I had not at any time suggested to Kathleen that O'Donnell might attempt to kidnap her, and nor had the Langfords. We have no wish to trouble her with a discussion of such a notion, since this can serve no purpose, and she will clearly have thought of it herself. We have merely said that she should never walk alone beyond the property: a precaution that all our neighbours are observing. Now I tightened my hand on hers, which tightened in response, and she gave me one of those quick, impulsive smiles by which I'm charmed: a smile with closed lips, accompanied by a single nod, causing her eyes to narrow, and wrinkles to fan out at their corners – jaunty and faintly comical.

We sat for a time in silence, watching the sunset deepen. Many small birds had begun their evening chatter. Miss Tibbs, the grey tabby cat, came through the gate into the field at a meditative pace, pretending not to look at us. She had followed us here, as she does every evening: she is a cat with dog-like habits, and dotes on Kathleen. She disappeared into the grass under the poplars, where various native flowers have appeared with the Spring. As I watched, she re-emerged, sniffing at the cream, tube-like flowers of a cotton bush. Then she passed on to a clump of white iris, intruding her nose into the long, dark green stalks, delicate and enquiring. Did she perhaps ask herself what she was doing here, among these strange plants of Van Diemen's Land? That I can set down their names I owe to Kathleen, who puts them in vases in our bedroom. She has made me see a beauty in them, and I begin to be fond of the delicate native iris in particular, whose flowers resemble a white-and-yellow butterfly. Sometimes I pick a bunch, and bring them to her.

– Listen, I said now. We may be soon out of this prison, you and I. I have something to tell you, dearest. In six months' time, we should be far beyond the reach of Denison and his gaolers, and of all crazed rogues such as O'Donnell. What do you say to that?

She looked up swiftly and frowned.

– In six months? How? What can you mean, Robert?

I had wanted for some time to tell her of our escape plans – but had decided to postpone doing so until an answer came from the New York Directory. Now I had spoken on impulse, unable to hold the news back any longer. I was full of elation, and expected her to be so too; but instead, as I spoke, I saw a kind of alarm dawn in her face: an alarm that was mingled with regret.

– I cannot come with you, she said.

I stared at her. The thickening light went dark between the hop towers, and on the furrows of brown soil.

– Cannot? Why? Are you afraid?

She looked down into her lap, picking at her thumbnail, and shook her head.

– I am not afraid. It is not that.

I took her by the shoulders.

– Do you fear that I will take you to America and then desert you? I will never desert you, Kathleen. I have told you that we will marry. We will marry before we go, if you wish it.

– It is not that. I know you'll not betray me. I would wish to come with you anywhere. But I cannot.

She had tilted her head back to look at me, and I studied her face. What I saw there now was the transparent imprint of another face: that of a woman much older; a woman both stern and despairing, whom she might some day become.

– Then tell me, I said. Tell me why you say this, Kathleen.

– I cannot come *then*, she said. I cannot come in six months. It could not be done then because it's then I will be having a baby. May is when it will be born.

And now she looked up at me directly, with a mingling of expressions. Apprehension struggled against joy; and her lips were daringly parted, as though in readiness to smile.

I asked her how long she had known.

– I am two months gone, she said. I did not feel sure until now. Are you sorry, Robert? Are you angry?

I smiled, and put my arms around her; I felt her smallness, and the frailness of her waist.

– I am not angry, I said. You are having our baby, and I love you: how can I be angry?

Her arms went about me, and she rubbed her cheek against mine.

– Ah, I was afraid you would not want it, she said. You make me so glad. But now we cannot escape, and I know how sad that will make you. Can it not be a little later? Our baby must be old enough to travel.

Perhaps, I told her. But it all depended on our comrades in New York, and no other time might be possible. There was also Barry to consider.

– If we must stay for a time, could you not be happy here? I'm sorry you want to go, Robert. I love the farm, and I love this land, now. What would we do, in America? It frightens me, the thought of that country.

I took her hand. Yes, we would be happy here, I said. America must wait.

But as I watched the darkening hop-field, disappointment lay heavy on my chest. Part of me wanted to enter into that delight which was as yet more hers than mine; and part of me eventually would do so, no doubt. But for now, I was digesting the fact that escape with Paul Barry had become impossible; that escape was indefinitely postponed.

Kathleen had prayed for this baby, I felt sure. Nothing else could finally have healed that sorrow in her heart and in her womb left there by the loss of her first child. And to ask her to leave here now seemed almost perverse: a folly. She had put down roots, in this alien soil – she who had known little else but misery and starvation on her own – and now, in this Spring of the Antipodes, when our hop-bines were climbing again, she was pregnant, and the gladness of the season was her gladness. It is a Spring that does not explode, as it does in Europe; it comes in from the edges, almost unnoticed, like the small native flowers among the bush grass: a casual, sly fecundity. I was glad for Kathleen that she carried our baby; and in time I would no doubt be as glad of the child as she was, and be proud of it. But our child was not yet real to me, except as a fatal encumbrance. Ever since Barry's news, I had been filled with an exultancy that surprised me: a fierce and powerful impatience to be gone. Now, it seemed, I must turn back from the brink.

The hills turned from olive to black; and my earthbound love laid her head on my shoulder, and sighed with pure contentment.

October 20th

A letter from Paul Barry today, carrying dreadful news: news I've already learned from the *Advertiser*.

Two weeks ago, Liam Kinane was arrested and brought to trial in Hobart Town, charged with having left his police district without permission. This, of course, was the consequence of his journey to join us at the Lakes. Someone had informed on him; and a couple of convict constables testified that he had been seen on horseback in the Hamilton district.

At first, Barry tells me, it seemed that Liam would get off lightly. The magistrate merely reprimanded him, and made him give a promise that he would not go out of the Hobart Town district again without applying for leave. But then the matter turned monstrous.

The next day, Kinane was taken into custody by the police on the direct order of Governor Denison – who personally sentenced him to three months' hard labour at Port Arthur. Within days of his arrival on the Tasman Peninsula, he was removed to a nearby probation station where conditions are even more harsh than at Port Arthur: the Saltwater River. He has written a letter to Barry which describes his situation. He does so without comment, since his letters are read by the authorities. Deep in the bush, he labours in all weathers beside thieves and murderers, clad in the magpie dress of a convict and no doubt subjected to every kind of petty indignity his guards can devise.

Barry is of the opinion that Denison has felt free to visit this outrage on Kinane because he imagines that Kinane has no powerful friends, as we have. But the Governor will find he is wrong: Barry and O'Neill are writing letters to every possible quarter, drawing attention to the injustice – and so am I. Meanwhile, Father Brennan is writing a memorial to the Governor, asking that Kinane be pardoned, and that his incarceration be cut short. The *Advertiser*, and every other newspaper in the colony, is also protesting at Denison's harshness – and they are saying that the Governor has gone outside the law in inflicting this punishment, when a magistrate had issued a judgment that called for no such sentence.

Will the tyrant listen? I doubt it; and my mind keeps dwelling on our poor, reckless Liam, labouring in the yellow and grey, wearing the hideous leather cap of the Vandemonian convict on his unruly black curls. This is the price he has paid for that evening of fellowship which began so well for him, and ended so badly; and a rush of shame fills me when I think of the way I spoke to him.

Meanwhile, I'm forced to take stock of what such an outrageous official action means. It means that none of us is safe, no matter what friends we may have. The colonial tyrant has at last shown his claws – and will do so again, should the chance present itself. Our 'comparative freedom' is an illusion.

October 22nd
Yesterday, they came.

They came when I wasn't ready. The night before, for the first time in nearly a year, I had endured an asthma attack. It was not very severe, but it left me in that debilitated and somewhat dream-like state which is generally the aftermath of the enemy's visits.

Perhaps this was a blessing in disguise. The progress that took place seemed to me as it descended to have no more consequence than a dream: one which I viewed with a dreamer's blank detachment.

Waking today, however, I find that everything has changed.

They came at around two-thirty: that time of eternal pause when day still stands on its height, and the slow descent into evening has not yet begun.

It was unseasonably hot, for October. Glare was established in the valley again, giving us a taste of the Summer to come. It probed every dry-grassed hollow; it leaked like a thin and tasteless soup into every stony crevice where the weeds grew, and into every seamed and weathered grey plank on fences, barns and stables. The house's ochre bricks were baking and shimmering, and there was a shimmering in the air above the roof. Emptiness droned in the yard, and down in the hop fields; it droned on the road, and in the mournful little gully of the nettles, on the western side of the house. It droned behind those tall western hills which seem always to brood, like

552

sombre, grey-green Titans locked in some paralysing spell.

Its other name was boredom; and boredom promised nothing. Yet its droning seemed to warn of something ill, and should have been heeded.

It was not heeded: Langford and I were too busy.

We were down in the second hop garden that James had prepared during the Winter, poling the new rows of hops. I set the tea-tree stakes in place, while Langford guided the young shoots around them: a gentle occupation, and one I found soothing, in my state of languid convalescence. A little way off up the field, Richardson and O'Leary were spreading cow manure from a handcart.

Langford and I spoke little. Bending and straightening in the sun, absorbed by the work, we did not see Bess Langford coming between the rows.

– James, she said.

She had suddenly materialised behind us: bareheaded, and wearing her usual print dress of faded blue. Her eyes were fixed on Langford, and their gleaming whites seemed more prominent than usual: they appeared almost to bulge, and their customary glint of humour was absent. Squatting, we both squinted up at her in surprise, and our brown mongrel dog Rufus, who had been watching us work, jumped up and wagged his tail. Bess seldom came down to the fields, and never showed signs of hurry; but today it was evident that she had run here all the way. She had not removed the sacking apron she wore for work in the kitchen, and her bosom rose and fell; a single brown strand of hair, escaped from its bun, hung down beside her face, and her neck was flushed.

– Hello Bess, said Langford. What's in the wind?

– O'Donnell and his mates, Bess said. That's what's in the wind. The bastards are here, Jim.

Both of us rose quickly to our feet and began to question her, speaking at once. But she held up her hand.

– We ain't got much time, she said. So listen, both of you. They ain't moving, at present: they're camped in those hills up the back of us, only a mile or so off. Old Tom saw them. He sneaked up and spied on them: they was resting their horses and eating.

There's three of them, he says, and one looks like O'Donnell – he knew him from the descriptions. Big cove; red hair. Maybe it's not O'Donnell, but Tom thinks it is – and all of them had guns. Tom rode down to tell me.

Old Tom is an aged and solitary man who was once a shepherd, and before that a Lincolnshire burglar. Now he's a hermit. There are many such ex-felons in the bush, without women or family, spending their last years alone. He lives in a bark hut on the edge of our property, and survives by growing a few vegetables and keeping some hens and goats. Bess has made it her business to supply him with extra food, and with comforts such as sugar and tea. She often gives him meals in the kitchen. He is taciturn; he seldom speaks to James or me, but I've grown used to the sight of him about the place, followed by an aged sheep dog – or else hunched over our kitchen table in his dark pea jacket, his yellowish, long white hair hanging about his face.

– So they're not coming down here just now, Bess said. Or they wasn't, when Tom saw them.

– But they could do, at any moment, Langford said.

– They could, she said. Why else would they be here?

She was calm, looking at him, still breathing deeply. Her large red hands hung steady at her sides, fingers loosely curled as though in readiness for action, like a man's. He and she stared at each other with an expression that was hard, intimate and calculating. No doubt they had looked at each other in just this way in that criminal past of theirs, when disaster was their constant pursuer: always to be duped and outrun, working in marital harmony.

My heart was pounding; the rows of hop-poles and the distances of the field had become unreal, and I grabbed Langford's arm.

– We must go to the house, I said. And quickly.

– We must, James said. We want them guns. You get up to the house with Bess, and wait for me there. Load up that Manton of yours, Robert, and make sure them shot and powder flasks are full. I'll get Richardson and O'Leary. It's important that everyone knows what they have to do.

He looked cheerful; his air had become brisk and military, as he issued these orders. He actually smiled, as though savouring the prospect of some imminent enjoyment. I turned to Bess.

– Where's Kathleen?

– Up at the house, Bess said. I told her to stay there, and keep all the doors locked. She's safe enough, for now.

– My God, I said. Do you think that they can't break in?

And I began to run.

And now the dream began: that dream which I recall in fragments, not in the connected sequences of sane and ordinary life.

Running through the hop rows and across the white road, running up the drive and into the farmyard, I saw the world in pieces, unconnected: clods of dark earth breaking under my boots; a white cabbage butterfly hanging from a grass-stalk; the way our open red gate leaned on its hinges; the dusty new leaves on the oak trees, and their shadows spangling the ground; a bottle someone had dropped in the grass. Running, I wheezed and rattled, and my head began to swim: the sun wavered in the sky. The asthma, as usual, had left me feeble and breathless; my excellent health of the past year had foundered, just when I needed it most. I made myself run faster, cursing. I had to get to Kathleen. But the pounding of my heart was telling me already that I was probably too late.

Entering the farmyard, I found it deserted, with no sign of life but a few scratching hens. We had no other dog but Rufus, and I regretted it, now. The ash tree, the stables, the hop kiln's grey spire: all were familiar, but only as memories are familiar; their present existence was dubious. Emptiness reigned: that afternoon monotony whose droning had not been heeded, and at whose heart lay something ill. Hurrying on to the verandah, I saw instantly what it was. The green kitchen door hung half off its hinges: its lock was shot away, and it had been kicked in.

I ran inside, calling Kathleen's name, knowing there would be no answer. Silence. The eternal buzzing of flies up near the ceiling; the smell of bread that had been baking. I went through every room, still calling her name; then I came back to the kitchen and stood absolutely still, trembling and recovering my breath. I found I had become quite calm; but underneath this calm was rage: rage of a kind I had never known before.

I went to the bedroom and put on an old, navy-blue pilot coat. I took out the Colt from its drawer in the study, capped it, loaded its six chambers, and thrust it into an inner pocket of the coat. Then I returned to the kitchen. When James and Bess and our two farmhands came in, I was setting out the replenished shot and powder flasks on the table. Bess cried out when she saw the broken door; then she began to curse with a masculine luridness that startled me. Langford stood in silence, eyes narrowed, rubbing his chin. Then he asked:

– She's gone?

– Of course she's gone, I said. And I must go after them. Will you come with me, James?

Langford stared at me, his eyes gone pale and empty in that way they had when his mood was about to turn threatening.

– You don't need to ask that, he said. I'm not leaving those grass-combing buggers all to you – I wouldn't get none of that reward. Besides, you're likely to miss some, with that bloody Manton. Now let's get these guns loaded.

He winked, cancelling his tone of aggression, and I felt a surge of love for him. I went and picked up my shotgun, propped it at an angle, and began to pour a portion of powder from the flask into the barrel.

– We must hurry, I said. Hurry.

– They've not got more than ten minutes on us, he said. We'll find them, never fear.

He turned to lift his Kentucky rifle from the wall, while I used the ramrod to pack down the wadding and powder in the Manton. My fingers were trembling, but not too badly for what they had to do. I picked up my leather shot flask, held it over the barrel and released the plunger. Richardson and O'Leary were silent; they stood against the wall and stared at Langford, who had begun to load powder into his own gun, tilting his brass flask. Bess was also watching him, standing in the middle of the room, hands on her hips. Her dark blue eyes had a fixed and glassy look that was intimidating.

– Take care, Jim, she said, and he looked up quickly.

– Don't you worry, Bess, he said.

She came up to him, looking at him as though no-one else was present. She laid a big red hand on his shoulder, and he paused to put his own hand on hers.

– These ain't nothing but low dogs, he said. A picnic, this'll be, Bess. You know me, love.

He loaded a single, cotton-wrapped musket ball into his rifle, and then began the delicate task of capping the gun, pointing the barrel to the floor. As he did so, Bess's expression grew stern.

– I know you, old man – but there's always bad luck. We didn't want this now, Jim.

– We didn't want it, but we've got it. You look after things here. Richardson and O'Leary will watch out for you. So will Rufus. Keep him on the chain outside, and you'll know if anything's near.

I stared at Langford in surprise. I had thought we would bring at least one of the servants with us; but I decided not to question his wish. He now began to issue orders to them. O'Leary was to find a way to block up the kitchen door, and was to stay close by Bess. Richardson was to load a shotgun that stood in the store-room, and stand guard; but first, he was to run out to the stables, and saddle our horses.

– Move, now. Waste not a minute, Langford told him.

His martial manner had become more pronounced: he had taken command, but I didn't resent it. In this situation, he was the one most competent to do so, and my gladness at having him with me was keeping my fears for Kathleen at bay, and giving me savage hope. He attached his shot and powder flasks to his belt, as I had done, slammed on his hat, and tucked the giant rifle under his arm.

– Come now, Robert, he said. What are you loitering about for, partner?

Side by side, we rode at a trot up the slope past the pickers' huts: that hillside to the west of the house where Kathleen and I had wandered in happiness.

Langford rode Major, a quiet bay horse. I was on Fleur-de-lis, a pretty little chestnut filly I bought quite recently, and of whom I've grown extremely fond. The smell of her coat rose into my nostrils, warm and dusty and innocent in the sun, like the smell of a child, and I was troubled by the thought that she might come to harm. The sun was stronger than ever, and I tilted the brim of my cabbage-tree hat low over my eyes. I urged Fleur forward in the muffled afternoon quiet, and debilitated calm enfolded me.

Something resembling a gauze curtain lay between myself and the border of the gum-forest in front of us, where the cleared, open hillside ended. I had entered the dream once more, and I saw that this hillside had always been the place where Kathleen would disappear. It had rained the previous night, and the ground was not quite dry; the tracks of at least three horses could be discerned, coming down the slope and returning.

Langford pointed to them. Then he pointed at a break in the gums up ahead, where the hoof-prints disappeared. We would not follow the tracks from this point, he said: instead, we would ride on to the forest-covered ridge above the valley, and move in the same direction.

– But we could lose them, I said. We can only guess at their direction.

Langford reined his horse in, and I did the same. He spoke low and fast, leaning forward over Major's neck and fixing me with his gaze, as though he intended to quarrel with me.

– Now hear me speak a word, Robert. That's a risk we've got to take, is how I see it. They'll probably keep to the floor of the gully – and I know the way this gully runs. We'll be moving above 'em, with the advantage of high ground, and a chance of surprising the buggers. See? We must be crafty, but not too bold. We must also go quiet, and not speak. Surprise is everything. That's why I had no use for them servants. They'd be noisy, and they don't love fire-arms. Well? Do you agree?

I agreed. Langford, with his martial and criminal abilities, was now in undisputed command. He nodded once, turned away, and spurred Major fast up the slope between the trees. I followed, riding inside the dream's false calm.

Soon, as the scrub grew dense, we were no longer able to keep our horses at a trot. We rode carefully among the trees, passing in and out of sun and shadow, forcing our way through prickly, sack-coloured undergrowth, watching out for rocks on which the horses might stumble. I placed my hand on Fleur's neck, and her sun-hot coat gave me an irrational sense of comfort and normality. But the odour of her coat had been joined by others, belonging to those territories of tedium that had now begun to engulf us, and which apparently went on without end: hot dry reek of eucalyptus leaves; of ants; of the fallen bark of gum trees. Waves of warmth, like those of a living body, came up to me from the ground.

This uneasy progress went on for perhaps a quarter of an hour. It seemed much longer, and I spoke inside the dream to *Herr Doppelgänger*, telling him that O'Donnell and his men were cunning enough to have escaped, that the floor of the gully was empty, and that Kathleen was lost to me. But then Langford reined in again, and held up his hand.

I brought Fleur to a halt beside him. She nervously shook her head from side to side, and I stroked her neck to soothe her. Still Langford said nothing; instead, he pointed through the narrow aisles of gums towards the gully. And now I detected sounds of male voices, and of jingling harness. Langford nodded, and jerked his head for me to follow. We rode on, making as little noise as possible. But if we can hear them, I thought, surely they can hear us.

They did not, it appeared. Soon we heard their voices and the sound of their harness and hoofs below us: quite close at hand, although they were made invisible by a screen of trees and bushes. From the sound of the hoofs, they were walking their horses, not trotting them – which seemed to me extraordinary. Was O'Donnell so sure of himself that he didn't believe we would pursue him? Or was the terrain too difficult for them to go any faster? Laughter rose, and a slurred Irish voice, quite loud. A possible explanation presented itself: they were drunk.

I looked at Langford. He pointed again, indicating that we

should go forward. He nudged Major's ribs with his heels, urging him into a gentle trot. I followed suit, moving close behind him. We came to a small, grassy clearing, skirted by wattle and she-oak. Here Langford dismounted, and I did the same. Frowning at me for silence, he began to tether Major to the trunk of a wattle, indicating that I should do likewise. We then took our guns, and moved into the belt of the trees.

On the other side, we came to the edge of a slope of dry grass that ran down into the gully. It was a peaceful, untouched place, lost in the hum of mid-afternoon. Langford was grinning, and his narrow eyes glinted. He pointed to a large, flat rock, and we threw ourselves down in the grass behind it, resting the barrels of our guns on it and pointing them down into the gully. James leaned close to my ear, so that his breath fanned it. He spoke rapidly, instructing me again as he'd done when we carried out our target practice, his eyes never leaving the gully. His voice had grown hoarse and throaty.

– Just what I wanted: a lovely spot. These rocks make a perfect cover. We can hit 'em, and they can't hit us. I'll take care of O'Donnell first – but then I'll need two minutes to reload. So use your two barrels right, Robert – hold your fire and aim careful, and try and bring them other two bastards down. But don't fret your eyelids if it don't go how we plan.

I nodded: I was disinclined to speak. Both of us fixed our eyes on the clearing, guns fully cocked, sighting along the barrels at the trees. There was a moment of pause that resembled reverie. I would have liked to sleep, and drift away; and yet I was fully alert. I found that my hands were sweating, and they were like someone else's hands. A magpie warbled suddenly, and the sounds of the invisible gang came closer: harness jingling, voices loud and careless as before, like those of revellers in a tap-room. Yes, surely they were drunk; and it occurred to me that I had only a rough idea of what O'Donnell looked like, and had read no descriptions of the appearance of the other two – whose names, according to the newspapers, were O'Hegarty and Lynch. I glanced at Langford. He lay utterly still as though meditating, the handsome, maple-wood stock of his

Kentucky rifle nestled into his shoulder, his thick index finger inside the trigger guard, his pale gaze fixed and unblinking. His face, in profile, now appeared distinct as though seen under a magnifying glass: the rough, sun-reddened skin; the bristling, brown and grey moustache, which twitched once as I watched; a cut on his chin from shaving. Soon, he or I or both of us might be dead, and this face of his seemed suddenly of inestimable value.

O'Donnell and his bushrangers entered the gully below, emerging from a line of gums some twenty yards away.

They rode out from under the glinting, dark green canopy like great, straggling fish coming up from the depths of a pool. O'Donnell, I saw instantly, held Kathleen on the saddle in front of him, his arm about her waist. Her hands, held in front of her, were tied at the wrists. A tingling began in my brain, and my heart hammered in my throat.

– God rot the fucking son of a bitch, I heard Langford whisper. I can't pick him off, with her in between. Hold your fire, Robert. Wait.

I did not take my eyes from O'Donnell; nor did I move.

He was a big man, and I would have known instantly that this was my enemy, even had he not held Kathleen. I had looked for the red hair: it was covered by a wide-brimmed felt hat, of the same olive-drab hue as the bush, but he had a full red beard, and was mounted on a handsome black thoroughbred which I guessed to be the one he had stolen at Green Ponds. To my considerable surprise, he wore spectacles. I had scarcely imagined a bushranger in spectacles.

In the seconds that followed, as he and his companions rode forward, they sprang into life with great clarity. They seemed to me a sorry-looking lot, this last band of outlaws to defy Van Diemen's Land's wish for respectability; these final inheritors of atrocity, and of quaint outlaw gallantry. They in no way resembled the bold, romantic bushrangers portrayed in books for London consumption which I had read on the *Raffles*. In fact, they appeared more like a trio of sottish, dissolute louts, strayed here from one of the taverns of St Giles – which of course is what they were. Their looks were threatening enough – each man having a double-barrelled shotgun slung from his harness – but they were so bedraggled and tattered, and got up in such an extraordinary collection of garments, that I would have found them comical, had the circumstances been otherwise.

'Captain' O'Donnell wore a tattered brown jacket trimmed with kangaroo fur, a dirty yellow neckerchief, moleskin trousers with a tear in one knee, and leather leggings. Next to him rode a fellow even bigger than himself, with a huge jaw and broken nose. His dirty red overshirt was strapped round the waist with a leather belt, and he wore a cap of kangaroo skin. Combined with his brutish features, this ugly and primitive headgear made him vaguely resemble some Tartar from the Central Asian steppes; but as he rode forward, I recognised him. O'Hegarty: I had not connected the name with my night in the Black Bull. 'Ballybunion Tim' had turned outlaw; and I wondered fleetingly whether Liam Kinane had maintained some connection with him, and perhaps with O'Donnell as well. The man riding just behind O'Hegarty must be Lynch: a small, sallow gnome with narrow features and lank hair, in a blue serge shirt and incongruous, light buckskin trousers (no doubt stolen from a gentleman's residence), soiled and torn and creased beyond repair. He looked like a stable-hand, rather than a bushranger. Perched on his head was a Scotch cap with a tassel on top.

Were we really to kill such clodhoppers as these?

But then I looked back at Kathleen. Riding side-saddle, bent sideways in O'Donnell's grasp, she frowned. She neither seemed to struggle nor to consent to his embrace; she stared straight ahead, like someone locked in illness. She was bare-headed, and had on a dress of white cotton, printed with a design of mauve flowers. It was a gown I had given her as a present; now it was creased and pulled awry by O'Donnell's gross hand.

Langford suddenly shouted, making me jump.

His resonant, parade-ground voice called on the group to halt – the single, sharp syllable echoing off the hill on the far side of the gully. His rifle was trained on O'Donnell.

The trio reined in their horses. O'Hegarty and Lynch pulled out their shotguns, staring wildly upwards. They could see little else but our faces, and the barrels of our guns. O'Donnell drew Kathleen closer, circling his horse so that he faced us more directly, placing Kathleen between us. He had drawn a huge pistol from a saddle-holster: from the size of it, a Colt Dragoon. But his movements and position were awkward. In order to take the gun in his right hand, he had been forced to hold the reins in his left – and his left arm must also secure Kathleen, pressing her against him. Should the hack become restive, it would be very difficult for him to control it, in such a posture. And it seemed to be skittish: it stamped and jerked its head nervously, so that O'Donnell was forced to keep a tight rein.

Now Langford was shouting again, in the same parade-ground voice, measured and unhurried.

– Listen to me, you coveys. We can kill all three of you. We can do it without reloading. But we'll give you another choice. Throw down them guns, and we'll take you alive to the traps. But you must be smart about it. Come, now: what's it to be?

On the upturned faces of the men, a similar expression had appeared: an amazement that resembled severity. This was succeeded by the slow and baffled outrage of drunkenness. They stared; and in those seconds, there was a return of silence, broken only by the soft and restless stamping of hoofs, and a snort from O'Donnell's thoroughbred. I saw O'Hegarty say something to O'Donnell, while the gnomish Lynch stared up at our position as though hypnotised, his gun resting on his pommel. O'Donnell shook his head, as though denying O'Hegarty something; but then a progress began which I viewed in disbelief.

Ballybunion Tim spurred his horse, and set it at a gallop up the hillside, directly towards us.

As he came, he roared: a sound which at first bore no resemblance to human speech. Then I realised that he was shouting in Irish, though not a word was comprehensible to me. His cavernous mouth gaped, revealing a few remaining teeth like those of a dog; his red, unshaven face was a mask of rage, under its hideous kangaroo-skin cap. He had apparently reverted to savagery, in the bush: a creature of the wilderness, driven by ungovernable wrath.

He raised his shotgun to his shoulder, and fired.

Langford and I put our heads down behind the rock. The shot sprayed overhead, and now I found James shouting in my face, spacing his words with care.

– Leave him to me. Take care of the other little bastard.

He raised himself from behind the rock, the Kentucky rifle at his shoulder, and sighted along the barrel with unhurried care. I lifted my head in time to see that O'Hegarty had almost reached us, his horse labouring on the slope; he had his shotgun raised, ready to fire his second barrel. But Langford fired first, and O'Hegarty threw up his hands. The ball had hit him in the chest: it blew him backwards off his horse, and I had time to see that he lay motionless on his back in the bush-grass, his eyes still glaring, his mouth still gaping in a furious and passionate shout. Then his huge head and red shirt were obscured by the cloud of white-blue smoke that had come from Langford's rifle. Another cloud, from O'Hegarty's gun, hung a little further off: the air was very still, and the clouds did not disperse or move.

Langford was up on one knee now, given some protection by the gunsmoke. He was calmly reloading, his powder flask over the barrel, and glanced across at me quickly.

– Get away from the smoke, he shouted. Get to where you can see, and don't bloody miss. But leave O'Donnell. We can't touch O'Donnell.

I crawled quickly through the grass towards a second group of rocks. As I did so, I heard a shotgun fired from below: that would be Lynch, but I was not even aware of any shot passing me. Now Lynch had one barrel left. I raised my head and found O'Donnell in the same position as before, facing us, with Kathleen shielding his body, his big black horse frantically pawing the ground and rearing: it clearly hated noise. He aimed his pistol at me, and fired; but controlling the horse and keeping his grip on Kathleen made it impossible to be accurate, at this distance, and the bullet went wide. He then fired through the smoke towards Langford, but missed there as well. Lynch, in his ridiculous Scotch cap, had ridden forward a few paces and had his shotgun raised, also aiming towards

Langford. But James, I saw, continued to calmly reload, squatting now, still partly screened by the smoke.

Lynch's shotgun discharged again, and Langford barely glanced up as the shot passed overhead. Until he reloaded, Lynch was now defenceless; there was only O'Donnell. Through my gauze veil, I saw Lynch scrabbling at his powder flask, and Kathleen staring up at us, while the black horse stamped and whinnied. O'Donnell, his pistol impotently raised, seemed to be considering his position.

Now fury drove me. I raised myself, looking down the barrel of the shotgun; I got Lynch in my sights, conscious of the advantage that elevation gave me. His scream after I fired was appalling: an accusation I had not anticipated.

Breathing in the biting reek of gunpowder, crawling through the grass to get away from the new cloud of smoke that hung stationary in front of me, like a curtain drawn over my deed, I looked from behind another rock to see that the small man had fallen from his horse and was lying in the grass, his Scotch cap beside him. He was embracing himself, holding himself about the middle, and even from this distance, the blue shirt and the light Summer trousers could be seen to be saturated with blood: I had hit him in the abdomen, and the pellets had opened a wound for the full width of his body. He did not cease to cry out, but continued at intervals, the falsetto sound both protesting and incredulous, like that of a child whose injury was beyond anything it had ever been led to expect.

– *Hah*, he said. *Hah. Hah. Hah.*

The sound was hateful, and monstrously comic, and I wanted it to stop; but it would not stop. No doubt his liver and intestines were riddled with my pellets, and his pain must have been appalling. But then I stopped thinking about Lynch: I cocked the hammer on my second barrel, and trained the gun on O'Donnell. I wouldn't be able to fire if he remained as he was; but I hoped for some unexpected mishap that would expose him, and force him to abandon Kathleen as a shield. It would be better that Langford should deal with him, though, since the single ball from his rifle could do it cleanly; my shot would spray over such an area that there would always be danger of hitting her.

– Good. Hold your fire, Langford muttered. You done well, partner. You done well.

He had appeared beside me, crawling on his belly, his rifle reloaded. Both of us stared down at O'Donnell, whose horse still stamped and circled and tried constantly to rear. Both of us sighted along the barrels of the guns that we dared not fire. Flies hummed, and sweat ran down my forehead, from under my hat.

– Har, Har, cried Lynch. *Help me. Oh Jesus and Mary, help me.*

Grasping Kathleen, his pistol still raised, O'Donnell was absurdly like a man posing for an equestrian statue. He did not look down at Lynch. The stallion shook its head and began to rear again, and we heard him curse it.

– We've got him in a nice bloody pickle, Langford whispered. He ain't got three hands, and if that horse gets really skittish, he has to let go of our Kathleen – or else of his pistol. And he can't afford to make a run. I'll pick the bastard off, if he does.

Baffled – or so it seemed – O'Donnell turned his head to and fro, the sun flashing on his spectacles, Kathleen pressed ever closer against him. Then he turned the giant pistol sideways, and put it to her temple.

She squinted, and I saw her mouth open. O'Donnell threw back his head, his red beard jutting, and began to shout at us. He had a voice as resonant as Langford's. From his accent, I guessed him to be from Ulster.

– Lay down your guns. Lay them down, or she dies. And then stand up. Do ye hear?

Langford and I looked at each other. James's mouth was thin, and his face had suddenly become drawn. He nodded at me.

– He's in earnest, the bugger. Do as he says, Robert: we don't have a choice. But keep that little barker ready in your pocket – unless you'd like me to have it?

I shook my head, and stood up. The sweat was running down my cheeks.

– Come down with raised hands, O'Donnell called. Come down slow, you sons of bitches, and let you not think of anything cute – or I swear to you by Christ, she dies.

We obeyed, walking down the slope past the body of O'Hegarty, who silently roared at the sky. I noticed idly that he had a large, ugly sore on his cheek: he had probably been diseased in some way. The birds remained silent, as we trudged. In the huge and monotonous stillness, every sound was magnified; Lynch had fallen silent, and all we heard was the creak and chink of O'Donnell's harness, and the restless, intermittent stamping of his horse's hooves.

We came on to the floor of the gully. Lynch lay some distance off, still embracing himself, while his horse quietly grazed in the bushes. I glanced at him fleetingly, as we passed, and saw that dark blood covered a remarkable area of his shirt and trousers, and was soaking into the patch of dusty ground where he lay. Why did I feel guilty? I felt guilty. His face was white as plaster, and his dark eyes met mine without accusation: he seemed instead to be concentrating on some terrible, unsolved problem. As we approached O'Donnell I looked only at Kathleen, who sat passive in his grip, her bound hands held in front of her, the pistol still pressed to her temple. O'Donnell's left hand, its red-gold hairs glinting in the sun, covered most of her waist. She stared back at me without expression, and without a sound. The colour of her eyes was drained by the unappeasable light which enveloped us all, and from which none of us could escape. She seemed scarcely to recognise me: she waited, like a rare and intelligent animal caught in a trap. I saw that there was a bruise on her left cheekbone, and my heart began to beat unevenly.

– Stop there, now, O'Donnell said. Don't drop your hands.

Langford and I obeyed, halting some four yards off from him, our hands still raised.

O'Donnell looked only at me, and grinned through his un-trimmed beard, whose coppery mass had the same gold lights in it as the hairs on the backs of his hands. He examined me from head to foot, looking through his small, round spectacles. He must have been quite short-sighted: they magnified his close-set eyes, which were a paler blue than Kathleen's. He had a long face, a sun-reddened, upturned nose, and thin lips. I hated him, but he was not entirely as I had expected. He was physically large and crude, but not the same species of brute that O'Hegarty had been. Probably because of the spectacles, he reminded me of a schoolmaster from the peasantry: one of those muscular, down-at-heel pedagogues who keep hedge schools, beating their pupils with a hazel bush. Finally, he addressed me.

– *Nach labhrann tú Gaeilge?*

– No, I told him. I don't speak Irish.

He shook his head, clicking his tongue, and smiled down insultingly from his tall black horse. The magnified blue discs of his eyes, behind their glasses, were fixed on me unwinkingly, as though I were a zoological specimen. He swayed a little, in the saddle. He had certainly been drinking: I could smell the rum on him even from where I stood, mingling with the odours of gunpowder and sweat: his horse's and his own. When he spoke again, his voice was heavily sarcastic, and sought to instruct me. Despite the slight slurring produced by the liquor, it was the voice of a rural pedant: a type often encountered among Ribbonmen.

– *Níl Gaeilge ar bith agat, mar sin,* he said. *Muise, nach aisteach é sin.* Yes: this is a queer thing, that Robert Devereux speaks no Irish. It's one of our great leaders, and he speaks no Irish! But isn't it a Protestant you are, and one of the bloody quality? Well, I say you've never been Irish. Do you hear? Not you nor your ancestors, whom I piss on: the God-damned Old English who stole our estates, and destroyed and ruined our lords. Do you think I know nothing of that butcher Essex, sent by the bloody whore Elizabeth? Your ancestor, Devereux! Your pox-ridden English ancestor!

I stood, my thoughts revolving slowly, as thoughts in dreams always do. Did he intend to shoot us, after his harangue? If so, I wished to keep him talking as long as possible, in the hope of some last opportunity to reverse things. But I knew there was little hope, and that Langford and I were probably doomed to die within minutes. Deliberately, I avoided looking at Kathleen, who still made no sound.

Suddenly, Langford spoke.

– When you've done with your history, mate, will you tell us what you're intending to do? We might be able to come to an arrangement.

– Shut your fucking English mouth, O'Donnell said. You that have shot Tim O'Hegarty, who was a better man than you will ever be. You will pay for that soon. *Gheobaidh tú bás, geallaimse dhuit.*

He had not even glanced at Langford; he went on looking at me. I saw that he had more to say to me, that he had probably been preparing it for some time, and that it was partly for Kathleen's benefit. Now I understood the emptiness of the eyes behind their spectacles: they looked inward, contemplating endless and repeated themes of grandeur, dispossession and revenge. The man was a fanatic, as Ribbonmen often are, driven by a hatred made splendid in their minds by myths of a lost nobility, when the estates of the gentry were rightfully theirs. His next words confirmed this.

– You may think that I bow before you, Devereux, as so many of our people do. I do not. I spit on you and yours, who were nothing but English robbers. And I bow to no man. I am a Ribbonman, and a descendant of kings. I am Daniel O'Donnell from Donegal, and a descendant of Red Hugh O'Donnell.

He lifted his long chin, and displayed the great red fan of his beard; head thrown back, he looked down his nose at me, with fatuous, alcoholic pride. He was not merely drunk, I saw, but mad, as Kathleen had said.

– The O'Donnell was a great man, I said. I honour him as you do, and you are surely of noble descent. Now can we not negotiate? Let Kathleen go, O'Donnell, and ride off: we will not attempt to follow. You have my word on it.

He laughed loudly, with every appearance of amusement. Then, just as quickly, he was stern again.

– The word of a bloody Protestant landlord, is it? Haven't I had sorrow enough from you, Devereux? You stole Kathleen away from me – but you'll do it no more, you high and mighty bastard. I know the lies and blather you've been telling her. Marriage, is it? Your kind never marry ours. You tell them that to get between their legs – but marry them you'll never do. Kathleen is not for you: she's too good for you. An O'Rahilly – of the same blood as the great bard! She has better Irish blood than yours, Devereux – and Kathleen is my woman. If she's not, she dies.

He lowered his head towards Kathleen with an expression of deranged fondness, the pistol held tenderly to her head. His arm pressed her closer while he grinned at me, and her body moved in her dress.

Suddenly she spoke, her voice clear and resigned.

– I must go with him, Robert. Tell him you agree – then he won't kill you.

But I said nothing, and O'Donnell looked down at her and frowned.

– I won't kill him, is it? And when did I promise you that, joy? Here's Tim O'Hegarty dead, and Thomas Lynch dying. Sure, I'll kill these two bastards both, I promise you.

Kathleen twisted her head to look up into his face. She pursed her mouth and squinted as I'd sometimes seen her do on the farm, when she was lifting a heavy bucket or churn.

– I'll come with you, Dan, she said. But I'm telling you, you'll not murder these two men. If you do, my curse on you for ever. Do you hear? *Má dhéanann tú é sin, mo mhallacht ort go deo.*

She did not implore, and the gaze she turned on him made the pistol pressed to her head seem like a foolish toy. She showed no sign of fear, and was clearly in the grip of something transcending fury: that Delphic force which sometimes visits women, reflecting the light of a truth which they are able to meet without flinching, but in front of which the male quails away. O'Donnell did so now. He blinked at her, in drunken bafflement; then he frowned, darting quick, warning glances at Langford and me. But Kathleen continued to stare at him, the dark blue bruise on her cheekbone like a brand: not pitiful but ominous, like the evidence of a crime whose consequences he would never escape.

There was a pause, as though neither Langford nor I existed. In it, I heard another moan from Lynch, some distance off on our left. O'Donnell answered Kathleen in Irish: too fast and slurred for me to understand a word. She shook her head; then she began to answer him, also in Irish. But she did not finish. As she spoke, Lynch set up a new outcry: a sudden wailing of extraordinary loudness, made unnerving by the fact that it now resembled that of a deranged and tormented woman. He screamed: and the screaming had a gurgling in it, no doubt because my pellets had penetrated his lungs, as well as his stomach. He must have been in great agony, and it was all I could do to refrain from looking across to where he lay. But I kept my eyes on O'Donnell, as I had done from the beginning.

– Dan, Lynch cried. Dan! Help me! Ah Jesus, Dan – won't you help me? Am I to die, Dan? It hurts! It hurts!

Then he began to scream again; and as he did so, O'Donnell's big stallion shook its head and whinnied in distress. It was never meant to be in such a situation, this nervous, stolen thoroughbred; it rolled its eyes in protest as Lynch's screams continued; it neighed loudly, showing its teeth and pink gullet, on a note that matched the small man's screaming. Then, while O'Donnell cursed it, it reared.

It reared to an extraordinary height, while he shouted his commands, and while he tried with one hand to bring it under control. Black, terrific and frenzied, it towered high above us, like some airborne, ancient horse-demon come to punish us for our crimes; and now I saw that O'Donnell could no longer pinion Kathleen with the hand that held the reins, though he still held the pistol to her head. She was sliding out of his grasp, while the horse, with infinite slowness, began to return to earth; she was twisting her body about and had thrown herself free, plunging sideways to the ground. I did not make the mistake of following her with my eyes. My pilot coat hung open; I had been conscious by its weight of exactly where the Colt sat, and now it was in my hand.

O'Donnell roared at Kathleen in Irish. He began to turn back towards Langford and me, the gun in his hand describing an arc towards us, like a clumsy club. But I had taken careful aim, pointing at that spot on the shabby, kangaroo-trimmed jacket which I judged to be the location of the heart. When I squeezed the trigger, the report was so loud that my head rang; and it was from inside the zone of that ringing that I saw O'Donnell jerk, as though twitching at the end of a rope.

For some seconds, he stared at me through his glasses, in a sort of dull surprise: or seemed to stare, since the life may already have left him. I had time, before he swayed to one side, to note the dark

571

patch on his chest; then he crumpled in on himself, dropping to the ground to lie on his face, his hat fallen in the grass. The thump he made was loud. His spectacles had come off too, and lay in the grass in the sun, one of the lenses glaring in its rays like a diamond. The black horse cantered away, making for the edge of the clearing.

The tedious silence of the land resumed, broken only by another wail from Lynch, as though in hopeless protest. The smoke from my pistol hung on the motionless air. Then I saw that Kathleen was on her feet, and was walking towards O'Donnell. She stood over the body in silence. She did not try to touch him, but merely stared, as though at a fallen tree.

I felt powerful arms go about me, and tobacco-smelling breath on my face. It was Langford, embracing me. He thumped me on the back, laughing with delight, and I saw his face greatly enlarged, inches from mine. I had never before seen in it such an expression of powerful joy – not even when I agreed to buy the farm with him. Nor had I ever seen such affection there.

– I knew you wasn't white-livered, he said. I knew it, Robert. What a shot! You and me – we're real partners *now*, eh? No, by God, we're brothers – ain't we?

Yes, we were brothers: dimly, I knew that was true, since we had beaten back death together. I wanted to share his joy; and I wanted more than anything to walk over to Kathleen and take her in my arms. But I found myself for the moment unable to move. Despite the whirring heat that still enclosed us, I was strangely cold. I stood frozen, the pistol hanging loosely from my hand. Langford saw my state, and asked:

– Is something wrong, partner?

– I have killed a man, I said. And he was one of my own.

He looked at me, his bright grey gaze puzzled and concerned. I turned, and began to walk towards Kathleen.

5. WRATH

November 6th

Yesterday to Hobart Town, and made my way as usual to Lenoir's little shop in Limbo.

I sat in my accustomed place, beside his roll-top desk under the storage platform. Twilight was gathering, and the shop grew steadily dimmer. There were few customers. Outside the door, odours made fouler by the growing warmth of Summer were drifting up the lane from the Rivulet. Despite the warmth, Monsieur Lenoir wore his ancient blue pilot coat, and a rusty neckerchief. But he had dispensed with the Russian cap, freeing his abundant grey hair, a lock of which fell over his forehead. He had turned himself sideways at his desk to face me, and grinned.

– So you are now a hero to the colony, he said. The past month's newspapers have had a good deal to say about your exploit. You reveal a talent for violence, Devereux – not surprising, I suppose, in a revolutionary terrorist.

He was teasing me, and smiled slyly; but I did not smile back. Though a month has gone by, the killing of O'Donnell is still not a matter I find I can easily speak of.

Bloodshed was not something from which I gained any satisfaction, I told Lenoir. Nor did I regard an affray with a sordid set of ruffians as something to take pride in. Moreover, it was James Langford who had done most to overcome O'Donnell and his gang, displaying his skills as an ex-soldier. What gave me great satisfaction was that the convict authorities had now informed Langford that for his part in the affair, he would be given a free pardon.

Lenoir fingered his beard, looking at me over his spectacles.

– Yes, I read of this, he said. But there will be no free pardon for *you*, I believe.

– Of course not.

– Of course not. There is something of an irony in this, is there not? It was you who killed O'Donnell, but you are too important to be pardoned. You will be given the reward, though, I trust?

James and I would share it, I told him, and it would all be put into the farm. We would put in a pump for the irrigation system, and make other improvements.

Lenoir nodded, tugging at his beard. I knew this mood of his; he had things he wished to impart to me, and would do so in his own time. Finally he said:

– This public service you have performed does not make Governor Denison love you more, of course – he loves you even less. I wonder that he did not make it an excuse to meet you face to face, and satisfy his curiosity about you. But it was bad enough for him, I'm sure, that he was forced to make a statement praising your action. It was even worse that it was celebrated in the press, both here and in the other Australian colonies.

He mused, and the flies up near the ceiling droned and dipped and circled, like some swarm of pygmy warriors whose numbers made their victory inevitable. Then he said:

– It is a dread I can understand: the more one hates an invisible foe, the more he grows into something more than human. Or *less* than human. I have had some experience of this phenomenon.

His tongue ran over his top lip, and he squinted as though tasting something unpleasant. His eyes wandered to the far end of the shop, where the Emperor brooded on the street, and where two well-dressed gentlemen were turning over books. As a precaution (which we'd sometimes adopted before), we now spoke in French, very low.

– You exaggerate, monsieur, I told him. I doubt that our Governor of convicts gives so much thought to me.

– I have told you before – he does, and you must not under-estimate his loathing. He was put in a rage by the agitation that you

574

and Mr Barry carried out for the release of Mr Kinane – and by the support given to you by the newspapers. It was doomed to failure of course – Kinane will serve out his sentence until Christmas. And the Governor is now determined to destroy him. Did you know that our friend ran an article in the *Exile* on your bushranger O'Donnell some time ago, speaking of him as an Irish patriot, driven to crime by the cruelty of English rule? Folly, my dear – folly! This was the last straw for Denison: and it will mean the end of the *Exile*.

– Will it? But London has always refused to give Denison his way in this.

Lenoir picked up a steel-nibbed pen from the desk and began to examine it, turning it over and over as though it were one of his molluscs. He sighed; when he spoke again it was in English, but so softly that I had to lean forward.

– I have told you, my dear: I have warned you. And yet you will not seem to listen. But you should listen now. The journalist Casey is your greatest enemy. I have told you of the game he plays with Kinane: now it has succeeded, and Casey has taken over as editor and publisher of the *Exile*.

I stared at him in astonishment; then I glanced at the far end of the shop. The two gentlemen had gone; we were alone here, and the place was almost dark, since Lenoir had lit no lamps.

– Taken over the *Exile*? How can that be? And how do you know this?

He looked up from the pen between his fingers as though prompted by a sudden noise, and his blue-green gaze held mine with an unwavering shrewdness which I imagined must have characterised him in his prime.

– If you repeat what I am going to tell you, I shall deny it, he said. Do you understand, young fellow?

– Certainly. But you shouldn't tell me, monsieur, if you don't trust me.

He smiled, and his expression came as close to affection as any expression of his could do.

– I trust you, he said. But I know you to be impetuous. So please be discreet.

He put down the pen, and steepled his ink-stained fingers.

– You know that I have acquaintances at official level, both in the Royal Society and as customers. As I have told you before, these gentlemen do not guard their tongues – and what I learn is this. Before going to Port Arthur, Mr Kinane executed a deed assigning the proprietorship of the *Exile* to Mr Casey – so that Casey might carry on the paper until Kinane was released to take up the editorship again. But Casey acts on the Governor's orders – and Kinane will never regain his paper. Casey will first draw its teeth – then he will destroy it.

I sat silent for a moment. Then I said:

– Christ. Liam is such a fool. He would listen to none of our warnings against Casey. But Matthew is exceedingly good at ingratiating himself, and appearing to be a devoted servant. Kinane needed such a person, I suppose.

– What will you do?

– About the paper? Nothing. I'm glad to see an end to it, monsieur. I found it an embarrassment, as you know.

Lenoir was looking out the door on to the lane, studying a rumbling dray that was going by. Laden high with crates, bound for the warehouse of Nathan and Moses, the lamp by the driver's seat already lit and glowing, it presented a complex silhouette. After it had gone, Lenoir said slowly:

– When Mr Kinane returns from Port Arthur and discovers that Casey has betrayed him, I fear for what he may do. This paper gave his life purpose, and Casey will have taken it away – as well as revealing himself as a traitor. Mr Kinane is even more impulsive than you, Devereux – and certainly more violent. I hear of him brawling in taverns, and attracting the attention of the police. He is highly intelligent, but his emotions rule him. You do see what I am driving at, don't you?

– Of course I do. My comrades and I will have to run Casey to earth before Liam does. That Judas will have to be dealt with.

My voice must have betrayed my anger. Lenoir threw up his hands – an uncharacteristically demonstrative gesture – and cast his eyes upwards to the circling flies.

– *Mon Dieu*, Devereux, you will put *yourself* at risk – as much risk as Kinane! Don't you see, if you do Casey a harm, you will at last give the Governor his excuse? He will arrest and incarcerate you.

– I am not such a fool, monsieur; and I assure you again, I am not a violent man. Of course I will offer Casey no physical harm.

Lenoir sat back, with an appearance of relief; but his eyes, returning to mine, remained dubious. Then he began to laugh: a high, wheezing giggle.

– You are not a violent man: I see. You are feared by the authorities as a terrorist, and you have just shot and killed two men – but you are not a violent man.

Seeing my expression, he ceased to laugh, drew a handkerchief from his pocket and wiped his eyes. Then he said:

– Well, well, I believe you. I know that you are far more disciplined than your friend Kinane. Forgive me for becoming agitated on your behalf – it was foolish of me, and none of my business. Human beings will always destroy themselves in their own way – I was forgetting that, for a moment. This is why I attend to my molluscs and my books: they are far more reliable than dangerous young fellows like you.

His eyes wandered off about the dark shelves, and I saw that he had gone away from me, in space and in time. I remained tactfully silent for a moment; then I said:

– I am honoured by your interest, nevertheless, Monsieur Lenoir – and very grateful for your confiding in me as you have. I promise you, I shall do nothing to jeopardise my situation. I intend to remain at liberty until the time comes to leave.

He came back, glancing at me quickly.

– To leave? You are planning an escape?

I wanted to trust him – to tell him of my determination to abscond next year, as soon as Kathleen and the child could travel. But I knew I would be foolish to trust him this much. Although I thought it unlikely, he might one day talk too freely to one of his official friends at the Royal Society; and I had no right to put Barry at risk, as well as myself. So I said:

– Not yet. Some day, perhaps.

– I shall miss you, *mon cher*, when that time comes. There are few men who can divert me, among these cold British officials and the brutish wretches they guard. But what will you do about your little passholder?

– She is my future wife. I shall take her with me.

– Yes, yes, of course – your future wife. And when do you intend to marry her?

– I doubt that I shall marry her in this colony, I said. I have no wish to humiliate myself by going cap in hand to Denison for permission, like a common convict.

– Ah. I see. Then the little one may have to wait a long time to be wed, he said.

We were now sitting almost in darkness. He struck a match and lit the oil lamp on his desk, and his hawkish, deeply seamed features sprang into relief, tinted orange by the light. For a moment, it was the visage of another man: one somewhat younger, of unswerving and formidable will, from a distant place and time.

– But perhaps this situation suits you, he said.

– I assure you, monsieur, it does not. I will marry Kathleen.

– Come, Devereux – don't be starchy. Of course I don't question your intentions – but forgive me if I say that intentions are always cheap. And I wonder – may I be frank? – if you may not be taking a direction which is at odds with your innermost nature. You have told me often that you love the people – but I have noticed you are very fastidious. To love people *en masse* is easy; but to love them at close quarters, with all their more tiresome or difficult features, is difficult. *I* could not do it – and I wonder if you are able to. You are the Christian, I the Jew – but I think that your instincts are Pagan.

– Where is all this leading, monsieur?

– Not to any condemnation, Devereux – just an old man's observations. You stand at life's mid-way point: you are thirty-five, no? The steps you take now will have consequences for ever: and I wish that I had known this, at your age. This girl is from the people – very well. But are you seeking a partner in life – or do you seek to prove through her how you love her kind? You have rescued her from servitude; rescued her from rape by a brute. Good;

578

very satisfying, for a man of romantic instincts. I understand. But is this what you truly want: to shelter a victim?

He suddenly grimaced, and stood up from his chair.

– You will pardon me, he said. I must go out and piss. One of the joys of my time of life is a constantly demanding bladder. One becomes an infant again.

As he moved off, he looked at me over his shoulder, and his expression grew stern.

– Do not take for granted your young and obedient body, Devereux: it will soon enough humiliate you. And do not take for granted that you can make what mistakes you please, and then discard them. Human beings in particular cannot be discarded. They remain in some way to haunt us.

He shuffled away from the lamplight, passing into the darkness between his tenements of books.

We are both of us exiles, Jacob Lenoir and I, and I think he sees himself in me, uttering warnings that his lost self can't heed. Whether this old bookseller is actually fond of me, as I am of him, is difficult to tell. Old men's feelings are seldom on show: their eyes and their hearts are dry. Perhaps he mourns his late wife. Perhaps he regrets that life left behind for ever, on the civilized side of the globe. Monsieur Lenoir has retired from the world, indifferent to its opinion as a hermit, wearing his dinginess like a mask; and if dinginess repels the crass and superficial, so much the better, from his point of view. Dinginess is a test, ridding him of those with whom he doesn't care to deal. His consolations now are his rare editions; his fine bindings; his works on conchology.

The dust of his books is perfume to him, and has settled in his soul.

November 7th

Monsieur Lenoir's questions continue to trouble my mind.

Am I a man of violence? Certainly I'm not the same man, since I shot O'Donnell and Lynch. Or rather, another man has been discovered inside me. I didn't speak truthfully about this to Lenoir – nor have I done so to anybody else.

Lynch didn't live long: he was dead by the time the police whom Richardson had fetched from New Norfolk rode up into the gully. The bodies of the three were taken into the town on a cart – where they were viewed by crowds of sightseers gathered outside the police office – and later conveyed to Hobart Town. Langford and I are now heroes in the district. We have had to endure speeches in our praise from the magistrate, Mr Whitford, and from the district constable and other worthies. There was even talk of a dinner in our honour; but mercifully, this has not eventuated. One or two people asked us if we could not have shot to wound the bushrangers, rather than to kill – but they were very quickly ridiculed, and made to hold their peace. There was general relief among the constabulary, I believe, that we had done their work for them, since O'Donnell's reputation was an intimidating one; they weren't inclined to question our methods.

Langford was amused by all this, and rather enjoyed it. But my mind kept returning to O'Donnell's enlarged eyes, looking from behind their spectacles when I shot him: an outraged village schoolmaster. On that hot afternoon when we accompanied the police and the bodies in to New Norfolk, I wished only to get away from the people who pressed around us, and the greedily curious eyes that examined us. I wanted to consider in solitude exactly what I had done.

I go double; I go double.

One of my two selves, I discover, is distressed by the fact that I have taken life. He accepts the fact that I'm not actually guilty, since the killing was done in self-defence – and yet he still feels like a murderer. Lynch's cries, like the anguished cries of a child, sound in my head before I sleep, while O'Donnell still stares, in the moment when his heart explodes, and falls again and again from his horse. My first self is horrified, and wishes to pick up the bushranger's fallen spectacles, and to explain to him why his death is necessary. But my second self feels differently. Fury drove him, and will no doubt drive him again. He not only wished to kill O'Donnell: he exulted in it. This was the truth; but I told it to no-one.

This second self alarms me, and makes me understand that I can never be quite the same man that I have been: a man who has always passed as gentle, except in his ideas. But have I ever been that man? My second self has been waiting to emerge, it seems; and I have now begun to ask myself whether Martin Fitzgibbon was right, in his bitter accusation at the Lakes. Is it true that I lust for blood and destruction? That I have urged them on the Irish people not just as a last resort, but also because I exult in them?

No. No. That is certainly unjust.

Lenoir's second challenge occupies my mind even more. It reduces to a single question: do I seriously intend to wed Kathleen?

The question drags in its train all those others which Barry and O'Neill have put to me. Have I really faced what Barry pointed out to me: that should I go back to Ireland, I could never be received again in Dublin society? And am I truly prepared to spend my life with a woman of only the barest education?

I answer these questions with conviction.

Yes, Kathleen is relatively uneducated – although she reads well enough to study each issue of poor Kinane's *Exile*, which she stubbornly insists on admiring, despite my explaining the folly of it – and she has read my essay on the Famine, and wept over it. True, I cannot discuss with her the poets and novelists whom I once discussed with Catherine Edgeworth, nor the current state of European affairs – and sometimes, in using the vocabulary that I would have done without thinking in speaking with Catherine, I will see Kathleen frown, and know that I must stop and explain a word or phrase to her. She has no knowledge of Greek or Roman mythology; she has never heard of Sophocles or Dante. But what of that? She knows very well who Queen Maeve was, and who the Fianna were, and she has recited to me the story of Dermot O'Dyna of the love-spot, and his doomed love of Grania, in a way that made my hair stand up. What she was reciting had come down to her directly, through generations of our people – and although she spoke in English, she spoke with the rhythms of the bards. In contrast with this rich, mysterious beauty, whose sources she and I share as our inheritance, my polite conversations with Catherine about literature seemed thin and dry and pointless indeed.

A comparison of the two women, in fact, told heavily in Kathleen's favour. The one was a sheltered young Anglo-Irish gentlewoman who had been educated well enough to express sentiments and judgments of literature, art and music that were always unsurprising, and always secondhand – learned from her books and teachers. The other was truly a daughter of the soil of Erin: an O'Rahilly who may well, as O'Donnell claimed (although Kathleen herself knows nothing of it), be an actual blood relation of that wonderful Egan O'Rahilly who lamented the death of the Gaelic order, and who created the inspired form of *aisling* in which Ireland herself is the woman of the poet's vision. Which woman made me truly the richer, in conversing with me? With whom would I rather converse? I no longer have any doubts.

Catherine belongs in the fussy Dublin drawing rooms of Protestant gentlefolk, where the careful talk and careful, temperate responses all suit her, and where my intemperate and dangerous behaviour would always be a source of alarm. Kathleen could scarcely be at ease in those salons (even to picture it makes me cringe for her sake) – and it's true that I would never be received in them with her at my side. But for this I care little. It's unlikely I'll be able to return for many years; perhaps never. We'll make a new life in America, she and I, where the old ways and the old snobberies mean little, and a new life will be possible for us both.

Kathleen gives me loyalty and passion. In return, I will give her my name, my protection, my life. When she speaks with me on any topic – whether it be animals or crops or flowers, or the dilemmas that my comrades and I face – it is her own mind that she opens for me, and not someone else's. And her mind looks as naturally beyond the visible world as her physical gaze does across a wall.

Each night before we sleep, she kneels by the bed in her nightgown, makes the Sign of the Cross, puts her face in her joined hands, and prays beneath her breath, her Rosary beads dangling from her fingers. These beads, so important to Roman Catholics, were bought in Hobart Town, replacing a set that was taken from her when she became a prisoner. When she prays, I think of Biddy Kearney, who must be dead for many years.

Biddy was a servant at 'Deerpark', in those placid years when debt had not yet begun to threaten my parents' lives, and when I believed, as my ancestors had done, that the house and the estate would be ours for ever. Kathleen brings Biddy back with sudden clarity: a plump, kindly, calm-faced woman in her sixties, with a high colour, a double chin, and white hair worn in a bun. I was fond of her as a child, and she of me, I believe: through Biddy, perhaps, I first came to love the people. She had a trick of giving definite little nods when she was pleased, and smiling with a triumphant expression; Kathleen does the same, and might almost be Biddy's grand-daughter. Biddy would occasionally put me to bed and hear my prayers. After I had said the Lord's Prayer, Biddy would say the Hail Mary over me; and she taught me to make the Sign of the Cross. My parents knew nothing of this, and would scarcely have given their approval to these Roman Catholic rites of Biddy's – though I doubt that they would much have minded, being relatively tolerant. Now I hear Biddy's voice again, drawling the words of the prayers in the brogue of the Clare countryside, and giving me her own personal blessing at the end:

– *Ask our Blessed Mother to keep you from all sin. She will always protect you from harm, joy. And may your Guardian Angel watch over you as you sleep, and guard you from the wiles of the Devil.*

The Guardian Angel – who stood just behind my bed, according to Biddy – came to interest me very much. I recall that I mentioned him one day to my father at breakfast, at the end of the meal, when the two of us were alone. I asked my father if he was real. I see us sitting at the big round table in the dining room, with its white linen cloth. A sunny Summer morning; outside the window, a glimpse of the kitchen garden: the old apricot tree which I would climb to pick the fruit when it was out in leaf; a section of tall stone wall. My father sits erect as always, in his dark frock coat and perfect cravat, dabbing at his mouth with his napkin, his eyes (which are mine), examining me with amusement.

– Papist superstition, he says; and goes on to explain that we don't believe in such things.

In that moment, at eight years old, I saw two truths: that Biddy was credulous and simple but also full of reverence for the mystery behind appearances; and that my elegant father, who never got excited about anything, God love him, knew nothing of the invisible world – which I still remain certain exists, as the Guardian Angel exists. And I dimly perceived the limits of his rational, Protestant mind.

Kathleen has told me that she prays every night that I'll rejoin the church of my ancestors. It feels odd, to be prayed for; I don't resent it, but I contemplate her kneeling figure with a mixture of affection and unease. I asked her recently what else she prayed for, and she told me that she prayed for my comrades: for Barry, O'Neill, Fitzgibbon and Kinane. She prays for their deliverance from this gaol colony, and their safe return to Ireland. She prays especially for Liam Kinane. Now that he's gone to Port Arthur, she urges me to help him if I can: she has a premonition, she says, that he'll be utterly destroyed. I fear it may be accurate.

Part of me wants to kneel beside Kathleen, and to pray to the Man of Sorrows who succeeded Prometheus as saviour of our race; even to pray to Our Lady, as Kathleen calls the Virgin. It would be fitting for me to join that Church which is the spiritual refuge of the Irish people – but alas, I remain as full of doubt as most men of my kind, in our age of science and rationalism. And Lenoir may be right: I may well be a Pagan, in my instincts.

When Kathleen goes to Sunday Mass at St Peter's, I now meet her afterwards, to drive her home. Generally I wait in the gig; but last week I decided to creep into the back of the church at the end of the service.

The congregation consisted almost entirely of Irish passholders, from farms about the district. It was Communion time. The Latin intoned by the red-haired missionary priest, the odour of the incense, and the statues of the Virgin and of the bleeding figure on the cross, here in this crude little chapel in Van Diemen's Land, made an atmosphere just as strange to me as the one I'd once experienced when I wandered into Notre Dame in Paris. United by that faith which no amount of persecution has ever made them give up, and which is only just tolerated even now, the people shuffled up the aisle to Communion: the men with their hair carefully combed, the women in their finest gowns, heads covered by bonnets or shawls. But Kathleen was not among them.

While they went up to the altar she knelt alone in her pew, head bowed in its straw bonnet. And I viewed her with sadness, and with something like guilt. She could not take the sacraments, she had told me, until she confessed to the sin that she was committing; and the Church had taught her that such a confession could not be a true one unless she was prepared to give up the sin. She might lie to the priest; but not to God. Only when we were married would she be able to return to the sacraments.

She told me this without any hint of reproach, or of implied demand. It was simply a fact, and she was strangely sanguine about it. Kathleen has a core of fatalistic independence and strength that surprises me. I detected a faint shadow of apprehension, but saw no sign of the divided feelings that one might have expected her to be torn by, as an obedient daughter of the Church. She has made a decision in favour of our love: her debt to the Devil was put from her mind, her account with God lay waiting to be adjusted; and there was an end to it.

If she died now, she once told me, she would go to Purgatory. Perhaps even to Hell, if no priest was available to hear her last Confession.

– Promise me, Robert, she said, that you would get me a priest, then.

I knew that she was thinking of her asthma attacks: we who are attended by this enemy know that he can always overwhelm us. I dismissed her fears; but I gave her my solemn promise. At the same time, I asked her whether she wished to stop sharing my bed until we were able to marry – since she must otherwise live with her fear and guilt.

– No, she said, and threw her arms about me. I could not bear that. God will forgive me, after we are married. All will be as it should be, then – and our baby will have your name.

Within our household, she lives as my wife without question –

sharing with Bess the status of mistress of the house, and in every way conducting herself as a free woman. We have hired a house-maid, and Kathleen has started a vegetable garden over beside the stables, spending much of her time there planting and weeding. This is where she seems most content. The Langfords treat her with great respect, and the fiction is carried on that she is no longer a pass-holder: a kindness for which I love them. She and I drive into New Norfolk together and walk on the streets of the township arm in arm, like man and wife. On these occasions, in the handsome gowns I've bought her, she turns many heads as we go; and we know what the gossip must be, in this small, malicious town.

So why do I not put aside my pride, and formally apply to the Governor for permission to marry?

I have given Kathleen my reasons. I have told her that to take such a step in Van Diemen's Land, within this hateful convict system, would humiliate me: in my view, would humiliate us both. To apply for permission to marry, from the Government that imprisons us! To petition my enemy, the colonial gaoler Denison, like a medieval serf his lord, asking him to allow me to wed a fellow-prisoner! This would sadly demean me, I told her – not only as a man, but as an Irish leader. The mockery in the English press, as my comrades have pointed out, is all too easy to imagine. I prefer that we marry in freedom, in America.

Nevertheless, I have said, if she truly wishes me to petition for marriage here, I will.

But she told me she did not. We must wait to reach America, she said.

For her, the United States is clearly a country of myth, and one which she is half afraid of. But her spirit is not only generous; it shares with mine the sort of Irish pride that makes a petition to the convict authorities repellent. Meanwhile, all that matters to her is our life on the farm, which she loves, and the coming of the baby. So long as we're together, she says, all will be well; and her smile is like a bright, searching light, filling my vision and dazzling me.

And I swear to myself that nothing will prevent my marrying her, as soon as we reach the shores of freedom.

November 9th

Kathleen kneels in the grass under the ash tree, in the sun of early morning. I come across the yard to her, and see that she is examining a newly-hatched brood of chickens.

The mother hen watches with suspicious sideways glances, its head darting. Kathleen picks up one of the scurrying yellow balls, holding it in her cupped palms, and the hen sets up drawling and unctuous protests, head cocked. I squat down, and Kathleen looks up at me and smiles, the sun making her squint. She holds the chicken out to me, and invites me to hold it. I do so, and see its beak open and shut as it cheeps to be released, and feel it pulse in my hand. Kathleen says:

– Do you feel the life in the little creature? That's the life of the world.

At twilight, I come out the door on to the back verandah. Kathleen stands alone at the far end, turning the handle of the butter churn.

As she does so she sings, unconscious that anyone is here. I have heard her sing before, under her breath; but now she sings out strongly, her voice untrained and husky, yet true. The words are in Irish and the air is strange, coming from outside the ordered world. In it, I glimpse a country that is lost to me, its horizons far off in time; and Kathleen's face, in the dusky, dying light of the milk-smelling verandah, seems no longer the face that I know, but that of a woman from antiquity: lovely, barbaric and chaste.

As I watch, she breaks off and straightens from the churn. She stands dreaming, staring across to the hop kiln and the dark native trees beyond, her hands lying lightly across her stomach. She has not begun to swell – yet she holds her belly as though she has, and seems to listen.

December 29th

Liam Kinane is free.

Barry came down on the coach from Ross to welcome him, having been granted a request to visit Hobart Town to purchase books. He arrived yesterday evening, putting up at the Ship in a room next to mine. After a pleasant hour or so over refreshments in the coffee room, he and I walked up Goulburn Street to Kinane's little cottage in St Giles.

Liam's appearance shocked us. He lay under a worn grey blanket, on the sofa that served him as a bed, his head supported by the same greasy cushion that I remembered from my previous visit. He stared at us as though from the bottom of a pit, his forehead dewed with sweat, his face a sickly white in the candle-light, its pallor made more pronounced by the blue-black shadow of his beard. He had clearly not shaved for days.

– A merry Christmas to you, boys, he said. My greeting's a few days late, but still I wish you both a right merry Christmas. Jesus, it's good to see you.

Side by side on hard kitchen chairs, Barry and I gazed down at him. He had been discharged from the Saltwater River convict station four days ago, on Christmas eve. He had been in the settlement's infirmary for a week before his release, he told us, suffering from a stomach complaint. We shook hands with him, returning his Yuletide greeting. His hand was cold and clammy, despite the warmth of the night; he was a good deal thinner, and there wasn't the usual strength in his grip. Clad in a dirty blue shirt, he had the musty odour of illness about him, made worse by the closeness of this box-like, low-ceilinged room – as hot in the Summer as it had been cold in Winter, the bluebottle flies that plagued Hobart Town in the warm months circling and droning in its corners.

Otherwise, all was the same here as before. The table in the centre, where two tall candles burned, was still strewn with galley proofs – but they were over two months old, dating from the period before Kinane was sent to serve his sentence. Paul and I had covered these sheets with gifts: pastries, fruit, preserves, coffee and a ham, bought from the best confectioners in Murray Street – as well as a bottle of whiskey, and a pile of newly-arrived books from Tegg's, on Wellington Bridge. Liam had eyed the books and the whiskey with avidity, and had declared himself grateful for the provisions; but it was clear that at present he was too ill to enjoy much food.

588

– What is the nature of your complaint? Barry asked. Is it an infection, do you think?

– It's a bloody flux, Kinane said. The God-damned doctors can tell me nothing, and do nothing for me – but it was caused by the food in that place, sure. A lot of those burglars and murderers thought themselves quite well fed there, after what they'd been used to – but I tell you, they are rations only stomachs like theirs can bear. In the end, I could not face the filthy, thin skilly any more – nor the rotten pork or salt beef. It made me vomit. So I ate only vegetables, or starved.

Barry frowned.

– It must have been unpleasant there, old fellow.

Kinane looked up at him in silence for a moment; and his face seemed to grow more haggard. He pushed the blanket down and clasped his hands, and his gaze went from one to the other of us. When he spoke again, it was in a hoarse whisper.

– I could not go back there. It would destroy me. I didn't dream what it would be like. I warn you, gentlemen – you must be sure that Denison doesn't find a way to get *you* there.

We began, gently, to question him. Had he been persecuted? Had he been flogged? Was the work very hard?

– It was not the work that was so bad, he said. Cutting timber in the bush I didn't mind – it was clean and healthy work enough. Can't you see me, boys, in my handsome grey uniform and leather cap? Sure, the floggings went on all the time, but I managed to avoid those punishments by being wary: it's only the stupid or the mad that get punished. Mind you, emptying tubs of convict piss was not so pleasant – and they did give me that to do.

Paul exclaimed in anger, and brought his fist down on his knee.

– That bastard Denison. We will make him pay for this, he said.

– Ah, even *that* I could stand, Kinane said. No – it was the nights I couldn't bear. Then I had to sleep with the others.

He broke off, and we looked at him in puzzlement. He propped himself on his elbow, his face working.

– I didn't know how foul they were – how *foul*, God damn them! Thirty in a dormitory: thieves, murderers, pickpockets, rapists: the worst London scum. I can smell them still. And there are some who are constantly buggering each other: sure, *that* is what I wasn't prepared for. Imagine it, in that horrible shed, with no partitions between the beds, and their grunting and their stinks and their bullying of the weak. All night I had to listen to those brutes – and always to be watching, should I need to fight them off. One of them I deprived of a few of his teeth – he didn't report me though, the dog. And there are *gentlemen* among them, poor devils: forgers and debtors and the like. Christ, it's terrible for men like those, who can't use their fists as I can. One of them had been a clergyman: I saved him from being buggered by two of them, and he broke down and cried like a baby. Do you want to know what Hell is like, gentlemen? It is a convict dormitory at night, on the Saltwater River, with the black bush all around, and nowhere to escape to.

Now we said nothing, but simply sat looking at him. After a time, in a weaker voice, he continued.

– All that helped me to survive it was prayer. I would pray as I lay on my palliasse at night: I would ask Christ to give me the strength to bear it, as he endured the Cross, and I would ask forgiveness for my sins – because I believe it was my sins that put me there.

He was breathing hard, and his sweating had increased. His weakness seemed to overcome him: he lay back feebly on the cushion, his eyes staring off into the darkness in a corner of the room. Barry and I glanced at each other; then I leaned forward.

– Nonsense, Liam. It was certainly not your sins that gave our English friends the chance to put you in chains – it was your rashness, my dear fellow. You must not be rash again: promise me. You must never give Denison an excuse to send you back. And now you must let Barry and me help you. Don't be proud: we can let you have some money until you're back on your feet – and we'll find a good doctor to attend you.

And I placed an envelope on the table. Kinane looked at it, and at the two of us; his lips trembled, and his eyes filled with tears.

– Ah, no. God bless you for darling boys, but I could not take your money, he said. There is no telling how long I would take to repay you.

Barry leaned forward and took Kinane's hand. As he held it, I was struck by the contrast he made with our stricken comrade. Dressed for town in a well-cut grey frock coat and gleaming white cravat, he looked exactly as he would have done in a club or a drawing room at home: at ease with his place in the world, and confident that it held in store for him every good thing possible.

– We beg you to take it, old fellow, he said. *I* beg you: and paying it back is of no importance; we don't give a damn if you *never* repay it. You are our comrade, and we love you. No man was more brave in '48: you were a tower of strength to Fitzgibbon, and Ireland owes you a debt. Take it, Liam, or you'll shame us.

Kinane drew a handkerchief from under the blanket, and blew his nose hard. When he spoke, his voice was gruff.

– Very well, and I thank you both, he said. But if you truly want to help me, so that I can go on earning my living and repay you, it's your support in another way I'm needing.

With an effort, he raised himself to a sitting position, his hard-lidded, bloodshot eyes narrowing. He breathed hard, surveying us both, and raised a pointing finger.

– Help me to destroy that bastard Matthew Casey, he said. Help me to get back my newspaper.

We stared at him. Both of us, I believe, were at a loss for words in that moment; and he mistook this for incomprehension. His pallor was replaced by a flush, and his eyes bulged.

– You don't *know*? he shouted. Can it be possible that you don't know? Has nobody told you? I wrote O'Neill a letter. Did he not –

– Yes, Barry said soothingly. We know, old fellow, we know. O'Neill wrote to us both.

Kinane turned to me.

– Ah, Devereux, how right you were when you warned me against that smiling, red-whiskered cur! Matthew Casey, a traitor! A Dublin Castle spy – and now a scheming tool of this bloody colonial Government! That arse-licking, scheming bugger! He was *Denison's* dog, all this time – and now he does Denison's dirty work, and steals away the *Exile*! What a damned, stupid fool I've been!

What a fool! But he made himself my friend. He posed as my greatest ally – and I believed him because I wanted to believe him. I *needed* such an ally! Do we not all need just one faithful friend? Sure, then we have the strength to bear exile, and the loss of those we love. Fool! Bloody fool that I was!

His eyes filled with tears again; but this time they were tears of rage, and he raised his big fist before his face.

– He was always so convincing, he said. So comforting and soft and flattering in his manner. That Judas! How did we not twig to him in Dublin, in the days when he was sneaking about in the St Patrick Club, and at Conciliation Hall?

Barry and I made speeches of sympathetic indignation, and urged Kinane to rest, and not excite himself. We had all been gullible, we said. We had not examined Casey closely enough – but he was a man whom one talked to and then forgot. He had seemed so ordinary; now we marvelled at his treachery. How could he betray his own?

– Easily, Kinane said bitterly. We have many such, and that is why the British still rule us. But now I'm asking you, brothers – will you help me to defeat him? To get my newspaper back?

It was Barry who answered him, his voice somewhat drawling, and neutral.

– My dear chap, how would that be possible? As I understand it, you signed a legal document: a deed assigning the proprietorship of the *Exile* to Casey. It's horrible, but that's the position – and I don't see how it can be changed.

Kinane began to shout again, at this. He had executed the deed, he said, only so that Matthew Casey could carry on the paper in trust until he, Kinane, returned from prison, and regained his Ticket-of-Leave. That was understood between them. Many of his advertisers and subscribers had been in arrears with their payments, and it had been vital to keep the paper going in his absence in order to press for these payments, and to liquidate the paper's debts. And this had been achieved, apparently. When Kinane arrived back in Hobart Town, a letter from Casey awaited him at the printery in lower Collins Street, where the *Exile* was produced: it announced that the debt was cleared, and that the paper was once more making a profit. But the letter also told him that Casey had been informed by the Comptroller-General of Convicts that Kinane was unlikely to be allowed the freedom to continue editing the paper: he might well be transferred to another police district, which would make it impossible. Therefore, Casey said, he thought it best to continue his editorship until things became clearer for Kinane. He would, of course, welcome articles from him.

Old Mr Harris, the printer, could not say where Casey was. Nor was Matthew to be found at his Melville Street lodgings, when Kinane went looking for him there. This had been on Boxing Day. For the rest of that day, and yesterday as well, he had continued to search for Casey all about the town, going back to Melville Street continually; but the door was always locked, he said, and the land-lady knew nothing of her lodger's whereabouts. Today, Liam's illness had grown worse, and had confined him here in his cottage.

– The bastard is hiding from me, sure, he said. Once I had a glimpse of him coming out of the printery. I ran after him, but he jumped into a cab. By Jesus, though, he won't get away from me for ever: the town's too small.

– What do you hope to achieve? I asked.

– That's just the point. We must put the fear of God into him, Kinane said. We must shame him, and expose him to the world as the Judas he is.

– I doubt that will make him let go of the paper, Barry said. He is Denison's creature. He's secure, so.

– Then in that case, he must be tracked down, Kinane cried. If he won't be shamed, he must be thrashed!

– Liam, Liam, I said. If you do that, you will find yourself back at the Saltwater River – and for a much longer time. Is that what you want?

The effect of these words surprised me. He stared at me for a moment; then he drew in his breath and fell back on the sofa as though his bones had collapsed, a hand laid over his closed eyes. When he opened them again, I saw a hopelessness in his face that I had never seen there before; and I began to realise fully the extent of his anguish.

His voice, when he spoke, was hoarse and weak and drained.

– Sure, you're right, he said. Of course you're right. So I'm finished.

– Come, Barry said, that's nonsense. A brave man like you is never finished, Liam. We –

But Kinane interrupted him.

– The *Exile* was not just a living for me, he said. It was giving me money to send home, to my wife and boys. They'd been dependent on the charity of friends, entirely: do you see how that put shame on me? The *Exile* was also my reason to go on in this place, and I was proud of it. Well, I am paying for my sins. Lust and adultery and drunkenness and anger: I am paying for them all.

He made the Sign of the Cross, staring up into the fly-humming murk near the ceiling; he no longer looked at us, and tears ran unheeded from the corners of his eyes. Barry laid a hand on his arm.

– Liam, old fellow, he said. God will forgive every sin that you repent of: you and I both know that. Don't give way to despair. Despair's a sin too, my boy. Come: you are far from home and ill, and you've been shamefully used by these English bastards. But when you grow better, it will all look differently.

Kinane shook his head, drawing a shuddering breath, and continued to look at the ceiling. His face was grey, and I began to wonder whether his illness might be more serious than he knew. I put a hand on his shoulder, and he turned and looked at me.

– Listen to me, Liam, I said. You will not go near Casey: you would only do something foolish. I've already begun to deal with him: I'm writing an article for the *New Nation*, exposing his treachery to all Ireland. And I'll find him and confront him. Barry will come with me, I'm sure.

Barry nodded; and Kinane smiled at me eagerly, hope returning to his face.

– Ah, Devereux, he said. I knew that you would. And when *you* face that bastard traitor, he will never be able to resist you! God bless you!

We stayed with him until he grew tired enough to sleep; then we walked back down the hill towards the Ship, and a late supper. For a time, we walked in silence. Then Barry said:

– Dear God, how that man suffers. I almost begin to wonder if execution would have been worse than what he now endures.

January 26th, 1851

The new year has begun in tragedy. I'm numb, as I write these words. Van Diemen's Land has claimed its first victim from our ranks: our sad, incorruptible Fitzgibbon.

Two letters bring me this news, and are spread on the desk in front of me: one from Thomas O'Neill; the other from Fitzgibbon himself.

Oh, Martin! You ruined your life for our suffering country – you who had no need to do so. Now you've been hounded to your death by those prim English settlers who posed as your friends; by those heartless officials who hold us all in their grip; by the criminal degenerates who are their informers and their creatures.

I'm filled with useless remorse. I've wept for you, and will no doubt do so again. Ashamed of our disputes now, and of my frequent heartless levity at your expense, I beg your forgiveness. Too late! You cannot forgive me now; you have gone beyond the incompatibilities of spirit that marred our relationship in life; now, you are a true Irish martyr.

I am writing to your family to place before them in confidence the truth of what has happened. Meanwhile, I've begun an article for the *New Nation* which will declare to the world that England's excessive vengefulness has taken the life of one of Ireland's most selfless patriots. My article will record that your exile in this gaol colony was a constant humiliation to your proud, fastidious spirit, and that your long separation from your loved wife and children was breaking your heart.

Your persecutors now have the means in their claws to sully your name for ever, should they wish; but I'm determined that if they try to do so, they will fail. I will make the truth known, if need be, and expose the lie.

∾

595

Only a week has gone by since we three sat together in the parlour of Glengarry Cottage: O'Neill, Fitzgibbon and I. After dinner, we drew up our chairs as usual about the fireplace – though no fire burned in it now, the Summer nights being mild.

I had ridden up to Bothwell from New Norfolk on Fleur-de-lis, to stay for two days – doing so in response to a letter from O'Neill that was both troubling and enigmatic. It told me that Fitzgibbon had quit 'Grasmere' because of trouble with the Morton family, and had moved back into Glengarry Cottage. But it gave no details – except to say that the matter was very serious, and might even reach the ears of the colonial authorities. O'Neill thought my presence and advice would be a comfort and a help to Fitzgibbon, who was in deep distress. All would be explained when I spoke with him.

I had only arrived a few hours ago, and had still to learn what had happened. I had noted that Fitzgibbon was pale, reserved and tense, and even more solemn than usual; but he had maintained a polite affability during dinner, and our talk had remained general. Now, with glasses of brandy in our hands, we shot glances at each other, knowing that the matter must soon be broached. I was intensely curious. What could have gone wrong? Martin had been so content at 'Grasmere'. I recalled his bitter description of himself as 'a nursery governor', in our argument up at the Lakes – but I assumed that this had been said in anger, rather than reflecting his true state of mind.

O'Neill leaned back in his rocking chair, saying nothing. Fitzgibbon had lit a cigar, and was staring into the empty fireplace – apparently unaware of my scrutiny. At last I grew impatient, and spoke to him abruptly. I had come here to learn about his trouble, I said, and if possible to help. Would he not tell me what had taken place?

He raised his eyebrows, and seemed to consider.

– Yes, I will tell you, he said slowly. But I beg that you will allow me to acquaint you with the situation in my own way. I must ask O'Neill's pardon for subjecting him to the story again. It's very important to me that you should both understand the situation exactly – since what I am accused of is so very monstrous.

It was as though he addressed a magistrate, rather than two friends. He put down his cigar in an ash-tray on the sea-chest and cleared his throat. Only the vertical frown-mark that stood between his brows gave evidence of his unease: it had deepened a little. He began in a prosy enough manner; but I see now that the poor fellow was defending both his character and his position – not only to us, his comrades, but to certain accusers in his head. As he spoke, my impatience drained away, and was replaced by an appalled fascination. I set down his account – and he grew very eloquent, in the end – to the best of my ability to recall it.

He had always honoured teachers, he said. Their vocation was surely one of the noblest and most useful that a man or woman could pursue. To impart the gifts of civilization to the next generation; to quicken the imagination of the intelligent child; to mould the character of such a child – these were functions that must surely command respect, and which carried a high responsibility. For this reason, he had undertaken the education of the Morton children not only with pleasure, but with a serious sense of duty. But after a time, his contentment grew less.

– It had never before fallen to my lot to be a tutor, he said. Much less a tutor to young children. Nor would such a fate ever have befallen me had I not been transported here. And I had not anticipated its drawbacks. Had I been a tutor to older children, I might not have become discontented so quickly; but giving most of my time each day to instructing two lads of eight and ten years, dinning such things as the elements of grammar and mathematics into them when this could just as easily have been done by some limited village schoolmaster – this very quickly lost its charm. Ralph and John were my principal responsibility, since the Mortons didn't expect their daughter to be given an education of the breadth and depth required for boys. And the two boys, although nice enough young fellows, were of very average ability indeed. Unlike Edith, they had little imagination, and their minds were not enquiring. I struck few sparks.

597

– Have you any idea how dispiriting it is to repeat the same thing over and over, in order to fix it in the minds of children such as these? And how discouraging it is to see that no matter how much effort you give, their minds are elsewhere – outside the window, usually, where such mundane delights as riding their ponies and fishing and kangaroo-hunting are awaiting them? That is how it was with the Morton boys – and I began to consider what I'd come to. I have spent thirty years unflaggingly cultivating my mind at the highest level. I have devoted myself to the study of classical antiquity – a field in which I've made some small contribution – as well as giving of my best in the struggle for our country's freedom: making speeches, writing articles and persuading, all for the benefit of our people. Now, I was reduced to acting as a pedagogue to the dullard sons of a colonial sheep farmer – and for this, my salary was little more than that of the governess who instructs my daughter Jane. It not only became tedious; it became humiliating.

In this situation, he told us, his one consolation was little Edith – who displayed an understanding far beyond her years. There was nowhere that his mind might rove and beckon that hers could not follow, he said; she was so much more gifted than her brothers that she might have sprung from different stock. He and she continued to go on their drawing expeditions in the open air – to which Fitzgibbon added lessons in botany.

– Let me be entirely honest about this, he said – since a great deal depends on it. Our drawing expeditions were not merely outdoor lessons: they came under the heading of recreation, and companionship. I saw nothing wrong in these little outings, and Mrs Morton was very pleased by them; she said many times how fortunate Edith was to have my extra attention in this way. She also remarked one day that it was good of me to give Edith so much of my spare time, since the child saw very little of her father, and her brothers would spend little time with her, being devoted to outdoor pursuits from which they excluded her.

– I had noticed this situation, and how it affected her. Mr Morton was constantly busy about the property, and his free time was mostly given to his sons – whom he would take away fishing up the river, or hunting kangaroo in the hills. Edith, though she was always occupied, and although she spent some leisure time with her mother, was clearly lonely. She had little in common with her brothers, whose recreation was entirely physical; and I believe she lacked affection from her father. Charles Morton is a pleasant, gentlemanly fellow; but he is reticent, and essentially cold. His smile made one easy, I found, yet kept one at a distance. He spoke always sparingly, and avoided personal topics. He would make brief observations at dinner about rural matters, or convict servant problems, and he and I would sometimes discuss events in Europe, when the newspapers came. That was the extent of his conversation with me; and I scarcely came to know him, at any depth. I once saw Edith throw her arms about his neck and put up her lips to be kissed – and he merely pecked her absently on the cheek. The fleeting expression of hurt that crossed her face is still with me. I could not have treated my own daughter so: and it pained me to recall the affectionate embraces I used to exchange with Jane – as well as with my sons.

– So you two gentlemen will understand, I hope, when I tell you now that Edith had begun to give to me that affection which her father would not receive from her. Yes, this is what was happening, and I see now that perhaps it should not have been – blameless though it seemed. I am trying to approach what took place, and to account for it; please bear with me. I have said that Edith was far in advance of her age in intelligence; she was perhaps also precocious in her emotions. Certainly she was becoming romantic, at nearly twelve: romantic as a young lady of sixteen or so. She had begun to dote on stories of the love between knights and ladies; and I sought these out for her, and watched her face dream as I read. Was this wrong? I swear to you, it didn't seem so at the time. It didn't seem anything but a light-hearted game when she said to me that I was her knight, and should take her away to a castle in the hills behind Bothwell. All of it seemed innocent – including the affection that she showed me. And it was; I still believe that it was.

Their sketching expeditions took place in the late afternoons, he told us – in a little space of time after lessons were over, before the children had their tea at half-past five. Edith and he would meet always at four o'clock; and that period when they were together, as the light slowly declined, became his day's destination, apparently: impatiently awaited. These meetings with a child were his greatest solace; that became clear, as he talked, and I looked at him now with a sort of pity.

– I've already told you of the regular meeting place that she and I had established on the river bank, he said. It was about a quarter of a mile from the house: the grove of wattle and gum trees that was her special childish retreat. I set out towards this grove, on the afternoon I'm describing, in my usual state of happy anticipation. But just as I left the house, an incident occurred which somewhat marred my mood.

He had come out through the back courtyard, he said, carrying his satchel of drawing materials and small folding stool, and was proceeding along a flagstone path that passed between two small, whitewashed outbuildings – one of which was a laundry, the other a dairy. As he passed the door of the dairy, he heard the clanging of pails, and saw two of the male convict servants at work inside, washing and sweeping the floor. One of them, Henry Jobbins, the most senior of the servants, Fitzgibbon described as having a bitter, thin-lipped face, and cunning eyes. His companion was Billy Fowler, a young fellow from Yorkshire: a coarse, empty-headed lout, Fitzgibbon said.

– I bade them good afternoon, he said, but they barely acknowledged me – merely grinning in an odd, unpleasant manner. This is typical: they are often surly and insolent, and their rudeness can be quite extraordinary. Before I came to Van Diemen's Land, I had the notion that the convict passholders were in total subjection to their masters. The opposite is the case, as you both know. These men find a multitude of ways to be idle; many are frequently drunk during the day, and some are slyly rude to their masters – going as far as they dare, short of absolute defiance. I had seen these two fellows behave rudely to Mr Morton; he merely sighed and shrugged, having rebuked them, and did no more. If Morton made an issue of every petty matter, sending them to the Bothwell magistrate for punishment, he would end by getting little support from the authorities; and so he put up with it.

Now Fitzgibbon discovered that he must put up with it too. As he walked on down the flagstone path, he was pursued by sniggering, and by voices raised deliberately for his benefit.

– Good afternoon, schoolmaster! Your lordship the school-master!

This from the youth Fowler. Then he heard the thin, cracked voice of old Jobbins.

– He's going dror-ing, the schoolmaster is. Going a-walkin' with the little mistress!

Then Fowler again:

– Schoolmaster! But he's really a lag like us. A teacher with a Ticket!

This was followed by more insolent sniggering; and he halted. Anger seized him: an anger that made him tremble, he said. It wasn't the first time that he'd been given a glimpse of the malignity of the convict class in Van Diemen's Land.

– You know that malignity, he said. It's to be found among the free population here, as well – and it expresses itself in a hatred and scorn of all that is highest in human nature. There is a particular hatred of intellectual gifts and aspirations, of the arts, and in fact of all the accomplishments of high civilization. All that is valued here is money – money and the base appetites. Hence the universal drunkenness and licentiousness. Well, you both know this. One sees the sneer everywhere, in the villages and in the streets of Hobart Town; one hears everywhere the jeering voice that derides culture; and it fills me with loathing. The mockery directed at me had a double edge, of course: these two saw me as a felon like themselves, and they resented the social standing I was allowed here. They would drag me down into their sty, if they could.

He turned, he told us, walked back up the path, and stood in the doorway, confronting his mockers. They seemed surprised, and bent over their brooms, their eyes avoiding his. He rebuked them thoroughly, telling them that if they offered him such insolence again, he would report them to Mr Morton. They said nothing, their heads cast down, and he went on his way.

And now he pictured that late afternoon for us: the weather and the scenes through which he moved, along the river bank. He did so in loving detail – speaking sadly, nostalgically, and with what seemed to me an extraordinary desire to portray it all exactly. It was as though he believed that the place and the weather had fashioned the fate that lay in wait for him.

It was hot and calm and golden, he said; but the highlands air, as always, was clear and in no way oppressive. A faint breeze came and went. The shadows of the trees already grew long, but the sun had not lost its strength. The sky was a deep, superb blue, except for a flotilla of white clouds lying low in the east. Delighting in the day's perfection, and in the serenity of the level, open landscape – in which no other human being was to be seen – he soon put the incident at the dairy behind him.

– I love the Summer afternoons of this latitude, he said. They dissolve into slanting twilights as lingering as those in Europe – have you noticed? I walked beside the Clyde – which is nothing but a shallow little brook, at this time of year – and my pleasure in my surroundings and at the prospect of meeting little Edith were one. The space and the silence up here are immense, are they not? You will know their effect. At times they can work a spell – and this was one of those times.

The only sounds were the calls of magpies and crows, the far bleating of sheep, and the soft bubbling of the stream. The grass-flats where he was walking were those that were flooded in Winter, and they were still quite green, in the surrounding Summer dryness. Beyond, on the flood-plain that continued on the opposite bank of the river, and which was now quite drained of moisture, miles of yellow tussocks waved in the breeze, stretching to a point in the flatness where a line of distant gums could be seen, and patches of dark gorse. Beyond these, on the ultimate horizon, lay the mauve and violet hills. These seemed more enigmatic than usual; and he fancied himself drawn on by a great, soundless music. It was the music of Apollo, he said, the power of whose rays enveloped him.

He had not been looking at us as he spoke; his voice was soft, and he seemed almost to be speaking to himself. But now he looked up.

– Do you despise this as foolishness, gentlemen? But have you never been so foolish yourselves – seizing on any illusory happiness or fancy that lonely exile has to offer? You, Devereux? Have you not done so with your Kathleen, investing her, perhaps, with an otherworldly beauty? I thought of Apollo and the Muses: that was the spell I was under.

He had been teaching the Greek myths to Edith, he told us, and acquainting her with the attributes of the old Hellenic gods and figures of fable – taking care, he said, to omit their more gross erotic exploits, or else clothing these in terms that were indirect, and suitable for a well-bred young lady to hear. The light, in these highlands of Van Diemen's Land, seemed to him in Summer to bear a quite uncanny similarity to the light he had experienced on his trips to Greece. So when he discussed Apollo with his pupil, and the Muses that were connected with the cult of the god, these deities seemed very close, hovering on those rises and nearby rocky cliffs that were the rim of wilderness. Apollo, he explained, favoured such stony mountain regions as this; and his attributes were many. God of light, he was also a shepherd god, who protected flocks of sheep like those at 'Grasmere'. God of music, who played upon a lyre, his closest companions were the Muses: goddesses of memory and poetry.

– I brought out books from my own little library, he said. I showed Edith a picture of Apollo pursuing Daphne, as she fled into the earth. I also showed her a drawing of the Muses, copied from the sarcophagus in the Louvre. She was fascinated, and seemed actually to recognise them – and I was tempted to agree with Plato and Goethe, and to believe in Metempsychosis, and the transmigration of souls. Edith had lived before, I thought, and had known the Muses in some earlier existence. Her soul was so highly charged!

His voice trembled; yet it had now become curiously toneless. His cigar had gone out, and he held it unheeding in his fingers, looking at the floor, and no longer at us. And I studied him with a baffled concern. He seemed actually to wish to re-enter that afternoon which had brought him to his ruin.

She was not in the grove when he entered it, he said: not sitting, as she usually was, on the fallen gum. This had never happened before: she was always here ahead of him. Uneasy, yet still in the spell of the great, golden peace lying everywhere on the river flats – the peace of the solar god – he walked on aimlessly by the river bank. He was conscious of the heat, which seemed to increase. He came shortly to a bend in the river where a clump of willows grew, hiding what lay beyond. Walking slowly around them, empty of thought, he turned his eyes upstream. And then he saw a Naiad.

She was naked, as Naiads are, he said. Some ten yards off, she stood up to her knees in the water of the stream, a little way out from the bank. Seeming to dream, she stared into the distance beyond the river flats, most of her weight on one foot, the other knee bent. Her hands hung lax at her sides, hiding no part of her body. She had clearly been swimming, just before he came: her hair fell to her shoulders in twisted, dark-gold ropes, and the water-droplets glistened on her whiteness.

He halted in amazement, and did not turn away. Would *we* have turned away? Her beauty might have been carved by Pheidias, he said; and in those few moments, he simply did not know that he was looking at Edith Morton.

He was very insistent about this. Edith was a child; but this was an exquisite young woman, with high, small breasts. His thoughts flew about for an explanation; and he decided that she was some village girl from Bothwell, trespassing on the property. Such a conclusion was natural for another reason, he told us: it was not to be imagined that a girl of Edith Morton's upbringing would bathe naked in the river – even in a place as secluded as this.

But now she began to walk from the water; and when she stepped on to the bank, it was Edith who turned her head towards him. She paused, her face quite blank. Then she smiled, looking across the space of grass between them; and her smile held no confusion, or even surprise. Instead, it seemed happily to confide in him. She calmly walked on, to where her clothes were scattered in the grass; and at last he recovered his wits. He retreated, hurrying along the river bank in the direction from which he'd come.

When he reached the grove again, he sat on the fallen gum and waited. He was guilty of no wrongdoing, he said; he had come upon her accidentally, after all, and had not even recognised her. Yet he sat in growing disquiet, troubled by the memory of her smile.

Within a few minutes she came into view, walking along the bank in her white muslin dress, her satchel of drawing materials slung over her shoulder. Her long, damp hair hung from under her wide-brimmed straw hat, and she carried in one hand a sodden petticoat. As she approached him, he found that she no longer smiled, but wore an expression that was strangely pleading. She came to a halt in front of him, and he stood up.

– Please don't tell, she said.

He asked her what she meant.

– Please don't tell my parents I was bathing, she said. They have said that I mustn't do it. But it's so awfully hot, and I wanted to so much. The boys do it – why shouldn't I?

Boys were different, he told her. It wasn't modest for a young lady to bathe naked.

– But there was no-one to see, she said. No-one but you, Mr Fitzgibbon. And I thought *you'd* understand.

A sort of alarm stole over him now, and he answered her in the stern tones of a tutor. He didn't think that her mother would have approved, he said. She hadn't even a towel with her: how had she managed to get dry?

– With one of my petticoats, she said. Look, I can spread it to dry on the grass. Mother will never know. Oh, Mr Fitzgibbon, please don't tell!

She dropped the wet petticoat and her satchel, and took both his hands in hers. He told her he would say nothing to cause her trouble, and she threw her arms about his neck and kissed him.

Gently, he pushed her away. She must not do that again, he told her. If she did, they could not meet like this any more.

Her eyes filled with tears, and her face became stricken. When she spoke, he said, he knew that she mimicked some heroine in one of her books.

– Oh, Mr Fitzgibbon, don't *you* desert me! I hate my brothers, and my parents care nothing for me. It's all been different since you came. You are so wonderful. I should be miserable without you!

He reassured her, still in the most formal tone that he could muster. After that, they did a little sketching, mostly in silence. Then, as five-thirty approached, they gathered up their things and walked slowly back along the river bank.

Nearing the house, they passed the two convict servants, Jobbins and Fowler. They were riding on a cart that was drawn by a draught horse – moving across the grass-flats some two hundred yards off, bringing back a load of firewood. They stared at Fitzgibbon and Edith across the distance; and although their faces were too far off to read, there was something worryingly furtive, he said, about the way that they ducked their heads down. He saw Jobbins make a remark to Fowler, and the stable-hand laughed with his hand across his mouth.

– Perhaps you may think that I began then to anticipate what was to come, he said. I can assure you that I did not. Even in my worst moments, I could never have imagined such a thing.

Fitzgibbon broke off and sat silent, staring into the fireplace. He laid a hand across his eyes, and sighed. He looked suddenly a good deal older.

O'Neill broke the silence, speaking gently.

– If you can bear it, Martin, I think you should tell Robert as simply as possible what you have been accused of. No need to go into detail; I know how painful it is. Just the bare facts.

For a moment longer, Fitzgibbon remained in the same attitude, with his eyes covered. When he took his hand away, his face was drawn. He glanced at us quickly, and then addressed the fireplace.

– I am accused of molesting Edith Morton, he said. I am accused of lustfully misusing her.

– Dear God, I said. By whom? Who made this accusation?

I strove to appear both surprised and outraged. My outrage was

genuine, but my surprise was not – since I had half-feared this catas-
trophe for some time. I believed Fitzgibbon to be innocent, of
course; I believed every word that he had said, and still do. But this
doom had been awaiting him, it seemed to me, ever since his
enchantment with the Morton child began.

In a voice that was entirely toneless, like a man talking in his
sleep, Fitzgibbon now concluded his account of that ill-fated
evening.

There was little conversation at dinner, he told us: both Mr and
Mrs Morton were unusually silent. When he went into the parlour
after dinner, Mr Morton was absent, and Mrs Morton was reading
a book. The children had gone to bed. Mrs Morton had barely
glanced at him, and had made little response to his attempts at conversation. Such a thing had never happened before; and her manner
seemed strained and nervous. Soon afterwards, she excused herself,
and went to bed. It was then that he noticed that his framed sketch
of Edith had been taken down from the wall.

In his small, snug bedroom that night, Fitzgibbon lay awake,
a hollow in the pit of his stomach. Something had gone wrong,
and clearly it related to Edith. Yet he could not see how this could
be so.

He was enlightened early the next morning.

At ten o'clock, Mr Morton asked Fitzgibbon to come to a room
at the back of the house which he used as an office. The proprietor
seated himself, in a somewhat official manner, at a big roll-top desk,
and turned himself sideways in order to face Fitzgibbon, whom he
invited to sit down in a small chintz armchair close by.

The convict servant Jobbins was standing beside the desk at
attention, like a soldier. When he saw Fitzgibbon, his eyes narrowed, and a faint, triumphant expression crossed his face. And now
at last, Fitzgibbon told us, he began to understand, and the knowledge froze his vitals.

Mr Morton, whose face was working with nervous unease,
began immediately to make his accusation. Clearly, Fitzgibbon told
us, nothing so unpleasant had ever happened to this gentleman

before, and Morton was finding it difficult to control his feelings. In a shaking voice, he informed Fitzgibbon that he had been seen by Jobbins and Fowler watching Edith bathe naked in the river, and continuing to watch her when she emerged from the water. He then turned to Jobbins and asked him to confirm it.

– That's right, sir, Jobbins said. Naked as the day she was born, and him a-standing and a-staring. Spying on her, he was.

Morton then asked Fitzgibbon if he denied this, and Fitzgibbon said he did not. He attempted to begin an explanation, but Morton cut him short. Jobbins and Fowler had seen something much worse a short time later, he said. Edith, now clothed, was sitting beside Fitzgibbon on a log, and they were embracing and kissing.

– They was kissing, and worse, Jobbins said. The schoolteacher had his hand up under her dress. Both of us seen it. Lust and abomination was what we seen.

At this, Fitzgibbon said, he lost his temper entirely. He shouted at Jobbins, calling him a lying, malicious felon; but Morton cut him short.

– If you please, Mr Fitzgibbon, I would prefer now that we discuss this matter alone, he said. I have asked Jobbins to tell you to your face what he accuses you of, and he has done so. I thought that only fair.

And with this, Fitzgibbon said, Mr Morton dismissed Jobbins.

The interview that followed, Fitzgibbon said, was the most painful of his life. Clearly, Charles Morton thought him guilty in some way; but equally clearly, the proprietor did not know how much to believe or to imagine. Mr Morton was a man who found frank or intimate discussion difficult, and to discuss the possible ruining of his young daughter was clearly almost beyond him. He was trembling – whether from anger or nervousness it was difficult for Fitzgibbon to tell.

– I told him exactly what had happened, Fitzgibbon said, and I told him of the way in which I had responded. I gave him my word as a gentleman that what I said was true, and that Jobbins and Fowler were lying out of spite – and I saw that he wanted to believe me. He wanted to believe, but he could not quite bring himself to do so. He is weak; weak. He kept shaking his head, and muttering how he and his wife had trusted me absolutely – as though I had abused that trust. He told me how difficult it was for him to confront me with such a thing – 'a man of my position and standing, despite all my misfortunes'. That was how he put it.

– So how has it ended? I asked.

Fitzgibbon looked at me, and what his face expressed now was utter despair.

– It ended with the Mortons asking me to leave the house the next day, he said. Even if I were blameless, they said, they could not see how things could continue as they were.

– Well then, I said, perhaps it's all for the best. They have made no complaint to the authorities, I presume: so you can put it all behind you.

But Thomas O'Neill was shaking his head, his concerned face warning me of something.

– No, Devereux, he said. It is not so simple.

Fitzgibbon's eyes had been closed, as though in pain. Now he opened them again, and looked at me.

– Mr Morton has not reported this to the authorities, he said. But there is someone who will. Morton saw fit to summon a medical man from Bothwell: a doctor named Williams, who has connections with the Government in Hobart Town. Doctor Williams came to the estate the next day, before I had left. They had asked him to examine little Edith, to see if she had lost her virginity. Yes: this is what they did. And then Doctor Williams asked to see me alone. He was a cold, offensive creature, and his manner fell just short of insolence. He informed me that I would be pleased to hear that Edith was *virgo intacta*, and that the worst suspicions against me were therefore removed. But he advised me, damn him, to put aside any idea of acting as a tutor in the colony in future.

He looked at me, twisting his empty brandy glass in his fingers.

– You do see what this means, he said. O'Neill has learned that Williams is a Government spy, who has worked in the past at Port Arthur and various convict stations. So this creature of the Government will put in a report to the Comptroller of Convicts. He is also likely to inform some jackal in the press. My honour is gone, you see, Devereux. I am ruined.

Setting the glass down on the sea-chest, he suddenly covered his face with his hands. The look of his bent shoulders, in their well-cut coat, filled me with pity; but I could only regard him helplessly, finding no words of comfort.

It was O'Neill, of the tender heart, who got up and put his arm about him.

What is in O'Neill's letter to me, which arrived yesterday, I shall now set down.

It tells me that Fitzgibbon has drowned himself in the Clyde. This took place two days ago, on Wednesday – the day after my return here to 'Clare'.

Fitzgibbon went out early in the morning, O'Neill says. He was quiet and subdued, and said that he was going on a walk about the district. He shook O'Neill's hand, which was unusual in parting so briefly; but O'Neill put this down to the emotion which enclosed them both, like a cloud. By evening, Fitzgibbon had not returned, and Thomas became alarmed. He informed the police in the village, who searched for Fitzgibbon in vain that night. The next morning, his body was found by two constables: it was floating by a bend in the stream not far from Nant Lane, trapped in some willow roots.

That it was suicide was not in doubt for O'Neill. During the night, he had entered Fitzgibbon's bedroom and had found three sealed letters on the bedside table. The first was addressed to Fitzgibbon's wife, Charlotte. A pencilled note on top of it asked that O'Neill post it to her in Ireland. The second letter was for O'Neill; the third was for me. The letter to O'Neill was concise. Fitzgibbon informed him that he intended to end his life: not just because of the shameful charge which hung over him, but because he faced so many more years as a prisoner in this colony. Sunk as he would be in disgrace, his honour and standing wrecked, he would not be able to endure his sentence. He begged O'Neill's pardon for leaving him to deal with the conse-quences of his suicide – at the same time knowing that no other friend would do so with the tact and forgiveness that Thomas would show.

Fitzgibbon's confidence was justified to a degree that he could not have imagined. O'Neill's fearless actions on our comrade's behalf have been extraordinary – and may well have saved Fitzgibbon's memory from dishonour.

The first of these actions was to persuade the rector of the Church of England in Bothwell to give Fitzgibbon a proper Christian burial. O'Neill achieved this by telling the rector that Martin's drowning was through misadventure while bathing, not suicide. It's unlikely that the rector believed him: it was already common gossip in the village that Fitzgibbon drowned himself, and the authorities are in no doubt of it at all – knowing as they do that the body was clothed, and having viewed the letter to O'Neill. But the rector is a sympathetic man, who knew and liked Fitzgibbon, and he has chosen to accept Thomas's fiction.

The authorities in Hobart Town have been only too happy to agree to a funeral in Bothwell. A modest burial in a remote hamlet will be very acceptable to them, rather than a funeral in Hobart Town, with all the public interest that such an event would invite. So a ceremony in the highlands will take place on Sunday. O'Neill is in charge of the arrangements, and has managed to delay the burial for this long so that Barry and I may travel there to attend it – if our turnkeys give us their permission.

Our exquisite gaoler Mr Laird, the Assistant-Comptroller of Convicts, went personally to Bothwell, accompanied by other officials, to make enquiries into the death on behalf of the Governor. He stayed for some days; and he interviewed Thomas O'Neill privately. His report will no doubt have gone to Denison; and I can imagine the tyrant's dismay, and the fluttering and cursing in Government House. Far from being gleeful over Fitzgibbon's death, Sir William will be deeply uneasy – since he will realise the effect of the news around the world, and the certainty that Fitzgibbon will be seen as a martyr – dying as a result of British persecution. So the fiction of Fitzgibbon's drowning by accident suits the authorities very well at present, even though the fact of his suicide will no doubt come out eventually. A secret inquest has already been held in Bothwell, and the official conclusions and the evidence of

Fitzgibbon's letter to O'Neill cannot be suppressed for ever. A report that Fitzgibbon took his own life must surely make its way into the newspapers here before long – and hence into the press overseas. At present, though, thanks to Thomas O'Neill, no word of the accusation made against Fitzgibbon by Mr Morton's servants has emerged.

O'Neill achieved this by calling on both Mr Morton and Doctor Williams, and discussing the charges against Fitzgibbon. He did so before the inquest was held. He accused both Mr Morton and Doctor Williams of hounding Fitzgibbon to his death, and of doing so through the use of lying accusations made by convicts, against a gentleman whose good name had never been questioned: a fond husband and father, and a patriot of world renown. Fitzgibbon's followers in Ireland and America would rise up in rage should the matter ever become known, he said, and demand justice for what had been done to him.

Doctor Williams, he says, was cold and uneasy. But Charles Morton was deeply distressed and agitated. Morton now blames himself for Fitzgibbon's death; his daughter Edith is inconsolable; and both he and Mrs Morton wish only to make amends. Mr Morton and Doctor Williams ended by assuring O'Neill that the matter would be made known to no-one.

It was after this that O'Neill had his private interview with the Assistant-Comptroller of Convicts, in the Bothwell police office. He discussed the Edith Morton incident with Mr Laird, and found him equally anxious that it should remain secret. Again, the reasons are not difficult to imagine. Should it become known that the unproven accusations of convict servants drove Fitzgibbon into taking his own life, there would be enormous anger at home among those who esteem and love him, as well as among the general public. There would also be those who would sneer and believe the worst, no doubt; and there would be demands in the press for an investigation. This is an outcome our convict authorities will do anything to avoid, since they fear influential opinion – and fear London's anger as well, should Denison's Government be seen to have bungled the affair. So O'Neill had his way.

I have always been aware of the steel under Thomas's gentle exterior. Yet it still surprises me when it surfaces – and it has never done so before to such powerful effect.

Fitzgibbon's letter to me is also quite short. I transcribe it here.

My dear Devereux,

You are stronger than I am; I have always known that. You are also harsher; but that is another matter, and I no longer judge you for it. Your cold resoluteness will enable you to survive, no matter what twist of fortune puts you to the test, and no matter how tyranny may try you. I lack that quality; perhaps this is why I was not meant for a revolutionary. Perhaps that is why our exile has broken me.

I can see your frown at this – and at what I shall have done when this letter reaches you. Try not to judge me; our disputes are at an end now. Try when I am gone to understand. I miss my wife unendurably; I miss my daughter and my sons. Had I survived here, they would have been eleven years older when I saw them again. Time would have robbed me of my children's youth, and brought my wife and myself into our old age. I can no longer endure that prospect. I am lonely; so lonely.

I was flung into this hellish colony because I loved my country, as you do. I love Ireland still, and weep that I shall not see her hills again in this world. My other love was beauty – and this love has brought me to destruction.

I write this to say farewell, and also to say: fly!

This island is beautiful, but demons lurk in its forests and streams – and the British have brought demons of their own. On the banks of that little highland river, a demon led me to my doom: and he did so, as demons so often do, through the lure of beauty.

I am remembering Hylas, who was drawn into the depths to his death.

Fly from this island, Devereux! You are right to do so, you and Barry: this is the only way you will save yourselves, and what is left of your youth and your great dreams. Fly to America, both of you – and God bless and speed you both. As you go, remember me in your prayers.

Your comrade and friend,
Martin Fitzgibbon

February 3rd

Ever since Paul Barry and I made our visit to Liam Kinane, over a month ago, I have been attempting to keep my promise to track down Matthew Casey. I go to Hobart Town only seldom, and it has scarcely been an intensive search; but I've done my best. He's moved from his lodging in Melville Street, and his landlady there couldn't say where he'd gone – or had perhaps been instructed to pretend ignorance. He's also left his job on the *Independent*, and has left no address there either. Nor could Harris the printer enlighten me. Casey's address was unknown to him, he said; he only saw him when he came in with some copy for the *Exile*.

It was almost as though Casey had made himself invisible; but yesterday, I encountered him unexpectedly.

I had come down to Hobart Town for a day's shopping. At four in the afternoon, I walked out the door of Tegg's bookshop on to Wellington Bridge, and paused under the awning. I was surveying the crowds on the Block, as I often do, and was about to move on, when Casey appeared among them. He was moving towards me, coming over the bridge from the Liverpool Street side, clad in a dark tail coat and tall grey hat, and looking remarkably like a Government official. When he saw me, he made no attempt to evade me. Instead he advanced with extended hand, his face breaking into a grin that showed not a trace of unease.

– Devereux, he said. What an unexpected pleasure!

– I will not shake the hand of an enemy, I said.

He blinked and lowered the hand, and his grin faltered. But when he replied, his voice had an insolent confidence.

– A surprising assumption, sir. On what do you base it?

– Come, I said. Let us play no more games, Matthew. What you are is now known to us: you work for Sir William Denison. And you have taken away the *Exile* from Kinane. I have been looking for you this past month, and I have a request to make of you. I make it on Liam's behalf, not for myself. If you have any decency left, hand his newspaper back to him.

Casey looked at me now with an indulgent expression, as

though I were a child. Then he began to shake his head; but I went on before he could answer.

– God knows I don't approve of that damned paper. But Liam created it, and made it successful; he has put his whole heart into it, and his very survival depends on it. He gave it into your care while he was imprisoned: he did not expect that you would seize it. He is a sick man, with a family depending on him. I ask you to restore it to him, Matthew.

He raised his eyebrows and pushed his lips out, seeming to consider. His manner when he answered was reasonable and placatory.

– Well now, I'll tell you what it is, Devereux. What I have done is for Kinane's own good. He is uncontrolled, and his articles and editorials were growing more and more seditious. It would have ended in his being sent back to Port Arthur for a very long time. I have saved him from that, and I have saved the paper.

– At the behest of your master Denison, I said.

He stared at me. As he did so, two middle-aged gentlemen in tail coats walked by, wearing those expressions of quiet self-congratulation common to public officials. Casey greeted them with eager warmth, exchanging a few words with them about some forthcoming meeting. He was very much a member of Hobart Town's establishment, it seemed, and at home on the Block. When he turned back to me, his tone had changed. For the first time, the ingratiating note was absent; in its place was one of self-important rebuke.

– Sir William Denison is the Governor of this colony, he said. Yes, he is my master – as he is yours, Devereux – and my work brings me into contact with him. I see nothing wrong with that.

– You work as a Judas, I said. How much silver does he put into your palm? And how much did Lord Clarendon put there, while you pretended to be one of us in Dublin?

He ceased to smile now, and his amber eyes went blank behind their spectacles.

– You cannot prove these things, he said. Be careful of what you say.

Anger seized me now like intoxication. I moved a fraction closer to him, and what he saw in my face made his eyes widen, and begin to glance about as though for help.

– Careful? I'll be careful of nothing, I said. How do you have the insolence to come grinning to me and holding out your hand? Did you think you'd still gull me, you treacherous son of a bitch? Let me assure you, Casey, you'll gull no-one, from now on. I have sent off an article exposing you as a traitor to Ireland, which will be published this month in Dublin. All will be known: that while you were a member of the St Patrick Club, and sneaking about the Irish Confederation, you were reporting all our plans to Clarendon, and whispering in the ears of his police detectives. When it's published, I doubt that you will ever contemplate returning home – since your life there will be not worth a penny.

– I advise you against publishing such an article, Casey said. You will regret it.

He had merely whispered this, but his stare had an insolent malevolence.

– You may keep your advice, I said, and be damned to you. The article will be published, depend on it. There is only one thing I should like to hear from you, Casey, before you and I sever our connection for ever. How could you pretend to be one of us, and sell us to the English? How could you sell your country?

Casey said nothing for a moment. The cold-fingered breeze of afternoon was blowing up Elizabeth Street from the south, coming by way of the port; he put up a hand to secure his tall hat, holding it by the brim. Then his eyes went past me, looking south towards the junction with Macquarie Street. The gates of Government House could be seen there, with a red-coated soldier in a sentry box. Perhaps the sight of him bolstered Casey's courage; when he turned back to me, his face showed a hard and open bitterness.

– We were never comrades, he said. You merely tolerated me at Trinity – you and O'Neill. What was I? A butcher's son. You allowed me to join your company like a privileged servant; I was never one of you. You secretly despised me – as you despise that poor fool Kinane.

I began to speak, but he held up his hand. The words rattled out of him now: measured and precise, like a long-prepared speech.

– And I have *not* sold my country, he said. I have *protected* it – from people like you. I told you once you were a dangerous man, Devereux. What you urged – which your comrades at least did not – was a resort to atrocities. The tearing up of train lines; violence in the streets of the cities; the peasants to take up arms. And your comrades listened – and the people listened. You threaten civil order, Devereux: you threaten the pact of civilization. There will always be brutes who threaten it: barbarians and criminals; idle, bloodthirsty rogues like the Ribbonmen. But you! You are one of the ornaments of that pact, and you betrayed it! *You* are the traitor, not I!

I listened with fascination, and I saw that he was utterly sincere.

– I see, I said.

– Young Ireland! he said, and curled his top lip. What did it really offer to our people? You and your comrades are irresponsible fops who are *playing* at revolution – ready to sacrifice the lives of a people who are starved and worn out. What future do you offer them? What does your nationalism *mean*, with its poems and songs? Of what use is it, all your rhetoric about your soil; your hills; your myths? It's all out of books! Let me tell you, Devereux, one hill is the same as another to me – there or here.

– At least you make me understand you, I said. You have no perception of our country's soul, since your own soul is stunted. You are like a blind man: I pity you. And you believe in nothing – except your own ambition, of course.

– There you are wrong, sir. What I believe in is the destiny of the British Empire. Yes: the Empire! You and your political club can do nothing for the Irish people: it is British wealth and the British sense of duty that ensures their survival. Good Lord, most of them cannot even *farm* efficiently! Is Britain responsible for that? What hope is there for Ireland without England? A country of peasants, and of feckless Irish gentry like you! I have *always* believed in the Union: that is what I have worked for. Union with Britain, and with an Empire greater than Rome's: *that* is the future, Devereux – the Empire! Look about you; look at what Britain has done, right across the globe. Peace, prosperity and equality under the law, wherever she colonises!

He waved his hand at Elizabeth Street and its shops, and at the Union Jack that fluttered on its staff above Government House; and I stared in pure amazement. At last I understood. There was a force in him I had not dreamed possible: a force that drew on this larger source, feeding on it like a parasite.

– Men like me are the men of the modern age, he said. Men who know what global power is all about, and are able to profit by it. You and Barry and O'Neill are men of the past, sir: your posturing, fanatical nationalism is outdated and provincial – suitable for such people as Hungarians. What matters now is the larger, civilising entity, which reaches to the ends of the earth, and contains such little provinces within it. To be a citizen of the Empire is to be a citizen of the world – at home wherever the flag flies. And that is what *I* am, Devereux: a citizen of the Empire and the world. Perhaps poor Fitzgibbon began to realise the truth of these things: perhaps that is why he took his life. Unless you give up your childish dreams, *you* might as well do the same.

My fists were clenched. Controlling myself, I said softly:

– If it were possible, Casey, I'd demand satisfaction of you.

The words sounded foolish as soon as they were out, and I saw Casey's grin return.

– You prove my point, sir. You are a man of the eighteenth century; a walking anachronism. I wish you would do it: I wish you would assault me. I could have you in Port Arthur immediately. But I will have you there anyway, in the end.

– I doubt that, I said.

– You would be foolish to, he said. Let me give you my good news. The Assistant-Comptroller of Convicts, Mr Laird, is returning to England in a week's time. I have been appointed in his place.

He turned on his heel abruptly, and began to walk on towards Macquarie Street, and Government House. As he did so, he grinned at me over his shoulder, one hand steadying his tall, important hat. It was not malicious, this grin; it was triumphant.

At Barry's Cottage, Lake Sorell
April 22nd

I write this very late, and cannot sleep. Terrible news has been brought to us this evening by Father Kevin Brennan: Liam Kinane is dead.

It's as though some force is moving to destroy us one by one: Denison has only to wait, and the work is done for him.

I came up here to spend three days with my comrades. The occasion was Paul Barry's birthday, and he and Thomas O'Neill and I celebrated with a happy and boisterous dinner last night. Father Brennan was to have come up from Hobart Town to join us, arriving yesterday afternoon – but he didn't appear before dark, and we knew then that we could no longer expect him.

Instead, he arrived late today, riding on a hired horse from Green Ponds, and his absence of the night before was soon explained. At the very time of Paul's birthday dinner, Father Brennan had been giving Liam Kinane the last rites. He had held our comrade's hand as he died, down there in Hobart Town.

I see that nearly three months have passed since my last entry in this journal. In that time, many misfortunes overtook Kinane. It might be said that these disasters were of his own making; but a more just way of putting it would be to say that he was destroyed by English tyranny – that tyranny against which he hurled himself without thought of the consequences; which he defied until it crushed him. We called this foolishness, my comrades and I; now we grow ashamed, and call it heroism.

After Barry and I had visited him at Christmas, Kinane made something of a recovery from the illness that had sapped him during his imprisonment. But his fortunes did not improve. His Ticket-of-Leave was renewed; but without his newspaper, he had no way of supporting himself. He looked for employment as a clerk with various Hobart Town solicitors, but none of them would employ him. He would have starved, or been forced into the convict hiring depot, had it not been for the funds that Barry and I had given him; but having to accept these funds had been humiliating to him, and he would take no more – though we pressed him very hard to do so, and pleaded with him to realise that such support was no more than his due. As for his wife and boys in Ireland, they were being kept alive through subscriptions donated by generous Irish settlers – not only in Van Diemen's Land, but in the colonies of New South Wales and Victoria. Many of these supporters wrote offering money to Kinane; but he would not accept. He was too proud; this despite the fact that he could no longer pay the rent for his house in Goulburn Street.

He moved out, and was only saved from starving in the streets by Father Kevin Brennan. Father Brennan officiates at a small Catholic church called St Virgil's Chapel. It stands in Patrick Street, half-way up a hill on the northern side of the city, and has a presbytery next door: a two-storeyed brick cottage where Father Brennan lives, attended by a housekeeper. He took Kinane in there, giving him a bedroom on the upper floor, and assured him that he could lodge there without rent for as long as he wished. Father Brennan is a true Christian, and Barry and O'Neill and I were grateful to him; it was a relief to know that Kinane had a refuge, and we began to tell one another that our difficult comrade was out of trouble.

But we were wrong. In the cottage, Father Brennan told us, Liam had little to do but brood. He also began to drink again: he would seek out his old companions in the taverns of St Giles, and disappear for days at a time; then he would return to the presbytery contrite and ashamed, and swear to remain sober. He wanted an occupation, Father Brennan said; he wanted his pride and his newspaper back, and the two were linked. Kinane sent out letter after letter, seeking support: to backers, to dignitaries such as the Catholic and Anglican bishops; to lawyers whom he asked to represent him in making a case against Casey, and recovering the debts that were owed to him. But the dignitaries, though they expressed polite sympathy, showed no inclination to do anything for him; and the lawyers soon realised that he had no money. They also realised that in going into court against Casey, they would be going into court against the Governor. So even had Kinane had any funds, it's unlikely that any of them would have touched his case.

In early February, following my meeting with Casey on the

Block, I felt it necessary to call on Kinane, and to tell him of our treacherous compatriot's appointment as Assistant-Comptroller of Convicts. I warned him of how dangerous an enemy Casey had thus become, and urged him to give up his pursuit of the man. But he refused, and his rage was majestic to see. This official appointment, whereby Casey became one of our gaolers, was of course the final confirmation of the man's amazing treachery – and it made Liam's hatred of him into an obsession. It was an obsession which we all understood, and with which we sympathised; but it now drove Kinane into acts that were reckless to the point of being deranged.

The first of these was his exploit with the dog. This was reported in the newspapers – the *Hobart Town Independent* and the Launceston *Examiner* both carrying stories which made the most of the incident's comic appeal – and it created great amusement among the citizens.

In mid-February, less than a week after Casey took up his appointment, a large, tawny-coloured mongrel dog appeared in the streets, and trotted about everywhere in the Block, evading attempts to catch it. About its neck hung a notice:

My name is MATTHEW CASEY, Assistant-Comptroller of Convicts. I am an Irish dog, who sells his comrades for money. Please send me back to my master, Sir William Denison.

The dog was finally apprehended by some soldiers from the Barracks. No recriminations followed, since neither the dog nor the notice it carried could be traced back to Kinane. But a few days later, he launched a more direct attack.

A dwarf bellman now presented himself on the Block – hired by Liam at Long Lane's depot in Wapping – and marched about the streets hung with placards, vigorously ringing his bell. The placards were eloquent, and detailed. They denounced the new Assistant-Comptroller as a traitor to Ireland: a former member of the Young Ireland movement who had betrayed his comrades to the British authorities in Dublin, who was informing on them even now to the colonial Goverment, and who had illegally seized the *Irish Exile* in order to destroy it.

The dwarf was eventually seized by some constables, and hurried away and questioned. He was probably threatened with dire measures if he did not cooperate, since he told them who had hired him. Kinane was summoned to the police office in Murray Street, and told by the Police Magistrate that he was guilty of grave offences: among them the libelling of a public official, and the display of seditious matter. He would not be charged this time; but if such a thing happened again, his Ticket-of-Leave would be withdrawn, and he would be sent back in chains to Port Arthur.

Much though the incident gave us delight, all of us warned Kinane against ignoring this threat, and carrying his campaign against Casey any further. He would not listen. Instead, he pushed it to a new level – and so enabled Sir William Denison to take him into his power.

He still had a firm friend and admirer in Mr Davis, the owner of the *Hobart Town Independent*. Mr Davis now had a new printer, and did not feel able to remove the man in order to give Kinane his old job back – but he was prepared to publish almost anything our friend wrote. And Kinane now presented him with an article on Casey. It was entitled *An Irish Judas*, and was published on February 22nd. It dealt with Casey's entire history. It owed something to the piece I had sent to the *New Nation* at home, which I had allowed Liam to read in manuscript – but it went even beyond my own efforts in its exposure and vilification of Casey. Some of the more vivid phrases that I recall:

> *This loathsome, repellent traitor, with his hypocrite's smile . . . This associate of drunken Dublin police detectives and their rat-like informers . . . This lap-dog of his English masters; this hireling of the Convict Department, who betrayed his friends and their high and glorious cause, and sold into exile some of the finest patriots and most honourable gentlemen Ireland has seen . . . Even in a convict colony, who would sit down to table with such a creature?*

I groaned when I read it. I believed he had put into the hands of the officials the instrument that would enable them to silence and crush him once and for all – and I was quickly proved right.

The press has remarkable freedom in Van Diemen's Land, and no action was taken against Mr Davis the editor. But within days of the article's appearance, Kinane was arrested on the Governor's orders and charged with writing a seditious article. He was tried, convicted, and sentenced to six months' hard labour. Soon after this, on the last day of February, he was led in chains with other condemned felons aboard the Government steamer that would carry them to Port Arthur.

They took him from there to the Saltwater River again: the place he had come to dread. Clad in his uniform of mustard and grey, he was set to work cutting timber in the bush as before, and found himself choking over the dreaded skilly and salt beef once more. And once again (I imagine it must have seemed like a familiar nightmare, closing inexorably about him), he found himself at night in that dreaded, hateful dormitory with its thieves, murderers and sodomites. Letters reached us from him; they were inspected by the authorities at Hobart Town before being sent on, so he therefore said little by way of complaint. But he spoke constantly of illness and weakness; and eventually he became so ill with diarrhoea that he was removed to the hospital again. This was at the end of the first week in April.

Father Brennan was now given permission to visit him. The priest was so shocked at Kinane's wasted and enfeebled condition that he immediately wrote memorials to the Commandant of the Port Arthur settlement and to Sir William Denison, begging to be allowed to take Kinane back to the presbytery, and to arrange for medical attention there.

This was speedily agreed to. Father Brennan was surprised; but I was not. Liam Kinane was a state prisoner, after all, and the *Exile* had made him known throughout the Australian colonies, especially among the Irish. His death in the settlement would have been a considerable embarrassment, coming hard on the heels of the suicide of Martin Fitzgibbon. Articles enquiring about his treatment would have appeared in most of the Australian newspapers – and London would no doubt have questioned Sir William Denison closely, requiring him to justify Kinane's excessive sentence.

Ten days ago, on April 12th, Liam was installed in Father Brennan's presbytery again, where he took to his bed. He was never to get up from it, except to sit in an armchair by the window – from which, on the hillslope of Patrick Street, he could view the port. With what a wistful eye must he have looked at those masts and sails from the other hemisphere! He sat there, Father Brennan said, writing letters home: to his wife and sons and closest friends. None of us feared that his illness might be fatal, until Thomas O'Neill went down to see him.

He appeared like a skeleton, O'Neill said: dreadfully gaunt, with a yellowish colour. He had passed a great deal of blood; he was very weak and listless, all his fire gone, and could eat nothing except broth. The doctor who was attending him had diagnosed an irritation of the bowel, and had told Kinane that an internal tumour was possible: he wanted to operate and explore. But Kinane had a fear of the surgeon's knife, and begged that this be postponed. He would soon get well, he said, now that he had escaped the convict station; he only needed time to recover.

This was how things stood on the night of Barry's birthday dinner. We were hoping that Father Brennan would bring us good news: that we would learn that our comrade was on the mend.

It was about ten o'clock, I remember, when Barry proposed a toast to Kinane in his absence. We had now reached the port and cheese. The small crimson parlour was snug and delightful as always; a fire blazed in the stone fireplace, and flickered in reflection on the rows of books. Candles burned in a three-branched candelabrum on the table; another was alight on the mantel shelf.

– To our absent Liam Kinane, Barry said. God protect him: and may he soon be cured of his illness, and made free of all his troubles.

When we had drunk to him, we spoke of him with concern, discussing what the nature of his illness might be. It was O'Neill, I think, who uttered the opinion that Kinane's nervous system was wrecked: partly by his excesses, but mostly by the strain of his constant disappointment, and by an anger that could have no satisfaction. And his worry over his family's plight was unrelieved – as was the grief of separation from them. To make matters worse, his wife's letters had begun to reproach him, asking him why he had not considered what would become of them, when he took up arms against the British. The privations he had endured at the Saltwater River convict station had no doubt completed this process of deterioration, causing his body to break down. As to the possibility of a tumour, we could only hope that the doctor was wrong, as they so often are.

In those moments, a shadow of sadness fell across the cheerful little parlour. It seemed to me that I could hear Liam singing, his great voice filling the room with *Aileen Aroon*; then we turned to other things, and laughter and high spirits slowly returned.

Was Kinane dying as we spoke of him? When the soul fled his big, wasted body, did it travel up to these highlands to join us, entering this cottage where he had so much wanted to be? Did he stand behind us, in Barry's convivial parlour – bidding us goodbye before setting out on his longer journey? Is that what prompted us to speak of him?

Ah, Liam, forgive us all.

This evening after dinner, all four of us sat about the fire drinking whiskey: Paul Barry, Thomas O'Neill, Father Kevin Brennan and myself.

The priest wore his clerical collar, which he never removed, but sat in his shirt-sleeves and waistcoat, toasting his stockinged feet at the fire. His round, fresh face and shining bald head were flushed from the warmth and the liquor, and his large hazel eyes, usually alert for amusement, surveyed us now with a deep solemnity. His voice had taken on those elegiac rhythms which an Irishman of the people adopts at times of death or loss – and Kevin Brennan was a man of the people.

Kinane's funeral would be in two days' time, he told us – and he, Brennan, would conduct it. It would be in St Joseph's, the Catholic church in Macquarie Street, and would certainly be attended by most of the Irish population of Hobart Town. All of us swore to attend, whether given permission to leave our districts or not. Then the priest described Kinane's death to us. It caused us to look into the fire in silence, remaining so for some time.

That Liam was gravely ill had only become apparent in the last few days, Father Brennan said. He had begun to be in great pain, and to vomit, and his abdomen grew monstrously swollen. He could now take nothing but liquids, and had grown dreadfully wasted, with deep black rings under his eyes. Brennan and his housekeeper were now with him constantly; the doctor was called, and decided that his bowel was blocked. Unless he could operate, he told them, gangrene would set in. Kinane agreed, but asked for one more day: he was dreadfully afraid of the Government hospital. The doctor gave him laudanum, and left.

That night, at Kinane's request, Father Brennan gave him Extreme Unction. Another episode of vomiting followed; then Kinane lay still, in a sort of drifting peace, with the priest holding his hand. He knew that he was dying now, he said, and Father Brennan did not deny it. The smell of death had been very strong, he told us, and involuntarily wrinkled his nose. Kinane begged not to be taken to the hospital, but to be allowed to die in the presbytery; and he asked that his Young Ireland comrades look after his wife and sons.

We promised Brennan now that we would do so. Liam's widow would have an annuity for life: Barry, O'Neill and I would share the cost between us.

– Ah boys, Father Brennan said, it was not an easy death. But it was a holy death, of that I can assure you. He made a good Confession. His last words were: God bless my darling Bridget, and my poor boys. May they forgive me: I have given Holy Ireland my life.

He and Paul Barry looked at each other, and Barry nodded slowly. I have noticed that Catholics attach great importance to the manner in which death is met – and of course, to that last sacrament which Father Brennan had given Kinane.

O'Neill and I studied them both as though across a gap; the old religion and its rituals made them strangers to us for a moment. Then O'Neill gave a great sigh, and said:

– No man gave more to our cause, poor old fellow. He sacrificed his family, perhaps his sanity, and now his life. I begin to wonder if any cause is worth that.

– Not when the sacrifice is wasted, I said. It might have been more merciful had they hanged him in Dublin in '48.

I stood up, putting down my glass on the table, and saw all three firelit faces turn up to me with faintly shocked expressions. Suddenly I felt a disgust with the noble and useless sentiments that my friends and I felt obliged to express.

– It was all a waste, I said, God rest him. He was brave and loyal and foolish, and it was all a waste. Now, if you'll pardon me, gentlemen, I'm going to take the air.

I walked out of the parlour into the little hall, and so out the door onto the verandah that looks onto the lake.

It was a still, dark night, with very little cloud. A half moon had just risen, and there was a luminous path on the water. The black shapes of the trees on the other side were only just discernible. As always, the nearness of the white, blazing hosts of stars made my head spin. I took a deep breath, and the chaste, unsullied air cleared my brain. I leaned with both hands on the rail.

After a time, I heard a step behind me. Barry had come out, and handed me a cheroot in silence, taking one for himself as well. He struck a match and lit both; then he said:

– It's time to go, Devereux. You realise that, I'm sure. We must escape this God-damned island before we end in chains too.

I looked at him.

– You know that I can't, I said. Kathleen expects our child in only a month's time.

He looked at me, expelling smoke from his cheroot, and his eyes shone pale in the dimness, seeming suddenly to promise great things. Then he said:

– I hope to change your mind. Kentucky Callaghan has arrived.

At 'Clare'
April 28th

This afternoon, Langford and I sat working at our accounts in his office, at the end of the front verandah.

A large kitchen table serves him as a desk, and he and I now sat on either side of it, the account books between us. It's always pleasantly dry and still in here, smelling of paper and of James's cigar smoke. A door on its inner side leads into a store-room, where unwanted items of furniture have been stowed, together with boxes of papers and some of Bess's storage jars. The portrait Doctor Howard painted stands on a table there. I've not hung it up (although Kathleen urges me to), because something about the expression of the face discomposes me. Perhaps the gentleman in the picture is not myself after all, but *Herr Doppelgänger*.

To see Langford immersed in his paper-work, bare, muscular arms planted on the table, eyes narrowed suspiciously, always touches me. Clerical activity will never be natural to him. He's excellent at bargaining and selling; but he was a stranger to running a profit and loss account when we took up the farm. Here I've been able to help him, teaching him the fundamentals of book-keeping. I still help him to balance the accounts; and this is what I'd now been doing.

He slammed shut the calf-bound book he was holding, and sat back in his chair. We had done; the entries were balanced, and the story of the last six months was clear.

– We've done uncommon well, he said. That's a handy profit.

– We've done amazingly well, I said. What a crop we had, compared to last year's! We'll grow rich at this rate, James. And it's all owed to you. Your irrigation channels have worked wonders.

He smiled, and his face lit up like a boy's. Langford is not a vain man, but praise of his irrigation system is something he can't resist. It ranks with his great railway affair as a landmark in his career; it has attracted the attention of all the other growers in the district, and of the Agricultural Society in Hobart Town.

– Well, it *has* worked well, he said, I must say that. But don't talk bloody nonsense, Robert – things ain't all owed to me. I could never have done it without you.

– I've something to tell you, I said. You may have to do without me in the future. I've decided to leave Van Diemen's Land.

He took his cigar from his mouth and ceased to smile, looking at me hard.

– Go on, he said.

628

I outlined our plans for escape. A comrade had arrived here from New York, I told him, who was able to arrange passage to America. Paul Barry and I would be meeting him at Bridgewater next week. Barry would escape first, and I hoped to follow.

Langford narrowed his eyes and frowned, his body appearing to stiffen. He put down the cigar in the grimy saucer that served him as an ash tray, locked his hands in front of him, and sat forward.

– And Kathleen? She's near her time. Are you telling me that you'll leave her – and your child?

– Of course not. She and the child must come with me. I intend to marry her in New York.

He examined my face as though to find proof of what I'd said; then he seemed to relax a little. He unlocked his hands, resting them palms down on the table. But his frown remained.

– That won't be an easy caper, he said. Going on the run with a new baby.

– I'm not quite so foolish as that, I said. We shall have to wait. Perhaps for six months or so – perhaps more. It depends on the health of the baby.

– I see, he said. He sat staring at the table between his spread, outstretched hands; then he looked up.

– You won't let the girl down, Robert? I wouldn't want to see you do that, partner. Bess says she's a good 'un, your Kathleen – and Bess knows a lot about women.

I assured him once again that I would not desert her. He nodded, and looked down again. He seemed to ponder deeply, and there was silence in the little room. I found myself examining the freckles on his tanned, extended fore-arms; to my surprise, I was not only filled with sadness, but with a sense that what I was proposing was a sort of perverse betrayal. Yet I wasn't betraying Langford, surely: his fortunes would be secure without me. Outside, I could hear our distant cows lowing, coming in to be milked, and Rufus barking. When Langford spoke, he did so to the table.

– *She* won't want to go. She loves it here on the farm. She's told Bess so, often.

– Yes, it will make her sad to leave. It will make me sad too –

I shall miss you badly, James, and will always remember you. But please try and understand. I have to get back to that side of the world where I can carry on the fight, and where my friends and countrymen are organised. I should simply go mad here, in the end.

He looked up at me and rubbed his moustache, and I saw his face take on that blankness which was usually his response to a crisis of some kind.

– Ah, yes, he said. Your revo-*lushion*. I'd forgotten about that, I suppose – and I thought you had too, Robert. I thought you was as content here as I am.

– I *have* been content, I said. I've had great happiness here, James, believe me.

He stared at me. When he spoke again, his tone had grown harsh.

– And what about your share of the farm? You'll be wanting me to buy you out, I expect.

– Not at the moment, I said.

– Not at the moment? When, then?

– When you get really prosperous. When you can spare it. You can send it to me in America.

– But you ain't really rich – you told me so. You'll be needing that money now.

– When I need it, I'll send for it, I told him.

He looked at me with a wondering expression, wrinkling up his forehead. For a moment, he said nothing. His expression remained serious, but his tone softened.

– Well I call that handsome of you, Robert – but it ain't very sensible, is it? America's a long way off – and I might never pay you. You must really trust me.

– I do, James.

He gave a wheezy laugh which ended in a cough; his eyes watered, and he wiped them with the back of his hand.

– Not many men would. Not many ever have. Have you forgot I'm a robber? By Christ, you're never going to get rich, Robert – you ain't careful enough. But you don't want to live careful, do you?

– I suppose not. Being careful never seemed to me what life was about.

He stood up, and I did the same. He came around the table, making for the door to the verandah, and we faced each other.

– That's the way *I* thought, once, he said. Not any more. I don't need no more trouble, Robert – and to me, the Old Country just means trouble and misery. *I'll* never go back to that side of the world, I swear it. I like it here: even though London and the screws are still running the place. They won't be doing it much longer: this'll be a real country, in a few more years – and coves like me will be running it. Maybe I'm just slowing down, and getting old. Pains in my knee joints, lately. Stiffening up.

– You'll never slow down, James, I said. You'll make this the best property on the Derwent – and end by being mayor of New Norfolk.

For a moment, we stood in silence. He was poised to go out the door, but could not seem to do so; he stared out the window at the roses in Bess's garden. Then he shrugged, and pulled the door open. Pausing, he looked at me sideways.

– You can always come back, he said abruptly. You and Kathleen. The farm'll always be here for you. But you won't, will you? You'll go on with your bloody revo-lushion, and break your bloody heart. That's the way you're made. It's a pity – but it ain't my business. And now I must be off, and do some real work. Thanks for the help with them accounts, Robert. We made it all add up, didn't we?

He turned and strode off along the verandah, coughing as he went. I stood looking after him with a heaviness in my chest. I had thought him too hard to have anything but highly practical attachments. It seemed I'd been wrong.

May 3rd

The Black Snake Inn at Bridgewater, halfway between New Norfolk and Hobart Town, on the Main Road.

Barry and I sit in the parlour at a table by the window, drinking coffee. We are waiting for Kentucky Callaghan. Leaning back in his chair, Barry takes his watch from his waistcoat pocket, staring at it for perhaps the tenth time. He sighs.

– Six-fifteen. That bloody antique vehicle of theirs is over an hour late. One begins to ask if it ever left Launceston.

We are both in a state of high tension. Callaghan is coming on the coach from the north, which was due here at five o'clock. I murmur some sort of reassurance, but I'm beginning to have the same concern as Barry does. He and I are the only customers in the parlour; but raised voices and barks of laughter tell us that there's plenty of trade in the tap-room across the corridor. The New Norfolk coach changes horses at this inn, and the stage coaches for Hobart Town and Launceston stop here for refreshments. The Black Snake is a sombre, crudely-built barn of grey weatherboard and stone, with steeply-pitched gables at either end, and a high, dim verandah in front. The parlour we sit in is quite well-furnished, with a Turkey carpet on the floor and a gilded mirror over the mantel-shelf; but the place remains oppressive. In fact, the inn has an unaccountable atmosphere of foreboding, which I do my best to ignore.

We keep watch through the window. There's little to be seen on this side of the river at Bridgewater but a tiny scatter of houses, tall, dark hills nearby, and the rough stone buildings of an abandoned convict station. The Derwent is very wide at this point, pewter-coloured under an overcast sky, with an icy wind bending the reeds. It's spanned here by a long wooden bridge that takes the Main Road to the north, and we glance at this bridge continually, looking for the Launceston coach. Barry, who seldom shows impatience about anything, is drumming his fingers on the table. As the light dwindles, and the bridge fades, his hope seems to fade too.

– I believe that bloody coach isn't coming, he says. We're here for nothing, Devereux.

– It will come, I say. Wait a little longer.

Barry has made all the arrangements that have brought us here tonight: first, in letters between Van Diemen's Land and America, and then – when Callaghan arrived in Australia on a ship from San Francisco – in a final exchange with him between here and

Melbourne. All has been agreed to, by the New York Irish Directory: Callaghan comes equipped with ample funds to enable all three of us to escape, should we wish to – Barry, O'Neill and myself – and will act as our agent in dealing with receptive ships' captains. He is posing as a correspondent for the *New York Tribune*; and the colonial authorities are no doubt convinced, since he's written some articles for that paper. Already he has secretly arranged a ship for Barry in Melbourne: it sails for San Francisco on the 30th, so Paul's escape to the Australian mainland must be very soon.

In order to come to Bridgewater, Barry obtained permission from his magistrate in Ross to visit the Hobart Town district for two days. He travelled down yesterday, and today rode eleven miles back up the highway on a hired horse – while I came the nine miles from 'Clare' on Fleur-de-lis. Callaghan will stay the night at the Black Snake, and then go on alone to Hobart Town tomorrow, where he plans to take lodgings.

These elaborate arrangements are for secrecy. No-one must know who Callaghan is, or that we're in contact with him. We have chosen the Black Snake as a meeting place since we dare not risk being seen with him in Hobart Town – and this junction of the highway to the north and the road to New Norfolk, which scarcely even qualifies as a hamlet, is very quiet, with little likelihood of the presence of police or officials. It lies in the New Norfolk police district; so Barry is taking a calculated risk in coming out of the Hobart Town district, and must be back in the Ship Inn before his curfew at ten.

It's too dark now to watch the bridge. We talk, returning to a topic that we skirted some time ago.

– How soon? Barry asks. How soon after will you follow me, Robert? Callaghan will need to know that.

– I must wait at least six months, I say, for the sake of the child. I have promised Kathleen that.

Barry looks at me quickly, and his gaze seems to grow cold. But it's merely concerned, and empty of its usual humour.

– So long? You have promised her that?

– I have, and I must keep my promise. She is afraid of America, you know. It's like some monstrous dream, in her mind – and she has grown attached to Van Diemen's Land, and especially to the farm and the Langfords. She will miss her hens and her garden, she says, and the peace of our valley. So will I, to tell you the truth.

– Don't grow too attached, he says. Don't lose your resolve. Remember your own advice, Devereux: don't become a lotus-eater. Six months! Oh dear. We must hope that Callaghan can linger here that long.

He stares at the blackness out the window again. As he does so, we hear the rumble of wheels, the trotting of hoofs, and the sudden blaring of the coach guard's bugle. We both jump to our feet, and hasten into the hallway.

Coming out the doorway into the verandah, we blink in the light of the lamps of the tall yellow coach, whose four sweating bays are stamping and snorting. Six passengers step stiffly from its interior: four men, and two women. Their faces are obscure, since the lamp over the Black Snake's door is a feeble one; laughing and talking, they all pass into the house except for one man, who lingers for a moment.

– He's not here, Barry says. He wasn't aboard. Ah, Jesus.

I ask him whether the fellow who is hanging back might not be Callaghan; but he peers at him and shakes his head.

The man walks up onto the verandah and passes us without a glance. He wears a dark grey cape and a low-crowned white hat with a broad brim. We follow him into the hall, which is now empty, making our way back towards the parlour. But the man turns, blocking the way, and looks at us hard. An oil lamp hangs from the ceiling, and his features are now clear.

– Callaghan! Barry says. My dear Michael, it's you after all.

He laughs, and puts out his hand. Callaghan takes it, and smiles briefly. When he answers his voice is low, and his tone one of warning.

– Hullo Barry, old fellow. Sure, it's wonderful to see you again. But look here – do keep your voice down, will you? And don't use that name: my name in this place is MacMahon. I'd as soon not be arrested here first off.

He turns to me, and holds out his hand.

– And you are Robert Devereux, I take it. I'm honoured to meet you, sir. I bring greetings from Patrick Dwyer in New York. Now: where can we be private?

The landlord took us to a small private room with a fire, and with dark, forbidding wainscoting. He brought us a supper of broth, boiled beef and greengage pie, accompanied by bottled ale; and Callaghan ate eagerly.

– I've been sitting in that old-fashioned box since four o'clock this morning, he said. And it stopped at every God-damned hostelry on the way, so that the coachman and the guard and most of the passengers could drink brandy. Are they *all* drunkards here? And why don't they build a railroad in this pestiferous little island?

He laughed, and we both joined in – his laughter being both boisterous and infectious. He dissolved the sullen darkness of the inn, and filled the little room with his energy: an energy brought from that far side of the world where all things give off an electric intensity. He was in his mid-thirties, like ourselves: not particularly tall, but strongly built, with a broad chest and shoulders, copper hair, and a luxuriant red moustache. He had somehow acquired a broken nose, which gave him the appearance of a pugilist. His large, greenish eyes were constantly lit by the force of his energy, and had a way of fixing you so that you metaphorically stepped back under their stare. He had taken off his wide-brimmed hat – no doubt the favoured headgear of Kentucky landowners – and thrown his cape over a chair. He proved to be as much of a dandy in his dress as Barry, in a handsome blue riding coat, an embroidered waistcoat, and fine American riding boots. His accent was still Irish, but it had American overtones; he'd acquired their tricks of speech, and his deep, rattling voice had the American vitality and impatience. But perhaps he'd always had this last characteristic; he seems to have been very pushing and successful in his father's firm in Waterford, and now was just as successful with his stock farm near Lexington.

He spoke to us of the beauty of Kentucky, with its lush blue-grass pastures, and its wonderful thoroughbred horses: he and his partner were breeding some of the best, he said, and I saw that he was something of a boaster. He extolled the greatness of New York – which he called 'Knickerbocker City' – where he went for regular meetings with our Young Ireland comrades in exile. He conjured up the city's great bay, and its forest of ships' masts; he showed us teeming Manhattan. He took us along Broadway, with its omnibuses and phaetons, beautifully-dressed women, and handsome, red brick houses. He conducted us into the strange and dubious district called the Bowery, with its ready-made clothes, ready-cooked foods, oyster cellars and bar-rooms, and faces from all over the earth.

– I reckon it's *our* people who will run New York soon, he said. Why, a quarter of the population is Irish, and more are coming all the time. The Democratic party is the party for us, and full of Irish bosses. And our Young Ireland comrades are doing well, gentlemen, and are very popular there, as you know. The *New York Herald* has written much in favour of Young Ireland, and of *you* two gentlemen, and of our poor Martin Fitzgibbon, may God rest his soul. Pat Dwyer's *Irish Echo* is a great success: and *your* articles are quoted constantly, Devereux. Ah, we simply can't wait to see you both, gentlemen, walking down Broadway! By Godfrey, what a welcome you'll get!

The man was infectious, and Barry and I found ourselves laughing in pure elation. The three of us toasted each other in brandy and water, and Kentucky brought out a box of fine cigars and handed them out. Then he glanced at the door and leaned forward, lowering his voice with a care I found somewhat theatrical.

– Now then: can we get down to business? Is it safe to talk?

– Safe enough in this place, I said dryly. There are no police detectives in Bridgewater. Not much of anything, in fact.

Kentucky glanced at me quickly; then, reassured, he began to outline the plans for Barry's escape.

The American ship on which Barry would sail for San Francisco on the 30th was due in Melbourne shortly, Callaghan told us. Her captain was entirely sympathetic; a price had been arranged, and Barry would board her under an assumed name. So all would go smoothly once he reached Melbourne. The difficult part was to get to the Australian mainland from Van Diemen's Land. It would be far too dangerous to try and arrange a ship from Hobart Town, he said. In such a small city, with the Government's spies everywhere, and the police out looking for Barry once he withdrew his *parole*, betrayal would be inevitable. Callaghan had therefore made an arrangement with the captain of the *Petrel*, a trading steamer that was coming across to Launceston from Melbourne in three weeks' time. Again, it would be too risky for Barry to board her openly – even in that small city in the north. Instead, a more demanding course was necessary. Launceston lies on the Tamar River, a good way inland from the northern coast. When the *Petrel* sailed for Melbourne on the 24th, and had been cleared and searched by the port officials, she would turn a little way westwards along the coast after she cleared the mouth of the Tamar. There, she would lie off a lonely bay near a bluff called Badger Head, where Barry must be waiting. It was a wild stretch of country, but there were many fishermen living along the Tamar, and he should easily be able to hire a boat to ferry him there, and so out to the ship.

– Michael, you're an angel, Barry said. Your planning is a joy. Ah, we never dreamed at Clongowes when we were boys that you would some day deliver me from a place like this!

His lips were parted in a rapt smile. He was looking at Callaghan and yet not: he gazed into vistas of freedom. The little room, with its odours of ale and burning eucalyptus logs, became suddenly like a dungeon from which we'd burst free; became suddenly like Van Diemen's Land itself, shrunk to a single cell. But then Barry's face became sober.

– There's one more difficulty, he told Callaghan. We cannot in all honour escape while we hold our Tickets-of-Leave – that has been agreed. So I must officially withdraw my *parole*. My servant can ride down from Lake Sorell to deliver it in a letter to the magistrate at Ross. And then I must wait at the Lakes until the police come up from Ross to arrest me. Only then can I make my break.

Callaghan stared at him.

– Are you serious, man?

– I am. Otherwise I will be said to have escaped through a

trick – and I won't give the English and their press that weapon against me. Nor will Devereux, I believe.

Kentucky sat looking at us both, rubbing his chin. Then he began to laugh under his breath.

– Well, he said. Jesus. I ain't going to argue with you, Paul, and you may be right. But that makes it a blamed sight more close-run. I'll have to gather together a few Irish boys from Hobart Town to help us. And you can be sure I'll have *this* about me.

He opened his coat, and briefly drew from his pocket a Colt revolver, before thrusting it out of sight again.

– A great man is Colonel Colt, he said. One of America's finest minds. You both own weapons yourselves, I guess. Together, we can deal with any bunch of God-damned convict constabulary.

We all laughed; but there was something unreal, I found, about the drift of this discussion. Barry and Callaghan, it seemed, were calmly able to contemplate a gun battle with the police, the possibility of killing or wounding some of them, and their own deaths by gunfire or hanging should that battle turn against them. There was something weirdly casual about it, and I wondered if I would be as sanguine as Barry when my own turn for escape came. I found my thoughts turning to the quiet green rows of the hop glades, to the murmuring peace of the valley, and to Kathleen, swollen with our child, lying in bed waiting for me. But now Kentucky turned to me.

– Come, then, Devereux, we must talk about *your* case. I know that Thomas O'Neill won't agree to escape, and that's a shame – but Paul tells me *you* will, once that baby's born. But I have to warn you: I've not got unlimited time. So when can you be ready?

It would have to be in six months' time, I told him.

He frowned, and his eyes widened.

– That's impossible, he said. I can't stay in this colony that long. Two months – not six. Can't you make it then?

– I'm sorry, I said. I've given my word to Kathleen – and I won't make her take such a risky journey with an infant so young, when her strength is low. I'm delighted you're here, Callaghan, and we're all in debt to you for your daring and concern. I'm moved that the Directory in New York has acted for us with such generosity – but since you can't wait for me, I'm forced to say no.

Callaghan stared at me in silence, still frowning, apparently trying to probe my mind. He exhaled a long stream of smoke, and stubbed his cigar out. Then he said softly:

– That's an awful pity. I hope you may change your mind, Devereux. That's always difficult when a woman's involved, I know. She must be a very delightful young creature. But I beg you to try and persuade her. Even though travelling with a very young baby is hard, it ain't impossible. You've got to realise what's at stake here. Everyone in the Directory is going to be mighty disappointed – and God knows when they can arrange for someone else to come out here, or who that could be. I know *I* can't come again.

Suddenly, with a startling dispay of frustration, he drove his right fist into the palm of his left hand and swore under his breath, his wide green eyes still fixed on me.

– I'm sorry, he said, but this makes me mad. You're a great man, Devereux – and the Directory is counting on my getting you free. They'll be sick when they find I couldn't bring you back. For God's sake – think what you're giving up! When you reach America, our Government will protect you from any British attempts to extradite you, and every Irishman in New York will turn out to welcome you. You'll be able to tour the United States, lecturing on behalf of the cause, and you'll raise amounts of money that will astound you. All you need to do is *come!*

But I merely shook my head, conscious as I did so that Barry was watching us sadly.

– You'll never persuade him, he told Callaghan. Not when his mind's made up.

He drew his watch from his pocket.

– And now Robert and I must go, or be caught out after curfew.

Callaghan came out with us onto the inn's front verandah, while a servant brought our horses round from the stables. It had grown very dark; little could be seen but the river's faint gleam, and the tall black hills beside the road, rearing above us like ramparts. There was one of those pauses when men don't speak because there's little left to say – or else too much. Then, in the dimness, Kentucky Callaghan gripped my arm, bringing his face close to mine. When he spoke again, his tone had become almost hectoring in the force of its urgent, pent-up feeling.

– Damn it, Devereux, are you really going to risk staying for *years* in this miserable penal island? A bastard England, on the arse of the globe? For Christ's sake, come to your senses! Come to a land where men and women are free! Come back to the *world*!

But again I shook my head; and he sighed and dropped my arm.

– You're a damned stubborn man, he said. And this is a sad, sad business.

– Believe me, I said, it's saddest of all for me. Good night to you, Kentucky – we'll meet again soon, I hope.

I walked towards the stable-hand who was leading up Fleur-de-lis. The mare shook her head at me, and I murmured to her. At that moment, she had the consoling familiarity of a friend.

When I reached the farm I put Fleur into her stall, but didn't immediately go in. Instead, I stood quite still under the ash tree, in the silence of the yard.

Ah Christ, I said, *am I never to be free?*

And now I saw New York, printed on the night's icy blackness, and on the dark, sullen mask of the bush. I saw its crowds of ships and swarming buildings; I saw its webs of streets, as Callaghan had painted them; I saw its eager citizens jostling to their destinies, in that vast republic of freedom. And my body yearned to be *there*: in my lost, native zone of the North.

I stretched out my arms. I tilted my face to the sky, and groaned beneath my breath. And I was filled with pure hatred for this island, and for the whole of the accursed Antipodes.

6. FLIGHT OF THE EARLS

May 7th
Again it's the time of the late autumn ploughing. The hop glades
are destroyed as though a battle has swept over them, and the tea-
tree poles stand stacked among the furrows like the lances of a
broken cavalry. Rain storms lash the valley. When they cease, long
scarves of cloud hang low across the dark blue hills, hinting deceit-
fully at regions of romance. I keep to my study a good deal.

This morning was sunny, bright and piercing. Kathleen came
walking across the yard towards the back verandah, carrying a basket
of eggs. I stood watching her, knowing I would never love her
more. She wore a loose brown dress and a knitted blue bonnet: a
sort of tam-o'-shanter. She rocked as she walked, in a manner both
comical and touching, the basket held out from her side. The child
is due at any time now, and her belly has grown phenomenally
large, as is often the case with small women. Her complexion,
usually so pale, has taken on a rosy tinge, and this glowing face, as
she stared in front of her, wore a small half-smile. It was the smile
of pregnancy: witless yet wise, childish yet inscrutable.

When she's naked, her belly protrudes in front of her like a
great white urn, its navel like a closed eye, its curve both disfiguring
and majestic. I have knelt and put my hand there, and felt our child
kick; and the certainty in her face, looking down, was as awesome
as the look she gave O'Donnell.

May 10th
The child is born: a son. We have named him Thomas, after
Kathleen's father. It should also please O'Neill.

Kathleen's labour began at about eight o'clock last night, and the baby was born at seven o'clock this morning. When her pains began, I held her hand for a time, sitting with her in our bedroom; then Bess Langford ordered me out, and summoned in the midwife I had brought from New Norfolk.

I retired to the dining room down the hallway, where I sat throughout the evening with Langford, drinking coffee and brandy. Bess came and went, visiting Kathleen constantly. I have had no direct acquaintance with childbirth until now, and Kathleen's cries, which could clearly be heard in here, and which merely caused Langford to raise his eyebrows, greatly unnerved me. They were not like any sound that she had ever made before: they were the cries of another creature. They alternated with long fits of coughing; and this coughing worried me more than her groans.

I feared that she would have an asthma attack during the birth – and for this reason, I had made an arrangement with a doctor in New Norfolk named Wilson, who was to come should any complication occur: I would fetch him in the gig. At midnight, after James had gone to bed, a particularly long coughing bout was heard, and I could bear no more. I tapped on the bedroom door, called the midwife into the hallway, and asked after Kathleen's condition.

The woman frowned. She was a small, plump old Englishwoman: the wife of a tradesman in the town. The coughing was making Kathleen weak, she said, and did not bode well for the final stages of her labour: she would need all her strength to give birth to the child.

This was enough: I decided to go for Doctor Wilson. The notion of losing Kathleen made me wild with terror: I was trembling and sweating, scarcely knowing what I did or said. Standing in the dark, narrow hallway, I told the midwife that should the birth come on during my absence, and should there be any danger to Kathleen, she was to let the infant die. If she did not, she would be answerable to me. I believe my voice was raised: the woman drew back against the wall, staring at me with a horrified expression, as though I were mad. Perhaps I looked it.

It was as well that I brought Doctor Wilson when I did. He

was a serious, conscientious Scot, in whom I felt a grateful confidence. He stayed throughout the night, doing everything he could to ease Kathleen's breathing. Because of his concern about her lungs, he would not give her chloroform to ease the late stage of her labour, and she suffered greatly. But nothing must threaten her breathing, he said.

During the birth itself, his services became even more important, since she lost a good deal of blood.

Nine o'clock in the morning: two hours after the birth of our son.

Riding on Fleur-de-lis up the hillside past the cow pasture and the dairy and the pickers' huts – where Kathleen and I so often walked together, and where Langford and I rode after Daniel O'Donnell.

Frost on the grass, in patches not reached by the sun. A day of drifting vapours on bright air: the cows releasing steam from their nostrils, their fresh dung steaming in the grass; my breath and Fleur's rising white in front of us. The filly flicks her ears and snorts: glad to be released, as I am. Heartened more than usual by her chaffy fragrance, I talk nonsense to her, patting her neck as I ride.

I ride without purpose, wanting only to be outside and on the move: not to be in a room. When I visited Kathleen in our bedroom, I was full of joy and eagerness: and I shall soon be anxious to return to her. Yet now that I'm in the open air, I recall that once-familiar chamber as though escaping from something. It had become transformed: it was now a cavern of Gaea, where creation's awesome serums make the air dense with their odour; where the male draws back in dismay, in front of illimitable twilight.

Kathleen lay propped on the pillows, smiling at me. Her hair was brushed and her nightgown fresh, thanks to Bess and the midwife. Her eyes shone with feeling, and yet they appeared to be blind, since they were almost drained of colour: it was as though she gazed into a very bright light. We were alone together: the midwife had gone out and shut the door. The baby, wrapped in a blanket, was invisible, held in the crook of Kathleen's left arm. I paid it no heed but went straight across to her, bending to kiss her upturned face. Her right arm came up to encircle my neck; her

643

hand had been clutching her rosary beads, and now she put them by on the bedside table. I sat down in the chair beside the bed.

She was deathly white. I had expected it; but I had not been prepared for the degree of her pallor. Her face – this face that I never grow tired of studying – was reduced to its most essential lines, and looked almost transparent. The loving things we said I shall not record, even in these secret pages. I had discovered how precious she was to me: I gazed at her as though she had been restored to me from the dead, and stroked her hair.

With a movement that was both timid and proud, she opened the blanket and showed me the infant. At first I was disconcerted: the red, wizened face, whose eyes were closed, was so unformed. A mixture of pity and wonder filled me; I touched my son's cheek with one finger, while Kathleen smiled at me. Then I turned back to her, and asked her whether her asthma still troubled her.

She frowned, and drew a deep breath; as she did so, I could hear the rattling in her chest. She began to cough, turning away from the infant; the spasm shook her, but soon passed off. When she spoke, it was in a whisper.

– I'm sorry. The doctor has given me a medicine that makes me much better. You are not to worry.

I began to tell her that her asthma worried me greatly; but she shook her head.

– I will be all right. Are not your own attacks worse than mine?

We both laughed; but her laughter quickly turned into another bout of coughing. I put my arm about her shoulders until it passed, and she lay with closed eyes for a moment. Then she looked at me, and said:

– Will you not hold your son, Robert?

She had spoken above a whisper now, but her voice remained faint and low. She held up our son, in his blanket and long gown. Gingerly, I took the tiny creature in my hands, holding him like a parcel; as I did so, he began feebly to cry, his minute fists clenched, his face even redder. And an entirely unexpected emotion swept through me: a wave of yearning love for him. Suddenly I understood that I had a son in my hands, for whom I would have to care.

– He sounds like a creaky door, I said, and we both laughed again.

I gave the baby back to her; it was time for me to go, leaving her to nurse it. At the door I turned, and told her I'd soon return.

She was lying back on the pillows, smiling at me as she'd smiled when I first arrived; but now it seemed to me that her smile had grown weaker, that the emptying of the colour from her eyes had made them sightless discs, and that she drifted off in the arms of some dubious pleasure: one that took her strength, like a drug. The baby had ceased crying, and was fastened to her bared left breast, whose slope was traced with blue veins. In those few seconds, she bore very little resemblance to a healthy mother who gives her infant sustenance; instead, the infant appeared to be drawing her life from her, while the lids of her eyes grew tragic with fatigue.

I put the notion away, and hurried off to the stables.

May 14th

A letter from Paul Barry arrived for me at the New Norfolk post office today. It was posted at Ross, and is dated the 10th.

In it, Barry tells me that he intends to return his Ticket-of-Leave to the magistrate at Ross the next day. He will send it down from the Lakes by his passholding servant Brown, giving notice in a letter accompanying it of his immediate intention to escape. Brown is to post this farewell letter to me (and another to O'Neill), at the same time. That evening, Barry says, with the assistance of Michael Callaghan, he will attempt to begin his flight to the northern coast – dealing with whatever police opposition may show itself.

News of his escape also confronts me in the latest edition of the *Hobart Town Independent*.

The unsigned article was no doubt written by our old supporter Mr Davis – and the editor has adopted a tone of barely-concealed glee. He reports that the prisoner of state Paul Barry escaped on the 11th of this month, and asserts that in the opinion of the *Independent*, Barry has done so in a manner which preserves his honour – having resigned his Ticket-of-Leave and withdrawn his *parole* some five or six hours before making his departure. There are those who might say that Barry should have presented himself to a magistrate to withdraw his *parole* in person, Davis says – but surely this would be an objection which no fair-minded person could entertain. Barry gave the police every opportunity to arrest him. They failed; and there will be few who do not wish this gallant Irish gentleman well – since few agreed with the harshness of the sentence that exiled him from his native land. The article concludes by saying that many prominent settlers in the Campbell Town district will miss Mr Barry's company, and his infectious light-heartedness and wit.

The *Independent* also reports that an armed encounter occurred at night by the shores of Lake Sorell, as Barry made his escape. Four mounted constables had come up to the highlands to detain him; but Barry and an unknown group of supporters defied them. There was an exchange of fire; then Barry and his comrades rode off into the wilderness, and escaped. Fortunately, there was only one casualty in this affray: a constable wounded in the arm. The group supporting Barry has not been caught, and their identities remain unknown; since darkness effectively disguised them. Meanwhile, no-one knows whether Barry is still on Van Diemen's Land, or has escaped from the island by ship.

Here at my desk, I sit with my thoughts racing. I didn't anticipate this venture taking place so soon. Since the ship which will carry Barry to Melbourne will not be waiting off the island's northern coast until the 24th, I'd assumed that his journey from Lake Sorell would take place somewhat nearer to that time. But it has already begun, it seems, and is no doubt still in progress. He must cross a good deal of the island – a distance of a hundred and thirty miles or so – and the country he must pass through is very rough indeed. The Winter will make it even harsher.

I have read Barry's letter many times.

It combines sadness at our parting with his usual jaunty high spirits, and excitement at the leap he's about to take. He urges me to join him soon in New York. My pulses race as I read it, and my throat swells with grief and regret.

Midnight. The old wind of wilderness outside, searching and sighing through our valley, coming down from the grim Western

646

Tiers. How cold it must be in the mountains; how gloomy those miles of rain-wet bush that recede to the unknown west! Where is Barry tonight? Has he found a hearth in the home of some kindly Irish settlers? Or does he lie freezing out there, under the wings of this wind?

Yet why should I pity him? The wind sounds in my head like the wind of liberation: Barry's liberation, not mine.

Dear Paul, my pixy man, God speed and protect you!

May 21st

Two o'clock in the morning, and I cannot sleep.

I've come through to my study from the bedroom, closing the door so that the lamp on the desk won't wake Kathleen. Thomas is asleep in his crib, which stands on a trunk at the foot of our bed. From time to time he makes small snorting noises: sounds that are absurdly touching.

I have good reason for my sleeplessness. Kentucky Callaghan arrived here this evening, and lies sleeping in the guest bedroom next door. He brought news that has caused my thoughts to distract me ever since. Because of this news, I leave for Bridgewater at five o'clock this morning, to catch the day-coach for Launceston.

Callaghan came without warning, riding up the drive in a gig at six o'clock yesterday evening. He had travelled down to Bridgewater on the coach from Launceston, and had hired a servant at the Black Snake Inn to drive him up here. He brought news that Barry was safe: but he would not tell me more until after we had all dined together, and he and I had withdrawn to my study here alone. His insistence on secrecy seems extreme: but it's part of his manner of life, I suppose.

He sat in an armchair by the bookshelves; I sat sideways at my desk. He was tired from his journey, yet he still exuded a pent-up energy. There was a massiveness about him, with his big chest and shoulders: he made the room seem smaller. He lit a cigar and waved the match out; then he said abruptly:

– Barry's been wounded.

As I exclaimed, he raised a reassuring hand. But his expression was not reassuring.

– He ain't going to die, he said. But we still have to pray that he doesn't get worse. He's being hidden by some of our own: an old Irish farming couple called Mahoney. They have a little place at West Head, at the mouth of the Tamar – not far from Badger Head, where the ship will come in. Barry's tucked away in an attic. The arrangement still stands: the *Petrel* will be there three days from now. But whether Barry can board her depends on whether he gets well enough to travel around the coast.

I asked him just how badly Paul was hurt. I could not keep the anxiety from my voice, and he looked at me with a guarded expression.

– Well, it ain't good, he said. Though it seemed at first it was nothing. When we had that little shoot-out at Lake Sorell, a ball from a damned police rifle went through his thigh. It only went through the fleshy part, and hasn't done serious damage – but it caused him to lose a good deal of blood. As soon as we got away into the bush, I swabbed the wound with brandy, tore up a shirt and bound up his leg as best I could. Being Barry, he made pretty light of it – though I guess he was in some pain. And because it was only a flesh wound, neither of us worried too much. So then we started off on the ride to the coast.

I asked for details of this journey, which Callaghan now described with laconic brevity.

After the encounter with the police, the two young Irishmen whom Callaghan had recruited as troops had immediately returned to Hobart Town. Barry and he had then set out on the long ride off the plateau, accompanied by a guide: a bushman called Woods, whom they had paid to lead them through the wilderness to the lowlands. They were making for a hamlet there called Westbury. From Westbury, they would have only a day's ride to the coast, and Bass Strait. The district had many Irish settlers, and Callaghan had arranged sanctuary for Barry and himself on the farm of some loyal supporters: a family called Clancy.

On that first night, Woods took them towards the Lake River, riding through pitch-dark forests of towering stringybark gums, and down steep, dangerous mountainsides of broken and splintered rock. They came to the river late in the night, and were forced to camp on its banks in the bitter cold, lighting a fire and attempting to snatch some sleep on the rocky ground.

Next morning, they had breakfast in a shepherd's hut. Barry was now feverish and shivering; but they rode all that day to reach Westbury, arriving down there at dusk. That night they ate heartily and slept in warm beds; but Barry grew more and more ill, and the pain in his leg had increased. He never complained, Callaghan said, but he had begun to vomit, and his condition was clearly serious. Next day, Woods returned to Bothwell, and Barry and Callaghan stayed with the Clancys, resting their exhausted horses and hoping that Barry's condition would improve. They dared not leave the house by day, or even seek a doctor, since a warrant was out already for Barry's arrest, with a full description. Police were searching the district, they were told, and stations all along the coast were on the alert. Every boat that sailed from Van Diemen's Land was being searched, and had to be given clearance.

On the night of the 15th, Barry and Callaghan, accompanied by Mr Clancy and two of his sons, set out to ride to the coast under cover of dark. Passing through a land of dreary marshes, they came the next morning to the inlet of Port Sorell, where friends of the Clancys gave them shelter. On the following day the two of them set off alone, riding towards West Head and Port Dalrymple through an empty country of tea-tree and sand dunes. Within nine miles or so, they passed Badger Head, where the *Petrel* would rendezvous with Barry. A few miles further on, they came to the region of West Head: the bluff at the mouth of the Tamar, on its western shore.

The Mahoney farm was located on a rise above the Tamar's estuary, looking out over the river-mouth and the ocean. Below the rise lay sand dunes, and a long, curving beach. The district was called Green's Beach; but there were few signs of settlement. The estuary was wide: remote in the east, the opposite bluff called Low Head could just be made out, and the tower of a lighthouse. Over

649

there, ships passed by into the strait, after being cleared at a settle-ment called George Town; and there, the *Petrel* would be cleared. Then, instead of steering north into the strait, she would come west for her assignation with Barry.

Barry and Callaghan were welcomed by the Mahoneys – an old man and his wife who lived alone – and Barry was put to bed in their attic. He was now completely exhausted, and more feverish than ever; he had begun to be light-headed, and had barely been able to sit on his horse. He could no longer conceal the severity of the pain in his leg.

The next day, Callaghan borrowed a gig from old Mr Mahoney and drove to Launceston. The Mahoneys had recommended a trust-worthy Irish doctor there named Kennedy, who came back with Callaghan. He cauterised Barry's wound using a red-hot poker; then he dressed it, and ordered Barry to rest. He informed him that he had blood-poisoning, and that his situation was therefore quite dangerous. If care was not taken, he could develop gangrene. They could only wait and see.

Callaghan nodded, as I stared at him.

– Gangrene, he repeated. At best he'll lose the leg, if it sets in; and you know what the worst could be, Devereux. But Doctor Kennedy came back again and looked at the wound, and so far it's not got worse – so the doctor's quite hopeful. But the question is: will Paul be strong enough to get around the coast? Which brings me to the point. He's asking to see you.

– He wants me to go up there?

– He hopes you will. You and he are very close friends, ain't you? He'd greatly welcome it. He lies there in that attic, looking through the window at night towards the beam on Low Head – and he seems to drift away. I've never seen the dear old fellow so low. He's got three more days to wait, and he don't know whether he'll lose his leg or not – and even if he don't, whether he'll be strong enough to get to the *Petrel*.

– And you want me to help him do it?

That was exactly it, Callaghan said. He was hoping I would go up there without him, since Barry wanted to see me so badly. If I did, he would go on to Hobart Town instead, where he had other business to do. He suggested that I catch the morning coach to Launceston. I could then hire a boat to take me up the Tamar: there were plenty available.

– If Barry's well enough, he said, you can help him get away to the ship. And if not, you'll be there to console him. Will you do it?

I did not even pause to think. I would go, I told him.

But is it wrong of me to go?

Kathleen had a very bad asthma attack two nights ago. I sat up with her for hours, and began seriously to fear for her life. She's recovered – but Doctor Wilson tells me that her weakened condition from the birth makes such visits from the enemy very dangerous. My unease about this has done as much as Callaghan's visit to deprive me of sleep, and has sent me out here to my desk.

I told her of my intention to go north only after we had gone to bed.

– Go, she said. You must go to your friend since he needs you, and might even die. I know how fond you are of Paul Barry. You would never forgive yourself if you did not go.

– But I am worried about you.

– Don't be worried, my honey. Bess will look after me, and will send for Doctor Wilson if I am bad.

After I'd blown the candle out, we lay awake in the dark. Her face was upturned in profile, her eyes open, her hands folded on her breast. Suddenly, I saw that tears were on her cheeks. She was crying without a sound, and a pang went through me.

– I will not go, I said. You are truly not well enough for me to leave you.

She drew a shuddering breath, and turned her face towards me.

– It is not that. I will be all right. It's you, Robert. I'm thinking that those bastard English may capture you and Paul Barry both. Jesus help me, I could not bear that. I could not bear that you should be taken from me.

I reassured her, stroking her back. There would be no danger,

I said: Barry and I would be safe and secret enough in the Mahoneys' cottage. But I did not tell her that I would be going with him to the ship.

– Sure, I understand, she said. Go. *Go gcoinne Dia thú, a ghrá* – may God keep you. I will pray for you, so.

I held her in my arms until she went to sleep.

At West Head, on the Tamar
May 24th

Barry is gone. Free.

I write this by candlelight, at a miniature table, in the attic that sheltered him. Here I spend tonight, before returning south.

He did recover: the wound became clean, and no gangrene developed. When I arrived here, I found him weak but in good spirits, joking about his escape from spending his life on a wooden leg, and apologising for bringing me all this way without cause. But he was plainly very glad to see me, and both of us were full of a wistful joy.

It's a very small attic indeed here, with its pine walls and ceiling – a ceiling that slopes inches above my head. I understand now why Barry spent so much time at the window, looking out over the river's mouth. I have been doing the same: watching the racing waves on the beach, their lines breaking white in the dark; watching the far-off beam of the lighthouse on Low Head, which seems to search the darkness for Barry.

He's gone, our mercurial Paul: gone beyond the reach of Governor Denison and his gaolers; gone from this island prison. He sleeps on the *Petrel* tonight, far out on Bass Strait. And as is the case with all voyagers, his spirit will be winging ahead of his body, to hover in advance above his destination.

He is in America already.

The boat heeled over in the gale, and Barry and I clung hard to the gunwale on the weather side.

The craft we had hired was a crude, twenty-foot fishing boat, fitted with two pairs of oars and a patched, flimsy-looking gaff-rigged sail. It was owned by two brothers named Baxter: fishermen on the Tamar, and friends of the Mahoneys: tall, fair men with peaceful, stolid faces, whom Barry would pay well for their service. They had agreed to take us around to the beach under Badger Head where the *Petrel* would lie off-shore; then they would ferry Barry out to board her. When we left, at eight in the morning, the weather had been calm; but as soon as we came around West Head and into the open sea, an icy south-westerly blew up.

We found ourselves bucking through a squall: the choppy, foaming water wetting us through, the boat almost standing on its side. Barry seemed to enjoy it; he laughed and sang as the spray wet his face. The Baxters steered west along the coast, which was rugged and uninhabited and clothed with sombre bush. They had to keep tacking, and their tactic was to take the boat before the wind, north-west into Bass Strait, and then come back towards the shore in the teeth of the gale. Shouting, they explained that we faced two possible difficulties: being blown on to the lee shore, or being taken far out to sea. The second danger was the worst, since the seas in Bass Strait were treacherous, and had destroyed many small boats.

But neither of these things happened. A final tack into the wind brought us at last in sight of Badger Head, and carried us in to a quiet beach. The waves were low enough here for the brothers to bring the boat on to the sand with no trouble; the wind had died down a good deal, and the sky was a cold blue, with high, racing clouds. The place was as empty of settlement as it had no doubt been throughout time: nothing here but great granite rocks, dunes, and the curious low trees called boobialla, with their shining, bottle-green, rubbery leaves. Gulls wheeled and cried, and there was no other sound but the breeze. We made a signal fire, for the *Petrel* to know we were here; then we sat in front of it, trying to get dry. Barry took out a flask of rum and handed it about, and the Baxter brothers drank, wiped their mouths, and sighed appreciatively. Then, with a tact surprising in such men, they withdrew to the other side of the fire, murmuring to each other, leaving Barry and me to our farewells. He looked at me and laughed, as he'd done in the midst of the gale – his spirits like a reflection of the high, running clouds and bright blue air.

– Just as well we met no police boats, I said. You still look like a dandy, Barry.

The blue pea-jacket, fustian trousers and heavy boots he wore as a disguise were somehow not convincing: he made even these clothes look stylish, and his cap with its glazed peak was set at a jaunty angle. The only luggage he was carrying to New York was a small valise.

We talked feverishly, knowing that at any moment our talk might be ended. What did we speak of? I scarcely remember: of little things, mostly, while we watched the headland where the steamer must appear. Barry's tone was somewhat languid, so that something of his old foppishness returned. He had still not got back all his strength – though he seemed to be recovering by the hour. He spoke of New York, and of how he would set up a newspaper there; and a claw gripped my vitals. Meeting his smile, so full of careless certainty, I was affected for the last time by the expression of his gaze – that look both whimsical and eerily distant, making one believe that Barry is somehow invulnerable to the doubt and sorrow and hurt that are the lot of other human beings. And I wanted irrationally to detain him: to simply cry: *Stay!*

No doubt Mary McCormack had cried that word aloud, before he left Ross, and had seen in those restless, light blue eyes another expression altogether: the hardness of a spirit that insists on its freedom, no matter what the cost.

– I believe they are taking bets on me in Hobart Town, he said. Which ship I've caught; when I've left the island, and so on. You could make some money, my boy.

Then, surveying the landscape behind the beach, he said:

– Look at it. Queer; this place is so queer. One might almost be back in the coal age. I can scarcely believe that soon I'll be gone from it.

– But you will, I said. And then it will be like a bad dream.

– Damn it, Robert, why must you stay inside the dream? Why not come with me?

His smile had never been more joyful or more challenging, and I saw that he half meant it.

– Don't ask me that, I said. Or I may jump into the boat.

He looked quickly into my face, and saw the pain there. Then I laughed, and he joined in, and both of us pretended that a joke had been made. He reached out and put his hand on my shoulder.

– I should not have said that, he said. Even in jest. Forgive me, my dear boy. You'll follow; don't doubt it. You'll soon be there, in New York, you and your love and your baby: I know it. But I'd give anything –

He broke off, his eyes looking past me and widening. He didn't need to speak; I turned, and saw the steamer coming around the headland, a column of smoke rising from her tall black funnel.

I didn't go out to her with him. I stood on the beach and watched the Baxters row him out, ploughing and bucking through the waves. He sat in the stern, looking back; he waved his cap to me, his pale hair fluttering in the wind. He rose high and then plunged down, as white plumes of spray exploded all around him. There was something triumphant about it, something magnificent; and in my head, I heard him singing.

Turning, I looked with revulsion at the granite rocks of savagery; at the pale tussock grass; at the glinting boobialla trees.

The landscape droned and droned. The monotony of its droning enveloped me like a cloud, and I cried in my heart: *Come back!*

But the droning went on, and entered my head, and I knew myself marooned.

I turned and walked away up the beach, hands in pockets against the cold, my thoughts turning to Kathleen.

I think of her now, in this attic; I see her vivid gaze, lit with humour and with love. Gladness flows back into me, like the warmth from a draught of liquor. She waits; and as long as she does, no despair can claim me.

At 'Clare'
May 27th

Kathleen is dead.

She died on the night of the 25th, as I rode down on the coach from Launceston. I can write no more.

May 28th

She is dead. Her funeral will be on Sunday at St Peter's, where she went to Mass. I have spoken with the priest there, whose name is O'Dea. He believes she was simply a servant in our household, and I have let him continue to believe it. I have no wish to encounter some notion of her having died in mortal sin. She will have a good Catholic funeral: I am determined on that.

It was a pity, Father O'Dea said, that she could not have had the last rites. Bess tells me that Kathleen asked for this priest, but there was no time; she died only minutes later.

I was not here. I was not here.

I can write no more.

May 29th

Langford told me. He was waiting at Bridgewater when the Launceston coach came in, at seven in the morning.

As we'd come into the south, I had thought with gladness of Kathleen and our son. I had pictured her embrace, and her quick, humorous smile with closed lips, and her head cocked on one side to look at me. Now I shall picture it all my life.

It was frosty when we crossed the bridge over the Derwent. Pink paths of dawn lay across the river, which was dotted with dozens of black swans. Coming on to the road, we passed the crouching, abandoned stone convict station, and turned up the drive to the Black Snake Inn, on its rise above the highway. Langford sat in the gig near the top of the drive, erect and still as a soldier in a sober grey frock coat and his best white felt hat.

I knew immediately that something was wrong: it would normally have been Richardson who met me here. As the coach rolled by, James looked up at me through the window with a steady, serious gaze. I smiled and waved: he raised his hand, but did not smile back.

It was then that a chill gripped my bowels.

We sat side by side in the gig. The reins were in his hands, but he did nothing to start the horse. We sat there, and he told me. As he spoke, he stared out over the steely, pink-stained river, and I

656

saw that his eyes were bloodshot from lack of sleep. Then he turned and looked at me.

– We done all we could, he said. Bess and me.

At first, I said nothing. Then I began to question him, gripping his arm so that he winced, scarcely knowing what I said. Could nothing more have been done? Why had Doctor Wilson not been there? Why? Why?

– Now hear me speak a word, he said, and his voice was soft. It came on sudden, like I told you, Robert. Kathleen came to our bedroom near midnight, coughing so bad she couldn't speak. I drove for that doctor as fast as I could, and brought him back – but by then she was gone. Bess had been with her all the time. She gave her the Stramonium, and balsam to inhale, but it didn't ease it for long. She went very quick, Bess said. She couldn't breathe: she just couldn't breathe, poor girl. Ask Bess. You do trust *her*, don't you?

His eyes held mine, daring me to disbelieve him. Then he raised his fist, holding it close to my face.

– I'd have cut off this hand to save her for you, he said.

– I believe you, I said. I believe you. Forgive me, James: I wasn't here.

Then I began to weep, and he reached out and took my hand, gripping it hard. I tried to stop, embarrassed by the sounds I was making. But I could not; and the more I wept, the harder his calloused hand gripped mine.

So we sat, in the gig, in front of the Black Snake Inn, with no-one about to see us but a stable-hand, who was walking around to the back of the inn with a saddle over his shoulder. And now its sombre gables and high, dim verandah took on a new significance. There are certain buildings that warn us of disaster: of entrapment, or of a guilt like damnation. It's as though we are fated to ruin our lives for ever in their shadow, or within their cunning rooms. The Black Snake Inn was such a building. It had waited for me; now it watched my life drain itself of joy.

༄

At Jacob Lenoir's Bookshop, Hobart Town
July 19th

I am lying on the storage platform under the ceiling, directly above Lenoir's desk. The bookshop holds me prisoner. They are searching for me all through the city.

Four o'clock: I've just heard the chimes of St David's. They rang loudly in my head – louder than was natural. Voices below in the shop and the clattering of hoofs in the street also resound oddly in my brain. I am not well; but what it is that is wrong with me I neither know nor care.

Lenoir has taken the ladder away and concealed it, so that it will not occur to anyone that this platform can easily be reached, or to see it as anything but a storage space. Or at least, this is what he and I hope. When I lie down, I'm hidden from the shop below by a wall of boxes and books. I can actually stand upright if I wish to, my head coming within inches of the grimy, green-painted boards of the ceiling – but this I refrain from doing, as far as possible, for fear of being sighted by a customer.

The old bookseller has made me a little nest up here, where I can read and sleep and write. I recline in my shirt on an old, some-what lumpy palliasse, covered by two blankets and a possum-skin rug. I'm glad of these, since the mid-winter evening grows freezing; rain can be heard through the ceiling, lashing the shingle roof. My face is hot, but my hands are cold as ice: I'm gripped by regular bouts of shivering. On a soap box placed beside me are a candle in a bottle, a flask of water, and a copy of Charles Dickens' latest novel, which reached Lenoir recently from London. Monsieur Lenoir also brought me a cup of camomile tea not long ago, for my feverishness. I'm touched by all this – but touched in a way that is dull and unreal, as though my feelings are those of someone else, which I observe but fail to share. Even my gratitude at his sheltering me has the same numbed quality.

This has been my state for these past two months: ever since Kathleen's death. I must learn to convince people that the man they are dealing with has the normal human emotions, and is in fact alive – when in every way that matters, he has ceased to live. Life has become as jarring and inconsequential as the voices of the customers below; meaningless as the noises in the town.

These sounds now drift to me from a long way off – yet it's vital that I heed them. I must prick up my ears in order to survive, like an animal fleeing its predators.

All I've brought away with me is a single portmanteau, which stands at the foot of my palliasse. It contains some essential clothing, my diaries, my translations of Aeschylus and Theocritus, my revolver, and some ammunition.

All else is left behind.

My infant son is left behind, in the care of Bess Langford.

I've made gifts of my possessions to the Langfords: my library, my furniture, and Fleur-de-lis, whom Langford has promised to treat with special care. Her rack will never lack hay, he said; oats will always fill her manger.

I write to keep myself awake, since my fever brings me dreams. The voices from the shop get into these dreams, and other voices as well: voices which hector and accuse. Their owners are faceless and unknown, yet I believe in my dream that they're actually present, in this apple-green gloom near the ceiling: should I open my eyes, they would stand here to confront me. And indeed, when I do wake, faces and shapes from these phantasies seem to flee and dissolve among the boxes.

Three days ago, at six o'clock on a cold, clear evening, I boarded the stage coach for Hobart Town, in front of the Black Snake Inn. I was dressed as a Catholic priest, in an outfit obtained from Father Brennan: broad black hat, long black overcoat, *soutane* underneath, narrow white band about the neck. I was also quite clean-shaven.

There were two other men inside the coach. One was a stockman, in pea jacket and rough cord trousers. The other, seated directly opposite me, in a good grey tail coat and round hat, was Mr Harrington: a gentleman farmer from New Norfolk, who owns the largest hop garden on the banks of the Derwent. I had recently been introduced to him by Langford, in the main street of the town; James consulted him on hop varieties. I glanced at him, and found him glancing back at me. My heart thudded: if he recognised me, I was lost.

But no recognition showed in his face. He politely looked away, and I did the same. My absurd disguise was effective, it seemed. I took deep, careful breaths, in my corner by the window, watching the cobweb-coloured gables and dark, sly verandah of the Black Snake Inn recede for ever, as we swayed down the drive in the twilight.

– Are you posted to a parish in Hobart Town, Father?

A throaty, pompous voice. I turned my head swiftly, to find Mr Harrington leaning forward and smiling at me, his knees almost touching mine.

– Yes, I said, I shall be working in Hobart Town.

I spoke with a Jesuit's cold reserve, hoping that Mr Harrington had failed to notice that this clerical gentleman had brought no luggage on board. He was looking at me with vacuous insistence, smiling and plump-cheeked.

– I know your bishop well, he said. A fine man; a fine man. I'm an Anglican, of course; but I admire his qualities.

I agreed that the bishop was indeed a fine man, and took out a breviary from a pocket of my soutane and began pointedly to read it. A reassuring weight was in another inner pocket: my Colt revolver. In that moment, I told myself that I would shoot this fool Harrington if he recognised me, and flee the coach. Whether I would have done so, I'm now inclined to doubt; but fortunately, Harrington gave up his attempts at conviviality, and still showed no sign of suspicion. We rolled beside the river in silence.

I closed my eyes. A great deal had happened today, and this was the first time I'd sat still. So far, everything had gone successfully.

At nine o'clock that morning, mounted on Fleur-de-lis, I'd ridden in to New Norfolk from 'Clare', accompanied by Kentucky Callaghan. The puddles beside the road were still iced over, and the stalks of oat-pale grass looked stiff with cold. We rode side by side, speaking very little, our horse's hoofs clicking in the bright, early silence by the river. Kentucky had arrived at the farm the previous evening, and had once again stayed the night. He was mounted on a fine grey horse which he'd ridden up from Hobart Town: a part-

Arab called Hector, capable of great speed, lent to him by an Irish supporter in the city who knew what Hector would be required to do today. We were both armed. My Colt was concealed in the breast pocket of my riding coat; Callaghan wore the latest Colt Dragoon in a holster under his cape.

My inner state was odd. I knew very well that we might soon be using these weapons, but I contemplated the fact with indifference: the indifference I feel towards all things now. I rode frozen through a frozen, silent landscape, caring little whether I lived or died; whether I killed or was killed. And I carried in an inner pocket a copy of a letter as potentially dangerous as my revolver, which I had posted yesterday to Sir William Denison. Its contents were brief and to the point:

New Norfolk, 15th July, 1851

TO SIR WILLIAM DENISON,
LIEUTENANT-GOVERNOR OF VAN DIEMEN'S LAND
SIR,
    I hereby resign the 'Ticket-of-Leave' your Government has bestowed on me, and withdraw my parole. I intend to present myself immediately to the police magistrate of New Norfolk, Mr Whitford, to provide him with a copy of this note, and to give him the opportunity to take me into custody.

      Your obedient servant,
       ROBERT DEVEREUX

We dismounted in front of the police office in Bathurst Street: a plain brick cottage with a narrow verandah in front. Small groups of people were on the street: women in bonnets carrying baskets; old men gossiping outside the blacksmith's shop; boys and dogs dodging about the road, their breath steaming. A spring-wagon lurched by, filled with potatoes. We tethered our horses to the verandah rail: my hands were so cold that I was scarcely able to knot the reins. An armed constable stood on guard by the door as usual, in his belted, dark-blue uniform: he saluted me and greeted me by name, having seen me here often, when I reported to Mr Whitford. Most people in the town knew me now; since the episode of Daniel O'Donnell, I'd become quite popular with the constabulary.

We walked down the hall towards the courtroom, passing on the way one of the town's leading merchants, Mr Grant: a white-haired, decent old Scottish gentleman who is friendly with both myself and Langford. He greeted me, and looked curiously at Callaghan. We did not pause, but went on into the courtroom, each of us carrying his riding whip. The place smelled of furniture oil and documents; a low fire burned in the grate. The police magistrate was seated at his big cedar desk. Near him, at a smaller desk, the police clerk Mr Jenkins sat writing: a short, sandy man in spectacles whom I'd never heard say a word. The room was otherwise empty.

I marched straight across to Mr Whitford, who looked up at me and smiled. He too had become quite warmly disposed to me, and suspected nothing wrong. He was one of those men who become somewhat vague in their late middle age: a tall, stooped Englishman with a long grey moustache and watery blue eyes. He owned a little farm up the Derwent, and often spoke to me of rural matters.

I bade him good morning, and handed him the copy of the letter, already open.

– Good morning to you, Mr Devereux, he said. Cold, very cold, is it not? What's this? Hm? Something you want me to read?

– It's a copy of a letter I've sent to Sir William Denison, I said. Yes, sir: I believe you should read it.

He put on his spectacles and surveyed the letter, brows raised in polite enquiry. Then he began to frown. He said nothing, but turned his eyes next on Callaghan, clearly wondering who this man was and what he did here. Kentucky stood close behind me; he had pushed back his cape and his coat, exposing his pistol in its holster. His fingers tapped delicately on the walnut grip.

– As you see, Mr Whitford, I said, I have resigned my Ticket-of-Leave. And this means that the promise I gave is now revoked. My *parole* now ends – and I am giving you the opportunity to take me into custody, sir.

But Mr Whitford was still looking at Callaghan, mesmerised, apparently, by my comrade's tapping fingers. Mr Jenkins, at his small, schoolboy's desk, sat motionless, his pen suspended, regarding us both through his spectacles with a sort of respectful horror. There was a silence, as though some appalling mistake had been made: a mistake that might still be remedied. From out in the street, a boy's sudden shout floated in. With curious reluctance, Mr Whitford looked back at me.

– What? he said. You wish me to do what? You must have gone mad, Mr Devereux. And who *is* this gentleman, pray?

– A friend, I said. His name is of no importance.

Mr Whitford seemed bewildered; and I sensed that he wished to deny to himself what was happening. I expected that he would shout for a constable; but he did not. Still he remained seated at his desk, and so did Mr Jenkins. The clerk looked no longer at us, but somewhere out the window; perhaps he hoped that we would simply disappear, like figures from a stage.

– You don't wish to arrest me? Very well, I said. Then I bid you good morning, Mr Whitford.

I put my hat back on, and Kentucky did the same. We turned, and walked towards the door. It was only when we reached it, not looking back, that we heard Mr Whitford's quavering shout behind us.

– Stay! Stay! I order you to stay! Constables! Duncan, there! Skeggs!

We walked quickly down the hall. I looked over my shoulder; Mr Whitford had emerged from the courtroom, and a constable had appeared. Mr Whitford was shouting at him, pointing, ordering him to arrest us, in the Queen's name. But the man seemed to follow with great reluctance, making no attempt to overtake us. Out of the corner of my eye, I saw that Callaghan now had his pistol in his hand, and knew that the constable had seen this too. But this was not the sole reason he merely pretended to pursue: I was convinced of that now.

They don't wish to take us, I thought.

What followed seemed to bear this out. We emerged onto the verandah, where the constable by the door still stood erect as a sentry. He watched us hurry by, his expression one of slow, bemused interest. We were mounted in seconds, and went at full gallop down the street: Callaghan in front, on his big grey horse, cape flying, whip rising and falling. The boys playing in the road

663

laughed and pointed, as though we rode a race; some farm workers on the footpath did the same. It was all just a game to them – some sort of gentlemen's prank, without any penalty: certainly not Port Arthur. Ex-felons most of them, they loved to see the police made fools of, and there would be no-one who would try and obstruct us. Dreamlike, receding, Mr Whitford's high old cries and the confused shouts of the constables sounded faintly in my ears. Callaghan looked back over his shoulder and waved me to go faster, and I urged Fleur on with the whip in a way I'd never done before, bent low over her neck, the wildness of flight and the prospect of freedom filling me with a shadowy elation.

There was little need for the speed we showed, since there seemed to be no mounted pursuit. But we couldn't be sure that it would not materialise, and we flogged our horses hard, following out Callaghan's plan. In minutes, we had reached the edge of the town, and were crossing a high wooden bridge to the eastern bank of the Derwent, the hollow drumming of our horses' hoofs filling the air like cannon-fire. Once across, we turned south, following a track beside the river, and entered the shelter of the bush. Soon we were riding into those tall, thickly wooded hills that rose on the river's eastern shore.

Deep in the gum forest, some miles from the town, we reined in for a moment in a gully. We sat listening, while our horses sweated and panted. There were no sounds of pursuit: no distant voices, no hoofs. The scent of the gums was the odour of refuge, and the carolling of magpies a welcome. I put out my hand, and Kentucky gripped it and smiled. But we didn't pause for long. Moving on south, always out of sight of the Derwent and habitation, we rode for perhaps an hour, seeking out the home of an ally: a poor Irish farmer called Rooney.

This man was a patriot to whom Callaghan had been directed by supporters in Hobart Town. Kentucky had visited his farm yesterday, making the arrangements which would enable us to complete our escape. We came to the place on a green stretch of hillslope that was partially cleared of bush; through the trees, a bend of the Derwent could be glimpsed. The Rooney dwelling was the

664

usual slab-built cottage common among small farmers; as we rode up, some half a dozen children came out to stare at us. Then Rooney himself emerged from the doorway: a strongly-built man with a mop of black hair, a shotgun under his arm. When he recognised us, he smiled, and put the gun aside. His wife, appearing beside him, was clearly in her best: a dress with an embroidered collar, and a knitted shawl.

We dismounted, and Rooney and one of his sons took the reins of our horses. Rooney held out his hand to me, and his eyes shone.

– It's an honour to have you in my house, sir: an honour to be helping a hero.

I should have felt pleasure; instead, I felt ashamed. I wanted to tell him that he was wrong: that Robert Devereux was no hero, but a man who had left the woman he loved in the church-yard in New Norfolk. But I thanked him as warmly as I could, and went on into the house.

There, watched by two little boys, I stood in the kitchen over a basin of hot water, a small, dim mirror on a shelf in front of me, and proceeded to shave off my moustache with Rooney's razor. After that, I was conducted into the bedroom, where I changed into the priest's costume that had been donated by Father Brennan, and brought here by Callaghan yesterday – together with a stockman's outfit with which Kentucky intended to disguise himself. The clothing that we removed was stowed in our empty saddle-bags, together with bottles of ale and some bread and cheese, pressed on us by the Rooneys. Then, having drunk a glass of whiskey with Rooney and his wife, and having toasted them and thanked them many times, Callaghan and I rode southwards again, coming at last to the village of Bridgewater, on the Derwent's eastern side.

Here, on a knoll outside the village, sheltered by a grove of trees, we hid until sunset, drinking our bottled ale. The weather remained clear, with no rain. We could view the long bridge from our knoll, and the distant Black Snake Inn on the western bank, where I would catch the seven o'clock coach to Hobart Town. Callaghan, meanwhile, would return to 'Clare' with the horses, and come on to Hobart Town tomorrow. That evening, we would board the *Southern Queen*: a regular passenger brig bound for Sydney. And in Sydney, on August 15th, he and I would board the *Eliza Jane* together – an American barque bound for San Francisco.

When the time was up, and sunset coloured the river, we rode across the bridge: a nondescript stockman and a priest. A farmer in a dray stared after us curiously, but we were not challenged. On the other side, I was forced to farewell my little Fleur-de-lis, who had carried me to freedom today. Kentucky wished me luck, and set off up the New Norfolk road, mounted on Hector and leading Fleur behind. I stood and watched them go, a grief inside me that weighted my veins like lead. Callaghan was leading away the last living fragment of a life I might have lived; of a happiness I had never been prepared to accept, and which was now destroyed.

I was leaving my son with the Langfords, to be reared as their own until I cared to send for him. Bess had always wanted more children; she was already deeply attached to Thomas, and I was confident that he was better off with her and James than he was likely to be with me, in the foreseeable future. Meanwhile, I set down here what I have told to no-one: that since Kathleen's death, I have scarcely been able to look at him. I do not of course blame this innocent little creature for her death; but the fact remains that she died because she bore him, as surely as though she had died in childbirth. When I looked at him, I was visited by a double pain: the anguish of knowing that he had cost my dearest her life; and guilt at my inability to love him.

No doubt this will pass, some day, and he will join me in America. But not yet.

Now, with an effort, teeth clenched, I forced myself to walk across the road, and to move up the drive to the Black Snake Inn: a lone priest in a broad black hat, unencumbered by baggage.

It was dark when the coach drew up in Collins Street, outside the familiar Ship Inn. Bidding a muttered farewell to Mr Harrington, I stepped down onto the footpath and paused. Rain had begun, and I turned up the collar of my black clerical overcoat.

The usual crowd was gathered there: groups of travellers; idlers watching the arrival and departure of the mail coaches. I was looking for a gentleman I didn't know, and who was to have been here to meet me. His name was John Connell, and Callaghan had told me that he would be wearing a white rose in his buttonhole. Mr Connell was the agent in Hobart Town for Terence Paterson – a wealthy Irish shipowner in Sydney who is a passionate supporter of Young Ireland, an admirer of mine, and one of the New York Directory's loyal Australian allies. The *Southern Queen* was a Paterson ship, and Callaghan, on a visit to Sydney last month, had stayed at Mr Paterson's home there, arranging all the details of my escape.

A plan had been devised to avoid my being discovered by the port authorities. The agent would shelter me tonight in his own home, in the suburb of Sandy Bay, a few miles down the estuary of the Derwent. The following evening, after the brig had been cleared and had sailed, she would move down the estuary and lie off Sandy Bay in the darkness, where Connell himself would row me out to her, and smuggle me aboard. Kentucky Callaghan, since the authorities had no evidence against him of wrongdoing, would have boarded her openly at the New Wharf, and would travel under his own name. I would travel under the name of Mr Brown.

But I could not see a gentleman with a white rose in his lapel. I lingered, looking about me; then I heard my name called. I turned to find a priest at my elbow, dressed almost identically to myself. It was Father Kevin Brennan, and his expression was a curious one: it warned me not to speak.

He took my arm, and told me to come away with him. He led me off up Collins Street; then, when we were well away from the lights of the Ship, he stopped and drew me into a doorway.

– John Connell could not come, he said. The plan is blown sky-high.

St David's clock again, striking half-past six.

I stopped writing here about ten minutes ago: as soon as I did so, a cloud entered my brain, and I began to descend into dream.

But I can't afford to dream. Kathleen will come to me, as she came last night.

Voices down in the shop. A customer, to Lenoir:

– These volumes of Gibbon, sir. You have marked them at two guineas. Do you really want such a price?

– That is why I marked them so, my dear sir. If you want cheap rubbish, you may go to one of the stalls in the street.

A snort of outrage, and departing footsteps; I smile, and pick up the new Charles Dickens novel again, whose title is *David Copperfield*.

I find it quite affecting. There is a portrait of childish love in it between David Copperfield and the small, orphaned daughter of a Yarmouth fisherman – a girl called little Em'ly – which is perfectly sentimental and cloying, if one looks at it with the eye of maturity. But Mr Dickens has a genius for making one see things through the eyes of childhood; and seen through those eyes, little Em'ly has great charm, and a melancholy, teasing mystery. I find my mind dwelling on her, this bereft, gentle child of humble fisher-folk; I grow quite lachrymose, and I want to cry out to David Copperfield: *Cling to her; never abandon her; never let her go!*

Is this too part of my illness – this easy, silly emotion?

I drifted again just now, and dreamed. The dream of last night returned.

Kathleen came. She stood at the glass doors of our bedroom, and knocked on the pane with no sound. She was wearing her white night-gown, and hugged herself, shivering. I opened the doors, and a piercing wind came in from the verandah, going to the marrow of my bones. She looked up at me, her oblique eyes so pale they appeared almost blind; they looked through me, not seeing my self at all. Her lips were bent upwards by her quick, closed-mouthed smile: not truly a smile any longer, but a grimace of infinite sadness.

– *Ah, Robert*, she said. *Will you not take me into bed? Will you not keep me warm?*

I could not: my arms were paralysed. I wanted to hold her, to warm her: I wanted to take in my arms that body I adored. I could not; and I woke to find myself groaning.

I was not there, when she fought for life. Would she have fought harder to breathe, had I been leaning over her?

I was not there.

And I am guilty of much more. Dying before I married her, she believed herself to be in a state of sin; and she died without a last Confession. Did she see Purgatory waiting for her? Is that the final punishment that my pride has brought upon her? I should have made myself petition the hated Denison for permission to marry her. I know that, now: too late.

Lying on this platform, with its freezing, fugitive draughts, its odours of mildewed books and the droppings of rats and mice, I see her whenever I close my eyes.

Walking beside me, she laughs and holds my hand and glances sideways, her eyes narrowed, their light mingling humour and love.

She advances across the yard in her pregnancy, rocking as she walks, her face pink and glowing with a phantom good health.

She is seized by a bout of coughing, lying in bed. Panting, recovering her breath, she softly says: *Oh, dear.* It is said to herself, in her extremity; low and despairing, yet resigned and unprotesting: *Oh, dear.* And a pang goes through my heart that I can scarcely bear.

She follows me up the hill behind the pickers' huts, on that walk when I failed to wait for her. She dwindles among the gold-lit, pallid bush grass: short-legged as a child, head tilted jauntily in its peaked straw hat, smiling across the space between us. Then she stops, her hand on her chest, and begins to cough. She calls after me, frowning, her high voice infinitely distant. And now I'm filled with remorse, and a fear that she is left behind for ever. Still she calls after me, across that space of gold grass, and I cannot turn around and go back to her. I clench my hands until they hurt; I open my eyes, and call her name aloud.

She lies in the small Catholic cemetery in New Norfolk, behind St Peter's church. Bess will take flowers each week to her grave; the headstone cut to my orders is simple but fine. Her loved body begins to decay; yet her spirit comes each night, knocking at the closed glass doors.

When I cross fifteen thousand miles of sea, and when I reach at last the lost, other hemisphere of my ancestry – then will these dreams stop? Then will I cease to weep?

On the night of my arrival in Hobart Town, I spoke with Father Kevin Brennan about the state of Kathleen's soul. Or rather, I questioned him about the Church's view of her soul, since I had no fears for it myself.

After he had met me at the coach, Father Brennan had taken me to his presbytery in Patrick Street. I could shelter here, he told me, until a new plan for escape was made. Michael Callaghan would be sure to come visiting us tomorrow evening: as soon as he spoke with John Connell he would learn where I was, and how I had been betrayed. No doubt he would form some new plan to get me away. Meanwhile, I must hide myself here. I was welcome to the bedroom on the upper floor which had sheltered Liam Kinane.

That evening after supper, Father Brennan and I sat on each side of the fire in his parlour. We drank sherry, and ate small round biscuits. The atmosphere was ecclesiastical but comfortable. Above the fireplace hung an oil painting of the Virgin and child – an indifferent copy of a Raphael – and Father Brennan's missal sat on a polished table by his elbow, together with the plate of biscuits. I must have looked quite in harmony here, since I was still clad in my soutane. My portmanteau had been sent ahead from 'Clare' to John Connell's shipping office in the city, and was being held for me to collect tomorrow; meanwhile, I had no other clothing or personal effects. We must have made an odd pair, Brennan and I: the true priest and the false one.

I found myself speaking to him about Kathleen, without having intended to do so. Perhaps priests invite confession – even from Protestants. Father Brennan watched me across the fire in silence, in the manner that priests have: his face a pleasant mask, neither sympathetic nor unsympathetic. He bit delicately into a biscuit, and some crumbs fell on his soutane.

I asked for his tolerance, I said; I was something of a heretic in my personal beliefs, and did not expect him to agree with them. Although I believed in God, I took a different view of Him from the orthodox Christian one. It was not my belief that a merciful God would wish to punish Kathleen for living with me out of wedlock, nor for giving birth to our child, when we had loved each other dearly, and had been determined to marry. But Kathleen had of course believed otherwise, as a Catholic, and this troubled me. I wanted to know that she had not died in a state of dread, believing she was going to some fearsome region of punishment.

As I spoke, I became conscious that my voice was no longer even, and that I was occasionally twisting my hands together, in an effort to control my emotions. Father Brennan watched me, pulling at his sidewhiskers, saying nothing until I had done. Then he sat in thought. The fire was hot; he drew out a handkerchief and mopped his bald head. I began to be aware that he was uncomfortable. His face had lost its comical, humorous look: he was no longer the jolly little priest who had caroused with us at the Lakes. When he answered me, his voice was almost toneless.

– I understand entirely that a man like yourself would hate going cap in hand to the English authorities here for permission to marry. But you have asked me to be frank, Robert, and I must tell you that it would have been better for Kathleen's sake had you swallowed your pride and done so. Since you are not a Catholic – nor even a dutiful Protestant, by your own admission – you are possibly overlooking the seriousness with which my Church regards this sin. It is a mortal sin, and your Kathleen knew this. It's a thousand pities that she didn't have the chance for a last Confession, and the last rites.

– Are you saying to me that she died thinking that she would go to Purgatory? Even Hell?

My voice had risen in spite of myself, and he looked at me guardedly. What he saw in my face seemed to trouble him. He shook his head, and spoke now in a soothing tone.

– Never Hell, no, I am not saying that, Devereux. And only God knows what our fate will be after death. You tell me that she was a devout Catholic: so it's likely, when she knew she was dying, that she said an Act of Contrition, and offered God her repentance. In that case, He will have taken her to Himself. That is what I think likely – and it is also what you should think.

He brushed away the biscuit crumbs, and took a small sip of sherry.

– And the baby? he asked. What is to happen to your son? Why are you escaping just now, and leaving him here?

– I am escaping now because this may be the only opportunity I have – and I cannot bear to stay, with Kathleen gone. Nor can I bear to take charge of the child that cost her her life – even though he is my son. Bess Langford will be a good mother to him. Eventually, when I'm established in America, and he has grown a little older, Thomas will come to me – always providing that I succeed in this escape. I shan't be taken alive, Father. I prefer to die; in which case the Langfords are happy to adopt him.

– Don't speak so, Robert. Do not even think in this way.

He stood up, placing a small hand on my shoulder. It seemed to have less weight than other men's hands. Then he walked over to the fire and turned, looking down at me.

– You will have him baptised a Catholic? he asked. Kathleen would have wanted that.

I shook my head.

– He has already been christened in the Anglican church in New Norfolk, which the Langfords attend. They arranged it, and I was happy to agree, since they may have charge of him for some time. And after all, I am a Protestant, Father – however negligent.

– Ah, he said.

He closed his eyes, as though at a small stab of pain. Then he opened them again, and released a small sigh of resignation. He said nothing else for a time, but stared down at me: round-eyed, round-faced and inscrutable. Then he said softly:

– I shall pray for your Kathleen. I shall offer up a Mass for her. I shall pray for you too, Robert, since I see that your spirit is shipwrecked. You must not despair.

Slowly and carefully, as though administering some life-giving medicine, he poured more sherry into my glass.

The next afternoon, Kentucky Callaghan arrived at the presbytery, looking over his shoulder as he came through the front door.

He stood in the parlour with Brennan and me, refusing to sit down, telling us that he had no time to linger. He turned his big white hat in his hands, and cursed the unknown creatures who'd betrayed us. His coach from New Norfolk had just come in, and had been met by John Connell. The agent had told him that our scheme had leaked; but Connell didn't know how. He could only suspect that someone in his shipping office was a spy, and had gone to Matthew Casey or the police. Connell, being quite prosperous, was respected in society here; he was received at Government House, and valued such signs of official favour, despite his Irish origins. One of his trusted friends was a Government official, and had told him in secret that my intention to sail on the *Southern Queen* had been known to Governor Denison and the Comptroller of Convicts for a week – although they didn't know how I intended to slip on board. Nor did they know that Connell himself was to have sheltered me. Tomorrow evening, however, when the ship was due to sail from the New Wharf, she would be searched more thoroughly than usual; many extra police would be posted on the docks, and river police would be on watch in the Derwent as well.

Under these circumstances, Connell's nerve had failed him. He was sympathetic to our cause, and wished to oblige his master Terence Paterson; but he valued his position in society here, and did not want to be charged with aiding a felon to abscond. He was very relieved that his own part in the business was not known – and he would take no further risks.

So all was lost, I said.

But Callaghan shook his head. There was another chance, he said. On Saturday the 21st – in four days' time – another Paterson Line ship would be sailing from Hobart Town for Sydney: the brig *Isabella*. She would reach Sydney on the 27th; so there would still be ample time for me to sail on the *Eliza Jane* for San Francisco. Meanwhile, I must continue to hide here with Father Brennan, and contrive to hire a boatman who would ferry me down the river after the *Isabella* had been cleared. Father Brennan would no doubt find some loyal Irish fisherman who would be willing to do it, and to keep his mouth shut. This time the ship would go a little beyond

Sandy Bay before dropping anchor. John Connell would arrange for her to wait for me – but he would not take me out to her himself, or shelter me.

Kentucky was speaking rapidly, as usual; as always, he was in a hurry. I doubt that he ever slows down. As he stood there, rocking on his toes in his beautiful American boots, poised on the brink of flight, I knew that when he was gone, it would be almost as though I'd imagined him.

– I'm sorry, Devereux, but I won't be here to help you, he said. This town's getting too hot for me: I'm getting the Hell out. I aim to sail tonight on the *Queen* as planned – and I've only got a couple of hours before I go on board. John Connell tells me those arseholes of Government spies are wise to me – begging your pardon, Father. I'd be watched wherever I went, if I stayed, and they'd look for any excuse they could find to arrest me. But I ain't broken any laws that they know about – so they can't stop me from sailing.

I understood, I said. He must go while he could. And I thanked him for all he'd done.

– Sure, it's been an honour, he said. When you get to America, every true Irishman will thank me for it. We'll celebrate in New York for a week, by Godfrey! I'll see you in Sydney, Devereux. And if not, in the United States.

He winked, gave me his broad smile, shook Father Brennan's hand and mine, clapped his big white hat on his head, and was gone down Patrick Street.

I found myself smiling after him. Just for a moment, his words had made my heart lift, bringing back that hunger for the world which had almost died in me. But mere minutes after he vanished, the hunger had faded too.

Seven-thirty has just struck. In half an hour, Jacob Lenoir will bring the ladder, and I'll be able to climb down and join him for supper. I look forward to seeing his forbidding, bearded face appear above the platform.

What a friend Lenoir has been to me! Now that my position has grown desperate, it's he who's given me refuge, and has saved me from capture: this marooned, aged scholar who has no involvement in our cause, and has never expressed an opinion of it, one way or the other. And his risk continues. Today is Thursday, and the *Isabella* doesn't sail until Saturday evening. For over two days more – knowing that if I'm detected he will be charged with harbouring a fugitive who is a prisoner of state – he must work in his shop while I lie here overhead. The risk of my being looked for here is great, since I imagine Matthew Casey will have recorded my friendship with Lenoir in whatever secret dossier he keeps on me – and the police could decide at any time to visit the shop. But Lenoir and I are gambling on the notion that no-one would imagine that my platform can be reached from below, or is anything but a shelf for storing old boxes. They are much more likely to search his storeroom.

They are searching for me all through the island, and Lenoir has been told by his Royal Society associates that Sir William Denison is beside himself. A handbill carrying my description has been put up in every town and hamlet. It is outside all the police offices in Hobart Town, as well as the Post Office, the Customs House, and various shipping offices – including the office of the Paterson Line. In the description that is given, I recognise the verbal portrait that was composed by the skull-like and respectful Mr Vincent, when I first arrived here on the *Raffles*. Citizens are asked to look out for a man five feet eleven inches tall, with dark brown hair, blue eyes, a long nose and clean-shaven except for a moustache. (So they have even noted my moustache, which was not there when Mr Vincent did his work; I'm glad that I've now removed it.) There is a reward of two hundred and fifty pounds offered for information leading to my arrest – which is a great deal of money to most Van Diemen's Land citizens, and is no doubt a measure of Denison's rage.

I can't imagine what the penalties would be for Monsieur Lenoir should I be discovered here, but they surely wouldn't be light; and his business might well be ruined. Why has he done it? Perhaps I remind him of his own intemperate youth; he's sometimes hinted as much. As for me, I turned to him because I had nowhere else to turn.

I was forced to come to him yesterday, at eight o'clock in the evening, after a visit to the St Virgil's presbytery by two police constables.

They knocked on the front door, which was answered by the old Irish housekeeper. Father Brennan and I were sitting in the parlour. When the housekeeper came and told him who was there, the priest went sickly white. Fortunately, she had left the front door half closed, with the constables standing on the step, and I was able to move out through the hallway and upstairs to my bedroom without being seen. I waited there inside the door, my Colt in my raised hand, listening to the loud London voices below in the hall. They were questioning Father Brennan; I heard my name pronounced, and began to wonder wildly whether I might escape by the window, and over the rooftops.

But this was not necessary; the voices soon ceased, and the front door banged.

Father Brennan came up and sat in the chair by the window: the chair that the dying Kinane had sat in, looking down from this hillside street on to the distant port. The lamps of moored ships glimmered through the rain, beyond the city's grids of lights. I sat down on the bed, and the priest looked at the revolver in my hand. He seemed to wince; he knew, I think, that I'd been ready to fire on the police had they trapped me, rather than be taken. Such things show in the face, and I tried to adopt a milder expression.

– Please, he said, put away that gun. The police are gone. They were sent because the authorities know of my association with you. They don't suspect that you're here – or at least, they didn't ask to search. But they thought that I might know of your whereabouts. I told them I knew nothing, of course – but I don't think they believed me.

He licked his lips, and took off his spectacles and polished them with his handkerchief, and I saw that his fingers trembled. He was still very pale, and I realised then that Brennan, although a good and generous man, was not a very brave one. The situation was becoming unnerving for him; and in that instant, I knew that I must go.

– They'll come back, I said. They'll get a warrant to search here.

You've been very kind to me, Father Brennan, and I'm deeply in your debt for what you've done. But to stay here is no longer fair to you. I'll leave immediately.

He looked up at me quickly, with a mixture of unease and eagerness.

– But where could you go?

– I have a friend in the city, I said. He's already offered to hide me, if need be – I spoke with him this morning, and I trust him. I can go to him now. All you need do is to send my portmanteau round tomorrow. I'll give you the address.

Father Brennan licked his lips again, and his air became one of hangdog relief.

– If you're sure you can trust him, he said. I'm sorry, Devereux: I feel badly about this. I admire you so greatly as an Irish patriot – and I know that you are in a state of grief. To be hunted at such a time by these English villains is intolerable. May God bless you, and keep you safe. I only wish that *I* could. But if they did find you here, it would be very grave for me. The bishop –

I held up my hand, and told him that he had done more than I had a right to expect.

– God bless you, he said again, and sat blinking and wretched, while I went to the wardrobe and drew out my priestly disguise.

I had worn it this morning, and had slipped out into the town. I'd been confident, after my encounter in the coach with Mr Harrington, that my black clerical overcoat, white priest's collar and clean-shaven face would entirely protect me from being recognised – and my confidence had proved to be justified. I passed a number of police constables without encountering a single suspicious glance. Some of them – the Irish – touched their caps, and muttered: 'Good morning, Father'. I entered shops where they knew me, and there was no sign of recognition. I even stood reading one of the handbills of which I was the subject, outside the Post Office.

But I hadn't deceived Jacob Lenoir. At first, when I walked into the shop, he didn't know me. He was sitting at his desk, and glanced at me only briefly, as I moved among the tables. Finally, I went up to him, and bade him good morning. He squinted up at me.

– And what can I do for you, Father?

But before I had time to respond, he peered more narrowly, adjusting his spectacles. There was one other customer in the shop – an old gentleman over by the door, absorbed in reading – and Lenoir looked at him quickly. Then he looked back at me, lowering his voice.

– I think you had better come out the back.

I followed him out into the store-room, through the tall and crazy mazes of books. When we had reached the parlour-like section at its far end, he stopped in front of the fire and confronted me fiercely.

– Are you mad, Devereux? Do you realise you are being hunted for everywhere?

I defended the effectiveness of my disguise. Then I asked:

– How did you recognise me, monsieur? Nobody else has done.

– You forget: when you first walked into my shop, you were clean-shaven. If I remember, others will. You had better hide here with me. You should not be going about: you are a fool.

I explained my situation to him, while he looked at me dubiously, pulling at his beard.

– That is one of the first places they will look, he said. Your comrade Kinane was at St Virgil's presbytery; they will remember that. You would be better here.

July 20th

Ten o'clock in the morning. The chimes have just sounded: chimes that circumscribe my days.

I had thought, when I woke today, that my curious, fluctuating fever might be gone. But my forehead still burns, my attention comes and goes, and appearances keep changing. The most familiar objects (my portmantau, the dusty pine boxes on this platform), look unfamiliar.

Last night, after a supper of beefsteak and potatoes, Monsieur Lenoir and I sat before the fire together, in that store-room parlour of his. The dim little cavern was lit by only one candle, and its outer darkness, among the ramparts of books, had become impenetrable.

Should there be a knock on the door, it was agreed that I'd escape through the bath-house, and so into the lane by the Rivulet.

Much of our talk was carried on for me through speckled veils of fever. Even Lenoir's face – yellow as old paper against the gloomy Genoa velvet armchair in which he sat – kept fading from my vision and then returning, and grew smaller and then larger again.

– Why did you insist on handing in your Ticket, and courting arrest? I still don't understand this, he said. Madness! I know, I know: you worry about your honour as a gentleman. But why should you wish to remain a gentleman, Devereux? Why not go outside the code, in dealing with your enemy? Why not cheat him? Why not lie to him? You certainly don't belong inside his system. That is why I'm hiding you, my dear.

And:

– There is one thing that troubles me: circumstances have now made you willing to kill. Do not grow too willing. Many idealists like yourself begin by recommending killing on paper, for the sake of noble ends: then they begin to commit such acts themselves, and the ends are no longer noble. Forgive me, but I must say this to you, before we part for ever: be careful that you do not kill to revenge yourself on life, and on what life has done to you.

– I have no wish to do so, I said. You do me an injustice, monsieur.

– Perhaps. But this is what I fear in revolutionaries: this process. Revolution demands blood, and more blood. In this, it is a terrifying religion. I think it replaces the passion we should feel for God.

And:

– What is it that has actually driven you to this point, Devereux? How do you come to be sitting here? Are you really able to say?

I told him that his question surprised me: he knew what the beliefs and ideals were that governed my life, did he not?

He sighed and set down his coffee cup – raising his eyebrows and staring at it, as though he'd suddenly discovered that it was not fine china after all, but a thick and dirty vessel with a crack in it. He sniffed, and gave one of his brief, dry coughs.

– Ah yes, Ireland. Of course. Always Ireland. Nationalism.

He looked up at me, his blue-green eyes glinting in that way which usually preceded some cutting remark, or one of those deliberate insults with which he drove customers away.

– But is nationalism really what you worship, Devereux? You, and all the other young men in Europe who have made their countries into deities? I think they are female deities, you direct such passion towards them. And each of these deities is supposed to be more beautiful and perfect and virtuous than the others! How is one to choose among these ladies, if one is put in the position of Paris?

He chuckled.

– You salute the end of the Austrian Empire, he said. I am not so jubilant. It has been a fairly comfortable old empire, and it has given us much peace in Europe. What will they do, all these nation states of yours – each one of them convinced that it's more favoured by destiny than the others? Prussia! Italy! Hungary! Will they not fight each other? I think I see blood in the future, and I'm sometimes glad of the peace of this colonial island – I, who will see Europa no more. But you have still not answered my question.

– I will try, I said. The trappings of nationalism – the flags, the medals, the rhetoric – these scarcely interest me. I am interested in my country's soul, which can be seen in every stone and hillside. And when one people is under the subjection of another, and is forbidden by its conqueror even to speak its own language, or to tell its own stories – then its soul becomes stunted: a parody of itself. I want Ireland to regain her own soul.

Lenoir was nodding slowly, pulling at his beard. As he raised his hand, the flames from the fire glinted on his ruby ring and lit one side of his face, exaggerating its hollows and deep lines, and the arrogant blade of the nose. Finally he said:

– Yes. I see. I see how strongly you feel. It's as I suspected. You are not a politician; not even a political agent, in your heart. You are an artist-warrior. A very dangerous type: one who will take up the gun with joy, once he is convinced he is justified. And the men who follow and succeed you will be just as dangerous. Well, young fellow, I do not wish to lecture you. But I wish to utter a warning – uselessly,

I'm sure. I admire your collection of Irish fairy tales. I find them very beautiful – and beautifully written. It's your best self who wrote those, Devereux. And I must ask you: in your inmost mind, is the country you call Erin not the half-world of Faery? Is it not *there* that you wish to live?

I knew that these words were fanciful; merely rhetorical, in fact. Yet they had a peculiar effect on me: a cold tingling went through my body. Probably this was simply because my fever was growing worse; but it did not seem so at the time. As I looked back at the old bookseller, his face was no longer the one I knew, but a vexing, interrogating mask, peering out of darkness. When I tried to answer, I could not; and Lenoir went on speaking, his lips busily moving in their grey beard.

– You are actually more Celtic than one realises, at first. You long for the world of shadows; of invisible spirits. I know how much you loved her, my dear. But you can't follow; you can't go where she is. You must learn to turn away, and climb back towards the world. The more that you long for the dead, the more your live spirit will wither. Isn't that wisdom to be found in the legends you so admire?

He leaned forward and pointed at me, and his face had become intensely sad.

– Beware, Devereux! When I lost my dear wife – of whom I have never spoken to you, and of whom I will speak to no-one – I made the mistake I warn you against. I came here to the Antipodes – truly to the Underworld! – in order to die to the world. For fifteen years, I have lived among shadows. Now it's too late to go back. Soon I shall join her, in the true land of shadows. But you in your youth and strength – no. No, Devereux, you must not do this. Go: catch your ship, sail out of the Underworld, and live!

One of his knobby, arthritic hands was opening and closing, I saw, as though he were clutching something. I don't recall how I answered him. I was touched, even in my illness, and I tried to express this; but I believe I was somewhat incoherent. I found myself speaking of Kathleen's faith, and of my own lack of belief. I had difficulty in believing in a loving God, I said, and very little confidence in the benevolence of the universe. I thought often lately of Pascal's words: that he was terrified by the eternal silence of infinite space.

Lenoir was nodding and nodding like a doll, his expression mingling tolerance and impatience.

– Yes, yes, yes. You are adrift, you modern young men, he said. You are no longer sure that what your Christian Church offers you is true. You are no longer sure of your Messiah – or whether his divine intervention can be believed. Well, well, belief in that particular intervention is not permitted me. Yet *I* know that God's order can be trusted. If it is not, everything shrinks. That is what we must hold on to, Devereux. Perhaps you should read your Old Testament again. Perhaps you should read the Preacher.

He raised one hand, the fingers loose, almost as though he were blessing me, and began to quote.

– 'Vanity of vanities saith the preacher; all is vanity . . . Remember now thy Creator in the days of thy youth, while the evil days come not, nor the years draw nigh, when thou shalt say, "I have no pleasure in them".'

His hoarse old voice had taken on a new resonance. He had suddenly became a prophet, his seamed and wrinkled face gone dark with powerful warning.

– 'Let us hear the conclusion of the whole matter. Fear God, and keep his commandments: for this is the whole duty of man. For God shall bring every work into judgment, with every secret thing, whether it be good, or whether it be evil.'

He sat back, and his voice resumed its usual throaty monotone.

– Catch your ship, he said. Go back to the world, and learn to love it again. That is my advice, my dear, if only you will take it. And now we must help you to your hiding place: you are looking rather ill.

Journal Ends

LETTER FROM ROBERT DEVEREUX
TO THOMAS O'NEILL

Aboard the *ELIZA JANE*, at sea
October 2nd, 1851

My dear O'Neill,

This letter will be posted to you from San Francisco.

We are three weeks out from Tahiti, and should reach California in a few more days. The *Eliza Jane* is an American barque: when I boarded her in Sydney, I took off my hat in homage to the Stars and Stripes. The passengers, captain and crew are all Americans, so I seem already to be an inhabitant of the United States.

You will, I hope, have received my very brief note from Sydney, and will therefore know of the success of my escape, and of Michael Callaghan's part in it. He is with me here on board. God bless the man: he was waiting in Sydney when I arrived on the *Isabella*, and we both had safe accommodation with my benefactor, the ship-owner Mr Terence Paterson. 'Mr Brown' (as Mr Devereux was known at that stage), landed in Sydney without being recognised by local police, since he was taken ashore in the captain's own boat.

Boarding the *Isabella* in Hobart Town, however, hadn't been easy. I escaped from Van Diemen's Land in the guise of a labourer, carrying nothing but a single change of clothes – leaving behind my portmanteau, and even my diaries. (All these possessions, I'm glad to say, will by now be safely back at 'Clare', having been retrieved for me by James Langford.)

You know nothing of this episode, of course – and I've had no inclination until now to give you an account of it. Forgive me, dear Thomas, but since my departure, I've simply had no desire to write to you, or to anyone else. I've scarcely been able to read a book; instead, I've sat hour after hour on deck, staring at the ocean and at the long white line of our wake. Or else I've lain in my bunk, intelligently studying the cabin ceiling. Conversation with my fellow-passengers – many of them quite pleasant people, I'm sure – I find intolerable, and have politely avoided.

Kentucky Callaghan has tried to rouse me, with talk of the reception I'll have in New York, when we reach there from California. The festivities should go on for a week, he says; and he talks of a formal reception for me in the Brooklyn City Hall, and tells me that the Mayor of Brooklyn is planning to arrange a parade through the streets of the city in my honour. Among the New York Irish, it seems, I'm put forward as President-in-waiting of the future Republic of Ireland; and the newspapers wait to interview me, as soon as I step ashore. All this is flattering, yet quite unreal. I express my appreciation to the ebullient Michael Callaghan; but then have little more to say. No doubt he finds me very dull; but he's tactful enough not to show it.

Well, you know the reason – as he does. Ever since my loss, it's as though my mind and spirit have closed up. I've won my way to freedom, which is a great thing; but it's as though this has happened to someone else, in whom I have only a cursory interest. The new sights and sounds of Sydney; of this ship; of tropical Tahiti – all have left me indifferent.

A week ago, however, there was a slight but significant change. An American passenger, taking his constitutional around the deck, remarked to me that we had recently crossed the Tropic of Cancer. They are great ones for information, these Americans: mostly I'm bored by their garnering of facts, but this piece of intelligence caused a stirring in my heart. We were truly back in the northern hemisphere, and would soon be approaching the high, cool latitudes of civilization. As I stood there by the rail, I sensed a new freshness in the wind, and a change in the whole blue world we traversed. The very ship seemed to lift with expectation, and the breeze, snapping in the rigging, booming in the sails, became all at once electric. The Antipodes were finally left behind. Soon I would be back in my native zone: an exile no more. With this knowledge, my dullness lifted, and something was unlocked in me. My grief was not gone, but at least I was alive again.

∽

684

I departed Hobart Town in circumstances that were both outlandish and degrading. I'm speaking of my last twenty-four hours there, before I finally boarded the *Isabella*: the hours between the evening of Friday, July 20th and that of Saturday, July 21st, when the brig sailed from the Derwent.

I was suffering from a sort of fever, which I feared was the beginning of the *grippe*. This, thank God, did not eventuate; but the fever persisted. My body temperature rose and fell; my head was thick, and I was altogether wretchedly unwell. At one point I was subject to hallucinations; and these grotesqueries must be part of my account, since they were intertwined with what was real in a way that was deeply confusing. I'll report them all, without comment or explanation; and I fear that at times you'll find the recital distasteful. But I rely on your famous tolerance, and your sympathetic heart.

I waded though shit to escape Van Diemen's Land. I mean this literally, O'Neill. I was forced to navigate the Hobart Rivulet: a stream surely as foul as any of the rivers of Hades. You've passed it by often enough, I imagine, on your visits to the city – a handkerchief over your nose? That secret, vilely polluted brook, running behind the town's back, emerging in the centre at intervals, to offend the genteel? I compared it in my mind to Acheron, when I first walked past its banks. Now, I compare it to Lethe: the stream which robs us of memory.

I fled to the Rivulet at around half-past eight on the Friday night. I'd taken refuge, as I told you in my note from Sydney, with my good friend Jacob Lenoir, the Liverpool Street bookseller – and felt reasonably secure with him. I would lie for most of the day on a platform up near the ceiling of his shop, behind a pile of boxes. Lenoir and I half-anticipated a visit from the police; but since the ladder to the platform was hidden, except when I needed to descend, we believed it would not occur to them that anyone was up there. Well, we were wrong.

I was lying on the platform in my makeshift bed when they came. I'd been waiting for old Lenoir to bring the ladder, and fetch me down to supper. The bookshop had been closed for half an hour, and the door into the lane at the side – the shop's only entrance – was closed and locked. There was a sudden knocking on this door, causing me to sit bolt upright. I knew immediately who it was, though my brain was vague with fever, and I'd been drifting in and out of sleep. I was clad at the time in a shirt, waistcoat and trousers. I heard Lenoir shuffle to the door and shout through it, demanding to know who it was.

A hoarse voice shouted: *Police*. But still the old man didn't open to them. He told them contemptuously that he was closed, and to come back tomorrow.

But the ugly London voice outside became belligerent. It shouted that they had a warrant to search the shop, and that Lenoir was to open up immediately, or the door would be broken in.

I heard Lenoir mutter to himself in French – the word *canaille* being the only one audible – and then there was a jingling of keys, and the sound of the lock being turned. Meanwhile, I was forcing myself to concentrate, and to bring my swimming senses into focus. Crawling about on my hands and knees, so as not to be seen above the barricade of boxes, I had put on my shoes and drawn on a frock coat, an overcoat and a cap. I then stealthily opened my portman- teau, searched out my pocket Colt, and loaded and capped it. My fingers were trembling so violently, both from alarm and illness, that I almost despaired of completing this operation. But eventually it was done.

Meanwhile, voices were rising to me from below.

First policeman: – We're informed, sir, that you're a friend of Mr Robert Devereux, the escaped political exile. That's so, isn't it, sir?

Lenoir: – We're acquainted. He's a regular customer here. That's no offence, I assume?

First policeman: – No, sir. But if you are harbouring him here – *that* would be an offence. Is he here, sir?

Lenoir: – He is not. That is quite ridiculous. Now I suggest that you men both leave. You are causing me annoyance.

Second policeman: – I'm sorry sir, but we must carry out a search – and it will be very thorough, I assure you. What's up on that platform?

Lenoir: – As you can see, boxes. You surely don't imagine I

686

have a wanted Irish gentleman crouched up there? You are wasting my time, constable – and your own.

Second policeman: – We'll be looking there, nevertheless. Would you have a ladder somewhere?

Lenoir: – No. It was borrowed some time ago.

First policeman: – We'll find a way. Damn my eyes, we'll have our work cut out here. What a precious mess these books is in!

Lenoir: – 'Of making many books there is no end; and much study is a weariness of the flesh.'

Second policeman: – What's that you say, sir?

Lenoir: – Never mind, constable. Go on, if you must. And I'm sure I'll be able to tell my friend the Colonial Secretary how efficient and respectful you both were.

Second policeman (suddenly cautious): – I'm sure you will, sir. Now what's out the back there?

Lenoir: – My living quarters. I trust you're not proposing to invade them?

First policeman: – I'm afraid we must, sir. Smartly, Carson. That's where he'll be, if he's here.

Their feet tramped away into the store-room: then I peeped below. The shop was empty, and it wasn't too difficult for me, even in my illness, to slide down one of the wooden pillars supporting the platform. I paused at the foot of it, listening to the voices from the store-room. Lenoir (probably on purpose), had drawn the door almost shut behind them, and I was able to creep unseen across the shop to the street door, and so out into the lane.

Hobart Town was freezing, that night. Colt in hand, turning up the collar of my overcoat, I tiptoed down the cobbled lane – which was empty, and very dark. I had no clear thoughts, except that I would shoot if pursued. The big stone warehouse of Nathan and Moses reared dim and high on my left, showing no lights. The only light here, which glowed like the eye of a nocturnal animal, was a single small window in the side of Lenoir's building. I left it behind, passing between paling fences, entering deeper darkness, and pocketing my revolver. I was making for the Rivulet, whose reek reached me already, intimately woven into the lane's obscurity. The only sounds were distant ones: wheels and hoofs and voices out in Liverpool Street, and the barking of a dog. Icy air burned on my burning face; then I became aware that it was snowing. Light, spinning flakes came down out of the black sky, settling on abandoned crates and barrels, and on the shingled, misshapen roofs of a set of weatherboard hovels that succeeded the warehouse building. I came to the end of the lane, and paused.

There was no moon, the darkness was almost impenetrable, and I peered to see where I was. I knew I'd reached the Rivulet mainly by the sound: a swift rushing and bubbling, somewhere below me. I moved nearer, and tripped over a box, and my heart pounded. I looked behind me, but there were no pursuing figures in the lane, where the snow had laid down a threadbare fabric. I found myself standing on the edge of a stone retaining wall, some twelve feet high. Below me, an occasional glint of water showed, and the reflection of some lights on the other side of the stream, not more than a dozen yards away. These, I knew, came from the backs of the buildings in Collins Street.

I squatted down, squinting against the snow flakes, and lowered myself over the wall. I hung by my hands and let myself drop, landing in the water up to my knees, my boots sinking in slime, the stench rising into my nostrils with a new and vile authority. And now I commenced my journey to freedom, wading down the edge of the Rivulet.

When I'd come out into the air, my fever had quickly grown worse: I was trembling in regular spasms, and was becoming more and more dizzy. But these symptoms had little interest for me at the time. My one aim was to move forward, and to be far from my pursuers; and my only concern was that the Rivulet might become too deep to wade in. You'll be wondering, Thomas, where I thought I was moving to – and why I'd made for this pestilential brook that had become a common sewer: breeder of crime and cholera. Well, I had sound enough reasons, despite my confused state. Clearly, I couldn't risk going the other way, and out into Liverpool Street. I was safer in that squalid, secret town which lies behind the respectable city – and whose thoroughfare is the Rivulet.

And the Rivulet went to the port, which was where I wanted to go.

Where I would spend the night, I had no idea. Perhaps I'd beg shelter in some poor prostitute's crib, and pay for her hospitality. How I would get aboard the *Isabella*, I didn't know either: I would think about that tomorrow. My notion now was to move down the Rivulet towards Wapping, and the region behind the Old Wharf where it flowed out into the port. I would know where I was by the bridges: first, Wellington Bridge across Elizabeth Street, at the town's centre; then the bridge across Argyle Street; then the derisively-named Palladio at Campbell Street, where Long Lane's depot stood – that fence and ex-servant of mine at Bermuda of whom I sometimes spoke to you, seated in front of the fire in Glengarry Cottage.

Once a bloated dead dog bumped against my legs, and I cursed. It was mostly too dark, except when I passed lighted windows, to see what I was wading through. But I knew. Sewage, and a hundred other varieties of foulness: the wastes from various flour mills, distilleries and tanneries; soakage from the cess-pit at the Cascades female prison; discharges of blood and dung from slaughter houses. Ah, Thomas, truly the way was long, and uncouth was the road! Here was Inferno's ninth and final circle, where I would need to arm my heart. Here was the region of ice. The snow flurries flew in my face, and then turned into sleet; I shuddered, and my teeth began to chatter, but still I waded on. Strange noises entered my head (clanging, screams, and laughter), and the shapes I saw in front of me grew difficult to discern. Other noises came down from the buildings that I passed: shouts and drunken laughter, and sometimes the strains of a concertina or fiddle. But I'd seen no human beings in the Rivulet; and here above Elizabeth Street, the stream was too shallow and uncertain for boats.

As I approached Wellington Bridge, however, a man loomed up in front of me, wading in the other direction. He wore spectacles, a tall black beaver and a dark and mud-stained tail coat, and was carrying in his hand what appeared to be documents. He smiled at me with a venom that made me shudder; his lips moved, but I heard nothing; and then I saw that it was Matthew Casey. I lunged at him, but night and the stream swallowed him up.

Next an old woman in a shawl approached, carrying a burden in her arms. I recognised her as an old procuress whom I'd seen in the stews of St Giles, accompanied by a child prostitute. As she came level, I saw that she was carrying the body of this child, who was quite naked, her long hair hanging like weed, her white flesh tinged with blue. She was dead, and I came to a halt. The old woman looked at me, and grinned.

– *Yours for a sov*, she said.

I waded on, weeping, and heard her laugh behind me. And now I saw Hell's monarch, the Emperor who swayed this realm of sorrow, rearing on my left behind a group of shanties. A voice said: *Vexilla regis prodeunt inferni*; and here was Lucifer, rising some forty feet into the murk, his wings spread out, the great sails beating the terrified air, while the sleet lashed at them in vain. He had three faces, and his flesh was grey. His six huge eyes were human, and they brimmed with tears. Yes, he was weeping, as I was; yet even as he did so, he was chewing at a white and bloody corpse, the legs dangling from his mouth, the blood dripping on his chest. My body shrilled with fear, and my flesh turned to ice; but I averted my eyes and went on, the filth sucking stubbornly at my boots, my overcoat heavy and sodden, its hem coated with ordure.

Wellington Bridge was above me now, humped against sleety sky. A street lamp glimmered on top of it, and a few ghostly pedestrians could be seen, their heads and shoulders moving above the parapet. I waded underneath, into stinking darkness.

The rushing of the water echoed off slimy stone walls. I was guided by an archway ahead of me which framed a wan, grey light on the other side of the bridge. But as I waded, this archway appeared to recede, and I felt myself sinking deeper into mud, struggling for every step. Finally, I seemed no longer to be moving at all, but to be suspended in darkness. This went on for a time that had no measure, while the water rose above my knees. Panic engulfed me, and there was a buzzing in my head. Suddenly, however, I emerged through the archway, gasping like a man who escapes suffocation. The water had almost reached my waist now, soaking through my clothing and chilling my private parts. Was I to be utterly submerged in the icy defilement of Dis?

I should explain to you at this point, Thomas, that my second self was watching these misfortunes with a kind of detachment, looking down on the soaked and desperate wretch who had once been Robert Devereux. It was this self who had enough wit left to take stock of his surroundings. I found that I was alone here, on the other side of the bridge. There was no-one on the bank above the retaining wall, and no-one was looking down from the parapet – though sounds of hoofbeats and wheels were floating through the sleet. Some yards ahead of me, at the foot of a flight of stone stairs, was a landing stage. A skiff was tied to a post there, and a pair of oars had been left in it. I remember hearing myself laugh. This boat was clearly waiting for me, I said.

I waded towards it, only to find the bottom shelving more and more steeply. I was up to my waist; then up to my chest. Foul things bobbed around me, and the sounds I made were like the outraged protests of a child. I reached the skiff with the water just below my chin, my mouth tightly closed. I was now very weak: it took all my strength to haul myself over the gunwale, almost upsetting the boat. But I achieved it, and still had enough rationality left to know that I must cast off the line very quickly, before I was seen.

No-one called out. I drifted away down Lethe's bubbling stream, the buzzing still loud in my head, clumsily attempting to ply the oars: wet to the skin, my overcoat and trousers covered in nameless filth, and in what my nose told me only too well was human ordure. I was unbearable to myself, and groaned as I rowed, carried by the stream, trying mainly to prevent the boat from being swept onto a bank. Faint lights glimmered though the sleet on either side, but if any human beings were there, they were invisible. I passed another skiff with the shapes of two men in it: they stared, but didn't challenge me. I was carried under the bridge at Argyle Street, and was soon approaching the Palladio.

It was then that the notion came to me to throw myself on the mercy of my former convict servant, Arthur Lane.

I hear you laugh, O'Neill – or perhaps exclaim. As you know, not only was Lane a vicious and perverse criminal, but he had reason to wish to take revenge on me, for the way in which I'd dealt with him at Bermuda. As well, the reward that Governor Denison had placed on my head was a sum that Lane would no doubt have found more than tempting. So why did I even think of taking refuge in his thieves' kitchen? I can only say to you again that I'd now reached a point where rational thought was gone, and where even my second self had lost control. As the skiff came out from under the bridge, and I saw on my left against the sleet the outline of that narrow, two-storeyed old house which seemed to lean sideways – the dubious rooming-house of which Lane was sole owner and proprietor, and which I described to you after my visit there with Langford – I gazed at it with feelings of longing, like a drowning man thrown a rope who has little concern as to who has thrown it.

I pulled hard on the oars, and brought the skiff in towards Long Lane's 'depot', as he called it: the peculiar, cabin-like structure projecting from the main body of the house, and supported by piles above the Rivulet. I managed somehow to come alongside the boat landing there, ship the oars, tie the skiff to a post, and climb the rickety ladder to the platform above, my foul and sodden overcoat like a leaden weight about me. The buzzing in my head had grown worse, and when I reached the platform at the top, I swayed and tottered, close to losing consciousness altogether. But my arm was now seized in a painful grip, and I found myself held by a heavily-built man wearing a dark blue naval officer's cap, who thrust his suet-coloured face close to mine. It wasn't a face I liked, being brutal and morose. He was a sort of guard, I imagine, whose function it was to watch Lane's back door, and to warn him of visits from the police. He spoke in a London accent, asking me what I thought I was doing here. I managed to say that I wished to see Arthur Lane. He asked me what my business was with Mr Lane – but I was now incapable of answering, and he dragged me through the door.

I blinked in the light, and was gratefully aware of being enclosed by a dense, stuffy warmth. Slowly, Long Lane's depot came into view:

the long, shadowy room with its mingled odours of cooking, unwashed bodies, tobacco smoke, and whale-oil from the lamps hung overhead – aromas which I inhaled as incense, after the stench of the Rivulet outside. All was as before: the crowds of shabby men and women clustered about in corners; the deal tables piled with goods; the clothing hung to dry on lines. I looked about for Lane; but there was no need. The guard was already dragging me towards him.

He was seated alone at a handsome oak table, close to the fire at the far end of the room. As we came closer, I saw that a large number of pocket watches lay on the table, which Lane appeared to be sorting and examining. He had on a pair of steel-rimmed spectacles, which I'd not seen him wear before. I won't say that they made him look respectable – nothing could do that – but they gave him an appearance of dubious authority, like the manager of some large but questionable business concern. As we approached, he looked up over their tops, without any change of expression. He was expensively if flashily dressed, in a blue frock coat, an embroidered waistcoat, a gleaming choker collar, and a cravat of sky-blue silk, fastened with a diamond pin. Seated nearby, on the floor by the hearth, were two boys of about sixteen years. One, with short, straw-yellow hair, was sorting through a basket containing women's jewellery and bracelets, arranging them into two piles; the other, who had curling black hair like a gypsy, was going through a box of clothing, folding the garments with care. They stopped their work when they saw me, and stared with great curiosity; then the straw-haired one laughed.

All this I saw with great clarity; but saw it like a picture, or like something through a screen, so that it seemed unlikely that I would ever be able to converse with these people. When the guard brought me up to him, Lane removed his spectacles and continued to study me blankly.

– I found this here cove on the landing, I heard the guard say. And by Christ, don't he stink! He says as how he knows you, Mr Lane.

Long Lane's dark eyes widened. When he spoke, his voice seemed to come from a distance.

– Why, it's Mr Robinson, ain't it? Mr Robinson, of *course*! That's all right, Bill – he's a pal of mine. You may leave us for now, Bill.

The guard bowed his head submissively, and shambled from Lane's presence; and Lane then addressed the two boys.

– You must cut along for now, my coveys. Mr Robinson and me have important matters to talk about.

When we were alone, he leaned forward, his eyes narrowing, and spoke in a rapid whisper. It was a whisper that mingled surprise with a sort of gloating.

– I gave you that name because if a sneak in this room was to hear your true one, they'd be off to the peelers very smartly, with the price *you've* got on your head. On the run, ain't you, sir? Is that why you've come to me?

You will understand my state when I say that I was childishly reassured. I had not made a mistake in coming to Lane, I told myself: he gave everybody a refuge. But when I tried to answer him, I found I could not: my dizziness had increased, and Lane's large eyes grew larger, shining like those of the horse he resembled. I looked helplessly about me. On a bench on the other side of the fire, an old, white-haired man was playing some mournful sailor's song on the concertina, singing dolefully below his breath. Behind him sat a red-haired young woman with her back to me, a rust-coloured shawl drawn about her shoulders. I seemed to know her, and looked harder; and a surging and terrible excitement shook me. *Kathleen*, I thought, and tried to call her name; but all I made was a croaking noise. Then she turned her head, and showed me the drink-bloated features of a prostitute.

Long Lane was speaking to me again; but I no longer heard what he said. A dark, waving curtain descended on my vision, and I fell towards the floor. I have a memory of hands coming out to catch hold of me.

I must have been semi-conscious through what followed, since I dimly remember being carried, and hearing above me the voices of Lane and the guard, who had hold of my arms and legs respectively.

– Bath him, I heard Lane say. And get rid of these shitty clothes. Old Betty will clean 'em up. Get him a nightshirt.

There were other voices and noises, but I could neither identify nor understand them. My next memory is a strange one: I was lying naked in a bath of hot water, in a narrow, candle-lit room. Charlie Porter, the black-haired dwarf, was bustling about like a laundress, a cake of soap in his hand, a towel tied about his waist. He poured fresh hot water over me from a jug, while Long Lane stood grinning in the background, surveying me through the steam. Then the dwarf began to soap my back. The hot water was delicious, and I wanted to tell them both so; but still I couldn't speak, and my head buzzed. I remembered my pocket-book, which held a large sum of money, and my watch and revolver. Were they stolen? No: I caught sight of them lying on a chair beside the bath, and pointed to them. I tried to tell Lane to give them to me; I tried to say the dwarf was a thief, who had stolen from me before. But Lane merely smiled and nodded – either in agreement or mockery. Then, without transition, I was enclosed by sleep.

I woke to find myself in a bed, between coarse but clean sheets. The room was small, and smelled musty: its walls were a dusky pink. There was a tall cedar wardrobe here, and a chair and a table beside the bed, on which a candle burned in a gin bottle. My pocket-book, watch and revolver lay beside the candle. I had just enough strength to examine them: to my amazement, all the money seemed safe. The Colt, however, had been emptied of its bullets. I drifted in and out of sleep, and it continued to be night. I was no longer in any world I knew, and this made me quite uneasy; but I was glad to be warm and dry.

Long Lane appeared, and sat on the chair beside the bed.

– You're worth two hundred and fifty quid, if I shop you, he said. And yet you come to *me*, Mr Devereux. I'm honoured by that, sir. I take it as a rare compliment.

He reached out and put his hand on my forehead.

– You're pretty sick, he said. Ain't you? You've got a fever, I believe. Here – drink this.

He handed me a glass of white liquid, and I drank it without question.

– I'm going to see you safe, he said. And you know why?

– No, Lane, I said faintly. Why?

He grinned, fingering the diamond pin in his cravat.

– For fun, he said. And because I don't need the money.

Then the grin vanished, and was replaced by an expression of piety.

– Leaving all jokes aside, he said, I'd never give a handsome man like you to the fucking traps. *You* ain't wanted for thieving or murder – and you ain't been lagged because of anything you tried to get for yourself. I admire that, Mr Devereux, I truly do. And I'm going to see you get clear because I *love* you, see? Even though you despised me for that, on the bloody old *Medway*. You think I'm not able to love true, I expect? But I can, and I'll show you that I can.

He stood up, looking down at me. The twitching I recalled had come back into his cheek, and there was an ancient anxiety in his eyes, mingling with his earnestness. This man Arthur Lane was a villain, O'Neill; please don't think that I imagined otherwise. Yet he was haunted, I believe, by some hazy vista of goodness: a land whose border he knew to be closed to him, but for which in certain moods he yearned. It was my good fortune, perhaps, that he did so now. Still standing over me, he seemed to try and read my thoughts; then he broke into a snigger, and held up his hand palm outwards.

– *Don't* worry, sir, he said. Even though I tell you I love you, I ain't going to do nothing nasty while you sleep. I've got all the boys I need for that, with lovely tight bottoms – and the choicest doxies on the game, when I feel like a change. So you can rest easy.

Then he touched my forehead again, with an almost timid care.

– You're safe here, Mr Devereux: I swear it by my mother. Your money's safe too – but do put it under your pillow, won't you?

He was gone, and I drifted into sleep.

When I woke, he was sitting beside me again; the candle had burned low, and the room had grown tall and different. Lane's face too had changed: it had the suffering refinement I had seen in it when he was flogged on Bermuda. He was questioning me, I found.

– What can Love be, then? he asked. A mortal?

– Far from it, I said.

– Well, what?

– He is half-way between mortal and immortal, I said.

– What sort of being is he, then?

– He is a great spirit, I said. He is half-god and half-man.

He nodded at me, satisfied; then I passed into peaceful sleep.

At seven the following evening, when darkness had closed in, I was sitting in the stern of a skiff, being rowed down the Rivulet towards the port. My ferryman was another of Lane's creatures: Ralph, the boatman, who would take me down the estuary to where the *Isabella* lay at anchor. Her captain would wait for me until half-past eight.

My clothing had been restored to me: cleaned, ironed and brushed and as good as new. It was packed in a handbag at my feet (given to me by Lane), together with such necessaries as a change of underclothing and a razor. I was clad in a set of old clothes from his vast store: a battered, low-crowned felt hat, a dark pea jacket, and corduroy trousers. In addition, I'd made my face grimy with coal dust. If we were stopped by the water police, I doubted that I'd be recognised. Fishing gear lay in the stern, to give our journey an apparent purpose.

I had lain all day in the pink bedroom, recovering my strength. Charlie Porter had brought me broth, and cups of tea; I'd had no appetite for anything else, but my fever was gone. Long Lane visited me at mid-morning. I told him of my assignation, and asked him to help me to reach the *Isabella*. When he agreed, and told me that Ralph would ferry me, I took out my pocket book and withdrew two hundred and fifty pounds.

– I want you to have this, I said. It's the amount that's on my head. So you see, you won't lose it after all.

He examined it, and an expression like pain crossed his face. But it was mixed with the excitement of avarice, and he licked his lips.

– You don't have to pay me, sir, he said. No.

– But I want to, I said. Don't refuse. I'm deeply thankful, Lane:

without your help, I'd be off in chains to Port Arthur. Why shouldn't the reward go to you?

He glanced at the banknotes and then back at me, and gave his neighing laugh. Then he put out his hand.

– Well now, if you put it that way, he said. You've got a big heart, Mr Devereux. I suppose I'm more deserving than a bloody grass – and we've fooled fucking Denison, ain't we? They'll never put the cat across *your* back, I've made sure of that.

As he tucked the notes away, his eyes grew cold; then, with a convulsive movement, he embraced me. I smelled his pomade, as well as onions on his breath; but I smiled, and thanked him again, and wished him farewell.

I had almost no money left, now: a hundred pounds was waiting in a bank in Sydney, and that was the last of my inheritance. I would have to find ways to make more in the United States. Perhaps the New York Bar would allow me to practise there.

The skiff was now well clear of the port, and out into the broad, quiet estuary. It was a calm, frosty night: overcast, but with no rain. Hobart Town's lights twinkled on the hills behind us, and I could dimly make out the black, decapitated cone of Mount Wellington, with a spectral cap of snow. Small fishing boats passed us, and once a big Norwegian whaler. Every ship's lamp was like a searcher; every voice that carried across the water made me flinch. It was now seven-fifteen; Ralph had a long haul in front of him, and I began to fear that we wouldn't reach the ship in time; that she'd give me up, and sail.

Ralph said little; he rowed, and grunted. Finally, he pointed to some lights on our right.

– Sandy Bay, he said. We must come to your ship soon. That's if she's here at all.

His one grey eye looked at me suspiciously, as he leaned back on the oars. But now I'd seen the lit stern windows of a brig, anchored not far ahead. We drew near, and I made out the green and yellow house flag of the Paterson Line, fluttering from her masthead.

We came up on her starboard side, and Ralph shipped his oars and picked up a boathook. I thrust five sovereigns into his fist, and he saluted me without smiling. I now had four sovereigns left in my purse. Two figures looked over the rail at us: one of them in the dark blue cap of an officer. A voice softly hailed us, asking if I was Mr Brown. When I said that I was, a rope ladder was let down, and a line for Ralph to attach to my handbag.

I stepped on to the deck and was greeted by the man in the cap, who proved to be the *Isabella*'s captain. He was bearded and quietly-spoken, and his voice matched the hush of the night-time river.

– Good evening, Mr Brown, he said. You were almost too damned late.

Farewell, Father O'Neill, my friend and gentle confessor! You remain in exile: a prisoner of that cursed and lovely island which confined us all, and which now holds the bones of our martyrs: Fitzgibbon and Kinane.

And yet I know you are not confined in your spirit. Wandering with your sketchbook and notepad, you've discovered that contentment which my friend James Langford has achieved – but which seemed to me like surrender, and so could not be mine. You hear an unknown music in the Roaring Forties winds; you are lulled by a crooning in the bush. I see you sitting by your fire, your kangaroo dogs at your feet, these pages in your hands. We had much contentment in your cottage, and I'm standing by your elbow as you read, inhaling the fumes from the eucalyptus logs. That you'll be freed in the end by our enemies, and that you and I will meet again in Ireland, will be my constant prayer. I'll be working in America to that end, so that the Directory and the United States Government will bring all their weight to bear on your behalf.

But I see you smile, O'Neill, and raise your monk-like brows – and I wonder if you've come to prefer being out of the world? If the door should open, would you actually leave your Antarctic forests and mountains? Or will you remain content there, among those easy colonial settlers for whom Bothwell and their flocks are the cosmos?

It's late at night, and I've just come down from the deck, where I stood alone in the bows. In the breeze was a sober hint of cold: we are entering the northern Autumn. Underneath my feet was the ship's lift and drop: buoyant and remorseless, bearing me into my future. I gripped the rail, which was wet with spume, and its bland, smooth wood seemed my only link with the actual. I tilted back my head to the stars.

The southern constellations were gone: lost below the globe's hidden rim. Above me, the Milky Way's hordes went streaming from west to east; ahead shone Charles's Wain, and the North Pole Star. And greeting Polaris again, that unwavering northern light which was hidden throughout my exile, I was seized by a cold, pure joy.

O North! I am home, I said.

It seems that I lost everything in the Antipodes, except for my infant son, and that all I came away with was grief. Yet is this really true? My grief has become a memory of grief: an echo of bad dreams.

EDITOR'S NOTES

PART TWO
CHAPTER 1

Page 220: *The excerpt from Cicero quoted by Monsieur Lenoir is from the speech given on the occasion of the flight of Catiline. It runs:*

'I was grieved, Fathers and Senators, grieved that the Republic once saved by your exertions and mine should be doomed so shortly to perish . . .'

Devereux's comment:

'This is true. We can still learn from Cicero how integrity and good government can be sold, and once sold, never regained.'

Lenoir's reply:

'You are a scholar, sir. Your Latin is excellent.'

CHAPTER 2

Page 259: *Mo bhrón!* Alas!

PART THREE
CHAPTER 3

Page 531: *Kinane's speeches in Gaelic, in the order in which they appear, may be translated as follows:*

'Are you there, Captain?'

'I'm your man.'

Cál ceannann is a dish based on potatoes and cabbage.

Uisce beatha (water of life), is whiskey.

CHAPTER 4

Pages 568 and 569: *Dan O'Donnell's speeches in Gaelic, in the order in which they appear, may be translated as follows:*

'Don't you speak Irish?'

'So you speak no Irish. Well, this is a strange thing.'

'You are going to die, I promise you.'

Page 570: *Kathleen's speech in Gaelic runs:*

'If you do, my curse on you for ever.'

CHAPTER 6

Page 690: 'The banners of Hell's Monarch do come forth towards us.'

Devereux is quoting here the opening line of Canto XXXIV of Dante's Inferno: *itself a parody of the opening line of a hymn by Fortunatus, sung in Catholic churches on the morning of Good Friday.*

Page 697: *Plainly, this dialogue was a product of Devereux's delirium. It took me some time to locate its source: the conversation between Socrates and Diotima, in* The Symposium. *I imagine Devereux knew that O'Neill would recognise it immediately, since he doesn't identify it.*

R.B.

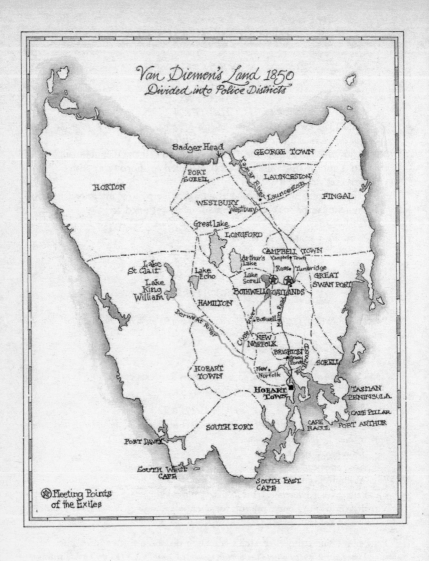

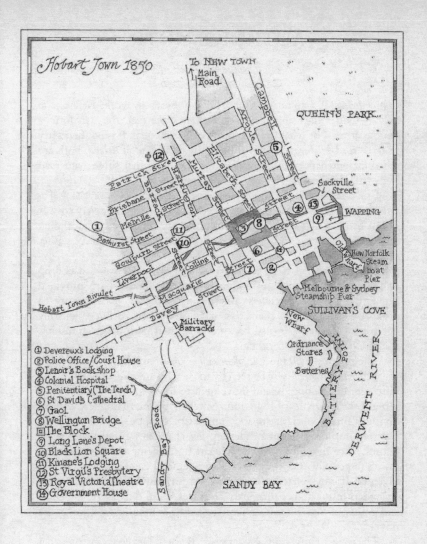

Hobart Town 1850

TO NEW TOWN
↑ Main Road

QUEEN'S PARK

Campbell Street

Argyle Street

Patrick Street

Elizabeth Street

Murray Street

Harrington Street

Bathurst Street

Brisbane Street

Melville Street

Goulburn Street

Liverpool Street

Collins Street

Macquarie Street

Davey Street

Sackville Street

WAPPING

Old Wharf

New Norfolk Steam boat Pier

Melbourne & Sydney Steamship Pier

SULLIVAN'S COVE

Hobart Town Rivulet

Military Barracks

New Wharf

Ordnance Stores

Batteries

BATTERY POINT

DERWENT RIVER

Sandy Bay Road

SANDY BAY

① Devereux's Lodging
② Police Office / Court House
③ Lenoir's Bookshop
④ Colonial Hospital
⑤ Penitentiary ("The Tench")
⑥ St David's Cathedral
⑦ Gaol
⑧ Wellington Bridge
▣ The Block
⑨ Long Lane's Depot
⑩ Black Lion Square
⑪ Kinane's Lodging
⑫ St Virgil's Presbytery
⑬ Royal Victoria Theatre
⑭ Government House

AUTHOR'S NOTE

Out of Ireland is a companion novel to my previous work, *Highways to a War*. Under the general title of *Beware of the Past*, the two form a double novel – or what I like to think of as a diptych. It is not necessary to have read *Highways to a War* before reading *Out of Ireland*: both are self-sufficient narratives. However, it's my hope that those who read both will see the larger pattern I've attempted to weave.

I may be asked why the present novel succeeds *Highways to a War* rather than preceding it, since it precedes *Highways* in time. My answer is that the enigmas of the present are often understood by descending into the past; and this is the progression which my dual narrative wishes the reader to follow.

In each novel, I have taken actual historical events as a backdrop for a work of fiction; and a number of real figures have provided inspiration for my characters. But having said that, it's necessary to point out that these characters have ended by being essentially fictitious – in their personal backgrounds, their personal relationships, and the events that befall them.

The political exiles in *Out of Ireland* – Devereux, Barry, Fitzgibbon, O'Neill and Kinane – will be seen by those who are acquainted with the history of the Young Ireland movement to have many resemblances to some of the real exiles of 1848: John Mitchel, Thomas Meagher, William Smith O'Brien, John Martin and Patrick O'Donohoe. However, I must warn against any attempt to identify my characters exactly with these figures, since in many ways they depart from them, and their personal stories (especially once they reach Van Diemen's Land), are very largely invented. If I am seen to have taken a liberty in drawing on the real Young Irelanders to create my imaginary creatures, I can only ask indulgence, and point out that this sort of liberty is a time-honoured tradition in the novel.

The case of my central character, Robert Devereux, is one that needs particular clarification.

He was inspired in many ways by John Mitchel, and shares a good many of Mitchel's ideas and features of character. But his origins and background are quite different. He shares his name and ancestry with a great-great uncle of mine of the same period, an Anglo-Irish gentleman who never came to Van Diemen's Land, but emigrated instead to

America, and of whom no more was heard. The events taking Devereux to Bermuda, and the facts of his circumstances there, are very similar to those experienced by Mitchel – but the people Devereux encounters on the *Medway* are fictitious. And once he reaches Van Diemen's Land, his circumstances and his fate become entirely different from Mitchel's. His character also changes, becoming somewhat different from that of the figure who was my starting-point.

All the other characters in the novel (except for the invisible Governor of Van Diemen's Land), are invented, with no historical models.

My primary sources in depicting the historical backgrounds and political issues in this story have been John Mitchel's *Jail Journal,* originally published in *The Irish Citizen* (New York, 1854); Mitchel's *The Last Conquest of Ireland (Perhaps),* (The Irishman Office, Dublin, 1861); *Meagher of the Sword,* the personal reminiscences and speeches of Thomas Francis Meagher, edited by Arthur Griffith (M.T. Gill, Dublin, 1916); and *To Solitude Consigned,* the Tasmanian Journal of William Smith O'Brien, edited by Richard Davis (Crossing Press, Sydney, 1995).

Among the many secondary sources consulted, those most essential were the *Life of John Mitchel* by William Dillon (Kegan Paul, London, 1888); *Young Ireland in Exile,* by Monsignor J.H. Cullen (Talbot Press, Dublin, 1928); *The Young Irelanders,* by T.F. O'Sullivan (The Kerryman Ltd., Tralee, 1944); *The Irish Exiles in Australia* by T.J. Kiernan (Burns & Oates, Melbourne, 1954); *William Smith O'Brien* by Blanche M. Touhill (University of Missouri Press, 1981); *Heart of Exile,* by Patsy Adam-Smith (Nelson, Melbourne, 1986); and *Revolutionary Imperialist: William Smith O'Brien,* by Richard Davis (Crossing Press, Sydney, 1998.) For the theory of Van Diemen's Land as a Panopticon, I've drawn on an essay by Peter Chapman: *The Island Panopticon* (Historical Records of Australia, 1990).

An historical novel such as this requires a good deal of help, in order to achieve some authenticity. I have been fortunate in the generosity of my helpers.

First and foremost, I am indebted to the Tasmanian historian Gillian Winter, who tirelessly guided me, over many years of work, through Van Diemen's Land in the 1850s, and helped me in my excavations of some strange, buried levels of my native city of Hobart.

I am grateful to Richard Davis, Emeritus Professor of History in the University of Tasmania, for discussing the Young Irelanders with me, and for his generous loan of the Smith O'Brien journals in type-script, long before he brought them to publication.

The Irish writer and historian Alf MacLochlainn, formerly Director of the National Library of Ireland, was kind enough to correspond with me on certain aspects of Irish background in this novel, and to send me some of his historical essays. His help was fundamentally valuable to me.

Des O'Malley, who lectures in Celtic Studies at Sydney University, assisted me with dialogue in Gaelic; the marine historian Mike Connell gave me expert advice on ships, and my friend Warren Reed acquainted me with the intricacies of 19th century firearms.

I should also like to acknowledge the help of Patrick O'Farrell, Professor of History at the University of New South Wales; of Margaret Glover, of the Archives Office of Tasmania, and of my friend Richard Connolly, broadcaster and composer, for his expert advice on matters ranging from nineteenth century wines to correct Latin usage.

Any errors of background or fact that may occur in the book will be my own, and not the fault of any of these experts.

Finally, I wish to thank my friends Jamie Grant and Margaret Connolly, for their sound advice and their belief in this novel over all the years it took to write.

In this Vintage edition, a number of typographical errors have been corrected.

Grateful acknowledgement is made to Penguin Books (UK) for per-mission to reprint excerpts from the following copyrighted works:

Aeschylus, 'Prometheus Bound', translated by Philip Vellacott.

Theocritus, 'The Cyclops', from *The Idylls*, translated by Robert Wells.

Plato, *The Symposium*, translated by W. Hamilton.

Acknowledgement is also made to Macmillan & Co. (UK) for the excerpt quoted from 'Remorse for Intemperate Speech', from the *Collected Poems* of W.B. Yeats.

The quotations from Dante's *Divine Comedy* are all from Henry Cary's translation, published by Everyman's Library.

The translation from the Prelude to *The Georgics* by Virgil is by John Dryden.